LAWRENCE SANDERS

Three Complete Novels

LAWRENCE SANDERS

Three Complete Novels

THE SIXTH COMMANDMENT

THE SEVENTH COMMANDMENT

THE EIGHTH COMMANDMENT

G. P. PUTNAM'S SONS · NEW YORK

G. P. Putnam's Sons
Publishers Since 1838
200 Madison Avenue
New York, NY 10016

Library of Congress Cataloging-in-Publication Data

Sanders, Lawrence, date
[Novels. Selections]
Three complete novels / Lawrence Sanders.
p.   cm.
Contents: The sixth commandment—The seventh commandment—The
eighth commandment.
ISBN 0-399-13972-9
1. Detective and mystery stories, American.   I. Sanders,
Lawrence,   Sixth commandment. 1994.   II. Sanders, Lawrence,
Seventh commandment.   1994.   III. Sanders, Lawrence,
Eighth commandment.   1994.   IV. Title.
PS3569.A5125A6   1994
813'.54—dc20   94-6726   CIP

Printed in the United States of America
1   2   3   4   5   6   7   8   9   10

Contents

THE SIXTH COMMANDMENT

Late November, and the world was dying. A wild wind hooted faintly outside the windows. Inside, the air had been breathed too many times.

"It's got nothing to do with your age," I said.

"Liar," she said.

I tried to groan. Swung my legs out of bed and lighted a cigarette. Sat there smoking, hunched over. She fumbled with my spine.

"Poor baby," she said.

I wouldn't look at her. I knew what I'd see: a small body so supple it twanged. Short brown hair cut like a boy's. All of her sleek. She had me in thrall. Soft swell to her abdomen. A little brown mole on the inside of her left thigh. Her ass was smooth and tight.

"All I'm saying," I said, "is that I've got to go away on a business trip. A week, two weeks, a month—who knows? I've *got* to; it's my job."

"I've got five weeks' vacation coming," she said. "I could get a leave of absence. I could quit. No problem."

I didn't answer.

Her squid arm slid around my neck. Even when she was coming, her flesh was cool. Did she ever sweat? Her skin was glass. But I could never break her.

"It's impossible," I said. "It wouldn't work."

She kneeled on the bed behind me. Put her arms about my neck. Pressed. Pointy little breasts. Very elegant. Pink bosses. All of her elegant. She worked at it: jogging, yoga, dance. I told her once that she even had muscles in her crap, and she said I was vulgar, and I said that was true.

"I'll be back," I said.

"No you won't," she said, and that was true, too.

I leaned forward to stub my cigarette in the ashtray on the floor. She leaned with me. For a moment I was supporting her naked weight on my back. Her warm breath was in my ear. I straightened slowly, pushing her back.

"At least," she said, "let's end things with a bang."

"You're outrageous," I said.

"Am I not?" she said.

See her in one of her tailored Abercrombie & Fitch suits, and you'd never guess. The Gucci brogues. Benjamin Franklin spectacles. Minimal makeup. Crisp. Aloof. All business. But naked, the woman was a god-damned tiger. Joan Powell. How I hated her. How I loved her. She taught me so much. Well, what the hell, I taught her a few things, too. I must have; why else had she endured my infidelities and shitty moods for three years?

"You'll call?" she said, and when I didn't answer, she said, forlornly, "You'll write?"

It wasn't her pleading that disgusted me so much as my own weakness. I wanted her so much, right then, that moment. After psyching myself for weeks, preparing for this break. If she had made the right gesture just then, the right touch, I'd have caved. But she didn't. Which meant she didn't want to, because she knew what the right gesture was, the right touch. She had invented it.

So I shrugged her off, got up, started to dress. She lay back on the rumpled sheets, watching me with hard eyes.

"The best you'll ever get," she said.

"I agree," I said. "Wholeheartedly."

She said she was forty-four, and I believed her. I said I was thirty-two, and she believed me. We didn't lie to each other about things like that. About facts. We lied about important things. It wasn't so much the difference in our ages that bothered me; it was the thralldom. I was addicted. She had me hooked.

I knotted my tie, looking at her in the mirror. Now she had one arm over her eyes. Her upper torso was supine, then, at the waist, her body curved over onto a hip. One knee drawn up. All of her in a sweet S curve, tapering. She kept a year-round tan. Milkier to mark the straps and little triangles of her string bikini. She liked me to shave her. I liked it, too.

"I'm going now," I said.

"Go," she said.

The Bingham Foundation wasn't the Ford or the Rockefeller, but it wasn't peanuts either. We gave away about ten million a year, mostly for scientific research. This was because the original Silas Bingham had been an ironmonger who had invented a new casting process. And his son, Caleb Bingham, had invented a cash register that kept a running total. *His* son, Jeremiah Bingham, had been a surgeon who invented a whole toolbox of clamps, saws, chisels, files, pliers, mallets, etc., for the repair of the human carcass.

Mrs. Cynthia, widow of Jeremiah, ran the Bingham Foundation. She looked like a little old man. The executive director was Stacy Besant. He looked like a little old woman. My name is Samuel Todd. I was one of several field investigators. The Bingham Foundation does not disburse its funds casually.

I was sitting in Besant's office on Friday morning, watching him twist a benzedrine inhaler up one hairy nostril. Fascinating. He unplugged it, with some difficulty, then sniffed, blinked, sneezed. He slid the inhaler into a vest pocket.

"A cold, sir?" I asked.

"Not yet," he said. "But you never know. You've reviewed the Thorndecker file?"

I flipped a palm back and forth.

"Briefly," I said. "I'll take it with me for closer study."

Actually, I had spent the previous night saying goodby to Joan Powell. I hadn't cracked the file. I didn't know who Thorndecker was. Moral: Ignorance really is bliss.

"What do you think?" Besant asked.

"Hard to say," I said. "The application sounds impressive, but all applications sound impressive."

"Of course, of course," he said.

Out came the inhaler again. Into the other nostril this time. Sniff. Blink. Sneeze.

"He's asking for a million," he said.

"Is he, sir?" I said. "They always double it, knowing we'll cut it in half, at least. It's a game."

"Usually," he said. "But in this case, I'm not so sure. He comes highly recommended. His work, I mean. Won a third of a Nobel at the age of thirty-eight."

"What was that for, sir?"

His eyes glazed over. Hunching across the desk toward me, he looked like a Galapagos tortoise clad in Harris tweed.

"Uh, it's all in the file," he said. "The science people are very high on him. Very high indeed." Pause. "His first wife was my niece."

"Oh?"

"Dead now. Drowned in the surf on the Cape. Terrible tragedy. Lovely girl."

I was silent.

The inhaler appeared again, but he didn't use it. Just fondled it. It looked like an oversize bullet. Something for big game.

"Go along then," he said. "Take as much time as you need. Keep in touch."

He held out his hand, and I moved it up and down. I thought again of a turtle. His flipper was dry and scaly.

Out in the gloomy corridor I met old Mrs. Cynthia. She was moving slowly along, leaning heavily on a polished cane. It had a silver head shaped like a toucan's bill. Handsome.

"Samuel," she said, "you're going up to see Doctor Thorndecker?"

"Yes, ma'am."

"I knew his father," she said. "Knew him well."

"Did you?"

"A sweet man," she said, and something that might have been pain pinched her eyes. "It was all so—so sad."

I stared at her.

"Does that mean you'd like me to approve the grant, Mrs. Cynthia?" I asked bluntly.

Her eyes cleared. She reached out a veined hand and tapped my cheek. Not quite a slap.

"Sometimes, Samuel," she said, "you carry lovable irascibility a little too far. I know you won't let my friendship with Doctor Thorndecker's father affect your judgment. If I thought that, I would never have mentioned it."

There didn't seem to be anything more to say. I went back to my broom-closet office, slid the Thorndecker file into my battered briefcase, and went home to pack. I planned to go over the research on Sunday night, and get an early start the next morning.

I should have slit my wrists instead.

Over the years the Bingham Foundation had developed a reasonably efficient method of processing grant applications. Unless they were obviously from nut cases ("I am on the verge of inventing perpetual motion!"), requests went to three independent investigative organizations that handled this type of work for private foundations and, occasionally, the federal government.

The firm of Donner & Stern, older even than Pinkertons, was too discreet to call their operatives "private detectives." They preferred "inquiry agents," and they provided personal background material on grant applicants. This included family history, education, professional employment record, personal habits (drinking? drug addiction?), and anything else of an intimate nature Donner & Stern felt would assist the Bingham Foundation in forming an opinion on the applicant's merit.

Lifschultz Associates conducted an inquiry into the applicant's financial status, his credit rating, banking history, investments, tax record, current assets, and so forth. The purpose here was to determine the applicant's honesty and trustworthiness, and to insure, as certainly as possible, that upon receipt of a Bingham Foundation grant, he wouldn't immediately depart for Pago Pago with his nubile secretary.

Finally, Scientific Research Records provided an unbiased analysis of the value, or lack of it, of the applicant's proposals: the reasons for which the subsidy was sought. The SRR report usually included a brief summary of similar work being conducted elsewhere, the chances for success, and a compilation of professional judgments on the applicant's intelligence and expertise by associates, colleagues, and rivals.

These three preliminary investigations eliminated about 90 percent of the hopeful scientists who approached the Bingham Foundation, hat in hand. The remaining applications were then handed over to Bingham's own field investigators.

Our job was to make an assessment of what Stacy Besant liked to call "the intangibles, human relations, and things known only to the applicant's priest, psychiatrist, or mistress."

First of all, we tried to discover if his family life was reasonably happy, if his relations with assistants and employees was troublefree, and if he enjoyed a good reputation in his neighborhood and community. If he was himself employed in a university or research facility, it was necessary to make certain the applicant had the confidence and respect of his superiors.

All this was fairly cut-and-dried, necessitating nothing more than talking informally to a great number of people and assuring them their comments would be off the record. But sometimes the results were surprising.

I remember the case of one renowned scientist, happily married, father of four, who applied for a grant for a research project into the nature and origins of homosexuality. During a final interview, the Bigham field investigator discovered the applicant himself was gay. His request was denied, not on moral grounds but because it was feared his predilection would prejudice his research.

In another case, a criminologist's request for funds was rejected when it was learned that he was an avid hunter and gun collector. It was a damaging revelation only because he had asked for the subsidy to make an in-depth analysis of "The Roots of Violence." Bingham decided to let some other foundation have the honor of financing the gunslinger's research.

"Field investigators" may have been our title, but "snoops" was more accurate. I had been doing it for almost five years, and if I was growing increasingly suspicious and cynical, it was because those were exactly the qualities the job required. It gave me no particular pleasure to uncover a weakness or ancient misstep that might mean the end of a man's dreams. But that was what I was being paid for, and paid well.

At least so I told myself. But occasionally, in moments of drunken enlightenment, I wondered if I enjoyed prying into other men's lives because my own was so empty.

The file on the application of Dr. Thorndecker was a fat one. Before I settled down with it, I put out a bottle of Glenlivet Scotch, pitcher of water, bucket of ice cubes. And two packs of cigarettes. I started something on the hi-fi—I think it was Vivaldi—the volume turned down so low the music was only a murmur. Then I started . . .

THORNDECKER, Telford Gordon, 54, BSCh, MD, MSc, PhD, etc., etc., member of this, fellow of that, Nobel Prize Winner for research in the pathology of mammalian cells. Father of daughter Mary, 27, and son Edward, 17. Presently married to second wife Julie, 23.

I took a swallow of Scotch at that. His second wife was four years younger than his daughter. Interesting, but not too unusual. About as interesting as the ten years difference in the ages of his two children.

I sat staring a few moments at the photograph of Dr. Thorndecker included in the file. It was an 8 × 10 glossy, apparently intended for publication; it had that professional type of pose and lighting. It was a head-and-shoulders shot, eyes looking into the camera lens, mouth smiling faintly, chin raised.

He was a handsome man; no doubt of that. Thick shock of dark, wavy hair; heavy, masculine features; surprisingly sensitive lips. Eyes large and widely spaced. High brow, a jaw that was solid without being massive. Smallish ears set close to the skull. Strong, straight nose, somewhat hard and hawkish.

In the photo, the fine lips were smiling, but the eyes were grave, almost moody. I wondered how his voice would sound. I set great store by the timbre of a man's voice. I guessed Thorndecker's would be a rumbling baritone, with deep resonance.

I read on . . . about his brilliant teaching career, and even more brilliant research into the pathology of mammalian cells. I am not a trained scientist, but I've read a great deal of chemistry and physics, and learned more on my job at Bingham. I gathered, from the SRR report, that Thorndecker was especially interested in the biology of aging, and particularly the senescence of normal mammalian cells. He had made a significant contribution to a research project that produced a statistical study of the reproduction (doublings) of human embryo cells *in vitro.*

After this pioneer work, Thorndecker, on his own, had followed up with a study of the reproduction of human cells *in vitro* from donors of various ages. His findings suggested that the older the donor, the fewer times the donated cells could be induced to reproduce (double). Thorndecker concluded that mammalian cells had a built-in clock. Aging and death were not so much the result of genetic direction or of disease and decay, but were due to the inherent nature of our cells. A time for living, and a time for dying. And all the improved medical skills, diet, and health care in the world could not affect longevity except within very definite natural parameters.

A jolly thought. I had another drink of Glenlivet on that. Then I turned to the report of Lifschultz Associates on the good doctor's finances. It was revealing . . .

Prior to the death of his first wife by drowning, Dr. Telford Thorndecker apparently had been a man of moderate means, supporting his family on his professor's salary, fees from speaking engagements, the Nobel Prize award, and royalty income from two college textbooks he had written: "Human Cells" and "The Pathology of Human Cells."

He had been sole beneficiary of his wife's estate, and I blinked my eyes when I saw the amount: almost a million dollars. I made a mental note to ask Stacy Besant the source of this inherited wealth. As the first Mrs. Thorndecker's uncle, he should certainly know. And while I was at it, I might as well ask Mrs. Cynthia what she had meant by her lament: "It was all so—so sad," when she mentioned knowing Thorndecker's father.

Shortly after the will was probated, Dr. Thorndecker resigned all his teaching, research, and advisory positions. He purchased Crittenden Hall, a 90-bed nursing and convalescent home located near the village of Coburn, south of Albany, N.Y. The Crittenden grounds and buildings were extensive, but the nursing home had been operating at a loss for several years prior to Thorndecker's purchase. This may have been due to its isolated location, or perhaps simply to bad management.

In any event, Thorndecker showed an unexpected talent for business administration. Within two years, a refurbishing program was completed, a new, younger staff recruited, and Crittenden Hall was showing a modest profit. All this had been accomplished in spite of reducing occupancy to fifty beds and converting one of the buildings to a research laboratory that operated independently of the nursing facility.

Thorndecker managed this by creating a haven for the alcoholic, mentally disturbed, and terminally ill members of wealthy families. The daily rates were among the highest in the country for similar asylums. The kitchen was supervised by a Swiss cordon bleu chef, the staff was large enough to provide a one-to-one relationship with patients, and a wide variety of social activities was available, including first-run movies, TV sets in every room, dances, costume balls, and live entertainment by visiting theatrical troupes. No basket weaving or finger painting at Crittenden Hall.

As chief executive of this thriving enterprise, Dr. Thorndecker paid himself the relatively modest salary of $50,000 a year. All profits of the nursing facility went to the Crittenden Research Laboratory which was, according to the prospectus distributed to potential donors, "Devoted to a continuing inquiry into the biology of aging, with particular attention to cellular morphology and the role it plays in productive longevity."

The Lifschultz Associates' report concluded by stating that the Crittenden Research Laboratory was supported by the profits of the nursing home, by grants and contributions from outside donors, and by bequests, many of them sizable and some of them willed to the laboratory by former patients of Crittenden Hall.

Dr. Thorndecker, I decided, had a nice thing going. Not illegal certainly. Probably not even immoral or unethical. Just nice.

I flipped the stack of records on the hi-fi, visited the can, mixed a fresh highball, lighted the last cigarette in pack No. 1, and settled down to read the original application submitted to the Bingham Foundation by the Crittenden Research Laboratory.

The petition was succinct and well-organized. It made it clear from the outset that despite similar names, the connection between Crittenden Hall, the nursing home, and the Crittenden Research Laboratory was kept deliberately distant. Each facility had its own building, each its own staff. Lab employees were not encouraged to associate with those of the nursing home; they even lunched in separate chambers. What the application was emphasizing was that no Bingham Foundation funds, if granted, would be used in support of Crittenden Hall, a profit-making institution. All monies would go to Crittenden Research Laboratory, a non-profit organization performing original and valuable investigation into the basic constitution of mammalian cells.

The specific purpose for which a million dollars was requested was a three-year study on the effects of the entire spectrum of electromagnetic radiation on human embryo cells *in vitro*. This would include everything from radio waves and visible light to infrared, X rays, ultraviolet, and gamma rays. In addition, the cells' reaction to ultrasound would be explored, as well as laser and maser emissions.

Preliminary experiments, the application stated, indicated that under prolonged exposure to certain wavelengths of electromagnetic radiation, human cells underwent fundamental alterations of their reproductive capabilities, the nature of which the basic research had not clearly revealed. But, it was suggested, the thorough study for which funds were requested could conceivably lead to a fuller understanding of the cause of senescence in mammalian cells. In effect, what the project was designed to discover was the cellular clock that determined the normal life span of human beings.

It was an ambitious proposal. The money requested would be used to pay the salaries of an enlarged staff and to purchase the expensive equipment and instruments needed. A detailed budget was submitted.

I shuffled the file back to the report of Scientific Research Records. It stated that while a great deal of work in this field had already been done by research facilities around the world, the information available was fragmented; no single study of this nature had ever been made, and no researchers, to the knowledge of SRR, had set out with this particular aim: to uncover exactly what it was in human cells that, within a finite time, made our eyesight dim, muscles weaken, organs deteriorate, and brought about aging and death.

That was the stated objective of Dr. Telford Gordon Thorndecker. I didn't believe it for a minute. Here was this brilliant, imaginative, and innovative scientist requesting funds to replicate the experiments of other men and perhaps identify the primary cause of senescence in mammalian cells. I just couldn't see Thorndecker limiting himself to such a goal. The man was a genius; even his rivals and opponents admitted that. Geniuses don't follow; they lead.

I thought I knew the secret ambition of Dr. Telford Thorndecker. It followed the usual pattern of research in the biological sciences: discover, analyze, manipulate. He could never be content with merely identifying and describing the factor in mammalian cells that caused aging and death. He had a hidden desire to control that factor, to stretch our three-score-and-ten, or whatever, and push back the natural limits of human growth.

I grinned, convinced that I had guessed the real motives of Thorndecker in applying for a Bingham Foundation grant. Which only proves how stupid I can be when I set my mind to it.

I took up Thorndecker's photograph, and stared at it again.

"Hello, Ponce de Leon," I said aloud.

Then I finished the whiskey. My own Fountain of Youth.

The First Day

When the alarm chattered at 7.00 A.M. on Monday, I poked an arm out from my warm cocoon of blankets and let my hand fall limply on the shut-off button. When I awoke the second time, I looked blearily at the bedside clock. Almost eleven. So much for my early start.

Thirty-two is hardly a ripe old age, but I had recently noticed it was taking me longer and longer to put it together and get going in the morning. Ten years previously, even five years, I could splurge a rough night on the town, maybe including a bit of rub-the-bacon, get home in the wee hours, catch some fast sleep, bounce out of bed at seven, take a cold shower and quick shave, and go whistling off to face the day's challenges.

That morning I moved slowly, balancing my head carefully atop my neck. I climbed shakily out of my warm bed with a grumbled curse. I stared at myself in the bathroom mirror, shuddering. I took a long, hot shower, but the cobwebs were made of stainless steel. Brushing my teeth didn't eliminate the stale taste of all those cigarettes the night before. I didn't even try to shave; I can't stand the sight of blood.

In the kitchen, I closed my eyes and gulped down a glass of tomato juice. It didn't soothe the bubbling in my stomach from all that whiskey I had consumed while reviewing the Thorndecker file. Two cups of black coffee didn't help much either.

Finally, while I was dressing, I said aloud, ''Screw it,'' went back into the kitchen and mixed an enormous Bloody Mary, with salt, pepper, Tabasco, Worcestershire, and horse radish. I got that down, gasping. In about ten minutes I felt like I might live—but still wasn't certain I wanted to.

I looked out the window. It was gray out there, sky lowery, a hard wind blowing debris and pedestrians along West 71st Street. This was in Manhattan, in case you haven't guessed.

A sickeningly cheerful radio voice reported a storm front moving in from the west, with a dropping barometer and plunging thermometer. Snow flurries or a freezing rain predicted; driving conditions hazardous by late afternoon. It all sounded so *good*.

I pulled on whipcord slacks, black turtleneck sweater, tweed jacket, ankle-high boots. I owned a leather trenchcoat. It was a cheapie, and the last rainstorm had left it stiff as a board. But I struggled into it, pulled on a floppy Irish hat, and carried my packed bags down to my Pontiac Grand Prix.

Someone had written in the dust on the hood: "I am dirty. Please wash me." I scrawled underneath, "Why the hell should I?" I got started a little after twelve o'clock. I wouldn't say my mood was depressed. Just sadly thoughtful. I resolved to stop smoking, stop drinking, stop mistreating my holy body. I resolved to—ahh, what was the use? It was *my* holy body, envelope of my immortal soul, and if I wanted to kick hell out of it, who was there to care?

I stopped somewhere near Newburgh for a lunch of steak and eggs, with a couple of ales. There was a liquor store next to the diner, and I bought a pint of Courvoisier cognac. I didn't open it, but it was a comforting feeling knowing it was there in the glove compartment. My security blanket.

Driving up the Hudson Valley was like going into a tunnel. Greasy fog swirled; a heavy sky pressed down between the hills. There was a spatter of hail against the windshield. It turned to rain, then to sleet. I started the wipers, slowed, and got a local radio station that was warning of worse to come.

There wasn't much traffic. The few cars and trucks were moving steadily but cautiously, lights on in the gloom. No one even thought of trying to pass on that slick highway, at least until the sand spreaders got to work. I drove hunched forward, peering into the blackness. I wasn't thinking about the storm. I wasn't even brooding about Dr. Telford Thorndecker. I was remembering Joan Powell.

I had met her three years ago, and there was a storm then much like this one. I wish I could tell you that we met like that couple in the TV commercial, on a hazy, sunlit terrace. We are sipping wine at separate tables, me red, her white. I raise my glass to her. She smiles faintly. The next thing you know, we're sharing the same table, our wine bottles nestling side by side. Don't like that? How about this one, from an old Irene Dunne-Cary Grant movie. We both run for the same cab, get in opposite sides. Big argument. Then the bent-nosed driver (Allen Jenkins) persuades us to share the cab, and we discover we're both going to the same party. You know how *that* turns out.

It wasn't like that at all. On a blowy, rancorous day, I had a late-afternoon appointment with my dentist, Dr. Hockheimer, in a medical building on West 57th Street. It was only for a checkup and cleaning, but

I'm terrified of dentists. The fact that Dr. Hockheimer gave all his patients a lollipop after treatment didn't help much.

Hockheimer shared a suite with two other dentists. The waiting room was crowded. I hung up my wet trenchcoat, put my dripping umbrella in the corner rack. I sat down next to a nice looking woman. Early forties, I guessed. She was holding a two-year-old copy of the *National Geographic* in shaking hands. The magazine was upside down. I knew exactly how she felt.

I sat there for almost five minutes, embarrassed to discover I had a lighted cigarette in each hand. I was tapping one out when a god-awful scream of pain came from one of the dentists' offices.

That was all I needed. I jerked to my feet, grabbed up trenchcoat and umbrella, headed for the door. The nice looking lady beat me out by two steps. At the elevator, we smiled wanly at each other.

"I'm a coward," she said.

"Welcome to the club," I said. "Need a drink?"

"Do I ever!" she said.

We dashed across Sixth Avenue, both of us huddling under my umbrella, buffeted by the driving rain. We ran into a dim hotel bar, laughing and feeling better already. We sat at a front table, about as big as a diaper, and ordered martinis.

"Was that a man or a woman who screamed?" I asked.

"Don't talk about it. Joan Powell," she said, offering a firm hand.

"Samuel Todd," I said, shaking it. "You a patient of Hockheimer's?" She nodded.

"We won't get our lollipops today."

"These are better," she said, sipping her drink.

She stared out the front window. Cold rain was driving in gusts. There was a flash of lightning, a crack of thunder.

She was a severely dressed, no-nonsense, executive-type lady. Sensible shoes. Tailored suit. High-collared blouse. Those crazy half-glasses. Good complexion. Marvelous complexion. Crisp features. A small, graceful, cool lady.

"You're a literary agent," I said. "An executive assistant to a big-shot lawyer. Editor of a women's magazine. Bank officer."

"No," she said. "A department store buyer. Housewares. You're a newspaper reporter. A computer programmer. An undercover cop. A shoe salesman."

"A shoe salesman?" I said. "Jesus! No, I'm with the Bingham Foundation. Field investigator."

"I knew it," she said, and I laughed.

The storm showed no signs of letting up, but I didn't care. It was pleasant in there with her, just talking, having another round. I never made a pass at her, nor she at me. It was all very civilized.

I figured her about ten years older than I. What I liked most about her was that she was obviously content with her age, made no effort to appear younger by dress, makeup, or manner. As I said, a very cool lady. Self-possessed.

After the second martini, she stared at me and said, "You're not the handsomest man I've ever met."

"Oh, I don't know," I said. "Last year I was runner-up in the Miss King of Prussia contest."

She looked down at her drink, expressionless.

"King of Prussia," I said. "A town in Pennsylvania."

"I know where it is," she said. "It wasn't a bad joke, but I very rarely laugh aloud. I chuckle inwardly."

"How will I know when you're chuckling inwardly?"

"Put your hand on my stomach. It flutters. Listen," she went on before I had a chance to react to that, "I didn't mean to insult you. About not being the handsomest man I've ever met. I don't particularly like handsome men. They're always looking in mirrors and combing their hair. You have a nice, plain, rugged face. Very masculine."

"Thank you."

"And you're polite. I like that."

"Good," I said. "Tell me more."

"Your eyes are good," she said. "Greenish-brown, aren't they?"

"Sort of."

"Was your nose broken?"

"A long time ago," I said. "I didn't think it showed."

"It does," she said. "Do people call you Sam?"

"They do. I don't like it."

"All right," she said equably. "Todd, may we have another drink? I'm going to split the check with you. Are you married?"

"No, Powell," I said. "Are you?"

"Not now. I was. Years ago. It was a mistake. Have you ever been married?"

"No," I said. "I was madly in love with my childhood sweetheart, but she ran off with a lion tamer."

"My childhood sweetheart *was* a lion tamer," she said. "Isn't that odd? You don't suppose . . . ?"

The rain had turned to sleet; the streets and sidewalks were layered with slush. There didn't seem much point in trying to get anywhere. So we had dinner right there in the hotel dining room. The food wasn't the greatest, but it was edible. Barely.

We talked lazily of this and that. She was from Virginia. I was from Ohio. She had come directly to New York after graduation from some girls' school. I had come to New York after a two-year detour in Vietnam.

"Army?" she asked.

"Not infantry," I said hastily. "No frontline action or anything like that. Criminal investigation. And there was plenty to investigate."

"I can imagine," she said. She stared down at her plate. "Tom, my younger brother, was killed over there. Marine Corps. I hate violence. *Hate* it."

I didn't say anything.

We had wine during the meal and vodka stingers afterward. I guess we were both more than a little zonked. We started chivying each other, neither of us laughing or even smiling. Very solemn. I don't know if she was chuckling inwardly—I didn't feel her stomach—but I was. What a nice, nice lady.

"Do you have a pet?" she asked. "Dog? Cat?"

"I have this very affectionate oryx," I said. "Name of Cynthia. I've trained her to sit up and beg. You have a pet?"

"A lemur named Pete," she said. "He can roll over and play dead. He's been doing it for a week now."

"Did you ever smoke any pot?"

"All the time. Takes me hours to scrub it clean with Brillo. You're not gay, are you?"

"Usually I'm morose."

And so on, and so on. I suppose it sounds silly. Maybe it was. But it was a pleasant evening. In today's world, "pleasant" is good enough.

After awhile we settled our bill—she insisted on paying half—and staggered out of there. We stood on the wind-whipped sidewalk for half an hour trying to get a taxi. But when a storm like that hits New York, empty cabs drive down into the subways and disappear.

We were both shivering under the hotel marquee, feet cold and wet. We watched the umpteenth occupied cab splash by. Then Joan Powell turned, looked into my eyes.

"The hell with this, Todd," she said firmly. "Let's get a room here for the night."

I stared at her, wondering again if she was chuckling inwardly.

"We've got no luggage," I pointed out.

"So?" she said. "We're a couple in from the suburbs. We've been to the theatre. Now we can't get home because the trains aren't running. Try it. It'll go like a dream."

It did.

I looked at her admiringly in the elevator. The bellhop, key in hand, was examining the ceiling.

"Call the babysitter the moment we get in the room, dear," I said. "Ask her to stay over with the children. I'm sure she'll oblige."

"Oh, she's obliging," Joan Powell said bitterly. "I'm sure you find that out when you drive her home."

The bellhop had a coughing fit.

The room was like our dinner: endurable, but just. A high-ceilinged, drafty barn of a place. A fake gas fireplace that wasn't burning. But a big radiator in the corner hissed steadily. Crackled enamel fixtures in the old-fashioned bathroom. One huge bed that sloped down to the center.

I gave the bellhop a five, and he was so grateful he didn't wink. He closed the door behind him, and I locked it. I turned to Joan Powell.

"Well, here we are, dear," I said. "Just married."

We could hear the world outside. Lash of hard rain against glass. Wail of wind. Thunder clap. Window panes rattled; the air seemed to flutter. But we were sealed off, protected. Warm and dry. Just the two of us in our secret, tawdry place. I didn't want to be anywhere else.

She undressed like an actress changing costumes. Off came the steel-rimmed spectacles, tailored suit, Gucci brogues, opaque pantyhouse. A bra so small it looked like two miniature half-moons.

"What size?" I asked hoarsely, staring at her elegant breasts.

"T-cup," she said.

She kept making sounds of deep satisfaction, "Mmm, mmm," when I put my lips and teeth to her. She was so complete and full. Not a dimple. All of her taut. Bulging hard. Trig, definitely trig. With strength and energy to challenge. I thought this was the real her. The other was role-playing. She was waiting to be free of the pretend.

What did we do? What did we not do? Our howls muffled the wind; our cries silenced the hissing radiator. She didn't give a damn, and after awhile I didn't either.

I topped her by a head, at least, but that can be interesting, too. I could look down with wonder at this cool, intent woman. She was very serious. It wasn't a your-place-or-mine thing. It had meaning for her. It was significant, I knew. And responded.

Sinuous legs came around my waist. Ankles locked. She pulled me deeper, fingernails digging. Her eyes were open, but glazed.

"Samuel," she said. "Samuel Todd."

"That's me," I said, and gave it my best shot.

I think it was enough. I hope it was enough. But it was difficult to tell. For a woman who hated violence, she was something.

The best part was when, sated, we lay slackly in each other's arms. Half-asleep. Murmuring and moaning nothing. That was nice, being warm and close, kissing now and then, rubbing. The storm was outside, growling, howling, but we were totally gone. Everything was quiet and smelled good.

Three years later I remembered that first night with Joan Powell. The storm was still howling and growling outside, but now I was alone. Well, that's the way I wanted it. Wasn't it?

My headlights picked up a sign through the snow's swirl: COBURN—1 MILE. I leaned forward to the windshield, peering into the darkness, searching for the turnoff. I found it, came down a long, winding ramp. There was a steel sign that had several holes blown through it, like someone had blasted away with a shotgun at close range. The sign said: WELCOME TO COBURN.

I was in the village before I knew it. An hour previously, I later learned, there had been a power failure; Coburn was completely without electricity;

all street lamps and traffic signals were out. I glimpsed a few flickering candles and kerosene lanterns inside stores and houses, but this deserted place was mostly black. I drove slowly, and when I saw a muffled pedestrian lumping along with a flashlight for company, I pulled up alongside him and cranked down the window.

"The Coburn Inn?" I yelled.

He motioned forward, in the direction I was heading. I nodded my thanks, sealed myself in, and started up again. For a few moments I thought I was stuck; my wheels spun. But I rocked the Grand Prix back and forth, and after awhile I got traction again and plowed ahead. I found the Coburn Inn dimly lighted with propane lamps. There were a lot of cars parked every which way in the courtyard: tourists who had decided to postpone their trips, to spend this broken night in the nearest warm, dry haven.

In the lobby it looked like most of the stranded travelers had decided to wait out the storm in the restaurant-bar. The flickering lamps gave enough light so I could see crowded tables and stand-up drinkers keeping two bartenders hustling.

There was a kerosene lantern on the front desk.

"Sorry," the bald clerk grinned cheerfully, "we're full up for tonight. The storm, y'know. But you can sit up in the lobby if you like. Plenty to eat and drink. Make a party of it."

"My name's Samuel Todd," I explained patiently. "My office called for a reservation."

"Sorry," he grinned. "No reservations for tonight. We're taking them first-come, first-served."

"I'm here at Dr. Thorndecker's request," I said desperately. "Dr. Telford Thorndecker of Crittenden Hall. He recommended this place. I'm meeting with him tomorrow."

Something happened to the grin. It remained painted on his face, mouth spread, teeth showing, but all the cheer went out of it. The eyes changed focus. I had the feeling that he wasn't seeing me anymore, that he was looking through me to something else. A thousand-yard stare.

"Samuel Todd," I repeated, to shake him out of his reverie. "Reservation. Friend of Dr. Thorndecker."

He shook his head in a kind of shudder, a brief, whiplike motion. His eyes slid down to the big register on the desk.

"Why didn't you say so?" he said in a low voice. "Samuel Todd, sure. Nice, big corner room. Sign here please. You got luggage?"

"Out in my car."

"You'll have to bring it in yourself. Half my people didn't show up tonight."

"I'll manage," I said.

He turned to a small bank of cubbyholes, took an old-fashioned skeleton key from 3-F. The key was attached to a brass medallion. He handed it to me, along with a sealed white envelope that had been in the box.

"Message for you," he said importantly. "See, it's got your name on it, and 'Hold for arrival.' "

"Who left it?"

"That I couldn't say."

"Well, when was it left here?"

"Beats me. It was in the box when I came on duty tonight. You might ask the day man tomorrow."

I nodded, and stuffed the envelope into my trenchcoat pocket. I went out into the storm again, and brought in my two suitcases and the briefcase containing the Thorndecker file. And the pint of brandy from the glove compartment.

The single elevator wasn't working. The bald clerk gestured toward the steep staircase. I went clumping slowly up, pausing on the landings to catch my breath. Kerosene lanterns had been set out in all the corridors. I found Room 3-F, and took one of the lanterns in with me. As far as I could see in the wavery light, it was a big corner room, just as the clerk had promised. Nothing palatial, but it seemed reasonably clean. It would do; I wasn't planning to settle permanently in Coburn.

I was peeling off my wet trenchcoat when I found the note that had been left for me. I took the envelope close to the yellowish lantern light to examine it. "Mr. Samuel Todd. Please hold for arrival." Neatly typed.

I opened the flap. A single sheet of white typing paper. I unfolded that. Two words:

"Thorndecker kills."

The Second Day

The storm passed over sometime during the night and went whining off to New England. When I awoke Tuesday at 7:30, power had been restored; I was able to use the electric shaver I carry in my travel kit. I noticed I had left about three fingers in the brandy bottle, demonstrating massive strength of character.

In daylight, my room looked old-fashioned, but okay. Lofty ceiling, raddled rug, sprung but comfortable armchairs. A small desk, the top tattooed with cigarette burns. Two dressers. The bed was flinty, but that's the way I like it. Biggest bathroom I had ever seen in a hotel, with a crackled pedestal sink, a yellowed tub on clawed legs, a toilet that flushed by pulling a tarnished brass chain hanging from an overhead tank. A Holiday Inn it wasn't, but there were plenty of towels, and the steam radiators were clanking away busily.

I took a peek outside. Instant depression. The sky was slate. Patches of sooty snow were melting; there wasn't a bright color in sight. No pedestrians. No life anywhere. Two of my five windows faced on what I guessed was Coburn's main street. I made a bet with myself that it was called Broadway. (It wasn't; it was called Main Street.) I saw the usual collection of small town stores and shops: Ideal Bootery, Samson's Drugs, E-zee Super-Mart, Bill's 5-and-10, Knowlton's Ladies and Gents Apparel, the Coburn *Sentinel*, Sandy's Liquors and Fine Wines.

Before sallying forth to take a closer look at this teeming metropolis, I spent a few minutes considering what to do about that anonymous billet-doux: "Thorndecker kills."

I was born a nosy bastard, and all my life I've been less interested in the how of things than in the why of people. I've had formal training in investigation, but you can't learn snoopery from books, any more than swimming, love making, or how to build the Eiffel Tower out of old Popsicle sticks.

Experience is what an investigator needs most. That, plus a jaundiced view of human nature, plus a willingness to listen to the palaver of old cops and learn by *their* experience.

Also, I have one other attribute of an effective shamus: I can't endure the thought of being scammed and made a fool of. I don't have that much self-respect that I can afford to let it be chipped away by some smart-ass con man. Con woman. Con person.

That dramatic note—"Thorndecker kills."—smelled of con to me.

In the groves of academe there's just as much envy, spite, deceit, connivery, and backbiting as in Hackensack politics. The upper echelons of scientific research are just as snaky a pit. The competition for private and federal funding is ruthless. Research scientists rush to publication, sometimes on the strength of palsied evidence. There's no substitute for being first. Either you're a discoverer, and your name goes into textbooks, or you're a plodding replicator, and the Nobel Committee couldn't care less.

So the chances were good that the author of "Thorndecker kills." was a jealous rival or disgruntled aide who felt he wasn't getting sufficient credit. I had seen it happen before: anonymous letters, slanderous rumors slyly spread, even sabotage and deliberate falsification of test results.

And the accusation—"Thorndecker kills."—wasn't all that shocking. All research biologists kill—everything from paramecia to chimpanzees. That's what the job requires. If the note had said: "Thorndecker murders," my hackles might have twitched a bit more. But all I did was slide the letter into an envelope addressed to Donner & Stern, along with a personal note to Nate Stern requesting a make on the typewriter used. I added the phone number of the Coburn Inn, and asked him to call when he had identified the machine. I doubted the information would have any effect on the Thorndecker inquiry.

That was my second mistake of that miserable day. The first was getting out of bed.

I waited and waited and waited for the rackety elevator, watching the brass dial move like it was lubricated with Elmer's Glue-All. When the open cage finally came wheezing down from the top (sixth) floor, the operator turned out to be a wizened colored gentleman one year younger than God. He was wearing a shiny, black alpaca jacket and a little skullcap something like a yarmulke. He was sitting on a wooden kitchen stool. He stopped the elevator five inches below floor level, creaked open the gate slowly. I stepped down and in.

"Close," I said, "but no cigar. How's life treating you this bright, sparkling morning?"

"It's hard but it's fair," he said, closing the gate and shoving the lever forward. "You checking out?"

"I just checked in."

"I thought you was one of those drummers the storm drove in."

"Not me," I said. "I'm here for a few days. Or maybe a few weeks."

"Glad to hear it," he said. "We can use all the customers we gets. My name's Sam. Sam Livingston."

"Sam's my name, too," I said. "Sam Todd. Glad to meet you, Sam."

"Likewise, Sam," he said.

We shook hands solemnly. About this time we were inching past the second floor.

"We'll get there," he said encouragingly. "I hop bells and hump bags and gets you room service, if you want. Like a jug late at night. A sandwich. I can provide."

"That's good to know," I said. "What hours do you work?"

"All hours," he said. "I live here. I got me a nice little place in the basement."

"Where were you last night when I needed you?"

"Hustling drinks in the saloon, I reckon."

"You busy, Sam?" I asked. "Many guests?"

"You," he said, "and half a dozen permanents. It's not our season."

"When is your season?"

He showed me a keyboard of strong, yellow teeth.

"We ain't got a season," he said.

We both laughed, and I looked down into the lobby as we slowly descended.

The floor was a checkerboard of greasy black and white tiles. There were a few small oriental rugs, so tatty the brown backing showed through. The couches and club chairs had once been sleek leather; now they were crackled, cushions lumped with loose springs. Alongside some of the chairs were round rubber mats with ancient brass cuspidors that had been planted with plastic ferns.

Fat wooden pillars, painted to imitate marble, rose from floor to vaulted ceiling. There was ornate iron grillwork around the elevator shaft and cashier's cage. Tucked in one corner was a glass cigar counter, presided over by a shimmering blonde wearing a tight turtleneck sweater punctuated by two Saturn nose cones.

The elevator bobbed to a stop. The gate squeaked open. I moved out. I had the feeling of stepping into the past, a scene of fifty years ago, caught and frozen. Old men slumped in dusty chairs stared at me over the tops of newspapers. The clerk behind the desk, another baldy, looked up from sorting letters into cubbyholes. The creampuff behind the counter paused in the act of opening a carton of cigarettes and raised her shadowed eyes.

It was not a memory, since I was too young to recall an ancient hotel lobby like that, smelling of disinfectant and a thousand dead cigars. I could only guess I remembered the set from an old movie, and any moment Humphrey Bogart was going to shamble over to the enameled blonde, buy a pack of Fatimas, and lisp, "Keep the change, thweetheart."

I shook my head. The vertigo vanished. I was staring at a shabby hotel lobby in a small town that had seen better days none of the citizens could recall. I went to the front desk . . .

"My name's Samuel Todd."

"Yes, Mr. Todd," the clerk said. "Room 3-F. Everything all right?"

He resembled the night clerk, but all bald men look like relatives.

"Everything's fine," I told him. "There was a letter waiting for me when I checked in last night. Could you tell me who left it?"

He shook his head.

"Can't say. I went back in the office for a few minutes. When I came out, the letter was laying right there on the register. Wasn't it signed?"

"Didn't recognize the name," I lied. "Where can I buy a stamp?"

"Machine over there on the cigar counter. Mailing slot's next to the door. Or you can take it to the post office if you like. That's around the corner on River Street. Go out a lot faster if you mail it from there. We don't get a pickup till three, four this afternoon."

I nodded my thanks, and walked over to the cigar counter. The machine sold me a 15-cent stamp for 20 cents. Nice business.

"Good morning, sir," brass head said throatily. "You're staying with us?"

She was something, a dazzle of wet colors: metallic hair, clouded eyes with lashes like inky centipedes, an enormous blooded mouth, pancaked cheeks. The red sweater was cinched with a studded belt wide enough for a motorcycle ride. Her skirt of purple plaid was so tight that in silhouette she looked like a map of Africa. Knee-high boots of white plastic. Tangerine-colored fingernails somewhere between claws and talons. A walking Picasso.

"Good morning," I said. "Yes, I'm staying with you."

I came down hard on the *you*, and she giggled and took a deep breath. It would have been cruel to ignore that. It would have been impossible to ignore that. I bought a candy bar I didn't want.

"Keep the change, sweetheart," I said.

The seediness was getting to me. All I needed was a toothpick in the corner of my mouth, and an unsmoked cigarette behind my ear.

I started for the doorway under the neon Restaurant-Bar sign.

"My name's Millie," the cigar counter girl called after me.

I waved a hand and kept going. Women like that scare me. I have visions of them cracking my bones and sucking the marrow.

One look at the Restaurant-Bar and I understood how the Coburn Inn survived without a season. There were customers at all twenty tables, and only two empty stools at the long counter. There were even three guys bellying up to the bar in an adjoining room, starting their day with a horn of the ox that gored them.

A few women, but mostly men. All locals, I figured: merchants, insurance salesmen, clerks, some blue-collar types, farmers in rubber boots and wool plaid shirts. They all seemed to know each other: a lot of loud talk, hoots of laughter. This had to be the *in* place in Coburn for a scoff or a tipple. More likely, it was the *only* place.

The menu was encouraging: heavy, country breakfasts with things like pork sausages, grits, scrapple, ham steaks, home fries, and so forth. I glanced around, and it looked like no one in Coburn ever heard of cholesterol. I had a glass of orange juice (which turned out to be freshly squeezed), a western omelette, hash browns, hot Danish, and coffee. When in Rome . . .

As I ate, the room gradually emptied out. It was getting on to 9:00 A.M., time to open all those swell stores I had seen, to start the business day thrumming. I figured that in Coburn, the sale of a second-hand manure spreader qualified as a thrum.

I was starting on my second cup of coffee when I realized someone was standing at my shoulder. I glanced around. A cop in khaki uniform under a canvas ranchers' jacket with a shearling collar. His star was on his lapel, his gun belt was buckled tightly. A long, tight man.

"Mr. Samuel Todd?" he asked. His voice was a flat monotone, hard. A pavement voice.

"That's right," I said. "I'm parked in a towaway zone?"

"No, sir," he said, not smiling. "I'm Constable Ronnie Goodfellow." He didn't offer to shake hands. "Mind if I join you?"

"Pull up a stool," I said. "How about a coffee?"

"No, sir. Thank you."

"No drinking on duty, eh?" I said. Still no smile. I gave up.

He took off his fur trooper's hat, opened the gun belt, took off his jacket. Then he buckled the gun belt about his waist again. He hung up hat and jacket, swung onto the stool alongside me.

While he was going through this slow, thoughtful ballet, I was watching him in the mirror behind the counter. I figured him for Indian blood. He was sword-thin, with dark skin, jetty hair, a nose that could slice cheese. He moved with a relaxed grace, but he didn't fool me. I saw the thin lips, squinny eyes. And his holster was oiled and polished.

I had known men like that before: so much pride they shivered with it. You see it mostly in blacks, Chicanos, and all the other put-downs. But some whites have it, too. Country whites or slum whites or mountain whites. Men so sensitive to a slight that they'll kill if they're insulted, derided, or even accidentally jostled. Temper isn't the reason, or merely conceit. It's a hubris that becomes violent when self-esteem is threatened. The image cannot be scorned. You don't chivy men like that; you cross to the other side of the street.

"Reason I'm here," he said in that stony voice, "is Dr. Telford Thorndecker asked me to stop by. Check to see you got settled in all right. See if there's anything you're wanting."

"That's very nice of you and Dr. Thorndecker," I said. "I appreciate your interest. But I'm settled in just dandy. No problems. And the western omelette was the best I've ever tasted."

"Introduce you to folks in Coburn, if you like," he said. "I know them all."

I blew across my coffee to cool it.

"Thorndecker tell you why I'm here?" I asked casually.

Then I turned to look at him. No expression in those tarry eyes.

"About the grant, you mean?" he said.

"The application for the grant," I said.

"He told me."

"That's surprising," I said. "Usually applicants like to keep it quiet. So if they're turned down, which they usually are, there's no public loss of face."

He looked down at his hands, twisted his thin wedding band slowly.

"Mr. Todd," he said, "Crittenden Hall is big business in Coburn. About a hundred people work out there, including the folks in the research lab. Biggest employer around here. They all live hereabouts, take home good paychecks, buy their needs from local stores. It's important to us—you know?"

"Sure," I said. "I understand."

"And with so many local people working out there, it would be pretty hard for Dr. Thorndecker to keep this grant business a secret. He didn't even try. There was a front-page story in the Coburn *Sentinel* a month ago. Everyone in town knows about it. Everyone's hoping it comes through. A million dollars. That would mean a lot to this town."

"Everyone's cheering for Thorndecker?" I said. "Is that it?"

"Just about everyone," he said carefully. "The best people. We're all hoping you give him a good report, and he gets the money. It would mean a lot to Coburn."

"I don't make the decision," I told him. "I just turn in a recommendation, one way or another. There are a lot of other factors involved. My bosses say Yes or No."

"We understand all that," he said patiently. "We just want to make sure you know how the people around here feel about Dr. Thorndecker and his work."

"The best people," I said.

"That's right," he said earnestly. "We're all for him. Dr. Thorndecker is a great man."

"Did he tell you that?" I said, finishing my coffee.

Those dark eyes turned slowly to mine. It wasn't a kindly look he gave me. No amusement at all.

"No," he said. "He didn't tell me. I'm saying it. Dr. Thorndecker is a great man doing fine work."

"Opinion received and noted," I said. "Now if you'll excuse me, Constable Goodfellow, I've got to go mail a letter."

"The post office is around the corner on River Street."

"I know."

"I'll be happy to show you the way."

"All right," I sighed. "Show me the way."

Goodfellow hadn't been exaggerating when he claimed to know all of Coburn. He exchanged greetings with everyone we met, usually on a first-name basis. We stopped a half-dozen times while I was introduced to Leading Citizens. After the Constable carefully identified me and explained what I was doing in Coburn, I was immediately assured that Dr. Telford Gordon Thorndecker was a prince, a cross between Jesus Christ and Albert Schweitzer—with maybe a little Abner Doubleday thrown in.

We mailed my letter. I had hopes then of ditching my police escort. It wasn't that he was *bad* company; he was no company at all. But I had underestimated him.

"Got a few minutes?" he asked. "Something I want to show you."

"Sure," I said, trying to sound enthusiastic. "I'm not on any schedule."

River Street was exactly that. It intersected Main Street, then ran downhill to the Hudson River. We stood at the top, before the street made its snaky descent to the water. The road was potholed, and bordering it were deserted homes and shops; crumbling warehouses, falling-down sheds, and sodden vacant lots littered with rubbish.

The slate sky still pressed down; God had abolished the sun. The air was shivery, wet, and smelled of ash. There was a greasy mist on the river. A current was running, I guess, but all I could see was floating debris, garbage, and patches of glinting oil. Empty crates, grapefruit rinds, dead fish. I don't think travel agents would push Coburn as "two weeks of fun-filled days and glamorous, romance-laden nights."

Constable Ronnie Goodfellow stood there, hands on hips, smoky eyes brooding from under the fur cap pulled low on his forehead.

"My folks lived here for two hundred years," he said. "This was a sweet river once. All the jumping fish you could catch. Salmon, bass, perch. Everything. The river was alive. Boats moving up and down. I mean there was commerce. Busy. Everyone worked hard and made a living. New York people, they wanted to go to Albany, they took the paddlewheel up. This was before trains and buses and airplanes. I mean the river was *important*. We shipped food down to the city by boat and barge. It all moves by truck now, of course. What there is of it. There were big

wharves here. You can still see the stubs of the pilings over there. This
town was *something*. It's all gone now. All different. Even the weather.
My daddy used to tell me the winters were so hard that the river froze
deep, and you could walk across the ice to Harrick. Or skate across. Hell,
Harrick doesn't even *exist* anymore. Lots of small farms around here then.
Good apples. Good grapes. Small manufacturing, like furniture, silver-
ware, glassware. Did you know there was a special color called Coburn
Blue? Something to do with the sand around here. They put it into vases
and plates. Known all over the country, it was. Coburn Blue. That must
have been something. The population was about five times what it is now.
The young people stayed right here. This was their home. But now . . .
This place . . . ''

His voice got choky. I began to like him.

"I'll tell you what," I said, "it's not only Coburn. It's New York City.
It's the United States of America. It's the world. Everything changes. You,
me, and the universe. It's the only thing you can depend on—change."

"Yes," he said, "You're right. And I'm a fool."

"You're not a fool," I told him. "A romantic maybe, but there's no
law against that."

"A fool," he insisted, and I didn't argue.

We walked slowly back to Main Street.

"You're married?" I said.

He didn't answer.

"Children?"

"No," he said. "No kids."

"Does your wife like Coburn?" I asked him.

"Hates it," he said in that hollow voice of his. "Can't wait to get out."

"Well . . . ?"

"No," he said. "We'll stay."

We didn't talk anymore until we were standing outside the Coburn Inn.

"Maybe you met my wife," he said, looking over my head. "Works
right here in the hotel. Behind the cigar counter. Name's Millie."

I nodded goodby, and marched into the Inn. I considered calling Dr.
Thorndecker, but I figured Constable Goodfellow would let him know I
was in town. To tell you the truth, I was miffed at the doctor. Not only
had he made his Bingham Foundation grant application a matter of public
knowledge—something that just isn't done—but he had sent an emissary
to greet me. Ordinarily I wouldn't have objected to that, but this agent
carried a .38 Police Special. I had a feeling I was being leaned on. I didn't
like it.

At this hour in the morning, getting on to eleven o'clock, there was
only one customer in the hotel bar. He was a gaffer wearing a checked
hunting cap, stained canvas jacket, and old-fashioned leather boots laced
to the knees. We used to call them "hightops" where I came from. You
bought a pair at Sears after your feet stopped growing, and they lasted for

the rest of your life, with occasional half-soling and a liberal application
of saddle soap or goose grease before you put them away in the spring.
The codger was hunched over a draft beer. He didn't look up when I came
in.

The bartender was another baldy, just like the desk clerks. A lot of
bald men in one small town. Maybe it was something in the water. I ordered a vodka gimlet on the rocks. He knew what it was, and mixed a
fine one, shaking it the way it should be made, not stirred. Most bartenders follow the recipe on the bottle, and make a gimlet tart enough to
pucker your asshole. But this one was mostly vodka, with just a flavor-
ing of the lime juice. Drink gimlets and you'll never get scurvy—right?
That's my excuse.

The bartender was wearing a lapel badge that read: "Call me Jimmy."

"Good drink, Jimmy," I said.

"Thank you, sir," he said. "I usually have some fresh lime to put in,
but that crowd last night cleaned me out. Maybe I'll have some more by
tomorrow, if you're still here."

"I'll be here," I said.

"Oh?" he said. "Staying in Coburn?"

"For awhile," I said.

The old character swung around on his barstool and almost fell off.

"What the hell for?" he demanded in a cracked, screaky voice. "Why
would anyone in his right mind want to stay in this piss-ass town?"

"Now, Mr. Coburn," the bartender soothed.

"Don't you 'Now, Mr. Coburn' me," the ancient grumbled. "I knowed
you when you was sloppin' hogs, and here you are still in the same line
of work."

I turned to look at him.

"Mr. *Coburn*?" I said. "Original settlers?"

"From the poor side of the family," he said with a harsh laugh. "The
others had the money and sense to get out."

"Now, Mr. Coburn," Jimmy said, again, nervously.

I saw the beer glass was almost empty.

"Buy you a drink, Mr. Coburn?" I asked respectfully.

"Why the hell not?" he said, and shoved the glass across the bar. "And
this time go easy on the head," he told the bartender. "When I want a
glass of froth, I'll tell you."

Jimmy sighed, and drew the brew.

"Mind if I join you, Mr. Coburn?" I asked.

"Come ahead," he said, motioning to the stool next to him.

When I moved over, I noticed he had a long gun case, an old, leather-
trimmed canvas bag, propped against the bar on his far side.

"Hunting?" I said, nodding toward the case.

"Was," he said, "but it's too damned wet after that storm. Ain't a
damned thing left worth shooting around here anyways. Except a few two-

legged creatures I could mention but won't. What you doing in town, sonny?''

There was no point in trying to keep it a secret, not after that tour of the village with Constable Goodfellow.

"I'm here to see Dr. Thorndecker," I said. "Of Crittenden Hall."

He didn't say anything, but something happened to that seamed face. Caterpillar brows came down. Bloodless lips pressed. Seared cheeks fell in. The elbow-chin jutted, and I thought I saw a sudden flare in those washed-blue eyes.

Then he lifted his glass of beer and drained it off, just drank it down in steady gulps, the wrinkled Adam's apple pumping away. He slammed the empty glass back down on the bar.

"Do me again, Jimmy," he gasped.

I nodded at the bartender, and motioned toward my own empty glass. We sat in silence. When our drinks were served, I glanced around. The bar was still empty. There were small tables for two set back in the gloom, and a few high-sided booths that could seat four.

"Why don't we make ourselves comfortable?" I suggested. "Stretch out and take it easy."

"Suits me," he grunted.

He picked up his beer and gun case, and led the way. I noticed his limp, a dragging of the right leg. He seemed active enough, but slow. He picked a booth for four, and slid onto one of the worn benches. I sat opposite him. I held out my hand.

"Samuel Todd," I said.

"Al Coburn," he said. His handshake was dry, and not too firm. "No relation to the Todds around here, are you?"

"Don't think so, sir," I said. "I'm from Ohio."

"Never been there," he said. "Never been out of New York State, to tell the truth. Went down to the City once."

"Like it?" I asked.

"No," he said. He glanced toward the bar where Jimmy was studiously polishing glasses, not looking in our direction. "What the hell you want with Thorndecker?"

I told him what I was doing in Coburn. He nodded.

"Read about it in the paper," he said. It was almost a Bostonian accent: "pay-puh." "Think he'll get the money?"

"Not for me to say," I said, shrugging. "You know him?"

"Oh, I know him," he said bitterly. "He's living on my land."

"*Your* land?"

"Coburn land," he said. "Originally. Was still in the family when my daddy died. He left me the farm and my sister the hill." Something happened to his eyes again: that flare of fury. "I thought I got the best of the deal. It was a working farm, and all she got was uncleared woods and a stretch of swamp."

"And then?" I prompted him.

"She married a dude from Albany. Some kind of a foreigner. His name ended in 'i' or 'o'. I forget."

I looked at him. He hadn't forgotten. Would never forget.

"He talked her into selling her parcels off. To a developer. I mean, she sold the *land*. Land that daddy left her."

I watched him raise his beer to his thin lips with a shaking hand. It means that much to some of the old-timers—land. It's not the money value they cherish. It's a piece of the world.

"Then what happened?" I asked him.

"The developer drained the swamp and cleared out most of the trees. Built houses. Sold the hill to a fellow named Crittenden who built the sick place."

"Crittenden Hall," I said.

"This was in the Twenties," he said. "Before the Great Depression. Before your time, sonny. Land was selling good then. My sister did all right. Then she and her foreigner upped and moved away."

"Where are they now?"

"Who the hell knows?" he rasped. "Or cares?"

"And what happened to your farm?"

"Ahh, hell," he said heavily. "My sons didn't take to farming. They moved away. Florida, California. Then I busted up my leg and couldn't get around so good. The old woman died of the cancer. I got tenants on the land now. I get by. But that Thorndecker, he's living on Coburn land. I ain't saying it's not perfectly legal and aboveboard. I'm just saying it's Coburn land."

I nodded, and signaled Jimmy for another round. But a waitress brought our drinks. There were three customers at the bar now, and from outside, in the restaurant, I could hear the sounds of the crank-up for the luncheon rush.

"You know Dr. Thorndecker, Mr. Coburn?" I asked him. "Personally?"

"I've met him," he said shortly.

"What do you think of him?"

His flaky eyelids rose slowly. He stared at me. But he didn't answer.

"Constable Goodfellow tells me all the best people in town are behind him one hundred percent," I said, pressing him. "That's Goodfellow's phrase: 'the best people'."

"Well, I ain't one of the best people," he said, "and I wouldn't trust that quack to cut my toenails."

He was silent a moment, then said sharply, "Goodfellow? How did you meet the Indian? My great-grandpa shot Indians hereabouts."

"He says Thorndecker sent him around. To see if I was settled in, if there was anything I needed, if I wanted to meet anyone in town."

Al Coburn stared down at what was left in his glass of beer. He was quiet a long time. Then he drained his glass, climbed laboriously to his feet, picked up his gun case. I stayed where I was. He stood alongside the table, looking down at me.

"You watch your step, Sam Todd," he said in that hard, creaking, old man's voice.

"Always do," I said.

He nodded and limped away a few steps. Then he stopped, turned, came back.

"Besides," he said, "I'm guessing it wasn't Thorndecker who sent Constable Goodfellow to see you. Thorndecker may be a fraud, but he ain't stupid."

"If not Thorndecker," I asked him, "then who?"

He stared at me.

"I reckon it was that hot-pants wife of his," he said grimly.

He was silent then, just standing there staring at me. It seemed to me he was trying to decide whether or not to say more. I waited. Finally he made up his mind . . .

"You know what they're doing out there?" he demanded. "In that laboratory of theirs?"

He pronounced it almost in the British manner: la*bor*atory.

I shrugged. "Biological research," I said. "Something to do with human cells."

"Devil's work!" he burst out, so forcibly I felt the spittle on my face. "It's devil's work!"

I sat up straight.

"What are you talking about?" I said harshly. "What does that mean—devil's work?"

"That's for me to know," he said, "and you to find out. Thank you kindly for the drinks."

He actually tipped that checked hunting cap to me. I watched him drag away.

I finished my drink, paid my tab, stalked out of the bar. That country breakfast had been enough; I didn't feel up to lunch. Went into the hotel lobby. Thumbed through magazines in a rack near the cigar counter. Waited until there were no customers. I wanted to talk to her alone.

"Hello, Millie," I said.

"Hi there!" she said, flapping her lashes like feather dusters. "Enjoying your visit to Coburn, Mr. Todd?"

So she had asked the desk clerk my name. I wondered if she had asked my room number, too.

"Lousy town," I said, watching her.

"You can say that again," she said, eyes dulling. "It died fifty years ago, but no one has enough money to give it a decent burial. Can I help you? Cigarettes? A magazine? *Anything?*"

She gave that "anything" the husky, Marilyn Monroe exhalation, arching her back, pouting. God help Constable Ronnie Goodfellow.

"Just information," I told her hastily. "How do I get to Dr. Thorndecker's place? Crittenden Hall?"

I tried to listen and remember as she told me how to drive east on Main Street, turn north on Oakland Drive, make a turn at Mike's Service Station onto Fort Peabody Drive, etc., etc. But I was looking at her and trying to figure why a hard, young Indian cop had married a used woman about five years older than he, and whose idea of bliss was probably a pound box of chocolate bonbons and the tenth rerun of "I Love Lucy."

When she ran down, I said, foolishly, "I met your husband this morning."

"I meet him every morning," she said. Then she added, "Almost."

She stared at me, suddenly very sober, very serious. Challenging.

I tried to smile. I turned around and walked away. I didn't know if it was good sense or cowardice. I did know I had misjudged this lady. Her idea of bliss wasn't the boob tube and bonbons. Far from it.

I found my car in the parking area, and while it was warming up, I scraped the ice off the windshield. Then I headed out of town.

I remember an instructor down in Ft. Benning telling us:

"You can stare at maps and aerial photos until your eyeballs are coming out your ass. But nothing can take the place of physical reconnaissance. Maps and photos are okay, but seeing the terrain and, if possible, walking over it, is a thousand times better. *Learn the terrain.* Know what the hell you're getting into. If you can walk over it before a firefight, maybe you'll walk out of it after."

So I had decided to go have a look at Dr. Telford Thorndecker's terrain.

By following Millie Goodfellow's directions, with a little surly assistance at Mike's Service Station, I found Crittenden Hall without too much difficulty. The grounds were less than a mile east of the river, the main buildings on the hill that had once belonged to Al Coburn's daddy.

The approach was through an area of small farms: stubbled land and beaten houses. Some of the barns and outbuildings showed light between warped siding; tarpaper roofing flapped forlornly; sprained doors hung open on rusty hinges. I saw farm machinery parked unprotected, and more than one field unpicked, the produce left to rot. It was cold, wet, desolate. Even more disturbing, there was no one around. I didn't see a pedestrian, pass another car, or glimpse anyone working the land or even taking out the garbage. The whole area seemed deserted. Like a plague had struck, or a neutron bomb dropped. The empty, weathered buildings leaned. Stripped trees cut blackly across the pewter sky. But the people were gone. No life. I ached to hear a dog bark.

The big sign read Crittenden Hall, and below was a small brass plaque: Crittenden Research Laboratory. There was a handsome cast iron fence at least six feet tall, with two ornate gates that opened inward. Inside was a guard hut just large enough for one man to sit comfortably, feet on a gas heater.

I drove slowly past. The ornamental iron fence became chain link, but it entirely enclosed the Thorndecker property. Using single-lane back roads, I was able to make a complete circuit. A lot of heavily wooded land. Some meadows. A brook. A tennis court. A surprisingly large cemetery, well-tended, rather attractive. People were dying to get in there. I finally saw someone: a burly guy in black oilskins with a broken shotgun over one arm. In his other hand was a leash. At the end of the leash, a straining German shepherd.

I came back to the two-lane macadam that ran in front of the main gate. I parked off the verge where I couldn't be seen from the guard hut. I got out, shivering, found my 7×50 field glasses in the messy trunk, got back in the car and lowered the window just enough. I had a reasonably good view of the buildings and grounds. The light was slaty, and the lens kept misting up, but I could see what I wanted to see.

I wasn't looking for anything menacing or suspicious. I just wanted to get a quick first impression. Did the buildings look in good repair? Were the grounds reasonably well-groomed? Was there an air of prosperity and good management—or was the place a dump, run-down and awaiting foreclosure?

Dr. Thorndecker's place got high marks. Not a broken window that I could see. Sashes and wooden trim smartly painted. Lawn trimmed, and dead leaves gathered. Trees obviously cared for, brick walks swept clean. Bushes and garden had been prepared for the coming winter. Storm windows were up.

All this spelled care and efficiency. It looked like a prosperous, functioning set-up with strong management that paid attention to maintenance and appearance even in this lousy weather at this time of year.

The main building, the largest building, was also, obviously, the oldest. Probably the original nursing home, Crittenden Hall. It was a three-story brick structure sited on the crest of the hill. The two-story wings were built on a slightly lower level. All outside walls were covered with ivy, still green. Roofs were tarnished copper. Windows were fitted with ornamental iron grilles, not unusual in buildings designed for the ill, infirm, aged, and/or loony.

About halfway down the hill was a newer building. Also red brick, but no ivy. And the roof was slated. The windows were also guarded, but with no-nonsense vertical iron bars. This building, which I assumed to be the Crittenden Research Laboratory, was not as gracefully designed as Crittenden Hall; it was merely a two-story box, with mean windows and a half-hearted attempt at an attractive Georgian portico and main entrance. Between nursing home and laboratory was an outdoor walk and stairway, a roofed port set on iron pillars, without walls.

There were several smaller outbuildings which could have been kitchens, labs, storehouses, supply sheds, whatever; I couldn't even guess. But everything seemed precise, trim, clean and well-preserved.

Then why did I get such a feeling of desolation?

It might have been that joyless day, the earth still sodden, the sky pressing down. It might have been that disconsolate light. Not light at all, really, but just moist steel. Or maybe it was Coburn and my mood.

All I know is that when I put down the binoculars, I had seen nothing that could possibly count against Dr. Telford Gordon Thorndecker and his grant application to the Bingham Foundation. Yet I felt something I struggled to analyze and name.

I stared at those winter-stark buildings on the worn hill, striving to grasp what it was I felt. It came to me on the trip back to Coburn. It wasn't fear. Exactly. It was dread.

After that little jaunt to the hinterland, Coburn seemed positively sparkling. I counted at least four pedestrians on Main Street. And look! There was a dog lifting his leg at a hydrant. Marvelous!

I parked and locked the car. What I wanted right then was—oh, I could think of a lot of things I wanted: vodka gimlet. Straight cognac. Coffee and Danish. Club sandwich and ale. Hot pastrami and Celery Tonic. Joan Powell. On rye. So I walked across Main Street to the office of the Coburn *Sentinel*.

It was a storefront with a chipped gold legend on the plate glass window: "Biggest little weekly in the State!" Just inside the door was a stained wooden counter where you could subscribe or buy a want-ad or complain your name was spelled wrong in that front-page story they did on the anniversary party at the Gulek Fat Processing Plant.

Behind the counter were a few exhausted desks, typewriters, swivel chairs. There was a small private office enclosed by frosted glass partitions. And in the rear was the printing area. Everything was ancient. Handset type, flatbed press. I guessed they did business cards, stationery, and fliers to pay the rent.

The place was not exactly a humming beehive of activity. There was a superannuated lady behind the counter. She was sitting on a high stool, clipping ads from old *Sentinels* with long shears. She had a bun of iron-gray hair with two pencils stuck into it. And she wore a cameo brooch at the ruffled neck of her shirtwaist blouse. She had just stepped off a *Saturday Evening Post* cover by Norman Rockwell.

Behind her, sitting at one of the weary desks, was a lissome wench. All of 18, I figured. The cheerleader type: so blond, so buxom, so healthy, so glowing that I immediately straightened my shoulders and sucked in my gut. Vanity, thy name is man. Miss Dimples was pecking away at an old Underwood standard, the tip of a pink tongue poked from one corner of her mouth. I'd have traded my Grand Prix for one—Enough. That way lies madness.

Farther to the rear, standing in front of fonts in the press section, a stringy character was setting type with all the blinding speed of a sloth on Librium. He was wearing an ink-smeared apron and one of those square caps printers fold out of newsprint. He was also wearing glasses with lenses like the bottoms of Coke bottles. I wondered about the *Sentinel*'s typos per running inch . . .

That whole damned place belonged in the Smithsonian, with a neat label: "American newspaper office, circa 1930." Actually, all of Coburn belonged in the same Institution, with a similar label. Time had stopped in Coburn. I had stepped into a warp, and any minute someone was going to turn on an Atwater Kent radio, and I'd hear Gene Austin singing "My Blue Heaven."

"May I help you?" the old lady said, looking up from her clipping.

"Is the editor in, please?" I asked. "I'd like to see him."

"Her," she said. "Our editor is female. Agatha Binder."

"Pardon me," I said humbly. "Might I see Miss, Mrs., or Ms. Binder?"

"About what?" she said suspiciously. "You selling something? Or got a complaint?"

I figured the Coburn *Sentinel* got a lot of complaints.

"No, no complaints," I said. I gave her my most winning smile, with no effect whatsoever. "My name is Samuel Todd. I'm with the Bingham Foundation. I'd like to talk to your editor about Dr. Telford Thorndecker."

"Oh," she said, "*that*. Wait right here."

She slid off the stool and went trotting back into the gloomy shop. She went into the closed office. She was out in a minute, beckoning me with an imperious forefinger. I pushed through the swinging gate. On the way back, I passed the desk of the nubile cheerleader. She was still pecking away at the Underwood, tongue still poked from her mouth.

"I love you," I whispered, and she looked up in alarm.

The woman sprawled behind the littered desk in the jumbled office was about my age, and fifty pounds heavier. She was wearing ink-stained painter's overalls over a red checkerboard shirt that looked like it was made from an Italian restaurant tablecloth. Her feet were parked on the desk, in unbuckled combat boots of World War II. There was a cardboard container of black coffee on the floor alongside her, and she was working on the biggest submarine sandwich I've ever seen. Meatballs.

Everything about her was massive: head, nose, jaw, shoulders, bosom, hips, thighs. The hands that held the sub looked like picnic hams, and her wrists were as thick as my ankles. But no ogre she. It all went together, and was even pleasing in a monumental way. If they had a foothill left over from Mt. Rushmore, they could have used it for her: rugged, craggy. Even the eyes were granite, with little sparkling lights of mica.

"Miss Binder," I said.

"Todd," she said, "sit down."

I sat.

Her voice was like her body: heavy, with an almost masculine rumble.

She never stopped munching away at that damned hoagie while we talked, and never stopped swilling coffee. But it didn't slow her down, and the meatballs didn't affect her diction. Much.

"Thorndecker getting his dough?" she demanded.

"That's not for me to say," I told her. How many times would I have to repeat that in Coburn? "I'm just here to do some poking. You know Thorndecker? Personally?"

"Sure, I know him. I know everyone in Coburn. He's a conceited, opinionated, sanctimonious, pompous ass. He's also the greatest brain I've ever met. So smart it scares you. He's a genius; no doubt about that."

"Ever hear any gossip about that nursing home of his? Patients mistreated? Lousy food? Things like that?"

"You kidding?" she said. "Listen, buster, I should live like Thorndecker's patients. Caviar for breakfast. First-run movies. He's got the best wine cellar in the county. And why not? They're paying for it. Listen, Todd, there are lots and lots of people in this country with lots and lots of money. The sick ones and the old ones go to Crittenden Hall to die in style—and that's what they get. I know most of the locals working up there—the aides, cooks, waitresses, and so forth. They all say the same thing: the place is a palace. If you've got to go, that's the way to do it. And when they conk off, as most of them eventually do, he even buries them, or has them cremated. At an added cost, of course."

"Yeah," I said, "I noticed the cemetery. Nice place."

"Oh?" she said. "You've visited Crittenden Hall?"

"Just a quick look," I said vaguely. "What about the research lab?"

"What about it?"

"Know anything about what they're doing up there?"

She kept masticating a meatball, but her expression changed. I mean the focus of her eyes changed, to what I call a "thousand-yard stare." Meaning she was looking at me, through me, and beyond. The same look I had seen in the eyes of the night clerk at the Coburn Inn when I had checked in and mentioned Thorndecker's name.

I had interrogated enough suspects in criminal cases in the army to know what that stare meant. It didn't necessarily mean they were lying or guilty. It usually meant they were making a decision on what and how much to reveal, and what and how much to hide. It was a signal of deep thought, calculating their own interests and culpability.

"No," she said finally, "I don't know what they're doing in the lab. Something to do with human cells and longevity. But all that scientific bullshit is beyond me."

She selected that moment to lean over and pick up her coffee cup. So I couldn't see her face, and maybe guess that she was lying?

"You know Thorndecker's family?" I asked her. "Wife? Daughter? The son? Can you tell me anything about them?"

"The wife's less than half his age," she said. "A real beauty. She's his second wife, you know. Julie comes into town occasionally. She dresses fancy. Buys her clothes on Fifth Avenue. Not your typical Coburn housewife.''

"Thinks she's superior?''

"I didn't say that,'' she said swiftly. "She's just not a mixer, that's all.''

"She and the doctor happy?''

Again she leaned away from me. This time to set the coffee container back on the floor.

"As far as I know,'' she said in that deep, rumbling voice. "You really dig, don't you?''

I ignored the question.

"What about the daughter?'' I asked. "Does she mix in Coburn's social life?''

"What social life?'' she jeered. "Two beers at the Coburn Inn? No, I don't see much of Mary either. It's not that the Thorndeckers are stand-offish, you understand, but they keep pretty much to themselves. Why the hell shouldn't they? What the fuck is there to do in this shithole?''

She peered at me, hoping I had been shocked by her language. But I had heard those words before.

"And the son?'' I asked. "Edward?''

"No secret about him,'' she said. "He's been bounced from a couple of prep schools. Lousy grades, I understand. Now he's living at home with a private tutor to get him ready for Yale or Harvard or wherever. I met him a few times. Nice kid. Very handsome. Like his pa. But shy, I thought. Doesn't say much.''

"But generally, you'd say the Thorndeckers are a close, loving American family?''

She looked at me suspiciously, wondering if I was putting her on. I was, of course, but she'd never see it in my expression.

"Well . . . sure,'' she said. "I suppose they've got their problems like everyone else, but there's never been any gossip or scandal, if that's what you mean.''

"Julie Thorndecker,'' I said, "the wife . . . she's a good friend of Constable Ronnie Goodfellow?''

The combat boots came off the desk onto the floor with a crash. Agatha Binder jerked toward me. Her mouth was open wide enough so I could see a chunk of half-chewed meatball.

"Where the hell did you hear that?'' she demanded.

"Around,'' I shrugged.

"Shit,'' she said, "that's just vicious gossip.''

"You just said there's never been any gossip about the Thorndeckers.''

She sat back, finished chewing and swallowing.

"You're a smartass, aren't you, Todd?''

I didn't answer.

She pushed the remnants of her sandwich aside. She leaned across the desk to me, ham-hands clasped. Her manner was very earnest, very sincere. Apparently she was staring directly into my eyes. But it's difficult to look steadily into someone else's eyes, even when you're telling the truth. The trick is to stare at the bridge of the nose, between the eyes. The effect is the same. I figured that's what she was doing.

"Look, buster," she said in a basso profundo rumble, "you're going to hear a lot of nasty remarks about the Thorndeckers. They're not the richest people hereabouts, but they ain't hurting. Anytime there's money, you'll hear mean, jealous gossip. Take it for what it's worth."

"All right," I said agreeably, "I will. Now how about Thorndecker's staff? I mean the top people. Know any of them?"

"I know Stella Beecham. She's an RN, supervisor of nurses and aides in Crittenden Hall. She practically runs the place. A good friend of mine. And I've met Dr. Draper. He's Thorndecker's Chief of Staff or Executive Assistant or whatever, in the research lab. I've met some of the others, but their names didn't register."

"Competent people?"

"Beecham certainly is. She's a jewel. Draper is the studious, scientific type. I've got nothing in common with him, but he's supposed to be a whiz. I guess the others in the lab are just as smart. Listen, I told you Thorndecker is a genius. He's a good administrator, too. He wouldn't hire dingbats. And the staff in the nursing home, mostly locals, do their jobs. They work hard."

"So Thorndecker's got no labor problems?"

"No way! Jobs are scarce around here, and he pays top dollar. Sick leave, pensions, paid vacation . . . the works. I'd like to work there myself."

"The hell you would," I said.

"Yeah," she said, grinning weakly. "The hell I would."

"You know Al Coburn?"

"That old fart?" she burst out. "He's been crazy as a loon since his wife died. Don't listen to anything *he* says."

"Well, I've got to listen to *someone*," I said. "Preferably someone who knows Thorndecker. Where does he bank?"

"Locally?" she said. "That would have to be the First Farmers & Merchants. The only bank in town. Around the corner on River Street. Next to the post office. The man to see is Arthur Merchant. He's president. That really is his name—Merchant. But the 'Merchants' in the bank's name has nothing to do with his. That means the bank was—"

"I get it, I get it," I assured her. "Just a fiendish coincidence. Life is full of them. Church? Is Thorndecker a church-goer?"

"He and his wife are registered Episcopalians, but they don't work at it."

"You're a walking encyclopedia of Coburn lore," I said admiringly. "You said, 'He and his wife.' What about the daughter? And the son?"

"I don't know what the hell Eddie is. A Boy Scout, I suspect."

"And the daughter? Mary?"

"Well . . . " she said cautiously. "Uh . . . "

"Uh?" I said. "What does 'Uh' mean?"

She punched gently at the tip of her nose with a knuckle.

"What the hell has that got to do with whether or not Dr. Thorndecker gets a grant from the Bingham Foundation?"

"Probably not a thing," I admitted. "But I'm a nosy bastard."

"You sure as hell are," she grumbled. "Well, if you must know, I heard Mary Thorndecker goes to a little church about five miles south of here. It's fundamentalist. Evangelical. You know—being born again, and all that crap. They wave their arms and shout, 'Yes, Lord!' "

"And speak in tongues," I said.

She looked at me curiously.

"You're not so dumb, are you?" she said.

"Dumb," I said, "but not so." I paused a moment, pondering. "Well, I can't think of anything else to ask. I want to thank you for your kind cooperation. You've been a big help."

"I have?" she said, surprised. "That's nice. I hope I've helped Thorndecker get his bread. He deserves it, and it would be a great help to this town."

"So I've heard," I said. "Listen, if I come up with any more questions, can I come around again?"

"Often as you like," she said, rising. I stood up too, and saw she was almost as tall as I am. A *big* woman. "Go see Art Merchant at the bank. He'll tell you anything you want to know. By the way, he's also mayor of Coburn."

"Fantastic," I said.

We were standing there, shaking hands and smiling idiotically at each other, when there was a timid knock on the door.

"Come in," Agatha Binder roared, dropping my hand.

The door opened hesitantly. There was my very own Miss Dimples. She looked even better standing up. Miniskirt. Yummy knees. Black plastic boots. A buttery angora sweater. I remembered an old army expression: "All you need with a dame like that is a spoon and a straw." She was holding a sheaf of yellow copy paper.

"Yes, Sue Ann?" the *Sentinel* editor said.

"I've finished the Kenner funeral story, Miss Binder," the girl faltered.

"Very good, Sue Ann. Just leave it. I'll get to it this afternoon."

The cheerleader dropped the copy on the desk and exited hastily, closing the door behind her. She hadn't glanced at me, but Agatha Binder was staring at me shrewdly.

"Like that?" she asked softly.

"It's okay," I said, flipping a palm back and forth. "Not sensational, but okay."

"Hands off, kiddo," she said in a harder voice, eyes glittering. "It's mine."

I was glad to hear it. I felt better immediately. The sensation of Coburn being in a time warp disappeared. I was back in the 1970s, and I walked out of there with my spirit leaping like a demented hart.

When I strolled into the lobby of the Coburn Inn, the baldy behind the desk signaled frantically.

"Where have you been?" he said in an aggrieved tone.

"Sorry I didn't check in," I said. "Next time I'll bring a note from home."

But he wasn't listening.

"Dr. Thorndecker has called you *three* times," he said. "He wants you to call him back as soon as possible. Here's the number."

Upstairs in my room, I peeled off the trenchcoat, kicked off the boots. I lay back on the hard bed. The telephone was on the rickety bedside table. Calls went through the hotel switchboard. I gave the number and waited.

"Crittenden Hall."

"Dr. Thorndecker, please. Samuel Todd calling."

"Just a moment, please."

Click, click, click.

"Crittenden Research Laboratory."

"Dr. Thorndecker, please. Samuel Todd calling."

"Just a monent, please."

Click, click, click.

"Lab."

"Dr. Thorndecker, please. Samuel Todd calling."

No clicks this time; just, "Hang on."

"Mr. Todd?"

"Yes, Dr. Thorndecker?"

"No. I'm sorry, Mr. Todd, but Dr. Thorndecker can't come to the phone at the moment. I'm Dr. Kenneth Draper, Dr. Thorndecker's assistant. How are you, sir?"

It was a postnasal-drip kind of voice: stuffed, whiny, without resonance.

"If I felt any better I'd be unconscious, thank you. I have a message to call Dr. Thorndecker."

"I know, sir. He's been trying to reach you all afternoon, but at the moment he's involved in a critical experiment."

I was trying to take my socks off with my toes.

"So am I," I said.

"Pardon, sir?"

"Childish humor. Forget it."

"Dr. Thorndecker asks if you can join the family for dinner tonight. Here at Crittenden Hall. Cocktails at six, dinner at seven."

"Be delighted," I said. "Thank you."

"Do you know how to get here, Mr. Todd? You drive east on Main Street, then—"

"I'll find it," I said hastily. "See you tonight. Thank you, Dr. Draper."

I hung up, and took off my socks the conventional way. I lay back on the bed, figuring to grab a nap for an hour or so, then get up and shower, shave, dress. But sleep wouldn't come. My mind was churning.

You've probably heard the following exchange on a TV detective drama, or read it in a detective novel:

Police Sergeant: "That guy is guilty as hell."

Police Officer: "Why do you say that?"

Police Sergeant: "Gut instinct."

Sometimes the sergeant says, "Gut feeling" or "A hunch." But the implication is that he's had an intuitive feeling, almost a subconscious inspiration, that has revealed the truth.

I asked an old precinct dick about this, and he said: "Bullshit."

Then he said: "Look, I don't deny that you get a gut feeling or a hunch about some cases, but it doesn't just appear out of nowhere. You get a hunch, and if you sit down and analyze it, you discover that what it is, is a logical deduction based on things you know, things you've heard, things you've seen. I mean that 'gut feeling' they're always talking about is really based on hard evidence. Instinct has got nothing to do with it."

I didn't have a gut feeling or a hunch about this Thorndecker investigation. What I had was more like a vague unease. So I started to analyze it, trying to discover what hard evidence had triggered it, and why it was spoiling my nap. My list went like this:

1. When a poor wife is killed accidentally, people cluck twice and say, "What a shame." When a rich wife is killed accidentally, people cluck once, say, "What a shame," and raise an eyebrow. Thorndecker's first wife left him a mil and turned his life around.

2. Thorndecker had released the story of his application for a Bingham Foundation grant to the local press. It wasn't unethical, but it was certainly unusual. I didn't buy Constable Goodfellow's story that it was impossible to keep a secret like that in a small town. Thorndecker could have prepared the application himself, or with the help of a single discreet aide, and no one in Coburn would have known a thing about it. So he had a motive for giving the story to the Coburn *Sentinel*. To rally the town on his side, knowing there'd be a field investigation?

3. Someone dispatched an armed cop to welcome me to Coburn. That was a dumb thing to do. Why not greet me in person or send an assistant? I didn't understand Goodfellow's role at all.

4. Al Coburn might have been an "old fart" to Agatha Binder, but I thought he was a crusty old geezer with all his marbles. So why had he

said, "You watch your step, Sam Todd?" Watch my step for *what*? And what the hell was that "devil's work" he claimed they were doing in the research lab?

5. Agatha Binder had called Thorndecker a "pompous ass" and put on a great show of being a tough, cynical newspaper editor. But she had been careful not to say a thing that might endanger the Bingham grant. Her answers to my questions were a beautiful example of manipulation, except when she blew her cool at my mention of the Julie Thorndecker-Ronnie Goodfellow connection. What the hell was going on *there*?

6. And while I was what-the-helling, just what the hell were Crittenden Hall (a nursing home) and the research laboratory doing with an armed guard and an attack dog patrolling the grounds? To make sure no one escaped from the cemetery?

7. That anonymous note: "Thorndecker kills."

Those were most of the reasons I could list for my "gut instinct" that all was not kosher with Dr. Thorndecker's application. There were a few other little odds and ends. Like Mrs. Cynthia's comment in the corridor of the Bingham Foundation: "I knew his father . . . it was all so sad . . . A sweet man." And the fact that the Crittenden Research Laboratory was supported, in part, by bequests from deceased patients of Crittenden Hall.

I agree that any or all of these questions might have had a completely innocent explanation. But they nagged, and kept me from sleeping. Finally, I got up, dug my case notebook from my suitcase, and jotted them all down, more or less in the form you just read.

They were even more disturbing when I saw them in writing. Something about this whole business reeketh in the nostrils of a righteous man (me), and I didn't have a clue to what it was. So I solved the whole problem in my usual decisive, determined manner.

I shaved, showered, dressed, went down to the bar, and had two vodka gimlets.

I started out for Crittenden Hall about five-thirty. At that time of year it was already dark, and once I got beyond the misty, haloed street lights of Coburn, the blackness closed in. I was falling down a pit, and my low beams couldn't show the end of it. Naked tree trunks whipped by, a stone embankment, culvert, a plank bridge. But I kept falling, leaning forward over the steering wheel and bracing for the moment when I hit bottom.

I never did, of course. Instead of the bottom of the pit, I found Crittenden Hall, and pulled up to those ornate gates. The guard came ambling out of his hut and put a flashlight on me. I shouted my name, he swung the gates open, I drove in. The iron clanged shut behind me.

I followed the graveled roadway. It curved slowly through lawn that was black on this moonless night. The road ended in a generous parking area in front of Crittenden Hall. As I was getting out of the car, I saw portico lights come on. The door opened, someone stepped out.

I paused a moment. I was in front of the center portion of the main building, the old building. The two wings stretched away in the darkness. At close range, the Hall was larger than I expected: a high three stories, mullioned windows, cornices of carved stone. The style was vaguely Georgian, with faint touches—like narrow embrasures—of a castle built to withstand Saracen archers.

A lady came forward as I trudged up to the porch. She was holding out a white hand, almost covered by the ruffled lace cuff of her gown.

"Welcome to Crittenden, Mr. Todd," she said, smiling stiffly. "I'm Mary Thorndecker."

While I was shaking the daughter's cold hand and murmuring something I forget, I was taking her in. She was Alice in Wonderland's maiden aunt in a daisied gown designed by Tenniel. I mean it billowed to her ankles, all ribbons and bows. The high, ruffled collar matched the lace cuffs. The waist was loosely crumpled with a wide velvet ribbon belt. If Mary Thorndecker had breasts, hips, ass, they were effectively concealed.

Inside the Hall, an attendant came forward to take my hat and coat. He was wearing a short, white medical jacket and black trousers. He might have been a butler, but he was built like a linebacker. When he turned away from me, I caught the bulge in his hip pocket. This bucko was carrying a sap. All right, I'll go along with that in an establishment where some of the guests were not too tightly wrapped.

"Now this is the main floor," Mary Thorndecker was babbling away, "and in the rear are the dining room, kitchen, social rooms, and so forth. The library, card room, and indoor recreational area. All used by our guests. Their private suites, the medical rooms, the doctors' offices and nurses' lounges, and so forth, are in the wings. We're going up to the second floor. That's where we live. Our private home. Living room, dining room, our own kitchen, daddy's study, sitting room . . . all that."

"And the third floor?" I inquired politely.

"Bedrooms," she said, frowning, as if someone had uttered a dirty word.

It was a handsome staircase, curving gracefully, with a gleaming carved oak balustrade. The walls were covered with ivory linen. I expected portraits of ancestors in heavy gilt frames. At least a likeness of the original Mr. Crittenden. But instead, the wall alongside the stairway was hung with paintings of flowers in thin black frames. All kinds of flowers: peonies, roses, poppies, geraniums, lilies . . . everything.

The paintings blazed with fervor. I paused to examine an oil of lilac branches in a clear vase.

"The paintings are beautiful," I said, and I meant it.

Mary Thorndecker was a few steps ahead of me, higher than me. She stopped suddenly, whirled to look down.

"Do you think so?" she said breathlessly. "Do you *really* think so? They're mine. I mean I painted them. You *do* like them?"

"Magnificent," I assured her. "Bursting with life."

Her long, saturnine face came alive. Cheeks flushed. Thin lips curved in a warm smile. The dark eyes caught fire behind steel-rimmed granny glasses.

"Thank you," she said tremulously. "Oh, thank you. Some people . . . "

She left that unfinished, and we continued our climb in silence. On the second floor landing, a man stumbled forward, hand outstretched. His expression was wary and hunted.

"Yes, Mary," he said automatically. Then: "Samuel Todd? I'm Kenneth Draper, Dr. Thorndecker's assistant. This is a . . . "

He left that sentence unfinished, too. I wondered if that was the conversational style in Crittenden Hall: half-sentences, unfinished thoughts, implied opinions.

Agatha Binder had said Draper was a "studious, scientific type . . . supposed to be a whiz." He might have been. He was also a nervous, jerky type . . . supposed to be a nut. He shook hands and wouldn't let go; he giggled inanely when I said, "Happy to meet you," and he succeeded in walking up my heels when he ushered me into the living room of the Thorndeckers' private suite.

I got a quick impression of a high vaulted room richly furnished, lots of brocades and porcelains, a huge marble-framed fireplace with a blaze crackling. And I was ankle-deep in a buttery rug. That's all I had a chance to catch before Draper was nudging me forward to the two people seated on a tobacco-brown suede couch facing the fireplace.

Edward Thorndecker lunged to his feet to be introduced. He was 17, and looked 12, a young Botticelli prince. He was all blue eyes and crisp black curls, with a complexion so enameled I could not believe he had ever shaved. The hand he proffered was soft as a girl's, and about as strong. There was something in his voice that was not quite a lisp. He did not say, "Pleathed to meet you, Mithter Todd," it was not that obvious, but he did have trouble with his sibilants. It made no difference. He could have been a mute, and still stagger you with his physical beauty.

His stepmother was beautiful, too, but in a different way. Edward had the beauty of youth; nothing in his smooth, flawless face marked experience or the passage of years. Julie Thorndecker had stronger features, and part of her attraction was due to artifice. If Mary Thorndecker found inspiration for her art in flowers, Julie found it in herself.

I remember well that first meeting. Initially, all I could see were the satin evening pajamas, the color of fresh mushrooms. Full trousers and a tunic cinched with a mocha sash. The neckline plunged, and there was something in that glittery, slithery costume that convinced me she was naked beneath, and if I listened intently I might hear the whispery slide of soft satin on softer flesh. She was wearing high-heeled evening sandals, thin ribbons of silver leather. Her bare toes were long, the nails painted a crimson as dark as old blood. There was a slave bracelet of fine gold links around one slender ankle.

I was ushered to an armchair so deep I felt swallowed. Mary Thorndecker and Dr. Draper found chairs—close to each other, I noted—and there was a spate of fast, almost feverish small talk. Most of it consisted of questions directed at me. Yes, I had driven up from New York. Yes, Coburn seemed a quiet, attractive village. No, I had no idea how long I'd stay—a few days perhaps. My accommodations at the Inn were certainly not luxurious, but they were adequate. Yes, the food was exceptionally good. No, I had not yet met Art Merchant. Yes, it had certainly been a terrible storm, with all the lights off and power lost. I said:

"But I suppose you have emergency generators, don't you, Dr. Draper?"

"What?" he said, startled at being addressed. "Oh, yes, of course we do."

"Naturally," I nodded. "I imagine you have valuable cultures in the lab under very precise temperature control."

"We certainly do," he said enthusiastically. "Why, if we lost refrigeration even for—"

"Oh, Kenneth, please," Julie Thorndecker said lazily. "No shop talk tonight. Just a social evening. Wouldn't you prefer that, Mr. Todd?"

I remember bobbing my head violently in assent, but I was too stunned by her voice to make any sensible reply.

It was a husky voice, throaty, almost tremulous, with a kind of crack as if it was changing. It was a different voice, a stirring voice, an adorable voice. It made me want to hear her murmur and whisper. Just the thought of it rattled my vertebrae.

Before I had a chance to make a fool of myself by asking her to read aloud from the Coburn telephone directory, I was saved by the entrance of the gorilla who had taken my hat and coat. He was pushing a wheeled cart laden with ice bucket, bottles, mixes, glasses.

"Daddy will be along in a few minutes," Mary Thorndecker told us all. "He said to start without him."

That was fine with me; I needed something. Preferably two somethings. I was conscious of currents in that room: loves, animosities, personal conflicts that I could only guess from glances, tones of voice, turned shoulders, and sudden changes of expression I could not fathom.

Julie and Edward Thorndecker each took a glass of white wine. Mary had a cola drink. Dr. Draper asked for a straight bourbon, which brought a look of sad reproof from Mary. Not seeing any lime juice on the cart, I opted for a vodka martini and watched the attendant mix it. He slugged me—a double, at least—and I wondered if those were his instructions.

While the drinks were being served, I had a chance to make a closer inspection of the room from the depths of my feather bed. My first impression was reinforced: it was a glorious chamber. The overstuffed furniture was covered with brown leather, beige linen, chocolate velvet. Straight chairs and tables were blond French provincial, and looked to me to be antiques of museum quality. There was a cocktail table of brass and smoked glass, the draperies were batik, and the unframed paintings on the walls were abstracts in brilliant primary colors.

In the hands of a decorator of glitchy taste, this eclecticism would have been a disaster. But it all came together; it pleased the eye and was comfortable to a sinful degree. Part of the appeal, I decided, was due to the noble proportions of the room itself, with its high ceiling and the perfect ratio between length and width. There are some rooms that would satisfy even if they were empty, and this was one of them.

I said something to this effect, and Julie and Edward exchanged congratulatory smiles. If it was their taste reflected here, their gratification was warranted. But I saw Mary Thorndecker's lips tighten slightly—just a prim pressing together—and I began to glimpse the outlines of the family feuds.

We were on our second round—the talk louder now, the laughs more frequent—when the hall door banged open, and Dr. Telford Gordon Thorndecker swept into the room. There's no other phrase for it: he swept in, the President arriving at the Oval Office. Dr. Kenneth Draper jerked to his feet. Edward stood up slowly. I struggled out of my down cocoon, and even Mary Thorndecker rose to greet her father. Only Julie remained seated.

"Hello, hello, hello, all," he said briskly, and I was happy to note I had been correct: it was a rumbling baritone, with deep resonance. "Sorry I'm late. A minor crisis. Very minor! Darling . . ." He swooped to kiss his young wife's cheek. "And you must be Samuel Todd of the Bingham Foundation. Welcome to Crittenden. This *is* a pleasure. Forgive me for not greeting you personally, but I see you've been well taken care of. Excellent! Excellent! How are you, Mr. Todd? A small scotch for me, John. Well, here we are! This *is* nice."

I've seen newsreels of President Franklin Roosevelt, and this big man had the same grinning vitality, the energy, and raw exuberance of Roosevelt. I've met politicians, generals, and business executives, and I don't impress easily. But Thorndecker overwhelmed me. When he spoke to you, he gave the impression of speaking only to *you*, and not talking just to hear the sound of his own voice. When he asked a question, he made you feel he was genuinely interested in your opinion, he was hanging on your every word, and if he disagreed, he still respected your intelligence and sincerity.

The photograph I had seen of him was a good likeness; he was a handsome man. But the black-and-white glossy hadn't prepared me for the physical presence. All I could think of was that he was smarter, better looking, and stronger than I was. But I didn't resent it. That was his peculiar gift: your admiration was never soured with envy. How could you envy or be jealous of an elemental force?

He took command immediately. We were to finish our drinks at once, and file into the dining room. This is how we'd be seated, this is what we'd eat, these were the wines we'd find superb, and so forth. And all this without the touch of the Obersturmführer. He commanded with humor, a self-deprecating wit, and a cheerful willingness to bend to anyone's whims, no matter how eccentric he found them.

If the table in the rather gloomy dining room had been set to make an impression on me, it did. Pewter serving plates, four crystal wine glasses and goblets at each setting, a baroque silver service, fresh flowers, slender white tapers in a cast iron candelabrum.

I sat on Thorndecker's right. Next to me was Dr. Draper. Julie was at the foot of the table. On her right was Edward, and across from me was Mary, on Thorndecker's left. Cozy.

The moment we were seated, two waitresses with starched white aprons over staid black dresses appeared and began serving. We had smoked salmon with chopped onion and capers; a lobster bisque; an enormous Beef Wellington carved at the table; a potato dish that seemed to be mixed tiny balls of white and sweet potatoes, boiled and then sautéed in seasoned butter; fresh green beans; buttered baby carrots; endive salad with hearts of palm; raspberry sherbet; espresso or regular coffee.

I've had better meals, but never in a private home. If the beans were overcooked and the crust of the Wellington a bit soggy, it could be forgiven or forgotten for the sake of the wines Thorndecker uncorked and the efficiency of the service. Every time my wine glass got down to the panic level, one of the waitresses or the gorilla-butler was at my elbow to refill it. Hot rolls and sweet butter were passed incessantly. It seemed to me that I had only to wish another spoonful of those succulent potatoes, when presto! they appeared on my plate.

"Do your patients eat as well?" I asked Thorndecker.

"Better," he assured me, smiling. "We have one old lady who regularly imports truffles from the south of France. Two years ago we had an old gentleman who brought along his private chef. That man—the chef, I mean—was a genius. A genius! I tried to hire him, but he refused to cook for more than four at a time."

"What happened to him?" I asked. "Not the chef, the old gentleman."

"Deceased," Thorndecker said easily. "Are you enjoying the dinner?"

"Very much so," I said.

"Really?" he said, looking into my eyes. "I thought the beans overcooked and the Wellington crust a bit soggy. Delighted to hear I was wrong."

The conversation was dominated by Dr. Thorndecker. Maybe "directed" is a better word, because he spoke very little himself. But he questioned his children and wife about their activities during the day, made

several wry comments on their reports, asked them about their plans for
the following day. I had a sense of custom being honored, a nightly interrogation. If Thorndecker had planned to present a portrait of domestic
felicity, he succeeded admirably.

Between courses, and during Thorndecker's quizzing, I had an opportunity to observe the ménage more closely. I picked up some interesting
impressions to store away, for mulling later.

Edward Thorndecker had been reasonably alert and cheerful prior to his
father's appearance; after, he became subdued, somewhat sullen.

Julie wore her hair cut quite short. It was fine, silvered, brushed close
to her skull. It appeared to be an extension of her satin pajamas, as if she
was wearing a helmet of the same material.

Dr. Kenneth Draper drank too much wine too rapidly, looking up frequently to Mary Thorndecker to see if she was noticing.

Thorndecker himself had a remarkably tanned face. At that time of year,
it was either pancake makeup or regular use of a suntan lamp. When I
caught him in profile, it suddenly occurred to me he might have had a
face-lifting.

The servants were efficient, but unsmiling. Conversations between
servants and family were kept to a minimum. Instructions for serving were
given by Mary Thorndecker. I had the oddest notion that she was mistress
of the house. In fact, on appearance alone, she could have been Thorndecker's wife, and Julie and Edward their children.

Thorndecker's pleasantness had its limits; his elbow was joggled by one
of the waitresses, and I caught the flash of anger in his eyes. I didn't hear
what he muttered to her.

After his fourth glass of wine, Dr. Draper stared at Mary Thorndecker
with what I can only describe as hopeless passion. I was convinced the
poor mutt was smitten by her charms. What they were escaped me.

I wondered if Julie and Edward Thorndecker were holding hands under
the tablecloth, improbable as that seemed.

Dr. Thorndecker was wearing a cologne or after-shave lotion that I
found fruity and slightly sickening.

Mary Thorndecker, with her thin, censorious lips, seemed disapproving
of this flagrant display of rich food and strong drink. She ate sparingly,
drank nothing but mineral water. Very admirable, even if it was imported
water.

Julie was a gamine, with an inexhaustible supply of expressions: pouts,
smiles, moues, frowns, grins, leers. In repose, her face was a beautifully
tinted mask, triangular, with high cheekbones and stung lips. Occasionally
she bit the full lower lip with her sharp upper teeth, a stimulating sight.

Never once during the meal did Mary address Julie directly, or vice
versa. In fact, they both seemed to avoid looking at each other.

That was about all I was able to observe and remember. It was enough.

I was on my second cup of espresso, replete and wondering how I might cadge a brandy, when the butler-gorilla entered hurriedly. He went directly to Dr. Kenneth Draper, leaned down, whispered in his ear. I saw this happen. I saw Draper's Bordeaux-flushed cheeks go suddenly white. He looked to Dr. Thorndecker. If a signal passed between them, I didn't catch it. But Draper rose immediately, weaving slightly. He excused himself, thanking the Thorndeckers for the " 'nificent dinner," addressing himself to Mary. Then he was gone, and no one commented on it.

"A brandy, Mr. Todd?" Telford Thorndecker sang out. "Cognac? Armagnac? I have a calvados I think you'll like. Let's all move back to the living room and give them a chance to clean up in here and get home at a reasonable hour. All right, everyone . . . up and out!"

We straggled back into the living room: Julie, Edward, Thorndecker, me. Mary stayed behind, for housewifely chores I suppose. Maybe to make sure that no one swagged a slice of that soggy Beef Wellington.

The calvados was good. Not great, but good. Julie took a thimbleful of green Chartreuse. Edward got a stick in the eye.

"Don't you have homework to do, young man?" Thorndecker demanded sternly.

"Yes, father," the youth said. A crabbed voice, surly manner.

But he said his goodnights politely enough, kissing his stepmother and father, on their cheeks, offering me his limp hand again. We watched him leave.

"Good-looking boy," I offered.

"Yes," Thorndecker said shortly. "Now take a look at this, Mr. Todd. I think you'll be interested."

We left Julie curved felinely in a corner of the suede couch, running a tongue tip around the rim of her liqueur glass. Thorndecker showed me a small collection of eighteenth-century miniatures, portraits painted on thin slices of ivory. I admired those, and Sevres porcelains, a beautifully crafted antique microscope in gleaming brass, a set of silver-mounted flintlock duelling pistols, an ornate Italian mantel clock that showed the time of day, date, phases of the moon, constellations, tides and, for all I know, when to take the meatloaf out of the oven.

Thorndecker's attitude toward these treasures was curious. He knew the provenance of everything he owned. He was proud of them. But I don't think he really *liked* them. They were valuable possessions, and fulfilled some desire he had to surround himself with beautiful things of value. He could have collected Duesenbergs or rare Phoenician coins. It would be all the same to him.

"It's a magnificent room," I told him.

"Yes," he said, nodding, looking about, "yes, it is. A few pieces I inherited. But Julie selected most of them. She decorated this room. She and Edward. It's what I've wanted all my life. A room like this."

I said nothing.

We strolled back to his wife. She rose as we approached, finishing her

Chartreuse, set the empty glass on the serving cart. Then she did an incredible thing.

She lifted her slender arms high above her head and stretched wide, yawning. I looked at her with amazement. She was a small, perfectly formed woman: a cameo body. She stood there, weight on one leg, hipsprung, her feet apart. Her head was back, throat taut, mouth yawned open, lips wet and glistening.

Thorndecker and I stood there, frozen, staring at that strained torso, hard nipples poking the shining stuff. Then she relaxed, smiling at me.

"Please forgive me," she said in that throaty voice. "The wine . . . I think I'll run along to bed."

We exchanged pleasantries. I briefly held the sinewy hand she offered.

"Don't be long, darling," she said to her husband, drawing fingertips down his cheek.

"I—I—I won't," he stammered, completely undone.

We watched her sway from the room. The gleaming satin rippled.

"Another calvados?" Thorndecker said hoarsely.

"Another drink, thank you," I said. "But I see you have cognac there. I'd prefer that, if I may, sir."

"Of course, of course," he muttered.

"Then I'll be on my way," I promised him. "I'm sure you have a full day tomorrow."

"Not at all," he said dully, and poured us drinks.

We sat on the suede couch, staring into dying embers.

"I suppose you'll want to see the place?" he said.

"I would, yes," I acknowledged. "The nursing home and the lab."

"Tomorrow morning? And stay for lunch?"

"Oh no," I said. "Not after that dinner! I'll skip lunch tomorrow. Would—oh, say about one o'clock be convenient? I have things to do in the morning."

"One o'clock would be fine," he said. "I may not be able to show you around myself, but I'll tell Draper to be available. He'll show you everything. I'll make that very clear. Anything and everything you want to see."

"Thank you, sir," I said.

We were turned half-sideways to converse. Now his heavy eyes rose to lock with mine.

"You don't have to call me 'sir'," he said.

"All right," I said equably.

"If you have any questions, Draper will answer them. If he can't, I will."

"Fine."

Pause, while we both sipped our drinks daintily.

"Of course," he said, "you may have some personal questions for me."

I considered a moment.

"No," I said, "I don't think so."

He seemed surprised at that. And maybe a little disappointed.

"I mean about my personal life," he explained. "I know how these grant investigations work. You want to know all about me."

"We know a great deal about you now, Dr. Thorndecker," I said, as gently as I could.

He sighed, and seemed to shrivel, hunching down on the couch. He looked every one of his 54 years. Suddenly I realized what it was: this man was physically tired. He was bone-weary. All the youthful vigor had leaked out of him. He had put in a strenuous, stressful day, and he wanted nothing more at this point than to crawl into bed next to his warm, young wife, melt down beneath the covers, and sleep. To tell you the truth, I felt much the same myself.

"I suppose," he said, ruminating in a low voice, "I suppose you find it odd that a man my age would have a wife young enough to be my daughter. Younger than my daughter."

"Not odd," I said. "Understandable. Maybe fifty, or even thirty or twenty years ago, it would have been considered odd. But not today. New forms of relationships. The old prejudices out the window. It's a whole new ballgame."

But he wasn't listening to my cracker-barrel philosophy.

"She means so much to me," he said wonderingly. "So much. You have no idea how she has made—"

His confessions disturbed me and embarrassed me. I drained my drink and stood up.

"Dr. Thorndecker," I said formally, "I want to thank you and your wife and your family for your gracious hospitality. A very pleasant evening, and I hope we—"

But at that precise instant the hall door was flung open. Dr. Kenneth Draper stood rooted. He was wearing a stained white lab coat. He had jerked his tie loose and opened his collar. His eyes were blinking furiously, and I wondered if he was about to cry.

"Dr. Thorndecker," he said desperately, "please, can you come? At once? It's Petersen."

Thorndecker finished his drink slowly, set the glass slowly aside. Now he looked older than his 54 years. He looked defeated.

"Do you mind?" he asked me. "A patient with problems. I'm afraid he won't last the night. We'll do what we can."

"Of course," I said. "You go ahead. I can find my way out. Thank you again, doctor."

We shook hands. He smiled stiffly, moved brokenly to the door. He and Draper disappeared. I was alone. So, what the hell, I poured myself another small brandy and slugged it down. I took a final look around that splendid room and then wandered out onto the second floor landing. In truth, I was feeling no pain.

I had taken one step down the stairway when I heard the sound of running feet behind me. I turned. Mary Thorndecker came dashing up.

"Take this," she said breathlessly. "Don't look at it now. Read it later."

She thrust a folded paper into my hand, whirled, darted away, the long calico gown snapping about her ankles. I wondered if she was heading for a brisk run through the heather, shouting, "Heathcliff! Heathcliff!"

I stuffed the folded paper into my side pocket. I walked down that long, long stairway as erect and dignified as I could make it. The butler-gorilla was waiting below with my coat and hat.

"Nighty-night," I said.

"Yeah," he said.

I drove slowly, very, very slowly, around the graveled road to the gates. They opened magically for me. I turned onto the paved road, went a few hundred yards, then pulled off onto the verge. I switched off engine and lights. It was raw as hell, and I huddled down inside my leather trenchcoat and wished I had a small jug of brandy to keep me alive. But all I could do was wait. So I waited. Don't ask me what I was waiting for; I didn't know. Maybe I figured it was best not to drive on unfamiliar roads in my condition. Maybe I was just sleepy. I don't know what my motives were; I'm just telling you what happened.

The cold woke me up. I snapped out of my daze, shivering. I glanced at the luminous dial of my watch; it was almost 2:00 A.M. I had left Crittenden Hall before midnight. Now I was sober, with a headache that threatened to break down the battlements of my skull. I lighted a cigarette and tried to remember if I had misbehaved during the evening, insulted anyone, done anything to besmirch the Bingham Foundation escutcheon. I couldn't think of a thing. Other than developing an enormous lech for Julie Thorndecker—which no one could possibly be aware of, except, perhaps, Julie Thorndecker—I had conducted myself in exemplary fashion as far as I could recall.

I was leaning forward to snub out my cigarette when I saw the lights. One, two, three of them, bobbing in line from the rear of Crittenden Hall, heading out into the pitchy grounds.

I slid from the car, leaving the door open. I went loping along outside the chain-link fence, trying to keep the lights in view. They moved up and down in a regular rhythm: marching men carrying flashlights or battery lanterns.

The fence curved around. I ran faster to catch up, happy that whoever had planned the security of Crittenden had cleared the land immediately outside the fence. No bushes, no trees. I was running on half-frozen stubble, the ground resisting, then squishing beneath my feet.

I came up to them, raised a hand to shield my mouth so they might not spot the white vapor of my breath. Another light came on, a more powerful lantern. I moved along with them, hanging back a little, the fence between us, and the bare trees on the Crittenden grounds.

Four men, at least. Then, in the lantern's beam, I saw more. Six men, heavily muffled against the cold. Three of them were hauling a wheeled cart. And on the cart, a black burden, a bulk, a box, a coffin.

When they stopped, I stopped. Crouched down. Lay down on the frost-silvered grass. The beams of flashlights and lanterns concentrated. I could see an open grave. A mound of loose earth at one side. I had not seen that during my afternoon reconnaissance.

The load was taken off the cart. A plain box. I could hear the grunts of the lifting men from where I lay. The coffin was slid into the open hole. One end first, and then it was dropped and allowed to thump to the bottom. Shovels had been brought. Two men attacked the mound of loose dirt, working slowly but steadily. The first few shovelfuls rattled on the coffin lid. Then, as the grave filled, they worked in silence. All I could see were the steady beams of light, the lifting, swinging, dumping shovels. Then the flash of empty shovel blades.

The grave was filled, the loose earth smacked down and rounded. Squares of sod were placed over the raw dirt. Then the procession, still silent, turned back to Crittenden Hall. I watched them go, knowing a chill without, a chill within. The lights bobbed slowly away. They went out, one by one.

I lay there as long as I could endure it, teeth making like castanets, feet and hands lumpy and dull. Then I made a run for my car, hobbling along as fast as I could, trying to flex my fingers, afraid to feel my nose in case it had dropped off.

I got the heater going, held my hands in front of the vents, and in a few minutes reckoned I'd live to play the violin again. I drove away from there at a modest speed, hoping the gate guard and roving night sentinel (if there was one) wouldn't spot my lights.

I told myself that both Thorndecker and Draper were licensed MD's, and could sign a death certificate. I told myself that one of the shrouded figures with flashlight or lantern could have been a licensed mortician. I told myself all sorts of nonsense. The cadaver was infected with a deadly plague and had to be put underground immediately. Or, all burials were made at this hour so as not to disturb the other withering guests of Crittenden Hall. Or, the dead man or woman was without funds, without family, without friends, and this surreptitious entombment was a discreet way of putting a pauper to rest.

I didn't believe a word of it. Of any of it. That slow procession of shadowed figures and bobbing lights scared the hell out of me. I had a wild notion of giving Dr. Telford Gordon Thorndecker an A-plus rating and, as quickly as possible, getting my ass back to the familiar violence of New York City. A dreadful place with one saving grace: the dead were buried during daylight hours.

The lobby of the Coburn Inn did nothing to lift my spirits or inspire confidence in a better tomorrow. It was almost three in the morning; only a night light on the desk shed a ghastly, orange-tinted glow. The place was totally empty. I guessed the night clerk was snoozing in the back office, and Sam Livingston was corking off in his basement hideaway.

I looked around at the slimy tiled floor, the shabby rugs, the tattered couches and armchairs. Even the plastic ferns in the old brass spittoons seemed wilted. And over all, the smell of must and ash, the stink of age and decay. The Coburn Inn: Reasonable Rates and Instant Senescence.

I didn't have the heart to wake Sam Livingston to run me up, so I trudged the stairway, still bone-chilled, muscle-sore, brain-dulled. I got to room 3-F all right, seeing not a soul in the shadowed corridors. But there was enough illumination to see that the door of my room was open a few inches. I had left it locked.

Adrenaline flowed; I moved cautiously. The room was dark. I kicked the door open wider, reached around, flicked the light switch. Someone had paid me a visit. My suitcases and briefcase had been upended, contents dumped on the floor. The few things I had stowed away in closet and bureaus had been pulled out and trashed. Even my toilet articles had been pawed over. The mattress on that hard bed had been lifted and tipped. Chairs were lying on their sides, the bottom coverings slit, and the few miserable prints on the walls had been taken off their hooks and the paper backing ripped away.

I made a quick check. As far as I could see, nothing was missing. Even my case notebook was intact. My wallet of credit cards was untouched. So why the toss? I gave up trying to figure it, or anything else that had happened that black night. All I wanted was sleep.

I restored the bed to reasonable order, but left all the rest of the stuff exactly where it was, on the floor. I started undressing then, so weary that I was tempted to flop down with my boots on. It was when I was taking off my jacket that I found, in the side pocket, the folded paper that Mary Thorndecker had slipped me just before I left Crittenden Hall.

I unfolded it gingerly, like it might be a letter bomb. But it was only a badly printed religious tract, one of those things handed out on street corners by itinerant preachers. This one was headed: WHERE WILL YOU SPEND ETERNITY?

Not, I hoped, at the Coburn Inn.

The Third Day

Constable Ronnie Goodfellow stood with arms akimbo, surveying the wreckage of my hotel room.

"Shit," he said.

"My sentiments exactly," I said. "But look, it's no big deal. Nothing was stolen. The only reason I wanted you to know was if it fits a pattern of hotel room break-ins. You've had them before?"

Sleek head turned slowly, dark eyes observed me thoughtfully. Finally . . .

"You a cop?" he said.

"No, but I've had some training. Army CID."

"Well, there's no pattern. Some petty pilferage in the kitchen maybe, but there hasn't been a break-in here since I've been on the force. Why should there be? What is there to steal in this bag of bones? The regulars who live here are all on Social Security. Most of the time they haven't got two nickels to rub together."

He took slow steps into the room, looking about.

"The bed tossed?" he asked.

"That's right. I put it straight so I could get some sleep last night."

He nodded, still looking around with squinty eyes. Suddenly he swooped, picked up one of those vomit-tinted prints that had hung on the tenement-green wall. He inspected the torn paper backing.

"Looking for something special," he said. "Something small and flat that could be slid between the backing and the picture. Like a photo, a sheet of paper, a document, a letter. Something like that."

I looked at him with new respect. He was no stupe.

"Got any idea what it could be?" he asked casually.

"Not a clue," I said, just as off-handedly. "I haven't got a thing like that worth hiding."

He nodded again, and there was nothing in that smooth, saturnine face to show if he believed me or not.

"Well . . ." he said, "maybe I'll go down and have a few words with Sam Livingston."

"You don't think—" I began.

"Of course not," he said sharply. "Sam's as honest as the day is long. But maybe he saw someone prowling around late at night. He's up all hours. You say you got in late?"

I hadn't said. I hoped he didn't catch the brief pause before I answered.

"A little after midnight," I lied. "I had dinner with the Thorndeckers."

"Oh?" he said. "Have a good time?"

"Sure did. Great food. Good company." Then I added, somewhat maliciously: "Mrs. Thorndecker is a beauty."

"Yes," he said, almost absently, "a very attractive woman. Well, I'll see what I can do about this, Mr. Todd. Sorry it had to happen to a visitor to our town."

"Happens everywhere," I shrugged. "No real harm done."

I closed and locked the door behind him. He hadn't inspected that lock, but I had. No sign of forced entry. That was one for me. But he had seen that the object of the search had been something small and flat, something that could be concealed in a picture frame. That was one for him.

I knew what it was, of course. My visitor had been trying to recover that anonymous note. The one that read: "Thorndecker kills."

With only a half-dozen regulars and me staying at the Coburn Inn, the management didn't think it necessary to employ a chambermaid. Old Sam Livingston did the chores: changing linen, emptying wastebaskets, throwing out "dead soldiers," vacuuming when the dust got ankle-deep.

I was still trying to set my room to rights when he knocked. I let him in.

"I'll straighten up here," he told me. "You go get your morning coffee."

"Thanks, Sam," I said gratefully.

I handed him a five-dollar bill. He stared at it.

"Abraham Lincoln," he said. "Fine-looking man. Good beard." He held the bill out to me. "Take it back, Mr. Todd. I'd clean up anyways. You don't have to do that."

"I know I don't *have* to do it," I said. "All I *have* to do is pay taxes and die. I *want* to do it."

"That's different," he said, pocketing the bill. "I thank you kindly."

I took another look at him: an independent old cuss in his black alpaca jacket and skullcap. He had a scrubby head of grayish curls and a face as gnarled as a hardwood burl. All of him looked like dark hardwood: chiseled, carved, sanded, oiled, and then worked for so many years that the polish on face and hands had a deep glow that could only come from hard use.

"Live in Coburn all your life?" I asked him.

"Most of it," he said.

"Seventy-five years?" I guessed.

"Eighty-three," he said.

"I'll never make it," I said.

"Sure you will," he said, "you lay off the sauce and the women."

"In that case," I said, "I don't want to make it. Sam, I want to come down to your place sometime, maybe have a little visit with you."

"Anytime," he said. "I ain't going anywhere. The French toast is nice this morning."

I can take a hint. I left him to his cleaning and went down for breakfast. But I skipped the French toast. Juice, unbuttered toast, black coffee. Very virtuous. On my way out, I looked in at the bar but Al Coburn wasn't there. Just Jimmy the bartender reading the *Sentinel*. I waved at him and went out to the lobby. I stopped for cigarettes. I really did need cigarettes. Honest.

"Good morning, Millie," I said.

"Oh, Mr. Todd," she said excitedly, "I heard about your trouble. I'm so sorry."

I stared at her glassily, trying to figure which trouble she meant.

She was wearing the same makeup, probably marketed under the trade name "Picasso's Clown." But the costume was different. This morning it was a voluminous shift, a kind of muumuu, in an orange foliage print. It had a high, drawstring neckline, long sleeves, tight cuffs. The yards and yards of sleazy synthetic fell to her ankles. Hamlet's uncle could have hidden behind that arras.

Strange, but it was sexier than the tight sweater and skirt she had worn the day before. The cloth, gathered at the neck, jutted out over her glorious appendages, then fell straight down in folds, billows, pleats. She was completely covered, concealed. It was inflammatory.

"Your trouble," she repeated. "You know—the robbery."

"Burglary," I said automatically. "But the door didn't seem to be jimmied."

"That's what Ronnie said. He thinks whoever did it had a key."

So the Indian had caught it after all. That pesky redskin kept surprising me. I resolved never to underestimate him again.

Millie Goodfellow crooked a long, slender forefinger, beckoning me closer. Since the glass cigar counter was between us, I had to bend forward in a ridiculous posture. I found myself focusing on the nail of that summoning finger. Dark brown polish.

"A passkey," she whispered. "I told Ronnie it was probably a passkey. There's a million of them floating around. Everyone has one." Suddenly she giggled. "I even have one myself. Isn't that awful?"

I was in cloud-cuckoo land.

"*You* have a hotel passkey, Millie?" I asked. "Whatever for?"

"It gets me in the little girls' room," she said primly. Then she was back in her Cleopatra role. "And a lot of other places, too!"

I think I managed a half-ass grin before I stumbled away. My initial reaction had been correct: this lady was scary.

Wednesday morning in Coburn, N.Y. . . .

At least the sun was shining. Maybe not exactly shining, but it was there. You could see it, dull and tarnished, glowing dimly behind a cloud cover. It put a leaden light on everything: illumination but no shadows. People moved sluggishly, the air was cold without being invigorating, and I kept hoping I'd hear someone laugh aloud. No one did.

Around to River Street and the First Farmers & Merchants Bank. It had the flashiest storefront in Coburn, with panels of gray marble between gleaming plateglass windows, and lots of vinyl tile and mirrors inside. The foreclosure business must be good.

There were two tellers' windows and a small bullpen with three desks occupied by New Accounts, Personal Loans, and Mortgages. There was one guard who could have been Constable Ronnie Goodfellow fifty years older and fifty pounds heavier. I went to him. His side-holstered revolver had a greenish tinge, as if moss was growing on it.

I gave my name and explained that I'd like to see the president, Mr. Arthur Merchant, although I didn't have an appointment. He nodded gravely and disappeared for about five minutes, during which time two members of the Junior Mafia could have waltzed in and cleaned out the place.

But finally he returned and ushered me to a back office, enclosed, walled with a good grade of polished plywood. A toothy lady relieved me of hat and trenchcoat, which she hung on a rack. She handled my garments with her fingertips; I couldn't blame her. Finally, finally, I was led into the inner sanctum, and Arthur Merchant, bank president and Coburn mayor, rose to greet me. He shook my hand enthusiastically with a fevered palm and insisted I sit in a leather club chair alongside his desk. When we were standing, I was six inches taller than he. When we sat down, he in his swivel chair, he was six inches taller. That chair must have had 12-inch casters.

He was a surprisingly young man for a bank president and mayor. He was also short, plump, florid, and sweatier than the room temperature could account for. Young as he was, the big skull was showing the scants; strands of thin, black hair were brushed sideways to hide the divot. The face bulged. You've seen faces that bulge, haven't you? They seem to protrude. As if an amateur sculptor started out with an ostrich egg as a head form, and then added squares and strips of modeling clay: forehead, nose, cheeks, mouth, chin. I mean everything seems to hang out there, and all that clay just might dry and drop off. Leaving the blank ostrich egg.

We exchanged the usual pleasantries: the weather, my reaction to Coburn, my accommodations at the Inn, places of interest I should see while in the vicinity: the place where a British spy was hanged in 1777; Lovers' Leap on the Hudson River, scene of nineteen authenticated suicides; and the very spot where, only last summer, a bear had come out of the woods and badly mauled, and allegedly attempted to rape, a 68-year-old lady gathering wild strawberries.

I said it all sounded pretty exciting to me, but as Mr. Merchant was undoubtedly aware, I was not in Coburn to sightsee or visit tourist attractions; I had come to garner information about Dr. Telford Gordon Thorndecker. That's when I learned that Arthur Merchant was a compulsive fusser.

The pudgy hands went stealing out to straighten desk blotter, pencils, calendar pad. He tightened his tie, smoothed the hair at his temples, examined his fingernails. He crossed and recrossed his knees, tugged down the points of his vest, brushed nonexistent lint from his sleeve. He leaped to his feet, strode across the room, closed a bookcase door that had been open about a quarter-inch. Then he came back to his desk, sat down, and began rearranging blotter, pencils, and pad, aligning their edges with quick, nervous twitches of those pinkish squid hands.

And all during this *a cappella* ballet he was explaining to me what a splendid fellow Thorndecker was. Salt of the earth. Everything the Boy Scout oath demanded. Absolutely straight-up in his financial dealings. A loyal contributor to local charities. And what a boon to Coburn! Not only as the biggest employer in the village, but as a citizen, bringing to Coburn renown as the home of one of the world's greatest scientists.

"One of the *greatest*, Mr. Todd," Art Merchant concluded, somewhat winded, as well he should have been after that ten-minute monologue.

"Very impressive," I said, as coldly as I could. "You know what he's doing at Crittenden?"

It was a small sneak punch, but Merchant reacted like I had slammed a knee into his groin.

"What? Why . . . ah . . . " he stammered. Then: "The nursing home," he burst out. "Surely you know about that. Beds for fifty patients. A program of social—"

"I know about Crittenden Hall," I interrupted. "I want to know about the Crittenden Research Laboratory. What's going on in the lab?"

"Well, ah, you know," he said desperately, limp hands flailing. "Scientific stuff. Don't ask me to understand; I'm just a small-town banker. But valuable things—I'm sure of that. The man's a genius! Everyone says so. And still young. Relatively. He's going to do great work. No doubt about that. You'll see."

He maundered on and on, turning now to what an excellent business manager Thorndecker was, what a fine executive, and how rare it was to find that acumen in a doctor, a professor, a man of science. But I wasn't listening.

I was beginning to feel slight twinges of paranoia. I am not ordinarily a subscriber to the conspiracy theory of history. For instance, I do not believe an evil cabal engineered the deaths of the Kennedys and Martin Luther King, the disappearance of Jimmy Hoffa, or even the lousy weather we've been having.

I believe in the Single Nut theory of history, holding that one goofy individual can change the course of human affairs by a well-placed bomb or a well-aimed rifle shot. I don't believe in conspiracies because they require the concerted efforts of two or more people. In other words, a committee. And I've never known a committee that achieved anything but endless bickering and the piling up of Minutes of the Last Meeting that serve no useful purpose except being recycled for the production of Mother's Day cards.

Still, as I said, I was beginning to feel twinges. I thought Agatha Binder had lied to me. I thought Art Merchant was lying to me. These two, along with the Thorndeckers, Dr. Draper, and maybe Ronnie Goodfellow and a few other of the best people of Coburn, all knew something I didn't know, and wasn't being told. I didn't like that. I told you, I don't like being conned.

I realized Arthur Merchant had stopped talking and was staring at me, expecting some kind of response.

"Well," I said, rising to my feet, "that's certainly an enthusiastic endorsement, Mr. Merchant. I'd say Dr. Thorndecker is fortunate in having you and the other citizens of Coburn as friends and neighbors."

I must have said the right thing, because the fear went out of his eyes, and some color came back into those clayey cheeks.

"And we are fortunate," he sang out, "in having Dr. Thorndecker as a friend and neighbor. You bet your life! Mr. Todd, you stop by again if you have any more questions, any questions at all, concerning Dr. Thorndecker's financial affairs. He's instructed me to throw his books open to you, as it were. Anything you want to know. Anything at all."

"I've seen the report of Lifschultz Associates," I said, moving toward the door. "It appears Dr. Thorndecker is in a very healthy financial position."

"Healthy?" Art Merchant cried, and did everything but leap into the air and click his heels together. "I should say so! The man is a fantastic money manager. Fan-tas-tic! In addition to being one of the world's greatest scientists, of course."

"Of course," I said. "By the way, Mr. Merchant, I understand you're the mayor of Coburn?"

"Oh . . . " he said, shrugging and spreading his plump hands deprecatingly, "I guess I got the job because no one else wanted it. It's unpaid, you know. About what it's worth."

"The reason I mention it," I said, "is that I haven't seen any public buildings around town. No courthouse, no city hall, no jail."

"Well, we have what we call the Civic Building, put up by the WPA
back in 1936. We've got our fire department in there—it's just one old
pumper and a hose cart—the police station, a two-cell jail, and our city
hall, which is really just one big office. We have a JP in town, but if we
get a serious charge or trial, we move it over to the courthouse at the
county seat."

"The Civic Building?" I said. "I'd like to see that. How do I find it?"

"Just go out Main Street to Oakland Drive. It's one block south, right
next to the boarded-up A&P; you can't miss it. Not much to look at, to
tell you the truth. There's been some talk of replacing it with a modern
building, but the way things are . . . "

He let that sentence trail off, the way so many Coburnites did. It gave
their talk an effect of helpless futility. Hell, what's the point of finishing
a sentence when the world's coming to an end?

I thanked him for his kind cooperation and shook that popover with
fingers. I claimed hat and trenchcoat, and got out of there. No customers
in the bank, and the people at the desks marked New Accounts, Personal
Loans, and Mortgages didn't seem to have much to do. I began to appreciate how much a big, active account like Thorndecker's meant to First
Farmers & Merchants, and to Mayor Art Merchant.

Having time to kill before my visit to Crittenden at 1:00 P.M., I spent
an hour wandering about Coburn. If I had walked at a faster clip, I could
have seen the entire village in thirty minutes. I made a complete tour of
the business section—about four blocks—featuring boarded-up stores and
Going Out of Business sales. Then I meandered through residential districts, and located the Civic Building. I kept walking until vacant lots
became more numerous and finally merged with farms and wooded tracts.

When I had seen all there was to see, I retraced my steps, heading back
to the Coburn Inn. I had my ungloved hands shoved into my trenchcoat
pockets, and I hunched my shoulders against a whetted wind blowing from
the river. I was thinking about what I had just seen, about Coburn.

The town was dying—but what of that? A lot of villages, towns, and
cities have died since the world began. People move away, buildings
crumble, and the grass or the forest or the jungle or the desert moves back
in. As I told Constable Goodfellow, history is change. You can't stop it;
all you can do is try to keep from getting run over by it.

It wasn't the decay of Coburn that depressed me so much as the layout
of the residential neighborhoods. I saw three-story Victorian mansions
right next to leaky shacks with a scratchy yard and tin garage. Judging by
homes, Coburn's well-to-do didn't congregate in a special, exclusive
neighborhood; they lived cheek-by-jowl with their underprivileged breth-
ren.

You might find that egalitarian and admirable. I found it unbelievable.
There isn't a village, town, or city on earth where the rich don't huddle
in their own enclave, forcing the poor into theirs. I suppose this has a

certain social value: it gives the poor a *place* to aspire to. What's the point
of striving for what the sociologists call upward mobility if you have to
stay in the ghetto?

The problem was solved when I spotted a sign in a ground-floor window
of one of those big Victorian mansions. It read: "Rooms to let. Day, week,
month." Then I understood. *All* of the Incorporated Village of Coburn
was on the wrong side of the tracks. As I trudged back to the Inn, the sky
darkening, the smell of snow in the air, I thought this place could have
been the capital city of Gloom.

I went into the bar and asked the spavined waiter for a club sandwich
and a bottle of beer. While I waited, I looked idly around. It was getting
on to noon; the lunch crowd was beginning to straggle in. Then I became
aware of something else about Coburn, something I had observed but that
hadn't really registered until now.

There were no young people in town. I had seen a few schoolkids on
the streets, but no one in the, oh, say 18-to-25 age bracket. There was
Miss Dimples in the *Sentinel* office, but except for her, Coburn seemed
devoid of young people. Even the gas jockeys at Mike's Service Station
looked like they were pulling down Spanish-American War pensions.

The reason was obvious, of course. If you were an eager, curious, reasonably brainy 20-year-old with worlds to conquer, would you stay in
Coburn? Not me. I'd shake the place. And that's what Coburn's young
people had done. For Albany, New York, Miami, Los Angeles. Or maybe
Paris, Rome, Amsterdam, Karachi. *Any* place was better than home.

On my way out, I stopped at the bar for a quick vodka gimlet. I know
it was a poor choice on top of my luncheon beer. But after the realization,
"*Any* place was better than home," I needed it.

Once again I drove to Crittenden through that blasted landscape, and
was admitted by the gate guard. He was pressing a transistor radio against
his skull. There was a look of ineffable joy on his face, as if he had just
heard his number pulled in the Irish Sweeps. I don't think he even saw
me, but he let me in; I followed the graveled road to the front of Crittenden
Hall.

Dr. Kenneth Draper came out to greet me. I took a closer look at him.
You know the grave, white-coated, eye-glassed guy in the TV commer-
cials who looks earnestly at the camera and says, "Have you ever suffered
from irregularity?" That was Draper. As a matter of fact, he looked like
he was suffering himself: forehead washboarded, deep lines from nose to
corners of mouth, bleached complexion, and a furtive, over-the-shoulder
glance, wondering when the knout would fall.

"Well!" Draper said brightly. "Now what we've planned is the grand
tour. The nursing home first. Look around. Anything you want to see.
Meet the head staff. Then to the lab. Ditto there. Take a look at our setup,
what we're doing. Meet some of our people. Then Dr. Thorndecker would
like to speak with you when we're finished. How does that sound?"

"Sounds fine," I assured him. The poor simp looked so apprehensive that I think if I had said, "Sounds lousy," he would have burst into tears.

We turned to the left, and Draper hauled a ring of keys from his pocket.

"The wings are practically identical," he explained. "We didn't want to waste your time by dragging you through both, so we'll take a look at the west wing. We keep the door locked for security. Some of our patients are mentals, and we try to keep access doors locked for their protection."

"And yours?" I asked.

"What?" he said. "Oh yes, I suppose that's true, although the few violent cases we have are kept pretty, uh, content."

There was a wide, tiled, institutional corridor with doors on both sides.

"Main floor": Dr. Draper recited, "Doctors' and nurses' offices and lounges. Records and admitting room. X ray and therapy. Clinic and dispensary. Everything here is duplicated in the east wing."

"Expensive setup, isn't it?" I said. "For fifty patients?"

"They can afford it," he said tonelessly. "Now I'm going to introduce you to Nurse Stella Beecham. She's an RN, head nurse in Crittenden Hall. She'll show you through the nursing home, then bring you over to the lab. I'll leave you in her hands, and then take you through the Crittenden Research Laboratory myself."

"Sounds fine," I said again, trying to get some enthusiasm into my voice.

Stella Beecham looked like a white stump: squat, straight up and down. She was wearing a short-sleeved nurse's uniform, and I caught the biceps and muscles in her forearms and thick wrists. But nurses are usually strong; they have to be to turn a two-hundred-pound patient in his bed, or lift a deadweight from stretcher to wheelchair.

Beecham wasn't the prettiest angel of mercy I've ever seen. She had gross, thrusting, almost masculine features. No makeup. Her complexion was rough, ruddy, with the beginnings of burst capillaries in nose and cheeks. To me, that signals a heavy drinker. She had a faint mustache. On the left side of her chin, just below the corner of her pale mouth, was a silvery wen with two short, black hairs sticking out. It looked for all the world like a transistor, and I consciously avoided staring at it when I talked to her.

Dr. Kenneth Draper cut out, and Nurse Beecham took me in tow, spouting staccato statistics. It went like this, in her hard, drillmaster's voice:

"Fifty beds. Today's occupancy rate: forty-nine. We have a waiting list of thirty-eight to get in. Seven addicts at present: five alcoholics, two hard drugs. Six mentals. Prognosis: negative. All the others are terminals. Cancer, MS, emphysema, myasthenia gravis, cardiacs, and so forth. Their doctors have given up. About all we can do is try to keep them pain-free. A hundred and fifty meals prepared each day in the main kitchen, not counting those for staff, maintenance personnel, and security guards. Plus special meals. Some of our guests like afternoon tea or a late-night snack.

We have a chef on duty around-the-clock. These are the nurses' offices and lounges. The doctors' are across the hall.''

"You have MD's in residence?'' I asked—not that I was so interested, but just to let her know I was listening.

"Two assigned to each wing. Plus, of course, Dr. Thorndecker and Dr. Draper. They're both MD's. Two RN's around-the-clock in each wing. Plus a pharmaceutical nurse for each wing. Three shifts of aides and orderlies. Our total staff provides a better than one-to-one ratio with our guests. Here's the X-ray room. We have a resident radiologist. Therapy in here. Our resident therapist deals mostly with the addiction cases, particularly the alcoholics. Spiritual therapy, if desired, is provided by the Reverend Peter Koukla of the First Episcopal Church. We also have an Albany rabbi on call, when needed. Examination room here, dispensary here. Combined barber and beauty shop. This is handled by a concession. Dietician's office here. We send out all our laundry and drycleaning. I think that about completes the main floor of this wing.''

"What's in the basement?'' I asked, in the friendliest tone possible.

"Storage,'' she said. "Want to see it?''

"No,'' I said, "that won't be necessary.''

It was a short, brusque exchange—brusque on her part. She had the palest blue eyes I've ever seen, almost as colorless as water, and showing about as much. All they did was glitter; I could read nothing there. So why did I have the feeling that my mention of the cellar had flicked a nerve? Just a tensing, almost a bristling of her powerful body.

"Now we'll go upstairs,'' she said. "The vacant suite is in this wing, so I'll be able to show it to you.''

We had passed a few aides, a few orderlies. But I hadn't seen anyone who looked like a patient.

"Where is everyone?'' I asked. "The place seems deserted.''

She gave me a reasonable explanation:

"It's lunchtime. The dining room is in the rear of the main entrance hall. Most of our guests are there now, except for those who dine in their rooms. The aides and doctors usually eat in the dining room also. Dr. Thorndecker feels it helps maintain rapport with our patients.''

"I hope I haven't interrupted *your* luncheon,'' I said.

"Not at all,'' she said. "I'm on a diet. I skip lunch.''

That sounded like a friendly, personal comment—a welcome relief from the officialese she had been spouting—so I followed up on it.

"I met an acquaintance of yours,'' I said. "Agatha Binder. I had a talk with her yesterday.''

"Did you?'' she said. "Now you'll notice that we have no elevators. But during Dr. Thorndecker's refurbishing program, the stairways at the ends of the corridors were made much narrower, and ramps were installed. So we're able to move wheeled stretchers and wheelchairs up to the top floors without too much trouble. Actually, there's very little traffic. Non-ambulatory guests are encouraged to remain in their suites. What do you think of Crittenden Hall so far?''

The question came so abruptly that it confused me.

"Well . . . uh," I said. "I'll tell you," I said. "I'm impressed," I said, "by how neat and immaculate and sparkling everything is. I almost suspect you prepared for my visit—like sailors getting ready for a white-glove inspection on a U.S. Navy ship.''

I said it in a bantering tone, keeping it light, but she had no humor whatsoever—except, possibly, bad.

"Oh no," she said, "it's like this all the time. Dr. Thorndecker insists on absolutely hygienic conditions. Our cleaning staff has been specially trained. We've gotten highest ratings in the New York State inspections, and I mean to keep it that way.''

It was a grim declaration. But she was a grim woman. And, as I followed her up the narrow staircase to the second floor, I reflected that even her legs were grim: heavy, thick, with clumped muscles under the white cotton stockings. I wouldn't, I thought, care to be given a needle by Nurse Stella Beecham. She was liable to pin me to the goddamned bed.

"I won't show you any of the occupied suites," she said. "Dr. Thorndecker felt it might disturb our guests unnecessarily.''

"Of course."

"But he wanted you to see the one vacant suite. We have a guest arriving for it tomorrow morning.''

"Was it occupied by a man—or maybe it was a woman—named Petersen?" I asked.

I don't know why I said that. My tongue was ahead of my brain. I just said it idly. Nurse Beecham's reaction was astonishing. She was standing on the second-floor landing, three steps above me. When I said, "Petersen," she whirled, then went suddenly rigid, her lumpy features set in an ugly expression that was half fear, half cunning, and all fury.

"Why did you say that?" she demanded, the "say" hissed so that it came out "ssssay.''

"I don't know," I told her honestly, staring up at her transistor-wen. "But I was at the Thorndeckers for dinner last night, and late in the evening Dr. Thorndecker was called away by Dr. Draper. I got the impression it involved some crisis in the condition of a patient named Petersen. Dr. Thorndecker said he was afraid Petersen wouldn't last the night.''

The gorgon's face relaxed, wax flowing. She took a deep breath. She had an awesome bosom.

"He didn't," she said. "He passed. The empty suite is just down the corridor here. Follow me, please.''

She unlocked the door, and stood aside. I walked in ahead of her. It was a suite all right: sitting room, bedroom, bathroom. There was even a little kitchenette, with a waist-high refrigerator. But no stove. The windows faced the sere fields of Crittenden.

The rooms were clean and cheerfully decorated: chintz drapes and slipcovers. Bright, innocuous paintings on the warm beige walls. A new, oval-shaped rag rug. Windows were washed, floor polished, upholstery spotless, small desk set neatly with blotter, stationery, ballpoint pen, Bible. The bed had been freshly made. Spotless white towels hung in the bathroom. The closet door was open. It was empty of clothes, but wooden hangers were precisely arranged along the rod.

Nurse Beecham stood patiently at the hallway door while I prowled around. A quiet, impersonal suite of rooms. Nothing of Petersen showed, nor of any of the others who had gone before. No cigarette butts, worn slippers, rumpled pillows. No initials carved in the desk top. There was a faint scent of disinfectant in the air.

I stood at the window, staring down at the withered fields. It was a comfortable place to die, I supposed. Warm. Lighted. And he had been well cared for. Pain-free. Still, the place had all the ambience of a motel suite in Scranton, Pa. It had that hard, machine look, everything clean enough, but aseptic and chilling.

I turned back to Stella Beecham.

"What did he die of?" I asked. "Petersen?"

"Pelvic cancer," she said. "Inoperable. He didn't respond to chemotherapy. Shall we go now?"

I followed her in silence down the stairway to the main floor. We stopped three times while she introduced me to staff: one of the resident MD's, the radiologist, and another RN. We all smiled and said things. I don't remember their names.

Nurse Beecham paused outside the back door of the west wing.

"It's a few steps to the lab," she said. "Would you like your coat?"

"No, I'll leave it here," I said. "Thank you for showing me around. It must be very boring for you."

"I don't mind," she said gruffly.

We walked out to that roofed port that led down the hill to the Crittenden Research Laboratory. It was a miserably rude day, the sun completely hidden now, air biting, wind slicing. But I didn't see Beecham hurry her deliberate tread or hug her bare arms. She just trundled steadily along, a boulder rolling downhill.

The side door of the lab was locked. Nurse Beecham had the key on an enormous ring she hauled from her side pocket. When we were inside, she double-locked the door.

"Wait here, please," she said, and went thumping down a wide, waxed linoleum corridor. I waited, looking around. Nothing of interest to see, unless closed doors excite you. In a few minutes, Dr. Kenneth Draper came bustling down the hall, rubbing his palms together and trying hard to look relaxed and genial.

"Well!" he said again. "Here we are! See everything you wanted in the Hall?"

"I think so," I said. "It appears to be a very efficient operation."

"Oh, it is, it is," he assured me. "Quality care. If you'd care to test the patients' food, just drop in unexpectedly, for any meal. I think you'll be pleasantly surprised."

"I'm sure I would be," I said. "But that won't be necessary, Dr. Draper. By the way, Nurse Beecham strikes me as being a very valuable member of your staff. How long has she been with you?"

"From the start," he said. "When Dr. Thorndecker took over. He brought her in. I understand she was the first Mrs. Thorndecker's nurse during a long illness prior to her—her accident. I don't know what we'd do without Beecham. Perhaps not the most personable, outgoing woman in the world, but she certainly does a job running the Hall. Keeps problems to a minimum so Dr. Thorndecker and I can devote more time to the lab."

"Where your real interests lie?" I suggested.

"Well . . . uh, yes," he said hesitantly, as if afraid of saying too much. "The nursing home is our first responsibility, of course, but we are doing some exciting things here, and I suppose it's natural . . . "

Another Coburnite who couldn't finish his sentences. I wondered how these people expressed love for one another. Did they just say, "I love . . . " and let it go at that?

"Now this is our main floor," Dr. Draper was saying. "Here you'll find our offices, records room, reference library, a small lounge, a locker and dressing room, showers, and a room we've equipped with cots for researchers who might want to sleep here after a long day's work or during a prolonged project. Do you want to see any of these rooms?"

"I'd like to glance at the reference library, if I may," I said. "Just for a moment."

"Of course, of course. Along here, please."

This place was certainly livelier than the nursing home. As we walked along the corridor, I heard voices from behind closed doors, hoots of laughter, and once a shouted argument in which I could distinguish one screamed statement: "You're full of shit!"

We stopped several times for Dr. Draper to introduce me to staff members hustling by. They all seemed to know who I was, and shook my hand with what appeared to be genuine enthusiasm. There were almost as many women as men, and all of them seemed young and—well, I think "keen" would describe them best. I said something about this to Draper.

"Oh, they're top-notch," he said proudly. "The best. Dr. Thorndecker recruited them from all over: Harvard, Duke, Berkeley, Johns Hopkins, Chicago, MIT. We have two Japanese, one Swede, and a kid from Mali you wouldn't believe, he's so smart. We pay them half of what they could be making with any of the big drug companies."

"Then why ... ?" I said. I was beginning to suffer from the Coburn Syndrome.

"Thorndecker!" Dr. Draper cried. "It's Thorndecker. The opportunity of working with him. Learning from him. They're very highly motivated."

"Or he's charmed them," I said, smiling.

Suddenly he was sober.

"Yes," he said in a low voice. "That, too. Here's our library. Small, but sufficient."

We stepped inside. A room about twenty by forty feet, lined with bookcases. Several small oak tables with a single chair at each, and one long conference table with twelve captain's chairs. A Xerox machine. The shelves were jammed with books on end and periodicals lying flat. It wasn't too orderly: the ashtrays filled, wastebaskets overflowing, books and magazines lined up raggedly. But after a visit to the late Mr. Petersen's abode, it was a pleasure to see human mess.

"Looks like it's used," I commented, wandering around.

"All the time," he told me. "Sometimes the researchers will get caught up in something, read all night, and then flop into one of those cots I told you about. Very irregular hours. No one punches a time clock. But if they do their jobs, they can work any hours they please. A very relaxed atmosphere. Dr. Thorndecker feels it pays off in productivity."

Meanwhile I was inspecting the titles of the books and periodicals on the shelves. If I had hoped they'd give me a clue to what was going on at the Crittenden Research Laboratory, I was disappointed. They appeared to me to be standard scientific reference texts, with heavy emphasis on human biology and the morphology of mammalian cells. A thick stack of recent oncological papers. One shelf of US Government publications dealing with demography, census, and public health statistics. I didn't see a single volume I'd care to curl up with on a cold winter night.

"Very nice," I said, turning to Draper. "Where do we go now—the labs?"

"Fine," he said. "They're on the second floor. On each side of the corridor is a large general lab used by the researchers. And then a smaller private lab used by the supervising staffers."

"How many supervisors do you have?"

"Well ... " he said, blushing, "actually just Dr. Thorndecker and me. But when the grant—*if* the grant comes through, we hope to expand. We have the space and facilities to do it. Well, you'll see. Let's go up."

Unlike nursing homes and hospitals, research laboratories don't necessarily have to be sterile, efficient, and as cozy as a subway station. True, I've been in labs that look like operating rooms: all shiny white tile and equipment right out of *The Bride of Frankenstein.* I've also been in research labs not much larger than a walk-in closet and equipped with not much more than a stained sink and a Bunsen burner.

When it comes to scientific research, there's no guarantee. A million dollars sunk into a palace of a lab with all the latest and most exotic stainless steel doodads can result in the earth-shaking discovery that when soft cheese is exposed to the open air, mold results. And from that little closet lab with roaches fornicating in unwashed flasks can come a discovery that remakes the world.

The second-floor working quarters of the Crittenden Research Laboratory fell about halfway between palace and closet. The space was ample enough; the entire floor was divided in two by a wide corridor, and on each side was a huge laboratory. Each had, at its end, a small, private laboratory enclosed by frosted glass panels. These two small supervisors' labs had private entrances from the corridor, and also etched glass doors leading into the main labs. All these doors, I noted, could be locked.

The main laboratories were lighted with overhead fluorescent fixtures, plus high-intensity lamps mounted near microscopes. Workbenches ran around the walls, with additional work tables in the center areas. Plenty of sinks, garbage disposal units, lab stools, metal and glass welding torches and tanks—from which I guessed they had occasional need to fabricate their own equipment.

But it was the profusion of big, complex, obviously store-bought hardware that bewildered me.

"I can recognize an oscilloscope when I see one," I told Draper. "And that thing's a gas diffusion analyzer, and that's a scanning electron microscope. But what's all this other stuff?"

"Oh . . . various things," he said vaguely. "The big control board is for an automated cell culture, blood and tissue analyzer. Very complete readings, in less time than it would take to do it by hand. Incidentally, in addition to our own work, we do all the tests needed by the nursing home. That includes blood, urine, sputum, stools, biopsies—whatever. We have pathologists on staff."

There had been half a dozen researchers working in the first lab we visited, and I saw about the same number when we walked into the lab across the hall. A few of them looked up when we entered, but most didn't give us a glance.

The second lab had workbenches along three walls. The fourth, a long one, was lined with stainless steel refrigerators and climate-controlled cabinets. Through the front glass panels I could see racks and racks of flasks and tubes of all sizes and shapes.

"Cell cultures?" I asked Dr. Draper.

"Mostly," he nodded. "And some specimens. Organ and tumor slices. Things of that sort. We have some very old, very valuable cultures here. A few originals. We're continually getting requests from all over the world."

"You give the stuff away?"

"Sometimes, but we prefer to trade," he said, laughing shortly. " 'Here's what we've got; what have *you* got?' Research laboratories do a lot of horse-trading like that."

"You have bacteria?" I asked.

"Some."

"Viruses?"

"Some."

"Lethal?"

"Oh yes," he nodded. "Including a few rare ones from Africa. They're in those cabinets with the padlocks. Only Dr. Thorndecker and I have the key."

"What are they all doing?" I said, motioning toward the researchers bent over their workbenches. "What's your current project?"

"Well, ah," he said, "I'd prefer you direct that question to Dr. Thorndecker. He specifically said he wished to brief you personally on our current activities. After we've finished up here."

"Good enough," I said. Just seeing the Crittenden Research Laboratory in action revealed nothing. If they were brewing up a bubonic plague and told me they were making chicken noodle Cup-a-Soup, I wouldn't have known the difference.

"The only thing left to see is the basement," Draper said.

"What's down there?"

"Mostly our experimental animals. A dissection room. Mainly for animals," he added hastily. "We don't do any human PM's unless it's requested by relatives of the deceased."

"Why would they request it?"

"For various reasons. Usually to determine the exact cause of death. We had a case last year in which a widow authorized an autopsy of her deceased husband, a mental who had been at Crittenden Hall for two years. She was afraid of a genetic brain disorder that might be inherited by their son."

"Did you find it?"

"Yes," he said. "And there have been some postmortems authorized by the subjects themselves, prior to their death. These were people who wished to donate organs: kidneys, corneas, hearts, and so forth. But these cases have been few, considering the advanced age of most of the patients in the nursing home. Their organs are rarely, ah, desirable."

And on that cheery note, we descended the stairway to the basement of the Crittenden Research Laboratory. Dr. Kenneth Draper paused with his hand on the knob of a heavy, padded steel door. He turned to me.

He seemed suddenly overcome by embarrassment. Spots of color appeared high on his cheeks. His forehead was pearled with sweat. Wet teeth appeared in a hokey grin.

"We have mostly mice, dogs, cats, chimps, and guinea pigs," he said.

"Yes?" I said encouragingly. "And . . . ?"

"Well," he said, tittering nervously, "you are not, by any chance, an anti-vivisectionist, are you, Mr. Todd?"

"Rather them than me," I said, and looked at him. But he had turned away; I couldn't see his face.

When we stepped inside, I heard immediately the reason for that outside door being padded. The big basement room was an audiophile's nightmare: chirps, squeals, barks, hisses, honks, roars, howls. I looked around, dazed.

"You'll get used to it," Draper shouted in my ear.

"Never," I shouted back.

We made a quick tour of the cages. I didn't mind the smell so much as that cacophony. I really am a sentimental slob, and I kept thinking the imprisoned beasts were making all that racket because they were suffering and wanted out. Not a very objective reaction, I admit; most of them looked sleek and well-fed. It's just that I hate to see an animal in a cage. I hate zoos. I see myself behind those bars, with a neat label: "Samuel Todd, Homus Americanus, habitat New York City. A rare species that feeds on vodka gimlets and celery stalks stuffed with anchovy paste."

There were a few aproned attendants around who grinned at us. One of them was wearing a set of heavy earphones. Maybe he was just blocking out that noise, or maybe he was listening to Mahler's Fifth.

After inspecting the spitting cats, howling dogs, barking chimps, and squealing mice, it was a relief to get into a smaller room closed off by another of those padded steel doors.

This one was also lined with cages. But the occupants were those animals being used in current experiments and were reasonably quiet. Some of them lay on their sides, in what appeared to be a comatose state. Some were bandaged. Some had sensors taped to heads and bodies, the wires leading out to a battery of recording machines.

And some of them—one young chimpanzee in particular—were covered with tumors. Great, monstrous growths. Blossoms of wild flesh. Red and blue and yellow. A flowering of raw tissue. The smell in there was something.

The young chimp was almost hidden by the deadly blooms. The eruptions covered his head, body, limbs. He lay on his back, spreadeagled, breathing shallowly. I could see his black, glittering eyes staring at the cage above him.

"Carcinosarcoma," Dr. Draper said. "He's lasted longer than any other in this particular series of tests."

"You infected him?" I asked, knowing the answer.

"Yes," Draper said. "To test the efficacy of a drug we had high hopes for."

"Your hopes aren't so high now?"

"No," he said, shrinking.

I felt like a shit.

"Forgive me, doctor," I said. "I know in my mind this kind of thing has to be done. I know it's valuable. I'd just prefer not to see it."

"I understand," he said. "Actually, we all try to be objective. I mean all of us—attendants, researchers. But sometimes we don't succeed. We give them names. Al, Tony, Happy Boy, Sue. When they die, or have to be destroyed, we feel it, I assure you."

"I believe you," I said.

I took a quick look at the dissecting room. Just two stainless steel tables, sinks, pots and pans for excised organs. Choppers. Slicers. Shredders. Something like a kitchen in a gourmet restaurant.

We walked back through the animal room. I was happy to get out of there. The stairway up to the main floor was blessedly quiet.

"Thank you, Dr. Draper," I said. "I'm sure you're a busy man, and you'll probably have to work late to catch up. But I appreciate your showing me around."

"My pleasure," he said.

Of course I didn't believe him.

"And now," I said, "I understand a meeting with Dr. Thorndecker is planned?"

"Correct," he said, obviously pleased that everything had gone so well, and one of his wild, young researchers hadn't dropped a diseased guinea pig's spleen down my neck. "I'll call Crittenden Hall from here. Then I'll unlock the back door, and if you'll just go back the way you came, someone will be at the Hall to let you in."

"Thanks again," I said, shaking his damp hand.

I figured him for a good second-level man: plenty of brains, but without the energy, ambition, and obsessive drive to make it to the top level. His attitude toward Thorndecker seemed ambivalent; I couldn't figure it. But he seemed enthusiastic enough about his work and the Crittenden Research Laboratory.

He made his phone call and was unlocking the back door when suddenly, on impulse, I asked him, "Are you married, Dr. Draper?"

His reaction reminded me of that analyzing computer I had just seen. Lights flashing, bubbles bubbling, bleeps bleeping; I could almost *see* him computing, wondering how his answer might affect a grant from the Bingham Foundation to the Crittenden Research Laboratory. Finally . . .

"Why no," he said. "I'm not."

"I'm not either," I said, hoping it might make him feel better. He might even get to like me, and start calling me Sam, or Happy Boy, like one of his experimental animals in that room of the doomed I had just seen.

Turned out into the cold, I trudged determinedly up the steps, back to Crittenden Hall. But then I realized how pleasant it was to be alone, even for a moment or two. It seemed to me I had been accompanied almost every minute I had been on the grounds. And it was possible I had been under observation for the few seconds I had been alone when Nurse Beecham went to fetch Dr. Draper.

I shook my head. Those paranoiac twinges again. But, looking around at the ruined day, the decayed fields of Crittenden, I figured they came with the territory.

A little, snub-nosed nurse's aide had the back door of Crittenden Hall open for me when I arrived. She escorted me down the corridor and delivered me to the white-jacketed goon in the entrance hall. He told me Dr. Thorndecker was awaiting me in his second-floor study, and waved me up the wide staircase. I went about halfway up, raised my eyes, and saw an aproned maid waiting for me on the second-floor landing. I glanced down to see the goon still watching me from the main floor entrance hall.

Then I was certain; it wasn't paranoia at all. They were keeping me in sight. Every minute. They didn't want me wandering around by myself. Who knew what closed door I might open?

Dr. Thorndecker's study was a rumpled warehouse of a room. It looked like an attic for furniture that wasn't good enough for the other rooms in Crittenden Hall, but was too good to give to the Salvation Army. No two chairs, styles, or colors matched. The desk was a scarred and battered rolltop. The lamps had silk shades with beaded fringe. The couch was one big, lumpy stain, and books and periodicals were stacked higgledy-piggledy on the floor. Some of the stacks had collapsed; there were puddles of magazines, scientific papers, spiral-bound notebooks. I had to step over them to get in.

Thorndecker made no apology for this mess, for which I admired him. He got me seated in a cretonne-covered armchair that had stuffing coming out one arm. I wriggled around cautiously until I could sit comfortably without being goosed by a loose spring. The doctor slumped in a swivel chair swung around from his desk.

"Your wife decorate this room?" I asked politely.

He laughed. "To tell you the truth, I like it just the way it is. It's my own private place. A hideaway. No one ever comes in here except the cleaning woman."

"Once every five years?" I suggested. "Whether it needs it or not?"

He laughed again. He seemed to enjoy my chivying. He had whipped off his glasses the moment I entered, but not before I had noted they made him look older. Not older than his 54 years, but just as old. He certainly looked younger without them.

The tanned complexion helped. Perfect teeth that I guessed were capped, not store-bought. Thick billows of dark hair; not a smidgen of gray. No jowls. No sagging of neck flesh. The skin was ruddy and tight, eyes clear and alert. He moved lithely, with an energetic bounce. If he had told me he was 40 years old, I might have thought he was shaving five years. But 54? Imfuckingpossible.

The clothes helped. Beige doeskin slacks, sports jacket of yummy tweed, open-collar shirt with a paisley ascot. Glittering, tasseled moccasins on his small feet. A very spiffy gentleman. When he spoke in that rich, fruity baritone, I could understand how he could woo whiz-kids away from drug cartels at half the salary. He had charm, and even the realization that it was contrived was no defense against it.

Suddenly I had a suspicion that not only the charm, but the man himself might be contrived. The artfully youthful look of bronzed skin, California whites, and hair unblemished by a speck of gray. That appearance might have been a perfectly natural bounty but was, more likely, the result of sunlamp, expensive dental work, facials, and hair dye. And those too-young clothes. I didn't expect Dr. Telford Gordon Thorndecker to dress like a mortician, but I didn't expect him to dress like a juvenile lead either.

Supposing my suspicions correct, what could possibly be his motive? The first one that occurred to me—the *only* one that occurred to me— was that this Nobel winner, this gifted scientist, this *genius* was trying to keep himself attractive and exciting to his young wife. The pampered body was for her. The elegant duds were for her. Even this mess of a room was to prove to her that disorder didn't faze him, that he was capable of whim and youthful nuttiness. He might be an amusing character, an original personality. But he was not a fuddy-duddy; *he was not.*

Irrational? No, just human. I don't mean my own suspicions; I mean Thorndecker's conduct. I had seen how swiftly his vigorous exuberance collapsed the night before when his wife was not present. I began to feel sorry for the man, and like him more.

He looked at me narrowly.

"The animals shake you up?" he asked.

"How did you know that?" I said.

"They usually do. But it must be done."

"I know."

"I have some brandy here. Join me?"

I nodded. He poured us small drinks from a bottle he took from a file drawer in his desk. He used plastic throwaway cups, and again made no apology or excuse. He took one of my cigarettes, and we lighted up.

"I'd be interested in hearing your reactions, Mr. Todd," he said. "On or off the record."

"Oh, on," I said. "I won't try to mislead you. I thought the nursing home a very efficient operation. Of course, it only has a peripheral bearing on your application, but it's nice to know you run a clean, classy institution. Good food, good care, pleasant surroundings, sufficient staff, planned social activities and all that stuff."

"Yes," he said, not changing expression, "all that stuff."

"From what I've read of our preliminary investigation reports, Crittenden Hall makes a modest profit. Which goes to the Crittenden Research Laboratory. Correct?"

He gestured toward the stacks of papers on his desk.

"Correct," he said. "And that's what I've been doing this afternoon, and why I couldn't show you around personally; I've been shuffling papers: bills, checks, requisitions, budgets, vouchers, salaries, and so forth. We have an accountant, of course; he comes in once a month. But I do the day-to-day management. It's my own fault; I could delegate the responsibility to Draper or Beecham—or hire a smart bookkeeper to do it. But I prefer doing it myself. I want to know where every penny comes from and where it goes. And you know, Mr. Todd, I hate it. Hate every minute of it. This paper shuffling, I mean. I'd much rather be in the lab with Dr. Draper and the others. Hard at work. The kind of work I enjoy."

It sounded swell: gifted scientist not interested in the vulgar details of making money, but only in pure research. For the benefit of mankind. What a cynical bastard I am! I said:

"That's a natural lead-in to my next question, Dr. Thorndecker. What kind of work? Everyone I saw in the lab seemed gung-ho and busy as hell. What's going on? What are you doing in the lab? I mean right now. Not if you get the grant, but what's going on *now*?"

He leaned back in his swivel chair, clasped his hands behind his head. He stared at plaster peeling off the high ceiling. His face suddenly contorted in a quick grimace, a tic that lasted no more than a second.

"Know anything about science?" he said. "Human biology in particular? Cells?"

"Some," I said. "Not much. I read your application and the report by our research specialists. But I'm not a trained scientist."

"An informed layman?"

"I guess you could say that."

"Anything in the application or report you didn't understand?"

"I caught the gist of it. I gather you're interested in why people get old."

His ceiling-aimed stare came slowly down. He looked directly into my eyes.

"Exactly," he said. "That's it in a nutshell. Why do people get old? Why does the skin lose its elasticity at the age of thirty-five? Why, at a later age, do muscles grow slack and eyesight dim? Why does hearing fail? Why should a man's cock shrink and his ass sink, or maybe shrivel up until there's nothing there but a crack on a spotted board? Why do a woman's breasts sag and wrinkle? Why does her pubic hair become sparse and scraggly? Why does a man go bald, a woman get puckered thighs? Why do lines appear? What happens to muscle tone and skin color? Did you know that some people actually shrink? They do, Mr. Todd, they *shrink*. Not only in body weight, but in their bone structure. Not to mention teeth falling out, a hawking of phlegm, an odor of the flesh like ash or loam, a tightening of the bowels."

"Jesus," I gasped, "I can hardly wait. Could I have a little more brandy, please?"

He laughed, and filled up my plastic cup. And his own, I noted. Once again I noted that sudden, brief twitching of his features. Almost a spasm of pain.

"I'm not telling you anything you didn't know," he said. "You just don't want to think about it. No one does. Mortality. A hard concept to grasp. Maybe even impossible. But the interesting thing about senescence, Mr. Todd, is that science was hardly aware of it as a biological phenomenon until the last—oh, let's say fifty years. Back in the Middle Ages, if you lived to the ripe old age of thirty or forty, you were doing well. Oh sure, there were a few oldsters of fifty or sixty, but most humans died in childbirth or soon after. If they survived a few years, disease, accidents, pestilence, or wars took them off before they really achieved maturity. Now, quite suddenly, with the marvelous advances in medical science, public health, hygiene, improved diet, and so forth, we have more and more people living into their sixties, seventies, eighties, nineties, and no one thinks it remarkable. It isn't. What is remarkable is that, in spite of medical care, diet, exercise, and sanitary toilets, very few humans make it to a hundred. Why is that, Mr. Todd?"

"Have no idea."

"Sure you do," he said gently. "They don't necessarily sicken. They don't get typhoid, the plague, smallpox, or TB. They just decay. They degenerate. The body not only stops growing, it simply stops. It's not a sudden thing; in a healthy human it takes place over a period of thirty or forty years. But we can see it happening, all those awful things I mentioned to you, and there's no way we can stop it. The human body declines. Heart, liver, stomach, bowels, brain, circulation, nervous system: all subject to degenerative disorders. The body begins to waste away. And if you study actuarial tables, you'll see there's a very definite mathematical progression. The likelihood of dying doubles every seven years after the age of thirty. How does that grab you? But it's only been in the past fifty years that science has started asking Why? Why should the human body decay? Why should hair fall out and skin become shrunken and crepey? We've extended longevity, yes. Meaning most people live longer than they did in the Middle Ages. But now we find ourselves up against a barrier, a wall. Why don't people live to be a hundred, two hundred, three hundred? We can't figure it out. No matter how good our diet, how efficient our sewers, how pure our air, there seems to be something in the human body, in our species, Mr. Todd, that decrees: Thus far, but no farther. We just can't seem to get beyond that one-hundred-year limit. Oh, maybe a few go a couple of years over, but generally a hundred years seems to be the limit for *Homo sapiens*. Why? Who or what set that limit? Is it something in *us*? Something in our physical makeup? Something that decrees the time for dying? What is it? What the hell *is* it? And that, Mr. Todd, is what those gung-ho, busy-as-hell young researchers you just saw in the Crittenden Research Laboratory are trying to find."

I must admit, he had me. He spoke with such earnestness, such fervor, leaning toward me with hands clasped, that I couldn't take my eyes from him, couldn't stop listening because I was afraid that in the next sentence he might reveal the miracle of creation, and if I wasn't paying attention, I might miss it.

When he paused, I sat back, took a deep breath, and drank half my brandy.

I stared at him over the rim of my plastic cup. This time the contraction that wrenched his features was more violent than the two I had previously noted. This one not only twisted his face but wracked his body: he stiffened for an instant, then shuddered as his limbs relaxed. I don't think he was aware that it was evident. When it passed, his expression was unchanged, and he made no reference to it.

"Wow," I said. "Heady stuff, even for an informed layman. And I don't mean the brandy. Are you saying that the Biblical three-score-and-ten don't necessarily have to be that? But could be more?"

He looked at me strangely.

"You're very quick," he said. "That's exactly what I'm saying. It doesn't *have* to be three-score-and-ten. Not if we can find what determines that span. If we can isolate it, we can manipulate it. Then it could become five-score-and-ten, or ten-score-and-ten. Or more. Whatever we want."

I was staggered. Almost literally. If that spring-sprung armchair hadn't clasped me close, I might have trembled. After reading his application, I had suspected Thorndecker wanted Bingham Foundation to finance a search for the Fountain of Youth. Everything I had seen of him up to that moment reinforced that suspicion. Older man-youthful wife. Cosseted body and the threads of a swinger. Contrived enthusiasm and the energy of a spark. It all made a kind of very human sense.

But now, if I understood him, he wasn't talking about the Fountain of Youth, of keeping smooth-skinned and romping all the days of our lives; he was talking about immortality—or something pretty close to it. I couldn't believe it.

"Dr. Thorndecker," I said, "let me get this straight . . . Are you saying there is a factor in human biology, in our bodies, that causes aging? And that once this agent—let's call it the X Factor—can be discovered and isolated, then the chances are that it can be manipulated, modified, changed—whatever—so that the natural span of a man's years could be increased without limit?"

He put his feet up on his desk. He sipped his brandy. Then he nodded.

"That's exactly what I'm saying."

I leaned back, lighted another cigarette, crossed my legs. I couldn't look at him. I was afraid that if I did, and he said, "Now jump out of the window," out I'd go.

Because I can't tell you how convincing the man was. It wasn't only the manner: the passionate voice, the deep, unblinking gaze. But it was the impression of personal confession he gave, as if he were revealing the secret closest to his heart, a secret he had never revealed to anyone but me, because he knew I would understand and be sympathetic. It was as moving as a murmured, "I love you," and could no more be withstood.

"All right," I said finally, "supposing—just supposing—I go along with your theory that there is something in human biology, in the human body, that determines our lifespan—it is just a theory, isn't it?"

"Of course. With some hard statistical evidence to back it up."

"Assuming I agree with you that we all have something inside us that dictates when the cock shrinks and the ass sinks, what is it? What is the X Factor?"

"You read my application, and my professional record?"

"Yes."

"Then you must know that I believe the X Factor—as you call it—is to be found in the cell. The human cell."

"Germ cells? Sex cells?"

"No, we're working with body cells. Heart, skin, lung."

"Why cells at all? Couldn't the X Factor, the aging factor, be a genetic property?"

He gave me a glassy smile.

"You *are* an informed layman," he said. "Yes, I admit many good men working in this field believe senescence has a genetic origin. That the lifespan of our species, of all species, is determined by a genetic clock."

"It makes sense," I argued. "If my parents and grandparents live into their eighties and nineties, chances are pretty good that, barring a fatal accident or illness, I'll live into my eighties or nineties, too. At least, the insurance companies are betting on it."

"You may," he acknowledged. "And the geneticists make a great point of that. Perhaps the X Factor exists in DNA, and determines the lifespan of every human born. And perhaps the X Factor in DNA could be isolated. Then what?"

I shook my head. "You've lost me. You speak of manipulating the X Factor in human cells, if and when it can be isolated. So . . . ? Why couldn't it be manipulated if found in the genetic code? I understand gene splicing is all the rage these days."

"Oh, it's the rage," he said, not laughing. "But recombination with *what*? If you isolated the senescence gene, what would you combine it with—the tortoise gene? They grow to a hundred and fifty, you know. As my son Edward might say, 'Big deal!' What I'm trying to say, Mr. Todd, is that, in this case, gene splicing does not offer anything but the possibility of extending the human lifespan by fifty years. I happen to believe that my cellular theory offers more than that. Much more. You ask if it's a theory, I reply that it is. You ask if I have any proof that the cellular

approach to senescence is viable, I reply that there is much proof that the
X Factor exists in human cells, but it has not been isolated. As of this
date. You ask if I have anything to go on, other than my own conviction,
that the X Factor can be isolated and manipulated, and I must reply in all
honesty: no, nothing but my own conviction.''

I took a deep breath.

"All right, Dr. Thorndecker," I said, "I appreciate your honesty. But
why in hell didn't you spell all this out in your application? Why did you
base it all on that crap about exposing human embryo cells to electromagnetic radiation?''

"First of all, that was accurate. We intend to do exactly that, in our
effort to isolate the X Factor. Second of all, if I had stated in the application that my ultimate aim was to make humans immortal, would the
Bingham Foundation even have bothered to process the application, or
would it have been immediately consigned to deep six?''

"You know the answer to that," I said. "If you had stated your true
reason for requesting the subsidy, I wouldn't be here now.''

"Of course not," he said.

I looked at him in wonderment.

"So why are you telling me now?" I asked him. "Aren't you afraid
I'll roll up my tent and go home?''

"It's a possibility," he acknowledged. "You could tell your superiors
I misled the Bingham Foundation. I didn't, of course. But I admit I was
not as totally forthright as I might have been. Still, my application is
entirely truthful. It is not dishonest.''

"You draw a fine line," I told him. I stared at that handsome, brooding
face a long time. "And you're confessing," I said, still marveling. "Are
you that sure of me?''

"I'm not sure of you at all," he said, somewhat testily. "But I think
you're a shrewd man. I'm paying you the compliment of not trying to
deceive you. You can report this conversation to your superiors or not, as
you please. The decision is yours.''

"You don't care?''

"Mr. Todd, I care a great, goddamned deal. That grant is important to
me. It's essential I get it. And it's vital, as I'm sure you're aware, to all
of Coburn. But as I say, the decision is yours.''

I drained my plastic cup, struggled out of that creaking armchair.

"You're certain," I said, "that the X Factor, the aging factor, will be
found in human body cells and not in the genetic code?''

He grinned at me. "I'm certain. No one else is.''

"Dr. Thorndecker, you stated there is hard statistical evidence to back
up your belief in the existence of the X Factor in human body cells.''

"That's correct; there is.''

"Could I take a look at it?''

"Of course," he said promptly. "It consists not only of my work, but the work of others in this field. I'll have it collected and prepared for you. It will be ready in a day or so.''

"Fine," I said. "Let's let it go until then. You've given me enough to think about for one day.''

He walked me out onto the second-floor landing, chatting amiably, hand on my shoulder. He held me fast, went on and on about this and that, and I wondered—why the stall? Then I saw his eyes flickering to the lobby below. Sure enough, when the white-jacketed goon-doorman appeared, Thorndecker released my shoulder, shook my hand, told me how much he had enjoyed our palaver—his word: ''palaver''—and gave me a smile of super-charm. I was becoming impervious to it. You can endure just so much charm in a given period. After that, it's like being force-fed a pound of chocolate macaroons.

I ambled slowly down that sweeping staircase. I was handed my coat and hat. I was ushered out the front door of Crittenden Hall.

I stood on the graveled driveway a moment, belting my trenchcoat, turning up the collar. Something odd was happening to that day: it was going ghostly on me. There was a cold mist in the air. At the same time, a whitish fog was rolling down.

Everything was silvered, swathed in the finest chain mail imaginable. It was a metallic mesh, wrapped around the physical world. I could see my car looming, but dimly, dimly, all glitter and glint. Beyond, even dimmer, the bare trunks of trees appeared, disappeared, appeared again, wavery in the hazy light. I could feel the wet on my face, and see it on my black leather coat.

I heard a weird chonking sound, and turned toward it. Then it became clopping. I heard the whinny of a horse, and out of the shivery mist, coming at a fast trot, rode Julie Thorndecker, sitting astride a big bay gelding. She pulled up alongside me. I stepped back hastily as the horse took a few skittering steps on the gravel, his eyes stretched. Then she quieted him, stroking his neck, whispering to him. I moved closer.

They had obviously been on a gallop. Steam came drifting from the beast's flanks and haunches; its breath was one long plume of white. It still seemed excited from the run: pawed the driveway, moved about restlessly, tossed its head. But Mrs. Thorndecker continued her ministering, solid in the English saddle. That was one hell of a horse. From my point of view, it seemed enormous, with a neck that was all glistening muscle, and a mouthful of teeth as big as piano keys.

Julie was wearing brown boots, whipcord jodhpurs, a creamy flannel shirt, suede jacket, gloves. There was a red silk scraf about her throat: the only splash of color in that somber scene. Her head was not covered, and the mist had matted down her fine hair so that it clung to her skull.

Before I could say, "Hi," or "Hello," or "Does he bite?" she had slipped from the saddle and landed lightly on her feet alongside me. She flipped the reins over the horse's head, then wrapped them around her hand.

"You always ride in the rain?" I asked her.

"It isn't raining," she said. "Just dampish. When the ground freezes, and the snow comes, I don't ride at all. Today was super."

"Glad to hear it."

"I have to cool him off," she said. "Take a little walk?"

"Sure," I said. "You walk between me and the horse."

"Are you afraid of horses?"

"Lady," I said, "I'm afraid of cocker spaniels."

So off we went, strolling slowly, that great beast following us like an equine chaperon.

"Have a nice visit?" she asked.

I hadn't forgotten that husky voice, that throaty, almost tremulous voice. It still seemed to promise everything a man might desire, and more. I began to warm under my trenchcoat.

"I like your hat," she said suddenly.

"Thanks," I said, flipping the limp brim at her. "It was made in Ireland, so I suppose it loves weather like this. Might even begin to grow. How long do we walk before that monster cools off?"

"A few minutes," she said. "Bored with me already?"

"No," I said. "Never," I vowed.

She laughed, a deep, shirred chuckle.

"Aren't you sweet," she said.

"I am," I acknowledged.

It seemed to me we were walking down a narrow road of packed earth. On both sides, indistinct in the fog, were the black trunks of winter-stripped trees, with spidery branches almost meeting overhead. It was like walking into a tunnel of smoke: everything gray and swirling. Even the light seemed to pulse: patches of pearl, patches of sweat.

"Did you have a good visit?" she asked again.

"Very good."

"And did you like what you saw?"

"Oh yes."

"Glad to hear it. You had a talk with my husband?"

"I did. A long talk. A long, interesting talk."

"Good," she said. "Perhaps he'll forgive me."

I turned to look at her. "Oh? For what?"

"For sending Ronnie Goodfellow to see you. I did that, you know. From the best motives in the world."

"I'm sure they were," I said.

"You aren't angry, are you?"

She stopped, I stopped, the horse stopped. She put a hand on my arm. She came a half-step closer, looked up at me.

"It won't hurt Telford, will it?" she breathed. "My sending Ronnie to see if you were settled in? It won't hurt our chances of getting the grant?''

That young face was as damp as mine. I remember seeing tiny silver beads of moisture on her long, black lashes. Her cheeks were still flushed from the gallop, and those ripe lips seemed perpetually parted, waiting. Everything about her seemed complaisant and yearning. Except the eyes. The eyes were wet stones.

Why, I wondered, with hard eyes like that, should she seem so peculiarly vulnerable to me? It was her crackly voice, I decided, and the little boy's hair-do, and the warmth of her hand on my arm, and the loose, free way she moved. The giving way.

"Of course not," I said. "You didn't do anything so awful. As a matter of fact, I liked Goodfellow. No harm done."

"Thank you," she said faintly. "You've made me feel a lot better." She came another half-step closer. "It's so important, you see. To Telford. To me. To all of us."

If, at that moment, she had looked into my eyes, batted her lashes, and murmured, "I'll do anything to get my husband that grant—*anything*," I think I would have burst out laughing. But she wasn't that obvious. There was just the warm hand on my arm, the two half-steps toward me, the implied intimacy in that furry scene of smoke, lustrous mist, shadowy trees, and a steaming horse making snorting noises behind us and beginning to paw impatiently at the earth.

We turned back, slowly. We walked a few minutes in silence. She hauled on the reins with both hands until the gelding's head was practically over her shoulder. She reached up to stroke that velvety nose.

"You darling," she said. "Darling."

I didn't know if she meant the horse or me. But then, at that moment, I suspected I might be happy.

We were about halfway back to the Hall when faintly, from far off, I heard the cry, "Julie! Julie!" Dimmed by distance, muffled by fog, that wailed cry stopped us dead in our tracks. It seemed to come from everywhere, almost howled, distorted: "Joo-lee! Joo-lee!" We looked around in the tunnel, trying to determine the direction. "Joo-lee! Joo-lee!" Louder now.

Then, first a drifting shade, then a dark presence, and then a figure wavering in the putty light, came running Edward Thorndecker. He pounded up to us, stood accusingly, hands on waist, chest heaving.

"Where *were* you?" he demanded of his stepmother. "You didn't come back from your ride and, my God, I was so worried! I thought you might have been thrown. Hurt. Killed! Julie, you've got to—"

"Edward," she interrupted sweetly, putting a hand on his arm (the same goddamned hand that had been on *my* arm!), "say hello to Mr. Todd."

"Hello, Mr. Todd," he said, not bothering to look at me. "Julie, you have no idea how frantic I was. My God, I was ready to call the cops."

"Were you, dear?" she said with that throaty chuckle. "You *must* have been upset if you were ready to call the cops."

I guessed it was an inside joke, because they both started laughing, he hesitantly at first, then without restraint. I didn't catch the enormous humor of it all, but it gave me a chance to take a closer look at him.

He was wearing a prep school uniform: dark blue blazer, gray flannel slacks, black shoes, black knitted tie. No coat, no hat. He was a beautiful, beautiful boy, clear cheeks flushed from running, red lips open, blue eyes clear and sparkling. And those crisp black curls, glittering with the wet.

"Julie," he said, "I've got to talk to you. Do you know what father—"

She leaned forward and pressed a gloved forefinger softly to his lips, silencing him. If she had done that to me, I'd have—ahh, the hell with it.

"Shh, Edward," she said, smiling with her mouth but not with her eyes. "We have a guest, and I'm sure Mr. Todd is not interested at all in a minor family disagreement. Mr. Todd, will you excuse us, please?"

Both looked at me, he for the first time. Since neither showed any indication of moving, I gathered I was being given the bum's rush.

"Of course," I said. I removed my sodden tweed hat and held it aloft. "Mrs. Thorndecker," I said. "Edward," I said.

I replaced the lid, turned, and plodded away from them. I trudged back to my car, resolved that I absolutely would not turn around to look back at them. I did about twenty steps before I turned around to look back at them.

I could see them glimmering through that scrim of fine chain mail. They were framed in the billowing fog between the rows of black trees and veiny, arching branches. Their figures wavered. I wiped a hand across my eyes, hoping to get a clearer look. But it was not clear. It was all smoke and shadow. Still, it seemed to me they were in each other's arms. Close. Close.

Somewhere, on the way back to Coburn, I pulled off the road. I left the motor running, the heater on. I lowered the window a bit so I wouldn't take the long, long sleep. I lighted a cigarette, and I pondered. I'm good at that. Not concluding, just pondering. In this case, my reflections were a mishmash: objective judgments of things I had observed that afternoon interspersed with subjective memories of parted lips, silvered hair plastered flat, husky laughs, and a loose, yielding way of moving.

Conclusions? You'll never guess. The only hard fact I came up with was that Al Coburn was a wise old owl. He had guessed Julie Thorndecker had sicced Constable Goodfellow onto me, and he had been right. Decision: cultivate Al Coburn and see what other insights the old fart might reveal.

As for the rest: all was confusion. But if you can't endure that, you shouldn't be in the snooping business. Sooner or later (if you're lucky), actions, relationships, and motives get sorted out and begin to make sense.

It might not be rational sense, but I was dealing with human beings—and who says people have to be logical? Not me. And I speak from self-knowledge.

But there was one thing I could nail down, and had to. So I finished my cigarette, flicked the butt into what was now a freezing rain, and completed my drive into Coburn. It was about four-thirty, and I hoped I'd get there before the place closed for the day.

I made it—but not by much. Art Merchant had been right: the Coburn Civic Building was definitely not a tourist attraction. It was a two-story structure of crumbling red brick, designed along the general lines of an egg crate. The fire department occupied the ground level in front, the police department the ground level in back. The second floor was the City Hall: one big, hollow room. A bronze plaque on the outside wall stated: "This building erected by the Works Progress Administration, 1936; Franklin D. Roosevelt, President." Some loyal Democrat should have destroyed that.

I tramped up a wooden stairway, steps dusty and sagging. The wall was broken by tall, narrow windows affording a splendid view of the boarded-up A&P. At the top of the stairs were frosted glass doors bearing the legend: "oburn ity all." The lettering was in black paint, which had lasted. I figured the capital letters had been in gilt which had flaked off years ago and had never been replaced.

In all that cavernous room there was one middle-aged lady spraying her blue hair with a long aerosol can that could have been "Sparkle-Clear" or "Roach-Ded," for all I knew. She looked at me disapprovingly.

"We're closed," she yelled at me from across the room.

I made a big business of looking at my watch.

"Nah," I called, smiling winsomely, "you wouldn't do that to me—would you? You've got to finish spraying your lovely hair, and then the nails to touch up, and a few phone calls to your girlfriends, and it's only fifteen minutes to five, and I swear what I want won't take more than two minutes. Three maybe. Five at the most. Look at me—a poor traveler from out of town, come to your fair city seeking help in my hour of need. Can you turn me away? In your heart of hearts, can you really reject me?"

I don't apologize for this shit.

"Real estate?" she guessed. "The plats are over on the left, and if you—"

"No, no," I said. "Something much sadder. An uncle of mine passed away in Coburn only last night. Poor man. I need copies of the death certificate. You know—for insurance, bank accounts, the IRS and so forth. I need about ten copies."

"Sorry," she sang out. We were shouting at each other across at least fifty feet of empty office. "Death certificates go to the county seat. The Health Department. They have fire-proof files."

"Oh," I said, deflated. "Well, thanks, anyway."

"Of course, we keep photocopies of Coburn deaths," she said. "They're in the Deceased file on your right, between Bankruptcies and Defaults."

"May I take a quick look, ma'm?" I asked politely. "Just to make sure there is a certificate filed on my uncle?"

"Help yourself," she called. "I have to make a phone call. Then I'm locking up, so don't be long."

"Won't take a minute," I promised.

She got busy on the phone. I got busy on the Deceased file. The photocopy of Petersen's certificate was easy to find; it was in front, the most recent Coburn death. Chester K. Petersen, 72, resident of Crittenden Hall. The certificate was signed by Dr. Kenneth Draper.

But that wasn't what I was looking for. My eyes raced to find Cause of Death. There it was:

Congestive heart failure.

I glanced at the blue-haired lady. She was still giggling on the phone. I fumbled through the file as quickly as I could. I managed to go back through the previous two years. There had been twenty-three death certificates filed that listed Crittenden Hall as place of residence. The certificates were signed by Dr. Kenneth Draper and several other doctors. I guessed they were the resident MD's in Crittenden Hall.

Item: Two years ago, there had been six certificates filed, signed by four different MD's, including Draper. There had been a variety of causes of death.

Item: During the past year, there had been eighteen certificates filed, including Petersen's. Of these, fourteen had been signed by Draper, the others by residents.

Item: Of the fourteen death certificates in the past year signed by Dr. Kenneth Draper, eleven listed congestive heart failure as cause of death. The other three noted acute alcoholism, emphysema, and leukemia.

Nowhere, on any of the death certificates, did the name Dr. Telford Gordon Thorndecker appear.

"Finished?" the blue-haired lady called.

"Yes, thank you."

"Find what you wanted?" she yelled.

I smiled, waved, and got out of there. Did I find what I wanted? What did I want?

Driving back to the Coburn Inn, I recalled the exact conversation:

Me: "What did he die of? Petersen?"

Nurse Stella Beecham: "Pelvic cancer. Inoperable. He didn't respond to chemotherapy."

Someone was lying. Beecham or Draper, who had signed the certificate stating congestive heart failure was the cause of death.

And all those other puzzling statistics . . .

I needed a drink.

So, apparently, did half of Coburn. The bar at the Inn was two-deep with stand-up drinkers, and all of the booths were occupied. I took a small table, and grabbed the harried waiter long enough to order a vodka gimlet and a bag of potato chips with a bowl of taco-flavored cheese dip. My brain was whirling—why not my stomach?

I was working on drink and dip, using both hands, when I heard a breathless . . .

"Hi! Buy a thirsty girl a drink?"

I lurched to my feet.

"Hello, Millie," I said, gagging on a chip. "Sure, sit down. What'll you have?"

"My usual," she said. "Chivas Regal and 7-Up."

I don't think she saw me wince. I shouted the order at the passing waiter, then looked around nervously; I don't enjoy being seen in public with a cop's wife. It's not a matter of morality; it's a matter of survival. But fortunately, there was an old John Wayne movie on the bar's seven-foot TV screen, and most of the patrons were staring at that.

"Don't worry," Millie laughed. "Ronnie's working a twelve-hour shift tonight: four to four."

I looked at her with respect, and began to revise my opinion. I pushed the dip toward her, and she dug in.

"Besides," she said, spraying me with little bits of potato chip, "he doesn't give a damn who I drink with."

"Besides," I added, "he'd be happy to know you're helping make my stay in Coburn a pleasant one. He wants me to be happy."

"Yeah," she said, brightening, "that's right. Am I really helping?"

"You bet your sweet patootie," I said. "Love that tent you're wearing."

She looked down at the flowered muumuu.

"Really?" she said doubtfully. "This old thing? It doesn't show much."

"That's what makes it so exciting," I told her. "It leaves everything to the imagination."

She leaned forward and whispered:

"Know what I've got on underneath?"

I knew the answer to that one, but I couldn't spoil her big yock.

"What?" I asked.

"Just perfume!" she shouted, leaned back and laughed like a maniac.

Her drink arrived, and she took a big gulp, still spluttering with mirth. It gave me a chance to take a closer look at her.

The face was older than the body. There were lines at the corners of eyes and mouth. Beneath the heavy makeup, the skin was beginning to look pouchy and tired. And there was something in her expression perilously close to defeat. But the neck was strong and smooth, firm breasts poked, the backs of her hands were unblemished. Nothing defeated about that body.

"Where do you and Ronnie live, Millie?" I asked idly.

"Way to hell and gone," she said sullenly. "Out on Fort Peabody Drive."

I thought a moment.

"Near Crittenden Hall?"

"Yeah," she said sourly, "right *near* it. Their fence runs along the back line of our property."

"What have you got—a house, farm, mobile home?"

"A dump," she said. "We got a dump. Could I have another one of these?"

I ordered another round of drinks.

"Tell me, Millie," I said, "where do the good citizens of Coburn go when they want to cut loose? Don't tell me they all come in here and watch television?"

"Oh, there's a few places," she said, coming alive. "Roadhouses. Out on the Albany post road. Nothing fancy, but they have jukes and dancing. Sometimes Red Dog Betty's has a trio on Saturday night."

"Red Dog Betty's?"

"Yeah. There's a big poodle in red neon outside the place. It's kind of a rough joint. A lot of truckers stop there. But loads of fun."

She looked at me hopefully, but I wasn't having any. I wasn't drunk enough for Red Dog Betty's and loads of fun.

"Tell me about the places you go to in New York," she said.

I didn't tell her about the places I go to; she'd have been bored silly. But I told her what I thought she wanted to hear, describing fancy restaurants, swinging bars, discos, outdoor cafes, beaches, pick-up joints and make-out joints.

Her face became younger and wistful. She asked eager questions. She wanted to know how the women dressed, how they acted, what it cost to live in New York, could she get an apartment, could she get a job.

"Could I have fun there?" she asked.

I felt like weeping.

"Sure, you could," I said. "Maybe not every minute. It can be the loneliest place in the world. But yes, you could have fun."

She thought about that a moment. Then the defeat came back in her eyes.

"Nah," she said mournfully. "I'd end up peddling my tail on the street."

It was another revelation. No dumbbell she. I had underestimated her. The clown makeup and the tart's costume she was wearing the first time I saw her had misled me. Maybe she wasn't intelligent, but she was shrewd enough to know who she was and what she was.

She knew that in Coburn she was *somebody*. Men came to the Inn lobby to buy their cigars and cigarettes and magazines and newspapers, just to wisecrack with her, to get a look at the finest lungs west of the Hudson River, to flirt, to dream. The femme fatale of Coburn, N.Y. As much a

tourist attraction as Lovers' Leap and the place where the British spy was
hanged. And in New York City, she'd end up hawking her ass on Eighth
Avenue, competing with 15-year-old hookers from Minneapolis, and she
knew it.

She knew it in her mind, but knowing couldn't entirely kill the dream,
end the fantasy. The wild, crazy, raucous, violent city drew her, beckoned,
lured, seduced. Loads of fun down there. *Loads* of fun.

The bar was emptying, the patrons going off grumbling to farms, homes,
wherever. There were several empty booths.

"Have dinner with me, Millie," I said impulsively. "You'd be doing
me a favor. I get tired of eating alone, and I'd—"

"Sure," she said promptly. "We'll eat right here. Okay? I hear the
meat loaf is very good tonight."

It was good, as a matter of fact. I think it was a mixture of beef, pork,
and lamb, very juicy and nicely seasoned. With it, they served thick slices
of potato that had been baked, then browned and crusted in a skillet.
Creamed spinach. We both had warm apple pie a la mode for dessert. I
figured if this Thorndecker investigation went on much longer, I was going
to need a new wardrobe, three sizes larger.

We had a bottle of New York State red with the meal, and brandy
stingers with our coffee. Millie Goodfellow sat there, chin propped on her
hand, a benign smile on her face, and I admit I was feeling the way she
looked: slack, satisfied, and grinny. The memory of those eleven congestive heart failures in the past year at Crittenden Hall slid briefly into my
mind, and slid right out again.

"You were talking about going to New York," I said. "Just you? Or
you and your husband?"

"What do you think?" she said scornfully. "He'll never leave this turd-
kicking town. He *likes* it here, for God's sake."

"Well . . ." I said, "it's his home. I understand his family have lived
her for years and years."

"That's not the reason," she said darkly. "The reason he won't get
out."

"Oh?" I said. "What is the reason?"

She put her two forefingers together and her two thumbs together, and
made an elongated spade-shaped opening. She looked down at it, then up
at me.

"Know what I mean?" she said.

"Yes," I said, "I think I know what you mean."

We were sitting across from each other in a highbacked booth. The
checkered tablecloth hung almost to the floor. Millie Goodfellow squirmed
around a bit, and before I knew it, she had a stockinged foot in my groin,
tapping gently.

"Hi there!" she said brightly.

"Uh . . . hi," I said, sliding a hand below the tablecloth to grip her ankle. It wasn't passion on my part; it was fear. One sharp kick would have me singing soprano.

"Sex is keeping him in Coburn?" I asked.

She winked at me.

"You said it, I didn't," she said.

"Let me guess," I said. "Julie Thorndecker."

She winked again.

"You catch on fast," she said. "She's got him hypnotized. He's in heat for her all the time. Walks around with his tongue hanging out. And other things a lady can't mention. He can't think straight. He runs errands for her. If she told him to, he'd jump in the river. He's gone nuts. He's out there all the time. I think they're making it in the back seat of his cruiser. Hell, maybe they're making it in our place while I'm working. She'd get a charge out of that: screwing my husband in my bed."

"Are you sure, Millie?"

"Sure, I'm sure," she said roughly. "But you think I give a damn? I don't give a damn. Because you know what the funny thing is?"

"What's the funny thing?"

"He thinks he's the only one, but he's only one of many, son. She's laying everything in pants. Maybe even that bull dyke Agatha Binder. Maybe even that sissy stepson of hers, that kid Edward. I wouldn't be a bit surprised. I'm telling you, Constable Ronald H. Goodfellow is in for a rude awakening one of these days. Oh yes. And I couldn't care less. But you know what burns my ass?"

"A flame about this high?" I asked, holding my palm at table level.

She was drunk enough to think that funny.

"What burns me," she said, still giggling, "is that I've got the reputation for being the fast one. Always playing around—you know? Cheating on my husband with every drummer and trucker who comes to town. That's what people think. And she's the re-*feened* Mrs. Lah-de-dah, wife of the big scientist, the first lady of Coburn. And she's just a randy bitch. She out-fucks me three to one. But I get the reputation. Is that fair? You know what I'm going to do? I'm going to hire a private detective and get pictures of them together. You know—naked as jaybirds and banging away. Then I'm going to sue Ronnie for divorce and smear her name and the pictures all over the place."

"No, Millie," I said, "you're not going to do that."

"No," she said dully, "I won't. I can't. Because Ronnie knows about me. Names, dates, places. He's got it all in that little goddamned notebook of his. He knows about me, and I know about him. Hey!" she said brightly. "What happened to our happy little party?" Her stockinged toes beat a rapid tattoo on my cringing testicles. "Let's you and me go up to your room. You show me the New York way, and I'll show you the Coburn way."

"What's the Coburn way?"

"Standing up in a hammock."

"Hell," I said laughing, "I don't even know the New York way. Unless it's impotence. I'm going to beg off, Millie. I appreciate your kind offer, but I'm somewhat weary and I'm somewhat drunk, and I wouldn't want to disappoint you. Another time. When I'm in tip-top condition."

The toes dug deeper.

"Promise?" she breathed.

"Promise," I nodded.

I paid the tab, we collected hats and coats, and I walked her out to her Ford Pinto in the parking lot. She was feeling no pain, but she was talking lucidly and wasn't staggering or anything. I believed her when she said she could get home all right.

"As a matter of fact," she said, "I'm practically stone cold sober. I might even stop by Red Dog Betty's and see if there's any action tonight."

"Don't do that, Millie," I urged. "Go home, go to bed, and dream of me. I'll go upstairs, go to bed, and dream of you. We'll have a marvelous dream together."

"Okay," she said, "that's what we'll do. You're so sweet, I could eat you up. Come in and sit with me a minute while the car warms up."

She pulled me into the car with her, started the engine, turned on the heater. I fumbled for a cigarette, but before I knew what was happening, she was all over me like a wet sheet. Her mouth was slammed against mine, a frantic tongue was exploring my fillings.

I knew it wasn't my manly charm. It wasn't even her physical wanting. It was misery and loneliness and hurt. It was despair. And the only way she could exorcise that was to cleave to a warm bod, any bod. I just happened to be the nearest.

She pulled her mouth away.

"Hold me," she gasped. "Please. Just hold me."

I held her, and hoped it was comfort. She took my hand and thrust it under her coat, under that long, voluminous skirt. She had been truthful: all she had on beneath the shift was perfume. She pressed my palm against a long, cool thigh. She just held it there and closed her eyes.

"Sweet," she whispered. "So sweet. Isn't it sweet?"

"Yes," I said. "Millie, I've—"

"I know," she said, releasing my hand and smiling bravely, "you've got to go. Okay. You'll be in town awhile?"

"Another few days at least," I said.

"We'll get together?" she asked anxiously.

"Sure we will."

"Listen, all that stuff I said about Julie Thorndecker—I shouldn't have said all that. It's all bullshit. None of it's true. I'm just jealous, that's all. She's so beautiful."

"And young," I said, like an idiot.

"Yes," she said in a low voice. "She's young."

I kissed her cheek and got out of there. I watched her drive away. When she turned onto Main Street, I waved, but I don't think she saw me. I hoped she wasn't going to Red Dog Betty's. I hoped nothing bad would happen to her. I hoped she'd be happy. I hoped I'd wake in the morning without a hangover. I hoped I'd go to Heaven when I died.

I knew none of these things was going to happen.

I went back into the bar. I had two straight brandies, figuring they'd settle the old tum-tum, and I'd be able to sleep without pills. Something was nagging at me. A memory was nagging, and I couldn't recall, couldn't define, couldn't pin it down. It had nothing to do with the Thorndecker investigation. It was a memory revived by something that had happened in the past hour, something that had happened with Millie Goodfellow.

It was more than an hour before I grabbed it. I was up in my room, hunched over on the bed, two boots and one sock off, when it came to me. I sat there, stunned, a wilted sock dangling in my fingers. The memory stunned me. Not the memory itself, but the fact that when it happened, I was convinced it would turn my life around, and I'd never forget it. Now it took me an hour to dredge it out of the past. So much for the woes of yesteryear.

What happened was this . . .

About two years previously—Joan Powell and I enjoying a sharp, hard, bright, and loving relationship—I was assigned a field investigation in Gary, Indiana: not *quite* the gardenspot of America.

An assistant professor in a second-rate engineering school had submitted an application for a modest grant. His specialty was solar energy, and he had been doing independent research on methods to increase the efficiency of solar cells. They're squares of gallium arsenide that convert sunlight directly to electricity. Even the types used in the space program were horribly expensive and not all that efficient.

The professor had developed, he said, a method of electronic amplification that boosted the energy output above that of fossil fuels at half the cost. Not only did I not know what the hell his diagrams and equations meant, but Scientific Research Records, who analyzed his proposals, more or less admitted they were stumped: "The claims made herein represent a totally new and unique approach to this particular problem, and there is nothing in current research to substantiate or refute the applicant's proposals." In other words: "We just don't know."

Lifschultz Associates reported the professor was small potatoes, financially speaking. He had a mortgage, a car loan, two kids in college, and a few bucks in the bank. Small insurance, small investments, small everything. Mr. Everyman.

Donner & Stern didn't have much to add of a personal nature. The professor had been married to the same woman for twenty-six years, had those two kids, drove a five-year-old car, didn't drink, gamble, or carouse, was something of an enigma to neighbors and colleagues. He was polite, quiet, withdrawn, didn't seem to have any close friends, and apparently his only vice was playing viola in a local amateur string quartet.

I went out to Gary to see him, and it was pretty awful. He had fixed up a basement lab in his home, but it looked like a tinkerer's workshop to me. He didn't talk much, and his dumpy wife was even quieter. I remember they served me a glass of cranberry juice, and put out a plate of Milky Ways cut into little cubes.

I thought he was a loser—the whole family were losers—and I guess some of this crept into my report. Anyway, his application was denied, and he got one of our courteous goodby letters.

A few days later he tried to swallow a shotgun and blew his brains all over his basement workshop.

I don't know why it hit me so hard. The professor wasn't rejected just on the basis of my report; the special investigators had been as unenthusiastic as I was. But I couldn't get rid of the notion that his suicide was my fault; I had done him in. If I had been a little kinder, more sympathetic, more understanding, maybe he'd have gotten his ridiculously small grant, and maybe his cockamamie invention would have proved out. Maybe the guy was another Edison. We'll never know, will we?

The night after I heard of his death, I had dinner with Joan Powell. We ate at a restaurant on West 55th Street that specialized in North Italian cooking. Usually I thought the food was great. That night the pasta tasted like excelsior. Powell knew my moods better than her own, and asked me what was wrong. I told her about the suicidal professor in Gary, Indiana.

"And don't tell me it wasn't my fault," I warned her. "Don't tell me that logically I have no business blaming myself. I don't want to listen to any logic."

"I wasn't going to serve you any," she said quietly.

"It goes beyond logic," I said. "It's irrational, I know. I just feel like shit, that's all."

"*Must* you use words like that?"

"You do," I reminded her.

"Not at the dinner table," she said loftily. "There is a time and place for everything."

I poked at my food, and she stared at me.

"Todd, you're really hurting, aren't you?"

"He was such a sad schlumpf," I groaned. "A little guy. And plain. His wife was plain, too. I mean they had nothing: no wit, no personality, and they weren't even physically attractive. Do you think that affected my judgment?"

"Probably," she said.

"You're a big help."

"Do you want advice or sympathy?"

"Neither," I said. "But five minutes of silence would be nice."

"Fuck you," she said.

"*Must* you use words like that?"

"I told you, there's a time and place for everything."

"Powell, what am I going to *do*?"

"Do? You can't do anything, can you? It's done, isn't it?"

"How long am I going to feel this lousy? The rest of my life?"

"Nooo," she said wisely, "I don't think so. A week. A month maybe. It'll pass."

"The hell you say," I growled. "Let's go."

"Go? Where?"

"Anywhere. I've got to get out of here."

"All right," she said equably. "You owe me half a veal cutlet Parmesan."

"Put it on my bill," I said.

"You're running up a big tab, buster," she said. "I'm not sure you're good for it."

If I had been in a better mood, I would have enjoyed that night: late September, with balm in the air over a little nip that warned of what was coming. I don't know how long we drove—an hour maybe. No, it was longer than that. We went up to the George Washington Bridge, turned around, and drove back down to the Battery. Not what you'd call a restful, bucolic drive. But working the traffic helped keep my mind off my misery. I don't think Joan Powell and I exchanged a dozen words during that trip. But she was there beside me, silent. It helped.

After we watched a Staten Island ferry pull in and pull out—about as exciting as watching grass grow—I drove back up the east side to Powell's home. She lived in one of those enormous high-rise luxury apartment houses that have an institutional look: hospitals, office buildings, or just a forty-story file cabinet.

There were two below-ground parking levels. Powell didn't own a car—didn't drive, as a matter of fact—but after I started seeing her, dating her, spending time in her apartment, including weekends, I persuaded her to rent a parking space. It cost fifty a month, and I paid it gladly. A lot easier than trying to find parking space on the street in that neighborhood. Plus the fact that my hubcaps were relatively secure.

Our parking space was down on the second level. A little like parking in the Lincoln Tunnel. It was a scary place: pools of harsh light and puddles of black darkness. Silent cars, heavy and gleaming. Concrete pillars and oil stains. I parked, switched off the motor. We lighted cigarettes, and were very alone.

I went through it all again. The schlumpfy professor, his crazy scheme, his mousy wife. The glass of cranberry juice and cubes of cut-up Milky Ways. The amateurish home laboratory, and how I couldn't understand what the hell he was mumbling about when he showed me his equations, demonstrated his equipment, and made an electric fan run on the power of a 100-watt lightbulb shining on a chip of white, glassy stuff.

Joan Powell let me gabble. She sat apart, hugging herself against the basement chill. A cigarette burned down in her lips. Her sleek head was tilted to keep the smoke from her eyes. She didn't say a word while I spun out my litany of woe and declaimed my guilt.

I ended my soliloquy and waited for a reaction. Nothing.

"Well?" I demanded.

"You know what I think you need right now?" she said.

"What?"

"A good fuck."

"Oh my," I said. "Listen to the lady."

We put out our cigarettes, turned to stare at each other. Powell was looking at me steadily, and there was something in her fine features I had never seen before: strength and knowing and calm acceptance. Maybe we're all created equal, in the sight of God and under the law, but there is quality in people. I mean human character runs the gamut from slug to saint. I realized, maybe for the first time, that this was one superior human.

And because I was feeling so deeply it embarrassed me, I had to say something brittle and smart-alecky. But I never did get it out. I choked on the words, and just came apart. I don't apologize for it; it had been coming on since I heard of the professor's messy death. But I wasn't mourning just for him; I was crying for all the sad, little schlumpfs in the world. For all of us. The losers.

Powell was holding me in her arms then, and I was gasping and moaning and trying to tell her all those things.

"Shh," she kept saying. "Shh. Shh."

I remembered she stroked my hair, kissed my fingers, touched my lips. She held me until I stopped shivering, pulling my head down to her warm breast. She rocked a little, back and forth, like a mother holding an infant. She smelled good to me, warm and fragrant, and I nuzzled my nose down into her neckline and kissed the soft skin.

It all went so slowly. After awhile it went in silence. I had the feeling, and I think she did too, that we were alone on earth. We were locked in a car, in an underground garage, the weight of an enormous building above, the whole earth below. We were in a coffin in a cavern in a mine. I had never known such sweet solitude, closed around like that.

And I had never known such intimacy, such closeness, not even naked on a sweated sheet. Without speaking, we opened to each other. I could feel it, feel the flow between us. My anguish was diluted by her strength; I suppose she took some of my hurt into her. Sharing eased the pain. When I kissed her, it was almost like kissing myself. A strange experience, but there it was. She was me, and I was her. It was peace. That's the only way I can describe it: it was total peace.

Well . . . that happened two years previously. I was convinced that night was going to remake my life, that I would suddenly become saintly and good, full of kindness and understanding. I didn't change, of course. The next day I was my normal shitty self, and a week later I had forgotten all about the dead professor, and a week after that I had forgotten all about an hour of total peace in an underground garage with Joan Powell when we had done nothing but hold each other and share. If I remembered it at all, it was to wonder why we hadn't screwed.

Now, two years later, sitting in a lonely room in Coburn, N.Y., the memory of that night came back. I knew what had triggered it: those few moments alone in the car with Millie Goodfellow. I had felt the stirring of the same emotion, the feeling of closed-in intimacy, of being the only survivors in the world, everything blocked out but the two of us, comforting, consoling.

I had been deceiving myself to think I was the only comforter, the lone consoler. She had given warm assurance to me as well, and when I waved goodby, the lights of her car fading into the black night, I was sorry to see her go. Because then I was really alone. And I was afraid.

I knew what it was. It all came back to Thorndecker. I could hear the name itself, boomed out by the Voice of Doom, with deep organ chords in the background: "Thooorn-deck-er. Thoorn-deck-er." It was like the tolling of a mournful bell. And even when I was in bed, covers pulled up, anxious for sleep to come, in my fear I heard that slow dirge and saw a dark funeral procession moving across frozen ground.

The Fourth Day

I woke suddenly, tasting my tongue, smelling my breath. I stared at the crackled ceiling and wondered how long I had been buried in Coburn, N.Y.

I had been through that mid-case syndrome before. In any investigation, the disparate facts and observations pile up, a jumble, and you'd like nothing better than to walk away whistling, tossing a live grenade over your shoulder as you go. Then you close the door carefully and— *boom!*—all gone.

I think, in my case, the discouragement comes from a hopeless romanticism. I want people to be nice. Everyone should be sweet-tempered, polite, considerate, and brush their teeth twice a day. There should be no stale breaths and furry tongues in the world. I like happy endings.

I stared morosely at my sallow face in the mirror of the bathroom medicine cabinet, and I knew the Thorndecker investigation wasn't going to have a happy ending. It saddened me, because I didn't dislike any of the people involved. Some, like Stella Beecham and banker Art Merchant, left me indifferent. But most of the others I liked, or recognized as fallible human beings caught up in fates they could not captain.

Except Dr. Telford Gordon Thorndecker. I couldn't see him as a willy-nilly victim. The man was master of his soul; that much was obvious. But his motives were wrapped around. At that dinner party—his youthful vigor and raw exuberance. A part he was playing? And then, in his study, another role: the serious, intent man of science, with a politician's use of charm and a secret delight in the manipulation of others. Which man was Thorndecker? Or was there another, another, another? A whole deck of Thorndeckers: Jack, Queen, King, and finally . . . the Joker?

I showered, shaved, dressed, and had a terrible desire to telephone Joan Powell, that complete woman. Not even to talk. Just to hear her say, "Hello?" Then I'd hang up. I didn't call, of course, I just mention it here to illustrate my state of mind. I wasn't *quite* out of the tree, but I was swinging.

Sam Livingston took me down in the ramshackle elevator. We exchanged mumbles. We both seemed to be in the same surly mood. If I had given him a bright, "Good morning, Sam!" he'd have kicked me in the jewels, and if he had sung out, "Nice, sunny morning," I'd have delivered a sharp karate chop behind his left ear. So we both just mumbled. It was that kind of a morning.

I saw Millie Goodfellow behind the cigar counter, and was pleased to know she was still alive. She was in one of her biddy's costumes again: a ruffled blouse cut down to the pipik, wide black leather belt, short denim skirt with rawhide lacing down the front, like a man's fly. She was also wearing dark, dark sunglasses.

I bought another pack of cigarettes I didn't need.

"Incognito this morning, Millie?" I inquired casually.

She lifted those dark cheaters, and I saw the mouse: a beauty. She had tried to cover it with pancake makeup, but the colors came through: glistening black, purple, yellow. The whole eye was puffed and bulging.

"Nice," I said. "Did you collect that at Red Dog Betty's?"

"No," she said, replacing the glasses, "this one was home-grown. I told him what I thought about him and his fancy lady."

I really didn't want to hear it. I didn't know if she was lying. I didn't know what the truth was. And on that feckless morning, I didn't care.

"See you around," I said, and started away.

A hand shot out, grabbed my arm.

"Remember what you promised last night?" she whispered.

That was last night, in another mood, another world, and before I knew her husband got physical.

"What?" I said. "Oh. Sure."

I stared at blank glass, not seeing her eyes.

"I remember," I said with a sleazy grin, more determined than ever to get my ass back to civilization as soon as possible.

I had another of those big, bulky country breakfasts. This one involved pancakes and pork sausages. I don't know what it did for my cholesterol count, but at least it took my mind off such topics as hanging, cyanide, and a long walk off a short pier. When I returned to the city, I decided, I'd diet, join a health club, exercise regularly, manufacture a hard stomach, and put the roses back in my cheeks. Is there no end to self-delusion?

On the way out, I detoured through the bar. Jimmy was behind the taps. I nodded at him. I didn't see anyone else, until I heard a rasped, "Todd. You there." I turned, and there was old Al Coburn sitting alone in a booth. He had a beer in front of him. I walked over.

"May I join you, Mr. Coburn?" I asked.

"No law against it," he said—as gracious an invitation as I've ever had.

I slid in opposite, called to Jimmy, pointed at Coburn's beer, and held up two fingers.

While we waited for our drinks to come, I said to him, "What's it like outside? Is the sun shining?"

"Somewhere," he said.

That seemed to take care of that. I stared at him. Have you ever seen bald land after a bad drought? Say the banks of a drained reservoir, or a parched river bed? That's the way Al Coburn's face looked. All cracks and lines, cut up like a knife had been drawn deep, the flesh without juice, squares and diamonds of dry skin.

But there was nothing juiceless about those washed-blue eyes. Looking into those was like staring into the Caribbean off one of the Bahamian cays. You stared and stared, seeing deep, deep. Moving things there, shifting shadows, sudden shapes, and then the clean, cool bottom. A few shells. Hard coral.

Maybe it was those pork sausages bubbling in my gut, but I felt uneasy. I felt there was more to Al Coburn than I had reckoned. I had misread Millie Goodfellow; there was more to her than the frustrated wife, the Emma Bovary of Coburn, N.Y. There was more to Al Coburn. If that was true, then it might be true of Agatha Binder, Art Merchant, Constable Goodfellow, Stella Beecham, Dr. Kenneth Draper—for the whole lot of them.

Maybe I was making an awful mistake. I was seeing them all (except Dr. Thorndecker) as two-dimensional cutouts. Types. Cardboard characters. But the longer I stayed around, the deeper I dug, the more they sprouted a third dimension. I was beginning to glimpse hidden motives and secret passions. It was like picking up Horatio Alger and finding William Faulkner. In *Coburn, N.Y.*!? A boggling thought, that in this brackish backwater there were characters who, if they didn't qualify for a Greek tragedy, were at least a few steps above, or deeper, than a TV sitcom.

We sipped our beers and looked vaguely at each other.

"How you coming?" Al Coburn asked in his scrawly voice.

"Coming?" I said. "On what?"

He looked at me with disgust.

"Don't play smarty with me, sonny," he said. "This Thorndecker thing. That's what I mean."

"Oh," I said. "That. Well, I'm making progress. Talking to people. Learning things."

He grunted, finished his old beer, started on the new.

"He's doing all right, ain't he," he said. "On Coburn land. Got a nice business going."

"It appears to be prosperous," I said cautiously. "Yes. I looked it over."

"That's what you think," he said darkly.

"What's that supposed to mean, Mr. Coburn?"

"The death of a man?" he said. "The world's heart don't skip a beat."

I shook my head, bewildered. I grabbed at a straw, and came up with nothing.

"Are you talking about Petersen?" I asked.

"Who?"

"Chester K. Petersen."

"Never heard of him."

"All right," I sighed. "You've lost me completely."

We drank awhile in silence. He glowered at his glass of beer, almost snarling at it. What a cantankerous old geezer he was. I watched him, damned if I'd give him another opening. If he had something to say, let him say it. Finally:

"Was he another?" he said.

"Petersen? I don't know. Another *what*?"

"Heart attack?"

"He died of congestive heart failure."

"Who says?"

"The death certificate says."

He smiled at me. I hope I never see another smile like it. It was all store teeth and blanched lips. A skeleton could smile with more warmth than that.

"The death certificate says," he repeated. "You believe *that*?"

This isn't original with me; I remember reading somewhere that the worst American insult, absolutely the *worst*, is to say, "Do you believe everything you read in the papers?" Al Coburn's last question had the same effect. I immediately went on the defensive.

"Well, uh, of course not," I stammered. "Not necessarily."

"Tell you a story," he said. More of a statement than a question.

I nodded, waved for two more beers, and settled back. I had nothing to lose but my sanity.

"Feller I knew name of Scoggins," he started. "Ernie Scoggins. We was friends from way back. Grew up together, Ernie and me. His folks had a sawmill on the river, but that went. They had an ice house, too. That was before refrigerators, you know, and them with all that sawdust to pack it in. Cut it on Loon Lake in the winter, and cover it over with burlap and sawdust in the ice house. Ernie and me used to sneak in there in the summer and suck on slivers of ice. I guess we was two crazy kids."

I could feel my eyeballs beginning to harden, and knew I was getting a glassy stare. I wanted to yelp, "Get on with it, for God's sake!" But

Al Coburn wasn't the kind of man you could hurry. He'd just shutter on me, and I'd never learn what he had on his mind. So I let him yabber.

"Bad luck," Coburn said. "Ernie sure had bad luck. His son got killed in Korea, and his two daughters just up and moved on. His wife died the same year my Martha went, and that brought us closer together, Ernie and me. Something in common—you know? Anyway, the sawmill went, and the ice house, of course. Ernie tried this and that, but nothing come out good for him. He took a lick at farming, and lost his crop in a hailstorm. Tried a hardware store, and that went bust. Put some money in a Florida land swindle, and lost that."

"Bad luck," I said sympathetically, repeating what he had said. But now he disagreed.

"Mebbe," he said. "But Ernie wasn't all that smart. I knew it, and I think sometimes he knew it. He just didn't have much above the eyebrows, Ernie didn't. Throwing his money around. But I'll tell you this: he was the best friend a man could have. Shirt off his back. Always cheerful. Could he tell a joke? Land! And a good word for everyone. Wasn't a soul in Coburn who didn't like Ernie Scoggins. Ask anyone; they'll tell you. Old Ernie Scoggins . . . "

He fell silent then, staring at his empty beer glass, ruminating. I took it for a hint, and signaled Jimmy for two more.

"What happened to him?" I asked Al Coburn. "Old Ernie Scoggins—is he still around?"

He didn't answer until Jimmy brought over our beers, collected the empty glasses, and went back behind the bar again.

"No, he ain't around," Coburn said in a low voice. "Not for almost a month now."

"Dead?"

He glanced at Jimmy, then leaned across the table to me.

"No one knows," he whispered. "Mebbe dead, mebbe not. He just disappeared."

"Disappeared?" I said incredulously. "You mean one fine day he just turned up missing?"

"That's right."

"Didn't anyone try to find him? His family?"

"Ernie didn't have no family," Coburn said, "rightly speaking. No one even knows where his two daughters are, if *they're* still alive. No brothers or sisters. I reckon you could say I was Ernie Scoggins' family. So after he didn't show up for a few days, I asked around. No one knew a thing."

"Did you report his disappearance to the police?"

Coburn snorted disdainfully, then took a long swallow of beer.

"To that Indian," he nodded. "Ronnie Goodfellow. The two of us went out to Ernie's place. He was living in a beat-up trailer out on Cypress Road. Goodfellow tried the door, it was open, and we went in. Everything looked all right. I mean the place wasn't broken up or anything like that. But most of Ernie's clothes was gone, including his Sunday-go-to-meeting suit, and a battered old suitcase I knew he owned. Goodfellow said it looked to him like Ernie just took off of his own free will. Just packed up and left.''

"Sounds like it," I said. "Did he have any debts in town?"

"Oh hell, Ernie *always* had debts. All his life."

"Well then? He just flew the coop. Got fed up and decided to try his luck somewhere else."

Al Coburn looked at me with a twisted face. I couldn't read it. Contempt there for me, and something else: indecision, and something else. Fear maybe.

"I'll tell you," he said. "The debts wasn't all that big. And for about two years before he disappeared, Ernie Scoggins had been working for Thorndecker out in Crittenden Hall."

"Oh," I said.

"It wasn't much of a job," Coburn said. " 'Maintenance personnel' was what they called it. Raking leaves, cutting down dead branches, taking care of the wife's bay gelding. Like that. But Ernie said it wasn't too hard, he was outside most of the time, you know, and the pay was good. I don't figure he ever paid a penny to Social Security in his life, and he needed that job. I can't see him just walking away from it. He wasn't any spring chicken, you know. My age."

I moved my beer glass around, making interlocking rings on the tabletop.

"What do you think happened?" I asked him. "Why did he leave?"

His answer was so faint I had to lean forward to hear his scratchy voice.

"I don't think Ernie Scoggins did leave," he said. "First of all, if he was taking off, he'd have stopped by to say so-long to me. I *know* that. Second of all, Ernie was in World War One, with the Marines. And he still had his helmet. You know, one of those pie-shaped hats with a brim. The old hunk of rusty tin was the one thing Ernie treasured. It was valuable to him. He never would have moved on without taking it with him. But when Goodfellow and I went into his place, the helmet was still there, setting on his little TV set."

"But his clothes were gone?"

"Most of them."

"And a suitcase?"

"Yes."

"And the door was open?"

He nodded.

I sat back, propped myself against the wall, put my feet up on the booth bench, sitting sideways to Coburn. I watched Jimmy polishing glasses behind the bar.

"I don't know," I said slowly. "I'll have to go along with Goodfellow. Ernie Scoggins packed some clothes and walked away. And left the door open because he wasn't coming back. He didn't take the helmet because there was no room for it in the valise. What's he going to do—wear it?''

He stared at me.

"Don't be a wisenheimer," he said.

I took a deep breath, blew it out, brought my feet down with a thump, and faced him.

"All right," I said, "you've obviously got more. What is it?''

"His car. It was still parked outside his trailer.''

"So he took a bus, a train, a plane.''

"He didn't," Al Coburn said. "I checked.''

"*You* checked? Didn't Constable Goodfellow check?''

"Not so's you know it.''

"Scoggins could have walked, or hitched a ride.''

"With his car there? Gas in the tank? You believe that?''

"No," I said unhappily. "All right, let's have it: what happened to Ernie Scoggins?''

When he didn't answer, I said:

"Look, Mr. Coburn, I've listened patiently to this sad story. You apparently think it's important enough for me to know about it. So I guess it's got something to do with Thorndecker. So why are you holding back? Is that all there is to the whole thing? An old boyhood pal of yours disappeared? What's the *point*?''

"Finish your beer," he said, finishing his.

I finished my beer. He jerked a thumb, got up, hobbled toward the exit. I paid Jimmy, then hurried after Coburn. He stumped his way through the lobby, out to the parking lot. We got in the cab of his dented Chevy pickup. I had time to note that it was a phlegmy day again, the sun hidden, an iron sky pressing down. And rawly cold.

"I think he's dead," Al Coburn said. "Ernie Scoggins. Dead and buried somewheres around here. I think they took some of his clothes and his suitcase to make it look like he just took off.''

"They?" I cried. "Who's *they*?''

He wouldn't answer that.

"Besides . . . '' he said. "Besides . . . ''

I held my breath. I had a feeling we had finally come to it. Coburn was gripping the steering wheel with bleached knuckles, leaning forward, staring unseeingly through the splattered windshield.

"Besides," he said, "about six months or so before he disappeared, Ernie gives me something to hold for him. A letter, in an envelope. If anything happens to me, he says, you open this and read it. Otherwise you just leave it sealed. He knew he could trust me, you see.''

The old man had gotten to me. It was damned cold in that pickup cab, but I could feel sweat trickling down my spine, a pressure under the sternum.

"All right, all right," I said tersely. "So something happened to him, and you opened it—right?"

He nodded.

"You read it?"

He nodded.

"Well, goddammit!" I exploded. "What the hell *was* it?"

He hunched forward a little further, still staring out that stupid windshield. I saw him in profile, saw what an ancient man he was: wattled and mottled, the jowls hanging slack, face cut and pitted deep. He looked terribly frail and vulnerable then. A strong wind might blow him away, a push crack a hip, a blow puddle the white, fragile skull showing through wisps of hair fine as corn silk.

"I haven't made up my mind," he said heavily. "Haven't decided."

"Is it a police matter?" I asked. "Should the cops know?"

"I can't," he said dully.

"Then show it to me, Mr. Coburn. Or tell me what it's all about. Maybe I can help. I think you need help."

"I've got notes at the bank," he said suddenly.

"What?" I said, bewildered by this new tack. "What are you talking about?"

"Notes," he said. "Loans with Art Merchant. He's given me one extension. I need another."

I caught on.

"And you think if you talk about what's in Ernie Scoggins' letter, you won't get your extension?"

"They'll crucify me."

"*They?*" I shouted again. "*They?* Who in God's name is *they?*"

"All of them," he said.

"Thorndecker?" I demanded.

But I couldn't get any more information out of him. All he'd say was that he had some thinking to do. The stubborn old coot! I slammed out of the cab and went back into the Inn, furious with him and furious with myself for listening to him. He didn't even thank me for the beers.

As usual, the lobby looked like the showroom of an undertaking parlor. The only thing lacking was a selection of caskets, lids open and waiting. I went over to the desk where one of the baldies was slowly turning the pages of *Hustler*, making "Tch, tch" sounds with tongue and teeth.

"I hate to interrupt your studies," I said, taking out my peevishness on him, "but I'd like to visit your local Episcopal Church. You got one?"

"Sure do," he said proudly. "First Episcopal Church of Coburn. My church. Nice place. The Reverend Peter Koukla. A marvelous preacher."

"How do I find it?"

"Easy as pie," he said happily. "East on Main Street to Cypress. Make a left, and there you are. You an Episcopalian?"

"Today I am," I said. "Thanks for the directions."

I started away.

"Mr. Todd," he said.

I turned back. He was looking somewhere over my head.

"Can I give you some advice, Mr. Todd?" he said in a low voice, in a rush.

"Sure. Everyone else does."

"I seed you with Al Coburn. You being a stranger in town and all, I got to tell you: Al Coburn is a nut. Always has been, always will be. I wouldn't pay no attention to anything he says, if I was you."

"Thank you," I said.

"A nut," he repeated. "He just shoots off his mouth. Everyone in town knows it. Senile, I guess. You know how they get."

"Sure," I said. "Thanks for the tip."

"Craperoo," he called after me. "He just talks craperoo."

I drove slowly east on Main Street, watching the rusted street signs for Cypress Road. Old Ernie Scoggins had lived on Cypress Road, I recalled. And the First Episcopal Church of Coburn was on Cypress Road. A coincidence that meant precisely nothing.

I was certain that sometime during the year, on favored days, blessed weeks, the sun shone on Coburn, N.Y. But I couldn't testify to it personally. It was now Thursday, and as far as I knew, there was a permanent shroud over the village. It seemed to have its own cloud cover. Sometimes, around the horizon, I could see a thin strip of blue sky and the sun shining on someone else. But an inverted bowl hung over Coburn. When it wasn't drizzling, it was misting, raining, snowing, sleeting. Or, as it was that day, just growly and frowning. It was only early December. What it might be like in January and February, I hated to think.

But the Episcopal Church was cheerful enough. Not a new building, but the weathered brick was warm and solid, wood trim white and freshly painted. A sign on the lawn gave the times for Sunday services, Sunday school, luncheon of the women's club, trustees' meeting, young folks' hootenanny, and so forth. Also, the subject of next Sunday's sermon: LOVE IS THE ANSWER. I wondered what the question was.

The wide front door was unlocked, and I walked into a big, pleasant nave. The most prosperous public setting I had seen in Coburn. Polished floor. Glistening pews. Well-designed altar and choir stall. Handsome organ. Everything clean and shipshape. A well-tended House of God, smelling faintly of Lemon Pledge.

I don't care how cynical you are, a church—any church—has a chastening effect. You find yourself speaking in whispers, walking on tiptoe, and trying very hard not to fart. Anyway, that's what church-going does to me. Religion is a language I don't understand, but I'm prepared to accept the fact that people communicate in it. Like Sanskrit.

I had the whole place to myself. If I knew how to fence new hymnals, I could have made a fine haul. I stepped gently up the center aisle, then heard the sound of hammering coming from somewhere. Bang, bang, bang. Pause. Bang, bang, bang. I followed the sound, through a side door, down a wide flight of iron steps. Bang, bang, bang. Louder now. There was a recreation room in the basement. Two Ping-Pong tables, and a sign on the wall: TRUST IN JESUS. Rather than a good backhand.

I walked down a cement corridor, and the banging stopped. He must have heard me coming because when I entered a small storage-workshop area, a man was facing the door with a hammer in his hand, raised.

"Beg your pardon," I said, "but I'm looking for the Reverend Peter Koukla."

"That's me," he smiled with relief, putting aside his weapon. "How may I be of service?"

"Samuel Todd," I said. "I'm here in—"

"Mr. Todd!" he cried enthusiastically, rushing forward to pump my hand. "Of course, of course! The Thorndecker grant! I heard you were in town. A pleasure. This *is* a pleasure!"

I don't know what I expected. A moth-eaten Moses, I suppose. But this Man of God was about my own age, or maybe a few years younger. He was shorter than me, and skinny as a fencer, nervy as an actor. Black hair covered his ears. Very long. Prince Valiant. A precisely trimmed black mustache and Vandyke beard. A white T-shirt that had IT'S FUN TO BE A CHRISTIAN printed on the front. Tailored, hand-stitched jeans that must have set him back a C-note, and Gucci loafers. But he wasn't wearing earrings; I'll say that for him.

We chatted of this and that for openers. Or rather, he chatted, and I listened, grinned, and nodded like one of those crazy dogs in the rear window of a car with Georgia license plates. The Reverend Peter Koukla was sure a talker.

He mentioned Dr. Thorndecker, Agatha Binder, and Art Merchant—all in one sentence. He commented on the weather, and assured me such muck was unusual, unique; usually Coburn, N.Y. enjoyed a blazing tropical sun cooled by the trade winds. He showed me what he had been hammering on: a miniature stable that was to become part of a crèche for the church's Christmas celebration.

"Ping-Pong is all very well," he informed me gravely, "but the traditions cannot be slighted. No indeed! The golden generation is heartened by this remembrance of the rituals of their youth, and the youngsters are introduced to the most sacred rites of their church."

Beautiful. I noted he had not repeated himself, using the words celebration, traditions, rituals, and rites. Guys who deliver a sermon every Sunday can do that: the Bible on their right hand, Roget's Thesaurus on their left.

"Do you have many youngsters in your congregation, Father?" I asked, a trifle nastily. "Pardon me, I'm not up on correct usage. Do I call you Father, Pastor, Padre, Reverend—or what?"

"Oh, call me anything you like," he laughed merrily. "But don't call me late for supper!"

He looked at me, suddenly stern, and didn't relax until I laughed dutifully.

"No," he said, "frankly, we don't have too many youngsters. Simply because Coburn is not a young community. Not too many young married couples. Ergo, not too many children. That is not to say the problems of our senior citizens are not of equal importance. Oh, I *am* enjoying this talk, and the opportunity to exchange opinions."

I wasn't aware that I had voiced any opinions, but I was willing to go along with him. He dusted off a shop stool, and made me sit down. He took a little leap and ended up sitting on his workbench, his legs dangling. I was bemused to note that he was wearing no socks inside those Gucci loafers. Very *in*. In Antibes and Southampton. A little uncomfortable, I guessed, in Coburn, N.Y., in early December.

"It's a challenge," he was saying. "The average age of our population increases every year. More and more of those over sixty-five. Can we ignore them? Discard them? Cut them off from the mainstream of American thought and culture? I say no! What do you think?"

"Very interesting," I said. "Your ideas. Refreshing."

"Refreshing," he repeated. "I like that. No, please, don't light a cigarette. We voted last year to ban the smoking of cigarettes, cigars, and pipes on church grounds. Sorry."

"My fault," I said, putting the pack back in my pocket. "It'll do me good to go without."

"Of course it will," he caroled, throwing back his head and shouting at Heaven. "Of course, of course!"

I don't know . . . maybe he was just high on God. If he had been a theatrical agent, I would have suspected cocaine, and if he had been an advertising copywriter, I would have suspected grass. But this guy was high on ideas. Loony ideas, possibly, but they were enough to keep him floating.

At the moment, the Reverend Peter Koukla was expounding on how the steady increase in the median age of the American population would affect national political attitudes. I was getting woozy with his machine-gun delivery: spouted words accompanied by a fine spray of saliva.

"Very interesting," I broke in. "A challenging concept. But I really came to talk to you about Dr. Thorndecker."

"Of course, of course!" he yelped, and changed gears in mid-course without a pause.

What followed were the same panegyrics I had heard from Ronnie Goodfellow, Agatha Binder, Art Merchant: that is, Dr. Telford Gordon Thorndecker was a prince of princes, one of God's noblemen. They were spreading it on thickly. Didn't the man have any warts? Koukla obviously didn't think so; he told me the doctor was a "great friend" of the church, lent his name and time to special activities, and made frequent and sizable contributions.

"I only mention this," the Reverend added, "to give credit where credit is due. The man is much too modest to tell you himself. I really don't know what we'd do without him."

"Attends services regularly, does he?"

"Frequently," Koukla said—which, I reflected, is a little different from "regularly."

"His wife and son, also?"

"They are members, yes."

"But not his daughter?"

"Ah . . . no. She has her own religious preferences, I understand. Somewhat more fundamental than our teachings."

"Is Draper one of your members? Dr. Kenneth Draper?"

"He was," Koukla said shortly. "I have not seen him at services recently. But we do get many staff members from the Hall and the research laboratory."

All his answers were bright, swift, delivered with every appearance of openness and honesty. It was hard to fault this perky little man. I went at him from another direction . . .

"Nurse Beecham told me that occasionally you are called to Crittenden Hall to provide spiritual comfort for some of the patients?"

"When they request it, yes. I had a discussion with Dr. Thorndecker about the possibility of providing a regular Sunday afternoon service, after my duties here are completed. But so many of the guests are bedridden, it probably wouldn't be a satisfactory arrangement. I do conduct a service in the Hall on Christmas and Easter, however."

"Reverend, I was surprised to learn that Crittenden has its own cemetery. When a patient dies, isn't the body usually claimed by his family? I mean, isn't he returned to his home for burial?"

"Usually," he said, "but not always. Sometimes the family of the deceased prefer burial on the Crittenden grounds. It's very convenient. Sometimes the deceased request it in their wills."

"Do you ever, ah, officiate at these burials?"

"Of course, of course! Several times. Sometimes the final service is held here at the church, and the casket returned to Crittenden for interment."

I nodded, wondering how far I might go without having my interest reported back to Dr. Thorndecker. The hell with it, I decided. Let Koukla report it. It just might stir things up. So I asked my question:

"Didn't attend the burial of a man named Petersen, did you? Chester K. Petersen?"

"Petersen?" he said. "No, I don't think so. When did he pass?"

"Two nights ago."

"Oh, no," he said, "definitely not. My last funeral service for a Crittenden guest was about a month ago. But if the deceased was of another faith—Catholic, perhaps, or Jewish—naturally I wouldn't be ... "

His sentence trailed off, in the approved Coburn manner. He had started his last speech with a confident rush, then slowed, slowed, until his final words were a doubtful drawl. I could almost see him begin to wonder if he wasn't talking too much, revealing something (in all innocence) that the church's "great friend" wouldn't want revealed.

I rose quickly to my feet, before he got the notion of asking what the death of Chester K. Petersen had to do with the Thorndecker grant.

"Thank you very much, sir," I said briskly, holding out my hand. "You've been very cooperative, and I appreciate it."

He hopped spryly off the workbench, and clasped my proffered hand in both of his.

"Of course, of course!" he said. "Happy to oblige. If you're still in town on Sunday morning, it would give me great pleasure to welcome you to our Sabbath services. I believe and preach the religion of joy. I think you'll find it invigorating."

"I might do just that," I nodded. "Well, I'm sure you're anxious to get back to your carpentry. Don't bother showing me out; I can find my way. Thanks again for your trouble."

"No trouble, no trouble!" he shouted, and waved a farewell.

I walked noisily down the cement corridor, then tramped heavily up the iron steps. At the top, I opened and slammed shut the side door leading to the church nave. But I remained inside, on the stairway landing, standing, listening, wondering if the hammering would commence again. It didn't. But I figured it wouldn't. I had seen the telephone in the Reverend Peter Koukla's workshop.

I went slowly down those iron steps again, moving as quietly as I could. I didn't have to go far along the cement corridor before I heard him speaking:

"This is Reverend Koukla," he was saying. "Could I talk to Dr. Thorndecker, please?"

I slipped silently away, and went out the side entrance into the church nave, easing the door shut behind me. I didn't have to listen to the rest of Koukla's conversation. I knew what he was going to say.

Walked out to my car, lighted a cigarette, took three fast, greedy drags. Nasty habit, smoking. So is drinking. So is burying dead men at two in the morning.

I felt I was running one of those Victorian garden mazes, my movements all false starts and retracings. The box hedges walled me around, higher than my head, and all I could do was wander, trying to find the center where I might be rewarded with a candy apple, or the hand of a princess and half the kingdom. I told you I was a closet romantic.

I was floundering and thinking crazy; I knew it. All I had was a hatful of suspicions, and there wasn't one of them I couldn't demolish with a reasonable, acceptable, *legal* explanation. I tried to convince myself that my mistrust was all smoke, and the smart thing for me to do was to stamp Thorndecker's application A-OK, and say, "Goom-by" to Coburn, N.Y.

So why did I sit in my car shivering, and not only from the cold? The hand holding the cigarette trembled. I had never felt so hollow in my life. It was a presentiment of being in over my head, up against something I couldn't handle, wrestling with a force I couldn't define and was powerless to stop.

I started the car and drove along Cypress Road, away from the business section. I left the heater off and cranked the window down a few inches, hoping the cutting air might blow through my skull and take the jimjams along with it. I drove slowly until the houses became fewer and fewer. Then I was in a section of scrabby wooded plots and open fields that looked like they had been shaved a week ago.

I drove past a sign that read: NEW FRONTIER TRAILER COURT, and kept on going. Then I braked hard, backed up, and read the smaller print: "Trailer parking by day, week, or month. All conveniences. Reasonable rates." In Coburn, N.Y., they still called it a "trailer court." The rest of the country called them "mobile home communities."

But it was on Cypress Road, and Al Coburn had said his old buddy, Ernie Scoggins, had lived in a trailer on Cypress Road. So I followed the bent tin arrow nailed to a pine stump, and rattled and jounced down a rutted dirt road to a clearing where maybe twenty trailers, camper vans, and mobile homes were drawn up in a rough circle. Maybe they were expecting an attack by Mohawks on the New Frontier.

I parked, got out of the car, looked around. God, it was sad. There wasn't a soul to be seen, and under that mean sky the place looked crumbling and abandoned. Maybe the Mohawks really had come through, scalped all the men, carried off the women and kids. Fantasy time. There were overflowing garbage cans, and lights on in some of the vans. People lived there; no doubt about it. Although "lived" might be an exaggeration. It looked like the kind of place where, if all the TV sets konked out simultaneously, they'd go for each other's throats. Nothing else to do.

I wandered around and finally found a mobile home that had a MANAGER sign spiked into the hard-scrabble front yard. There was another sign over the door with two painted dice showing seven, and the legend: PAIR-O-DICE. Those dice should have shown crap.

The steps were rough planks laid across piled bricks; they swayed when I stepped cautiously up. I knocked on the door. From inside I could hear the sound of gunfire, horses' hooves, wild screams. If it wasn't a TV western, I was going to skedaddle the hell out of there.

I knocked again. The guy who answered the door looked familiar. I had never met him, but I knew him. You'd have known him, too. Soiled undershirt showing a sagging beer belly. Dirty chinos. Unlaced work shoes over gray wool socks. A fat head with a cigar sprouting from the middle.

An open can of a local brew in his hand. He wasn't happy about being dragged away from the boob tube. It was filling the room behind him with flickering, blue-tinted light, and the gunfire sounded like thunder.

"Yeah?" he said, glowering at me.

"Who is it, Morty?" a woman shrieked from inside the room.

"You shut your mouth," he screamed, not bothering to turn his head, so for a moment I thought he was yelling at me.

"I understand there's a trailer out here for sale," I began my scam, "and I was—"

"What?" he roared. "Iola, will you turn that god-damned thing down? I can't hear what the man is saying."

We waited. The gunfire was reduced to a grumble.

"Now," he said, "you want a place to park? We got all modern conveniences. You can hitch up to—"

"No, no," I said hastily. "I understand there's a trailer out here for sale."

His piggy eyes got smaller, if possible, and he removed the sodden cigar from his mouth with an audible *plop*!

"Who told you that?" Morty demanded.

"Fellow I met in the bar at the Coburn Inn. Name of Al Coburn. He says a friend of his, name of Ernie Scoggins, lived out here. That right?"

"Well . . . yeah," he said mistrustfully. "He did."

"I understand this Scoggins took off, and his rig's up for sale."

He rubbed his chin with the back of his beer-can hand. I could hear the rasp of the stubble.

"I don't know about that," he said. "I ain't even sure he owned the thing. He's got debts all over town. He took off owing me a month's rent. I'm holding the rig and his car until I get mine."

"Maybe we can work something out," I said. "The bank's holding the title. Al Merchant's willing to work a deal if I decide to buy. All I want to do is take a look at the thing."

"Well . . . " He couldn't decide. "What the hell you want Scoggins' pisspot for? It ain't worth a damn."

"Just for summer," I said hurriedly. "You know—holidays and weekends in the good weather. I figure it would be cheaper than buying a cottage."

"Oh, hell," he said heavily, "it'd be cheaper than buying an outhouse. Well . . . it's your money. It's that gray job over there. The one with the beat-up VW parked alongside. Take a look if you want to; the door ain't locked."

"Thank you very much," I said, turned carefully on those rickety steps, started down.

"Hey, listen," he called after me, "if you decide to buy, I got to get that month's rent he owes me."

"Off the top," I promised him, and he seemed satisfied. He went back in, slammed the door, and in a few seconds I heard the thunder of gunfire again.

I took a look at the VW first. Either Scoggins had been a lousy driver, or he had bought it fourth-hand after it had endured a series of horrendous accidents. You could see the geography of its history: dents, scars, scrapes, nicks, cuts, patches of several-colored paints, rust spots, places where bare metal showed through. All the hubcaps were missing. The front trunk lid was wired shut to the bumper with a twisted coat hanger.

I looked through one of the dirty windows. Nothing to see but torn upholstery, rags on the floor, some greasy road maps, and a heap of empty Copenhagen snuff tins. I would have liked to unbend that coat hanger and take a look in the trunk, but I was afraid Morty might be watching me from one of his windows.

Scoggins' trailer was exactly that: a trailer, not a mobile home. It was an old, *old* model, a box on wheels, narrow enough and light enough to be towed by a passenger car on turnpikes, highways, or secondary roads. It was a plywood job, with one side door and two windows that were broken and covered with tacked shirt cardboards.

It had been propped up on cement blocks; the wheels were missing. A tank of propane was still connected, and a wire led to an electrical outlet in a pipe that poked above the ground at every parking space. There was a hose hookup to another underground pipe, for water.

There were no stairs; it was a long step up from ground to doorway. The door was not only unlocked, it was ajar an inch or so. I pushed it open, stepped up and in. A cold, damp, musty odor: unwashed linen and mouldering furniture. There was a wall switch (bare, no plate), and when I flicked it, what I got was a single 60-watt bulb hanging limply from the center of the room.

And it was really one room. There was a small alcove with waist-high refrigerator, small sink, a grill over propane gas ring, plywood cupboard. No toilet or shower. I hoped the New Frontier offered public facilities. The bed folded up against the wall. Mercifully, it was up. Judging by the rest of the interior, I really didn't want to see that bed. One upholstered armchair, torn and molting. A twelve-inch, portable TV set on a rusted tubular stand. A varnished maple table with two straight-back kitchen chairs. An open closet with a few scraps of clothing hanging from wall hooks. A scarred dresser with drawer knobs missing.

That was about all. The World War I helmet was still where Al Coburn had said it was, atop the TV set. There were some unwashed dishes in the sink, clotted and crusted. Brownish water dripped from the tap. The plywood floor squeaked underfoot. The only decoration was last year's calendar from Mike's Service Station, showing a stumpy blonde in a pink bikini. She was standing on a beach, one knee coyly bent, with palm trees in the background. She had an unbelievable mouthful of teeth, and was holding a beachball over her head.

"A little chilly in here, honey?" I asked her.

Compared to that place, my room at the Coburn Inn was the Taj Mahal. I looked around, trying to imagine what it was like for old Ernie Scoggins—wife dead, son dead, daughters moved away—to do a hard day's work at Crittenden Hall, and then to lump home to this burrow in his falling-apart VW. Take off his shoes, fry a hamburger, open a beer. Collapse into the sprung armchair in front of the little black-and-white screen. Drink his beer, munch his hamburger, and watch people sing and dance and laugh.

I tried to imagine all that, but it didn't work. It was like trying to imagine what war was like if you had never been there.

I went through the Grand Rapids dresser but found nothing of interest. A pair of torn longjohns, some gray, unpressed handkerchiefs, a blue workshirt, wool socks that needed toes, junk. I figured Constable Goodfellow or Al Coburn had taken the old man's papers away, if there were any. I found nothing.

I poked around in the cabinet over the sink. All I found were a few cockroaches who stared at me, annoyed at being interrupted. One interesting thing: there was an eight-ounce jar of instant coffee, practically new, with no more than one or two teaspoonsful taken out. The jar still bore the supermarket pricetag: $5.45. Odd that a poor old man would take off for parts unknown and leave that treasure behind.

I didn't unlatch the bed, let it down, and paw through it. I just couldn't.

So that was that, I figured. Nothing plus nothing equals nothing. I stood in the doorway, my finger on the light switch, taking a final look around. My God, that must have been a cold place to live. There was a small electric heater set into one wall, and I suppose he used the propane stove for added warmth, but still . . . The chill came right up through that bare, sagging plywood floor and stiffened my toes inside my boots.

Maybe the trailer had been carpeted when it was new. But now the only piece of rug was under the old man's armchair. It was about a three-foot square, with ravelled edges. It looked like a remnant someone had thrown out, a piece left over after a cheap wall-to-wall carpeting job had been completed.

I stared at it, wondering why I was staring. Just a ragged piece of rug in a shit-brown color. It was under the armchair and stuck out in front where his feet would rest when he gummed his hamburger and watched TV. Keep his tootsies relatively warm while he stared at young, handsome people winning Cadillacs and trips to Bermuda on the game shows.

It made sense; that's why the rug was there. So far so good. But why wasn't the rug scarred and scuffed and stained in front of the armchair, where his feet rested and he dribbled food while guffawing at the funny, funny Master of Ceremonies? It wasn't scarred or scuffed or stained. It looked new.

I took my finger off the light switch. I went back to the armchair, got down on my knees, peered underneath. The portion of the rug *under* the chair was scarred and scuffed and stained.

"Shit," I said aloud.

I stood, lifted the armchair, set it aside. He could have turned the rug, I acknowledged. Shortly before he departed, he noticed the rug under his feet was getting worn and spotted. So he just turned it around. Then the worn part would be under the chair, and he'd have a nice, new, thick pile under his feet in front of the chair.

Except . . . Except . . .

There were special stains on the portion of the rug that had been under the armchair. I got down on my knees again, put my nose right down to them. They didn't look like food stains to me. They were reddish-brown, crusted. There were several heavy blobs with crowns of smaller stains radiating around them. Like the heavy blobs had fallen from a distance and splashed.

I smelled the stains. It wasn't a scientific test, I admit, but it was good enough for me. I knew what those stains were. They weren't Aunt Millie's Spaghetti Sauce.

I replaced the armchair in its original position, switched off the light, got out of there. I didn't look toward the manager's mobile home. I slid into the Grand Prix, jazzed it, spun away.

They didn't have much time: that's what I was thinking as I drove back to the Coburn Inn. They were in a hurry, frantic, afraid of being seen by Manager Morty or some other denizen of the New Frontier Trailer Court. So they did what they had come to do. And then they got him out of there—what was left of him—with some clothes thrown hastily into his old suitcase, trying to make it look like he had scampered of his own free will. And because the blood was ripe and thick and glistening in front of the armchair, they had turned the rug around so the stains would be hidden under the chair.

Time! Time! They were working so fast, so anxiously. Maybe even desperately. They just wanted him snuffed and out of there. What about his car? Maybe it was one killer, and he couldn't handle the VW and the car he came in. Maybe it was two killers, and one couldn't drive. Fuck the car. And fuck the helmet; they didn't know it was his most prized possession. And they didn't have time to search the place and find that almost-full jar of coffee. They didn't have time, they didn't plan it well, they weren't thinking. Amateurs.

I went at it over and over again. The final thought as I pulled into the parking lot of the Coburn Inn: they couldn't have known that he had written a letter, or they would have tossed the place to find it. And Al Coburn had said, " . . . the place wasn't broken up, or anything like that."

I felt so goddamned smug with my brilliant ratiocination. My depression was gone. I walked into the lobby humming a merry tune. I should have been droning a dirge. I was so wrong, so *wrong*!

But at the moment I was in an euphoric mood, bouncing and admiring the way the overhead fluorescent lights gleamed off the nude pate of the guy behind the desk. *Another* baldy!

"Oh, Mr. Todd," he called in a lilting, chirpy voice, and held up one manicured finger.

In my new humor, I was willing to accommodate; I walked over for my message.

"The Reverend Koukla has called you *twice*," he breathed, in hushed and humble tones. "Such a *fine* man. Could you call him at once, *please?*"

"I'm going in for lunch," I said. "I'll call him as soon as I'm finished."

"Please, *please*," he said. "It sounded so *urgent*. You can talk to him right here on the desk phone. I'll put it through for you."

"Okay," I said, shrugging, "if it's so important."

"I'm not supposed to let people use the desk phone for personal calls," he whispered. "But it's the *Reverend Koukla!*"

"Have you caught his walking-on-the-water act?" I asked him. "A smash."

But he was already inside the office, where the switchboard was located, and I don't think he heard me.

Koukla came on immediately.

"Mr. Todd," he said briskly, "I owe you an apology."

"Oh?"

"Yes indeedy!" he said, then went on with a rush: "I'm afraid I was not as hospitable as I should have been to a visitor to Coburn, a stranger in our midst. As a matter of fact, I'm having some people in this evening for good talk and a buffet supper. No occasion; very informal. Just a friendly get-together. The Thorndeckers will be here, and Art Merchant, Agatha Binder, others you've met, and people who would like to meet *you*. Could you possibly join us? About sixish? For refreshments and talk and then a cold supper later? It should be fun."

That had to be the most quickly arranged buffet supper in the annals of Coburn's social life. I figured Dr. Thorndecker had put the Reverend up to it, and sometime during the evening I'd get a casual explanation of what happened to Chester K. Petersen.

"Sounds good to me," I said. "Thank you for the invitation. I'll be there."

"Good, good, good," he gurgled, making it sound like, "Googoogoo." "I'm in the Victorian monstrosity just west of the church. You can't miss it; the porch light will be on."

"See you at six," I said, and hung up.

I went into the bar a little subdued, a little thoughtful. It seemed to me Thorndecker was over-reacting. If there was nothing fishy about Petersen's death and burial, he didn't have to do a thing until I inquired, and then he could set me straight. If it was a juggle, then he had to go on the con, preferably in an atmosphere of good cheer, of bonhomie. That's the way I figured he figured it, and I resented it. They were taking me for an idiot.

The bar was full, and the restaurant was crowded: all seats taken. I gave up, came back to the lobby, and asked Sam Livingston if he could get me a club sandwich and a bottle of Heineken, and bring it up to my room. He said it might take half an hour, and I said no problem. He went immediately to the kitchen, and I tramped up the stairs to Room 3-F.

Skinned off damp hat, damp trenchcoat, damp boots. Lighted another cigarette. Stood in my stockinged feet at the window, staring down at Main Street but not seeing it. Thinking. I wish I could tell you my thoughts came in a neat, logical order. They didn't; I was all over the place. Something like this:

1. Maybe they tried to take Scoggins's car, but it was locked.

2. Why didn't they roll up the blood-stained rug and take it with them? I could brainstorm a lot of reasons for that. Maybe Al Coburn and other friends had seen that cheap scrap of carpet many times, and would wonder at its absence. Maybe it was just easier and faster to turn the carpet front to back. They figured no one would notice, and no one did. Not investigating officer Constable Ronnie Goodfellow, not best friend Al Coburn.

3. Why was I using the mysterious pronoun "they," when I had become so furious when Al Coburn used it?

4. Those debts of Al Coburn at the bank . . . Was he afraid of Art Merchant? Or was it Thorndecker, working through Merchant?

5. How could Nurse Beecham tell me Petersen died of cancer when the death certificate, signed by Dr. Draper, listed congestive heart failure as cause of death? Was one of them innocent, and one of them lying? Or were they both in on it, and just got their signals crossed?

6. What color were Julie Thorndecker's eyes?

At this point Sam Livingston knocked and came in with my club sandwich and Heineken. I signed, slipped Livingston a buck, and locked the door behind him. I went back to my station at the window, chomping ravenously at a quarter-wedge of sandwich and swilling the beer. The rambling went on . . .

7. If Al Coburn was right, and Ernie Scoggins was "buried somewheres around here," where would be the logical place to put him under? Easy answer: in the Crittenden cemetery. Who'd go digging there?

8. Something's going on in that lab that's not quite kosher, and Scoggins tumbled to it.

9. Just what in hell was in that letter Scoggins left with Al Coburn? It couldn't be a vague accusation; it had to be hard evidence of some kind if it had that effect on Coburn. A photograph? Something lifted from the Crittenden Research Laboratory? A photocopy of someone else's letter? A microfilm? What?

10. Was Julie Thorndecker really making it with her stepson?

11. How was I going to get out of my promise to Millie Goodfellow?

12. Who killed Cock Robin?

I had finished the beer and sandwich, and was licking mayonnaise off my fingers, when the phone rang. I wiped my hands on the back of an armchair slipcover and picked up the handset.

"Todd," I said.

"Nate Stern," the voice said.

"Nate. Good to hear from you. How're the wife, kids, grand-children?"

"Fine," he said. "You?"

Nate Stern, a man of few words, was boss of Donner & Stern. Lou Donner had been shot dead by a bank officer who had been dipping in the till. Lou made the mistake of trying to get back some of the loot before turning the guy over to the blues.

"I'm surviving, Nate," I said.

"Switchboard?" he asked.

"Yes," I said, beginning to talk just like him.

"That sample . . . "

"Yes?"

"Olympia Standard, about five years old."

"Thanks."

"Any help?"

"Not much. Be talking."

"Sure."

We both rang off.

In case you forgot, we were talking about that anonymous note: "Thorndecker kills." I had tried to get a look at the typewriters out at Crittenden. I hadn't seen any in the nursing home. The two I saw in the research lab were both IBM electrics. So? So nothing.

There was a telephone call of my own I had to make. I admitted that maybe I had been putting it off because I was afraid it might cause pain to the people I had to talk to. But I couldn't postpone it any longer. It couldn't go through the hotel switchboard, where the desk baldy might be listening in, nodding, and busily taking notes.

So I pulled on damp boots, damp trenchcoat, damp hat again. I crossed Main Street to Samson's Drugs, and crowded myself into an old wooden phone booth. I made a person-to-person call, collect, to Mr. Stacy Besant at the Bingham Foundation in New York City. I knew he'd be in; he never went out to lunch. He always brought a peanut butter sandwich from home in a Mark Cross attaché case.

"Samuel," he said, "how are matters progressing?"

"Slowly," I said, "but surely."

Something in my voice must have alerted him.

"Problems?" he asked.

Problems! The man asked if I had problems! I was *selling* problems.

"Some," I said, "yes, sir."

I heard a long, sniffing wheeze, and figured he had jammed that inhaler up his nose again.

"Anything we can do at this end?"

"Yes, Mr. Besant," I said. "I have a few questions. You said the first Mrs. Thorndecker was your niece. Was she older than Thorndecker?"

There was a silence a moment. Then, quietly:

"Does that have a bearing on your investigation?"

"Yes, sir, it does."

"I see. Well, the first Mrs. Thorndecker, Betty, was approximately ten years older than her husband."

It was my turn to say, "I see." I thought a moment, then asked Besant: "Thorndecker inherited a great deal. Could you tell me the source of the first Mrs. Thorndecker's wealth?"

"Old money," he said. "Pharmaceuticals. That's how Thorndecker met Betty. He was running a research project for her company."

"That takes care of that. Could you tell me a little more about the circumstances of her death?"

Again I heard the sniffing wheeze.

"Well . . . " he said finally, "Betty had a drinking problem, and—"

"Pardon the interruption, sir," I said, "but did she have the problem before she married Thorndecker, or did it develop afterward."

Silence.

"Sir," I said. "Are you there?"

"I'm here," he said in a low voice. "I had never considered that aspect before, and I am attempting to search my memory."

"Take your time, Mr. Besant," I said cheerily.

"Do not be insolent, Samuel," he said sharply. "I am not as senile as you sometimes seem to think. I would say that prior to her marriage, Betty was an active social drinker. Her marriage appears to me now to have exacerbated her problem."

"She became an alcoholic?"

The old man sighed. "Yes. She did."

"And exactly how did she die?"

"It was summer. The family went to the Cape. She had the habit, Betty did, when she was, ah, in her cups, so to speak, to take midnight swims. Or in the early hours of the morning."

"Cold sea at the Cape. Even during the day."

"Oh yes," the old man mourned. "Everyone warned her. Husband, daughter, son—everyone. But they couldn't lock her up, could they? When possible, someone went with her. No matter what the hour. But she would sneak away, go off by herself."

"Asking for it?"

"What?"

"Was she courting death, sir? Seeking it? Did she want to die?"

Silence again. Then a heavy sigh.

"Samuel," he said, "you are a very *old* young man. The thought had never occurred to me. But perhaps you're right, perhaps she was courting death. In any event, it came. One morning she wasn't there when the household awoke. Her body was found in the surf."

"Uh," I said, "any signs of—you know?"

"Just minor bruises and scrapes. Things to be expected in such a death. No unusual wounds, no abnormalities. Salt water in the lungs."

"Was she a good swimmer?"

"An excellent swimmer. When sober."

"How about Thorndecker?" I asked. "A good swimmer?"

"Samuel, Samuel," he groaned. "I have no idea. *Must* you be so suspicious?"

"Yes, sir," I said, "I must. Any evidence of his having something on the side? You know—mistress? Girlfriend? Anything like that?"

He cleared his throat.

"No," he said.

"You're sure?"

"As a matter of fact," he said, and I could almost see that tortoise head ducking defensively, "I made a few discreet inquiries of my own."

"Oh-ho," I said. "And he was pure?"

"Absolutely."

"Where was he the night his wife died? Home in bed?"

"No," he said. "At a medical conference in Boston. He had departed that evening. His presence in Boston that night was verified."

"Oh," I said, deflated. "I guess he *was* pure. Unless . . . "

"Unless what, Samuel?"

"Nothing, sir. You're right; I *am* very suspicious. I was just imagining a way he could have jiggered it."

The old man shocked me.

"I know," he said. "A drug in her bottle. He had easy access to drugs."

I sucked in my breath.

"You're right again, sir," I said. "I do tend to underestimate you, and I apologize for it. Were the contents of her bottle analyzed?"

"Oh yes," he said. "Everything was done properly; I saw to that. The contents were just gin; no foreign substances. But, of course, by the time the body was found, the authorities called, and the investigation started, Thorndecker had been summoned back to the Cape from Boston."

"What you're saying is that he could have switched bottles, or replaced the contents?"

"There is that remote possibility, yes."

"Do you think he did?"

The silence lasted a long time. It was finally ended by another deep sniff, then another: a two-nostril job.

"I would not care to venture an opinion," Mr. Stacy Besant said gravely.

"All right," I said. "It's a moot point anyway. Barring a confession, we'll never know, will we?"

"No," he said, "we never will."

"One final question, sir. I'm puzzled by the dates and ages involved. Particularly the ten-year difference between Mary and Edward, Thorndecker's two children. A little unusual, isn't it?"

"A simple explanation," he said. "Betty was a widow when Thorndecker married her. Mary is her daughter by her first husband. Edward is the son of Betty and Telford Thorndecker. So Mary and Edward are really half-brother and half-sister."

"Thank you, sir," I said. "That explains a great deal."

"Does it?" he said surprised.

"Mr. Besant," I said, "I wonder if you'd be kind enough to switch me to Mrs. Cynthia, if she's available."

"Of course," he said. "At once. Hang on."

I'll say this for the old boy: he wouldn't dream of asking why I wanted to talk to the boss-lady of the Bingham Foundation. If she wanted him to know about her conversation with me, she'd tell him.

He had my call switched, and in a few seconds I was talking to Mrs. Cynthia. We exchanged news about the states of our health (good), and the weather (miserable), and then I said:

"Ma'am, just before I came up here, I met you in the corridor, and you mentioned you had known Dr. Thorndecker's father."

"Yes," she said, "so I did."

"You also said he was a sweet man—those are your words, ma'am—and then you added, 'It was all so sad.' What did you mean by that?"

"Samuel," she said, "I wish I had your memory."

"Mrs. Cynthia," I said, "I wish I had your brains and beauty."

She laughed.

"You scamp," she said. "If I was only fifty years younger . . . "

"If I was only fifty years older," I said.

"You will be, soon enough. Yes, I knew Dr. Thorndecker's father. Gerald Thorndecker. Gerry. I knew him quite well."

She didn't add to that, and I didn't pry any deeper. The statement just lay there, given and accepted.

"And what was so sad, Mrs. Cynthia?"

"The manner of his death," she said. "Gerald Thorndecker was killed in a hunting accident. Shocking."

"A hunting accident?" I repeated. "Where was this?"

"In Maine. Up near the border."

"How old was his son at the time?"

"Telford? Thirteen perhaps. Fourteen. Around there."

"Thank you," I said, ready to say goodby.

"He was with him when it happened."

It took me a second to comprehend that sentence.

"The son?" I asked. "Telford Thorndecker? He was there when his father was killed in a hunting accident?"

"That is correct," she said crisply.

"Do you recall the details, Mrs. Cynthia?"

"Of course I recall the details," she said sharply. "I'm not likely to forget them. They had flushed a buck, and—"

"They?" I said. "Gerald Thorndecker and his son?"

"Samuel," she said, sighing, "either you let me tell this story in my own, old woman's way, or I shall ring off this instant."

"Sorry, ma'am," I said humbly. "I promise not to interrupt again."

"The hunting party consisted of Gerald Thorndecker, his young son Telford, and four friends and neighbors. Six in all. They flushed a buck, spread out on a line, and pressed forward. Later, at the coroner's inquest, it was stated that Gerald Thorndecker walked faster than the rest of them. Trotting, moving out ahead of them. I believe it. He was that kind of man. Eager. In any event, the others were behind him. They heard a crashing in the brush, saw what they thought was the buck doubling back, and they fired. They killed Gerald. Now you may ask your questions."

"Thank you," I said, without irony. "How many of the hunters fired at Gerald?"

"Three, I believe."

"Including the son, Telford?"

"Yes."

"Were ballistics tests made?"

"Yes. He had been hit twice."

"Including a bullet from his son's rifle?"

"Yes. And another."

I should have known. You think that in any investigation, criminal or otherwise, you get the facts, put them together, and the whole thing opens up like one of those crazy Chinese lumps you drop in water and a gorgeous blossom unfolds? Not so. Because you rarely deal with facts. You deal with half-facts, or quarter-, eighth-, or sixteenth-facts. Little bitty things that you can't prove or disprove. Nothing is ever sure or complete.

"All right," I said to Mrs. Cynthia, "Gerald Thorndecker was killed by two bullets, one fired by his son. What about the mother?"

"Her name was Grace. She died of breast cancer when Telford was just a child. I think he was three. Or four. His father raised him."

"Money?"

"Not much," she said regretfully. "Gerald was foolish that way. He squandered. He had a standard of living and was determined to maintain it. He inherited a good income, but it goes fast when nothing new is coming in."

"What did he do? Did he have a job or profession?"

"Gerald Thorndecker," she said severely, "was a poet."

"A poet? Oh my God. I can understand why the money went. Was he published?"

"Privately. By himself." Then she added softly, "I still have his books."

"Was he any good?" I asked.

"No," she said. "His genius was for living."

"Telford was an only child."

"How did you know?"

"He *looks* like an only child. He *acts* like an only child. Mrs. Cynthia, just let me recap a moment to see if I've got this straight. Dr. Thorndecker is an only child. His mother dies when he's three or four. He's brought up by his father, a failed poet rapidly squandering his inheritance. The father is killed accidentally when the boy is thirteen."

"Or fourteen," she said.

"Or fourteen," I agreed. "Around there. Now, what happened to the boy? Who took him in?"

"An aunt. His father's sister."

"She put him through medical school?"

"Oh no," Mrs. Cynthia said. "She was poor as a church mouse. Telford never would have made it without his father's insurance. That's all he had. The insurance saw him through medical school and his post-graduate work."

"Wow," I said.

"Wow?" she said.

"He wanted to be a doctor all along?" I asked.

"Oh yes. For as long as I can remember. Since he was just a little boy."

"Mrs. Cynthia, I thank you," I said. "Sorry to take up so much of your time."

"That's quite all right, Samuel," she said. "I hope what I've told you may be of some help in your inquiry. If you see Dr. Thorndecker, please give him my love. He may remember me."

"How could he forget you?" I said gallantly.

She made a humphing sound, but I knew she was pleased. She really was a grand old dame, and I loved her and didn't want to hurt her. Which is why I didn't make a snide comment about the extraordinary coincidence of two violent deaths in the life of Dr. Telford Thorndecker, both of which he might possibly have caused, and from both of which he had profited handsomely. But maybe it wasn't an extraordinary coincidence; maybe it was just a plain coincidence, and I was seeing contrivance where only accident existed.

I walked slowly back to the Inn. One good thing about Coburn: you didn't have to look about fearfully for traffic when you crossed the street.

Stacy Besant and Mrs. Cynthia had given me a lot to think about. Now

I knew much more; my plate was full. A full plate, hell; my platter was overflowing. The investigation was slowly becoming two: the history, character, personality, and ambitions of Dr. Telford Gordon Thorndecker; and the strange events that had taken place in and around Crittenden during the past month. That the two would eventually come together, merge, and make some kind of goofy sense, I had no doubt. But meanwhile I didn't know what the hell to do next.

What I did was to go back across Main Street to Sandy's Liquors and Fine Wines. I bought a fifth of a twelve-year-old Scotch. It came all gussied up in a flashy box. Carrying that in a brown paper sack, I returned to the Coburn Inn. I looked around for Sam Livingston, but he was nowhere to be seen. The lobby was enjoying its early afternoon siesta. Even Millie Goodfellow was somnolent, filing slowly at her talons behind the cigar counter.

I walked down the stairway into the basement, pushed through a fire door, and wandered along a cement corridor lined with steam and water pipes. I found a door with a neat sign that read: SAMUEL LIVINGSTON. PLEASE KNOCK BEFORE ENTERING. I knocked, but I didn't enter; I waited.

He came to the door wearing his usual shiny, black alpaca jacket and little skullcap. He also had on half-glasses and was carrying a closed paperback novel, a forefinger marking his place. I took the bottle of Scotch from the sack and thrust it at him.

"Greeks bearing gifts," I said. "Beware."

His basalt face warmed in a slow smile.

"For me?" he said. "Now I take that kindly of you. Come in, get comfy, and we'll sample a taste of this fine sippin' whiskey."

He had a snug little place down there. One low-ceilinged room with kitchenette, and a small bathroom. Everything neat as a pin. A sleeping sofa, two overstuffed armchairs, a table with ice cream parlor chairs. A chest of drawers. No TV set, but a big bookcase of paperbacks. I took a quick look. Barbara Cartland. Frank Yerby. Daphne du Maurier. Elsie Lee. Like that. Romantic novels. Gothics. Edwardians. Regencies. Women with long, glittering, low-cut gowns. Men with mustaches, wearing open, ruffled shirts and carrying swords. Castles in dark mountains with one light burning in a high window. Well . . . what the hell; I read H. Rider Haggard.

He had me sit in one of the soft armchairs, and he brought us each a small glass of the Scotch.

"We don't want to hurt this with water," he said.

"Straight is fine," I agreed.

He lowered himself slowly into the other armchair, lifted his glass to me, then took a small sip. His eyes closed.

"Yes," he breathed. "Oh my yes." He opened his eyes, passed the glass back and forth under his nose, inhaling with pleasure. "How you finding Coburn, Sam? Slow and quiet enough for you?"

"You'd think so," I said, "judging from the surface. But I'm getting the feeling that underneath, things might be faster and noisier."

"Could be," he said noncommittally. "I hear you been doing some digging?"

"Just talking to people," I said. "I figured you might be able to help me."

"How might I do that?"

"Well, you've lived here a long time, haven't you?"

"Thirty years," he said. "And I figure to live out the rest of it right here. So you, being a smart man, won't expect me to bad-mouth any of the people I got to live with."

"Of course not," I said. "It's just that I've picked up some conflicting opinions, and I thought you could straighten me out."

He stared at me over the rim of his glass. It was a dried apple of a face: lines and creases and a crinkly network of wrinkles. Black and gleaming. The teeth were big and yellow. His ears stuck out like flags, and his eyes had seen everything.

"Tell you what," he said. "Supposin' you asks your questions. If I want to answer, I will. If I don't, I won't. If I don't know, I'll tell you so."

"Fair enough," I said. "My first question is about Al Coburn. You know him?"

"Sure, I know him. Everyone in town knows Al Coburn. His people *started* this place."

"You think he's a nut?"

He showed me that keyboard of teeth.

"Mr. Coburn?" he said. "A nut? Nah. Sly as a fox, that man. Good brain on him."

"Okay," I said. "That was my take, too. Art Merchant?"

"The banker man? He's just a banker. What do you expect?"

"You think that newspaper, the *Sentinel*, is making money?"

He took a sip of his drink, then looked at me reflectively.

"Just," he said.

"You think they've got loans from the bank?"

"Now how would I know a thing like that?"

"Sam," I said, "I got the feeling that there's not much going on in Coburn that you don't know about."

"Agatha Binder could have some notes at the bank," he acknowledged. "Most business folks in Coburn do."

"You know the Thorndeckers?"

"I've seen them," he said cautiously.

"To speak to?"

"Only Miz Mary. We're friends."

"Constable Goodfellow? You know him?"

"Oh sure."

I threw my curve.

"Anything between him and Dr. Thorndecker's wife?"

The curtain came down.

"I wouldn't know," he said.

"Ever hear any gossip about what's going on at the Crittenden Research Laboratory?"

"I never believe in gossip."

"But you listen to it?"

"Some."

"Ever hear about a man named Petersen? Chester K. Petersen?"

"Petersen? Can't say that I have."

"Scoggins? Ernie Scoggins?"

"Oh my yes, I knew Ernie Scoggins. He sat right where you're sitting many's a time. Stop by here to chew the fat. Bring me a jug sometimes. Sometimes he was broke, and I'd make him a little something to eat. Nice, cheerful man. Always joking."

"They say he just took off," I said.

"So they say," he nodded.

"Do you think he did?" I asked him.

He thought a long moment. Finally . . .

"I don't know what happened to Ernie Scoggins," he said.

"What do you *think* happened?"

"I just don't know."

"When was the last time you saw him?"

"Couple of days before he disappeared."

"He came here?"

"That's right."

"When? What time of day?"

"In the evening. When he got off work."

"Anything unusual about him?"

"Like what?"

"What was his mood? Was he in a good mood?"

"Yeah, he was in a good mood. Said he was going to get some money pretty soon, and him and me would go up to Albany and have a steak dinner and see the sights."

"Did you tell Constable Goodfellow this?"

"No."

"Why not?"

"He didn't ask."

"Did Scoggins tell you how much money he'd be getting?"

"No."

"But could you guess from what he said how much it'd be? A lot of money?"

"Anything over a five-dollar bill would be a lot of money to Ernie Scoggins."

"Did he tell you where the money would be coming from?"

"No, and I didn't ask."

"Could you make a guess where it was coming from?"

"I just don't know."

I went along like that, with his "I don't know's" getting more frequent. I couldn't blame him. As he said, he had to survive in Coburn; I was going home one blessed day. I knew he wouldn't reveal the town's secrets—until thumbscrews come back in fashion.

I ran out of questions, and accepted another small Scotch. Then we just sat there sipping, talking of this and that. I discovered he had a deadpan sense of humor so subtle, so hidden, that you could easily miss it if you weren't watching for it. For instance:

"Are you a church-going man?" I asked him.

"I certainly am," he said. "Every Saturday—that's my afternoon off here—I sweep and dust the Episcopalian Church."

Said with no smile, no lifted eyebrow, no irony, no bitterness. Apparently just an ingenuous statement of fact. Ingenuous, my ass! This gaffer was *deep*. He was laughing, or weeping, far down inside himself. If you caught it, fine. If it went over your head, that was also fine. He didn't give a damn.

But he could say profound things, too.

"What do you think of Millie Goodfellow?" I inquired.

He said: "She's lonely with too many men."

I asked him if he was the only black in town. He said no, there were two families, a total of nine men, women, and children. The men farmed, the women worked as domestics, the kids went to a good school.

"They doin' all right," Sam Livingston said. "I don't mess with them much."

"Why is that?"

"I don't mess with *anyone* much."

"No family of your own, Sam?"

"No," he said. "They all gone."

Whether that meant they were dead or had deserted Coburn, I didn't know, and didn't ask.

"Sam," I said, "you say you and Mary Thorndecker are friends. How is that? I mean, does she visit you here? What opportunity do you have to talk to her?"

"Oh . . . " he said vaguely. "Here and there."

I stared at him, remembering what Agatha Binder had said about Mary Thorndecker going to an evangelist church about five miles south of Coburn. A fundamentalist church. The Reverend Peter Koukla had said something similar.

"Your church?" I asked Livingston. "You and Mary Thorndecker go to the same church? A born-again place about five miles south of here?"

The glaze came down over his ocherous eyes again.

"Sam," he said, "you do get around."

"I'd like to visit that church," I said. "How do I get there?"

"Like you said: five miles south. Take the river route, then make a left. You'll see the signs."

"You drive there?"

"No," he said, "I don't drive. Miz Mary, she stops by for me."

"When are services?" I asked. "Sunday?"

"Sunday, and every other night in the week. Every night at eight."

"I think I'll go," I said. "Good minister?"

"Puts on a good show," he said, grinning. "A joy to hear."

The Scotch was making me drowsy. I thanked him for his hospitality, and stood up to leave. He thanked me for the whiskey, and offered to take me up in the elevator. It came down into the basement, alongside his little apartment, and he could hear the bell from inside his room. I told him I'd walk up, the exercise would do me good.

I started down the cement corridor. He was still standing at his open door. A small, wizened figure, a frail antique. I had walked perhaps five steps when he called my name. I stopped, turned around. He didn't say anything more.

"What is it, Sam?" I asked him.

"It's worse than you think," he said, moved inside his room, and closed the door.

I stood there, surrounded by cement and iron, trying to decipher: "It's worse than you think." What did he mean by that? Coburn? The Thorndecker investigation? Or maybe life itself?

I just didn't know.

Not then I didn't.

I trudged slowly up the stairway to Room 3-F. I was pondering the sad fate of Ernie Scoggins. Thought he was coming into some money, did he? The hopeful slob. As Al Coburn had said, he just didn't have much above the eyebrows. After what Sam Livingston had told me, this was the scenario I put together:

Scoggins had seen something or heard something. Or both. Probably on his job at Crittenden Hall. If Constable Ronnie and Julie Thorndecker really did have the hots for each other, maybe Scoggins walked in on them while they were rubbing the bacon. Somewhere. In the woods. In the stall of that big bay gelding. In the back seat of Goodfellow's cruiser. Anywhere.

So Scoggins, having watched plenty of *Kojak*, *Baretta*, and *Police Woman*, thinks he knows just how to profit from this unexpected opportunity, the poor sod. He tries a little cut-rate blackmail (which in Coburn, N.Y., would be on the order of $9.95). If they don't pay up, Scoggins threatens to report their hanky-panky to Dr. Thorndecker. Who knows— maybe he's got some hard evidence: a tape recording, photograph, love letter—something like that.

But the lovers, realizing like all blackmail victims that the first demand is just a down payment, decided that Ernie Scoggins had to be scrubbed. I figured Goodfellow did it himself, driving his cruiser; he had the balls for it. And the Constable working alone would explain why Scoggins's car hadn't been taken away, and why Goodfellow had said nothing about the blood-stained rug when he "investigated" Scoggins's disappearance. It would also explain what was in that letter left with Al Coburn: the hard evidence of Julie and Ronnie putting horns on the head of the august Dr. Telford Gordon Thorndecker—photograph, love letter, tape recording, whatever.

That scenario sounded good to me. I could buy it.

And tomorrow, I reflected sourly, I would solve the riddle of Chester K. Petersen's death and burial, on Saturday I would discover what was meant by that note: "Thorndecker kills," and on Sunday I would rest.

Ordinarily I keep a case notebook during an investigation, filling it with observations, bits of dialogue, suggestions for further inquiries. The notebook is a big help when it comes time to write my final report.

But after the tossing of my room at the Coburn Inn, I hadn't put anything on paper. I kept it all in my pointy little head. It was a mess up there. Nothing seemed neat.

I couldn't get a handle on what the hell was going on. Or even know positively that anything *was* going on.

I sprawled on the hard bed, boots off, hands clasped behind my head. I tried to find a thread, an element, a theme that might pull it all together. I had been flummoxed like this on other investigations, and had devised a trick that sometimes worked for me.

What I did was try my damndest to stop *thinking* about the case. I mean, try to ignore who did what, who said what, and the things I had seen, done, guessed. Just wash the whole shmear out of my consciousness and leave myself open to emotions, sensations, instincts. It was an attempt to get down to a very primitive level. Reasoning was out; *feeling* was in.

When I tried to determine what I felt about the Thorndecker inquiry, what my subjective reactions were, I came up with an odd one: I suddenly realized how much this case was dominated by the conflicts of youth and age, the problems of senescence, the puzzles of natural and perverse death.

Start with the Thorndecker application. That was for a grant to investigate and, hopefully, isolate and manipulate the X Factor in mammalian cells that causes aging and the end of life.

Add a nursing home with a high death rate: normal for institutions that provided care of the terminally ill.

Add a middle-aged doctor married to a very young wife who, possibly, was finding her jollies elsewhere with, amongst others, a macho Indian cop and, maybe, a stepson younger than she.

Add a bedraggled covey of old, old men: Scoggins, Petersen, Al Coburn. Even Sam Livingston.

Add a staff of very young, whiz-kid researchers who might be long on talent and short on ethics.

Add a village that was a necropolis of fractured dreams. A village that seemed to be stumbling toward oblivion, that was not merely old but obsolete, showing its toothless mouth and sounding its creaks.

All these were notes in a player piano roll: holes punched in thin paper. And the discordant melody I heard was all about age, the enigma of age. I could understand Thorndecker's passion to solve it. Compared to what he hoped to do, a walk on the moon was a stroll to the corner drugstore. I mean the man wanted it *all*.

One other factor crept into my merry-go-round brain . . . Maybe *I* was obsessed with youth and age, their mysteries and collisions. I had rejected Joan Powell for what I imagined was a good and logical reason: the difference in our years. But was that really a rational reaction, or had I demonstrated an inherited response I was not even aware of? Something in my cells, or genes, that forced me to discard that good woman? Something to do with the preservation of my species?

I didn't, I decided, understand *anything*. All I knew was that right then, I wanted her, needed her. Loved her? Who said that?

I spent the late afternoon that way: stewing. It had been a yo-yo day: I was up, I was down, I was up, I was down. When it came time to shower and dress, preparing for the Reverend Peter Koukla's "friendly get-together," I had resolved to put in a token appearance, split as quickly as I reasonably could, and return to the sanctuary of Room 3-F with a jug of comfort provided by Sandy's Liquors and Fine Wines.

So much for high hopes and good intentions . . .

Koukla had been right; his place was easy to find. Not only was the porch light on, but the front door was open and there were guests standing outside, drinks in hand, even though it was a sharp night. Cars were parked in Koukla's driveway, and on both sides of the street. I took my place at the tail end of the line, about a block away, left coat and hat in my locked car, walked back to the party.

If he had organized that bash on short notice, the Reverend had done one hell of a job. I reckoned there were forty or fifty people milling about, drinking up a storm. But after I plunged into the throng, shaking hands and grinning like an idiot, I saw that most of the guests were researchers from the lab and off-duty staff from Crittenden Hall. In other words, Thorndecker had called out the troops.

Most of them were in civvies, but a few were wearing white trousers and short white jackets, as if they had just rushed over from nursing home or laboratory. I didn't see Mary Thorndecker, but the rest of the clan was there. And Agatha Binder, Art Merchant, Dr. Kenneth Draper, and Ronnie Goodfellow, self-conscious in his uniform. There were others whose names I had forgotten but whose faces were vaguely familiar: the "best people" Goodfellow had introduced on my first morning in Coburn.

There was a punch bowl, and white wine was available. No hard booze. But the kids out on the porch were puffing away like mad, and even inside the house the smell of grass was sweet and thick. Include me out. I had tried pot twice, with Joan Powell, and each time, at the crucial moment, I fell asleep. I'd rather have a hangover.

It was all genial enough, everyone talking, laughing, mixing. No one leaned on me, and Koukla didn't try to introduce me to everyone; just left me free to roam. I met some of the kid researchers and listened to their patter. The fact that I couldn't understand their sentences didn't bother me so much as the fact that I couldn't understand their *words*. I had a hazy notion of what "endocrinology" meant, but when they moved down the dictionary to "endocytosis," they lost me.

"Do you understand what they're talking about?" I asked Julie Thorndecker.

"Not me," she said, rewarding me with a throaty chuckle. "I leave all that to my husband. I prefer words of one syllable."

"Me, too," I said. "Four-letter words." Then, when she froze, I added, "Like 'love' and 'kiss'." I laughed heartily, signifying it was all a big yock, and after awhile her lips smiled.

"Enjoying your stay in Coburn, Mr. Todd?" she asked me.

"Not really. Quiet place. Lonely place."

"My, my," she said mockingly. She put a hand on my arm again. She seemed to have a need to touch. "We'll have to do something about that."

She was wearing a pantsuit of black velvet. Stud earrings of small diamonds. The gold-link ankle bracelet. She looked smashing. But she could have made a grease monkey's coveralls look chic.

In that crush, in the jabber of voices around us, it would have been possible to say the most outrageous things—make an assignation: "You do this to me, and I'll do that to you."—and no one would have heard. But actually we talked inconsequentialities: her horse, my car, her home, my job. All innocent enough.

Except that as we said nothing memorable, we were jammed up against each other by the mob. I could feel her heat. She made no effort to pull away. And while we yakked, our eyes were locked—and it was like being goosed with an icicle: painful, shivery, pleasurable, frightening, mind-blowing. The look in her eyes wasn't flirty or seductive; it was elemental, primeval. It was raw sex, stripped of subterfuge. No game-player she. My scenario sounded better to me; I could understand how a man could kill for such a woman.

"There you are!" Dr. Thorndecker said, slipping an arm about his wife's shoulders. "Entertaining our guest, are you? Splendid! Suppose we get a cup of that excellent punch?"

We worked our way over to the punch bowl. In the process, Julie Thorndecker moved away. If a signal had passed between the doctor and her, I hadn't caught it.

"A lot of your people here tonight," I mentioned, sampling a plastic cup of the punch and setting it carefully aside.

Later, thinking about it, I had only admiration for the way he used that offhand comment to lead into exactly what *he* wanted to say. I think if I had offered, "The price of soybeans in China is going up," he could have done the same thing. The man was masterful.

"Oh yes," he said, looking around, suddenly serious. "We should plan more social activities like this. These people work very hard; they not only deserve a break, they *need* it. It's not the happiest place to work. I refer to the nursing home, of course, not the lab."

"I can imagine," I murmured, pouring myself a paper cup of the white wine. That was a *little* better.

"Can you?" he said. "I'm not sure anyone not intimately associated with such an institution can even guess the emotional stress involved. We try to remain objective, to refrain from becoming personally involved. But it's impossible. We *do* become involved, intimately involved. Even with those we know have only a week, a month, a year to live. Some of them are such marvelous human beings."

"Of course," I said. "Maybe, when they accept their fate, know their days are numbered, maybe then they become superior human beings. More understanding. Kinder."

"You think so?" he asked. His dark eyes came down from the ceiling to focus on me. "Maybe. Although I'm not certain any of us is capable of believing in our own mortality. One effect I have noted, though: the closer to death our patients grow, the more exaggerated their eccentricities become. That's odd, isn't it? A man who might have sung aloud occasionally, just sung for his own amusement with no one else present, begins to sing constantly as death approaches. A vain woman becomes vainer, spending all her waking hours making-up and doing her hair. Whatever weakness or whim they might have, intensifies as death approaches."

"Yes," I agreed, "that *is* odd."

"For instance . . . " he said, almost dreamily.

No, not dreamily. But he was away from me, disconnected from his surroundings, off someplace I couldn't reach. It was not just that he was lying; I knew he was. But, while lying, he had retreated deep within himself, to a secret dream. I was seeing another facet of this many-sided man. Now there was almost a stillness in him, a certainty. His stare turned inward, and he seemed to be listening to his own falsehoods, with approval. He was so *sure*, so sure that what he was doing was right, that the splendid end justified any sordid means.

"He came to us a few years ago," he said, speaking in a steady voice, but so low that I had to bend close to hear him in that hubbub. Finally, he was almost whispering in my ear. "A man named Petersen. Chester K. Petersen. Pelvic cancer. Terminal. Inoperable. I talked to his personal physician. Petersen had always been a solitary. Almost a recluse. A wealthy man, unmarried, who had let his family ties dwindle. And as his illness worsened, his craving for solitude intensified. Meals were left outside his door. He refused to submit to medical examinations. He seemed anxious to end all human contact. It was as I told you: in the last stages, the eccentricity becomes a dreadful obsession. We've seen it—all of us who serve in this field—happen again and again.''

I knew it was a fairy tale, beautifully spun, but I had to hear it out. The man had me locked. I could not resist his certitude.

But in spite of my fascination with what he was saying, I have to tell you this: I was observing him. What I mean is that I was two people. I was a witness, spellbound by his resonant voice and intriguing story. I don't deny it. But at the same time I was an investigator, searching. What I was looking for was evidence of what I had seen in our previous meetings: the weariness that concluded the first, those racking spasms of pain I had noted during our second interview.

On that night, at that moment, I saw no indication of either: no weariness, no pain.

What I did see were preternaturally bright eyes, that secretive expression, and movements, gestures, that were slowed and glazed. It hit me: this man was drugged. Somehow. On something. He was so drawled out, so spaced and deliberate. He was functioning; no doubt about that. And functioning efficiently. But he was gone. That's the only way I can express it: he was gone. Off somewhere. Maybe he was dulling the weariness, the pain. I just didn't know.

"What became of him?" I asked. "This Petersen?"

"He left a will," Thorndecker said, smiling faintly. "Quite legal. Drawn by a local attorney. Signed and witnessed. In the event of his death, he desired to be buried late at night, or in the early morning hours. Between midnight and dawn. The wording of the will was quite specific. He was to be buried in the Crittenden cemetery. No religious service, no mourners, no funeral. With as little fuss as possible. He just didn't want the world to note his passing.''

"Weird," I said.

"Wasn't it?" he nodded.

"And you respected his wishes?"

"Of course."

"He died of cancer?"

"Well . . . '' Thorndecker said, pulling gently at the lobe of one ear, "the immediate cause of death was congestive heart failure. But, of course, it was the cancer that brought it on.''

He looked at me narrowly, tilting his head to one side. He had me, and I knew it. Try to fight that diagnosis and that death certificate in a court of law, and see how far you'd get.

He must have glimpsed confusion and surrender in my eyes, for he suddenly slapped me on the shoulder.

"Good Heavens!" he cried. "Enough of this morbidity! Let's enjoy this evening. Now I'll leave you to your own devices, and let you meet and talk with some of these fine young people. I'm happy you could attend the Reverend Koukla's party, Mr. Todd."

I put a hand on his arm to stop him.

"Before you go," I said, "I must tell you. Mrs. Cynthia Bingham asked me to give you her regards. Her love."

The change in him was startling. He froze. His face congealed. Suddenly he was looking back, remembering. He was alone in that crowded room.

"Cynthia Bingham," he repeated. I couldn't hear him, but I saw his lips move.

His features became so suddenly tragic that I thought he might burst out weeping.

"Can we ever escape the past, Mr. Todd?" he asked me.

I mean he really *asked* me. It wasn't a rhetorical question. He was confounded, and wanted an answer.

"No, sir," I told him. "I don't think we can."

He nodded sadly.

He disappeared into the crowd. What a great performance that had been. A bravura! The man had missed his calling; he should have been an actor, playing only Hamlet. Or Lear. He left me stunned, shaken, and almost convinced.

"Mr. Todd," Dr. Kenneth Draper said, with his nervous smile, "enjoying the party?"

"Beginning to," I said, pouring myself another cup of white wine. "I haven't seen Mary Thorndecker this evening. Is she around?"

"Ah, regretfully no," he said, wiping a palm across a forehead that as far as I could see was completely dry. "I understand she had a previous engagement."

"Lovely young woman," I said. "And talented. I liked her paintings."

He came alive.

"Oh yes!" he said. "She does beautiful things. Beautiful! And she's such a help to us."

"A help?"

"In Crittenden Hall. She visits our guests, talks to them for hours, brings them flowers. Things of that sort. She's very people-oriented."

" 'People-oriented'," I repeated, nodding solemnly. "Well, I guess that's better than being horse-oriented."

He didn't pick up on that at all, so I let it slide.

"By the way," he said, looking about, searching for someone, "Dr. Thorndecker asked us to prepare a report for you. A precis of the research that's been done to date on aging and its relationship to human cells."

"Yes, he said he'd get something together for me."

"Well, we've completed it. Mostly photocopies of papers and some original things we've been doing in the lab. Are you familiar with the term *in vitro*?"

"Means 'In glass,' doesn't it?"

"Specifically, yes. Generally, it means under laboratory conditions. That is, in test tubes, dishes, flasks—whatever. In an artificial environment. As opposed to *in vivo*, which means in the body, in living tissue."

"I understand."

"Most of the papers you'll receive report on experiments with mammalian cells *in vitro*."

"But you have experimented on living tissue, haven't you?" I said. "I saw your animals."

Also, at that moment, I saw the sudden sweat on his forehead.

"Of course," he said. "Rats, guinea pigs, chimps, dogs. It's all there. My assistant has the package for you. Linda Cunningham. She's around here somewhere."

He looked about wildly.

"I'll bump into her," I soothed him. "And if we don't get together, you can always drop the package off at the Coburn Inn."

"I suppose so," he said doubtfully, "but Dr. Thorndecker was most explicit about getting it to you tonight."

I nodded, and wandered away. Geniuses might be great guys: fun to read about, fun to know. But I'm not sure I'd care to work for one.

"*So* glad you could make it, Mr. Todd," the Reverend Peter Koukla said, clasping my hand in both of his. "You have a drink? Good. It's a *nice* white wine, isn't it?"

"Very nice."

"Excuse me, please. I must see to the chow."

I hadn't heard food called "chow" since Boy Scout camp. Unless, I reflected idly, Koukla was referring to his dog—the kind with a black tongue.

I worked my way across the room to where Agatha Binder and Nurse Stella Beecham were standing stolidly, close together, backs against the wall. They looked like a bas relief in mahogany.

"Ladies," I greeted them.

"Watch your language, buster," Agatha Binder said, grinning. "So you made it, did you? Well, what would a party be without a guest of honor?"

"Is that what I am?" I asked, smiling with all my boyish charm at Nurse Beecham.

If looks could kill, I'd have been bundling with Chester K. Petersen.

"Mr. Todd!" Art Merchant caroled, twitching. "Nice to see you again. How is your investigation progressing?"

"Leaps and bounds," I said, turning to him. "Tell me something, Mr. Merchant . . . Do you ever lend money on trailers?"

"Trailers?"

"Mobile homes."

"Oh," he said. "Well . . . it depends."

"Thank you," I said.

I moved away. I'm tall enough to see over heads. I saw Dr. Telford Thorndecker crowding his wife into a corner. He was all over her, not caring. His hands were on her shoulders, arms, stroking her hip, touching her hair. Once he put a finger to her lips. Once he leaned down to kiss her ear. Another role: Dr. Telford Thorndecker, sex fiend.

"They seem very happy," I said to Constable Ronnie Goodfellow, who was watching the same scene. "Not drinking? Oh . . . on duty, are you?"

"Yes," he said, staring at the Thorndeckers. "Just stopped in to say hello."

"Something I've been meaning to ask you," I said. "You're not the only cop in town, are you?"

He turned those black eyes to look at me. Finally . . .

"Of course not," he said. "We've got the county sheriff's deputies and the state troopers."

"No," I said, "I mean here in Coburn. Are you the only constable?"

"No, sir," he said. "Four constables. I work mostly nights."

"Who's top man?"

"Chief Constable? That's Anson Merchant."

"Merchant?" I said. "Related to Art Merchant, the banker?"

"Yes," Ronnie Goodfellow said shortly, turning his eyes back to the Thorndeckers loving it up in the corner. "The chief is the mayor's brother."

"Are you Mr. Todd?" she asked breathlessly.

A plump, little butterball. A Kewpie doll. She was holding out a sealed manila envelope.

"And you must be Linda Cunningham," I said. "Dr. Draper's assistant."

"Right on!" she cried, slapping the envelope into my hand. "And here's your report. Now you tell Kenneth you got it, y'hear? He was so *nervous*!"

"I'll tell him," I promised. "But what if I have questions about it? Who do I contact?"

"Me," she said, giggling. "My name, address, and phone number are on the report."

"Super," I said, getting high on her breath. "You may be hearing from me."

"Super," she said, still giggling.

I folded the heavy envelope lengthwise and jammed it into my jacket pocket. I was prepared to talk nonsense to her a little longer, just to hear her giggle, but a long drink of water in a lab coat dragged her away. I looked around the crowded room. Most of the guests were straggling into the dining room where I could see a table laid with cold meats, potato salad, dishes of this and that. I saw Thorndecker talking to the Reverend Koukla. I turned back to Constable Goodfellow, but he was gone.

"Hello, Mr. Todd," Edward Thorndecker said in his half-lisp. "Going to get something to eat?"

"Soon," I said. "How are you, Edward?"

"Okay, sir," he said politely. "I wanted to get Julie a plate. Have you seen her?"

"Not recently." I said.

"She's around here somewhere," he said fretfully, his beautiful eyes anxious. "I saw her, and then she just disappeared."

"You'll find her," I said.

He moved away without replying. I watched the mob at the buffet, and decided I wasn't all that hungry. I wandered out onto the porch to smoke a cigarette. The tobacco kind. But a flock of chattering guests came after me, juggling filled paper plates and plastic cups of coffee. I didn't want noisy company; I wanted quiet, solitude, and the chance to sort things out.

I stepped down from the porch. Cigarette in my lips, hands jammed into pockets, shoulders hunched against the cold, I sauntered slowly down the deserted street.

What happened next was a scene from an Italian movie: as wildly improbable.

There were street lights on both corners: orange globes with dim and flickering halos. But mid-block, sidewalks and street were shadowed, black as sin and not half as inviting. I was moving toward my parked Grand Prix. Across the street I could see, dimly, the official cruiser of Constable Ronnie Goodfellow. In 1976, it had been painted in a gaudy Bicentennial design. Now the bold stars were faded, the brave stripes mud-encrusted and indistinct.

It seemed to me, as I glanced at the cruiser, that slender white arms were beckoning me from the back seat. I spat out my cigarette, ground it out quickly. I slipped farther back into the gloom, behind a tree. I waited until my eyes became accustomed to the dark. I peered cautiously around. I saw . . .

Not slender white arms, but bare feet, ankles, calves. The window frame cut off the legs at mid-thigh. A woman's legs, waving in the air as languidly as a butterfly's wings. A slave bracelet glinted about one ankle. I watched without shame. I could make out a man's shirted back bent between those stroking legs. The image, in that somber light, had the eerie and stirring quality of a remembered dream.

I glanced back toward Koukla's house. I saw the lights, the guests on the porch. I heard faintly the tinkle of talk and laughter. But the two in the car were oblivious to everything but their own need. The broad back rose and fell, faster and faster. The slender white legs stretched and flexed in response.

I caught something in peripheral vision: the brief flare of a lighted match. I turned slowly . . .

I was not the only silent stalker, the only bemused witness. Halfway between me and the lighted Koukla home, Dr. Telford Gordon Thorndecker stood back from the sidewalk, observing the scene in the cruiser, quiet and contemplative while his wife was being done. There was no mistaking his massive frame, his leonine head. He smoked his cigarette with care and deliberation. Nothing in his manner or posture showed anger or defeat. Resignation, possibly.

Then I moved, as silently and stealthily as I could. I slid down the row of trees to my car. I unlocked the door, pulled it quietly shut behind me. I started the engine, but didn't turn on the lights. I backed up to the corner, so I wouldn't have to pass that busy official cruiser of the Coburn constabulary.

On my way back to the Inn, I did not reflect on Thorndecker's hurt or on the lovers' scorn. All I could think was that if they had dared it, in such a place, at such a time, then they knew he was aware. And his knowledge had no significance for them. They just didn't care.

And if he knew, and they didn't care, then why was Ernie Scoggins snuffed? My beautiful scenario evaporated.

It was not until I had parked in the lot of the Coburn Inn, and was stumbling across Main Street to Sandy's Liquors and Fine Wines, that the squalidness of the scene I had just witnessed bludgeoned me. I saw again that calm, silent husband watching his wife getting it off with a man half his age. I saw again the frantically pounding back, the jerking, naked legs.

Did he love her that much? Did they both love her that much?

I wanted to weep. For their misery and doomed hopes. For the splintered dreams of all of us.

I had no desire for food, wasn't sure I ever wanted to eat again. But I did want to numb my dread. I drank warm vodka from a bathroom glass caked with Pepsodent around the rim.

I sat in one of the gimpy armchairs, pulled a spindle lamp close. I began going through the report Linda Cunningham had delivered. I think I mentioned that I've had no formal education or training in science, so most of the research papers meant little to me. But I could grasp, hazily, the conclusions.

They weren't very startling, because I had read much the same in the preliminary investigation of Dr. Thorndecker's work by Scientific Research Records for the Bingham Foundation. It had been found that normal human body cells reproduced (doubled) a finite number of times *in vitro*. There seemed to be a significant correlation between the number of doublings and the age of the donor.

When normal human embryo cells were nurtured and reproduced *in vitro*, about fifty doublings could be expected. As donor age increased, the number of doublings decreased. The normal cultured cells did not die, exactly, but after each doubling became less differentiated and simpler, until they bore little resemblance to the original normal cells.

All this argued forcibly, as Dr. Thorndecker had said, for a "cellular clock," an X Factor that determined how long a normal human cell remained viable. When I read the reports on reproduction *in vitro* of normal mammalian cells other than human, the same apparently held true. So, obviously, each species had a built-in lifespan that was reflected in the lifespan of each body cell of which it was composed. When the cells completed their allotted number of doublings and died, the organism died.

"I'll drink to that," I said aloud, and took another hefty belt of Pepsodent-flavored vodka.

One thing bothered me here. It concerned a paper on original research done by the Crittenden lab on the morphology of normal chimpanzee body cells. The conclusions were consistent with the research on normal body cells of other species.

But there was nothing in the report concerning the testing of an experimental cancer drug on chimps. Yet I had seen that young, comatose specimen in the basement of the Crittenden Research Laboratory. He had been a mass of putrescent, cancerous tumors, and Dr. Draper had stated that the animal had been deliberately infected, then treated, and the experimental drug had failed.

There was nothing of this in the report I received. But after thinking about it awhile, I could understand why it might not be mentioned. The lab was undoubtedly engaged in several research projects. One of them might be the development of drugs efficacious against sarcomas and carcinomas. But information on this project was not included in the report prepared for me simply because it was extraneous. It had nothing to do with Dr. Thorndecker's application for funds to investigate the cause of aging. It had nothing to do with my inquiry.

That made sense, I told myself.

Finally, the report tossed aside, vodka in the bottle getting down to the panic level, I closed my eyes, stretched out my legs, and tried to determine exactly what it was in that report that was nagging at me. There was a question I wanted answered, and for the life of me I couldn't determine what it was.

Sighing, I picked up the report and skimmed it through again. It told me nothing more, but the feeling persisted that I was missing something. It was something that wasn't stated in the report, but was implied.

I gave up. I capped the vodka bottle. I went into the bathroom. I peed. I washed hands and face in cold water. I combed my hair. I slapped cologne on my jaw. I decided to go down to the bar. Maybe Millie Goodfellow was lounging about, and I could buy her a drink. After all, it was only what any other normal, red-blooded American boy would—

I stopped. "Normal, red-blooded American boy." The key word was "normal." I rushed back to the living room. I grabbed up the research report from the floor. I flipped through it wildly.

It was as I remembered. *Now* I remembered. It was all about *normal* body cells, *normal* mammalian cells, *normal* human embryo cells, *normal* chimpanzee cells. In every instance, in every report on reproduction, doubling, aging, the qualifying adjective "normal" had been used to describe the cells *in vitro*.

I took a deep breath. I didn't know what the hell it meant, but I thought it had to mean something. I found the phone number of Linda Cunningham.

"Hi!" she said, and giggled. "Whoever you are."

"Samuel Todd," I said. "How're you doing?"

"Super!" she said, and I believed her. I could hear punk rock blaring in the background—it sounded like the Sex Pistols—and there was a lot of loud talk, yells, groans, screams of laughter. I figured she had invited a few friends to her home, for something a little stronger than fruit punch and white wine.

"Sorry to interrupt your party," I said, "but this will just take a minute. Linda? Linda, are you there?"

"Super!" she said.

"Linda, in that report—you know what report I'm talking about, don't you?"

"Report?" she said. "Oh sure. Report. Who is this?"

"Samuel Todd," I repeated patiently. "I'm the guy you gave the report to earlier tonight at the Reverend Koukla's party."

"Oh wow!" she cried. "Harry, don't you *ever* do that again! That *hurt*."

"Linda," I said desperately, "this is Sam Todd."

"Super!" she said.

There was a louder blast of music, then the sound of scuffling. A male voice came on the phone.

"Are you an obscene phone caller?" he asked drunkenly. "I can breathe heavier than you."

More scuffling sounds. Crash of dropped phone. I heard Linda say, "Now stop it. You're just *awful*."

"Linda!" I yelled. "Linda? Are you there?"

She came back on the line.

"Who is this?" she said. "Who—whom are you calling?"

"This is Samuel Todd. I am calling Linda Cunningham, that's whom."

"Mr. Todd?" she cried. "Really? Super! Come on right over. We have a marvelous party all our—"

"No, no," I said hastily. "Thanks very much, but I can't come over. Linda, I have a question about the report. You said I could contact you if I had a question about the report."

"Report? What report?"

"Linda," I said as calmly as I could, "tonight at Koukla's party you gave me a report. Dr. Draper prepared it on orders of Dr. Thorndecker."

"Oh," she said, suddenly sober. "*That* report. Well, yes, sure, I remember. This is Mr. Todd?"

"Right," I said gratefully. "Just one little question about the report, and then I'll let you get back to your party."

"Super party," she said, giggling.

"Sounds like it," I said, hearing glass smashing in the background. "Sounds like a jim-dandy party. I wish I could join you, I really do. Linda, in that report you keep talking about normal cells. Normal embryo cells, and normal mammalian cells, and so forth. All the statistics have to do with normal cells—right?"

"Right," she said, and it came out "Ri." She giggled. "All normal cells. Normal body cells."

"Now my question is this:" I said. "Do all those statistics hold true for *ab*normal cells, too? Do abnormal cells decay or die after a limited number of reproductions?"

"Abnormal cells?" she said, beginning to slur. "What kind of abnormal cells?"

"Well, say cancer cells."

"Oh no," she said. "No no no no. Cancer cells go on forever. *In vitro*, that is. They never die. Harry, I *told* you not to *do* that again. It's really very embarrassing."

"Cancer cells never die?" I repeated dully.

"Didn't you know?" she said, giggling. "Cancer cells are immortal. Oh wow, Harry, do *that* again. That's super!"

I hung up softly.

I didn't go down to the bar that night. I didn't finish the quart of vodka either, though I put a hell of a dent in it. But the more I drank, the more sober I became. Finally I undressed and got into bed. I didn't know when sleep would come. Maybe in about ten years.

Didn't you know? Cancer cells are immortal.

I had a vision of a pinhead of pulsing jelly. Becoming something about as large as a dried pea. Discolored and wrinkled. Growing. Swelling. Expanding. The tiny wrinkles becoming folds and valleys. The discolorations becoming blobs of corruption. Larger and larger. A tumor as big as the Ritz. Taking over. Something monstrous. Blooming in wild colors. Runny tissue. The stink of old gardenias. Spreading, oozing, engulfing. And never dying. Never, never, never. But conquering, filling a slimed universe.

Immortal.

The Fifth Day

I don't know what your life is like, but sometimes, in mine, I just don't want to get out of bed. It's not a big thing, like I've suddenly come to the conclusion that life is a scam. It's a lot of little things: Con Edison just sent me a monthly bill for $3,472.69; a new shirt was missing when my laundry was returned; a crazy woman on the bus asked me why my nose was so long; a check from a friend, in repayment of a loan, promptly bounced. *Little* things. Maybe you could cope with them one at a time. But suddenly they pile up, and you don't want to get out of bed; it just isn't worth it.

That's how I felt on Friday morning. I looked toward the light coming through the window. It was the color of snot; I knew the sun wasn't shining. I wasn't hung over. I mean my head didn't ache, my stomach didn't bubble. But I felt disoriented. And I had all these problems. It seemed easier to stay exactly where I was, under warm blankets, and forget about "taking arms against a sea of troubles." Hamlet's soliloquy. Hamlet should have spent a week in Coburn, N.Y. He'd have found a use for that bare bodkin.

But why the hassle? There was no reason, I told myself, why I *should* get out of bed. What for? No one I wanted to see. No one I wanted to talk to. Events were moving smoothly along without my intervention. Corpses were getting shoveled into the ground at two in the morning, old geezers were disappearing, young wives were cuckolding their husbands in the back seats of police cars, cancer cells were reproducing like mad. God's in His Heaven; all's right with the world. What could I do?

It went on like that until about ten in the morning. Then I got out of bed. I wish I could tell you it was from stern resolve, a conviction that I owed myself, my employers, and the human race one more effort to tidy up the Thorndecker mess. It wasn't that at all. I got out of bed because I had to pee.

This led to the reflection that maybe the memorable acts of great men were impelled by similarly basic drives. Maybe Einstein came up with $E=MC^2$ while suffering from insomnia. Maybe Keats dashed off "Ode on a Grecian Urn" while he was constipated. Maybe Carnot jotted down the second law of thermodynamics while enduring an attack of dyspepsia and awaiting the arrival of Mother Tums. It was all possible.

I record this nonsense to illustrate my state of mind on that Friday morning. I may not have been hung over, but I wasn't certain I was completely sober.

Breakfast helped bring me back to reality. A calorie omelette, with a side order of cholesterol. Delicious. Three cups of black coffee.

"*Another?*" the foot-sore waitress asked when I ordered the third.

"Another," I nodded. "And a warm Danish. Buttered."

"It's your stomach," she said.

But it wasn't. It belonged to someone else, thank God. And my brain was also up for grabs.

I came down to earth during that final black coffee. Then I knew who I was, where I was, and what I was doing. Or trying to do. Caffeine restored my anxieties; I was my usual paranoiac self. Stunned by what I had seen and heard the previous evening. Wanting to put the jigsaw together, and looking frantically for those easy corner pieces.

I signed my breakfast tab, then wandered through the bar on my way to nowhere.

"Hey you, Todd," Al Coburn called in his raspy voice. "Over here."

He was seated alone in one of the high-backed booths. I slid in opposite, and before I looked at him, I glanced around. Jimmy was behind the bar, as usual. Two guys in plaid lumberjackets were drinking beer and arguing about something. I turned back to Al Coburn. He was drinking whiskey, neat, with a beer wash.

I jerked my chin at the booze.

"Taking your flu shot?" I asked.

"They killed my dog last night," he said hoarsely. "Poisoned her."

"Who's 'they?' Who poisoned your dog?"

"I come out this morning, and there she was. Stiff. Tongue hanging out."

"You call a vet?"

"What the hell for?" he said angrily. "Any fool could see she was dead."

"How old a dog?"

"Thirteen," he said.

"Maybe she died of natural causes," I said. "Thirteen's a good age for a dog. What makes you think she was poisoned?"

He tried to get the full shot glass up to his lips, but his hand was trembling too much. Finally, he bent over it and slurped. When he straightened up, whiskey dripped from his chin. He hadn't shaved for a few days; I watched drops run down through white stubble.

"Two nights ago," he said, "someone fired off a rifle, through my windows."

"Joy-riding kids," I said.

"That hound," he said, choking. "The best."

This time he got the shot glass to his mouth, and drained it. I went over to the bar and bought him another, and a beer for me. I carried the drinks back to the booth.

Grief must have mellowed him; this time he thanked me.

"You tell Goodfellow about this?" I asked him.

He shook his head. His rough, liver-spotted hands were still trembling; he gripped the edge of the table to steady himself.

"You tell any cop about it?"

"What's the use?" he said despairingly. "They're all in on it."

"In on what?"

He wouldn't answer, and we were back on the merry-go-round: vague hints, intimation, accusations—and no answers.

"Mr. Coburn," I said, "why would anyone want to poison your dog?"

He leaned across the table. Those washed-blue eyes were dulled and rheumy.

"That's simple, ain't it? A warning to me to keep my trap shut. A sign of what might happen to me."

"Why you?" I asked him. "Because you were Ernie Scoggins's best friend?"

"Maybe just that," he said. "Or maybe they looked for that letter, couldn't find it, and figured Ernie give it to me. Listen, maybe they *hurt* him, and he *told* them he give me the goddamned letter. Ernie, he wouldn't do anything to cause me harm, but maybe he told them I had the letter, hoping it would keep them from killing him. But it didn't. Now they're after me."

"What are you going to do?"

He sat back, folded his twitchy hands in his lap, stared down at them.

"I don't know," he muttered. "Killed my dog. Shot out my windows. I don't know what to do."

"Mr. Coburn," I said, as patiently as I could, "if you feel your life's threatened because of the Scoggins letter, why don't you do this: put the letter in a safe deposit box at the bank. Then tell it around town how Scoggins gave you that letter, and it's in a safe place, and it will only be opened in the event of your death. That's a good insurance policy."

"No," he said, "I don't trust the bank. That Art Merchant. How do I know them boxes are safe?"

"They can't open the box without your key."

He laughed scornfully. "That's what *they* say."

I didn't try to argue. He was so spooked, so irrational, that compared to him, my paranoia seemed like a mild whim.

"All right," I said, "then show me the letter. Let me read it. Tell everyone in town I've seen it. They're not going to kill both of us."

"What makes you think so?" he said.

I didn't even have sense enough to be frightened. All I could think of was that I was drinking beer with a psychotic old man who kept talking about how "they" poisoned his dog, shot holes in his windows, and wanted to kill him. And I was going right along with him as if what he was saying was real, logical, believable.

"The hell with it," I said suddenly.

"What?" he said.

"Mr. Coburn, I've had it. I've enjoyed our little chats. Interesting and instructive. But I've gone as far as I can go. Either you tell me more, or I'm cutting loose. I can't go stumbling along in the dark like this."

"Yeah," he said unexpectedly, "I can see that."

He took his upper denture from his mouth, wiped it carefully on a cocktail napkin, slipped it back in. A jolly sight to see.

"Tell you what," he said. Then he stopped.

"What?" I asked. "Tell me what?"

He went through the same act with the lower plate. His way of gaining time, I suppose. I would have preferred finger-drumming or a trip to the loo.

"Maybe I can get this whole thing stopped," he said. "If I can, then there's no need to worry."

"And if you can't?"

He looked up sharply. Bleached lips pressed tighter. That elbow chin jutted. Resolve seemed to be returning.

"You figuring on being here tomorrow?" he asked.

"Sure. I guess so. Another day at least."

"I'll see you. Here at the Inn."

"I may not be in."

"I'll leave a message."

"All right. Are you sure you don't want to tell me now what this is all about?"

"Maybe tomorrow," he said evasively. "I'll know by tomorrow."

I wanted to nail it down. "And if you don't get the whole thing stopped, like you said, then you'll show me Ernie Scoggins's letter?"

"You'll see it," he said grimly.

Later, when it was all over, I realized I should have leaned on him harder. I should have leaned on all of them harder, bulldozing my way to the truth. But hindsight is always 20–20 vision. And at the time, I was afraid that if I came on too strong, they'd all clam, and I'd have nothing.

Besides, I doubt if what I did or did not do had much effect on what happened. Events had already been set in motion before I arrived in Coburn and visited Crittenden Hall. Perhaps my presence acted as a catalyst, and the Thorndecker affair rushed to its climax faster simply because I was there. But the final outcome was always inevitable.

Al Coburn went stumping off, and I went thoughtfully out into the hotel lobby. Millie Goodfellow beckoned me over to the cigar counter. She was wearing a tight T-shirt with a road sign printed on the front: SLIPPERY WHEN WET.

"How do you like it?" she said, arching her back. "Cute?"

"Cute as all get out," I said, nodding.

The dark glasses were still in place, the black eye effectively concealed.

"I know something you don't," she said, making it sound like a 6-year-old girl taunting her 8-year-old brother.

"Millie," I said, sighing, "*everyone* knows something I don't know."

"What will you give me if I tell you?" she asked.

"What do you want—a five-pound box of money?"

"I could use it," she giggled. "But I want you to keep your promise, that's all."

"I would have done that anyway," I lied. "What do you know that I don't know?"

She glanced casually about. The lobby was in its usual state of somnolence. A few of the permanent residents were reading Albany newspapers in the sagging armchairs. The baldy behind the desk was busy with scraps of paper and an old adding machine.

Millie Goodfellow beckoned me closer. I leaned across the counter, which put my face close to that damned road sign. I felt like an idiot, and undoubtedly looked like one.

"You remember when someone broke into your room?" she said in a low voice, still watching the lobby.

"Of course I remember."

"You won't tell anyone will you?"

"Tell anyone what?"

"Tell anyone that I told you."

It would have been laughable if it wasn't so god-damned maddening.

"Told me *what*?" I said angrily.

"My husband," she whispered. "I think it was Ronnie who did it."

I stared at her, blinking. If she was right, that Indian cop had done a hell of an acting job when he came up to "investigate" the break-in.

"Why do you think that, Millie?"

"He took my keys that night. He thinks I didn't notice, but I did. I told you I've got a passkey. And the next morning my keys were back."

"Why didn't you tell me this before?"

She lifted the black glasses. The mouse under her eye was a rainbow.

"I didn't have *this* before," she said. "You won't tell him I told you, will you? I mean about the keys?"

"Of course I won't tell him," I said. "Or anyone else. Thank you, Millie."

"Remember your promise," she called after me.

The elevator door bore a hand-printed sign: NOT WORKING. That would do for me, too, I thought glumly, walking up the stairs. Oh, I was working—but nothing was getting done. Bits and pieces—that's what I was collecting: bits and pieces. I wondered, if Constable Goodfellow *had* been my midnight caller, how he had learned of that anonymous note and why he was so anxious to recover it. Every time I got the answer to one question, it led to at least two more. The whole damn thing kept growing, spreading. Of course I made the comparison to cancerous cells *in vitro*. No end to it.

When I got to my room, the door was open, and I discovered why the elevator was out of operation: Sam Livingston was in 3-F, sweeping up, making the bed, setting out a clean drinking glass and fresh towels.

"Morning, Sam," I said grumpily.

"Morning, Sam," he said. He held up the quart vodka bottle. Maybe two drinks were left. "You have friends in?" he asked.

"No, I did that myself."

"My, my. Someone must have been thirsty."

"Someone must have been disgusted. Have a belt, if you like."

"A little early in the morning for me," he said, "but I thank you kindly. What you disgusted about?"

He kept moving around the room, emptying ashtrays, rearranging the dust.

"You want a complete list?" I asked him. "The weather, for starters. With this lousy town running a close second."

"Nothing you can do about the weather," he said. "God sends it; you take it."

"That doesn't mean I can't bitch about it."

"As for this town, I don't reckon it's much worse than any other place. Trouble is, it's so small, you see it clearer."

"I'm not tracking, Sam."

"Well, like in New York City. Now, you got a lot of rich, powerful people running that town—right?"

"Well . . . sure."

"And maybe some of them, you don't even know their names. Like bankers maybe, newspaper editors, preachers, union people, big property owners, businessmen. They really run the town, don't they? I mean, they got the muscle."

"I suppose so."

"I know so. And you don't even know who they are, because that city is so big, and they like to keep their names out of the papers and their faces off the TV. They want to be invisible. They can do that in a great big city. But in Coburn, now, we're small. Everyone knows everyone else. No one can keep invisible. But otherwise it's the same.''

"You mean a small group of movers and shakers who run things?''

"Pretty much,'' he said. ''Also, this town's in such a bad money way—no jobs around, the young folks moving out, property values dropping—that these here people they got to stick together. They can't go fighting amongst themselves.''

I stared at him, saw that old, black face deliberately expressionless. It was a mask that had been crumpled up, then partly smoothed out. But the wrinkles were still there, the scars and wounds of age.

"Sam,'' I said softly to him, ''I think you're trying to tell me something.''

"Nah,'' he said, ''I'm just blabbing to pass the time whilst I tidy up in here. Now you get a lot of people in a lifeboat, and they all got to keep rowing and bailing, bailing and rowing. If they don't want the whole damn boat to go down.''

I thought about that pearl of wisdom for a moment or two.

"Sam, are you hinting that there's a conspiracy? Amongst the movers and shakers of Coburn? About this Thorndecker grant?''

"Conspiracy?'' he said.

"What does that mean—a bunch of folks get together and make a plan? Nah. They don't have to do that. They all know what they got to do to keep that lifeboat floating.''

"Rowing and bailing,'' I said.

"Now you got it,'' he said. ''These people, they don't want to get wet, floating around out there in the ocean, boat gone, not a prayer. So they go along, no matter what they hear or what they guess. They *gotta* go along. They got no choice, do they?''

"Self-preservation,'' I said.

"Sure,'' he said cheerfully. ''That's why you finding it so tough to get people to talk to you. No one wants to kick holes in the boat.''

"Are things really that bad in Coburn?'' I asked.

"They ain't good,'' he said shortly.

"Well, let me ask you this: would the 'best people' of Coburn, the ones who run the town, would they go along with something illegal, something criminal or evil, just to keep the boat floating?''

"You said it yourself,'' he said. ''Self-preservation. Mighty powerful. Can make a man do things he wouldn't do if he don't have to. Just to hang onto what he's got, you understand.''

"Yes, I do understand,'' I said slowly. ''Thank you, Sam. You've given me something else to think about.''

"Aw hell,'' he said, gathering up broom, mop, pail and rags, ''I'd have thought you'd have figured that out for yourself.''

"I was getting to it,'' I said. ''I think. But you spelled it out for me.''

He turned suddenly, looked at me with something like alarm in his face.

"What did I say?'' he demanded. ''I didn't say nothing.''

I turned my eyes away. It was embarrassing to see that fear.

"You didn't say anything, Sam," I assured him. "You didn't tell me word one."

He grunted, satisfied.

"I got a message for you," he said. "From Miz Thorndecker."

"Mary?"

"No," he said, "the married one."

I couldn't tell if his "Miz" meant "Miss" or "Mrs."

"Mrs. Julie Thorndecker?" I asked.

"That's the one," he said. "She wants to meet with you."

"She does? When did she tell you this?"

"She got the word to me," he said vaguely.

"Where does she want to meet?"

"There's a place out on the Albany post road. It's—"

"Don't tell me," I said. "A roadhouse. Red Dog Betty's."

"You know it?" he said, surprised. "Yeah, that's the place. It's got a big parking lot. That's where she'll meet you. She don't want to go inside."

"When?"

"Noon today," he said. "She drives one of these sporty little foreign cars."

"She would," I said. "All right, I'll meet her. Thanks again, Sam."

He told me how to get to Red Dog Betty's. I gave him five dollars, which he accepted gratefully and with dignity.

I had more than an hour to kill before my meeting with Julie Thorndecker. There was only one thing I wanted to do: I got into the Grand Prix and drove out to Crittenden. I didn't have anything planned; I just wanted to look at the place again. It drew me.

It was another lost day: someone had destroyed the sun and thrown a gauzy sheet across the world. The sky came right down—you wanted to duck your head—and the light seemed to be coming through a wire strainer, and a rusty one at that. Damp wood smell, and the river, and frosted fields. The melancholy of that place seeped into my bones. The marrow shriveled, and if someone had tapped my tibia, I'd have gone *ting!* Like a crystal goblet.

Nearing Crittenden, I passed a Village of Coburn cruiser going the other way. The constable driving wasn't Ronnie Goodfellow, but he raised a hand in greeting as we passed, and I waved back. I was happy to see another officer. I was getting the idea that the Indian worked a twenty-four-hour shift.

I drove slowly around the Crittenden grounds. The buildings looked silent and deserted. I had the fantasy that if I broke in, I'd hear a radio playing, see hot food on the tables, smell hamburgers sizzling on the grill—and not a soul to be found. A new *Marie Celeste* mystery. All the signs of life, but no life.

I saw a blue MGB parked on the gravel before the main entrance of Crittenden Hall, and figured it was Julie's "sporty little foreign car" that Sam Livingston had mentioned. But I didn't see her, or anyone else.

I drove around the fenced estate. Fields and woods dark and empty under the flat sky. No guard with shotgun and attack dog. Just a vacant landscape. I came up to the cemetery, still rolling gently, and then I saw someone. A black figure moving quietly among the tombstones, not quite sauntering.

There was no mistaking that massive, almost monumental bulk: Dr. Telford Gordon Thorndecker surveying his domain, a shadow across the land. He was overcoated, hatless; heavy brown hair fluffed in gusts of wind. He walked with hands clasped behind him, in the European fashion. His head was slightly bowed, as if he was reading the tombstones as he passed.

Something in that wavery air, that tainted light, magnified his size, so that I imagined I was seeing a giant stalking the earth. He tramped the world as if he owned it, as indeed he did—at least that patch of it.

He was doing nothing suspicious. He was doing nothing at all. Apparently just out for a morning stroll. But his posture—bowed head, slumped shoulders, hands clasped in back—spoke of deep, deep thoughts, heavy pondering, dense reflection. A ruminative figure.

Even at a distance, seeing him as a silhouette cut from black paper and pasted against a frosty scene, the man dominated. I thought of how we all revolved around him, whirling our crazy, uncertain courses. But he was the eye of the storm, the sure calm, and everyone looked to him for answers.

I had a wild desire to walk alongside him through that home of the dead and ask him all the questions that were troubling me:

Did you shoot your father deliberately, Dr. Thorndecker?

Did you contrive your first wife's death?

Why did you marry such a young second wife, and how are you able to endure her infidelities?

Why are you obsessed with the problems of aging, and do you really hope to unlock the secret of immortality?

He might, I dreamed, tell me the whole story: father, wife, love, dream—everything. In grave, measured tones, that resonant baritone booming, he would tell me the complete story, leaving nothing out, and the tale would be so wondrous that all I'd be able to say would be, "And then what happened?"

And nothing in his story would be vile or ugly. I wanted it all to be the chronicle of a hero, moving from triumph to triumph. I wanted him to succeed, I really did, and hoped all my doubts and suspicions were due to envy, because I could never be the man he was, never be as handsome, know as much, or have the ability to win a woman as beautiful as Julie.

I had spent only a few hours in the man's company, but I had come under his spell. I admit it. Because he was endless. I could not get to his limits, couldn't even glimpse them. The first colossus I had ever met, and it was a chastening experience.

I didn't want to stop the car to watch him, and after awhile he and the graveyard were hidden behind a copse of bare, black trees stuck in the hard ground like grease pencils. I completed the circuit of Crittenden. As I headed for the Albany post road, the Coburn constabulary cruiser passed me again.

This time the officer didn't wave.

The place wasn't hard to find. There was a big red neon poodle out in front, and underneath was the legend: RED DOG BETTY'S. Even at noontime the sign was flashing on and off, and there were three semi-trailers and a score of private cars parked in the wide blacktop lot. I made a complete circle, and then selected a deserted spot as far from the roadhouse as I could get. I parked where I had a good view of arrivals and departures. I switched off, opened the window a bit, lighted a cigarette.

It was larger than I had imagined: a three-story clapboard building with a shingled mansard roof and dormer windows on the top floor. I couldn't figure what they needed all that space for, unless they were running games upstairs or providing hot-pillow bedrooms for lonely truckers and traveling salesmen. But maybe those upper floors were something as innocent as the owner's living quarters.

There were neon beer signs in the ground floor windows, and I could hear a juke box blaring from where I sat. As I watched, another semi pulled into the lot, and two more private cars. That place must have been a gold mine. Over the entrance was a painted sign: STEAKS, CHOPS, BAR-B-QUE. I wondered how good the food was. The presence of truckers was no indication; most of those guys will eat slop as long as the beer is cold and the coffee hot.

I sat there for two cigarettes before the blue MGB turned off the road and came nosing slowly around. I rolled down the window, stuck out my arm, and waved. She pulled up alongside, and looked at me without expression.

"Your place or mine?" she called.

Funny lady.

"Why don't you join me?" I said. "More room in here."

She came sliding out of her car, feet first. Her skirt rode up, and I caught a quick flash of bare legs. If she wanted to catch my attention, she succeeded. She took the bucket seat next to me, and slammed the door. I lighted her cigarette. Her hands weren't shaking, but her movements were brittle, almost jerky.

"Mrs. Thorndecker," I said, "nice to see you again."

"Julie," she said mechanically.

"Julie," I said, "nice to see you again."

She tried a small laugh, but it didn't work.

She was wearing a white corduroy suit. Underneath was a white turtle-neck sweater, a heavy Irish fisherman's sweater. Her fine, silvered hair was brushed tight to the scalp. No jewelry. Very little makeup. Maybe something around the eyes to make them look big and luminous. But the lips were pale, the face ivory.

She was one beautiful woman. All of her features were crisp and defined. That heavy suit and bulky sweater made her look fragile. But there was nothing vulnerable in the eyes. They were knowing and, looking at her, all I could see was a gold slave bracelet glittering on a naked ankle high in the back seat of a cop's car.

"Been here before?" she said absently.

"No, never," I said. "Looks like an okay place. How's the food?"

She flipped a palm back and forth.

"So-so," she said. "The simple stuff is good. Steaks, stews—things like that. When they try fancy, it's lousy."

I wasn't really hearing her words. I was hearing that marvelous, husky voice. I had to stop that, I decided. I had to listen to this lady's words, and not get carried away by her laughing growls, murmurs, throaty chuckles.

I didn't give her any help. I didn't say, "Well?" Or, "You wanted to see me?" Or, "You have something to say?" I just waited.

"I like Coburn," she said suddenly. "I know you don't, but I do."

"It's your home," I observed.

"That's part of it," she agreed. "I never had much of a home until I married. Also, I think part of it is that in Coburn I'm a big frog in a little pond. I don't think I could live in, say, Boston or New York. Or even Albany. I know. I've tried. I was lost."

"Where are you from, Julie? Originally?"

"A little town in Iowa. You never heard of it."

"Try me."

"Eagle Grove."

"You're right," I said. "I never heard of it. You don't speak like a midwesterner."

"I've been away a long time," she said. "A long, *long* time. I wanted to be a dancer. Ballet."

"Oh?" I said. "Were you any good?"

"Good enough," she said. "But I didn't have the discipline. Talent's never enough."

"How did you meet your husband?"

"At a party," she said. "He saved my life."

She said that very simply, a statement of absolute fact. So, of course, I had to joke about it because I was embarrassed.

"Choking on a fishbone, were you?" I said lightly.

"No, nothing like that. It was the last party I was going to go to. I had been to too many parties. I was going to have a good time, then go back to my fleabag and eat a bottle of pills."

I couldn't believe it. She was young, young, young. And beautiful. I just couldn't make the connection between suicide and this woman with the cameo face and limpid body who sat beside me, filling the car with her very personal fragrance, a scent of warm breath and fresh skin.

All I could think of to say was: "Where was it? This party?"

"Cambridge. Then Telford came over to me. He had been staring at me all evening. He took me aside and told me who he was, how old he was, what he did, how much money he had, how his wife had died a few months before. He told me everything. Then he asked me to marry him."

"Just like that?"

"Just like that," she said, nodding. "And I said yes—just like that. The shortest courtship on record."

"You think he knew?" I asked her. "What you intended to do?"

"Oh yes," she said in a low voice. "I didn't tell him, but he knew. I didn't tell him a thing about myself, but he knew. And asked me to marry him."

"And you've never regretted it?"

"Never," she said firmly. "Never for a minute. Do you have any idea of what kind of man he is?"

"I've been told he's a genius."

"Not his work," she said impatiently. "I mean *him*?"

"Very intelligent," I said cautiously. "Very charming."

"He's a great man," she said definitely. "A *great* man. But I have a problem."

Sure you do, I thought cynically; you fuck Indian cops: that's your problem.

"His daughter," she went on, leaning forward to peer out the fogged windshield. "Mary. She's really his stepdaughter. His first wife was a widow when she married Telford."

I didn't tell her this was old news to me. I lighted cigarettes for us again. She was slowly calming, her movements and gestures becoming easier, more fluid as she talked. I wanted to keep her talking. I was conscious of that suggestive voice, but I was listening to her words now.

"Mary is older than me," she said. "Four years older. She loves her stepfather very much."

She suddenly turned sideways on the seat. She drew up her legs so those bare knees were staring at me. They were round, smooth, hairless as breasts.

"*Very* much," she repeated, staring into my eyes. "Mary loves her stepfather *very* much. So she resents me. She hates me."

I made a sound. I waved a hand.

"Surely it's not that bad," I said.

"It's that bad," she said solemnly. "And also—I don't know whether you know this or not—Mary is a very, uh, disturbed woman. She's into this religious thing. Goes to some outhouse church. Shouts. Reads the Bible. Born again. The whole bit."

"Maybe she's sincere," I said.

She put a soft hand on my arm, leaned closer.

"Of *course* she's sincere," she whispered. "Believes every word of that shit. That's one of the reasons she hates me. Because I took her mother's place. She thinks I'm committing adultery with her father."

I was bewildered.

"But Thorndecker isn't her father," I said.

"*I* know that. *You* know that. But Mary is so mixed up, she thinks of Telford as her father. She thinks I stole her father from her and her dead mother. It's very complex."

"The understatement of the year."

"Sex," Julie Thorndecker said. "Sex has got a lot to do with it. Mary is so in love with Telford, she can't think straight. She thinks we—she and I—are competing for the love of the same man. That's why she hates me."

"What about Dr. Draper? Where does he fit into all this?"

"He'd marry Mary tomorrow if she'd have him. She never will. She wants Telford. But Draper keeps tagging after her like a puppy, hoping she'll suddenly see the light. I feel sorry for him."

"And for Mary?"

"Well . . . yes. I feel sorry for Mary, too. She's so mixed up. But also, I'm scared of her."

"Scared?" I said. "I can't picture you being frightened of anything or anyone."

"I thank you, kind sir," she said, tilting her head, giving me a big smile, tightening her grip on my arm.

She shouldn't have said that. It was a false note. She was not the flirty, girlish type of woman who says, "I thank you, kind sir." I began to get the idea that I was witnessing a performance, and when she finished, the audience would rise, applauding, and roses would be tossed.

"Why are you frightened of Mary?" I asked her.

She shrugged. "She's so—so unbalanced. Who knows what she might do? Or say? Oh, don't get me wrong. I'm not frightened of what she might say about me. That's of no importance. But I'm afraid for my husband. I'm afraid crazy Mary might endanger his career, his plans. That's really why I asked you to meet me here today, to have this talk."

"You're afraid Mary might—well, let's say slander her stepfather?"

If she had said, "Yes," then I was going to say, "But why should Mary endanger Thorndecker's career and his plans if she loves him as much as you say?"

But Julie didn't fall into that trap.

"Oh, she'd never do or say anything against Telford. Not directly. She loves him too much for that. But she might slander *me*. Say things. Spread stories. Because she hates me so much. Not realizing how it might reflect on Telford, how it might affect the grand dreams he has."

I leaned forward to stub out my cigarette. The movement had the added advantages of removing my arm from Julie's distracting grasp and tearing my eyes away from those shiny knees.

"What you're saying," I said slowly, "is that you hope whatever Mary might say about you will not affect Dr. Thorndecker's application for a Bingham Foundation grant. Isn't that it?"

"Yes," she said, "that's it. I just wanted you to know what a disturbed woman she is. Whatever she might say has absolutely nothing to do with my husband's application or his work."

Then we sat without speaking. I became more conscious of her scent. I'm sensitive to odors, and it seemed to me she was exuding a tantalizing perfume that was light, fragrant, with an after-scent, the way some wines have an after-taste. Julie's after-scent was deep, rich, musky. Very stirring. I thought of rumpled sheets, howls, and wet teeth.

I came back to this world to see the Coburn constabulary cruiser move slowly by. It drove up behind us, passed, made the turn behind the roadhouse, and disappeared. The officer driving, the same one I had twice met near Crittenden, didn't turn his head as he drove by. I don't know if he saw us sitting together or not. It didn't seem important. But we both watched him as he went by.

"I love my husband," Julie Thorndecker said thoughtfully.

I was silent. I hadn't even asked her.

"Still . . . " she said.

I said nothing.

"You're not giving me much encouragement," she said.

"When did you ever need encouragement?" I asked her.

"Never," she said. "You're right. Could I have a cigarette, please?"

We lighted up again. I ran the window down to get rid of the smoke.

"Too cold for you?" I said.

"Yes," she said, "too cold. But not the weather. Leave the window down. The trouble is . . . "

Another Coburnite. The unfinished sentence.

"What's the trouble?" I said.

She turned her head slowly to stare at me. I could read nothing in her eyes. Just eyes.

"I'd like to fuck you," she said steadily. "I really would. The trouble is, you'd think I was flopping so you'd give Telford a good report."

I don't care how much experience you've had, what a hot-shot cocksman you are. You're still going to feel fear when a woman says, "Yes."

"That's exactly what I'd think," I said. "What I'm thinking."

"Too bad," she said. "It's not like that at all. If you picked me up in a bar . . . ?"

"Or met you at a party? A different can of worms."

"A lovely figure of speech. Thank you."

"You know what I mean," I said. "In another place, another time."

She looked at me shrewdly.

"You're sure you're not making excuses?" she said.

"I'm not sure," I said. "I'm not sure of anything. I'm especially not sure of a woman who makes an offer like that right after she's told me she loves her husband."

She looked at me in astonishment.

"What has one got to do with the other?" she asked.

She wasn't dissembling. She meant it.

There's so much about living I don't understand.

"Mrs. Thorndecker," I said. "Julie. I'm not making any value judgment. I'm just saying it's impossible. For me."

"All right," she said equably. "I can live with it. What about Millie Goodfellow?"

"What about her?"

"She's married. Is your fine sense of propriety working there?"

"Not much point to this conversation," I said. "Is there?"

"You're something of a prig, aren't you?" she said.

"Yes," I said. "Something. I'll just have to live with it."

She opened her door, then turned back.

"About Mary," she said. "She *is* disturbed. Please remember what I told you."

"I'll remember," I said.

She gave me a brief smile. Very brief. I watched her drive away. I took a deep breath and blew it out slowly. I felt like a fool. But I've felt like that before, and will again.

I put up the window. I scootched far down on the seat. I tilted my lumpy tweed hat over my closed eyes. I wasn't dreaming of my lost chance with Julie Thorndecker; I was remembering a somewhat similar incident with Joan Powell. It had started similarly; it had ended differently.

We had spent a whole Saturday together, doing everything required of an unmarried couple on the loose in Manhattan: wandering about Bloomingdale's for an hour, lunch at Maxwell's Plum, a long walk over to the Central Park Zoo to say hello to Patty Cake, then a French movie in which the actors spent most of their time climbing sand dunes, dinner at an Italian place in the Village, and back to Powell's apartment.

It should have been a great day. The sun was shining. Garbage had been collected; the city looked neat and clean. I think Joan enjoyed the day. She acted like she did. She said she did. But sometime during the afternoon, it began going sour for me. It wasn't the movie or the restaurants. It wasn't Joan. It was just a mood, a foul mood, without reason. I couldn't account for it; I just knew I had it.

Powell assumed we'd end our busy day in bed. A reasonable assumption based on past experience. When we got back to her place, she went into the bathroom for a quick shower. She came out bareass naked, rubbing her damp hair with a big pink towel.

Joan Powell is something to see naked. She really fits together. Nothing extra, nothing superfluous. She's just there, complete. She's a small woman, but so perfectly proportioned that she could be tarnishing in the garden of the Museum of Modern Art.

I was sitting on the edge of her Scarpa sofa, leaning over, hands clasped between my knees.

"How about mixing us something?" she suggested.

"No," I said. "Thanks. I think I better take off."

She looked at me.

"Sick?" she said.

"No," I said, "just lousy. I don't know what it is. Instant depression. I think I better be alone. I don't want to bore you."

"That's what I want you to do," she said. "Bore me."

"When you get out of those Gucci loafers," I said, "you can be incredibly vulgar."

"Can't I though?" she said cheerfully. "Take off your clothes."

"Oh God," I groaned, "haven't you understood a thing I've said? I just don't *feel* like it."

She tossed the towel aside. She moved naked about the room. Lighted her own cigarette. Mixed her own Cutty and soda.

"You don't feel like it," she repeated. "So what?"

"So what?" I said, outraged. "I've just said I don't feel like fun and games tonight. What are you going to do—rape me? For God's sake, it's got nothing to do with you. I just don't feel like a toss, so I'm taking off."

"Go ahead," she said. "Take off. But don't come back."

This was during a time when the last thing in the world I wanted was to lose her. We were just in the process of working out a sweet, easy, take-it-as-it-comes relationship, and I thought I could be completely honest with her.

"I can't believe you," I said. "One night—*one* night; the first time— I don't want to rub the bacon, and you're ready to call it quits."

She looked at me narrowly.

"It's been more than one time for me, kiddo," she said.

Then she may have seen in my face what that did to my ego, because she came over to sit beside me and slid a cool arm around my neck.

"Look, Todd," she said, "there have been times when I've climbed between the sheets with you when I didn't feel like it. Because you wanted to. Because I love you. And doing something you wanted to do, and I didn't want to, was a sacrifice that proved that love. More important, it turned out to be the best sex we've ever had—for me. Because I was proving my love. And in addition to the physical thing, I was feeling so warm and tender and giving. Try it; you'll like it."

She was right. It was the best sex we ever had—for me. I told you she taught me a lot.

But I didn't think it would work that way with Julie Thorndecker. There was no love between us; I wasn't ready to make a willing sacrifice so she could be happy. And something else kept me away from her. Maybe she was right; I was a prig. Maybe I was just a hopeless romantic. It had to do with Thorndecker. Screwing his wife would be like throwing mud at a statue.

Just to complicate matters further, there was an additional factor involved in my rejection of Julie Thorndecker.

As you've probably gathered by now, I'm a fantasist. I could get twenty years in the pokey for what I dream in one day. For instance, I've had a lot of sexual daydreams about Joan Powell. Some I told her about; some I didn't. I even had some recent fantasies about Millie Goodfellow.

But I found myself totally incapable of fantasizing about Julie Thorndecker. God knows I tried. But the dreams just slid away and dissolved. It wasn't all due to the fact that she was married to a man I admired. It was that she was so beautiful, the body so young and tender, that I couldn't dream about her.

Fantasies, to be pleasurable, must have *some* relation to reality. Even daydreams must be *possible* to be stirring. You can't, for instance, successfully fantasize about hitting the sheets with Cleopatra because a part of your brain keeps telling you that she was smooched by an asp centuries ago, and any fantasy involving her would be a waste of time.

I could fantasize about Joan Powell and Millie Goodfellow because those daydreams were possible. But when I attempted a sexual fancy involving Julie Thorndecker . . . nothing. I told myself it was because of her husband and her superbeauty.

But there was another reason. Powell and Goodfellow were living, breathing, warm, eager women. Julie Thorndecker was not. She was, I thought, a dead lady.

After all that heavy thinking, I decided that if I didn't get a drink immediately I might shuffle off to Buffalo from a hyperactive cerebellum. So I got out of the car, locked up, stomped over to Red Dog Betty's.

Inside, the place looked like it had originally been a private home: a dozen connecting rooms. The doors had been removed, but the hinge butt plates were still there, painted over. The wall between what I guessed were the original living room and parlor had been knocked down to make a long barroom. The other rooms, smaller, were used for dining. It was an attractive arrangement: a lot of intimate nooks; you didn't feel like you were eating in a barn, and the jukebox in the barroom was muffled to an endurable decibel level.

The barroom itself wasn't fake English pub, or fake fishermen's shanty, or fake anything. The decorations didn't look planned; just accumulated. A few Tiffany lamps shed a pleasantly mellow glow. The long, scarred mahogany bar was set with stools upholstered in black vinyl. There were a few battered oak tables with captain's chairs. A wall of booths had table candles stuck in empty whiskey bottles covered with wax drippings.

The light was dim, the air redolent of stale beer. There was no chrome or plastic. A snug place, with no cutesy signs. In fact, the only sign I saw bore the stern admonition: BE GOOD OR BE GONE. There was a big array of liquor bottles behind the bar—much larger than the selection at the Coburn Inn—and I was happy to see they kept their "garbage" on the bar, in plain view.

"Garbage" is what bartenders call their little containers of cherries, olives, onions, lemon peel, lime wedges, and orange slices. Keeping these garnishes atop the bar is a tip-off to a quality joint; you know you're getting fresh fixings in your drinks. When the "garbage" is kept below the bar, out of sight, that olive in your martini was probably the property of a previous martini drinker who either forgot to eat it, ignored it, or tasted it and spit it back into his empty glass. A schlock bar can keep one olive going a week that way.

I hung up my coat and hat on a brass tree, gratified to note the absence of a hatcheck attendant. I swung onto one of the barstools and looked around. Sitting near me were three guys who looked like traveling salesmen. They were working on double martinis and exchanging business cards. Down the other end were two truckers in windbreakers, wearing caps decorated with all kinds of metal badges. They had boilermakers on the bar in front of them, and were already shaking dice in a cup to see who'd pay for the next round.

There were no other customers in the barroom; all the action was in the dining areas. They were crowded, and there was a crew of young, fresh-faced waitresses serving drinks, taking orders, lugging in trays of food from the kitchen in the rear.

There was one black bartender doing nothing but working the service section of the bar, preparing drinks for the diners as the waitresses rushed up with their orders. The other bartender, the one who waited on me, was a heavy woman of 50–55, around there. She was comfortably upholstered, wearing a black silk dress two sizes too tight for her. She had a ring on every finger—and she hadn't found those in Crackerjack boxes. Her face was at once doughy and tough. A lot of good beef and bourbon had gone into that complexion.

She flashed diamond earrings, and a doubled strand of pearls. A brooch of what looked to me like rubies in the shape of a rose bloomed on her awesome bosom. Her black wig went up two feet into the air, and was pierced with long, jeweled pins. As the ad says: if you got it, flaunt it.

Like a lot of heavy people, she was light on her feet, and worked with a skillful economy of movement that was a joy to watch. When I ordered Cutty and soda, she slid a napkin in front of me, poured an honest shot-glass to the brim, uncapped a nip of soda, placed a clean twelve-ounce glass on the napkin, and half-filled it with ice from a little scoop. All this in one continuous, flowing motion. If I owned a bar, I'd like to have her working for me.

"Mix?" she asked, looking at me.

"Please," I said.

She dumped the Scotch into the tall glass without spilling a drop, added an inch of soda, then waited until I took a sip.

"Okay?" she asked. Her voice was a growl, low and burred.

"Just what the doctor ordered," I said.

"What doctor is that?" she said. "I'd like to send him a few of my customers. You passing through?"

"Staying a few days in Coburn," I told her.

"We all got troubles," she said philosophically, then went down the bar to the truckers to pour them another round. A chubby little waitress came up to the bar to whisper something to her. She walked back to the three salesmen. "Your table's ready, boys," she rasped. "The waitress will bring your drinks."

"Thanks, Betty," one of them said.

I waited until they disappeared into one of the dining rooms. The dia-mond-studded barmaid began washing and rinsing glasses near me.

"Your name's Betty?" I asked.

"That's right."

"*The* Betty? You own the place?"

"Me and the bank," she growled. She dried her hand carefully and stuck it over the bar. I shook a fistful of silver, gold, and assorted stones. And not, I bet, a hunk of glass in the lot. "Betty Hanrahan," she said. "You?"

"Samuel Todd."

"A pleasure. I don't want to hustle you, Mr. Todd, take your time, but I just wanted you to know that if you're alone and thinking of eating, we can serve you right here at the bar."

"Thanks," I said. "I might do that. But maybe I'll have another first."

"Sure," she said, and refilled the shotglass with one swift, precise mo-tion. She also gave me a fresh highball glass and fresh ice. I was beginning to like this place.

"What's with the red dog?" I asked her.

"I had a poodle once," she said. "Reddish brown. A mean, miserable bitch. When I took this place over, I thought it would be like a trademark. Something different."

"Looks like it worked out just fine," I said, nodding toward the crowded dining rooms.

"I do all right," she acknowledged. "You should stop in some night, if you're looking for action."

"What kind of action?" I said cautiously.

She polished glasses for a few moments.

"Nothing heavy," she said. "Nothing rough. I run a clean joint. But at night, after the dinner crowd clears out, we get a real friendly drinking bunch. A lot of local girls from the farms and small towns around here. Not hookers; nothing like that. Just out for a good time. Have a few drinks, dance a little. Like that."

"And sometimes a trio on Saturday nights?" I asked.

She stopped polishing glasses long enough to look up at me.

"Who told you that?" she asked curiously.

"A loyal customer of yours," I said. "Millie Goodfellow. Know her?"

"Oh hell yes, I know her. Millie's a lot of woman. Life of the party."

"I figured," I said. "Can I buy you a drink?"

"Not till the sun goes down," she said.

"It's been down for the past five days," I said.

She considered that thoughtfully.

"You got something there," she said. "I'll have a short beer, and thank you."

"My pleasure."

She drew herself a small brew from the Michelob tap. She planted herself in front of me and lifted her glass.

"Health," she said, drained off the glass, and went back to her washing, drying, and polishing chores.

"How well do you know Millie?" she asked casually.

"Not very well. Just to talk to. I'm staying at the Coburn Inn."

She nodded.

"I know she's married to a cop," I added. "Ronnie Goodfellow."

Betty Hanrahan looked relieved.

"Good," she said. "As long as you know it."

"I'm not likely to forget it."

"Millie does," she said. "Frequently."

"It doesn't seem to bother him," I said.

"Uh-huh," she said. "Now I'll tell you a story. The same story I told Millie Goodfellow. Thirty years ago I was married—for the first and last time. His name was Patrick Hanrahan. My unmarried name is Dubcek, Betty Dubcek from Hamtramck, Michigan. Anyway, Pat turned out to be a lush, and I turned out to be Miss Roundheels of Detroit. I was a wild one in those days; I admit it. Pat knew about it, and didn't seem to mind. It went on like that for almost two years, with him trying to drink the breweries dry, and me making it with anyone who had a Tootsie Roll between his legs. I thought Pat just didn't care. Then one night he came home stone-cold sober and gave me this . . . ''

She lifted a corner of that heavy wig. I saw a deep, angry scar that seemed to run across the top of her skull down to her left ear.

"He damned near killed me," she said. "After two years of taking it, and telling himself it didn't matter, and he couldn't care less, he blew up and damned near killed me. I should have known it would get to him eventually; he was a prideful man. They're like that. It may bubble along inside them for a long while, but sooner or later . . . ''

"What happened to him?" I asked.

"Pat? He just took off. I didn't try to find him. Didn't even make a complaint to the cops; I had it coming. After ten years I got a legal divorce. But the reason I'm telling you this is because that Ronnie Goodfellow is the same kind of prideful man as Pat was. Millie thinks he doesn't care. Maybe he doesn't—now. Some day he will, mark my words, and then biff, bam, and pow.''

"Thanks for the warning," I said. "Maybe I'll have some lunch now. What's good?''

"Try the broiled liver and bacon," she said. "Home fries on the side.''

It was served to me right there on the bar, with slices of pumpernickel and sweet butter, and a small bowl of salad. It wasn't a great meal, but for a roadhouse like that, in the middle of nowhere, it was a pleasant surprise. I had a Ballantine ale, and that helped. And Betty Hanrahan mixed me some fresh Colman's mustard to smear on the liver. It was hot enough to bring the sweat popping out on my scalp. That's the way to eat broiled liver, all right.

I was on my second black coffee, wondering if I wanted a brandy or something else. Betty Hanrahan was down at the end of the bar near the door, checking her bottled beer supply. A guy came in wearing a fleece-collared trucker's jacket. He was still wearing his gloves, and didn't bother removing his badge-encrusted cap. He spoke to Betty for a few minutes, and I could see him gesturing toward the outside, toward the parking lot. Then the owner turned and stared at me. She came slowly down the bar.

"Mr. Todd," she said, "you don't, by any chance, drive a Grand Prix, do you?''

"Sure, I do," I said. "A dusty black job. Why?''

"You got trouble," she said. "Someone slashed your tires. All four tires.''

"Son of a bitch!" I said bitterly.

Betty Hanrahan said she'd call the cops. I walked out to the parking lot with the trucker, and he told me what had happened. He had pulled his semitrailer onto the lot, and parked three spaces from my Pontiac. He and his mate got down from the cab, locked up, started for the roadhouse. They had to walk by the Grand Prix, and the mate was the first to see the tires had been slashed.

When we reached my car, the mate was hunkering down, examining one of the tires. He looked up at me.

"Your car?"

I nodded.

"Someone did a job on you," he said in a gravelly voice. "Looks to me like a hatchet, but it could have been a heavy hunting knife—something like that. One deep cut in every tire, except the left rear. That has two cuts, like the guy who did it started there, didn't cut deep enough on the first slash and had to swing again."

"How long do you figure it took?" I asked him.

The two truckers looked at each other.

"A couple of minutes, Bernie?" the mate asked.

"No more than that," the other said. "Just walked around the car hacking. The balls of the guy! In broad daylight yet. You got any enemies, mister?"

"Not that I know of."

"Haven't been sleeping in any strange beds, have you?" Bernie asked, and they both laughed.

I moved slowly around the Grand Prix. The car wasn't exactly on its rims, but it had settled wearily and was listing.

We heard the growl of a siren, and looked up. The Coburn constabulary cruiser, the same car I had seen thrice before, was pulling into the parking lot. One of the truckers waved his arms; the cruiser turned away from the roadhouse, came cutting across the lot toward us, pulled to a stop about ten feet away. The constable cut his flashing light and got out, tugging on his cap. He strutted toward us.

"What have we got here?" he demanded.

"Someone did a hatchet job on this man's tires," Bernie said. "All four of them."

The constable circled the Grand Prix. He was a short, hard bantam with a slit mouth and eyes like licked stones. He came back to join us and stood staring at the car, hands on his hips.

"Jesus," he said disgustedly, "ain't that a kick in the ass."

"I figure a hatchet," the mate said. "Hell, maybe it was an ax."

The constable stooped, fingered one of the cuts.

"Could be," he said. "Or a heavy knife. But I'd say you're right: a hatchet. No sign of sawing with a knife. Just one deep slash. Who discovered it?"

"We did," the mate said. "Pulled in, locked up, and started for the roadhouse. Then I seen it, and Bernie went on ahead to tell Betty, and I stayed here."

"How long ago was this?"

"Not more'n ten minutes. Right, Bernie?"

"About that. Fifteen tops."

The constable turned to me.

"Your car?"

"Yes, it's mine."

"How long you been parked here?"

I looked at my watch.

"Two hours," I said. "Give or take ten minutes."

"You were inside all that time? In the restaurant?"

He stared at me, waiting. The son of a bitch, he *had* seen Julie Thorndecker and me.

"Not all the time," I said. "I smoked a cigarette out here first, then went in. I'd say I was in the bar about an hour and fifteen minutes. Something like that."

He kept staring at me, eyes squinted. But he didn't ask why it took me forty-five minutes to smoke a cigarette or why I hadn't gone into the roadhouse right after I parked.

"See anyone hanging around?" he asked me. "Anyone acting suspicious?"

"No," I said. "No one."

"I came through here a little after noon," he said, "just on routine patrol, you understand, and I didn't see anyone either." He paused thoughtfully. "Come to think of it, I don't recollect seeing your car."

"I was here," I said.

"Well," he said, "what the hell. A lot of cars here; I can't be expected to remember everyone I seen." He sighed deeply. "Crazy kids, I expect. Just doing something wild. We've had a lot of vandalism lately." He paused again, looking at me without expression. "Unless you got some idea of who'd do a thing like this to you?"

"No," I said. "No idea at all."

"Well, I'm sorry this had to happen, Mr. Todd," he said briskly. "It's a damned shame. I'll have to make out a report. Could I see your license and registration, please?"

"We'll be in the bar if you need us," Bernie said.

The constable waved a hand.

"Sure, boys, you go along. I'll drop by in a few minutes to get your names and addresses."

He used the hood of the Pontiac as a desk to copy information into a small notebook he took from a leather pouch strapped to his gunbelt.

"Some of these rotten kids," he said as he wrote, "you wouldn't believe the things they do. Smash windshields, rip off radio antennas, sometimes run a nail down a car they're walking by. Just to ruin the finish, you understand. No rhyme or reason to it. Damned troublemakers."

He replaced the notebook in his gunbelt, handed the license and registration back to me. We started walking toward the roadhouse.

"New York City—huh?" he said. "I guess you're used to shit like this. I hear the place is a jungle."

"Oh, I don't know," I said. "There are places just as bad. Maybe worse."

"Yeah," he said in a flat, toneless voice, "ain't it the truth? Well, you'll be needing a wrecker, I expect. Know any garages around here?"

"How about Mike's Service Station?" I asked. "Could they handle the job?"

"Oh hell, yes. They got a tow car. A job like this, I figure you won't get it today. Maybe tomorrow, if they put a rush on it. My name's Constable Fred Aikens. Mike knows me. Mention my name, and maybe he'll shave the price a little. But I doubt it," he added with a dry laugh.

We paused just inside the entrance of the roadhouse.

"We'll do what we can, Mr. Todd," Constable Aikens said, "but don't get your hopes up. A malicious mischief job like this, probably we'll never catch who done it unless they pull it again, and we get something to go on."

"I understand," I said.

"Besides," he said, "you got insurance—right?"

"I have insurance," I said, "but I'm not sure it covers malicious mischief. I'll have to call my agent."

"Well, I'm sorry it happened, Mr. Todd," he said again. "But at least no one got hurt—right? I mean, no bodily harm done. That's something to be thankful for, ain't it?" He smiled coldly. "Well, I got to find those truckers and get their names and addresses. You'll be hearing from us if we come up with anything."

He waved a hand, started toward the back of the bar where Bernie and his mate had joined the two truckers who had been there since I had first entered. All four of them were drinking boilermakers.

The black bartender was alone, and motioned me over.

"Miss Betty is upstairs in the office," he told me. "She'd like to see you up there, if you got a minute. Take that door over there, and it's at the head of the stairs."

"Thanks," I said. "I'll go up."

"She says maybe you better bring your hat and coat with you."

"Yeah," I said sourly, "maybe I better."

The door of the office was open. Betty Hanrahan was on the phone. She motioned me to come in, and pointed to a wooden armchair alongside her cluttered desk. I sat down, took out my cigarettes, offered the pack to Betty. She took one, and I lighted it for her as she was saying, "Yes, Dave . . . Yes . . . I understand, but I've never made a single claim before . . . "

I lighted my own cigarette and looked around. It was about as big as a walk-in closet, with just enough room for a desk, two chairs, a scarred metal file cabinet, and a small, old-fashioned safe shoved into one corner: a waist-high job on big casters with a single dial and brass handles.

Betty Hanrahan leaned back in her oak swivel chair and parked her feet

up on the desk. Good legs. Her rhinestone-trimmed shoes had heels at
least four inches high, and I wondered how she could wait bar on those
spikes. I also realized that in her stockinged feet, she'd be a small one. In
length, not in width.

"Okay, David love," she was saying, "do what you can . . . Fine . . .
Let me know as soon as you hear."

She leaned forward to hang up the phone. As she did, she looked at
her skirt and tugged it down a bit over her knees.

"Nothing showing, is there?" she said.

"I didn't see a thing," I assured her.

"Well, what the hell, I'm wearing pants."

She opened a side drawer and pulled out a half-full bottle of Wild
Turkey. She also set out a stack of paper cups.

"Build us a couple," she said.

I rose and began pouring the bourbon into two cups.

"I'll get you some water," she said, "if you want it."

"This'll do fine."

"I need a shot," she said. "I don't like rough stuff on my property. It
scares me, and gives the joint a bad name. That was my insurance agent
I was talking to. He thinks I'm covered against malicious mischief. But
even if I'm not, I want you to know I'm picking up the tab."

"I appreciate that, Betty," I said. "But I may be covered myself. I'll
wait till I get back to New York, and check it out."

"New York," she said, shaking her head. "That's funny. I had you
pegged for Chicago. You don't talk like a New Yorker."

"Transplanted," I said. "Ohio originally. Could I use your phone? I
want to call Mike's Service Station and see what they can do about my
car."

"Let me call Mike," she said. "I know how to handle that old crook."

She took her feet off the desk, rummaged through a drawer, came up
with a dog-eared business card. She had to put on a pair of glasses to
read the number. The frames of the spectacles were sparkling with little
rhinestones and seed pearls.

I listened to her explain to Mike what had happened. She told him
she wanted the car picked up immediately, and new tires installed by
5:00 P.M. I heard an angry crackle on the phone. She screamed back,
and finally agreed on the job being finished before noon on Saturday.
Then they started talking cost, and another argument erupted. I didn't
catch what the final figure was, but I do know she beat him down, and
concluded by yelling, "And you make sure I get the bill, you goddamned pirate."

She slammed down the phone and grinned at me. She took off her
glasses and put her feet back on the desk again. This time she didn't bother
tugging down her skirt. She was right; she was wearing pants.

"They'll pick it up right away," she told me. "He claims he just can't get to it today. But they'll have it ready for you by noon tomorrow. They'll deliver it to the Coburn Inn. Okay?''

"Thanks, Betty," I said gratefully. "But you don't have to pay the bill. It wasn't your fault.''

"It happened on my property, didn't it?'' she said. "I'm responsible for the safety of my customers' cars.''

"I'm not sure you are,'' I said. "Under the law.''

"Fuck the law,'' she said roughly. "I feel responsible, and that makes it so. Got any idea who did it?''

I had a lot of ideas.

"I have no idea,'' I said.

"Haven't been leaving your shoes under a strange bed, have you?''

"That's what one of the truckers suggested. But it just isn't so. As far as I know, I have no enemies in these parts. Maybe it was an accident. I mean that my car was hit. Maybe some joy-riding kids just picked on me because my heap was parked by itself, way down at the end of the lot.''

"Maybe,'' she said doubtfully.

"That's what Constable Fred Aikens thinks. Claims you've had a lot of vandalism by wild kids lately.''

"Constable Fred Aikens,'' she said with great disgust. "He couldn't find his ass with a boxing glove.''

"Betty,'' I said, "tell me something . . . When you called the cops, when I went out to look at my car, did you tell them my name? Did you say the car was owned by Samuel Todd?''

She thought a moment, frowning.

"No,'' she said definitely. "I just told them a customer had gotten his tires slashed. I didn't mention your name.''

"When Aikens showed up and was inspecting the car—this was before he checked my license and registration—he called me Mr. Todd. I just wondered how he knew who I was.''

"Maybe he saw you around Coburn and asked who you were. Or maybe someone pointed you out to him.''

"That's probably what it was,'' I said casually. "Someone pointed me out to him.''

"Ready for another?'' she asked, nodding toward the bottle.

"Sure.''

"Use fresh cups. They begin to leak if you use them too long.''

I poured us two more drinks in fresh cups. She drank hers with no gasps, coughs, or changes of expression. I hardly saw her throat move; she just tilted it down. No way was I going to try keeping up with this lady.

"You're in Coburn on business, Mr. Todd? If you don't mind my asking?''

"I don't mind,'' I said, and I told her, briefly, about the Bingham

Foundation, the Thorndecker application, and how I had come to Critten-den to make a field investigation.

"I know that Crittenden bunch," she said. "The Thorndeckers have been over two or three times for dinner. That wife is a doll, isn't she?"

"Yes," I said. " A doll."

"And we get staff from the nursing home, and a lot of the young kids from the lab. Usually on Saturday and Sunday nights. A noisy bunch, but they mean no harm. Drink up a storm. Mostly beer or wine."

"Mary Thorndecker ever show up?"

"Never heard of her. Who is she?"

"Thorndecker's daughter. Stepdaughter actually. Twenty-seven. Spin-sterish looking."

"I don't think I've ever seen her."

"How about Draper? Dr. Kenneth Draper?"

"Him I know. A loner. He comes in two or three nights a week. Late. Sits by himself. Drinks until he's got a load on. A couple of times he got a crying jag."

"Oh?" I said. "That's interesting. How about Stella Beecham? She's chief nurse at Crittenden Hall."

"Yeah," Betty Hanrahan said scornfully, "I know that one. I had to kick her ass out of here. She was hustling one of my young waitresses. Listen, I'm strictly live and let live. I don't care who screws who. Or how. But not on my premises. I got a license to think about. Also, this waitress's folks are friends of mine, and I promised to keep an eye on the kid. So I had to give that nurse the heave-ho. That's one tough bimbo."

"Yes," I agreed, "she is. Betty, I don't want you telling any tales out of school, but did Julie Thorndecker, the doll, ever come in with any man but her husband?"

"No," she said promptly. "At least not while I was working, and I usually am. You want me to ask around?"

"No, thanks. You've done plenty for me already, and I appreciate it. Could I call a cab—if there is such a thing around here? I've got to get back to the Inn."

"I'll do better than that," she said. "You need wheels until Mike fixes up your car. I can take care of that. Not a car exactly. I drive a Mark Five; you can't have that, but we got a wreck, an old Ford pickup. We use it for shopping and put a plow on it to clear snow off the parking lot. It's not much to look at, but it goes. You're welcome to use it until you get your own car back."

I didn't want to do it, but she wouldn't take No for an answer. I kissed her thankfully. Much woman.

So there I was, twenty minutes later, rattling back to Coburn in the unheated cab of an ancient pickup truck that seemed to be held together with Dentyne and Dill's pipe cleaners. But it rolled, and I was so busy figuring out its temperamental gearbox, trying to coax it to do over thirty-five, and mastering its tendency to turn to the right, that I was back at the Coburn Inn before I remembered that I had forgotten to pay my lunch tab at Red Dog Betty's. When I returned to New York, I resolved, I would send Betty Hanrahan a handsome gift.

Something encrusted with rhinestones, seed pearls, and sequins. She'd like that.

Up in my room, I glared balefully at those two drinks lying quietly in the bottom of the quart vodka bottle, not doing anyone any harm. Not doing anyone any good either. I got my fresh bathroom glass and emptied the bottle. I flopped down and took a sip. So far that day I had swilled beer, Scotch, ale, bourbon and vodka. How had I managed to miss ouzo, sangria, and hard cider?

I drank morosely. I was not feeling gruntled. The slashing of my tires seemed such a childish thing to do. I knew it was intended as a warning— but how juvenile can you get?

I figured it had to be Constable Fred Aikens, acting on orders from Ronnie Goodfellow. I could even imagine how it went:

Aikens makes a routine patrol of the parking lot at Red Dog Betty's. Or maybe he's been tailing me since he saw me nosing around Crittenden Hall. Anyway, he spots me parked outside the roadhouse, thigh-to-thigh with Julie Thorndecker. If Aikens didn't actually see her face, he sure as hell recognized her blue MGB nuzzling my Grand Prix. So he hightails it to the nearest public phone. It must have gone something like this:

"Ronnie? Fred. Did I wake you up?"

"That's okay. What's going on?"

"I just spotted your girlfriend's car. Parked in the lot at Red Dog Betty's."

"So?"

"Right next to a black Grand Prix. She's sitting in the front seat of the Pontiac with this tall dude. Thought you might want to know."

Silence.

"Ronnie? You there?"

"I'm here. That son of a bitch!"

"You know him?"

"A snoop from the City. A guy named Todd. He's here to investigate Thorndecker about that grant."

"Oh. It's okay then? Them being together?"

Silence.

"I just thought you might want to know, Ronnie."

"Yeah. Thanks. Listen, Fred. Could you fix that smartass bastard?"

"Fix him?"

"Just his car. Don't touch him. But if you get the chance, you could do a job on the car."

"What for, Ronnie?"

"Just to give him something to think about."

"Oh, yeah, I get it. You know that hatchet you took away from Abe Tompkins when he was going to brain his missus?"

"I remember."

"The hatchet's still in the trunk. If I get the chance, maybe I can chop down that Grand Prix."

"Thanks, Fred. I won't forget it."

"You'd do the same for me—right?"

"Right."

I figured it went something like that. But solving the Mystery of the Slashed Tires gave me no satisfaction. Small mystery; small solution. It had nothing to do with the Thorndecker investigation.

I thought.

I sat there, trying to make the vodka last, glowering at nothing. In any inquiry there is an initial period during which the investigator asks, listens, observes, collects, accumulates, and generally lets things happen to him, with no control.

Then, when certain networks are established, relationships glimpsed, the investigator must start flexing his biceps and make things happen. This is the Opening Phase, when all those sealed cans get their lids peeled off, you lean close to peer in—and usually turn away when the stench flops your stomach.

It was time, I decided, to get started. One thing at a time. I chose the first puzzle of the Thorndecker inquiry. It turned out to be ridiculously easy.

But the simple ones sometimes take the most time to unravel. I remember working a pilferage case in a two-story Saigon warehouse. This place stored drugs for front-line medical units and base hospitals. An inventory turned up horrendous shortages.

The warehouse had three entrances. I had two of them sealed up; all military and civilian personnel had to enter and exit from one door. I doubled the guards, and everyone leaving the place had to undergo a complete body search. The thefts continued. I checked for secret interior caches, for tunnels. I even had a metal detector set up, the kind airports use, in case someone was swallowing the drugs in small metal containers, or getting them out in capsules up the rectum.

Nothing worked. We were still losing drugs in hefty amounts, and I was going nuts trying to figure how they were getting the stuff out of the place.

Know how I solved it? One day I was sitting at my desk in the security office. I took the last cigarette out of a pack. I crumpled the empty pack in my fist and tossed it negligently out an open window. I then leapt to my feet and shouted something a little stronger than "Eureka!"

That's how they were doing it, all right. A bad guy was dropping the stuff out a second-story window, right into the arms of a pal standing in an alley below. Simple? Sure it was. All the good scams are. Took me three weeks to break it.

But finding the author of the note, "Thorndecker kills," wasn't going to take me that long. I hoped.

I grabbed up my hat and trenchcoat, and went back down to the lobby, using the stairs. Twice as fast, I had learned, as waiting for Sam Livingston's rheumatic elevator.

I glanced toward the cigar counter, but Millie Goodfellow had a customer, one of the antediluvian permanent residents. He was leaning over the counter, practically falling, trying to read the sign on the front of her tight T-shirt.

"What?" I heard his querulous voice. "What does it say? I left my reading glasses upstairs."

I went to the desk, and the baldy on duty looked up, irritated at being interrupted in his contemplation of the *Playboy* centerfold.

"Yes?" he said testily.

"I need a new typewriter ribbon," I said. "You got any place in town that sells office supplies?"

"Of course we do," he said in an aggrieved tone, angry because he thought I doubted Coburn could provide such an amenity.

He told me how to find Coburn Office Supplies, a store located one block north of the post office.

"I'm sure they'll have everything you need," he said stiffly.

I thanked him, and started away. Then my eyes were caught by the right shoulder of his blue serge suit. He saw me staring, and twisted his head and looked down, trying to see what I was looking at. I reached out and brushed his shoulder twice with the edge of my hand.

"There," I said. "That looks much better."

"Thank you, Mr. Todd," he said, humble and abashed.

There was nothing on his shoulder, of course. God, I can be a nasty son of a bitch.

I found Coburn Office Supplies, a hole-in-the-wall with a dusty window and a sad display of pencils, erasers, faded stationery, and office gadgets already beginning to rust. The opening door hit a suspended bell that jangled in the quiet of the deserted store. I looked around. The place was a natural for a Going-Out-of-Business Sale.

And the little guy who came dragging out of the back room was perfectly suited to be custodian of this mausoleum. All I remember about him was that he wore shredded carpet slippers and had six long strands of hair (I counted them) brushed sideways across his pale, freckled skull.

"Yes, sir," he sighed. "Can I help?"

That last word came out "hep." In fact, he said, "Kin ah hep?" Southern, I thought, but I couldn't place it exactly. Hardscrabble land somewhere.

I had intended to waltz him around, but he was so beaten, so defeated,

I had no desire to make a fool of him. Life had anticipated me. So I just said:

"I want to bribe you."

The pale, watery eyes blinked.

"Bribe me?"

I took out my wallet, extracted a ten-dollar bill. I dangled it, flipping it with my fingers.

"This is the only office supply store in town?"

"Wull . . . sure," he said, eyeing that sawbuck like it was a passport to Heaven, or at least out of Coburn.

"Good," I said. "The ten is yours for a simple answer to a simple question."

"I don' know . . . " he said, anxious and cautious at the same time.

"You can always deny you talked to me," I told him. "No one here but us chickens. Your word against mine."

"Yeah," he said slowly, brightening, "thass right, ain't it? Whut's the question?"

"Anyone in town buy ribbons for an Olympia Standard typewriter?"

"Olympia Standard?" he said, licking his dry lips. "Only one machine like that in town as I know of."

"Who?"

"Mary Thorndecker. She comes in ever' so often to buy—"

I handed him the ten.

"Thanks," I said.

"Mebbe ever' two months or so," he droned on, staring down at the bill in his hand. "She always asks—"

The bell over the door jangled as I went out.

I strutted back to the Coburn Inn, so pleased with myself it was sickening. As a reward for my triumph, I stopped off at Sandy's and bought another quart of Popov, a fine Russian-sounding vodka distilled in Hartford, Conn. But by the time I entered Room 3-F, my euphoria had evaporated; I didn't even open the bottle.

I lowered myself gingerly into one of those grasping armchairs and sat sprawled, staring at nothing. All the big problems were still there. Mary Thorndecker may have written the note, and Ronnie Goodfellow may have tried to recover it. An interesting combo. Tinker to Evers to Chance. But who was Chance?

How's this?

Mary Thorndecker types out a note, "Thorndecker kills," and leaves it for me. What's her motive? Well, maybe she's driven by something as innocent as outrage at the vivisection being practiced at the Crittenden Research Laboratory. If she's a deeply religious woman, a fundamentalist, as everyone claims, she could be goaded to write, "Thorndecker kills." Anyway, she writes the note, for whatever reason.

Now, who might Mary tell what she had done? She could tell Dr.

Kenneth Draper. But I doubted that; he was deeply involved in the activities of the research lab. She might tell her half-brother, Edward Thorndecker. That made more sense to me. She wants to protect Edward from what she conceives to be an evil existing in Crittenden.

Let's say she does tell Edward, and hints to him that she intends to end what she sees as wickedness pervading the tiled corridors of Crittenden. But Edward, smitten by Julie's beauty and sexuality—I had observed this; it was more than a crush—tells his stepmother what Mary is up to. Especially the note left in my box at the Coburn Inn.

Julie, wanting to protect her husband, the "great man," before the letter can be used as evidence to deny Thorndecker's application for a grant, asks Constable Ronnie Goodfellow to recover the damned, and damning thing. For all Julie knows, it could be a long bill of particulars signed by Thorndecker's stepdaughter.

And because he is so pussy-whipped, Goodfellow gives it the old college try (using his wife's passkey), and strikes out. Only because I had already mailed the note to Donner & Stern for typewriter analysis.

All right, I admit it: the whole thing was smoke. A scenario based on what I knew of the people involved and how they might react if their self-interest was threatened. But it all made sense to me. As a matter of fact, it turned out to be about 80 percent accurate.

But it was that incorrect 20 percent that almost got me killed.

I had something to eat that evening. I think it was a tunafish salad and a glass of milk; the size of my gut was beginning to embarrass me. Anyway, I dined lightly and had only two vodka gimlets for dessert at the Coburn Inn bar before I climbed into Betty Hanrahan's pickup truck, drove happily out of Coburn, and rattled south on the river road. I was heading for Mary Thorndecker's church. It wasn't that I was looking for salvation, although I could have used a small dollop. I just wanted to touch all bases. I wanted to find out why a young, intelligent woman seemed intent on destroying a man she reportedly loved.

I've attended revival meetings in various parts of the country, including a snake-handling session in a tent pitched on the outskirts of Macon, Georgia. I've heard members of fundamentalist churches speak in tongues, and I've seen apparent cripples throw away their crutches or rise from wheelchairs to dance a jig. I'm familiar with the oratorical style of backwoods evangelists and the fervor of their congregations. This kind of down-home religion is not my cup of vodka, but I can't see where they're hurting anyone—except possibly themselves, and you won't find anything in the Constitution denying a citizen the right to make a fool of himself.

So I thought I knew what to expect: a mob of farmers, rednecks, and assorted blue-collar types shouting up a storm, clapping their hands, and stomping their feet as they confessed their piddling sins and came forward to be saved. All this orchestrated by a leather-lunged preacher man who knew all the buzzwords and phrases to lash his audience to a religious frenzy.

I was in for a surprise.

The First Fundamentalist Church of Lord Jesus was housed not in a tent or ramshackle barn, but in a neat, white clapboard building with well-kept grounds, a lighted parking area, and a general appearance of modest prosperity. The windows were washed, there were bright boxes of ivy, and the cross atop the small steeple was gilded and illuminated with a spotlight.

I had expected a junkyard collection of battered sedans, pickup trucks, rusted vans, and maybe a few motorcycles. But the cars I saw gave added evidence of the economic well-being of the congregation: plenty of Fords, Chevys, VW's, and Toyotas, but also a goodly sprinkling of imported sports cars, Cadillacs, Mercedes-Benzes, and one magnificent maroon Bentley. I parked Betty Hanrahan's heap amongst all that polished splendor, feeling like a poor relation.

They were singing ''Jesus, Lover of My Soul'' when I entered. I slid into an empty rear pew, opened a hymnal, and looked around. A simple interior painted an off-white, polished walnut pews, a handsome altar covered with a richly brocaded cloth, an enormous painting of the crucifixion on the wall behind the altar. It was no better and no worse than the usual church painting. Lots of blood. The seated congregation was singing along with music from an electronic organ up front against the left wall. There was a door set into the opposite wall. I assumed it led to the vestry.

There wasn't any one thing about the place that I could label as definitely fake or phony. But I began to get the damndest feeling that I had wandered into a movie or TV set, put together for a big climactic scene like a wedding or funeral, or maybe the church into which the bullet-riddled hero staggers to cough his last on the altar, reaching for the cross.

Trying to analyze this odd impression, I decided that maybe the *newness* of the place had something to do with it. Churches usually look used, worn, comfortably shabby. This one looked like it had been put up that morning; there wasn't a nick, stain, or scratch that I could see. It even smelled of paint and fresh plaster.

Maybe the congregation had something to do with my itchy feeling that the whole thing was a scam. There were a few blacks, but most of them were whites in their twenties and thirties. The men favored beards, the women either pigtails or hair combed loosely to their waist. Both sexes sported chain necklaces and medallions. Most of them, men and women, wore jeans. But they were French jeans, tailored jeans, or jeans with silver studs, appliques, or designs traced with bugle beads and seed pearls.

All I could do was guess, but I guessed there was a good assortment of academics, writers, artists, musicians, poets, and owners of antique shops. They looked to be the kind of people who had worked their way through Freudian analysis, high colonics, est, Yoga, TM, primal scream, communal tub bathing, and cocaine. Not because they particularly needed any of these things, but because they had been the *in* things to do. I'd make book that the First Fundamentalist Church of Lord Jesus was only the latest brief enthusiasm in their fad-filled lives, and as soon as they all got "born again," the whole crowd would decamp for the nearest disco, with shouts of loud laughter and a great blaring of horns.

The hymn came to an end. The congregation put their hymnals in the racks on the pew backs in front of them. A young man in the front pew stood up and faced us. "Faced" is an exaggeration; he had so much hair, beard, and mustache, all I could see were two blinking eyes.

"Welcome to the First Fundamentalist Church of Lord Jesus. My name is Irving Peacock, and I am first vestryperson of your church. Most of you I know, and most of you know each other. But I do see a few brothers and sisters who, I believe, are here for the first time. To these newcomers, may I say, 'Welcome! Welcome to our family!' It is our custom, at the beginning of the service, for each sister and brother to turn to the right and left and kiss their neighbors as a symbol of our devotion to the love and passion of Lord Jesus. Now, please, all kiss. On the lips now! On the lips!"

The congregation stood. I rose along with them, wondering what kind of a nuthouse I had strayed into. I watched, fascinated, as men and women turned right and left, embracing and kissing their neighbors. A great smacking of lips filled the room.

I was alone in the rear pew and figured I was safe. But no, a grizzly bear of a man in the pew in front of me kissed right and left, then turned suddenly and held out his arms to me.

"Brother!" he said.

What could I do—say, "Please, not on the first date?" So I kissed him, or let him kiss me. He had a walrus mustache. It tickled. Also, he had just eaten an Italian dinner. A cheap Italian dinner.

After this orgy of osculation, the congregation sat down, and Irving Peacock announced the offertory. Contributions would be accepted by vestrypersons John Millhouse and Mary Thorndecker, and we were urged to give generously to "support the splendid work of Father Michael Bellamy and to signify our faith in and love for our Lord Jesus."

The two vestrypersons started down the center aisle. Brass trays, velvet-lined to eliminate the vulgar sound of shekels clinking, were passed along each pew, hand-to-hand, then returned to the aisle. I saw that Mary Thorndecker was collecting on the other side. I slipped across the aisle, into the empty rear pew on her side. I watched her approach, features still and expressionless.

She was wearing an earth-colored tweed suit over a death-gray sweater. Opaque hose and flat-heeled brogues. Her hair was drawn back tightly, pinned back with a barrette. No jewelry. No makeup. I wondered if she was making herself as unattractive as possible in reaction to Julie's obvious charms.

She moved slowly down the aisle toward me, not looking up. Even when she took the brass tray from the pew in front of me, she still hadn't seen me. I had time to note the plate contained a nifty pile of coins and folding money. Father Michael Bellamy was doing all right.

Then she was at my pew. Her eyes rose as she proffered the tray.

"Why . . . Mr. Todd!" she said, not quite gasping, her face flushing.

I looked at her. I may have smiled pleasantly.

"Thorndecker kills?" I said.

Down went the brass tray. Coins clanged, bounced, rolled. Bills fluttered to the floor. For a moment I thought she was going to cave. Her face went putty-white, then greenish. A pale hand fluttered up to her hair, and just hung there, waving futilely.

Then she was gone, dashing out the double-door. I thought I heard a sound: a sob, a moan. I let her go. I helped others gather up the spilled coins, the scattered bills. I added a fin of my own. Atonement.

The collection plates were returned to the first vestryperson; everyone settled down. A few moments passed while the congregation gradually quieted. Nothing happened. But I felt the expectation, saw heads turning toward the vestry door. Still nothing. A very professionally calculated stage wait. Tension grew.

Then the effete lad at the Hammond organ played something that sounded suspiciously like a fanfare. The vestry door was flung open. Father Michael Bellamy, clad in flowing white robes, swept into the nave, arms outstretched to embrace his followers.

"Blessings on my children!" he intoned.

"Blessings on our father!" they shouted back.

He stood before the altar, arms wide, head thrown back, eyes turned heavenward.

"Let us pray together a moment in silence," he declaimed. "Let our souls' voices merge and rise to Lord Jesus, asking love, understanding, and redemption for our sins."

All heads bowed. Except mine. I was too busy studying Father Michael Bellamy.

A big man, maybe six-four. Broad shoulders and chest. I couldn't see much more because of those robes, but got an impression of a comfortable corporation. A marvelous head of wavy, snow-white hair. If it wasn't a carpet, it had enjoyed the attentions of an artful coiffeur. No one's hair could be that white or that billowy without aid.

The hair was long enough and full enough to cover what I guessed were big, meaty ears. I reckoned that from the rest of his face, also big and meaty. A nose like a sausage, a brow like a rare roast, chin and jowls like beef liver. The man was positively appetizing. Stuck in all this rosy suet were glistening eyes, round and hard as black marbles.

The voice was something; it made the electronic organ sound like a twopenny whistle. Orotund, booming, it not only filled the church but rattled the windows and, for all I knew, browned the ivy in the outside window boxes. That voice conquered me; it was an instrument, and if a good soprano can shatter a wine glass, this guy should have been able to bring down the Brooklyn Bridge.

"Children," he said, and his praying family looked up, "tonight we shall speak of sin and forgiveness. We shall speak of the unutterable lusts that corrupt the human heart and soul; and how we may all be washed clean in the blood of our Redemptor, Lord Jesus Christ of Nazareth."

Then he was off. I had heard the sermon before, but never so well delivered. The man was a natural, or practiced preacher. His magnificent voice roared, whispered, entreated, scorned, laughed, hissed, wailed. There was nothing he could not do with that voice. And the gesturings and posturings! Waves, flappings, pointings, clenched fists, pleading palms, stoopings, leaps, stridings from one side of the platform to the other. And tears. Oh yes. The eyes moist and brimming on demand.

Did they listen to his words? I wasn't sure. I found it difficult to listen, so overwhelming was his physical performance. He was a whirlwind, white robes streaming in the tempest, and what he said seemed of less importance than the presence of the man himself. Behind him, on the wall, Christ bled and died on the cross. And Father Michael Bellamy, the white-haired prophet incarnate, stamped the boards before this image and mesmerized his trendy flock with a performance worth four Oscars, three Emmys, two Grammys, one Ike, and a platinum record. The man was a master.

As I said, the sermon was familiar. He told us that the human heart was a fetid swamp, filled with nasty crawling things. We were all sinners, in thought or in deed. We betrayed the best impulses of our souls, and turned instead to lechery, lust, and lasciviousness. (The Father was big on alliteration.)

He gave a fifteen-minute catalogue of human sins of the flesh, listened to attentively by the congregation who, I figured, wanted to find out if they had missed any. This portion of the sermon was all stern denunciation, a jeremiad against the permissiveness of our society which condoned conduct that in happier times would have earned burning at the stake, or at least a holiday weekend in the stocks.

And where was such lewdness and licentiousness leading us? To eternal damnation, that's where. To a hell which, according to Father Bellamy's description, was something like a Finnish sauna without the snowbanks.

But all was not lost. There was a way to redeem our wasted lives. That was to pledge our remaining days to the service of Lord Jesus, following in His footsteps. It was being born again, finding the love and forgiveness of the Father of Us All, and dedicating our lives to walking the path of righteousness.

Up to this point, the sermon had followed the standard revivalist pattern: scare 'em, then save 'em. But then Bellamy got into an area that made me a little queasy.

He said there was only one way to prove sincere relinquishment of a wicked life. That was by full public confession, acknowledgment of past sins, and wholehearted and soul-felt determination to make a complete break with the past, to seek the comforting embrace of Lord Jesus and be saved.

"O, my children!" cried Father Bellamy, throwing his gowned arms wide like a great white bat. "Is there not one among ye willing to stand now, this moment, and confess your most secret vices openly and honestly in the presence of Lord Jesus and these witnesses?"

As a matter of fact, there was more than one amongst us; several leaped to their feet and clamored for attention. What followed convinced me that this mob had come to church directly from a grass-uppers-LSD buffet, or was on leave from a local acorn academy.

A young woman, tears streaming down her cheeks, described, graphically, how she had been unfaithful to her husband on "myriad occasions," and how she was tortured by the memories. During this titillating recital, her hand was held by the young man seated beside her. He was, I presumed, the betrayed husband. Or he could have been one of the tortured memories.

A young man, twisting his fingers nervously, told how he had been seduced by his aunt when he was wearing his Boy Scout uniform, and how the relationship continued until he was wearing a U.S. Army uniform, at which time the aunt deserted him, leaving him with a seared psyche and a feeling of guilt that frequently resulted in nocturnal emissions.

Three witnesses, in rapid succession, testified to how much they hated their mother/father/brother/sister, and wished them dead.

A woman confessed to unnatural sex acts with a dalmatian owned by her local fire company.

A stuttering lad, desperately sincere, confessed to a secret passion for Madame Ernestine Schumann-Heink, who died in 1936. He had come across her photograph in an old magazine, and her image had haunted his waking hours and dreams ever since.

A wispy blond girl, eyes glazed and enormously swollen, said she had this "thing." She could never get rid of this "thing." She thought about it constantly and she wanted Lord Jesus, or at least Father Michael Bellamy, to exorcise this "thing."

It went on and on like that: a litany of personal confessions that had me squirming with shame and embarrassment. I am, by nature, a private man. I could match anyone of them sin for sin, depravity for depravity, in dream or in deed, but I'd be damned if I'd stand voluntarily before a jury of my peers and spill my guts. It was just none of their business. I

don't think I could do it in a confessional booth either. I can't even watch
TV talk shows. Listen, if we all told one another what we really did,
thought, and dreamed, the world would dissolve into mad laughter, helpless with despair, and then who would have the strength and resolve to
plan wars?

So I rose quietly from the rear pew and slipped out the church door,
just as an older, bearded man was describing how he had been abusing
himself ever since he picked up a weight-lifting magazine in a barber shop
and, as a consequence, had become a chronic bed-wetter.

I climbed into the dank cab of the pickup. I turned up the collar of my
trenchcoat and slouched down. I lighted a cigarette and waited. I wasn't
bored; I had a lot of questions to ponder.

Like: were those idiots inside who were stripping themselves naked in
front of friends and strangers really sincere about this confession and redemption jazz? Or was it just another kick like Zen or rolfing?

Like: had any bright young sociologist ever written a PhD thesis on the
remarkable similarities between bucolic American revival meetings and
sophisticated American group therapy sessions? Both had a father-leader
(preacher/psychiatrist). Both demanded public confession. Both promised
salvation.

Like: where did Mary Thorndecker run after I jolted her? I figured she'd
have to call me, that night or Saturday morning. I put my money on a
morning call, after she had a desperate night wondering how I had fingered
her as the author of the anonymous note.

Three cigarettes later, the service ended. The congregation of the First
Fundamentalist Church of Lord Jesus streamed forth into the cold night
air, presumably cleansed and rejuvenated. I had been right: there were
bursts of raucous laughter and a great tooting of horns as they roared away
from the parking lot. Kids let out of school.

Still I sat there in Betty Hanrahan's broken wreck. The spotlight illu-
minating the steeple cross went out. The interior lights of the church went
out. Only one car remained in the parking area: that impressive maroon
Bentley. Of course, it would be his.

I got out of the truck slowly, being careful not to slam that tinny door.
I made a slow circuit of the church building. Lights still burned in a side
extension of the nave: the vestry. I went back to the main entrance. The
double-door was still unlocked. I slid in, tiptoed up the aisle. Even in
broad daylight a church is a ghostly place. At night, in almost total darkness, it can spook you. Don't ask me why.

The only illumination was a thin bar of light coming from the interior
door of the vestry. I heard laughter, the clink of glasses. I pulled down
my tweed hat to shadow my eyes, stuck my hands deep in the trenchcoat
pockets. All I needed was a Lone Ranger mask.

I shoved the door open with my foot and stalked in. I was thinking of
a joke a cop had told me: this nervous robber goes into a bank on his first

job and pulls out a gun. "All right, you mother-stickers," he snarls. "This is a fuck-up."

There were two of them in there. Father Michael Bellamy had doffed his pristine robes. Now he was wearing a beautifully tailored suit of soft, gray doeskin with a Norfolk jacket, lavender shirt, knitted black silk tie. I had time to eyeball his jeweled cufflinks: twin Kohinoors. He was seated behind a desk, counting the night's collection. Piling the coins in neat columns, tapping the bills into square stacks.

The other gink was the limp young man I had seen playing the organ. He was a washed-out lad with strands of lank blond hair falling across his acned forehead. The acne was hard to spot under the pancake makeup. He was wearing a ranch suit: faded blue jeans and jacket. With high-heeled western boots yet. He looked as much like a Wyoming cowpoke as Joan Powell looks like Sophie Tucker.

There was a bottle of Remy Martin on the desk. Bellamy was taking his straight in a little balloon glass. The organist was diluting his cognac with a can of Pepsi, which is like blowing your nose in a Gobelin tapestry.

The effete youth was first to react to my entrance. He jerked to his feet and glared at me, not knowing whether to shit, go blind, or wind his watch.

Bellamy didn't pop a capillary.

"Easy, Dicky," he said soothingly. "Easy now." Then to me, brightly: "Yes, sir, and how may I be of service?"

I gave them the silent treatment, looking at them, one to the other, back and forth.

"Well?" Bellamy said. "If it's spiritual advice you're seeking, my son, I must tell you I conduct personal sessions only on Tuesdays and Thursdays, beginning at twelve noon."

I said nothing. He leaned forward a little to stare at my shadowed face.

"At the service tonight, weren't you?" he said in that rich, rolling voice. "In the rear pew, left side?"

"Keen eyes," I said. "What were you doing, counting the house?"

I had been keeping watch on nervous Dicky. But as I spoke, he relaxed back in his chair, apparently reassured. But he never took his glittering eyes off me.

"If this is a robbery," Father Bellamy said steadily, "you're welcome to everything you see before you. Just don't hurt us."

"It isn't a robbery," I told him, "and why should I want to hurt you?"

That Bellamy was one cool cat. He sat back comfortably, took out a pigskin cigar case, and went through all the business of selecting, cutting off the tip, and lighting it with a wooden match. The whole ceremony took about two minutes. I waited patiently. He took an experimental puff to see if it was drawing satisfactorily. Then he blew a plume of blued smoke at me.

"All right," he said, "what's this all about?"

"It's a grift, isn't it?" I asked him.

"Grift?" he said perplexedly. "I don't believe I'm familiar with that term."

"Bullshit," I said. "You're in the game. It's all a con."

"A con?" he said. "Could you possibly be implying trickery? That I, as an ordained minister of the First Fundamentalist Church of Lord Jesus, am running a confidence game designed to deceive and defraud my parishioners?"

"Tell you what," I said, "you call the cops and tell them I'm threatening you. I'll wait right here until they come. No rough stuff, I promise you. Then, when they take me in, I'll ask them to run a trace. The Feds should have you in their files. Or someone, somewhere. They'll find out about the outstanding warrants, skips, and like that. Well? How about it?"

He looked at me with a beatific smile, rolling the cigar around in his plump lips.

"Mike, for Christ's sake!" Dicky cried. "Let's throw this turd out on his ass."

"Now, sonny," I said, "be nice. Have a little respect for a seeker of the truth. How about it, Mr. Bellamy?"

He sighed deeply, running a palm lightly over his billowy white hair.

"How did you tumble?" he asked me curiously.

"You're too good," I said. "Too good for the come-to-Jesus scam. With your looks and voice and delivery, I figure you for Palm Beach or Palm Springs, peddling cheesy oil stock. Or maybe in a Wall Street boardroom, trading conglomerates. You don't belong in the boon-docks, Mr. Bellamy."

The Father smiled with great satisfaction. He raised his brandy snifter to me.

"Thank you for those kind words, sir," he said. "Did you hear that, Dicky? Haven't I told you the same thing?"

"Lots of times," Dicky grumbled.

"But I haven't asked your name, sir," Bellamy said to me.

"Jones," I said.

"To be sure," he said. "Very well, Mr. Jones. Assuming—just assuming, mind you—that your false and malicious allegations are correct, where do we go from here?"

"Mike, what are you doing?" the organist yelled. "Can't you see that this crud—"

Bellamy whirled on him.

"Shut your trap!" he said in a steely voice, the black eyes hard. "Just sit there and drink that loathsome mixture and don't say word one. Understand?"

"Yes, Mike," the youth said meekly.

"As I was saying," Bellamy went on blandly, turning back to me, "where do we go from here?"

I was still standing. There were two empty chairs in the room, but he didn't ask me to sit down. That was okay. Oneupsmanship. You keep a guy standing in front of your desk, he becomes the inferior, the supplicant.

"I don't want to blow the whistle on you," I assured him. "You got a nice thing going here, and as far as I'm concerned, you can milk it until you run out of sinners. I just want a little information. Whatever you can tell me about one of your vestrypersons."

He took a sip of cognac, a puff of his cigar. Then he dipped the mouth of the cigar in the brandy and took a pull on that. He looked at me narrowly through the smoke.

"Are you heat?"

"No. Just a concerned citizen."

"Aren't we all?" he said, smiling again. "Who do you want?"

"Mary Thorndecker."

"Mike, will you stop it?" the damp youth agonized. "You don't have to tell this creep anything, except to get lost."

"Sonny, sonny," I groaned, "can't you be civilized? The Father and I have reached a cordial understanding. Can't you see that? Now just let us get on with our business, and then I'll climb out of your hair, and you can go back to counting the take. Won't that be nice?"

"Listen to the gentleman, Dicky," Bellamy rumbled. "He is obviously a man of breeding and a rough but nimble wit. Mary Thorndecker, you said? Ah, yes. A plain jane. And yet I have the feeling that with the advice and assistance of a clever hairdresser, corsetiere, and dress designer, our dull, drab Mary might blossom into quite a swan indeed. Do you share that dream, Mr. Jones?"

"Could be," I said. "But what I really came to find out is anything you know about her private life, especially her family. Has she ever had one of those private consultations with you on Tuesdays and Thursdays, beginning at noon?"

"On occasion."

"And?"

"A very troubled young woman," he said promptly, staring over my head. "A difficult family situation. A stepmother who is younger and apparently much prettier than Mary. A man who wishes to marry her and who, for some reason she has not revealed to me, she both loves and loathes."

"And?" I said.

"And what?"

"That's it? That's all she talked about in those private sessions?"

"Well . . ." he said, waving a hand negligently, "she did confess to a few personal peccadilloes, a few minor misdeeds that could hardly be dignified as sins. Would you care to hear them?"

"No," I said. "And that's all there is?"

He smoked slowly, frowning in an effort to remember conversations in which, I was sure, he had no interest whatsoever. He leaned forward to pour himself another cognac. I licked my lips as obviously as I could. It won me an amused smile, but no invitation.

"Mike," Dicky said loudly, "you've told this jerk enough. Let's bounce him."

"Sonny," I said, "I'm trying very hard to ignore you, but it's a losing battle. If you'd like to—"

"Now, now," Bellamy interrupted smoothly, raising a palm. "There is no room for animosity and ill-feeling in God's house. Calm down, you two; I detest scenes." He took another sip of brandy, closing his eyes, smacking his wet lips. Then he opened his eyes again and looked at me thoughtfully. "She did say something else. Ask something else. In the nature of a hypothetical question. To wit: what is the proper course of conduct for a child of Lord Jesus who becomes aware that her loved ones are involved in something illegal? They are, in fact, not only sinning but engaged in a criminal activity."

"Did she tell you who the loved ones are?"

"No."

"Did she tell you the nature of the criminal activity?"

"No."

"What did you tell her to do?"

"I suggested she report the entire matter to the police," he said virtuously. "I happen to be a very law-abiding man."

"I'm sure you are," I said.

I decided not to push it any further; he was obviously tiring. After his physical performance at the church service that evening, considering his age it was a wonder he wasn't in intensive care.

"Nice doing business with you, Father," I said, "Keep up the good work. By the way, I put a finif in the plate tonight. You and sonny have a drink on me."

"Don't call me sonny!" the infuriated youth screamed at me.

"Why not?" I said innocently. "If I had a son, I'd want him to be just like you." I paused at the door, turned back. "Father, just out of curiosity, is Mary Thorndecker a heavy mark?"

"She is generous in contributing to God's work on earth," he said sonorously, rolling his eyes to heaven.

"Could you give me a ballpark figure?" I asked him.

He inspected the soaked stump of his cigar closely.

"It is a very large ballpark," he said.

I laughed and left the two of them together. They deserved each other.

I chugged back to Coburn, glad I couldn't coax any more speed out of that groaning heap, because I had some thinking to do. Up to that moment I had vaguely suspected Dr. Telford Gordon Thorndecker might be cutting corners in that combined nursing home-research-lab organization of his. I was thinking along the lines of unethical conduct: not an indictable offense but serious enough to put the kibosh on his application for a grant. Something like trying out new drugs without an informed consent agreement. Or maybe persuading doomed patients to include a plump bequest to the Crittenden Research Laboratory in their wills. Nasty stuff, but difficult, if not impossible, to prosecute.

But Mary Thorndecker hinted at something illegal. A criminal activity. I couldn't guess what it was. I did know it was heavy enough to get Ernie Scoggins chilled when he found out about it. And heavy enough to give Al Coburn the shakes when *he* found out about it.

I must have dreamed up a dozen ugly plots on my way back to Coburn. I had Thorndecker rifling the bank accounts of guests, hypnotizing them into signing over their estates, working on biological warfare for the U.S. Army, trying to determine safe radiation dosages with human subjects, even raping sedated female patients. I went wild, but nothing I imagined really made sense.

I pulled into the parking lot at the Coburn Inn. It was a paved area, lighted with two floods on short poles. They cast puddles of weak yellowish illumination, but most of the lot was either in gloom or lost in black shadow. Still, that was no excuse for what happened next. After the Great Slashed Tire Caper, I should have been more alert.

I parked, got out of the truck, turned to struggle with a balky door lock. The next thing I knew, I was face down on cold cement. That was the sequence: I went down first, and *then* I felt the punch that did it, a slam in the kidneys that spun me around and dumped me. Strange, but even as I realized what had happened, I remember thinking, "That wasn't so bad. It hurt like hell, but this guy is no pro." Probably the last thoughts of every man who's been killed by an amateur.

On the ground, I went into the approved drill: draw up the knees to protect the family jewels, bend neck, cover face and head with folded arms, make yourself into a tight, hard ball. All this to endure the boot you've got to figure is coming. It came, in the short ribs mostly. And though it banged me something fierce, there wasn't any crushing force, and I never came close to losing consciousness. I remember the other guy breathing in wheezing sobs, and thinking he was as much out of condition as I was.

So there I was, lying on my side on a hard bed, curled into a knot. After a few ineffectual kicks to my crossed arms, thighs, and spine, I began to get annoyed. At myself, not the guy who was trying so hard and doing such a lousy job of messing me up.

I recalled an army instructor I had who specialized in unarmed combat. His lecture went something like this:

"Forget about trying to fight with your fists. Forget about those roundhouse swings and uppercuts you see in the movies and on TV. All that'll get you is a fistful of broken knuckles. While you're trying the Fancy Dan stuff, an experienced attacker will be cutting you to ribbons, even if you're a Golden Gloves champ. Rule Number One: hug him. If he's a karate or judo man, and you stand back, he'll kill you. So get in close where he can't swing his arms or legs. Rule Number Two: there are no rules. Forget about fair play and the Marquis of Queensberry. A guy is trying to murder you. Murder him first. Or at least break him. A knee in the nuts is very effective, but if he's fast enough, he'll turn to take it on his thigh. A punch to the balls is better. A hack at the Adam's apple gets good results. If you can get behind him, put two fingers up his nostrils and yank up. The nose rips. Very nice. Also the eyes. Put in a stiff thumb and roll outward. The eyeball pops out like a pit from a ripe peach. And don't forget your teeth. The human jaw can exert at least two hundred pounds of pressure— enough to take off an ear or nose. Shin kicks are fine, and if you can stomp down on the kneecap, you can get his legs to bend the wrong way. Pretty. Pulling hair comes in handy at times, and fingers bent backward make a nice snapping sound.''

He went on and on like that, telling us what we could do to stay alive. So after taking a series of nondisabling kicks, I peeked out from under my folded arms, and the next time I saw a stylish black moccasin flashing for my ribs, I reached out, grabbed an ankle, and pulled hard. He landed on his coccyx, and his sharp yelp of pain was music to my ears.

Then I swarmed all over him. A hard knee into the testicles. A knuckled chop at his throat. I stiffened my thumb and started for the eyes when I suddenly saw that if I carried through, Edward Thorndecker would need a cane and tin cup.

''Oh for God's sake,'' I said disgustedly.

I dragged myself to my feet, tried to catch my breath. I dusted myself off. I left him lying there, weeping and puking. After my breathing re- turned to normal, and I had satisfied myself that I had no broken bones or cracked ribs, just bruises and wounded pride, I dug the toe of my boot into his ass.

''Get up,'' I told him.

''You keep away from her,'' he croaked, in rage and frustration. ''If you go near my stepmother again, I'll kill you. I swear to God I'll kill you!''

All in that half-lisp of his, sobbed out, coughed out, spluttered out. All in a cracked voice after that hack on his voice box.

I reached down, got a good grip on his collar, hauled him to his feet. I propped him back against the door of the pickup and patted him down. Just in case he was carrying a lethal weapon, like a Ping-Pong paddle or a lime Popsicle. Then I opened the door, shoved him inside, and climbed in after him. I rolled down the windows because he had upchucked all over himself. I lighted a cigarette to help defuse the stench.

I smoked patiently, waiting for his snuffling and whimpering to fade away. I wasn't as calm as it sounds. Every time I thought of how close I came to wasting that young idiot, I'd get the shakes and have to go to deep breathing to get rid of them. I handed over my handkerchief to help him clean himself. But he was one sad looking dude, hanging onto his balls and bending far over to cushion the hurt.

We must have sat there in the damp cold for at least fifteen minutes before he was able to straighten up. He didn't know which part of his anatomy to massage first. I was glad he was aching; his attack had scared me witless. I had thought it was Ronnie Goodfellow, of course. But if *he* had punched me in the kidneys, I'd have been peeing blood for three weeks. After I came to.

"All right," I said, "let's get to it. What makes you think I'm annoying your stepmother?"

"I don't want to talk about it," he said sullenly.

I turned sideways, and laid an open palm against his chops. His head snapped around, and he began crying again.

"Sure you want to talk about it," I said stonily. "Unless you want another knock on the cojones that'll have you singing soprano for the rest of your life."

"She said so," he mumbled.

"Julie told you I made a pass at her?"

"She didn't tell me. She told father. I heard her."

I didn't doubt him.

We sat there in silence. I gave him a cigarette and lighted another for myself. He began to feel a little better; his nerve came back.

"I'm going to tell my father that you beat me up," he said angrily.

"Do that," I told him. "Tell your father that we met by accident in the parking lot of the Coburn Inn, at an hour when you should be home studying, and I suddenly attacked you for no reason at all. Your father is sure to believe it."

"Julie will believe me," he said hotly.

"No one will believe you," I said cruelly. "Everyone knows you're a sack of shit. The only thing you've got going for you is that you're young enough to outgrow it. Possibly."

"Oh God," he said hollowly, "I want to die."

"Love her that much, do you?" I said.

"I saw her naked once," he said, in the same tone of wonderment someone might use to say, "I saw a flying saucer."

"Good on you," I said, "but she happens to be your father's wife."

"He doesn't appreciate her," he said.

What's the use? You can't talk to snotty kids. They know it all.

"All right, Edward," I said, sighing. "I could tell you that I never propositioned your stepmother, but I know you wouldn't believe me. Now you tell me something: what's going on in the research lab?"

"Going on?" he said, puzzled. "Well, you know, they do experiments. I don't understand that stuff. I'm not into science."

"Oh? What are you into?"

"I like poetry. I write poems. Julie says they're very good."

Full circle. Thorndecker's father was a poet. Thorndecker's son was a poet. I hoped the son wouldn't die as his grandfather had.

"And you've got no idea of anything strange going on out there?"

"I don't know what you're talking about."

I believed him.

He said he had "borrowed" Julie's sports car and parked it a block away. I told him that if he was smart, he'd drive directly home, soak in a hot tub, and keep his mouth shut about what had happened.

"I'm here to check on your father's qualifications for a grant," I said. "I don't think he or Julie would be happy to hear you tried to dent my head tonight."

I don't believe he had thought of that. It sobered him. He got out of the truck, then turned back to stick his head through the open window.

"Listen," he said, "my father's a great man."

"I know," I said. "Everyone tells me so."

"He wouldn't do anything wrong," he said, then walked away into the shadows. I watched him go. After awhile I got out, locked up, trotted to the Inn.

I'd had my fill of parking lots for one day.

Up in Room 3-F, I stripped down and inspected the damage. Not too bad. Some scrapings, bruises, minor contusions. I took a shower as hot as I could stand it, and that helped. Then I cracked that bottle of vodka I had purchased ten years ago and bought myself a princely snort.

I sat there in my skin, sipping warm Popov, and wondering why Julie Thorndecker had done it. Why she had told her husband that I had, ah, taken liberties. I couldn't blame it on the "woman scorned" motive; she was more complex than that.

This is what I came up with:

She was preparing ammunition in case I gave Thorndecker a negative report, as she feared I might. Then, having reported my churlish behavior to her husband, she might prevail upon him to write the Bingham Foundation claiming that my reactions were hardly objective, but had been colored by my unsuccessful attempt to seduce his wife.

I could imagine the response of Stacy Besant and Mrs. Cynthia to such an allegation. They might not believe it entirely; they'd tell me they didn't believe it. But they might think it wise to send a second field investigator to check out the Thorndecker application. An older investigator. More mature. Less impetuous. And on the strength of *his* report, Thorndecker might squeak through.

I believed Julie was capable of such a Byzantine plot. Not entirely for her husband; self-interest was at work here. In Coburn, she had said, I'm a big frog in a little pond—and that was true. Most women are conservative by nature; she, in addition, was conservative by circumstance. The little she had let drop about the rackety life she led before she met Thorndecker convinced me that she enjoyed and cherished the status quo, didn't want it to change. She had found a home.

Having settled the motives of Julie Thorndecker, and resolving to meet with her husband as soon as possible to see how much damage she had done, I got back to my favorite topic: what was going on at the Crittenden Research Laboratory? I came up with another choice assortment of wild and improbable scenarios:

Thorndecker was developing a new nerve gas. Thorndecker was a Frankenstein, putting together a monster from parts of deceased patients. Thorndecker was engaged in recombinant genetic research, combining the DNA of a parrot with that of a dog, and trying to breed a schnauzer who talked. The more Popov I inhaled, the sappier my fantasies became.

What gave me nightmares for months afterward was that I had already come up with the solution and didn't know it.

The Sixth Day

The phone woke me up the next morning. I have a thing about phones. I claim that when I'm calling someone who isn't at home, dialing a number that no one will answer, I can tell after the second ring. It has a hollow, empty sound. Also, I think I can judge the mood of anyone who calls me by *their* ring: angry, loving, good or bad news. Tell me, doctor, do you think I . . . ?

In this case, coming out a deep, dreamless sleep, the ring of the phone sounded desperate, even relayed through the hotel switchboard. I was right. It was Mary Thorndecker, and she had to see me as soon as possible. It couldn't be at the Coburn Inn. It couldn't be at Crittenden Hall. It couldn't be anywhere in public. I figured that left the Carlsbad Caverns, but she insisted on the road that led around the Crittenden grounds, in the rear, past the cemetery. She said eleven o'clock, and I agreed.

I got out of bed feeling remarkably chipper. Unhungover. You can usually trust vodka for that. After all, it's just grain alcohol and water. Very few congeners. Drink vodka all your life, and everything will be hunky-dory—except you may end up with a liver that extends from clavicle to patella.

A shower, a shave, a fresh turtleneck—and I was ready for a fight or a frolic. When I went out into the hall, the brass indicator showed the elevator was coming down. I rang the bell, waited, watched Sam Livingston come slowly into view in his cage: feet, ankles, knees, hips, waist, shoulders, head. A revelation. The elevator shuddered to a stop. I stepped in.

"Sam," I said, "you suckered me."

He knew immediately what I meant.

"Nah," he said, with almost a smile, "I just told you he puts on a good show."

"The guy's a phonus-balonus," I said.

"So? He gives the folks what they want."

"Aren't you ashamed of yourself? You got Mary Thorndecker driving you out there. She thinks she's bringing in another convert, and all the time you're laughing up your sleeve."

"Well . . . " he said solemnly, "it's better'n TV. Hear you had a little trouble with your car."

"Good gracious me," I said, "word does get around. Mike's is delivering it with new tires, I hope, at noon today. If I'm not here, will you ask them to leave the keys at the desk? No, scratch that. Will you keep the keys for me?"

He explained that he expected to leave by 1:00 P.M., to take care of his cleaning chores at the Episcopal church. He'd keep my car keys until then. If I hadn't returned by one o'clock, he'd leave the keys on the dresser in my room. I said that would be fine.

We descended slowly past the second floor. In the old Greek plays, the gods must have come down out of heaven in their basket at about our speed.

"Sam," I said, "you know Fred Aikens? The constable?"

"Seen him around," he said cautiously.

"What's your take?"

He didn't answer.

"I wouldn't want to stroll down a dark alley with him," I offered.

"No," he said thoughtfully, "don't do that."

"Is he buddy-buddy with Ronnie Goodfellow?"

The old man turned to stare at me with his yellowish eyes.

"You ever know two cops who weren't?" he asked. "And they don't even have to *like* each other."

We inched our way down to the lobby. Millie was chatting it up with two customers at the cigar counter, and didn't notice me as I sneaked into the restaurant. It was practically empty, which surprised me until I remembered it was Saturday morning. I assumed the bank and a lot of offices and maybe some stores were closed. Anyway, I was able to get a table to myself and spread out.

After that tunafish salad for dinner the night before, I was ravenous. I shot the works with an Australian breakfast: steak and eggs, with a side order of American home-fries and a sliced tomato that tasted like a tomato. First one like that I had eaten in years.

I started my second cup of black coffee, and looked up to see Constable Ronnie Goodfellow standing opposite. From where I sat, he looked like he was on stilts. Did I tell you what a handsome guy he was? A young Clark Gable, before he grew a mustache. Goodfellow was as lean and beautiful, in a tight, chiseled way. I'm a het, and have every intention of staying that way. But even the straightest guy occasionally meets a man who makes him wonder. This is what I call the "What-if-we-were-marooned-on-a-desert-island Test." I don't think there's a man alive who could pass it.

"Morning," I said to him. "Join me for a cup?"

"I'd like to join you," he said, "but I'll skip the coffee, thanks. Four cups this morning, so far."

He took off his trooper's hat, and sat down across from me. He removed his gloves, folded them neatly inside the hat on an empty chair. Then he put his elbows on the table, scrubbed his face with his palms. He may have sighed.

"Heavy night?" I asked him.

"Trouble sleeping," he said. "I don't want to start on pills."

"No," I said, "don't do that. Try a shot of brandy or a glass of port wine."

"I don't drink," he said.

"One before you go to sleep isn't going to hurt you."

"My father died a rummy," he said, with no expression whatsoever in his voice. "I don't want to get started. Listen, Mr. Todd, I'm sorry about your car."

I shrugged. "Probably some wild kids."

"Probably. Still, it doesn't look good when it happens to a visitor. I stopped by Mike's Service Station. You'll have your car by noon."

"Good."

Then we sat in silence. It seemed to me we had nothing to say to each other. I know I didn't; he'd never tell me what I wanted to know. So I waited, figuring he had a message to deliver. If he did, he was having a hard time getting it out. He was looking down at his tanned hands, inspecting every finger like he was seeing it for the first time, massaging each knuckle, clenching a fist, then stretching palms wide.

"Mr. Todd," he said in a low voice, not looking at me, "I really think you're prying into things that are none of your business, that have nothing to do with your investigation."

Then he raised those dark eyes to stare at me. It was like being jabbed with an icepick.

I took a sip of coffee that scalded my lips. I moved back from the table, fished for my cigarettes. I lighted one. I didn't offer the pack to him.

"Let me guess," I said. "That would be the Reverend Father Michael Bellamy reporting in. Sure. How could a grifter like him operate around here without official connivance? Tell you about our little conversation, did he?"

"I don't know what you're talking about," he said, face impassive.

"Then what are *you* talking about?"

"As I understand it, you came up here to take a look around, inspect

Dr. Thorndecker's setup, make sure it was what he claimed it was. Is that
right?''

"That's about it."

"Well? You've looked over the place. It's what he said it was, isn't
it?''

"Yes."

"So? Why are you poking into things that have nothing to do with your
job? Private matters. You get some kind of a kick trying to turn up dirt?
You really shouldn't do that, Mr. Todd. It could be dangerous."

What I said next I know I shouldn't have said. I knew it while I was
saying it. But I was so frustrated, so maddened by hints, and eyebrow-
liftings, and vague suggestions, and now so infuriated by this cop's implied threat, that I slapped cards on the table I should have been pressing
to my chest.

I made a great show of sangfroid, old nonchalant me: sipped coffee,
puffed cigarette, stared at him with what I hoped was amusement, inso-
lence, secret knowing—the whole bit.

"I get kicks out of a lot of things," I told him. "Of seeing a guy
named Chester K. Petersen being stuck in the Crittenden cemetery at
two in the morning. Of being told by one person that he died of internal
cancer, and by another person that he died of congestive heart failure.
Of discovering that a remarkable number of patients at Crittenden Hall
have died of congestive heart failure, with most of the death certificates
signed by the same doctor. Let's see—what else? Oh yes—the mysterious disappearance of one Ernie Scoggins, a Crittenden employee. With
blood stains on the rug in his trailer. Did you spot those during your
investigation, *Constable* Goodfellow? Anything more? Not much—except rumors and hints and insinuations that something unethical, illegal,
and probably criminal is going on out at Crittenden. I suppose I could
add a few things, but they're mostly supposition. Like Dr. Thorndecker
owns this village and every soul in it. I use the word 'soul' loosely.
That Thorndecker has a finger in every pie in town. That this place is
dying, and if he goes down, you all go down. That's about all I've got.
Private matters? Nothing to do with my job? You don't really believe
that, do you?''

I'll say this for him: he didn't break, or gulp, or give any indication
that what I was saying was getting to him. He just got harder and harder,
turned to stone, those black eyes glittering. Maybe he got a little paler.
Maybe the hands spread out on the table trembled a little.

But he made no reply, no threat. Just stood, pulled on gloves and hat
with precise movements, staring at me all the time.

"Goodby, Mr. Todd," he said tonelessly.

And that was enough to set my nerve ends flapping. "Goodby." Not
So-long, or See you around, or *Ciao*, baby. Just "Goodby." Final.

I was glad I hadn't mentioned anything about Al Coburn. That was the only thing I was glad about. It didn't help. I had talked too much, and knew it. I tried to persuade myself that I had told Goodfellow all that stuff deliberately, to let everyone know what I knew, to stir them up, spook them into making some foolish move.

But I couldn't quite convince myself that I had just engineered an extremely clever ploy. All I had done was blab. I got up, signed my check, and strolled into the bar whistling. Like a frightened kid walking through a graveyard on his way home.

The restaurant may have been dying, but that bar was doing jim-dandy business for an early Saturday morning. Most of the stools were taken; three of the booths were occupied. The customers looked like farmers killing time while their wives shopped, had their hair done, or whatever wives did in Coburn on a Saturday morning. I finally caught Jimmy's eye, ordered a stein of beer, took it over to a small table away from the babble at the bar.

I had started the day in a hell-for-leather mood, but my little confabulation with Constable Goodfellow had brought that to a screeching halt. A new Samuel Todd record: one hour from manic to depressive. I sipped my beer and reflected that Coburn and the Coburnites had that effect: they doused the jollies, and nudged you mournfully into the Slough of Despond. I think I've already reported that I heard no laughter on the streets. Maybe, I thought, the Board of Selectmen had passed an anti-giggling ordinance. "Warning! Levity is punishable by a fine, imprisonment, or both."

I watched one of the customers climb down from his bar stool, waddle over to the door of the Men's Room, and try to get in. But the room was occupied; the door was locked. The guy rattled the knob angrily a few times, then went growling back to the bar. A very ordinary incident. Happens all the time. The only reason I mention it is that seeing the customer rattle the knob on the locked door inspired, by some loony chain of thought, a magnificent idea: I would break into Crittenden Hall and the Crittenden Research Laboratory late at night and look around.

My first reaction to that brainstorm was a firm conviction that I was over the edge, around the bend, and down the tube. First of all, if I got caught, it would mean my job, even if I was able to weasel out of a stay in the slammer. Second, how could I get over that high fence, avoid the armed guards, and gain entrance to the locked buildings? Finally, what could I possibly hope to find that I hadn't been shown on my tour of the premises?

Still, it was an enticing prospect, just the thing to keep me awake and functioning until it was time to drive out for my meet with Mary Thorndecker.

The more I chewed on it, the more reasonable the project seemed to me. I could get over the fence with the aid of a short ladder. There were only three guards I knew of: the rover with shotgun and attack dog, the guy on the gate, and the bentnose inside the nursing home. A sneaky type like me shouldn't find it too difficult to duck all three.

The stickler was how to get inside the locked buildings without smashing windows or breaking down doors. That business of opening a lock with a plastic credit card—beloved by every private eye on TV—works only when there's no dead bolt. And, I had noted on my visit, the doors at Crittenden had them. I'm no good at picking a lock, even if I owned a set of picks, which I don't. Also, I don't wear hairpins. That left only one impossible solution: keys.

But even assuming I got inside undetected, what did I expect to find? The answer to that was easy: if I knew what I'd find, a break-in wouldn't be necessary. This would be what the sawbones call an exploratory operation. It really was the only way, I acknowledged. Waiting for one of the cast of characters to reveal all was getting me nowhere.

I bought myself another beer, and went into the campaign a little deeper. Dr. Kenneth Draper had mentioned that his eager, young research assistants sometimes worked right through till dawn. But surely there wouldn't be many in the labs on Saturday or Sunday night. Even whiz-kids like to relax on weekends, or so Betty Hanrahan had said. As for the nursing home, it would probably be quiet at, say, two in the morning, with a skeleton night staff drinking coffee in offices and labs when they weren't making their rounds.

See how easy it is to talk yourself into a course of action you know in your heart of hearts is dangerous, sappy, and unlikely to succeed? Talk about Father Bellamy being a grifter! His talents were nothing compared to the skills we all have in conning ourselves. Self-delusion is still the biggest scam of all.

I know it now, I knew it on that Saturday morning in Coburn. I told myself to forget the whole cockamamie scheme.

But all I could think about was how I could get the keys to those locked Crittenden doors.

"Hey, Todd," Al Coburn said in his cracked voice, kicking gently at my ankle. "You dreaming or something?"

"Or something," I said. "Pull up a chair, Mr. Coburn."

He was carrying his own beer, and when I pushed a chair toward him, he flopped down heavily. His hands were trembling. He wrapped them around his beer glass and held on for dear life.

"*Mister* Coburn," he said, musing. "You got manners on you for a young whipper."

"Sure," I said. "I'm also trustworthy, loyal, friendly, brave, clean, and reverent. Boy Scout oath."

"Yeah," he said, looking around absently. "Well, you remember what we were talking about before?"

"The letter from Ernie Scoggins?"

"What happened was this: I got in touch with the, uh, party concerned, and maybe it was all like a misunderstanding."

I looked at him, but he wouldn't meet my eyes. His vacant stare was over my head, around the walls, across the ceiling.

"You're a lousy liar," I said.

"No, no," he said seriously. "I just gabbed more than I should. That Ernie Scoggins—a crazy feller. I told you that. He blew it all up. Know what I mean? So I'm having a meeting late this afternoon, and we'll straighten the whole thing out. Everything's going to be fine. Yes. Fine."

I felt sick. I leaned across the table to him, tried to hold his gaze in mine. But he just wouldn't lock eyes.

"Your notes at the bank?" I said. "They got to you?"

I was doing it: using the word "they." Who? The CIA, the FBI, the KGB, the Gold Star Mothers, the Association for the Investigation of Paranormal Phenomena? Who?

"Oh no," he said, very solemn now. "No no no. This has nothing to do with my notes. Just a friendly discussion. To come to an agreement for our mutual benefit."

That wasn't Al Coburn talking. "An agreement for our mutual benefit." I knew he was quoting someone. It smelled of con.

"Mr. Coburn," I said slowly and carefully, "let's see if I've got this right. You're going to meet someone late this afternoon and talk about whatever is in that letter Ernie Scoggins left you? Is that it?"

"Well . . . yeah," he said, looking down into his beer. "It'll all get straightened out. You'll see."

"Want me to come along?" I asked him. "Maybe it would be better if you had—you know, like a witness. I won't say a word. I won't do anything. I'll just *be* there."

He bristled.

"Listen, sonny," he said, "I can take care of myself."

"Sure you can," I said hastily. "But what's wrong with having a third party present?"

"It's confidential," he said. "That was the agreement. Just him and me."

I grabbed that.

"Him?" I said. "So you're meeting just one man?"

"I didn't say that."

"No, you didn't. I guessed it. Am I wrong?"

"I'm tired," he said fretfully.

I looked at him, and I knew he was telling the truth: he *was* tired. The head was bowed, shoulders slumped, all of him collapsed. Tired or defeated.

"I don't want no trouble," he mumbled.

What was I to do—hassle a weary old man? The years had rubbed away at him. As they do at all of us. Will slackens. Resolve fuzzes.

Worst of all, physical energy leaks out. We just don't have the verve to cope. A good bowel movement becomes life's highest pleasure, and we see a tanned teenager in a bikini and think bitterly, "Little do you know!"

I wanted to take his stringy craw in my fists and choke the truth from him. Who was the guy he was going to meet? What was in Scoggins's letter? What were they going to agree about? But what the hell could I do—stomp it out of him?

I'm pretty good at self-control. I mean I don't rant and rave. The stomach may be bubbling, but the voice is low, level, contained.

"Look, Mr. Coburn," I said, "this meeting of yours—I hope it comes out just the way you want it. That everything is solved to your satisfaction. But just in case—in *case*, you understand—things don't turn out to be nice-nice, don't you think you should have an insurance policy? An ace in the hole?"

Then, finally, he looked at me. Those washed-out eyes focused on my stare, and I knew I had him hooked.

"Like what?" he said.

I shrugged. "A copy of Scoggins's letter. Left some place only you and I know about. Doesn't that make sense? Gives you a bargaining point, doesn't it? With the guy you're meeting? A copy of the letter, or the original, left in someone else's hands. In case . . . "

True to the Coburn tradition, I didn't finish that sentence. I didn't have to. He understood, and it shook him. I started from the table to buy him another beer, but he wagged his head and waved me back. All he wanted to do was think, ponder, figure, reckon. He may have been an old man, but he wasn't an old dummy.

"Yes," he said at last. "All right. I'll go along with that. It'll be in the glove compartment of my pickup. In case. But I won't need to use it; you'll see. I'll call you right after the meeting. You'll be here?"

"What time are you talking about?"

"Five, six this evening. Around there."

"Sure," I said, "I'll be here. If not, you can always leave a message. Just tell me everything's okay."

He nodded, nodded, like one of those Hong Kong dolls, the spineless head bobbing up and down.

"That's a good way," he said. "I'll call you to tell you everything's okay. Hey, maybe we can eat together tonight. Listen, Todd, I made a good stew last night. You come out and eat with me. I'll tell you about stew: you cook it, and then you let it cool, and you eat it the next day, after it's got twenty-four hours of soaking. Tastes better that way."

"Sounds good to me," I said. "I'll wait for your call. Then I'll come out, and we'll have the stew. What's in it?"

"This and that," he said.

I began to have second thoughts. Not about the stew, but about the arrangements we had made. Too many things could go wrong. Murphy's Law.

"Well, look," I said, "I expect to be in and out all day, so maybe you'll call and I won't be here, and those nut-boys at the desk will forget to deliver your message. So why don't you give me your phone number now, and tell me how to locate your place?"

He wasn't exactly happy about that, but I finally got his phone number and directions on how to find his home. He said he lived in a farmhouse not too far from the foot of Crittenden Hill, and if I looked for a clumsy clapboard house set on cinder blocks, that was it. I'd know it by a steel flagpole set in cement in the front yard. He flew Old Glory day and night, no matter what the weather. When the flag got shagged to ribbons, he bought a new one.

"If I get six months out of a flag," Al Coburn said, "I figure I'm lucky. But I don't care. I'm patriotic, and I don't give a damn who knows it."

"Good for you," I said.

I watched him stumble out of there. He was trying to keep his shoulders back, chest inflated. I wanted to be like that when I was his age: cocky and hopeful. None of us can win the final decision. But, with luck, we can pick up a few rounds. I hoped old Al Coburn would pick up this round.

That blighted week . . . The sharpest memory I have is my Saturday morning phone call to Dr. Telford Thorndecker. I planned it: what I would say, what he might say, what I would reply.

I got through to Crittenden Hall with no trouble, but it took them almost five minutes to locate Thorndecker. Then I was told he was in his private office at the Crittenden Research Laboratory, and didn't wish to be disturbed except in case of emergency. I said it was an emergency. A string of clicks, and he finally came on the line. Angry.

"Who is this?" he demanded.

I told him.

"Oh yes," he said. "Mr. Todd. Did you get that report I promised you?"

"I did," I said, "and I want to—"

"Good," he said. "Then I presume the grant will be forthcoming shortly."

"Well, not exactly. What I really—"

"The skeptics," he said disgustedly. "The nay-sayers. Don't listen to them. We're on the right track now."

"Dr. Thorndecker," I said, "I was wondering if—"

"Of course there's a lot to be done. We've just scratched the surface. No one knows. No one can possibly guess."

"If you could—"

"I don't know when I've been so optimistic about a research project.

I mean that sincerely. It just seems like everything is falling into place. The Thorndecker Theory. That's what they'll call it: the Thorndecker Theory.''

All this in his booming baritone. But I missed the conviction the words should have conveyed. The man was remote: that's the only way I can describe it. I didn't know if he was trying to convince me or himself. But I had a sense of him being way up there in the wild blue yonder, repeating dreams.

"Dr. Thorndecker," I said, trying again, "I have some questions only you can answer, and I was hoping you might be able to spare me a few moments this afternoon.''

"Julie," he said. "She'll be so proud of me. Of course. What is it you wanted?''

"If we could meet," I said. "For a short time. This afternoon.''

"Delighted," he shouted. "Absolutely delighted, Now? This minute? Are you at the gate? I'm in my lab.''

"Well . . . no, sir," I said. "I was thinking about this afternoon. Maybe three o'clock. Around there. Would that be all right?''

There was silence.

"Hello?" I said. "Dr. Thorndecker? Are you there?''

"What's this about?" he said suspiciously. "Who is this?''

Once more it occurred to me that he might be on something. In never-never land. He wasn't slurring; his speech was distinct. But he wasn't tracking. He wasn't going from A to B to C; he was going from K to R to F.

I tried again.

"Dr. Thorndecker," I said formally, "this is Samuel Todd. I have a few more questions I'd like to ask you regarding your application to the Bingham Foundation for a grant. Could I see you at three this afternoon?''

"But of course!" he said heartily. Pause. "Perhaps two o'clock would be better. Would that inconvenience you?''

"Not at all," I said. "I'll be out there at two.''

"Excellent!" he said. "I'll leave word at the gate. You come directly to the lab. I'll be here.''

"Fine," I said. "See you then.''

"And Mary and Edward," he said, and hung up.

It was Loony Tunes time. I figured I might as well be equipped. I found a hardware store that was open, and bought a three-cell flashlight with batteries, a short stepladder, 50 feet of cheap clothesline, and a lead sash weight. They didn't have any ski masks. I stowed my new possessions in Betty Hanrahan's pickup and headed out to Crittenden to meet Mary Thorndecker. If she had showed up in a Batman cape, I wouldn't have been a bit surprised. The whole world had gone lunatic. Including me.

She wasn't hard to find. Parked off the road in a black car long enough to be a hearse. I pulled up ahead of her, figuring I might want to get away in a hurry and wouldn't want to be boxed in. I got out of the pickup, ready to sit in her limousine. It had to be warmer in there. The Yukon would be warmer than Betty Hanrahan's pickup.

But Mary Thorndecker got out of her car, too. Slammed the door: a solid *chunk* muffled in the thicker air. Maybe she didn't want to be alone with me in a closed space. Maybe she didn't trust me. I don't know. Anyway, we were both out in the open, stalking toward each other warily. High Noon at Crittenden.

But we waded, actually. Because there was a morning ground fog still swirling. It covered our legs, and we pushed through it. It was white smoke, billowing. The earth was dry ice. And as we breathed, long plumes of vapor went out. I glanced around that chill, deserted landscape. Bleak trees and frosted stubble. A blurred etching: fog, vapor, my slick trench-coat and her heavy, old-fashioned wrap of Persian lamb. I hadn't seen one of those in years.

She wore a knitted black cloche, pulled down to her eyes. Her face was white, pinched, frightened. Everything that had seemed to me mildly cu-rious and faintly amusing about the Thorndecker affair suddenly sank to depression, dread, and inevitability. Her demonic look. Bleached lips. Her hands were thrust deep into her pockets, and I wondered if she had brought a gun and planned to shoot me dead. In that lost landscape it was possible. Any cold violence was possible.

"Miss Thorndecker," I said. "Mary. Would you—"

"How did you know?" she demanded. Her voice was dry and gaspy. "About the note? That I wrote the note?"

"What difference does it make?" I said. I stamped my feet. "Listen, can we walk? Just walk up and down? If we stand here without moving for fifteen minutes, we'll never dance the gavotte again."

She didn't say anything, but dug her chin down into her collar, hunched her shoulders, tramped beside me up the graveled road and back. Behind the fence was the Crittenden cemetery. On the other side were the winter-shredded trees. Not another car, a sound, a color. We could have been alone on earth, the last, the only. Smoke swirled about us, and I wanted a quart of brandy.

"Why did you write it?" I asked her. "I thought you loved your father. Stepfather."

She tried to laugh scornfully.

"*She* told you that," she said. "I hate the man. *Hate* him! He killed my mother."

"Can you prove that?"

"No," she said, "but I *know*."

I wondered if she was out to lunch, if her fury had corroded her so deeply that she was lost. To me, herself, everyone.

"Is that why you wrote: 'Thorndecker kills'? Because you think he murdered your mother?"

"And his father," she said. "I know that, too. No, that's not why. Because he's killing, now, in that lab of his."

"Scoggins?" I suggested. "Thorndecker killed him?"

"Who?"

"Scoggins. Ernie Scoggins. He used to work at Crittenden. A maintenance man."

"Maybe," she said dully. "The man who disappeared? I don't know anything about him. But there were others."

"Petersen?" I asked. "Chester K. Petersen? They buried him a few days ago. Pelvic cancer."

"No," she said, "he was a heart patient. That's why he came to Crittenden Hall. I saw his file. Angina. No close relatives. A sweet old man. Just a sweet old man. Then, about three months ago, he began to develop tumors. Sarcomas, carcinomas, melanomas. All over his body. On his scalp, his face, hands, arms, legs. I saw him. I visited him. He rotted away. He smelled."

"Jesus," I said, looking away, remembering the dying chimp.

"But he was only the latest," she said. "There were others. Many, many others."

"How long?" I demanded. "How long has this been going on?"

She thought a moment.

"Eighteen months," she said. "But mostly in the past year. Patients with no medical record of cancer. Cardiacs, mentals, alcoholics, addicts. Then they developed horrible cancers. They decayed. He's doing it to them. Thorndecker is. I *know* it!"

"And Draper?" I said softly. "Dr. Kenneth Draper?"

A hand came swiftly out of her coat pocket. She gnawed on a chalky knuckle.

"I don't know," she said. "I ask him. I plead with him. But he won't *tell* me. He cries. He worships Thorndecker. He'll do anything Thorndecker says."

"Draper is in on it," I told her flatly. "He's the physician in attendance. He signs the death certificates. But *why* are they doing it? For the bequests? For the money the dead patients leave to the lab?"

The question troubled her.

"I don't know," she said. "That's what I thought at first, but that can't be right. Some of them didn't leave the lab anything. Most of them didn't. I don't know. Oh my God . . . "

She began weeping. I put an uncomfortable arm about her shoulders. We leaned together. Still stamping back and forth, wading through that twisting fog.

"All right," I said, "let's go over it . . . A patient checks in. A cardiac case, or a mental, drugs, alcoholic, whatever. Young or old?"

"Mostly old."

"Then after awhile they develop cancer and die of that?"

"Yes."

"The same way Petersen died? Or internal cancer, too? Lung cancer? Stomach? Spleen? Liver?"

"All ways," she said in a low voice.

"In how long a time? How long does it take them to die of the cancer?"

"At first, when I became aware of what was going on, it was very quick. A few weeks. Lately it's been longer. Petersen was the most recent. He lasted almost three months."

"And they're all buried here on the grounds?"

"Or shipped home in a sealed coffin."

"But all of them tumorous?"

"Yes. Decayed."

"And no complaints from relatives? No questions asked?"

"I don't know," she said. "Probably not. People are like that. People are secretly relieved when a sick relative dies. A problem relative. They wouldn't ask questions."

"You're probably right," I said sadly. "Especially if they're inheriting. And Draper hasn't told you a thing about what's going on?"

"He just claims Thorndecker is a genius on the verge of a great discovery. That's all he'll say."

"He loves you."

"He says," she said bitterly, "but he won't tell me anything."

We paced back and forth in silence. It was the pits, absolutely the pits.

"What will you do to find out?" I asked her finally.

"What? I don't understand."

"How far will you go to discover what's going on? How important is it to you to stop Thorndecker?"

Suddenly she came apart. Just splintered. She stopped, jerked away from my shielding arm, turned to face me.

"That cocksucker!" she howled. Her spittle stung. I took a step back, shocked, bewildered. "That murderer!" she screamed. "Turdy toad! Wife killer! You think I don't—And he—with that slimy wife of his rubbing up against everything in sight. He has no right. No right! He must suffer. Oh yes! Skin flayed away. Flesh from his bones. Rot in the deepest, hottest hell. Vengeance is mine, sayeth the Lord! Naked! The way she dresses! Licking up to every male she meets. Edward! Oh my God, poor, young, innocent Edward. Yes, even him. What does she *do* to them? And he, *he*, lets her go her way, his life destroyed by that wanton with her filthy ways. Ruining him. Her body there. For everyone! Oh yes, I know. Everyone knows. The whore! The smirking whore! Den of iniquity. That house of wickedness. Oh God, strike down the evil. Lord Jesus, I beg you! Smite this filth. Root out—"

She went on and on, using words I could hardly believe she knew. The schoolteacher gone berserk. The spinster wrung by an orgasm. Obscenity, jealousy, sexual frustration, religious frenzy: it was all in her inchoate shouts, words tumbling, white stuff gathering in the corners of her mouth something leaking from her eyes.

And love there. Oh yes; love. Julie hadn't been so wrong. This woman had to love Thorndecker to damn him so viciously, to want him so utterly destroyed. Every woman deserves one shot at the man she loves, and this was Mary's, this wailed revilement, this hysterical abuse that frightened me with its intensity. The vapor of her screams came at me in spouts of steam smelling of acid and ash.

I wondered if I might shake her, slap her, or take her in my arms and say, "There, there," and commiserate over her wounded soul, lost hopes, wasted life. Finally, I did nothing but let her rant, rave, wind down, lose energy, become eventually silent, just standing there, mouth open, trembling. And not from cold, I knew, but from pain and shame. Pain of her hurts, shame for having revealed it to another.

I put a hand on her arm as gently as I could, and led her back to her car. She came willingly enough, and let me get her seated behind the wheel. I pulled up her collar, folded the coat carefully over her knees, did everything but tuck her in. I offered her a cigarette, but I don't think she saw it. I lighted up, with shaking fingers, smoked like a maniac. I finally had to open the window on my side just a crack.

When, after a few moments, I turned to look at her, I saw her eyes were closed, her lips were moving. She was praying, but to whom or for what, I did not know.

"Mary?" I said softly. "Mary, can you hear me? Are you listening to me?"

Lips stopped moving, eyes opened. Head turned, and she looked at me. The focus of her eyes gradually shortened until she saw me.

"I can help you, Mary," I whispered. "But you must help me do it."

"How?" she said, in a voice less than a whisper.

I laid it out for her:

I wanted to know the number of exterior and interior security guards on duty Sunday night. I wanted to know their schedules, when the shift changed, their routines, where they stayed when they weren't patrolling.

I wanted to know everything she could find out about alarms, electric and electronic, and where the on-off switch or fuse box was located. Also, the location of the main power switches for the nursing home and the research laboratory.

I wanted to know the number of medical staff on duty Sunday night in Crittenden Hall and who, if anyone, might be working in the laboratories.

Finally, most important, I wanted that big ring of keys that Nurse Stella Beecham carried. If she wasn't on duty late Sunday night—say from midnight till eight Monday morning—she probably left the keys in her office. I wanted them. If Beecham was on duty, or if she handed over her keys to a night supervisor, then I needed at least two keys: to the Hall and to the research lab. If those were impossible to obtain, then Mary Thorndecker would have to let me in from the inside of the nursing home, and I'd have to get into the lab by myself, somehow.

It took me a long time to detail all this, and I wondered if she was listening. She was. She said dully: "You're going to break in?"

"Yes. I'm going to find out about those cancer deaths."

"You're going to get the evidence?"

I felt like weeping. But I had no compunction, none whatsoever, about using this poor, disturbed woman.

"Yes," I said, "I'm going to get the evidence."

In my own ears, it sounded as gamy and cornball as if I had said, "I'm going to grab the boodle and take it on the lam."

"All right," she said firmly, "I'll help you."

We went over it again in more detail: what I wanted, what she could get, what we might have to improvise.

"How will you get over the fence?" she asked.

"Leave that to me."

"You won't hurt anyone, will you?"

"Of course not. I don't carry a gun or a knife or any other weapon. I'm not a violent man, Mary."

"All you want is information?"

"Exactly," I said, nodding virtuously. "Just information. Part of my investigation of Thorndecker's application for a grant."

That seemed to satisfy her. Made the whole scam sound more legal.

We left it like this: she was to collect as much of what I wanted as she could, and on Sunday she was to call me at the Coburn Inn.

"Don't give your real name to the switchboard," I warned her. "Just in case they ask who's calling. Use a phony name."

"What name?"

"Joan Powell," I said instantly, without thinking. "Say your name is Joan Powell. If I'm at the Inn, don't mention any of this over the phone. Just laugh and joke and make a date to meet me somewhere. Anywhere. Right here would be fine; it's deserted enough. Then we'll meet, and you can tell me what you've found out. And give me the keys if you've been able to get them."

"What if I call the Coburn Inn, and you're not there?"

"Call every hour on the hour. Sooner or later I'll be there. Any time before midnight on Sunday. Okay?"

We went over the whole thing once more. I wasn't sure she was getting it. She was still white as paper, and every once in awhile her whole body would shudder in a hard fit of trembling. But I spoke as quietly and confidently as I could. And I kept touching her. Her hand, arm, shoulder. I think I made contact.

Just before I got out of the car, I leaned forward to kiss her smooth, chill cheek.

"Tell me everything's going to be all right," she said faintly.

"Everything's going to be all right," I said.

I knew it wasn't.

I drove back to Coburn as fast as Hanrahan's rattletrap would take me. I kept watching for a public phone booth. I had a call to make, and didn't want it to go through the hotel switchboard. My paranoia was growing like "The Blob."

I found a booth on Main Street, just before the business section started. I knew the offices of the Bingham Foundation were closed on Saturday, so I called Stacy Besant at his home, collect. He lived in a cavernous nine-room apartment on Central Park West with an unmarried sister older than he, three cats, a moth-eaten poodle, and a whacking great tank of tropical fish.

Edith Besant, the sister, answered the phone and agreed to accept the call.

"Samuel!" she caroled. "This *is* nice. Stacy and I were speaking of you just last night, and agreed you must come to us for dinner as soon as you return to New York. You and that lovely lady of yours."

"Well, ah, yes, Miss Edith," I said. "I certainly would enjoy that. Especially if you promise to make that carrot soup again."

"Carrot vichyssoise, Samuel," she said gently. "Not soup."

"Of course," I said. "Carrot vichyssoise. I remember it well."

I did, too. Loathsome. But what the hell, she was proud of it.

We chatted of this and that. It was impossible to hurry her, and I didn't try. So we discussed her health, mine, her brother's, the cats', the poodle's, the fishes'. Then we agreed the weather had been miserable.

"Well, my goodness, Samuel," she said gaily, "here we are gossiping away, and I imagine you really want a word with Stacy."

"Yes, ma'am, if I could. Is he there?"

"Of course he is. Just a minute."

He came on so quickly he must have been listening on the extension.

"Yes, Samuel?" he said. "Trouble?"

"Sir," I said, "there are some questions I need answers to. Medical questions. I'd like to call Scientific Research Records and speak to one of the men who worked on the Thorndecker investigation."

"Now?" he asked. "This minute? Can't it go over to Monday?"

"No, sir," I said. "I don't think it can. Things are moving rather rapidly here."

There was a moment of silence.

"I see," he said finally. "Very well. Wait just a few minutes; I have the number somewhere about."

I waited in the closed phone booth. It was an iced coffin, and I should have been shivering. I wasn't. I was sweating.

He came back on the phone. He gave me the number of SRR, and the name of the man to talk to, Dr. Evan Blomberg. If SRR was closed on

Saturday, as it probably was, I could call Dr. Blomberg at his home. The number there was—

"Mr. Besant," I interrupted, "I know this is an imposition, but I'm calling from a public phone booth for security reasons, and I just don't have phone credit cards, although I have suggested several times that it would make your field investigators' jobs a lot easier if you—"

"All right, Samuel," he said testily, "all right. You want me to locate Dr. Blomberg and ask him to call you at your phone booth. Is that it?"

"If you would, sir. Please."

"It's that important?"

"Yes," I said. "It is."

"Let me have the number."

I read it off the phone. He told me it would take five minutes. It took more than ten. I was still sweating. Finally the phone shrilled, and I grabbed it off the hook.

"Hello?" I said. "Dr. Evan Blomberg?"

"To whom am I speaking?" this deep, pontifical voice inquired. I loved that "To whom." Much more elegant than, "Who the hell is this?"

I identified myself to his satisfaction and apologized for calling him away from his Saturday relaxation.

"Quite all right," Dr. Blomberg said stiffly. "I understand you have some questions regarding our investigation of the application of Dr. Telford Gordon Thorndecker?"

"Well, ah, in a peripheral way, doctor," I said cautiously. "It's just a general question. A general medical question."

"Oh?" he said, obviously puzzled. "Well, what is it?"

I didn't want to say it. It was like asking an astronomer, "Is the moon *really* made of green cheese?" But finally I nerved myself and said:

"Is it possible to infect a human being with cancer? That is, could you, uh, take cancerous cells from one human being who is suffering from some form of the disease and inject them into a healthy human being, and would the person injected then develop cancer?"

His silence sounded more shocked than any exclamation.

"Good God!" he said finally. "Who would want to do a thing like that? For what reason?"

"Sir," I said desperately, "I'm just trying to get an answer to a what-if question. Is it possible?"

Silence again. Then:

"To my knowledge," Dr. Evan Blomberg said in his orotund voice, "it has never been done. For obvious reasons. Unethical, illegal, criminal. And I can't see any possible value to any facet of cancer research. I suppose it might be theoretically possible."

Try to get a Yes or No out of a scientist. Hah! They're as bad as lawyers. Almost.

"Then you could infect someone with cancer cells, and that person would develop cancer?"

"I said theoretically," he said sharply. "As you are undoubtedly aware, experimental animals are frequently injected with cancer cells. Some host animals reject the cells completely. Others accept them, the cells flourish, the host animal dies. In other words, *some* animals have an immunity to *some* forms of cancer. By extension, I suppose you could speculate that *some* humans might have or develop an immunity to *some* forms of cancer. It is not a chance I'd care to take."

"I can understand that, Dr. Blomberg, but—"

"Different species of animals are used for different kinds of cancer research, depending on how similar they are to humans insofar as the way they react to specific types of cancer. Rats, for instance, are used in leukemia research."

"Yes, Dr. Blomberg," I said frantically, "I can appreciate all that. Let's just call this speculation. That's all it is: speculation. What I'm asking is if healthy humans are infected with cancer cells from a diseased human, will the healthy host develop cancer?"

"Speculation?" he asked carefully.

"Just speculation," I assured him.

"I'd say the possibility exists."

"Possibility?" I repeated. "Would you go so far as to say 'probability'?"

"All right," he said resignedly. "Since we're talking in theoretical terms, I'm willing to say it's probable the host human will develop cancer."

"One final question," I said. "We have been talking about injecting a healthy human host with cancerous cells from a live but diseased human donor. You've said it's probable the host would develop cancer. Does the same hold true of abnormal cells that have been cultivated *in vitro*?"

"Good God!" he burst out again. "What kind of a nightmare are you talking about?"

I wouldn't let him off the hook. "Would it be possible to infect a healthy human being with cancerous cells that have been grown *in vitro*?"

"Yes, goddammit," he said furiously, "it would be possible."

"In fact—probable?" I asked softly. "That you could infect a healthy human being with cancerous cells grown in a lab?"

"Yes," he said, in such a low voice that I could hardly hear him. "Probable."

"Thank you, Dr. Blomberg," I said, hung up gently and wondered if I had spoiled his weekend. The hell with him. Mine was already shot.

I drove the rest of the way into Coburn, reflecting that now I knew it could be done, what Mary Thorndecker feared. But why? *Why?* As Blomberg had said, who would want to do a thing like that? For what reason?

The Grand Prix was waiting for me in the parking lot of the Coburn Inn. Not only had it been equipped with new radials, but the car had been washed and waxed. I walked around it, kicking the tires with delight. But gently! Then I transferred my new purchases from the pickup to the trunk of the Pontiac.

In the lobby, a tall, skinny gink with "Mike's Service Station" stitched on the back of his coveralls was leaning over the cigar counter, inspecting Millie Goodfellow's cleavage with a glazed stare. He had a droopy nose and looked like a pointer on scent. Any minute I expected him to raise a paw and freeze.

I interrupted their tête-à-tête—and guessing the subject of their conversation, that's the only phrase for it. I asked the garageman about the bill for the tires and wax job. He said Betty Hanrahan had picked up the tab; I didn't owe a cent. I handed him a ten for his trouble, and he looked at it.

"Jesus, Mr. Todd," he said, "Betty told me I wasn't to take any money from you *a*-tall. She find out about this, she'll bite my ass."

He and Millie laughed uproariously. At last—Coburn humor. The hell with the quality; people were laughing, and after the way I had spent the last two hours, that was enough for me.

"I won't tell Betty if you don't," I said. "Can you get her pickup back to the Red Dog?"

"Sure," he said happily. "No problem. Hey, Millie, I'm a rich man now. Buy you a drink tonight?"

"I'll be there," she nodded. "For the ten, you can look but don't touch."

He said something equally as inane, and they gassed awhile. It was that kind of raunchy sexual chivying you hear between a man and woman who have been friends a long time and know they'll never go to bed together. I listened, smiling and nodding like an idiot.

Because I can't tell you how comforting it was. Their smutty jokes were so *normal*. There was nothing deep, devious, or depraved about it. It had nothing to do with cancerous cells and fluorescent tumors. No one dying in agony and pushed into frosted ground. That stupid conversation restored a kind of tranquillity in me; that's the only way I can describe it. I felt like an infantryman coming off the front line and being handed a fresh orange. Fondling it, smelling it, tasting it. Life.

I waved goodby and went up to my room. I had an hour to kill before my meeting with Dr. Thorndecker. I didn't want to eat or drink. I just wanted to flop on my bed, dressed and booted, and think about the man and wonder why he was doing what he was.

I think that investigators work on the premise that most people act out of self-interest. The kicker is that a lot of us don't know, or can't see, our true self-interest. Case in point: my breaking up with Joan Powell. I thought I acted out of concern for my own well-being. All I got was a galloping attack of the guilts and a growing realization that I had tossed away a relationship that was holding me together.

What was Telford Gordon Thorndecker's self-interest—or what did he *think* it was? Not merely avarice, since Mary had said the lab didn't profit from the deaths of many of the victims. Then it had to be some kind of human experimentation that might result in professional glory. A different kind of greed.

I tried that on for motive. Mary had reported that Dr. Draper had said Thorndecker was a genius on the verge of a great discovery. Thorndecker himself had admitted to me that human immortality was his true goal. So far the glory theory made sense. Until I asked myself why he was injecting cancer-free patients with abnormal cells. Then the whole thing fell apart. The only fame you achieve by that is on the wall of a post office.

The man was such a fucking enigma to me. Inspired scientist. Paterfamilias. Skilled business administrator. Handsome. Charming. Energetic. And remote. Not only from me, I was convinced, but from wife, children, friends, staff, Coburn, the world. Either he had something everyone else was lacking, or he lacked something everyone else had. Or perhaps both.

Have you ever seen one of those intricately carved balls of ivory turned out by Oriental craftsmen? It only takes about ten years to make. The artist starts with a solid sphere of polished ivory. The outer shell is carved with fanciful open designs, and within a smaller sphere is cut free to revolve easily. That second ball is also carved with a complex open design, and a third smaller ball cut free to revolve. And so on. Until, at the center, is a ball no larger than a pea, also intricately incised. Spheres within spheres. Designs within designs. Worlds within worlds. The carving so marvelously complicated that it's almost impossible to make out the inscription on that pea in the center.

That was Dr. Telford Gordon Thorndecker.

Who had carved him?

But all that was purple thinking, ripe fancy. When I came back to earth, all I saw was a big man standing in the shadows, watching his young wife's bangled ankle flashing in the back of a cop's cruiser. And the man's face showing no defeat.

An hour later I was on my way out to Crittenden again. The only pleasure I had in going was being behind the wheel of the Grand Prix. After bruising my kidneys in Betty Hanrahan's junk heap, the Pontiac's ride felt like a wallow in a feather bed. I took it up to seventy for a minute or two, just to remind myself what was under the hood. The car even smelled good to me. More important, the heater worked.

I had no trouble at the gate. The guard came out of his hut when I gave the horn a little *beep.* Apparently he recognized the car; he didn't ask for identification. I watched his routine carefully. He had a single key attached by a chain to a length of wood. He opened the tumbler lock. The gates swung inward. After I drove through, I glanced in my rearview mirror.

He swung the gates back into place, locked up, went back into his hut. He was a slow-moving older man wearing a pea jacket. No gun that I could see. But of course it could have been under the jacket or in the hut.

I didn't like the idea of those iron gates opening inward. I would have preferred they swung outward, in case I had to bust through in a hasty exit. But you can't have everything. Some days you can't have *anything*.

The gate guard must have called, because when I got to the front door of the Crittenden Research Laboratory, Dr. Kenneth Draper was waiting for me. He looked like a stunned survivor. He was staring at me, but I wasn't sure he saw me.

"Dr. Draper," I said, "you all right?"

He came out of his trance with a slight shake of his head, like someone trying to banish an ugly dream. Then he gave me a glassy smile and held out his hand.

He was wearing a white laboratory coat. There were dark brown stains down the front. I didn't even want to wonder about those. His hand, when I clasped it, was cold, damp, boneless. I think he tried to press my fingers, but there was no strength in him. His face was white as chalk, and as dusty. When he led me inside, his walk was stumbling and uncertain. I thought the man was close to collapse. I didn't think he'd suddenly fall over, but I had an awful vision of him going down slowly, melting, joints loose and limbs rubber. Then he'd end up sitting on the floor, knees drawn up, head down on his folded arms, and weeping softly.

But he made it up to the second floor, painfully, dragging himself hand over hand on the banister. I asked him if many staff were working on Saturday. I asked him if his research assistants worked through the weekend. I asked him if lab employees worked only daylight hours, or was there a night shift. I don't think he heard a word I said. I know he didn't answer.

So I looked around, peeked into the big laboratories. There were a few people at the workbenches, a few peering through microscopes. But not more than a half-dozen. The entire building had the tired silence of a Saturday afternoon, everything winding down and ready to end.

Draper led me to the frosted glass door of one of the small private labs. He knocked. No answer. He knocked again, louder this time, and called, "Dr. Thorndecker. Mr. Todd is here." Still no reply.

"Maybe he fell asleep," I said, as cheerfully as I could. "Or stepped out."

"No, no," Dr. Draper said. "He's in there. But he's very, uh, busy, and sometimes he . . . Dr. Thorndecker! Mr. Todd is here."

No one answered from inside the room. It was getting embarrassing, and just a little spooky. We could see lights burning through the frosted glass door, and I thought I heard the sounds of small movements.

Finally Draper hiked the skirt of his lab coat, fished in his pants pocket, and came out with a ring of keys which he promptly dropped on the floor.

He stooped awkwardly, recovered them, and pawed them nervously, trying to find the one he wanted. He unlocked the door, pushed it open cautiously, peeked in. My view was blocked.

"Wait here," Draper said. "Please. Just for a moment."

He slipped in, closed the door behind him. I was left standing alone in the corridor. I didn't know what was going on. I couldn't even guess. I didn't think about it.

Draper came out in a minute. He gave me a ghastly smile.

"Dr. Thorndecker will see you now," he said.

He brushed closely past me. I caught an odor coming from him, and wondered if it was possible to smell of guilt.

The laboratory was small, with minimal equipment: a blackboard, workbench, a fine compound microscope, stacks of books and papers, a slide projector and screen, a TV monitor.

Dr. Telford Gordon Thorndecker was seated in a metal swivel chair behind a steel desk. He didn't rise when I entered, nor did he smile or offer to shake hands. He was wearing a laboratory coat like Draper's, but his was starched and spotless. In addition, he was wearing white cloth gloves with long, elasticized gauntlets that came to his elbows.

I did not think the man looked well. His face was pallid, but with circles of hectic flush high on his cheeks, and lips almost a rosy red. I think what startled me most was that his head was covered with a circular white cloth cap, similar to the type worn by surgeons. But the cap did not cover his temples, and it was apparent that Thorndecker was losing his hair in patches; the sideburns I remembered as full and glossy were almost totally gone.

But that resonant baritone voice still had its familiar boom.

"What is of paramount importance," he said sternly, "is the keeping of careful, accurate, and detailed records. That is what I have been doing: bringing my journal up to the present, to this very minute."

"Yes," I said. "May I sit down, Dr. Thorndecker?"

He gestured toward the book in which he had been writing. It was a handsome volume bound in buckram.

"More than two hundred of these," he said. "Covering every facet of my professional career from the day I entered medical school."

I slid quietly into the tubular chair alongside his desk. He was looking down at the journal, and I couldn't see his eyes. But his voice was steady, and his hands weren't trembling.

"Dr. Thorndecker," I said, "I have a few questions concerning your work here at the research lab."

"Two hundred personal diaries," he mused. "A lifetime. I remember a professor—who was he?—telling us how important it was to keep precise notes. So that if something should happen, an accident, the work could be continued. Nothing would be lost."

Then he raised his eyes to look at me. I saw nothing unusual in the pupils but it seemed to me the whites were clouded, with a slight bluish cast, like spoiled milk.

"Mr. Todd," he said, "I appreciate your coming by. I regret I have not been able to spend more time with you during your visit, but I have been very involved with projects here at the lab. Plus the day-to-day routine of Crittenden Hall, of course."

"Dr. Thorndecker, when I spoke to you on the phone this morning, you seemed excited about a potential breakthrough in your work, a development of considerable importance."

He continued to stare at me. His face was totally without expression.

"A temporary setback," he said. "These things happen. Anyone in scientific research learns to live with disappointment. But we are moving in the right direction; I am convinced of that. So we will pick ourselves up and try a new approach, a different approach. I have several ideas. They are all here." He tapped the open pages of his journal. "Everything is here."

"Does this concern the X Factor, Dr. Thorndecker? Isolating whatever it is in mammalian cells that causes aging and determines longevity?"

"Aging . . . " he said.

He swung slowly in his swivel chair and stared at the blackboard across the room. My eyes followed his gaze. The board had been recently erased. I could see, dimly, the ghost of a long algebraic equation and what appeared to be a few words in German.

"Of course," he said, "we begin dying at birth. A difficult concept to grasp perhaps, but physiologically sound. I always wanted to be a doctor. Always, for as long as I can remember. Not necessarily to help people. Individually, that is. But to spend my life in medical research. I have never regretted it. Never."

This was beginning to sound like a valedictory, if not a eulogy. I knew I was not going to get answers to specific questions from this obviously troubled man, so I thought it best to let him ramble.

"Aging," he was saying again. "Perhaps rather than study the nature of senescence, we should study the nature of youth. My wife is a very young woman."

I wondered if he would now mention what his wife had told him about my alleged advances. But he made no reference to it. Perhaps he was inured to his wife's infidelities, real or fancied. Anyway, he kept staring at the erased blackboard.

"Are you a religious man, Mr. Todd?"

"No, sir. Not very."

"Nor I. But I do believe in the immortality of the human race."

"The *race*, Dr. Thorndecker? Not the individual?"

But he wasn't listening to me. Or if he was, he disregarded my question.

"Sacrifices must be made," he said quietly. "There can be no progress without pain."

He had me. I knew he was maundering, but the shields were coming down; he was revealing himself to me. I wanted to hear more of the aphorisms by which he lived.

"Did I do wrong to dream?" he asked the air. "You must dare all."

I waited patiently, staring at him. I had an odd impression that the man had shrunk, become physically smaller. He was effectively concealed by the lab coat and long gloves, of course, but the shoulders seemed narrower, the torso less massive. The back was bowed; arms and legs thinner. Perhaps his movements gave the effect of shriveled senescence. They had slowed, stiffened. The exuberant energy, so evident at our first meeting, had vanished. Thorndecker appeared drained. All his life force had leaked out, leaving only a scaly husk and dry memories.

He said nothing for several minutes. Finally I tried to provoke him . . .

"I hope, Dr. Thorndecker, you have no more surprises for me. Like admitting your application to the Bingham Foundation was not as complete as it should have been. I haven't yet decided what to do about that, but I wouldn't care to discover we have been misled in other things as well."

Still he sat in silence, brooding. He looked down at his closed journal, touched the cover with his gloved fingertips.

"I could never take direction," he said. "Never work under another man's command. They were so slow, so cautious. Plodders. They couldn't fly. That's the expression. None of them could fly. I had to be my own man, follow my instincts. What an age to live in. What an age!"

"The past, sir?" I asked. "The present?"

"The future!" he said, brightening for the first time since I had entered the room. "The next fifty years. Oh! Oh! It's all opening up. We're on the edge of so much. We are so close. You'll see it all within fifty years. Human cloning. Gene splicing and complete manipulation of DNA. New species. Synthesis of human blood and all the enzymes. Solution of the brain's mysteries, and mastery of immunology. And here, in my notebooks, the ultimate secret revealed, human life extended—"

But as suddenly as he had become fervent, he dimmed again, seemed to dwindle, retreat, lose his glowing vision of tomorrow.

"Youth," he said, and his voice no longer boomed. "The beauty of youth. She made me so happy and so wretched. On our wedding night we . . . The body. The youthful human body. The design. The way it moves. Its gloss and sweet perfume. A man could spend his life in . . . The taste. Did you know, Draper, that a—"

"Todd, sir," I said. "Samuel Todd."

"A proved diagnostic technique," he said. "Oh yes. Taste the skin. Acidity and—and—all that. So near. So close. Another year perhaps. Two, at most. And then . . . "

"You think it will be that soon, sir?"

"Please let me," he said. "Please."

I had a sudden feeling of shame listening to him. Watching the statue crumble. Nothing was worth witnessing that destruction. I stood abruptly. He looked up at me in surprise.

"Finished?" he said. "Well, I'm glad we've had this little chat, and I'm happy I've been able to answer your questions and clear up your doubts. Could you give me some idea of when the grant might be made?"

He was serious. I couldn't believe it.

"Difficult to say, sir. I turn in my report, and then the final decision is with my superiors."

"Of course, of course. I understand how these things work. Channels, eh? Everything must go through channels. That's why I . . . Forgive me for not seeing you out, Mr. Todd, but—"

"That's perfectly all right."

"So much to do. Every minute of my time."

"I understand. Thank you for all your help."

Again he failed to rise or offer to shake hands. I left him sitting there, staring at an erased blackboard.

I had hoped I might have the chance to snoop around the labs unattended, but Linda Cunningham, Draper's chubby assistant, was waiting for me in the corridor.

"Hi, Mr. Todd," she said brightly. "I'm supposed to show you the way out."

So that was that. I was in the Pontiac, warming the engine, when suddenly Julie Thorndecker was standing alongside the window. I don't know where she came from; she was just there. She was wearing jodhpurs, tweed hacking jacket, a white shirt, ascot, a V-necked sweater. I turned off the ignition, lowered the window.

"Mrs. Thorndecker," I said.

Her face was tight, drawn. Gone were the pouts and moues, the sensuous licking of lips. I glimpsed the woman underneath: hard, wary, merciless.

"We're not getting the grant, are we?" she said.

"For God's sake," I said roughly, "get your husband to a doctor."

"For God's sake," she replied mockingly, "my husband *is* a doctor."

I was in such a somber mood, so confused and saddened, that I didn't trust myself to speak. I watched her put a thumb to her mouth and bite rapidly at the nail, spitting little pieces of matter onto the gravel. I had the feeling that if I could look into her brain, it would not be a cold, gray, convoluted structure; it would be a live lava bed, bubbling and boiling, with puffs of live steam.

"Well," she said finally, "it was nice while it lasted. But all good things must come to an end."

"Also," I said, "a stitch in time saves nine, and a rolling stone gathers no moss."

She looked at me with loathing.

"You're a smarmy bastard," she said, her face ugly. "When are you leaving?"

"Soon. Probably Monday."

"Not soon enough," she said, turning away.

I was less than a mile outside the gates when I passed a Coburn police cruiser heading toward Crittenden. Constable Ronnie Goodfellow was driving. He didn't look at me.

When I got back to Coburn I realized that on the big things, my mind wasn't working. It wouldn't turn over. But on the little things, it was ticking right along. It knew that the next day was Sunday, and liquor stores would be closed. So off I went to Sandy's to pick up a quart of vodka, a fifth of Italian brandy, and a fifth of sour mash bourbon. The vodka and brandy were for me. The sour mash was for Al Coburn. Somehow I figured him for a bourbon man, and I saw us having a few slugs together before digging into that stew he promised. And a few shots after. I also picked up two cold six-packs of Ballantine ale. I reckoned I might need them early Sunday morning.

I carted all these provisions back to the Coburn Inn. I stopped at the desk long enough to ask if there were any messages for me. There weren't, but then I didn't expect any; it was barely 3:30, too early to expect Al Coburn to call. So up I went to 3-F. I put the six-packs out on the windowsill. If they didn't slide off and brain a passing pedestrian, I could count on cold ale for Sunday breakfast. I opened the brandy, and had a small belt with water from the bathroom tap. It tasted so good that I had another to keep it company. Then I fell asleep.

It wasn't that I was tired; it was emotional exhaustion. If I've given you the impression that investigative work is a lark, I've misled you. The physical labor is minimal, the danger is infinitesimal. But what gets you— or rather, what gets *me*—is the agitation of dealing with people. I don't think this is a unique reaction. Doctors, lawyers, psychiatrists, waiters, cab drivers, and shoe clerks suffer from the same syndrome. Anyone who deals with the public.

People exert a pressure, deliberately or unconsciously. They force their wills. Their passion, wants, angers, lies, and fears come on like strong winds. Deal with people, and inevitably you feel you're being buffeted. No, that's no good. You feel like you're in a blender, being sliced, chopped, minced, ground, and pureed.

The problem for me was that I could appreciate the hopes and anxieties of everyone in Coburn I had interviewed. I could understand why they acted the way they did. I could *be* them. And everyone of them made sense to me, in a very human way. They weren't monsters. Cut anyone of them, and they'd bleed. They were sad, deluded shits, and I had such empathy that I just couldn't take any more pain. So I fell asleep. It's the organism's self-defense mechanism: when stress becomes overwhelming, go unconscious. It's the only way to cope.

I awoke, startled, a little after five. It took me a moment to get oriented. It was early December. I was in Coburn, N.Y. I was staying at the Coburn Inn, Room 3-F. My name was Samuel Todd. After that, everything came flooding back. I grabbed up the phone. The desk reported no messages. Al Coburn hadn't called.

I splashed cold water on my face, dried, looked at my image in the bathroom mirror. Forget it. The Monster Who Ate Cleveland. I went downstairs and told the baldy on duty that I'd be in the bar if I got a call. He promised to switch it.

The bar was almost empty. But Millie Goodfellow was sitting alone at one end.

"Join you?" I asked.

"Be my guest," she said, patting the stool alongside her.

She was wearing a white blouse with a ruffled neckline cut down to her two charlotte russe. She had obviously gussied up after getting off work; her hair looked like it had been worked on by a crew of carpenters, and the perfume was strong enough to fumigate a rice warehouse. She was trying.

She drank crazy things like Grasshoppers, Black Russians, and Rusty Nails. That night she was nibbling on something called a Nantucket Sleighride. I don't know exactly what it was, except that it had cranberry juice in it and enough *spiritus frumentum* to give the 2nd Airborne Division a monumental hangover.

I ordered her a new one, and a vodka gimlet for me.

"Millie," I said, gesturing toward her tall glass, "I hope you know what you're doing."

"I don't know," she said, "and I don't care."

"Oh-ho," I said. "It's like that, is it?"

"What are you doing tonight?" she asked.

I took out my cigarettes and offered her one. She shook her head. She waited until I lighted up, then took out her own pack of mentholated filtertips. She put one between her lacquered lips and bent close to me.

"Light my cold one with your hot one," she said.

It was so awful, so *awful*. But obediently, I lighted her cigarette from mine.

"How can you drink those things?" I asked, when Jimmy brought our drinks.

"One is an eye-opener," she said, swinging around to face me, putting a warm hand on my knee. "Two is a fly-opener. Three is a thigh-opener."

Oh God, it was getting worse. But I laughed dutifully.

"You didn't answer my question," she said. "What are you doing tonight?"

"Right now? Waiting for a phone call. Haven't seen Al Coburn around, have you?"

"Not since this morning. You're waiting for a phone call from *him*?"

"That's right. I'm supposed to have dinner with him."

"Instead of *me*?"

"It's business," I said. "I'd rather have dinner with you."

She wasn't mollified.

"*You* say," she sniffed. "What if he doesn't call?"

"Then I guess I better call him. Right now, in fact. Excuse me a minute."

I used the bar phone. It went through the hotel switchboard, but I couldn't see any danger. Anyway, Al Coburn didn't answer. No one answered.

I sat at the bar with Millie Goodfellow for another hour and two more drinks. I called Coburn, and I called him, and I called him. No answer. I was surprised that I wasn't alarmed, until I realized that I never did expect to hear from him.

"Millie," I said, "let's have dinner together. But I've got an errand to run first. Take me maybe an hour. If I can't get back, I'll call you here at the bar. You'll be here?"

"I may be," she said stiffly, "and I may not."

I nodded and turned away. She grabbed my arm.

"You won't stand me up, will you?"

"I wouldn't do that."

"And if you can't make it, you'll call?"

"I promise."

"You promise a lot of things," she said sadly.

That was true.

So there I was, back in the Grand Prix, heading out toward Crittenden for the third time that day. I felt like a commuter. My low beams were on, and I drove slowly and carefully, avoiding potholes and bumps. I had the bottle of bourbon on the seat beside me.

It was a sharp, black night, and when I thought of complaisant Millie Goodfellow waiting for me back in that warm bar, I wondered just what the hell I thought I was doing. I knew what I'd find at Al Coburn's place.

I've read as many detective-mystery-suspense paperbacks as you have—probably more—and there was only one ending to a situation like this:

I'd walk into Coburn's house and find him dead. Bloodily dead. Horribly mutilated maybe, or swinging on a rope from a rafter in a faked suicide. His home would be turned upside down because his killer would have tossed the place for that letter left by Ernie Scoggins.

I knew that was what I'd find. The only reason I was going out was the skinny hope that the old man had done what he promised: left the Scoggins letter or a copy in the glove compartment of his pickup. If he had the strength to withstand the vicious torture he had undergone.

Dramatic? You bet. Maybe I was disappointed, because it wasn't like that at all.

I could have driven past Al Coburn's farmhouse a dozen times without picking it out of the gloom if it hadn't been for that flagpole in the front-yard. Old Glory was hanging listlessly, barely stirring. I pulled into a gravel driveway and looked around. No lights anywhere. And no pickup truck.

I left my headlights beamed against the front door and got out of the car, taking the bourbon with me. I found my new flashlight, switched it on, started toward the house. I got within a few yards before I noticed the door was open. Not yawning wide, but open a few inches.

I pushed the door wider, went in, switched on the lights. It was a surprisingly neat home, everything clean and dusted. Not luxurious, but comfortable and tidy. And no one had turned it upside down in a futile search.

I didn't find the Scoggins letter. I didn't find evidence of murder most foul. I didn't find Al Coburn either. I found nothing. Just a warm, snug home with an unlocked door. I went through it slowly and carefully, room to room. I looked in every closet and cupboard. I poked behind drapes and got down on my knees to peer under beds and couches. I opened the trap to the unfinished attic and beamed my flashlight around in there. Ditto the half-basement.

Nothing.

No, not quite nothing. In the kitchen, on an electric range, a big cast-iron pot of stew was simmering. It smelled great. I turned off the light.

I went outside and made three circuits of the house, each one a little farther out. I found nothing. I saw nothing that might indicate what had happened to Al Coburn. He was just gone, vanished, disappeared. I came back into the house and lifted his phone. It was working normally. I called the Coburn Inn, identified myself, asked if anyone had called me. No one had.

I stood there, in the middle of the silent living room, looking around dazedly at the maple furniture with the cretonne-covered cushions. "Al Coburn!" I yelled. "Al Coburn!" I screamed. "Al Coburn!" I howled.

Nothing.

I think the quiet of that empty house spooked me more than a crumpled corpse. It was so like what had happened to Ernie Scoggins: now you see him, now you don't. Only in this case there wasn't even a blood-stained rug as a tipoff. There was nothing but a pot of stew simmering on a lighted range.

What could I do—call the cops and tell them a man hadn't phoned me as he promised? Ask for a search, an investigation? And then have Al Coburn waltz in with two quarts of beer he had gone to buy for our dinner?

But I knew, I *knew*, Al Coburn was never going to waltz in on me or anyone else, that night or any night. He was gone. He was just gone. How it had been managed I couldn't figure. It had to be some kind of a scam to get him out of the house. To get rid of him and his pickup truck. If the man he met had threatened, Al Coburn would have fought; I was convinced of that. And I would have found evidence of violence instead of just a pot of simmering stew. So he had been tricked. Maybe he had been conned to drive his truck himself to some other meeting place, some deserted place. And there . . .

I left the unopened bottle of bourbon in the kitchen. To propitiate the Gods? I turned off the lights inside the house. I closed the door carefully. I looked up at the flag still drooping from the staff. Patriotic Al Coburn. His folks had founded the town.

Then I drove slowly back into Coburn.

When I entered the lobby of the Inn, a gaggle of permanent residents was clustered about the desk, chattering excitedly. As I walked by, the clerk called out, "Hey, Mr. Todd, hear the news? They just found Al Coburn and his truck in the river. He's deader'n a doornail."

They had heard about it in the bar. "You won't be having dinner with Al Coburn," Millie Goodfellow said. "No," I said. "He probably had one too many and just drove in," Jimmy said. "Yes," I said. "Another gimlet?" he asked. "Make it a double," I said. "Just vodka. On the rocks."

That's where I was—on the rocks. I won't pretend to remember all the details of that Walpurgisnacht. But that's how it began—on the rocks. Millie and I drank at the Coburn Inn for another hour or two. I wanted her husband to come in and catch us together. I don't know why. I think I had some childish desire to bend his nose.

"Why don't we go out to Red Dog Betty's for dinner?" Millie suggested.

"Splendid idea."

I drove, and not too badly. I mean I wasn't swarming all over the road, and I didn't exceed the limit by more than five or ten. Millie snuggled against me, singing, "You Light Up My Life." That was okay with me. I might even have joined in. Anything to keep from thinking.

Betty's joint was crowded, but she took one look at us, and hastily shoved us into a booth in a far dining area.

"Get your car all right?" she asked me.

"Did indeed," I said. "For which much thanks."

I leaned forward to kiss her.

"If you can ditch Miss Tits," she said, "I'll be around."

"Hey, wait a minute," Millie protested, "I saw him first."

Betty Hanrahan goosed her, and went back to the bar. Millie and I ordered something: skirt steaks I think they were. And we drank. And we danced. I saw people from Crittenden, including Linda Cunningham. I waved at her. She stuck her tongue out at me. I like to think it was more invitation than insult.

We kept chomping a few bites, finishing our drinks, then rushing back to the dance floor when someone played something we liked on the juke. Millie was a close-up dancer. I mean she was *close*.

"Carry a Coke bottle in your pocket?" she asked.

"Something like that."

"Come on," she yelled gaily in my ear. "Have fun!"

"Sure," I said.

So I had fun. I really did. I drank up a storm. Told hilariously funny stories. Asked Betty Hanrahan to marry me. Sang the opening verse of "Sitting One Night in Murphy's Bar." Bought drinks for Linda Cunningham's table. And threw up twice in the men's room. Quite a night.

Millie Goodfellow must have seen worse. Anyway, she stuck with me: conduct above and beyond the call of duty. She'd leave occasionally to dance with a trucker she knew, or with the tall, skinny gink from Mike's Service Station. But she always came back to me.

"You're so good to me," I told her, wiping my brimming eyes.

"You're not going to pass out on me, are you?" she asked anxiously.

Betty Hanrahan came back to persuade me to switch to beer. I agreed, but only, I told her, because she had bought me four "radical" tires. I may have kissed her again. I was in a kissing mood. I kissed Millie Goodfellow. I kissed Linda Cunningham. I wanted to kiss the black bartender, but he said he was busy.

Millie drove us back to Coburn.

"What a super car," she said.

"Super," I said.

"You need some black coffee," she said.

"Super," I said. "Millie, you drop me at the Inn, and then you go home."

"You really want me to go home?"

"No," I said.

"Super," she said.

It was then, I estimate, about 2:00 A.M. The lobby of the Coburn Inn was deserted, but the bar was still open. Millie sat me down in one of the spavined armchairs and disappeared. I sat there, content and giggling, until she returned with a cardboard container of black coffee. She helped me to my feet.

"Up we go," she said.

"Up we go," I said.

We took the stairs. It didn't take long, no more than a month or so, but eventually we arrived in Room 3-F. Millie locked the door behind us.

"Madam," I said haughtily, "do you intend to seduce me?"

"Yes," she said.

"Excuse me," I said suddenly, grabbed the black coffee, ran for the bathroom, and just did make it. I had let myself think about Al Coburn. So I threw up for the third time that night. Brushed my teeth. Showered. For some reason I'll never know, washed my hair and shaved. Finished the coffee. Put on a towel. Came out feeling mildly human. Millie Goodfellow was still there.

"You've very patient," I told her. "For a seductress."

"I found the brandy," she said cheerfully. "It's very good. Want one?"

"Do I ever!" I said.

She was using my sole glass, so I drank from the bottle. Not elegant, but effective.

"I'm sorry," I told her.

"What for? You weren't so bad."

"Bad enough. Did I pay the tab at Betty's?"

"Of course you did. And left too much tip."

"It couldn't have been too much," I groaned. "Betty and I are still friends?"

"She loves you."

"And I love her. Nice lady."

"Who was the little butterball you were slobbering over?"

"Linda Cunningham? She works at the Crittenden lab."

"You like her?"

"Sure. She's nice."

"You love her?"

"Come on, Millie. Tonight was the third time I've seen her. Just an acquaintance."

"I'm jealous."

I picked up her hand and kissed her fingertips.

"I like that," I said, grinning. "You jealous! You've got every guy in Coburn popping his suspenders."

"It's just a game," she said. "You play the game, and you get the name."

"And don't do the crime if you can't do the time."

"That's very true," she said seriously.

There I was in my towel. She was still fully clothed, sitting rather distantly in one of the sprung armchairs. I poured her another brandy.

"I talked to Al Coburn just this morning," I said. "Hearing he was dead hit me hard."

"I figured," she said. "You okay now?"

"Oh sure. I'm even sober. Sort of."

"I am, too," she said. "Sort of. I think Ronnie's going to leave me."

I tilted the brandy bottle again. I wasn't gulping. I was tonguing the opening. Little sips. It was helping.

"What makes you think that?" I asked her.

"I just know," she said. "A woman's instinct," she said virtuously.

"Well . . . if he does, how do you feel about it?"

"It's that chippy," she burst out. "It's because of her."

"Julie? Julie Thorndecker?"

"She'll be the end of him." Millie Goodfellow said. "He's pussy-whipped. If he wanted to leave me for some nice, sweet homebody who likes to cook, I could understand it, and wish him the best. But that hoor? She'll finish him.''

I looked at her with awe. You never know people. Never. You think you've got them analyzed and tagged. You think you know their limits. Then they surprise you. They stagger you and stun you. They have depths, complexities you never even imagined. Here was this nutty broad mourning her husband's infidelity, not for her own injury, but because of the pain he would suffer. I admired her.

"Well, Millie," I said, "I don't think there's a thing you can do about it. He's got to make his own mistakes."

"I suppose so," she said, staring into her glass of brandy. "If I come to New York, could you do anything for me? I don't mean money—nothing like that. I mean introduce me to people. Tell me how to go about getting a job. Would you do that?"

"Of course," I said bravely.

"Oh hell," she said, shaking her head. "Who am I kidding? I'll never leave Coburn. You know why?"

"Why?"

"Because I'm scared. I watch television. I see all these young, pretty, bright girls. I'm not like that. I sell cigarettes at the Coburn Inn. They could put in a coin machine, but I bring guys around to eat in the restaurant and drink at the bar. Think I don't know it? But I'm safe here. I'll never leave. I might dream about it, but I know I'll never leave. I'll die in Coburn."

I groaned. I went down on my knees, put my head in her lap. I took up her hand again, kissed her palm.

"You'll be nice to me, won't you?" she asked anxiously. It was a pleading, little girl's voice. "Please be nice."

I nodded.

From the way she dressed and the way she came on, I expected her to be sex with four-wheel drive, a heaving, panting combination of Cleopatra, Catherine the Great, and the Dragon Lady. But she undressed with maidenly modesty, switching off all the bedroom lamps first, leaving only the bathroom light burning with the door open just wide enough to cast long shadows across the softly illuminated bed.

She turned her back to me when she took off her clothes. I think she was humming faintly. I watched her in amazement. She didn't come diving eagerly between the sheets like a chilled swimmer entering a heated pool. She slid in next to me demurely, her back still turned. All cool indifference.

I pulled her over to face me.

"Be nice," she kept murmuring. "Please be nice."

That Picasso clown makeup ended at her neck. On almost a straight line. Above was the painted, weathered, used face of a woman who's been through the mill twice: seams and wrinkles, crow's feet and puckers, worried eyes and a swollen, hungry mouth. She looked like she had been picked up by the heels and dipped in age.

But below the pancake makeup line, from neck to toes, her body was fruit, as fresh and as juicy. It was a revelation. She was made of peach skin and plum pulp: a goddamned virgin.

"Millie," I said. "Oh Millie . . ."

"Please be nice," she said.

Nice? I was in bed with a white marble Aphrodite, a faintly veined Venus. Having sex with her was like slashing a Rubens or taking a sledge to a Michelangelo. Screwing that woman was sheer vandalism.

I made love to her like an archeologist, being ever so careful. I didn't want to break or mar anything. After a while she lay on her back, closed her eyes, and stopped saying, "Be nice," for which I was thankful. But she gave me no hint, no clue as to what I might do that would bring her pleasure. She made small sounds and small movements. If she felt anything, it was deep, deep, and there were few outer indications that she might not be falling asleep.

It became evident that I could do anything to her or with her, and she would slackly submit. Not from desire or unendurable passion, but simply because this was what one did on Saturday night in Coburn, N.Y., after a drunken dinner at Red Dog Betty's. It was ritual.

But something happened to me. I think it was caused by the texture of her skin: fine-pored, tight and soft, firm and yielding. Joan Powell had skin like that, and holding a naked Millie Goodfellow in my arms, putting lips and tongue to her warm breast, I thought of Powell.

"Aren't you going to *do* anything?" she breathed finally.

So I knew that if I did not *do* something, Europe would be the less. She expected tribute; denial would have demolished what little ego survived. Almost experimentally, and certainly deliberately, I began a long, whispered hymn of love.

"Oh Millie," I declaimed into her ear, "I've never seen a woman like you. Your body is so beautiful, so beautiful. Your breasts are lovely, and here, and here. I want to eat your sweetness, take all of you into me. This waist! Legs! And here behind your knees. So soft, so tender. This calf. These toes . . ."

On and on. And as I reassured her, she came alive. Her magnificent body warmed, began to twist and writhe. Her sounds became stronger, her pulse beat more powerfully, and she pressed to me.

"How lovely," I carried on, "how wonderful. You have a perfect body. Perfect! Never have I seen nipples so long. And this slender waist! Look, I can almost put my hands around it. And down here. So warm, so warm and loving."

It wasn't my caresses, I knew. It was the con, the scam. Is it so awful to be wanted? She awoke as if my words were feathers between her thighs. Her eyes opened just a bit, wetly, and I thought she might be weeping from happiness.

"Don't stop," she told me. "Please don't stop."

So I continued my sexual gibberish as she became fevered and bursting beneath me. In all things I was gentle, and hoped it was what she meant by, "Be nice." And all the time, delivering my cocksman's spiel, I was remembering Joan Powell, tasting *her* skin, kissing *her* skin, biting *her* skin. I loved Millie Goodfellow, and loving her, loved Joan Powell more.

I'll never understand what it's all about.

The Seventh Day

I guess it was the clanking of the radiator that woke me up Sunday morning. Of course it might have been the clanking in my head, but I didn't think so; I wasn't hissing and spitting.

It was nice in that cocoon of warmed sheets and wool blankets. For the second time since I arrived in Coburn, I debated the wisdom of staying there for the rest of my life. I could pay Sam Livingston to bring me bologna sandwiches and take away the bedpan. What I had to do that day offered no hope of jollity. Maybe it's a sign of age (maturity?) when the future holds less than the past.

I turned to look at the other pillow, still bearing the dent of Millie Goodfellow's architectural hairdo. I leaned across to sniff. It still smelled of her scent but, faded, it didn't seem as awful as it had the night before. Now it seemed warm, fragrant, and very, very intimate. I kissed the pillow like a demented poet.

We had dressed shortly before what laughingly passes for dawn in Coburn, N.Y., and I had escorted Millie down to her car in the parking lot. An affecting parting. We clung to each other and said sappy things. It wasn't the world's greatest love affair—just a vigorous one-night stand—but we liked each other and had a few laughs.

Then I had returned to my nest for five good hours of dreamless sleep. When I awoke, other than that crown of thorns (pointed inward) I was wearing, the carcass seemed in reasonably efficient condition: heart pumping, lungs billowing, all joints bending in the proper direction. Bladder working A-OK; I tested it. Then I rescued a cold ale from the windowsill. See how rewarding careful planning can be?

Sat sprawled naked, sipping my breakfast calories, and tried to remember what goofy things I had done the night before. But then I gave up on the self-recriminations. I've played the fool before, and will again. You'd be surprised at how comforting that acknowledgment can be.

Finished the ale, went in to shave and discovered I had shaved the night before. In fact, at about two in the morning. Beautiful. So I showered and dressed, happy to feel the headache fading to a light throb. Went to the window again, not expecting to see the sun, and didn't. Had another chilled ale while planning the day's program. I didn't want to stray too far from the hotel in case Mary Thorndecker called. But there was one thing I decided I had to do: try to convince the local cops to let me take a look at Al Coburn's pickup truck, especially the glove compartment. It wasn't a job I was looking forward to, but I figured I had to make the try.

Went down to the lobby to discover the restaurant and bar didn't open until 1:00 P.M. I decided that a day-long fast wouldn't hurt me. After my behavior the night before, maybe a week-long penance would be more appropriate.

Sam Livingston came to my rescue. He found me in the lobby, trying to get a newspaper out of a coin machine. Sam showed me where to kick it. Not only did you get your newspaper, but your money came back. Then I accepted his invitation to join him in his basement apartment for coffee and a hunk of Danish.

It was snug in that warm burrow, and the coffee was strong and hot. We sat at the little table with the ice cream parlor chairs, drank our coffee, chewed Danish, and grunted at each other. It wasn't till the second cup and second cigarette that we started talking. That may have been because this wise old man was putting a dollop of the 12-year-old Scotch in the drip brew. Coffee royal. Nothing like it to unglue the tongue on a frosty Sunday morning.

"I keep hearing things," he told me.

"Voices?" I asked idly.

"Nah. Well . . . them too. I was talking about gossip."

"Thought you didn't believe in gossip?"

"Don't," he said stoutly. "But this was about something you asked me, so I listened."

"What did you hear?"

He poured us each a little more coffee, a little more whiskey. It was warming, definitely warming. The headache was gone. I began to expand.

"I should have been a detective," he said. "Like you."

"I'm not a detective; I'm an investigator."

"There's a difference?"

"Sometimes. Sometimes they're the same. But why should you have been a detective?"

"Well, you've got to know that in a place small like this, we ain't got too much to talk about. Small town; small talk. Like Mrs. Cimenti had her hair dyed red. Aldo Bates bought a new snow shovel. Fred Aikens bounced a bad check at Red Dog Betty's. Little things like that.''

"So? What did you hear?''

"On Friday, one of the regulars here told me he stood behind Constable Ronnie Goodfellow at the bank, and Goodfellow closed out his account. More'n three hundred dollars. Then that fellow from Mike's Service Station, he told Millie Goodfellow that her husband had brought in their car for a tune-up. Then one of the clerks from Bill's Five-and-Dime happened to mention that Ronnie Goodfellow stopped in and bought the biggest cardboard suitcase they got. Now you put all those things together, and what do you get?''

I grinned at him.

"A trip,'' I said. "Constable Goodfellow is cutting loose.''

"Yeah,'' he said with satisfaction, taking a sip of the coffee royal, "that's what I figured.''

"Thanks for telling me,'' I said. "Any idea where he's going?''

"Nope.''

"Any idea who he's going *with*?''

"Nope, except I know it ain't his wife.''

"Sam,'' I said, "why would Goodfellow go about planning this trip so openly? He must know how people talk in this town. Is it that he just doesn't give a damn?''

That seamed basalt face turned to me. He showed the big, yellowed teeth in what I supposed was intended as a smile. The old eyes stared, then lost their focus, looking inward.

"You know what I figure?'' he said. "I figure it's part what you say: he don't give a damn. But why don't he? I tell you, I think since he took up with that woman—or she took up with him—he ain't been thinking straight. I figure that woman scrambled his brains. Just stirred him up to such a hot-pants state, he don't know if he's coming or going. I hear tell of them two . . . ''

"All right,'' I said, "that fits in with what I've heard. Sam, you think he'd kill for her? You think he'd do murder for a woman he loves?''

He reflected a moment.

"I reckon he would,'' he said finally. Then he added softly, "I did.''

I froze, not certain I had heard him aright.

"You killed for a woman?''

He nodded.

I glanced briefly at his bookcase of romantic novels. I wondered if what he was telling me was fact or fiction. But when I looked at him again, I recognized something I had never before put a name to. That unreadable, inward look. Speaking with a minimum of lip movement. The ability to turn a question. The coldly suspicious, standoffish man-

ner. Friendly enough, genial enough. To a point. Then the steel shutter
came rattling down.

"You've done time," I told him.

"Oh yes," he said. "Eleven years."

"Couldn't have been manslaughter. Murder two?"

He sighed. "My woman's husband. He was a no-good. She wanted
him gone. After awhile, I wanted him gone, too. I'd have done anything
to keep her. Anything. Murder? Sheesh, that wasn't nothing. I'd have
cut my own throat to make her happy. Some women can do that to
you."

"I guess," I said. "Did she wait for you?"

"Not exactly," he said. "She took up with others. Got killed when a
dancehall burned down in Chicago. This happened a long time ago,
whilst I was inside."

He just said it, without rancor. It was something that had happened a
long time back, and he had learned to live with it. Memories blur. Pain
becomes a twinge. Can you remember the troubles you had five years
ago?

"So you think Goodfellow would do it?"

"Oh, he'd do it; no doubt about that. If she said, 'Jump,' he'd just
say, 'How high?' You think he did?"

I started to say yes, started to say I thought Ronnie Goodfellow had
murdered both Ernie Scoggins and Al Coburn. But I shut my mouth. I
had nothing to take to a D.A. Nothing but the sad knowledge of how
a tall, proud Indian cop might become so impassioned by sleek, soft
Julie Thorndecker that the only question he'd ask would be, "How
high?"

We finished our coffee. I thanked Sam Livingston and left. He didn't
rise to see me out. Just waved a hand slowly. When I closed the door,
he was still seated at the table with empty cups and a full ashtray. He
was an old, old man trying vainly to recall a dim time of passion and
resolve.

When I got up to the lobby, the desk clerk motioned me over and
said I had a call at ten o'clock. A Miss Joan Powell had called.

I was discombobulated. Then insanely happy. Joan Powell? How had
she learned where I was? What could she—? Then I remembered: it
was the name Mary Thorndecker was to use.

"Did she say she'd call again?"

"Yes, sir, Mr. Todd. At eleven." He glanced at the wood-cased reg-
ulator clock on the wall behind him. "That'll be about twenty minutes
or so."

I told him I'd be in my room, and asked him to switch the call. Upstairs, I sat patiently, flipping the pages of my Sunday newspaper, not
really reading it or even seeing it. Just turning pages and wondering if
I'd ever meet a woman I'd kill for. I didn't think so. But I don't sup-

pose Sam Livingston or Ronnie Goodfellow ever anticipated doing what
they had done.

I remember meeting a grunt in Vietnam, a very shy, religious guy
who told me that during training he had given the matter a great deal of
painful thought, and had decided that if he got in a firefight, he'd shoot
over the heads of the enemy. He just believed it was morally wrong to
kill another human being.

Then, less than a week after he arrived in Nam, his platoon got
caught in an ambush.

"How long did it take you to change your mind?" I asked him.
"Five minutes?"

"About five seconds," he said sadly.

I grabbed up the phone after the first ring. I might have had my fingers crossed.

"Samuel Todd," I said.

"This is Joan Powell," Mary Thorndecker said faintly. "How are
you, Mr. Todd?"

"Very well, thanks. And you, Miss Powell?"

"What? Oh yes. Fine. I'm going to church this morning. The Episcopal church. The noon service, and I was wondering if you were planning to attend?"

"As a matter of fact, I am. The noon service at the Episcopal church.
Yes, I'll be there."

"Then maybe I'll see you."

"I certainly hope so. Thank you, Miss Powell."

I hung up slowly, and thought about it. I decided she was a brainy
woman. A crowded church service would offer a good opportunity to
talk. There's always privacy in mobs. I glanced at my watch and figured
I had about forty-five minutes to kill.

I wandered out to the vacant streets of Coburn. A drizzle was beginning to slant down from a choked sky. I turned up my collar, turned
down the hat brim. It seemed to me that my boots had been damp for a
week, and soggy pant and sleeve cuffs rubbed rawly. I passed a few
other Sunday morning pedestrians, hunched beneath black umbrellas. I
didn't see any cars moving. The deserted village.

I walked over to River Street, stood at the spot where Ronnie Goodfellow and I had paused a week ago to watch the garbage-clogged water
slide greasily by. Then I turned away and went prowling through the
empty streets. There were some good storefronts beneath the grime. A
few bore the date of construction: 1886, 1912, 1924.

A paint job and clean-up drive would have done wonders for Coburn.
Like putting cosmetics on a corpse. I had told Goodfellow that if history
teaches anything, it teaches change. That people, cities, nations, civili-
zations are born, flourish, die. How fatuous can you get? That may be
the way things are, but knowing it doesn't make it any easier to accept.

Especially when you're a witness to the senescence of what had once been a vital, thriving organism.

Coburn was dying. Unless I had misread the signs, Dr. Telford Gordon Thorndecker was dying. If he went, the village would surely go, for so much of the town's hopes seemed built on his money, his energy, his dreams. They would vanish together, Thorndecker and his Troy.

I shouldn't have felt anything. This place meant nothing to me. It was just a mouldering crossroad on the way to Albany. But once, I suppose, it had been a busy, humming community with brawls and parades, good times, laughter, a sense of growth, and a belief it would last forever. We all think that. And here was Coburn now, the damp and the rot crumbling away brave storefronts and streaking dusty glass.

If this necropolis and the sordid Thorndecker affair meant anything, they persuaded me to feel deeply, cherish more, smell the blooms, see the colors, love, laugh at pinpricks and shrug off the blows. What do the Hungarians say? "Before you have time to look around, the picnic is over." The picnic was ending for Coburn. For Thorndecker. Nothing but litter left to the ants.

I plodded back to the Coburn Inn. I had a sudden vision of this place in twenty years, or fifty. A lost town. No movement. No lights. No voices. Dried leaves and yellowed newspapers blowing down cracked pavements. Signs fading, names growing dim. Everyone moved away or dead. Nothing but the rain, wind, and maybe, by then, a blank and searing sun.

You're as old as you feel? Bullshit. You're as old as you look. And you can't fake youth, not really. The pain is in seeing it go, grabbing, trying to hold it back. No way. Therefore, do not send to ask for whom the ass sinks; it sinks for thee. Forgive me, Joan Powell. I cast you aside not from want of affection, but from fear. I thought by rejecting an older mate I might stay young forever: the Peter Pan of the Western World. Why do we think of the aged as lepers when we are all registered for that drear colony?

So much for Sunday morning thoughts in Coburn, N.Y. Gloomsville-on-the-Hudson. But I met this emotional wrench with my usual courage and steadfastness. I rushed up to Room 3-F and had a stiff belt of vodka before setting out for the noon service at the Episcopal church.

My nutty fantasy of the morning had been the right one: I should have stood in bed.

I was a few minutes late getting to the church. But I wasn't the only one; others were hurrying up the steps, collapsing their umbrellas, taking seats in the rear pews. I stood a moment at the back of the nave, trying to spot Mary Thorndecker. A robed choir was singing "My Faith Is a Mountain," and not badly.

I finally saw her, sitting about halfway down on the aisle. Next to her were Dr. Kenneth Draper, Edward Thorndecker, and Julie. *Julie?!* I couldn't figure out what she was doing there, unless she was screwing the choir.

I noticed Mary was turning her head occasionally, glancing toward the rear of the church, searching for me. I moved over to one side, and the next time she looked in my direction, I raised a hand and jerked a thumb over my shoulder. I thought she nodded slightly. I went back outside. I wasn't about to sit through the service. If Mary could get out while it was going on, so much the better. If not, I'd wait outside until it was over.

I stood on the pillared porch, protected from the rain. I lighted a ciga- rette. The Reverend Peter Koukla had practically said it was a sin to smoke on church grounds. But it wasn't a 100 mm. cigarette, so it was really a *small* sin.

I was leaning against a pillar watching the rain come down—almost as exciting as watching paint dry—when an old guy came around the corner of the church. Another of Coburn's gnarled gaffers. He had to be 70, going on 80. Coburn, I decided, had to be the geriatric capital of the U.S.

This ancient was wearing a black leather cap, rubberized poncho, and black rubber boots. He was carrying a rake and dragging a bushel basket at the end of a piece of soggy rope. He was raking up broken twigs, sodden leaves, refuse, and dumping all the slop in his basket.

When he came close to me, I said pleasantly, "Working on Sunday?"

"What the hell does it look like I'm doing?" he snarled.

It was a stupid question I had asked, so I was willing to endure his ill- humor. I pulled out my pack of cigarettes and held it out to him. He shook his head, but he dropped rake and rope, and climbed the steps to join me on the porch. He fished under his poncho and brought out a blunt little pipe. The shank was wound with dirty adhesive tape. The pipe was already loaded. He lighted it with a wooden kitchen match and blew out an ex- plosion of blue smoke. It smelled like he had filled it with a piece of the wet rope tied to his bushel basket.

"No church service for you?" I said.

"Naw," he said. "I been. See one, you seen 'em all."

"You're not a religious man?" I asked.

"The hell I'm not," he said. He cackled suddenly. "What the hell, it don't cost nothing."

I looked at him with interest. All young people look different; all old people look alike. You see the bony nose, wrinkled lips, burst capillaries. The geezer sucked on his pipe with great enjoyment, looking out at the wet world.

"How come you ain't inside?" he asked.

"Like you," I said, "I been."

"I got no cause to go," he said. "I'm too old to sin. You been sinning lately?"

"Not as much as I want to."

He grunted, and I hoped it was with amusement. At that moment, a religious nut I didn't need.

"You the sexton?" I asked.

"How?"

"Sexton. Church handyman."

"Yeah," he said, "I guess you could say that. Ben Faber."

"Samuel Todd," I said.

His hands were under his poncho. He didn't offer to shake, so I lighted another cigarette and dug my chilled hands back into my trenchcoat pockets.

"You don't live hereabouts?" he said.

"No."

"Just passing through?"

"I hope so."

He grunted again, and then I was certain it was his way of expressing amusement.

"Yeah," he said, "it's a pisser, ain't it? Going down the drain, this town is. Well, I won't be here to see it."

"You're moving?"

"Hell, no," he said, astonished. "But I figure I'll be six feet under before it goes. I'm eighty-four."

"You look younger," I said dutifully.

"Yeah," he said, puffing away. "Eighty-two."

I was amazed at how this chance conversation was going, how it seemed a continuation of my melancholy musings of the morning.

"It doesn't scare you?" I asked him. "The idea of dying?"

He took the pipe out of his mouth long enough to spit off the porch into a border of shrubs tied up in burlap sacks.

"I'll tell you, sonny," he said, "when I was your age, it scared me plenty. But don't worry it; as you get along in years, the idea of croaking gets easier to live with. You see so many people go. Family. Friends. It gets familiar-like. And then, so many of them are shitheads, you figure if they can do it, you can do it. Then too, you just get tired. Nothing new ever happens. You've seen it all before. Wars and accidents. Floods and fires. Marriages. Murders. People dying by the billions, and billions of babies getting born. Nothing new. So just slipping away seems like the most natural thing in the world. Naw, it don't scare me. Pain, maybe. I don't like that. Bad pain, I mean. But as for dying, it's got to be done, don't it?"

"Yes," I said faintly, "it surely does."

He knocked the dottle from his pipe against the heel of his rubber boot. It made a nice mess on the porch, but that didn't seem to bother him. He took out an oilskin pouch, unrolled it, began to load the pipe again, poking the black, rough-cut tobacco into the bowl with a grimy forefinger.

"Want some advice, sonny?" he said.

"Well . . . yeah, sure."

"Do what you want to do," he said between puffs, as he lighted his pipe. "That's my advice to you."

I thought that over a moment, then shook my head, flummoxed.

"I don't get it," I told him. "I always do what I want to do."

The grunts came again. But this time he showed me a mouthful of browned, stumpy teeth.

"The hell you do," he said. "Don't tell me there ain't been things you wanted to do, but then you got to thinking about it. What would this one say? What would that one say? What if this happened? What if that happened? So what you wanted to do in the first place never got done. Ain't that right?"

"Well . . . I guess so. There have been things I wanted to do, and never did for one reason or another."

"I'm telling you," he said patiently. "I'm giving you the secret, and not charging for it neither. What it took me eighty-four years to learn. I ain't got a single regret for what I done in this life. But I'll go to my grave with a whole lot of regrets for things I wanted to do and never did. For one reason or another. Now you remember that, sonny."

"I surely will," I said. "Tell me, Mr. Faber, how long do you figure this service will last?"

"What time you got?"

I glanced at my watch. "About ten to one."

"Should be breaking up any minute now. The Ladies' Auxiliary, they're serving coffee and doughnuts in the basement. Think I'll get me some right now. You coming?"

"No, thanks. I'll stay here."

"Waiting for someone?"

"Yes."

"A woman?"

I nodded.

He cackled again, then clumped down the steps to pick up his rake and rope tow to the wet bushel basket.

"A woman," he repeated. "I don't have to fret about *that* no more. But you remember what I said: you want to do something, you just *do* it."

"I'll remember," I said. "Thanks again."

He grunted, and trudged away in the rain. I watched him go. I wasn't sure what the hell he had been talking about, but somehow I felt better. He had found a kind of peace, and if that's what age brought, it might be a little easier to endure varicose veins, dentures, and a truss.

I moved back toward the doors and heard the swelling sonority of the church organ. A few people came out, buttoning up coats and opening umbrellas. I stood to one side and waited. In a few minutes Mary Thorndecker came flying out, face flushed. The long Persian lamb coat was flapping around her ankles. She was gripping a black umbrella. She grabbed my arm.

"The others are having coffee," she said breathlessly. "I don't think they saw you. I only have a minute."

"All right," I said, taking the umbrella from her and opening it. "Let's go to my car."

"Oh no," she cried. "They may come out and see us."

"This was your idea," I said. "What do you want to do?"

"Let's walk across the street," she said nervously. "Away from the church. Just a block or two. It won't take long."

I took her arm. I held the big umbrella over both of us. We crossed the street and walked away from the church on the opposite sidewalk.

"There are three guards," she said rapidly. "The gate guard, one on duty in the nursing home, and a man with a dog who patrols outside. They come on at midnight. A day shift takes over at eight in the morning."

"No guard in the lab?"

"No. Each building has its own power switches and alarm switches. In the basements of both buildings. The switch boxes are kept locked."

"Shit," I said. "I beg your pardon."

"I can't get Nurse Beecham's keys," she went on. "She hands them over to the night supervisor, a male nurse. He carries them around with him."

"Listen," I said, "I've narrowed it down. There's only one place I want to go, one thing I want to see. Your stepfather's private office. On the second floor of the research laboratory."

"I can't get the keys."

"Sure you can," I said gently. "Dr. Draper has keys to the main lab building and to your stepfather's private lab. Get the keys from Draper."

"But how?" she burst out desperately. "I can't just ask him for them."

"Lie," I told her "Where does Draper live?"

"In Crittenden Hall. He has a little apartment. Bedroom, sitting room, bathroom."

"Good," I said. "Wake him up about two o'clock tomorrow morning. Tell him Thorndecker is working late in Crittenden Hall and wants his journal from the lab. Tell him anything. You're a clever woman. Make up some excuse, but get the keys."

"He'll want to get the journal himself."

"Not if you handle it right. Just get the keys. By fifteen minutes after two, I'll be inside the fence. I'll be waiting at the back entrance to the research lab. The door at the end of that covered walk that comes down the hill from the nursing home."

She didn't say anything, but I felt her shiver under my hand. I thought I might have thrown it at her too fast, so I slowed down and went over it once again. Get the keys from Draper at 2:00 A.M. Let me into the lab at 2:15.

"I'm not going to steal anything," I told her. "You'll be with me; you'll see. I just want to look in Thorndecker's journal."

"What for?"

"To see what he's been doing, and why. He said he keeps very precise, complete notes. It should all be there."

She was silent awhile, then . . .

"Do I have to be with you?" she asked. "Can't I just give you the keys?"

I stopped and turned her toward me. There we stood under that big, black umbrella, the rain sliding off it in a circular curtain. She wouldn't meet my eyes.

"You don't really want to know, do you?" I asked softly.

She shook her head dumbly, teeth biting down into her lower lip.

"Mary, I *need* you there. I need a witness. And maybe you can help me with the scientific stuff. You must know more of that than I do. Anyone would!"

She smiled wanly.

"And also," I said, "I need you with me for a very selfish reason. If we're caught, it'll be impossible to charge me with breaking-and-entering if I'm with a member of the family."

She nodded, lifted her chin.

"All right," she said. "I'll get the keys. Somehow. I'll let you in. I'll go with you. We'll read the journal together. I don't care how awful it is. I do want to know."

I pressed her arm. We started walking back toward the church. Her stride seemed more confident now. She was leading the way. I had to hurry to keep up with her. We stopped across the street from the church. We faced each other again.

"I know how to get the keys from Kenneth," she said, looking into my eyes.

"Good," I said. "How?"

"I'll go to bed with him," she said, plucked the umbrella from my hand, dashed across the street.

I just stood there, hearing the faint hiss of rain, watching her run up the church steps and disappear. And I had thought her prissy.

It was a few minutes before I could move. I felt the drops pelt my sodden tweed hat. I saw the rain run down my trenchcoat in wavery rivulets. I knew my boots were leaking and my feet were wet.

Simple solution: "I'll go to bed with him." Just like that. Maybe old Ben Faber was right. You want to do something, then *do* it.

I got back in my car, still in a state of bemused wonderment. I drove around awhile, trying to make sense of what was going on, of what people were doing, of what I was doing. What amazed me most was how Telford

Gordon Thorndecker, unknowingly, was impinging on the lives of so many. Mary. Dr. Draper. Julie. Edward. Ronnie and Millie Goodfellow. The "best people" of Coburn. And me. Thorndecker was changing us. Nudging our lives, for better or for worse. None of us would ever be the same.

The man was a force. It went out in waves, affecting people he didn't even know. Joan Powell, for example. Thorndecker was the reason I had come to Coburn. Coburn was changing the way I felt about Joan Powell. Her life might be turned around, or at least altered, by the influence of a man she had never met.

I wondered if all life was like this: a series of interlocking concentric circles, everything connected to everything else in some mad scheme that the greatest computer in the world would digest and then type out on its TV monitor: "Insufficient data."

It was a humbling thought, that we are all pushed and pulled by influences that we are not even aware of. Life is not a bowl of cherries. Life is a bowl of linguine with clam sauce, everything intertangled and slithery. No end to it.

Maybe that was the job of the investigators. We're the guys with the fork and the soup spoon, lifting high a tangle of the strands, twirling fork tines in the bowl of the spoon, and producing a neat, palatable ball.

It made me hungry just to think of it.

The Coburn Civic Building looked like it had shrunk in the rain. I didn't expect bustling activity on a Sunday afternoon, but I thought *someone* would be on duty in the city hall, minding the store. I finally found a few real, live human beings by peering through the dirty glass window in the wide door of the firehouse. Inside, four guys in coveralls sat around a wooden table playing cards. I would have bet my last kopeck it was pinochle. I also got a view of their equipment: an antique pumper and a hose truck that looked like a converted Eskimo Pie van. Neither vehicle looked especially clean.

I walked around the building to the police station in the rear. It was open, desolate, deserted. It smelled like every police station in the world: an awful amalgam of eye-stinging disinfectant, vintage urine, mold, dust, vomit, and several other odors of interest only to a pathologist.

There was a waist-high railing enclosing three desks. A frosted glass door led away to inner offices. This splintered room was tastefully decorated with *Wanted* posters and a calendar displaying a lady in a gaping black lace negligee. I thought her proportions highly improbable. She may have been one of those life-size inflatable rubber dolls Japanese sailors take along on lengthy cruises.

From somewhere beneath my feet, a guy was singing—sort of. He was bellowing, "Oh Dolly, oh Dolly, how you can love." That's all. Over and over. "Oh Dolly, oh Dolly, how you can love." From this, I deduced that the drunk tank was in the basement.

"Hello?" I called. "Anyone home?"

No answer. One of these days, some smart, big-city gonnif was going to drop by and steal the Coburn police station.

"Hello?" I yelled again, louder. Same result: none.

I pushed open the railing gate, went over to the frosted glass door, opened that, stepped into a narrow corridor with four doors. Three were unmarked; one bore the legend: Chief. One of the unmarked doors was open. I peeked in.

My old friend, Constable Fred Aikens. He was sprawled in a wood swivel chair, feet parked up on the desk. His hands were clasped across his hard, little pot belly. His head was thrown back, mouth sagging, and he was fast asleep. I could hear him. It wasn't exactly a snore. More like a regular, "Aaagh. Aaagh. Aaagh." There was a sheaf of pornographic photos spread out on his desk blotter.

I stared at Coburn's first line of defense against criminal wrongdoing. I had forgotten what a nasty little toad he was, with his squinchy features and a hairline that seemed anxious to tangle with his eyebrows. I had an insane impulse. I'd very carefully, very quietly tiptoe into the office and very slowly, very easily slide his service revolver from his holster. Then I'd tiptoe from the room, from the building, and drive back to the Coburn Inn where I'd finish the vodka while laughing my head off as I thought of Fred Aikens explaining to the Chief Constable how he happened to lose his gun.

I didn't do it, of course. Instead, I went back to the main room. I slammed the gate of the railing a few times, and I really screamed, "Hello? Hello? Anyone here?"

That did the trick. In a few minutes Aiken came strolling out, uniform cap squared away, tunic smoothed down, every inch the alert police officer.

"Todd," he said. "No need to bellow. How you doing?"

"Okay," I said. "How *you* doing?"

"Quiet," he said. "Just the way I like it. If you came to ask about those slashed tires of yours, we haven't been able to come up with—"

"No, no," I said. "This is about something else. Could I please talk to you for a couple of minutes?"

I said it very humbly. Some cops you can handle just like anyone else. Some you can manipulate better if you start out crawling. Fred Aikens was one of those.

"Why, sure," he said genially. "Come on into my private office where we can sit."

I followed him through the frosted glass door into his room. He jerked open the top desk drawer and swept the pornographic photos out of sight.

"Evidence," he said.

"Yes," I said. "Terrible what's going down these days."

"Sure is," he said. "You park there and tell me what's on your mind."

I sat in a scarred armchair alongside his desk, and gave him my best wide-eyed, sincere look.

"I heard about Al Coburn," I said. "That's a hell of a thing."

"Ain't it though?" he said. "You knew him?"

Those mean, little eyes never blinked.

"Well . . . sure," I said. "Met him two or three times. Had a few drinks with him at the Coburn Inn."

"Yeah," he said, "old Al liked the sauce. That's what killed him. The nutty coot must have had a snootful. Just drove right off the bluff into the river."

"The bluff?"

"A place we call Lovers' Leap. Out of town a ways."

"How did you spot the truck? Someone call it in?"

"Hell, no," he said. "Goodfellow saw him go over. Had been tailing him, see. Coburn was driving like a maniac, all over the road, and Ronnie was trying to catch up, figuring to pull him over. Had the siren and lights going: everything. But before he could stop him, Al Coburn drives right off the edge. There's been talk of putting a guard rail up there, but no one's got around to it."

I shook my head sadly. "Hell of a thing. Where is he now? The body, I mean."

"Oh, he's on ice at Markham's funeral parlor. We're trying to locate next of kin."

"You do an autopsy in cases like that?" I asked him casually.

"Well, hell yes," he said indignantly. "What do you think? Bobby Markham is our local coroner. He's a good old boy."

"Coburn drowned?"

"Oh sure. Lungs full of water."

"Was he banged up?"

"Plenty. Listen, that's more'n a fifty-foot drop from Lovers' Leap. He was a mess. Head all mashed in. Well, you'd expect that. Probably hit it on the wheel or windshield when he smacked the water."

I didn't say anything. He looked at me curiously. Something wary came into those hard eyes. I knew: he was wondering if he had said too much.

"What's your interest in this, Todd?"

"Well, like I said, I knew the guy. So when I heard he was dead, it really shook me."

"Uh-huh," he said.

"Also," I said, "something silly. I'm embarrassed to mention it."

He leaned back in his swivel chair, clasped his hands across his belly. He regarded me gravely.

"Why, you go right ahead," he said. "No need to be embarrassed. I hear a lot of things right here in this office, and it never gets past these walls."

I bet.

"Well," I said hesitantly, "I had a drink with Al Coburn yesterday morning. A beer or two. Then afterward, he wanted me to see where he lived. The flagpole and all."

"Oh yeah," he laughed. "Old Al's flagpole. That's a joke."

"Yes," I said. "Anyway, I own a gold cigarette lighter. Not very valuable. Cost maybe twenty, thirty bucks. But it's got a sentimental value—you know?"

"Woman give it to you?" he said, winking.

I tried a short laugh.

"Well . . . yeah. You know how it is. Anyhow, I remember using it while I was in Al Coburn's pickup. And then, a few hours later, after I got back to the Inn, it was missing. So I figure I dropped it in Coburn's truck. Maybe on the floor or back between the cushions. I was wondering where Coburn's pickup is now?"

"The truck?" he said, surprised. "Right now? Why, it's out back in our garage. We're holding it until everything gets straightened out on his estate and will and all. You think your gold cigarette lighter is in the truck?"

"I figured it might be."

"I doubt it," he said, staring at me. "When we went down to get Coburn out, we had to pry open the doors, and the river just swept through. Then we winched the truck out of the water. Nothing in it by then. Hell, even the back seat cushion was gone."

"Well," I said haltingly, "I was hoping you'd let me take a quick look . . . "

"Why not?" he said cheerily, jerking to his feet. "Never can tell, can you? Maybe your gold cigarette lighter got caught in a corner somewhere. Let's go see."

"Oh, don't bother yourself," I said hastily. "Just tell me where it is, I'll take a quick look and be on my way. I imagine you have to stick close to the phones and all."

"No bother," he said, his mouth smiling but not his eyes. "Nothing happens in Coburn on a Sunday. Let's go."

I had pushed it as far as I thought I could. So I had to follow him out of the station house, around to a corrugated steel garage. He unlocked the padlock, and we went in.

Al Coburn's pickup truck was a sad-looking mess. Front end crumpled, windshield starred with cracks, doors sprung, seat cushion soaked, steering column bent.

And the glove compartment open and empty.

"Stinks, don't it?" Aikens said.

"Sure does," I said.

I made a show of searching for a cigarette lighter. The constable leaned against the wall of the garage and watched me with iron eyes.

I crawled out of the sodden wreck, rubbing my palms.

"Ahh, the hell with it," I said. "It's not here."

"I told you," he said. "Nothing's there. The river got it all."

"I suppose," I said dolefully. "Well, thanks very much for your trouble."

"No trouble," he said. "I'm just sorry you didn't find what you were looking for."

"Yes," I said, "too bad. Well, I guess I'll be on my way."

"Leaving Coburn soon?"

That's what Julie Thorndecker had asked me. And in the same hopeful tone.

"Probably tomorrow morning," I said.

"Stop by and see us again. Happy to have you."

"Thanks. I might do just that."

We grinned at each other. A brace of liars.

Nothing's ever neat. The investigator who's supposed to twirl a tight ball of linguine with fork and spoon usually ends up with a ragged clump with loose ends. That's what I had: loose ends.

I didn't know how it was managed, but I knew Al Coburn never drove off that cliff deliberately. His truck was nudged over, or driven over with a live driver leaping out at the last second, leaving an unconscious or dead Al Coburn in the cab. An experienced medical examiner could have proved those head injuries were inflicted before drowning, but not Good Old Boy Bobby Markham.

Maybe the glove compartment had been searched before the truck was pushed over. Maybe after it was hauled out. Or maybe the river really did sweep it clean. It didn't make any difference. I knew I'd never see the letter Ernie Scoggins had left with Al Coburn.

I could guess what was in the letter. I could guess at a lot of things. Loose ends. But in any kind of investigative work, you've got to live with that. If you're the tidy type, take up bookkeeping. Business ledgers have to balance. Nothing balances in a criminal investigation. You never learn it all. There's always something missing.

I got out to Red Dog Betty's about 3:30 in the afternoon. That crawl through Al Coburn's death truck had affected me more than I anticipated. When I held out a hand, the fingertips vibrated like tuning forks. So I went to Betty's, for a drink, something to eat, just to sit quietly awhile and cure the shakes.

This time I parked as close to the entrance to the roadhouse as I could get, hoping it would discourage the Mad Tire Slasher from striking again. I hung up hat and coat, sat at the bar, ordered a vodka gimlet. I asked for Betty, but the black bartender said she wouldn't be in until the evening.

The barroom and dining areas had that peaceful, dimmed, hushed atmosphere of most watering places on a Sunday afternoon. No one was playing the juke. No voices were raised. The laughter was low-pitched and rueful. Everyone ruminating on their excesses of the night before. I knew that Sunday afternoon mood; you move carefully and slowly, abjure loud sounds and unseemly mirth. The ambience is almost churchlike.

I must have been wearing my head hanging low, because I saw them for the first time when I straightened up and looked in the big, misty mirror behind the bar. Sitting in an upholstered banquette on the other side of the room were Nurse Stella Beecham, editor Agatha Binder, and the cheerleader type from the *Sentinel* office, Sue Ann. Miss Dimples was seated between the two big women. They looked like massive walnut bookends pressing one slim volume of fairy tales.

If they had noticed me come in, they gave no sign. They might have been ignoring me, but it seemed more likely they were too busy with their own affairs to pay any attention to anyone else. Beecham was wearing her nurse's uniform, without cap. Binder had a clean pair of painters' overalls over a black turtleneck. The lollipop between them had on a pink angora sweater with a long rope of pearls. She kept nibbling on the pearls as the two gorgons kept up a running conversation across her. The older women were drinking beer from bottles, scorning their glasses. The young girl had an orange-colored concoction, with a lot of fruit and two long straws.

I stole a glance now and then, wondering what the relationship of that trio was, and who did what to whom. About 3:45, Nurse Beecham lurched to her feet and moved out from behind the table. She smoothed down her skirt. That was one hefty bimbo. Get an injection in the rump from her, and the needle was likely to go in the right buttock and come out the left.

She said something to the other women, bent to kiss them both. She took a plastic raincoat and hat from the rack, waved once, and was gone. I figured she was heading for Crittenden Hall, for the four-to-midnight shift.

The moment the nurse disappeared, Agatha Binder turned slightly sideways and slid one meaty arm across Sue Ann's shoulders. She leaned forward and whispered something in the girl's ear. They both laughed. Chums.

I saw Miss Dimples' drink was getting low, and the editor was tilting her beer bottle high to drain the last few drops. I got off my barstool and went smiling toward them.

"Hi!" I said brightly. "How are you ladies?"

They looked up in surprise. The nubile one with some interest, Agatha Binder with something less than delight.

"Well, well," the editor said, "if it isn't supersnoop. What are you doing here, Todd?"

"Recovering," I said. "May I buy you two a drink?"

"I guess so," she said slowly. "Why not?"

"Won't you join us?" Sue Ann piped up, and I could have kissed her.

I moved onto the seat vacated by Stella Beecham, ignoring Binder's frown. I signaled the waitress for another round, and offered cigarettes.

We all lighted up, and chatted animatedly about the weather until the drinks arrived.

"When are you planning on leaving Coburn?" Agatha asked. Same question. Same hopeful tone. It's so nice to be well-liked.

"Probably tomorrow morning."

"Find out all you need to know about Thorndecker?"

"More," I said.

We sampled our drinks. Sue Ann said, "Oh, wow," and blushed. She was so fresh, so limpid and juicy, that I think if you embraced her tightly, she'd squirt mead.

"Well, he's quite a man, Thorndecker," the editor said. "Very convincing."

"Oh yes," I said. "Very. I'll bet he could get away with murder."

She looked at me sharply. "What's that supposed to mean?"

"Figure of speech," I said.

She continued to stare at me. Something came into her eyes, something knowing.

"This is yummy," Miss Dimples said, sucking happily at her straws. Lucky straws.

"He's not going to get the grant, is he?" Binder demanded.

"When is your next edition coming out?" I asked her.

"We just closed. Next edition is next week."

"Then I can tell you," I said. "No, he's not going to get the grant. Not if I have anything to do with it, he isn't."

"Well . . . what the hell," she said. "I figured you'd find out."

"You mean you knew?"

"Oh Christ, Todd, everyone in Coburn knows."

I took a deep breath, sat back, stared into the air.

"You're incredible," I said. "You and everyone else in Coburn. Something like this going on under your noses, and you just shrug it off. I don't understand you people."

"Sometimes I have a Tom Collins," the creampuff giggled, "but I really like this better."

"You know, Todd, you're an obnoxious bastard," the editor said. "You come up here with your snobbish, big-city, sharper-than-thou attitude. You stick your beezer in matters that don't concern you. And then you condemn Thorndecker because of the way his wife acts. Now I ask you: is that fair?"

My stomach flopped over. Then I just spun away. My hand stopped halfway to my glass. I tried to slow my whirling thoughts. I had a sense of total disorientation. It took awhile. A minute or two. Then things began to harden, come into focus again. I understood: Agatha Binder and I had been talking about two different things.

"I tried beer a few times," Miss Dimples volunteered, "but I really didn't like it. Too bitter."

I drained my glass, motioned toward their glasses.

"Ready for another?" I asked hoarsely.

"Hell, yes," the editor said roughly.

Sue Ann said, "Whee!"

By the time my fresh gimlet arrived, I had it organized: how I would handle it.

"You think Thorndecker knows about it?" I asked cautiously.

"Oh hell," she said, "he has to know. Those trips to Albany and Boston and New York. Once to Washington. To talk to potential sponsors. Big-money guys who might dip into their wallets for the Crittenden Research Laboratory. Then Thorndecker would come back alone. Julie would return a day or two or a week later. And a day or two after *that*, the contribution would come in. It wasn't hard to figure out what was going on."

I nodded as if I was aware of this all along.

"I knew you'd catch on," Agatha Binder said morosely. "Listen, is what they do so bad? It's in a good cause. You talk like it's a federal case or something."

"No," I said thoughtfully, "it's not so bad. Maybe a little shabby, but I suppose it's done in other businesses every day in the week."

"You better believe it," she said, nodding violently.

"I'm hungry," Sue Ann said.

I mulled over this new information. An angle I hadn't even considered. Was this the "conspiracy" that all the Coburnites shared? Pretty sleazy stuff.

"A very complex woman, our Julie," I said wonderingly. "I'm just beginning to appreciate her. My first take was of a bitch with a libido bigger than all outdoors. But now it seems there's more to her than that. Why does she do it, Agatha? Is it the sex? Or just the money to keep her life-style intact?"

Binder punched gently at the tip of her nose with one knuckle. Then she took a deep swig from her beer bottle.

"When are we going to eat?" Sue Ann asked plaintively.

"A little of both," the big woman said. "But mostly because she loves Thorndecker. *Loves* him! And believes in him, in his work. She worships him, thinks he's a saint. She's really a very loving, sacrificing woman."

I literally threw up my hands.

"It's a masquerade," I said hopelessly. "Everyone wearing masks. Do you all take them off at midnight?"

"You come up here from the big city and think you're dealing with simple country bumpkins. It's obvious in your attitude, in your sneers and jokes. Then you act like we've been misleading you when it turns out that we're not cardboard cutouts, that we're as screwed-up as everyone else."

I thought about that for a few moments.

"You may be right," I admitted. "To some extent. I've underestimated most of the people here I've met; that's true. But not Thorndecker. I never sold him short."

"Oh, he's one of a kind," Agatha Binder said. "You can't judge him by ordinary standards."

"I don't," I said. "I just wonder what kind of a man would endure what his wife is doing. Encourage her to do it. Or at least accept it without objection."

"His work comes first," the editor told me. "That's his only test. Is it good or bad for his work?"

"A monomaniac?" I suggested.

"Or a genius," she said.

"Obsessed?" I said.

"Or committed," she said.

"Insensitive?" I said.

"Or totally dedicated," she said.

Then we were both silent, neither of us certain.

"Maybe a hamburger," Sue Ann said dreamily. "A cheeseburger. With relish."

I sighed and stood up.

"Feed the child," I told Agatha Binder, "before she collapses. Thanks for the talk."

"Thanks for the drinks."

Unexpectedly, she thrust out a hand, hard and horny. I shook it. I won't say we parted friends, but I think there was some respect.

I went back to the bar. I had intended to have something to eat there, but I decided to return to the Coburn Inn. I didn't want to look into a misty bar mirror and see Agatha Binder sticking her tongue in Sue Ann's ear. Then I knew I was getting old. It upset me to see things in public that people used to do only in bedrooms after the lights were out and the kids were asleep.

On the drive back to the Coburn Inn, I tried not to think of what the editor had told me about Julie Thorndecker. But it bothered me that what she had revealed came as such an unexpected shock. The whole Thorndecker business had been like that: unfolding slowly and painfully. I wondered if I stayed in Coburn another week, a month, a year, if it would all be disclosed to me, right down to the final surprise.

Agatha Binder's accusation rankled because it was true. Partly true. I *had* assumed that these one-horse-town denizens were a different species, made of simpler, evident stuff, their motives easily perceived, their passions casually analyzed. There was hardly one of them who hadn't proved my snobbery just by being human, displaying all the mysterious, inexplicable quirks of which humans are capable. I should have known better.

The dining room at the Coburn Inn was moderately crowded; I ate in the bar. Had two musty ales with broiled porkchops, apple sauce, a baked potato, green beans with a bacon sauce, and rum cake for dessert. Well, listen, the fast I vowed that morning had lasted almost nine hours. After all, I *am* a growing boy.

Went up to my room and began packing. I wasn't planning to leave until the following morning, but I was nagged by the feeling that after my criminal enterprise scheduled for 2:00 A.M., I might want to make a quick getaway. So I packed, leaving the two suitcases and briefcase open.

Then, using hotel stationery, I wrote out a precis of the Thorndecker affair. I tried to keep it brief and succinct, but included everything I had discovered, and what I hadn't discovered: Thorndecker's motive for infecting his nursing home patients with cancer.

It ran to five pages, front and back, before I had finished. I read it over, made a few minor corrections, then sealed it in an envelope addressed to myself at the address of the Bingham Foundation in New York. I remembered what Thorndecker had said about keeping precise, complete notes "in case of an accident." Then someone else could carry on the work.

If there was no "accident" (like driving off Lovers' Leap), I could destroy the manuscript when I got back to the office on Tuesday. If, for some reason, I didn't return, someone at the office would open the letter. And know.

Put on coat and hat again, went down to the lobby, bought stamps at the machine on the cigar counter.

"Mail that for you, Mr. Todd?" the baldy behind the desk sang out.

"No, thanks," I said. "I'll take a walk and drop it in the slot at the post office."

"Wet walking," he said.

"The farmers need it," I said.

I liked saying that. A Coburn tradition. A hurricane could hit, decimating Coburn and half of New York State, and someone was sure to crawl painfully from the wreckage, look up at the slashing, ripping sky, and croak, "Well, the farmers need it."

When I got back to Room 3-F, I shucked off wet coat, wet hat, wet boots, and fell into bed. I had heard that if you fall asleep concentrating on the hour you want to awake, you'll get up on the dot. So I tried it, thinking, "Get up at midnight, get up at midnight, get up at midnight." Then I conked off.

I awoke at 1:15, which isn't bad, considering it was my first try. But I did have to rush, making sure I was dressed completely in black, sneaking down the stairs, waiting until the lobby was deserted and the desk clerk was in the back office. Then I strode swiftly out to the parking lot. Still raining. I figured that was a plus. That roaming shotgun-armed guard with the attack dog would probably be inside someplace dry and warm, reading *Penthouse* or *The Wall Street Journal*. Something like that.

I drove out to Crittenden at a moderate speed. I didn't want to be late for my rendezvous with Mary Thorndecker—I doubted if her nerves could endure the wait—but I didn't want to be too early either, chancing discovery by one of the guards.

I cruised slowly by the gate. There were outside lights burning on the portico of Crittenden Hall, and I could see Julie Thorndecker's blue MGB parked on the gravel driveway. It seemed odd that the car wasn't garaged on a night like that.

There were a few lights burning on the main floor of the nursing home, none on the second and third floors. No lights in the laboratory. There was a dim bluish glow (TV?) coming from the gatekeeper's hut.

I passed the gate, followed the fence until it began to curve around toward the cemetery. Then I pulled well off the road, doused my lights, waited until my eyes became accustomed to the dark. I opened the car door cautiously, stepped out, closed the door but left it unlatched.

Gathered my equipment: stepladder, clothesline, sash weight, flashlight. I stuck the flash and weight in my hip pockets. My pants almost fell down.

Carried ladder and rope across the road to the fence. Still raining. Not hard, but steadily. Straight down. A rain that soaked and chilled.

Tied one end of the rope to the top of the aluminum stepladder. Threw the loose coils over the fence. Then I set up the ladder carefully, making sure the braces were locked. I climbed up.

You've seen movies where James Bond or one of his imitators goes over a high fence by leaping, grabbing the top, pulling himself up and over. Try that little trick some time. Instant hernia. It's a lot easier to carry your own stepladder.

I stood on the top rung, swung one leg over the fence, straddled, swung the other leg over and jumped, remembering to land with flexed knees. Then I pulled my rope, and the ladder came up the outside of the fence. It took me a few minutes to jiggle it over, but eventually it dropped down inside. I caught it, and set it up against the inside of the fence, ready for a quick escape.

Now I was inside the grounds. I had selected a spot where the bulk of Crittenden Hall came between me and the gate guard. I hoped I was right about the roving sentry keeping out of the rain. But just in case, I crouched a few moments in the absolute dark and strained to hear. A silence like thunder. No, not quite. I heard the rain hitting my hat, coat, the ground. But other than that—nothing.

Moved warily toward the nursing home and its outbuildings. Didn't use my flash, so twice I blundered into trees. Didn't even curse. Did when I tripped over a fallen branch and fell to my hands and knees.

Figure it took me at least fifteen minutes to work my way slowly around Crittenden Hall. A light came on briefly on the second floor, then went out. I hoped that was Mary Thorndecker with the keys, leaving the apartment of Dr. Kenneth Draper, starting down to meet me.

Sudden angry barking of a dog. I froze. The barking continued for a minute or two, then ended as abruptly as it began. I moved again. Slowly,

slowly. Trying to peer through the black, through the rain. Nightglow was practically nonexistent. I was in a tunnel. Down a well. Buried.

Came up to Crittenden Hall. Eased around it as noiselessly as I could, fingertips lightly brushing the brick. Reflected that I was no outdoorsman. Not trained for this open-country stuff. I could navigate a Ninth Avenue tenement better than I could a copse, stubbled field, meadowland, or hills.

Found the covered steps leading down from the nursing home to the back door of the Crittenden Research Laboratory. Kept off the paved walk, but moved in a crouch alongside it. Tried to avoid crashing through shrubbery or kicking the slate border.

Finally, at the door. No Mary. I hunkered down. Put flashlight under the skirt of my trenchcoat. Risked quick look at my wristwatch. About 2: 20. Sudden fear that I had missed her at 2:15, and she, spooked, had gone back to Draper's bed.

Waited. Hoping.

Heard something. Creak of door opening. Pause. Soft thud as it closed. Wiped my eyes continually, peering up the hill. Saw something lighter than the night floating down. Tensed. Watched it draw closer.

Mary Thorndecker. In white nightgown partly covered by old-fashioned flannel bathrobe cinched with a cord. Heavy brogues on bare feet. She was carrying the big umbrella, open. Beautiful. But I didn't feel like laughing.

She almost fell over me. I straightened up. She jerked back. I grabbed her, palm over her mouth. Then she steadied. I released her. Shoved my face close to hers under the umbrella.

"The keys?" I whispered.

Felt rather than saw her nod. Rings of keys pressed into my hand. I put my lips close to her ear.

"I'm going to give you the flashlight. Before you switch it on, put your fingers across the lens. We just want a dim light. A glimmer. Just enough to show the lock. Understand?"

She did just fine. We stood huddled at the door, blocking what we were doing with our bodies. She held the light, her fingers reducing the beam to a reddish glow. I tried three keys before the fourth slid in. I was about to turn it, then stopped. Still.

"What is it?" she said.

There had to be an alarm.

I left the keys in the lock. Took her hands in mine, turned the flashlight slowly upward along the jamb of the door. There, at the top, another lock taking a barrel key.

"Alarm," I breathed in her ear. "Got to be turned off first before we open the door. There's a barrel key on the ring. Let's hope it—"

At that moment. Precisely. Two sounds. Muffled. Indoors. From the nursing home. They were not snaps. More like dulled booms.

"What—?" Mary said.

I put a hand on her arm. We waited. In a few seconds, four more hard sounds in rapid succession. These were louder, more like cracks. They sounded closer.

"Handgun," I said in my normal voice, knowing it had all come apart. "Heavy caliber. You stay here."

"No," she said, "I'm coming with you."

I grabbed the flashlight from her. Took her hand. We went stumbling up the walk, the open umbrella ballooning behind us, a puddle of light jerking along at our feet.

Reached the back door of Crittenden Hall. Both of us panting.

The door was locked.

"The keys," I said.

"You left them in the door of the lab."

"What a swell burglar I am," I said bitterly.

I took out the sash weight, smashed the pane of glass closest to the lock. Hammered the shards away from the frame so I wouldn't slit my wrists. Then reached in, opened the door.

We ran into a brightly lighted corridor. Chaos. Alarms and excursions. Shouts and screams. People in white running, running. All toward the main entrance hall.

And a shriek that shivered me. A wailing shriek, on and on. Man or woman? I couldn't tell.

"That's Edward," Mary Thorndecker gasped. "Edward!"

We dashed like the others. Debouched into the lobby. Joined the jostling mob. All circling. Looking down.

The shriek was all wail now. A weeping siren. It rose and fell in hysterical ululation.

"Shut him up!" someone yelled. "Slap him!"

I pushed roughly through, Mary following. No one saw us. Everyone was looking at what lay on the marble floor, at the foot of the wide staircase.

They must have been shot while coming down the stairs. Then they fell the rest of the way. Ronnie Goodfellow, clad in mufti, hit first. He was prone, face turned to one side. His right leg snapped under him when he hit. A jagged splinter of bone stuck out through the cloth.

Julie Thorndecker had landed near him, on her back. One side of her head was gone. Her arms were thrown wide. Her coat was flung open, skirt hiked up. One naked, pale, smooth, beautiful leg was lying across Goodfellow's neck.

Two pigskin suitcases had fallen with them. One had snapped open on impact, the contents cascading across the floor. Blue panties, brassieres, a small jewel case, negligees, the silver evening pajamas and sandals she had been wearing the night I met her.

I don't think the first two shots killed them. But then he followed them down and emptied his gun. The blood was pooling, beginning to merge, his and hers, and trickle across the marble tiles.

Like the others, I stared at the still, smashed dolls. Dr. Draper knelt alongside, wearing a raincoat, bare shins sticking out. He fumbled for a pulse at their throats, but it was hopeless. Everyone knew it. He knew it. But his trembling fingers still searched.

When I first glimpsed them, Edward Thorndecker was sitting cross-legged on the floor, his stepmother's torn head in his lap. His head was back, face wrung, and that shrieking wail came out of his open mouth continuously, as if he needed no breath but only grief to produce that terrifying scream. Finally, hands reached down, pulled him away, took him off somewhere. They half-carried him, his toes dragging on the marble. The shriek faded, faded, then stopped suddenly.

Surprisingly, Mary Thorndecker took charge.

"Don't touch anything," she commanded in a loud, sharp voice. "Kenneth, you call the police. At once. Did anyone see where he went?"

Where *he* went. There was no doubt in her mind, nor in anyone else's, who had done this slaughter.

The gorilla-butler, with a shoulder holster and gun strapped across a soiled T-shirt, pushed forward.

"Out the back door, Miss Thorndecker," he said. "I heard the shots and come running. I seen him. Out the back door and onto the grounds."

Mary Thorndecker nodded. "Alma, you and Fred see to the patients. Some of them may have heard the commotion. Calm them down. Sedation, if needed. The rest of you get your hats and coats. Bring flashlights and lanterns. We must find him. He is not a well man."

I pondered that: "He is not a well man." And Hitler was "disturbed."

It took us maybe ten minutes to get organized. Mary Thorndecker ordered us around like a master sergeant. I couldn't fault her. She got us spread out on a ragged line, at about fifteen-foot intervals. Most of the beaters had flashlights or lanterns. One guy had a kerosene lamp. And all the interior lights of Crittenden Hall were switched on, cutting the gloom in the immediate vicinity.

At a command from Mary, we started moving forward, trying to keep the line intact. Once we were out of the Hall's glow, the dark night closed in. Then all I could see was a bobbing, wavering necklace of weak lights, shimmering in the rain.

"Thorndecker!" someone called in a quavery voice, and the others took up the cry.

"Thorndecker!"

"Thorndecker!"

"Thorndecker!"

Then it became a long, wailing moan: "Thooorndecker!" And we all, scarcely sane, went stumbling across the slick, frosted fields, lights jerking up and down, calling his name again and again, echoing his name, while the cold rain pelted a black and ruined world.

Oh yes, we found him. We had passed through the cemetery and were slowly, fearfully working the stand of bare trees on the far side. There was a shout, the wild swinging of a lantern in wide circles. We all ran, breathless and blundering, to the spot. We clustered.

He lay on his back, spreadeagled, face turned to the falling sky. He wore only pajama pants. He was almost completely bald; only a few wet tufts of hair were left. Bare feet were bruised and bleeding. His eyes were open. He was dead.

Arms, shoulders, torso, neck, face, scalp—all of him exposed to view was studded with suppurating tumors. Great blooms of red and yellow and purple. Rotting excrescences that seemed to have a vigorous life of their own, immortal, sprouting from his cooling flesh. They had soft, dough-like centers, and browned, crusted petals.

There was hardly an inch of him not choked by cancerous growths. Eyes bulging with necrosis, mouth twisted, nose lumped, the limbs swollen with decay, trunk gnarled with great chunks of putrescent matter. The smell was of deep earth, swamp, and the grave.

The trembling circles of light exposed the horror he had become. I heard a sobbing, was conscious of people turning away to retch. Someone began to murmur a prayer. But I was stone, transfixed, looking down at what was left of Dr. Telford Gordon Thorndecker, wanting desperately to find meaning, and finding nothing.

The butler-thug volunteered to remain with the body. The rest of us wandered back to Crittenden Hall. We moved, I noted, in a tight group, seeking the close presence of others to help hold back the darkness, to prove that live warmth still existed in the world. No one spoke. Silently we filed through the cemetery, gravestones glistening in our lights, and straggled across the stubbled fields to the brightness of Crittenden Hall, a beacon in the black.

A half-hour later I was seated with Dr. Kenneth Draper in Thorndecker's private office in the Crittenden Research Laboratory. I had left Mary Thorndecker to deal with the police. I had latched onto Draper—literally. I took him by the arm and would not let him go, not for an instant. I am not certain if any of us were acting rationally that night.

I marched Draper upstairs to his apartment and let him dress. Then I pulled him into that marvelous Thorndecker sitting room where I swiped a bottle of brandy, and thought nothing of it. I made Draper gulp a mouthful, because his face was melting white wax, and he was moving like an invalid. I took him and the brandy back to the research lab. Found the keys, turned off the alarm, opened the door, turned on the lights.

In Thorndecker's private lab, I pushed Draper into the chair behind the desk. I peeled off my soaked hat and coat. I found paper cups, and poured us each a deep shot of brandy. Some color came back into his face, but he was racked with sudden shivers, and once his teeth chattered.

Thorndecker's journal, the one he had been working on the last time I saw him alive, still lay open on the desk. I shoved it toward Draper.

"When did it start?" I asked him.

"What will they do to me?" he said in a dulled voice. "Will I go to jail?"

I could have told him that if he kept his mouth shut, probably nothing would happen to him. How could they prove all those Crittenden Hall patients had died other than natural deaths? I figured the Coburn cops would be satisfied that Thorndecker had killed his wife and her lover, then died himself from terminal cancer. It was neat, and it closed out a file. They wouldn't go digging any deeper.

But I wanted to keep Draper guilty and quivering.

"It depends," I told him stolidly, "on how willing you are to cooperate. If you spell it out for me, I'll put in a good word for you."

I didn't tell him that I had about as much clout with the Coburn cops as I do with the Joint Chiefs of Staff.

"All right," I said, in the hardest voice I could manage, "when did it start?"

He raised a tear-streaked face. I poured him another brandy, and he choked it down. He stared at the ledger, then began turning the pages listlessly.

"You mean the—the experiments?"

"Yes," I said, trying not to yell at him, "the experiments."

"A long time ago," he said, in a voice so low I had to crane forward to hear him. "Before we came to Crittenden. We started with normal mammalian cells. Then concentrated only on normal human cells. We were looking for the cellular clock that causes aging and death. Dr. Thorndecker believed that—"

"I know what Thorndecker believed," I interrupted him. "Did you believe in the cellular clock theory?"

He looked at me in astonishment.

"Of course," he said. "If Dr. Thorndecker believed in it, I *had* to believe. He was a great man. He was—"

"I know," I said, "a genius. But you didn't find it? The cellular clock?"

"No. Hundreds of experiments. Thousands of man-hours. It's extremely difficult, working with normal human cells *in vitro*. Limited doublings. The cells become less differentiated, useless for our research. We confirmed conclusively that the cell determines longevity, but we couldn't isolate the factor. It was—well, frustrating. During that period, Dr. Thorndecker became very demanding, very insistent. Hard to deal with. He could not endure failure."

"This was before you came to Crittenden?"

"Yes. Dr. Thorndecker's first wife was still alive. Most of our research was being done on small grants. But we had no exciting results to publish. The grant money ran out. But then Dr. Thorndecker's first wife was killed in an accident, and he was able to buy Crittenden and establish this laboratory."

"Yes," I said, "I know. And then?"

"We had been here only a short time, when one night he woke me up. Very excited. Laughing and happy. He said he had solved our basic problem. He said he knew now what our approach should be. It was an inspiration. Only a genius could have thought of it. A quantum leap of pure reason."

"And what was that?" I asked.

"We couldn't keep normal cells viable *in vitro*. Not for long. But cancer cells flourished, reproduced endlessly. Apparently they were immortal. Dr. Thorndecker's idea was to forget about finding the factor in normal cells that caused senescence and death, and concentrate on finding the factor in abnormal cells that caused such wild proliferation."

"The factor that made cancer cells immortal *in vitro*?"

"Yes."

I took a deep breath. There it was.

I knew what was coming. I could have stopped right there. But I wanted him to spell it out. Maybe I wanted to rub his nose in it.

"And you found the factor?"

He nodded. "But the problem was how to separate the longevity effect from the fatal effect. You understand? The cancer cells themselves simply grew and grew—forever, if you allowed them to. But they killed the host organism. So all our research turned to filtering out the immortality factor, purifying it in effect, so that the host's normal cells could absorb it and continue to grow indefinitely without harm. Very complex chemistry."

"It didn't work?" I said.

"It did, it did!" he cried, with the first flash of spirit he had exhibited. "I can show you mice and guinea pigs in the basement that have lived three times as long as they would normally. And they're absolutely cancer-free. And we have one dog that, in human terms, is almost two hundred years old."

"But no success with chimps?"

"No. None."

"So this essence of yours, this injection, wasn't always successful?"

"No, it wasn't. But animals are notoriously difficult to work with. Sometimes they reject the most virulent cancer cells. Sometimes a strain of rats supposed to be leukemia-prone will prove to be immune. Animals do not always give conclusive results, insofar as their reactions can be applied to humans. And animal experimentation is expensive, and takes time."

I leaned back and lighted a cigarette. Like most specialists, he tended to lecture when riding his own hobbyhorse. I probably knew as much about nuclear physics as he did, but bio-medicine was his world; he was confident there.

"Animal experimentation is expensive," I said, repeating his last words, "and it takes time. And Thorndecker never had enough money for what he wanted to do. But more than that, he didn't have the time. He was a man in a hurry, wasn't he? Impatient? Anxious for the fame the published discovery would bring?"

"He was convinced we were on the right track," Dr. Draper said. "I was, too. We were so close, so close. We had those animals in the basement to prove it—the ones who had doubled and tripled their normal life spans."

I rose and began to pace back and forth in front of the desk. Somehow I found myself with a lighted cigarette in each hand, and stubbed one out.

"All right," I said, "now we come to the worm in the apple. Whose idea was it to try the stuff on humans?"

He lowered his head and wouldn't answer.

"You don't have to tell me," I said. "I know it was Thorndecker's idea; you don't have the balls for it. I'll bet I even know how he convinced you. 'Look, Draper,' he said, 'there can be no progress without pain. Sacrifices must be made. We must dare all. Those patients in Crittenden Hall are terminal cases. How long do they have—weeks, months, a year? If we are unsuccessful, we'll only be shortening slightly their life span. And think of what they will be contributing! We can give their remaining days meaning. Think of that, Draper. We can make their deaths meaningful!' Isn't that what Thorndecker told you? Something like that?"

He nodded slowly. "Yes. Something like that."

"So you selected the ones you thought were terminal?"

"They were, they were!"

"You *thought* they were. You weren't sure. Doctors can never be sure; you know that. There are unexpected remissions. The patient recovers for no explainable reason. One day he wakes up cured. It happens. You know it happens."

He poured himself another cup of brandy, raised it to his pale lips with a shaking hand. Some of the brandy spilled down his chin, dripped onto his shirtfront.

"How many?" I demanded. "How many did you kill?"

"I don't know," he muttered. "We didn't keep—"

"Don't give me that shit!" I screamed at him. "Thorndecker kept very complete, precise records, and you know it. You want me to grab up this journal and all the others for the past three years, and take them to the cops? You think you can stop me? Try it! Just try it! How many?"

"Eleven," he said in a choked voice.

"And none survived?"

"No," he said. Then, brightly: "But the survival time was lengthening.

We were certain we were on the right track. Dr. Thorndecker was convinced of it. I was, too. We had purified the extract. A week ago we were absolutely certain we had made the breakthrough.''

''Why didn't you try it on another patient?''

Draper groaned.

''Don't you understand? If it had succeeded, how could Thorndecker publish the results? Admit experiments on humans? Fatal experiments? With no informed consent agreements? They'd have crucified him. The only way was to inject himself. He was so sure, so sure. He laughed about it. 'The elixir of life, Draper,' he told me. 'I'll live forever!' That's what he told me.''

I marveled at the man, at Thorndecker. To have such confidence, such absolute faith in your own destiny, such pride in your own skill. To dare death to prove it.

''What went wrong?'' I asked Draper.

''I don't know,'' he said, shaking his head. ''Initially, everything was fine. Then, in a short time, the first symptoms appeared. Hair falling out, skin blotches that signaled the beginning of tumors, sudden loss of weight, loss of appetite, other things . . . ''

''Thorndecker knew?''

''Oh yes. He knew.''

''How did he react?''

''We've spent the last few days working around the clock, trying to discover what went wrong, why the final essence not only didn't extend life but produced such rapid tumor germination.''

''Did you find out what it was?''

''No, not definitely. It may have been in the purifying process. It may have been something else. It could have been Dr. Thorndecker's personal immunochemistry. I just don't know.''

''Julie Thorndecker was aware of this?''

''She was aware that her husband was fatally ill, yes.''

''Was she aware of the experiments you two ghouls were carrying out?''

''No. Yes. I don't know.''

I sat down again. I slumped, so exhausted that I could have slept just by closing my eyes.

Dazed, not thinking straight, I wondered what I could do about this guy. I could have him racked up on charges, but I knew a smart lawyer could easily get him off. Do what? Exhume the corpses and find they had died of cancer? He'd never spend a day in jail. There might be a professional inquiry, and his career would be ruined. But so what? I wanted this prick to *suffer*.

''What about Ernie Scoggins?'' I asked him dully. ''Was Scoggins blackmailing Thorndecker?''

''I don't know anything about that,'' he mumbled.

"You goddamned shitwit!" I yelled at him. "You were Thorndecker's righthand man. You know about it all right."

"He got a letter from Scoggins," Draper said hastily, frightened. "Not mailed. A note shoved under his door. Scoggins was working here at the time. He helped out with the animals occasionally. And when we had burials in the cemetery. He guessed something was wrong. All those tumorous corpses . . ."

"Did he have any hard evidence of what was going down?"

"He stole one of Dr. Thorndecker's journals. It was—ah—incriminating."

"Then what happened?"

"I don't know. Dr. Thorndecker said he'd take care of it, not to worry."

"And he got the journal back?"

"Yes."

"And Ernie Scoggins disappeared."

"Dr. Thorndecker had nothing to do with that," he said hotly.

"Maybe not personally," I said. "But he had his wife persuade Constable Ronnie Goodfellow to take care of it. She persuaded him all right. It wasn't too difficult. She could be a very persuasive lady. And I suppose the same thing happened when it turned out that old Al Coburn had a letter from Scoggins recounting what was in Thorndecker's journal. So Al Coburn had to be eliminated, and the letter recovered. Constable Goodfellow went to work again, and did his usual efficient job."

"I don't know anything about Al Coburn," Draper insisted, in such an aggrieved tone that he might have been telling the truth.

I couldn't think of anything else to ask. Not only was my body weary, but my brain felt flogged. Too many strong sensations for one night. Too many electric images. The circuits were overloaded.

I stood up, pulled on my sodden coat and hat, preparing to leave. I had a sudden love for that bed in Room 3-F.

"What's going to happen to me?" Dr. Kenneth Draper asked.

"Keep your mouth shut," I advised him resignedly. "Tell no one what you've told me. Except Mary Thorndecker."

"I can't tell her," he groaned.

"If you don't," I said, " I will. Besides, she's already guessed most of it."

"She'll hate me," he said.

"Oh, I think she'll find it in her heart to forgive you," I told him. "Just like Lord Jesus. Also, she'll probably inherit, and she'll need someone to help her run Crittenden Hall and the lab."

He brightened a little at that.

"Maybe she will forgive me," he said, almost to himself. "After all, I just did what Dr. Thorndecker told me to."

"I know," I said. "You just obeyed orders. Now where have I heard that before? Goodnight, Dr. Draper. I hope you and Mary Thorndecker get married and live happily ever after."

There were two Coburn police cruisers, a car from the sheriff's office, and an ambulance in the driveway when I went outside. The gates were wide open. I just walked out, and no one made any effort to stop me.

Thirty minutes later I was snuggling deep in bed, purring with content. The last thing I thought of before I dropped off to sleep was that I had forgotten to pick up my aluminum stepladder before I left Crittenden. I was more convinced than ever that I just wasn't cut out for a life of crime.

The Eighth Day

I awoke about eleven Monday morning. I got out of bed immediately.
Showered, shaved, dressed. Finished packing and snapped the cases shut.
Took a final look around Room 3-F to make certain I wasn't forgetting
anything. Then I rang for Sam Livingston, and asked him to take the
luggage down to my car. I told him he could have what was left of the
ale and vodka. I took the remainder of the brandy with me.

The desk clerk wanted to talk about the terrible tragedy out at Crittenden. That was his label: "Terrible tragedy." I cut him short and asked
for my bill. While he was totaling it, I glanced over toward the locked
cigar stand. There was a sign propped on the counter. I went over to read
it.

"Closed because of death in the family."

I think that sad, stupid sign hit me harder than anything I had seen the
night before.

I paid my bill with a credit card, and said goodby to the clerk. Went
into the bar to shake Jimmy's hand, pass him a five and say goodby. Went
out to the parking lot and helped Sam Livingston stow the suitcases and
briefcase in the trunk. Put my hat, coat, and brandy bottle in the back
seat.

I gave Sam a twenty. He took it with thanks.

"Take care," I said, as lightly as I could.

That ancient black face showed nothing—no distress, sadness, sorrow.
Why should it? He had seen everything twice. Like Ben Faber, the old
sexton, had said: nothing new ever happens.

I got in the Grand Prix, slammed the door. I stuck my hand out through
the open window. The mummy shook it briefly.

"Sam," he said, "you ain't going to change this world."

"I never thought I could," I told him.

"Um . . . " he said. "Well, if you ever get up this way . . . "

I drove away. It seemed only right that the last words I heard in Coburn were an unfinished sentence.

It was a long, brooding drive back to New York. I wish I could tell you that once Coburn was behind me, the sky cleared, the sun came out, the world was born again. It would have been a nice literary touch. But nothing like that happened. The weather was almost as miserable as it had been a week ago, when I drove north. A wild west wind scattered snow flurries across the road. Dark clouds whipped in a grim sky.

I stopped for breakfast at the first fast-food joint I came to. Tomato juice, pancakes, bacon, three cups of black coffee. Nothing tasted of anything. Sawdust maybe. Wet wallboard. Paste. The fault may have been mine. Back in the car, I cleansed my palate with a belt of brandy.

I hit the road again, driving faster than I should have. It was all automatic: steering, shifting, braking. Because I was busy trying to understand.

I started with Julie Thorndecker. Maybe, as Agatha Binder said, she was a loving, sacrificing wife. But deserting a fatally ill husband to run away with a young lover is not the act of a loving, sacrificing wife. I thought that in all Julie's actions there was a strain of sexual excitement. I do not mean to imply she was a nymphomaniac—whatever that is. I just believe she was addicted to illicit sex, especially when it included an element of risk. Some people, men and women, are like that. They cannot feel pleasure without guilt. And they cannot feel guilt unless there is a possibility of punishment.

I think Julie Thorndecker had the instincts of a survivor. If Thorndecker hadn't saved her at that Cambridge party, someone else would have. She was too young, too beautiful to perish. Her reactions were elemental. When she saw her husband dying, she thought simply: the game is up. And so she planned to move on. She may have loved him and respected him—I think she did—but she just didn't know how to grieve. Life was too strong in her. So she made ready to take off with a hot, willing stud. I'm sure she loved him, too. Goodfellow, that is. She would love any man who worshipped her, since he was just giving her back a mirror image of her own infatuation with herself, her body, her beauty. A man's love confirmed her good taste.

Telford Gordon Thorndecker offered a more puzzling enigma. I could not doubt his expertise in his profession. I'd agree with everyone else and say he was a genius—if I was certain what a genius was. But I think he was driven by more than scientific curiosity and a desire for fame. I think his choice of his particular field of research—senescence, death; youth, immortality—was a vital clue to his character.

Few of us act from the motive we profess. The worm is always there, deep and squirming. A man might say he wishes to work with and counsel young boys, to give them the benefit of his knowledge and experience, to

keep them from delinquency, to help them through the agonies of adoles-
cence. That may all be true. It may also be true that he simply loves young
boys.

In Thorndecker's case, I think he was motivated by an incredible seductive, sexually active young wife as much as he was by the desire to
pioneer in the biology of aging. I think, perhaps unconsciously, the dis-
parity in their ages was constantly on his mind. He saw her almost every
day: youthful, live, energetic, vibrant, physically beautiful and sexually
eager. He recognized how he himself, more than twice her age, had
slowed, bent, become sluggish, his blood cooling, all the portents of old
age becoming evident.

The search for immortality was as much, or more, for himself as it was
for the benefit of mankind. He was in a hurry to stop the clock. Because
in another ten years, even another five, his last chance would be gone.
There could be no reversal; he knew that. He dreamt that, with hard work
and good fortune, he might never grow older while she aged to his level
and beyond.

You see, he loved her.

Although he could understand the rational need for her infidelity with
Goodfellow—his work must not be delayed!—jealousy and hatred can-
kered his ego. In the end, he could not endure the thought of those two
young bodies continuing to exist, rubbing in lubricious heat, swollen with
life, while he was cold mould.

So he took them with him.

Wild supposition, I know. All of it was. So I came to the dismal conclusion: how could I hope to understand others when I was a mystery to
myself. I wanted desperately to tell the saga of Dr. Telford Gordon Thorndecker to Joan Powell. That brainy lady had the ability to thread her way
through the tangles of the human heart and make very human sense.

It was raining in New York, too. I found a parking space only a half-
block away from my apartment, and wrestled my luggage into the lobby
in a single, shin-bumping trip. I collected my mail, and banged my way
up the narrow staircase. Inside, door locked and chained, I made myself
a dark Scotch highball and took it into the bathroom with me while I
soaked in a hot tub. My feet had been wet and cold for a week; I was
delighted to see the toes bend and the arches flex.

Came back into the living room, dressed casually, and went through the
accumulated mail. Bills. Junk. Nothing from Joan Powell. I unpacked, put
dirty laundry in the hamper, restored my toilet articles to the medicine
cabinet.

Put something low and mournful on the hi-fi, and sat down to prepare
an official report on the Thorndecker affair. The Bingham Foundation
supplied its field investigators with a five-page printed form for such reports. It had spaces for Personal Habits, Financial Status, Religious Affil-
iation, Neighbors' comments, etc., etc. I stared at the form a few minutes,

then printed APPLICANT DECEASED in big block letters across the top page, and let it go at that.

There was a can of sardines in the refrigerator, and I finished that with soda crackers. I also ate a few olives, a slice of dill pickle, a small wedge of stale cheddar, and a spoonful of orange marmalade. But that was all right; I wasn't hungry.

I watched the news on TV. All bad. I tried reading three different paperbacks, and tossed them all aside. I piled my outstanding bills neatly for payment. I sharpened two pencils. I smoked almost half a pack of cigarettes. I found a tin of rolled anchovies in the kitchen cupboard, opened it, and wolfed them down. And got thirsty, naturally.

About 9:30 P.M., on my third highball, I gave up, and sat down near the phone, trying to plan how to handle it. I brought over several sheets of paper and the sharpened pencils. I started making notes.

"Hello?" she would say.

"Powell," I'd say, "please don't hang up. This is Samuel Todd. I want to apologize to you for the way I acted. There is nothing you can call me as bad as what I've called myself. I'm phoning now to ask if there is any way we can get together again. To beg you. I will accept any conditions, endure any restraints, suffer any ignominy, do anything you demand, if you'll only let me see you again."

It went on and on like that. Abject surrender. I made copious notes. I imagined objections she might have, and I jotted down what my answer should be. I covered three pages with humility, crawling, total submission. I thought sure that, if she didn't hang up immediately, I could weasel my way back into her favor, or at least persuade her to give me a chance to prove how much I loved her and needed her.

And if she brought up the difference in our ages again, I prepared a special speech on that:

"Powell, the past week has taught me what a lot of bullshit the whole business of age can be. What's important is enjoying each other's company, having interests in common, loving, and keeping sympathy and understanding on the front burner, warm and ready when needed."

I read over everything I had written. I thought I had a real lawyer's brief, ready for any eventuality. I couldn't think of a single way she might react, from hot curses to cold silence, that I wasn't prepared to answer.

I mixed a fresh drink, drained half of it, picked up the phone. I arranged my speeches in front of me. I took a deep breath. I dialed her number.

She picked it up on the third ring.

"Hello?" she said.

"Powell," I said, "please don't hang—"

"Todd?" she said. "Get your ass over here."

I ran.

THE SEVENTH COMMANDMENT

◆

1

It was a swell year.

In January, her boss, Mike Trevalyan, sent Dora up to Boston to look into a claim on a homeowners' policy. This yuppie couple had gone to New York for the weekend and returned Sunday night to find their condo looted. They said. All their furniture and paintings had disappeared. They had made a videotape to record their possessions, and wanted the Company to fork over the full face value of the policy: $50,000.

It took her two days to discover that the yuppies were bubbleheads with a fondness for funny cigarettes. Every piece of furniture in their pad, every painting, had been leased; they didn't own a stick. They thought all they'd have to do was take out an insurance policy, pay the first year's premium, sell off their rented furnishings, and file a claim. Hah!

In February, Dora went to Portland to investigate a claim on a quilt factory that had been totaled by an early-morning fire. The local fire laddies couldn't find any obvious evidence of arson, but the quilt company was having trouble paying its bills, and that two-mil casualty policy the owner carried must have looked mighty sweet.

It took her a week to figure out how it had been done. The boss had pulled a wooden table directly under a low-hanging light bulb. He had heaped the table with cotton batting. Then he had draped the 150-watt bulb with gauze, switched on the light, and strolled away, humming ''Blue Skies.'' The heat of the bulb ignited the gauze, which fell onto the batting, and eventually the whole factory was torched.

In April, she went to Stamford to look into a claim for the theft of a Picasso pencil sketch from a posh art gallery. The drawing was valued at $100,000. She was in Stamford less than a day when the Company got a phone call from a man claiming to be the thief and offering to sell the artwork back for twenty-five grand. Trevalyan called Dora and told her to liaise with the FBI.

After several phone calls, she set up a meet with the crook in a shopping mall parking lot. She handed over the marked cash, received the drawing, and the FBI moved in. The artwork turned out to be a fake, and the "thief" turned out to be the lover of the art gallery owner who had filed the claim. He had engineered the whole deal and had the real Picasso sketch in his safe deposit box.

In May and June, every claim Dora investigated was apparently on the up-and-up. Everyone seemed to be honest, and it worried her; she feared she had overlooked something.

But things got back to normal in July.

It happened just outside of Providence at the summer home of a Wall Street investment banker. His wife said there had been a power failure shortly before midnight. The banker stumbled around in the darkness, found a flashlight, and started down the basement stairs to check the circuit breakers. The wife heard him shriek and the sound of his fall. A few moments later the lights came back on, and she had hurried to the basement to find her husband crumpled at the foot of the stairs. Broken neck. Very dead.

Dora got there a day after it happened, and the wife's story sounded fishy to her. It took on a more profound piscine scent when she noted, and pointed out to the investigating detectives, that although all the electric clocks in the house showed a loss of about twenty minutes, corroborating the wife's tale, the timing clock on their VCR hadn't been reset and showed the power had gone off at 9:30 P.M. that evening.

Questioning of neighborhood yentas suggested that the wife had been having a torrid affair with their part-time gardener, a husky youth who studied the martial arts and frequently competed in karate tournaments. The gardener might have been physically strong, but there was little between his ears. He broke first and admitted he had taken part in a murder plot devised by the wife.

She had smuggled him into the basement late that afternoon while her husband was out playing croquet. At 9:30 P.M., the lover cut the power at the main switch. The banker came cautiously down the basement stairs. The gardener caught his ankle and after he fell, broke his neck. Power was restored, and they let the electric clocks show a lapse of twenty minutes. But they forgot about the VCR timer. Their motive? The banker's life insurance, of course. And love, Dora supposed.

In September, she went to Manhattan where a local politico claimed his Hatteras 37 Convertible had been stolen from the 79th Street boat basin. It took Dora less than a week to discover he had *given* the yacht to his ex-mistress, a vengeful woman who had threatened to talk to the tabloids about his bedroom peccadilloes. These included, she said, a fondness for wearing her lingerie—and she had the Polaroids to prove it.

Dora found the boat moored at City Island. The ex-mistress had changed the name on the transom from *Our Thing* to *My Thing*.

October was filled with a number of routine cases, but in November Dora investigated the claim of a wizened dealer in autographs and signed historical documents. He said the gems of his collection, several rather raunchy letters from Samuel Clemens to his brother, had been stolen from his shop. The Worcester police told Dora that the store showed every evidence of a break-in, but they couldn't understand why other valuable items on display hadn't been taken, unless it was a contract burglary: The thief had been paid to lift the Mark Twain items and none others.

Dora came close to okaying the claim until she noticed ("You're a pain in the ass," Mike Trevalyan had once told her, "but you're observant as hell") that the office walls in the dealer's musty shop had recently been repapered. It seemed strange that the dealer would spend money to brighten his private sanctum while the remainder of his store looked like the loo in the House of Usher.

She hired a local PI with more nerve than scruples, and one dark night they picked the front door lock of the dealer's shop. It took them less than a half-hour to find the Samuel Clemens letters, in plastic slips, concealed beneath the new wallpaper in the back office. It turned out that the dealer was suffering a bad case of the shorts, having conceived an unholy passion for a tootsie one-third his age whose motto was "No pay, no play."

Dora returned home to Hartford to find her husband, Mario Conti, planning their Thanksgiving Day dinner. He had been a long-haul trucker when she married him, but had since been promoted to dispatcher. However, his real kingdom was the kitchen. He loved to cook and had the talents of a cordon-bleu, which was why Dora, who stood five-three in her Peds, usually weighed 150 pounds (or 145 during semimonthly diets). But Mario had never called her "dumpling" or "butterball," the darling man.

"Tacchino di festa!" he cried, and showed his shopping list.

"Salami?" she said, reading. "And sweet sausage? With turkey?"

"For the stuffing," he explained. "Trust me."

"Okay," she said happily.

They invited twelve guests, family and friends, and the dining room of their snug cottage was crowded. But everyone praised the turkey as Mario's masterpiece, and the numerous side dishes and gallons of jug wine made for a real *festa*.

There was enough food left over, Dora figured, for two more dinners, but it was not to be. Trevalyan called on Friday morning, although it was supposed to be a holiday.

"Better pack," he said, "and get down to the office. I'll brief you here."

"Where am I going?" she asked.

"Manhattan."

"For how long?"

"As long as it takes."

"How much is involved?"

"Three million," he said. "Whole life."

"Whee!" Dora said. "Natural death?"

"Not very," Trevalyan said.

2

Helene Pierce watched him dress. He had a good body—not great, but good. Flab was beginning to collect on his abdomen and his ass was starting to sink, but for a guy of forty-six, what did you expect?

"I wish you could stay," she said. "I could order up some food. Maybe that chicken you like with rosemary and garlic."

He was standing before the long mirror on the bathroom door, flipping his tie into a Windsor knot.

"No can do," Clayton Starrett said. "Eleanor wants me home early. Another of her charity bashes."

"Where?"

"At the Plaza. For children with AIDS. I had to buy a table."

"A party so soon after the funeral?"

He turned and shrugged into his vest. "You know Eleanor and her charity bashes. Besides, all the clichés are true: Life really does go on. He's been dead—how long? A week tomorrow. People used to mourn for a year. Women wore black. Or, if they were Italian, for the rest of their lives. No more. Now people mourn for a week."

"Or less," she said.

He stood before the mirror again, adjusting the hang of his jacket. Everything must be just so.

"Or less," he agreed. "You know who's taking it hardest?"

"Your sister?" Helene guessed.

He turned to look at her. "How did you know? Her eyes are still swollen. I've heard her crying in her room. I never would have thought it would hit her like that; Felicia is such a fruitcake."

"What about your mother?"

"You know her: strictly the 'God's-will-be-done' type. Since it happened, she's practically been living with that guru of hers. I'd love to know how much she's been paying him. Plenty, I bet. But that's her problem.''

"Have the police discovered anything new?'' Helene asked.

"If they have, they're not telling us. They still think it was a mugger. Probably a doper. Could be. Father was the kind of man who wouldn't hand over his wallet without a fight.''

"Clay, he was seventy years old.''

Starrett shook his head. "He could have been ninety, and he still would have put up a struggle. He was a mean, cantankerous old bastard, but he had balls.''

He took up his velvet-collared chesterfield. He came over to sit on the edge of the bed. He stared down at her. She was still naked, and he put one hand lightly on her tawny thigh.

"What will you do tonight?'' he asked.

"I'll call my brother and see if he's got anything planned. If not, maybe we'll have dinner together.''

"Good. If you see him, tell him everything is going beautifully. No hitches.''

"I'll tell him,'' she promised.

He leaned down to kiss a bare breast. She gasped.

"You're getting me horny again,'' she said.

He laughed, stood up, pulled on his topcoat. "Oh,'' he said, "I almost forgot.'' He fished into his jacket pocket, took out a small suede pouch closed with a drawstring. "Another bauble to add to your collection,'' he said. "Almost three carats. D color. Cushion cut. A nice little rock.''

"Thank you, Clay,'' she said faintly.

He started to leave, then snapped his fingers and turned back.

"Something else,'' he said. "The claims adjuster on the life insurance policy is in town asking questions. A woman. I've already talked to her, and she's planning to see mother, Eleanor and Felicia. It's possible she may want to talk to our friends. If she looks you up, answer all her questions honestly but don't volunteer any information.''

"I can handle it,'' Helene said. "What's her name?''

"Dora Conti.''

"What's she like?''

"Red-haired. Short and plump. A real butterball.''

"Doesn't sound like an insurance snoop.''

"Don't let her looks fool you,'' he said. "I get the feeling she's a sharpie. Just watch what you say. I'll call you tomorrow.''

She rose and followed him into the living room. She locked, bolted, and chained the door behind him. She brought the little suede pouch over to her corner desk and switched on the gooseneck lamp. She took a jeweler's loupe from the top drawer, opened the pouch, spilled the diamond onto the desk blotter.

She leaned close, loupe to her eye, and turned the stone this way and that. She couldn't spot a flaw, and it seemed to be an icy white. She held it up to the light and admired the gleam. Then she replaced the gem in the pouch and added it to a wooden cigar box, almost filled. Her treasures went into the bottom desk drawer.

She knew she should take the unset diamonds to her safe deposit box. She had been telling herself that for a year. But she could not do it, *could not*. She liked their sharp feel, their hard glitter. She liked to sit at her desk, heap up the shining stones, let them drift through her fingers.

She called Turner Pierce.

"He's left," she reported. "Going to a society bash at the Plaza with his wife. How about dinner?"

"Sure," he said. "But I'll have to split by ten. I'm meeting Ramon uptown at eleven."

"Plenty of time," she assured him. "Suppose I meet you at seven at that Italian place on Lex. The one with the double veal chops."

"Vito's," he said. "Sounds good to me. Don't get gussied up. I'm wearing black leather tonight."

"You would," she said, laughing.

They sat at a table in a dim corner, and three waiters fussed about them, knowing he tipped like a rajah. They both had Tanqueray vodka on ice with a lime wedge. Then they studied the menus.

"What did you get?" Turner asked in a low voice.

"Almost three carats," Helene said. "Icy white. Cushion cut."

"Nice," he said. "But you earned it."

"He said to tell you everything is going beautifully. No hitches."

"I'm glad he thinks so. I have a feeling Ramon isn't all that happy. I think he wants more action."

"I thought the idea was to go slowly at first, get everything set up and functioning, and then build up the gross gradually."

"That was the idea, but Ramon is getting antsy since his New Orleans contact was charged."

"Will he talk?"

"The New Orleans man? I doubt that very much. He had an accident."

"Oh? What happened?"

"His car exploded. He was in it."

She raised her head to stare at him. "Turner," she said, "watch your back with Ramon."

"I never drive my car to visit him," he said, grinning. "I always take a cab."

They had double veal chops, rare, and split orders of pasta all'olio and Caesar salad. They also shared a bottle of Pinot Grigio. They both had good appetites and finished everything.

"Not like Kansas City, is it?" Turner said, sitting back.

"Thank God," she said. "How many hamburgers can you eat? Listen,

Clayton said there's an insurance claim adjuster in town asking questions. A woman named Dora Conti. He thinks she's a sharpie and says she may want to talk to Lewis Starrett's friends.''

"No sweat," he said. "You know, I liked the old man. Well, maybe not liked, but I admired him. He inherited a little hole-in-the-wall store on West Forty-seventh Street, and he built it into Starrett Fine Jewelry. They may not be Tiffany or Cartier, but they do all right. How many shops? Sixteen, I think. All over the world. Plenty of loot there.''

"There was," Helene said, "until Clayton brought in those kooky designers. Then the ink turned red.''

"That was last year," Turner said. "He's on the right track now. Let's have espresso and Frangelico at the bar; I've got time.''

They sat close together, knees touching, at the little bar near the entrance.

"Felicia phoned me again," Turner said.

"Oh? What did she want?''

"You know.''

"Clayton called her a fruitcake.''

"That she is. In spades. But she could be a problem. So I'll play along.''

"Dear," she said, putting a hand on his arm, "how long have we got? A year? Two? Three?''

"Three, I hope. Maybe two. I'll know when it's coming to a screeching halt.''

"And then?''

"Off we go into the wild blue yonder. You know what my cut is. We'll have enough in one year, plenty in two, super plenty in three. And you'll have your rock collection. We deserve it; we're nice people.''

She laughed, lifted his hand to her lips, kissed his knuckles. "Dangerous game," she observed.

He shrugged. "The first law of investing," he said. "The higher the return, the bigger the risk.''

"Busy tomorrow?" she asked casually.

"I'm meeting Felicia for an early lunch. The afternoon's open.''

"Sounds good to me," she said.

3

The Company kept a corporate suite at the Hotel Bedlington on Madison Avenue, and that's where Dora stayed. She called Mario to tell him about the sitting room with television set and fully equipped wet bar, the neat little pantry, and the two bedrooms, each with a king-size bed.

"Great for orgies," Dora told him.

Mario lapsed into trucker talk, and she giggled and hung up.

The hotel had a cocktail lounge off the lobby and, in the rear, a rather frowsty dining room that seemed to be patronized mostly by blue-haired women and epicene older men who carried handkerchiefs up their sleeve cuffs. The food was edible but tasteless; everything lacked seasoning. They needed a chef, Dora decided, who had Mario's faculty with herbs and spices.

But that's where she had lunch with Detective John Wenden, NYPD. They met in the lobby and examined each other's ID. Then he inspected her.

"You know," he said, "if you lost thirty pounds you'd be a very attractive woman."

"You know," she said, "if you were Robert Redford you'd be a very attractive man."

He laughed and held up his palms. "So-ree," he said. "It was a stupid thing to say, and I apologize. Okay?"

"Sure," she said. "Let's go eat."

"You got a swindle sheet?"

"Of course."

"Then I'll have a steak."

"Take my advice and use plenty of salt and pepper. The food is solid but has no flavor."

"Ketchup covers a multitude of sins," he said.

The ancient maître d' showed them to a table against the wall. Detective Wenden looked around at the oldsters working on their watercress sandwiches and chamomile tea.

"Think I could get a Geritol on the rocks?" he said.

"Whatever turns you on," Dora said.

But he ordered a light beer with his club steak. Dora also had a beer with her chef's salad.

"You married?" Wenden asked her.

"Yes," she said. "Happily. You?"

"Divorced," he said. "All New York cops are divorced—didn't you know? Occupational hazard. How much was the Starrett insurance?"

"Three million."

"That's sweet. Who gets it?"

"Thirds; equal shares to his wife, son, and daughter. Hey, I'm supposed to be asking the questions. That's why I'm buying you a steak—to pick your brain."

"Not much to pick." He paused while the creaking waiter served their beers. Then: "You read the clips?"

She nodded. "A lot of nothing."

"That's all we've got—nothing."

His steak was served. He cut off a corner and tasted it cautiously. "You're right," he said. "Cardboard." He sprinkled the meat heavily with salt and pepper as Dora dug into her salad.

"You can talk with your mouth full, you know," she said. "I won't be offended."

"Okay," he said equably, "let me give you a quick recap.

"The victim is Lewis Starrett, seventy, white male, retired president of Starrett Fine Jewelry, Inc. But he's still chairman and principal stockholder. Shows up every working day for a few hours at their flagship store on Park Avenue. Lives in an eighteen-room duplex on Fifth Avenue with his wife, daughter, son and son's wife. Also two live-in servants, a butler and a cook-housekeeper, a married couple. The deceased was supposed to be a nasty, opinionated old bastard but everyone agrees he was fearless. His first mistake; it doesn't pay to be fearless in this city.

"Every evening at nine o'clock, Lewis Starrett takes a stroll. His second mistake; you don't walk at night in this city unless you have to. He goes down Fifth to Fifty-ninth Street, east on Fifty-ninth to Lexington Avenue where he stops at a cigar store and buys the one daily cigar his doctor allows.

"Then he continues north on Lex to Eighty-third Street, smoking his cigar. West on Eighty-third Street to his apartment house on Fifth. They say you could set your watch by him. His third mistake; he never varied his route or time.

"On the fatal night, as the tabloids like to say, he starts his walk at the usual time, buys his cigar at the Lexington Avenue shop, lights up and starts home. But he never makes it. His body is found facedown on the sidewalk between Lex and Park. He's been stabbed once, practically between the shoulder blades. Instant blotto. No witnesses. And that's it.''

Detective Wenden's timing was perfect; he finished his story at the same time he finished his lunch. He started to light a cigarette, but the maître d' came hobbling over to tell him the whole dining room was a no-smoking area.

''Unless you want dessert and coffee,'' Dora said, ''let's go into the cocktail lounge and have another beer. We can smoke in there.''

''You got a deal,'' he said.

They were the only customers in the bar. They sat on uncomfortable black vinyl chairs at a black Formica table, sipped their beers, smoked their cigarettes.

''Was he robbed?'' Dora asked.

Wenden looked at her curiously. ''Do you always go to this much trouble to check out an insurance claim?''

''Not usually,'' she admitted. ''But this time we've got three million reasons. The Company wouldn't like it if someone profits illegally from Starrett's murder.''

''You mean if one of the beneficiaries offed him?''

''That's what I mean.'' She repeated: ''Was he robbed?''

''Negative,'' Wenden said. ''He had all his credit cards and a wallet with about four hundred in cash. Also, he was wearing a gold Starrett watch worth fifteen grand and a man's Starrett diamond ring worth another thirty Gs.''

''But you figure it was a bungled robbery?''

''Not necessarily. Maybe a coked-up panhandler asks for a buck. Starrett stiffs him, maybe curses him, and turns away. His family and friends say he was capable of doing that. Then the panhandler gets sore, pulls out a blade, lets him have it and takes off.''

''Without pausing to lift his wallet or watch?''

''There were apparently no witnesses to the stabbing, but maybe the killer didn't want to push his luck by staying at the scene for even another minute. Someone might have come along.''

''I don't know,'' Dora said doubtfully. ''Seems to me there are a lot of maybes in your scenario.''

The detective stirred restlessly. ''Have you investigated many homicides?''

''A few.''

''Then you know that even when they're solved there are always a lot of loose ends. I've never worked a case that was absolutely complete with everything explained and accounted for.''

''Another beer?'' she asked.

"Why not?" he said. "I've got nothing to do this afternoon but crack four other killings."

"That much on your plate?"

"It never ends," he said wearily. "There's a lot of dying going around these days."

Dora went to the bar and brought back two more cold bottles.

"Why do I get the feeling," she said, "that you don't totally believe your own story of the way it happened."

"It's the official line," he said.

"Screw the official line," she said angrily. "This is just between you and me, and I'm not about to run off at the mouth to the tabloids. What do *you* think?"

He sighed. "A couple of things bother me. You ever investigate a stabbing?"

"No."

"A professional knifer holds the blade like a door key, knuckles down. He uses an underhanded jab, comes in low, goes up high, usually around the belly or kidneys. It's soft there; no bones to snap the steel. The blow that killed Starrett started high and came down low into his back. An amateur did that, holding the knife handle in his fist, knuckles up. And it was amateur's luck that the blade didn't break on the spine or ribs. It sliced an artery and punctured the heart—more luck."

"For the killer, not Starrett."

"Yeah. Ordinarily one stab like that wouldn't kill instantly."

"Man or woman?"

"A man, I'd guess. That shiv went deep. Plenty of power there. It cut through overcoat, suit jacket, shirt, undershirt, skin, flesh, and into the heart."

"A long blade?"

"Had to be. You talk to any of the family yet?"

"The son," Dora said. "Clayton."

"What was your take on him?"

"I got the feeling he wasn't exactly out of his mind with grief."

Wenden nodded. "I thought he was controlling his sorrow very well. From what I've been able to pick up, he and his father didn't get along so great. Clayton became president and CEO of Starrett Jewelry when the old man retired, and I guess they didn't see eye-to-eye on a lot of business decisions. Plenty of screaming arguments, according to the office staff. But that's not unusual when a father gives up power and a son takes over. The heir usually wants to do things differently, try new things, prove his ability."

Dora sighed. "I hate these family affairs. They always turn out to be snarls of string. It's so sad. You'd think a family would try to get along."

The detective laughed. "Most homicides are committed by a family member or a close friend. You talk to the attorney yet?"

"No, not yet."

"A nice old guy. He was Lewis Starrett's lawyer from the beginning."

"Who inherits?" Dora asked.

"The wife," Wenden said. "For tax reasons. About eighty million."

"Wow! Nothing to the son or daughter?"

"Well, you say they'll each be getting a million in insurance money. And I guess Lewis figured Olivia would leave everything to the children when she shuffles off."

"What's she like?"

"Olivia?" He grinned. "I'll let you make up your own mind. The daughter, Felicia, is the one to look out for. She's off the wall."

"How so?"

"Crazy. Runs with a rough downtown crowd. But I'll say this for her: She seems to be taking her father's death harder than any of the others."

"What about Clayton's wife?"

"Eleanor? A social butterfly. She's on a zillion committees. Always planning a party for this charity or that. She loves it. Maybe because she can never wear the same dress twice. Listen, I've got to split. Where do you live?"

"Hartford."

"Going home for the weekend?"

"I doubt it. My husband may come down if he can get away."

"What does he do?"

"He's a dispatcher for a trucking company. Works crazy hours."

"Well, if he doesn't show up, maybe we can get together for a pizza." She stared at him. "I told you I was happily married."

"And I heard you," the detective said. "What's that got to do with sharing a pizza?"

"Nothing," Dora said. "As long as we keep it on a professional level. Maybe we can compare notes and do each other some good."

"Sure we can," Wenden said. "Here's my card. If I'm not in, you can always leave a message. Thanks for the lunch."

"My pleasure," Dora said and watched him move away, thinking he was an okay guy but he really should get his suit pressed and his shoes shined. She knew he had to deal with a lot of scumbags, but he didn't have to dress like one.

4

The flagship store of Starrett Fine Jewelry, Inc., was located on Park Avenue just south of 57th Street. It occupied one of the few remaining town houses on the Avenue in midtown Manhattan, surrounded by steel and glass towers. The baroque six-story structure, built in 1896 as the family home of a shipping magnate, was designed by a student of Stanford White, and the exterior had been cited by the Landmarks Preservation Commission.

The jewelry selling area was on the ground level, with silverware, crystal, and china on the second. The third and fourth floors were designers' studios and shops for engraving and repairs. Executive offices filled the top two stories. Starrett's main workshop for the crafting of exclusive designs was in Brooklyn. The company also purchased quantity items and gold chains from independent suppliers in Taiwan and South Korea.

In addition to New York, Starrett stores were located in Boston, Chicago, Beverly Hills, San Francisco, Atlanta, Dallas, Palm Beach, London, Paris, Zurich, Hong Kong, Honolulu, Cancun, Rome, and Brussels. Starrett did not have a mail order catalogue but sometimes sent favored customers drawings of new designs before they were made up and offered to the general public. Many of these were one-of-a-kind pieces: brooches, bracelets, rings, necklaces, tiaras.

Generally, all the Starrett stores, worldwide, offered the same merchandise, although the mix was often varied. The general manager of each shop ordered the items from New York that he thought would sell best in his area. In addition, every Starrett store had its own workshop and was encouraged to produce jewelry on special order for valued clients, usually personalized items designed to the customer's specifications.

During the last year, Clayton Starrett's second as president and chief executive officer, he had replaced the general managers of nine of the sixteen Starrett stores. Some of these men (and one woman) had been with the company for ten, fifteen, twenty years, and their termination had been the cause of the violent disagreement between Clayton and his father.

The late Lewis Starrett claimed they were all experienced, loyal employees who had proved their competence, and firing them was not only an act of ingratitude but, more important, would have an adverse effect on revenues and net profits.

But Clayton was adamant. The veterans would have to go because, he said, they knew little about modern merchandising, advertising, promotion, and public relations. They were content to cater to an aging clientele and made no effort to attract a new generation of Starrett customers. The argument between father and son became so fierce that it began to affect the morale of personnel in the New York store. It was only resolved when Clayton, white-faced, threatened to resign and move out of his parents' apartment. Thereupon the old man backed down, and the son became the recognized and undisputed boss of Starrett Fine Jewelry, Inc.

The new general managers he hired for the subsidiary stores were mostly hard young men, smartly dressed, with an eye on the bottom line and a brusque manner with subordinates. A few were reputedly MBAs, and several were foreign-born. All seemed possessed of driving ambition and, shortly before his death, Lewis Starrett had to admit that revenues and net profits were increasing spectacularly.

When Lewis ran the company with iron fist and bellows of rage, he arrived for work each morning at 7:30 and frequently put in a twelve-hour day. Clayton's style of management was considerably more laid-back. He showed up around ten o'clock, took a lengthy lunch and, if he returned from that, was usually out of the office by five.

On this day he stepped from his chauffeured stretch limousine (a presidential perk) and entered the Starrett Fine Jewelry Building a few minutes before ten. He hardly glanced into the selling area, almost devoid of customers. He was not dismayed; Starrett's patrons were not early-morning shoppers; they preferred late afternoon.

A small, elaborately decorated elevator lifted him slowly to his private office on the top floor. His secretary, an English import hired more for her accent than her ability, took his homburg and chesterfield. A few minutes later she returned with a cup of black coffee and a toasted bagel. This minibreakfast was served on bone china in an exclusive Starrett pattern called Belladonna.

As he gnawed his bagel, he reviewed the day's schedule. There was nothing that seemed to him of monumental importance, and he wondered if, about four or four-thirty that afternoon, he might call Helene Pierce and ask if she was willing to receive him.

He was paying $5,400 a month for her apartment, giving her $1,000 a week walking-around money, and occasionally bringing her small diamonds for her collection. But in spite of this largesse, he had to obey her rules: no unexpected visits, limited phone calls, no questions as to how she spent her time. He accepted these dictates cheerfully because, he admitted to himself, he was obsessed. Helene was half his age, had a body that never failed to arouse him, and was so practiced in the craft of love that he never ceased to wonder how one so young could be so knowing and experienced.

His first task of the morning was to review, on his desktop computer, the previous day's sales at the sixteen Starrett stores. It was then the height of the Christmas shopping season, a period that usually accounted for thirty percent of Starrett's annual revenues. He punched the keys and watched intently as numbers filled the screen.

The computer showed not only current sales but provided comparison with income of the same week during the previous five years. The numbers Clayton studied showed that Starrett's business was essentially flat; the increase was barely enough to cover the inflation rate. He was now more firmly convinced than ever that Starrett could not depend solely on retail sales for continued profits and growth.

He then switched to a software program for which only he possessed the access code. Now the numbers shown on the screen were much more encouraging. Exciting, in fact, and he blessed the day Helene and Turner Pierce had come into his life. Helene had brought joy, and sometimes rapture; Turner had provided financial salvation.

His first meeting was with an in-house designer to go over proposed designs for a new line of sterling silver keyrings in the shapes of mythological beasts. They had a surrealistic discussion as to whether or not the unicorn was a phallic symbol and if so, what effect it might have on sales. Clayton eventually initialed all the sketches except for the centaur, which he deemed too suggestive for public display and sale.

He accepted a phone call from Eleanor and spoke with her for almost fifteen minutes, marveling (not for the first time) how his adulterous affair had made him a better husband, more patient with his wife and amenable to her wishes. She had called to remind him that they were to attend a charity dinner and fashion show at the Metropolitan Museum.

Eleanor was not directly involved, but the Starretts had subscribed ($1,000 a couple) because one of Eleanor's close friends had organized the affair. These endless charity parties were, Clayton knew, a world of mutual back-scratching. He submitted because they kept his wife busy and happy, and because they were good public relations. Also, he enjoyed wearing a dinner jacket.

He then met with an interior decorator and went over plans to redecorate his office. The day after his father's funeral, Clayton had moved into his office, the largest in the executive suite. But it was crammed with dark oak furniture, the windows overlooking Park Avenue half-hidden behind dusty velvet drapes, the walls covered with flocked paper. Clayton spent an hour describing exactly what he wanted: stainless steel, glass, Bauhaus-style chairs, bright Warhols on the walls, and perhaps a Biedermeier couch as a conversation piece.

He lunched at a Japanese restaurant, the guest of a Tokyo merchant who wanted Starrett to carry a choice selection of antique inro and netsuke. While they ate sashimi and drank hot sake, the exporter displayed a few samples of his exquisitely carved wares. Clayton was fascinated and agreed to accept a small shipment on consignment as a test of the sales potential.

He returned to his office, wondering if Starrett might emulate Gump's of San Francisco and offer imported curios, bibelots, and objets d'art. They could, he reckoned, be sold in the department now handling estate jewelry, and might very well find a market.

He dictated several letters to his secretary and, after she left, called Helene's apartment on his private line. But there was no answer, and he guessed she was out spending money. "Shopping," she had once told him, "is my second favorite pastime."

It was then almost 4:30, and Clayton decided to call his limousine, return home, and take a nap before he dressed for dinner. But then Solomon Guthrie phoned and asked if he could come up immediately. Guthrie was Starrett's chief financial officer, and Clayton knew what he wanted to talk about.

Sol was sixty-three, had worked for Starrett forty years, and called his bosses Mister Lewis and Mister Clayton. He had a horseshoe of frazzled white hair around a bald pate, and was possibly the last office worker in New York to wear celluloid cuff protectors. He had learned, with difficulty, to use computers, but still insisted in keeping a duplicate set of records in his spidery script in giant ledgers that covered half his desk.

He came stomping into Clayton's office carrying a thick roll of computer printout under his arm.

"Mister Clayton," he said aggrievedly, "I don't know what the hell's going on around here."

"I suppose you mean the bullion trades," Clayton said, sighing. "I explained it to you once, but I'll go over it again if you want me to."

"It's the paperwork," the CFO said angrily. "We're getting invoices, canceled checks, bills of lading, warehouse receipts, insurance premium notices—it's a snowfall! Look at this printout—one day's paper!"

"Just temporary," Clayton soothed him. "When our new systems integration goes on-line, the paperwork will be reduced to a minimum I assure you."

"But it never used to be like this," Sol complained. "I used to be able to keep up. All right, so I had to work late some nights—that comes with the territory. But with these bullion trades, I'm lost. I'm falling farther and farther behind."

"What are you telling me, Sol—that you need more people?"

"No, I don't need more people. By the time I tell them what to do, I could do it myself. What I want to know is the reason for all this. For years we were a jewelry store. Now suddenly we're gold dealers—a whole different business entirely."

"Not necessarily," Clayton said. "There's money to be made buying and selling bullion. Why should we let the dealers skim the cream? With our contacts we can buy in bulk and sell to independent jewelers at a price they can't match anywhere else."

"But where are we buying the gold? I get the invoices, but I never heard of some of these suppliers."

"All legitimate," Clayton told him. "You get the warehouse receipts, don't you? That's proof they're delivering, and the gold is going in our vaults."

"And the customers—who are they?"

"First of all, I plan to make all our stores autonomous. They'll be more subsidiaries than branches. I want them to do more designing and manufacturing on their own. New York will sell them the raw materials: gold, silver, gemstones, and so forth. At a markup, of course. In turn, the subsidiaries can sell to small jewelers in their area."

Guthrie shook his head. "It sounds meshugenah to me. And right now we got too much invested in bullion. What if Russia or South Africa dumps, and the market price takes a nosedive. Then we're dead."

Clayton smiled. "We're hedged," he said. "There's no way we can be hurt. Sol, you see the bottom line. Are we losing money on our gold deals?"

"No," the CFO admitted.

"We're making money, aren't we? Lots of money."

Sol nodded. "I just don't understand it," he said fretfully. "I don't understand how you figure to unload so much gold. I think our inventory is much, much too heavy. And your father, God rest his soul, if he was alive today, believe me he'd be telling you the same thing."

Clayton took a cigar from a handsome mahogany humidor on his desk. It was a much better brand than his father had smoked. But he didn't light the cigar immediately. Just rolled it gently between his fingers.

"Sol," he said, "you're sixty-three—right?"

"Yes."

"Retirement in two years. I'll bet you're looking forward to it."

"I haven't thought about it."

"You should, Sol. It isn't too soon to start training someone to take your place."

"Who? These kids—what do they know. They come out of college and can't even balance a checkbook."

"How about the new man I hired—Dick Satterlee?"

"He's a noodle!" Sol cried.

"Teach him," Clayton urged. "Teach him, Sol. He comes very highly recommended."

"I don't like him," Sol said angrily. "Something creepy about that guy. Last week I caught him going through my ledgers."

"So?" Clayton said. "How else is he going to learn?"

"Listen, Mister Clayton," the older man said, "those ledgers are private business. Everyone in my office knows—*hands off!* I don't want anyone touching them; they're my responsibility."

Starrett slowly pierced and lighted his cigar. "Sol," he said, "when was your last raise?"

Guthrie was startled. "Two years ago," he said. "I thought you knew."

"I should have remembered," Clayton said, "but I've had a lot on my mind. Father's death and all . . . "

"Of course."

"Suppose you take a raise of fifty thousand a year until you retire. With your pension, that should give you a nice nest egg."

The CFO was shocked. "Thank you, Mister Clayton," he said finally.

"You deserve it. And Sol, stop worrying about the gold business. Trust me."

After Guthrie left his office, Clayton put his cigar carefully aside and called Turner Pierce. The phone was lifted after the sixth ring.

"Hello?"

"Turner? Clayton Starrett."

"How are you, Clay? I was just thinking about you. I saw Ramon last night, and there have been some interesting developments."

"Turner, I've got to see you as soon as possible."

"Oh? A problem?"

"It could be," Clayton said.

5

Dora Conti, listing to port under the weight of an overstuffed shoulder bag, was admitted to the Starrett apartment at 2:30 P.M. The door was opened by a tall, bowed man she assumed was the butler, identified in newspaper clippings as Charles Hawkins.

He didn't look like a Fifth Avenue butler to her, or valet, footman, or even scullion. He seemed all elbows and knees, his gaunt cheeks were pitted, and a lock of dank, black hair flopped across his forehead. He was wearing a shiny gray alpaca jacket, black serge trousers just as shiny, and Space Shoes.

"Dora Conti," she said, "to see Mrs. Olivia Starrett. I have an appointment."

"Madam is waiting," he said in a sepulchral whisper, and held out his arms to her.

For one awful instant she thought he meant to embrace her, then realized he merely wanted to take her coat. She whipped off her scarf and struggled out of her heavy loden parka. He took them with the tips of his fingers, and she followed his flat-footed shuffle down a long corridor to the living room.

This high-ceilinged chamber seemed crowded with a plethora of chintz- and cretonne-covered chairs and couches, all in floral patterns: roses, poppies, lilies, iris, camellias. It was like entering a hothouse; only the scent was missing.

A man and a woman were sharing a love seat when Dora came into the room. The man stood immediately. He was wearing a double-breasted suit of dove-gray flannel, with a black silk dickey and a white clerical collar.

"Good afternoon," Dora said briskly. "I am Dora Conti, and as I explained on the phone, I am your insurance claims adjuster. Thank you for seeing me on such short notice.''

''Of course,'' the man said with a smile of what Dora considered excessive warmth. ''I hope you won't be offended if I ask to see your credentials.''

She made no reply, but dug her ID out of the shoulder bag, handed him card and letter of authorization.

He examined them carefully, then returned them, his smile still in place. ''Thank you,'' he said. ''You must understand my caution; so many newspaper reporters have attempted to interview family members under a variety of pretexts that we've become somewhat distrustful. My name is Brian Callaway.''

''*Father* Brian Callaway,'' the woman on the settee said, ''and I am Olivia Starrett.''

''Ma'am,'' Dora said, ''first of all I'd like to express my condolences on the death of your husband.''

''Oh, he didn't die,'' the woman said. ''He passed into the divine harmony. My, what beautiful hair you have!''

''Thank you.''

''And do construction workers whistle at you and shout, 'Hey, red!'?''

''No,'' Dora said. ''They usually whistle and shout, 'Hey, fatso'!''

Olivia Starrett laughed, a warbling sound. ''Men can be so cruel,'' she said. ''You are certainly not fat. Plump perhaps—wouldn't you say, Father?''

''Pleasingly,'' he said.

''Now then,'' the widow said, patting the cushion beside her, ''you come sit next to me, and we'll have a nice chat.''

She was a heavy-bodied woman herself, with a motherly softness. Her complexion was a creamy velvet, and her eyes seemed widened in an expression of continual surprise. Silvery hair was drawn back in a chignon and tied with a girlish ribbon. Her hands were unexpectedly pudgy, and her diamond rings, Dora estimated, would have kept Mario supplied with prosciutto for two lifetimes.

''Mrs. Starrett,'' Dora began, ''let me explain why I am here. If your husband had been ill and had, uh, passed away in a hospital, or even at home with a doctor in attendance, there probably would have been no need for our investigating the claim, despite its size. But because his, uh, passing was violent and unexpected, an investigation is necessary to establish the facts of the case.''

Father Callaway seated himself in an armchair facing the two women. ''Surely,'' he said, ''an investigation of that horrible crime is a job for the police.''

''Of course it is,'' Dora agreed. ''But right now all they have is a theory as to how and why the homicide was committed. It may or may not be correct. But until the perpetrator is caught, there are unanswered questions we'd like to see cleared up. Mrs. Starrett, I hope I am not upsetting you by talking of your husband's, uh, death."

"Oh, not at all," she said, almost blithely. "I have made my peace."

"Olivia is a strong woman," Callaway said.

"As you said at the service, Father: Faith conquers all."

"Just a few questions," Dora said. "First of all, can you tell me the whereabouts of family members at the time your husband, uh, passed away?"

"Now let me see," Mrs. Starrett said, staring at the ceiling. "Earlier that evening the entire family was here, and we were having cocktails and little nibbles. Helene and Turner Pierce stopped by."

"I was also present, Olivia," Callaway interrupted.

"Of course you were! Well, we had a few drinks, and then Clayton and Eleanor left to attend a charity affair at the Waldorf. And Felicia had a dinner date, so she left. And then the Pierces."

"And I left at the same time they did," the Father reminded her. He looked directly at Dora. "I have a small tabernacle on East Twentieth Street—and I like to be present at the evening meal to offer what spiritual solace I can."

"Tabernacle?" Dora said. "Then you are not Roman Catholic?"

"No," he said shortly. "I am the founder and pastor of the Church of the Holy Oneness."

"I see," Dora said, and turned to the widow. "So only you and your husband were in the apartment at dinnertime?"

"And Charles, our houseman, and Clara, our cook."

"Charles' wife."

Olivia's eyes widened even more. "Now how did you know that?"

"It was in the newspapers," Dora lied smoothly. "You had dinner, and then Mr. Starrett left to take his usual walk—is that correct?"

"Yes," Olivia said, nodding, "that's what happened. I remember it was threatening rain, and I wanted Lewis to take an umbrella and wear his rubbers, but he wouldn't." She sighed. "He was a very obstinate man."

Callaway corrected her gently. "Strong-minded, Olivia," he murmured.

"Yes," she said, "he was a very strong-minded man."

"Mrs. Starrett," Dora said, "do you know anyone who might wish to harm your husband? Did he have any enemies?"

The widow lifted her chin. "My husband could be difficult at times. At home and, I'm sure, at the office. I was aware that many people thought him offensive. He did have a temper, you know, and I'm sure he sometimes said things in anger that he later regretted. But no, I know of no one who wished to harm him."

"Was he ever threatened? In person or by letter?"

"Not to my knowledge."

"The police," Callaway observed, "believe he was killed by a stranger."

"Uh-huh," Dora said. "That's their theory. Mrs. Starrett, I don't want to take any more of your time. If I think of more questions, may I come back?"

Olivia put a warm hand on her arm. "Of course you may, my dear. As often as you like. Are you married?"

"Yes. We live in Hartford. My husband is a dispatcher for a trucking company."

"How nice! Does he love you?"

Dora was startled. "I believe he does. He says he does."

"And do you love him?"

"Yes."

Olivia nodded approvingly. "Love is the most important thing. Isn't it, Father?"

"The only thing," said Callaway, a broad-chested man who liked to show his teeth.

Dora stood up. The pastor rose at the same time and took a wallet from his inner jacket pocket. He extracted a card and handed it to her.

"The address of the Church of the Holy Oneness," he said. "Service every Friday evening at eight. But you'll be welcome anytime you wish to stop by."

"Thank you," she said, tucking the card in her shoulder bag. "I may just do that. Mrs. Starrett, it's been a pleasure meeting you, and I hope to see you again."

"And the insurance?" Callaway asked. "When may the beneficiaries expect to have the claim approved?"

Dora smiled sweetly. "As soon as possible," she said, and shook his hand.

Charles was waiting in the foyer, and she wondered how much of the conversation he had overheard. He helped her on with her parka.

"Thank you, Charles."

She thought he might have winked at her, but it was such an unbutler-like act that she decided he had merely blinked. With one eye.

6

Clayton Starrett could see no physical resemblance between Helene and Turner Pierce, yet they both showed the same face to the world: cool, somewhat aloof, with tight smiles and brief laughs. And both dressed with careless elegance, held their liquor well, and had a frequently expressed distaste for the commonplace. "Vulgar!" was their strongest term of opprobrium.

Sitting with them in the living room of Helene's apartment, sharing a pitcher of gin martinis, Clayton noted for the first time how pale both were, how slender, how languid their gestures. In their presence he felt uncomfortably lumpish, as if his energy and robust good health were somehow vulgar.

"And what was Guthrie's reaction when you gave him the raise?" Turner asked.

"He was surprised," Clayton said. "Perhaps shocked is a better word. I know he never expected anything like that. I did it, of course, to give him a bigger stake in the company. You might call it a bribe—to keep his mouth shut about the gold deals."

"You think it'll work?"

"I don't know," Clayton said worriedly. "Sol is an honest man— maybe too honest. In spite of the raise he may keep digging. I got the feeling he wasn't completely satisfied with my explanation."

"Helene?" Turner said.

"Don't do anything at the moment," she advised. "The money may convince him it would be stupid to make waves. But you better tell Dick Satterlee to keep an eye on him, just in case."

"Yes, that would be wise," Turner said. "Since his New Orleans contact was eliminated, Ramon wants to increase his investments elsewhere.

We'll be getting the lion's share, so the last thing we want right now is a snoopy accountant nosing around. I'll phone Satterlee at home and alert him." He glanced at his Piaget Polo, finished his martini, stood up. "I've got to run. Thanks for the drink, sis."

"I'll give you a call later," she said.

He swooped to kiss her cheek. "Much later," he said. "I won't be home until midnight."

"I hope you're behaving yourself," she said.

"Don't I always?" he said. "Clay, sometimes this sister of mine acts like she's my mother."

They all laughed. Turner gathered up his leather trench coat and trilby. "Clay," he said, "don't worry about Sol Guthrie. I'll take care of it."

"Good," Clayton said. "He's been with Starrett a long time and only has two years to go before he starts drawing a hefty pension. He'd be a fool to endanger that."

"Sometimes honest men do foolish things," Turner said. "You know the old saying: No good deed goes unpunished. I hope Mr. Guthrie knows it."

He waved a hand at them and left. Helene rose to bolt the door and put on the chain. "Another party tonight?" she asked Clayton.

He nodded. "The third this week. My wife is cohostess of this one. At the Pierre."

"For which charity?"

He shrugged. "Who the hell knows—or cares. For unwed mothers or to spay stray cats or *something.*"

"So you have to go home to dress?"

He smiled at her. "Not for an hour," he said.

"Time enough," she said. "We can go around the world in an hour."

If she seemed languid, almost enervated, when dressed and in the company of others, she displayed a totally different persona when naked and alone with him. Her strength was astonishing, her vigor daunting. Indifference vanished; now she was vital and determined. She gave Clayton credit for this transformation. "You make me a pagan," she told him.

He could scarcely believe his good fortune. This lovely, intense young woman seemed to have no wish but to give him pleasure. There was nothing he asked that she would not do, and their lovemaking became a new world for him. He was a sexual despot, and she his willing slave, eager to serve.

He thought he had never known an ecstasy to equal this, and only later did he begin to plot how he might change his life to insure that his happiness would endure forever.

7

Dora Conti had been trying for almost a week to pin down a meeting with Felicia Starrett. Two appointments had been made, but Felicia called at the last minute to cancel both, offering excuses that seemed trivial to Dora: she had to have her hands waxed, and Bloomies was having a panty hose sale.

Finally she agreed, positively, to meet Dora for a drink at the Bedlington cocktail lounge at 4:30 on Friday. She was only twenty minutes late.

She came sailing into the bar wearing a mink Eisenhower jacket that Dora would have killed for. Under the jacket she wore a white turtleneck sweater, and below was a skirt of black calfskin, short and tight. Her only jewelry was a solitaire, a marquise-cut diamond in a Tiffany setting. Five carats at least, Dora guessed.

Felicia shook hands, took off her mink and tossed it onto an empty chair. "Chivas neat," she yelled at the bartender. "Perrier on the side." She sat down across the table from Dora, looked around the cocktail lounge. "Ratty dump," she said.

"Isn't it," Dora said pleasantly. "Thank you for giving me a few minutes of your time, Miss Starrett. I appreciate it."

"I hope it's only a few minutes. I have an appointment for a trim and rinse at five-thirty, and if I'm late Adolph will probably scalp me. Who does your hair?"

"I do," Dora said. "Doesn't it look like it?"

"It's okay," Felicia said. "Like you don't give a damn how it looks. I like that. May I have one of your cigarettes?"

"Help yourself."

"I'm trying to stop smoking so I don't buy any. I'm still smoking but I'm saving a lot of money. Your name is Dora Conti?"

"That's right."

"Italian?"

"My husband is."

"How long have you been married?"

"Six years."

"Children?"

"No."

"That's smart," Felicia said. "Who the hell wants to bring kids into this rotten world. This is about the insurance?"

"Just a few questions," Dora said. "Your mother has already told me most of what I wanted to know. She said you were in the apartment having cocktails the evening your father was killed. But you left early."

"That's right. I had a dinner-date downtown. A new restaurant on Spring Street. It turned out to be a bummer. I told the cops all this. I'm sure they checked it out."

"I'm sure they did," Dora said. "Miss Starrett, do you know of any enemies your father had? Anyone who might have wanted to harm him?"

Felicia had been smoking with short, rapid puffs. Now tears came to her eyes, and she stubbed out the cigarette.

"Damn!" she said. "I thought I was finished with the weeping and wailing."

"I'm sorry I upset you."

"Not your fault. But every time I think of him lying there on the sidewalk, all alone, it gets to me. My father was a sonofabitch but I loved him. Can you understand that?"

"Yes."

"And no matter what a stinker he was, no one should die like that. It's just not right."

"No," Dora said, "it isn't."

"Sure, I guess he had enemies. You can't be a world-class bastard all your life without getting people sore at you. But no, I don't know of anyone who hated him enough to murder him."

"I met Father Callaway when I questioned your mother. He seems to agree with the police theory that your father was killed by a stranger."

"*Father* Callaway!" Felicia cried. "He's as much a Father as I am an astronaut. Don't pay any attention to what he says or thinks. The man's a phony."

"Oh?" Dora said. "How do you mean?"

"He's got this rinky-dink church in an empty store, and he cons money from a lot of innocent people like my mother who fall for his smarmy smile and bullshit about one world of love and harmony."

"Surely he does some good," Dora suggested. "He said his church runs a soup kitchen for the homeless."

"So he hands out a few cheese sandwiches while he's dining at the homes of his suckers on beef Wellington. My father had his number. Every time he saw Callaway in his preacher's outfit, he'd ask him, 'How's white-collar crime today?' ''

Dora laughed. "But your father allowed him in your home."

"For mother's sake," Felicia said wearily. "She's a true believer in Callaway and his cockamamy church."

"Is anyone else in your family a true believer? Your sister-in-law, for instance."

"Eleanor? All she believes in are the society columns. If she doesn't see her name in print, she doesn't exist. I don't know why I'm telling you all this; it's got nothing to do with the insurance."

"You never know," Dora said, and watched the other woman light another cigarette with fingers that trembled slightly.

She figured Felicia had already endured the big four-oh. She was a tall, angular woman, tightly wound, with a Nefertiti profile and hands made for scratching.

"I'll tell you something about Eleanor," she said broodingly. "We used to be as close as this . . . '' She displayed two crossed fingers. "Then she and Clay had a kid, a boy, a beautiful child. Lived eighteen months and died horribly of meningitis. It broke Eleanor; she became a different woman. She told everyone: 'No more kids.' That was all right; it was her decision to make. But—and this is my own idea—I think it also turned her off sex. After a while my brother started playing around. I know that for a fact. One-night stands, nothing serious. But who could blame him; he wasn't getting any at home. And then Eleanor got on the charity-party circuit, and that's been her whole life ever since. Sad, sad, sad. Life sucks—you know that?"

Dora didn't reply.

"Well, enough soap opera for one day," Felicia said, and rose abruptly. "I've got to dash. Thanks for the drink. If you need anything else, give me a buzz."

"Thank you, Miss Starrett."

She tugged on her mink jacket, stood a moment looking down at Dora.

"Six years, huh?" she said. "I've never been married. I'm an old maid."

"Don't say that," Dora said.

"Why not?" Felicia said, forcing a laugh. "It's true, isn't it? But don't feel sorry for me; I get my jollies—one way or another. Keep in touch, kiddo."

And with a wave of a hand she was gone. Dora sat alone, feeling she needed something stronger than beer. So she moved to the bar and ordered a straight Chivas, Perrier on the side. She had never before had such a drink, but Felicia Starrett had ordered it, and Dora wanted to honor her. Go figure it, she told herself.

She had the one drink, then went upstairs to the corporate suite and worked on notes that would be source material for her report to Mike

Trevalyan. Then she took a nap that worked wonders because she awoke in a sportive mood. She showered and phoned Mario while she was still naked. It seemed more intimate that way. Mario said he missed her, and she said she missed him. She made kissing sounds on the phone.

"Disgusting!" he said, laughing, and hung up.

She dressed, pulled on her parka, and sallied forth. It was a nippy night, the smell of snow in the air, and when she asked the Bedlington doorman to get her a cab, he said, "Forget it!"

So she walked over to Fifth Avenue and then south, pausing to admire holiday displays in store windows. She saw the glittering tree at Rockefeller Center and stopped awhile to listen to a group of carolers who were singing "Heilige Nacht" and taking up a collection for victims of AIDS.

She wandered on down Fifth Avenue, crisscrossing several times to inspect shop windows, searching for something unusual to give Mario for Christmas. The stone lions in front of the Library had wreaths around their necks, which she thought was a nice touch. A throng stood on line to view Lord & Taylor's animated windows, so she decided to see them another time.

She was at 34th Street before she knew it, and walked over to Herald Square to gawk at Macy's windows. It was then almost 7:30 and, having come this far, she suddenly decided to walk farther and visit Father Callaway's Church of the Holy Oneness.

It was colder now, a fine mist haloing the streetlights. She plodded on, hands deep in parka pockets, remembering what Detective Wenden had said about the stupidity of walking the city at night. She knew how to use a handgun but had never carried one, believing herself incapable of actually shooting someone. And if you couldn't do that, what was the point?

But she arrived at East 20th Street without incident, except for having to shoo away several panhandlers who accepted their rejection docilely enough. Stiffing them did not demonstrate the Christmas spirit, she admitted, but she had no desire to stop, open her shoulder bag, fumble for her wallet. Wenden didn't have to warn her about the danger of being fearless. She wasn't.

As Felicia Starrett had said, Callaway's church was located in a former store. It apparently had been a fast-food luncheonette because the legend TAKE OUT ORDERS was still lettered in one corner of the plate glass window. A wide venetian blind, closed, concealed the interior from passersby, but a sign over the doorway read CHURCH OF THE HOLY ONENESS, ALL WELCOME in a cursive script.

Dora paused before entering and suddenly felt a hard object pressing into her back. "Your money or your life," a harsh voice grated. She whirled to see Detective John Wenden grinning and digging a knuckle into her ribs.

"You louse!" she gasped. "You really scared me."

"Serves you right," he said. "What the hell are you doing down here by yourself?"

"Curiosity," she said. "What are *you* doing here?"

"Oh, I had some time to kill," he said casually, "and figured I'd catch the preacher's act. Let's go in."

"Let's sit in the back," she suggested. "Mrs. Starrett may be here, and I'd just as soon she didn't see me."

"Suits me," he said. "I hope the place is heated."

It was overheated. About fifty folding chairs were set up in a long, narrow room, facing a low stage with a lectern and upright piano. The majority of the chairs were occupied, mostly by well-dressed matrons. But there were a few young couples, a scatter of single men and women, and a couple of derelicts who had obviously come in to warm up. They were sleeping.

A plump, baldish man was seated at the piano playing and singing "O Little Town of Bethlehem" in a surprisingly clarion tenor. The audience seemed to be listening attentively. Conti and Wenden took off their coats and slid into chairs in the back row. Dora craned and spotted Mrs. Olivia Starrett seated up front.

The hymn ended, the pianist rose and left the stage, exiting through a rear doorway. The audience stirred, then settled down and waited expectantly. A few moments later Father Brian Callaway entered, striding purposefully across the stage. He stood erect behind the lectern, smiling at his audience.

He was wearing a long cassock of white satin, the sleeves unusually wide and billowing. The front was edged with purple piping, cuffs and hem decorated with gold embroidery. A diamond ring sparkled on the forefinger of his right hand.

"Father Gotrocks," Wenden whispered to Dora.

"Shh," she said.

"Good evening, brothers and sisters," Callaway began in a warm, conversational tone. "Welcome to the Church of the Holy Oneness. After the service, coffee and cake will be served, and you will be asked to contribute voluntarily to the work of the Church which, as many of you know, includes daily distribution of food to those unfortunates who, often through no fault of their own, are without means to provide for themselves.

"Tonight I want to talk to you about the environment. Not acid rain, the pollution of our air and water, the destruction of our forests and coastline, but *personal* environment, the pollution of our souls and the need to seek what I call the Divine Harmony, in which we are one with nature, with each other, and with God."

He developed this theme in more detail during the following thirty minutes. He likened greed, envy, lust, and other sins to lethal chemicals that poisoned the soil and foods grown from it. He said that the earth could not endure such contamination indefinitely, and similarly the human soul could not withstand the corrosion of moral offenses that weakened, debilitated, and would eventually destroy the individual and inevitably all of society.

The solution, he stated in a calm, reasonable manner, was to recognize that just as the physical environment was one, interdependent, and sacred, so the moral environment was one, and it demanded care, sacrifice, and, above all, love if we were to find a Divine Harmony with nature, people, and with God: a Holy Oneness that encompassed all joys and all sorrows.

He was still speaking of the Holy Oneness when Wenden tugged at Dora's sleeve.

"Let's split," he said in a low voice.

She nodded, and they gathered up their coats and slipped away. Apparently neither the pastor nor anyone in that rapt audience noticed their departure. Outside, the mist had thickened to a freezing drizzle.

"I've got a car," the detective said, "but there's a pizza joint just around the corner on Third. We won't get too wet."

"Let's go," Dora said. She took his arm, and they scurried.

A few minutes later they were snugly settled in a booth, breathing garlicky air, sipping cold beers, and waiting for their Mammoth Supreme, half-anchovy, half-pepperoni.

"The guy surprised me," Wenden said. "I thought he'd be a religious windbag, one of those 'Come to Jesus!' shouters. But I have to admit he sounded sincere, like he really believes in that snake oil he's peddling."

"Maybe he does," Dora said. "I thought he was impressive. Very low-key, very persuasive. Tell me the truth: How come you found time to catch him in action?"

Wenden shrugged. "I really don't know. Maybe because he's so smooth and has too many teeth. How's that for scientific crime detection?"

They stared at each other for a thoughtful moment.

"Tell you what," Dora said finally, "I'll ask my boss to run Callaway through our computer. But our data base only includes people who have been involved in insurance scams."

"Do it," the detective urged. "Just for the fun of it."

Their giant pizza was served, and they dug in, plucking paper napkins from the dispenser.

"How you coming with the Starrett family?" Wenden asked her.

"All right, I guess. So far everyone's been very cooperative. The net result is zilch. Why do I have a feeling I'm not asking the right questions?"

"Like what?" he said. "Like 'Did you kill your husband?' or 'Did you murder your father?' "

"Nothing as gross as that," she said. "But I'm convinced that family has secrets."

"All families have secrets."

"But the Starretts' secrets may have something to do with the homicide. I tell you, John—"

"John?" he interrupted. "Oh my, I thought you told me you were happily married."

"Oh, shut up," she said, laughing. "If we're going to pig out on a pizza together, it might as well be John and Dora. What I was going to say is that I mean no disrespect to the NYPD, but I think the official theory of a stranger as the murderer is bunk. And I think you think it's bunk."

He carefully lifted a pepperoni wedge, folded it lengthwise, began to eat holding a paper napkin over his shirtfront.

He had a craggy face, more interesting than handsome: nose and chin too long, cheekbones high and prominent, eyes dark and deeply set. Dora liked his mouth, when it wasn't smeared with pizza topping, and his hair was black as a gypsy's. The best thing about him, she decided, was his voice: a rich, resonant baritone, musical as a sax.

He wiped his lips and took a gulp of beer. "Maybe it is bunk," he said. "But I've got nothing better. Have you?"

She shook her head. "Some very weak threads to follow. Father Callaway is one. Clayton Starrett is another."

"What's with him?"

"Apparently he's cheating on his wife."

"That's a crime?" Wenden said. "The world hasn't got enough jails to hold all the married men who play around. What else?"

"You got anything on Charles Hawkins, the butler?"

He smiled. "You mean the butler did it? Only in books. You ever know a homicide where the butler was actually the perp?"

"No," she admitted, "but I worked a case where the gardener did the dirty work. I think I'll take another look at Mr. Hawkins. You going to drive me back to my hotel?"

"Sure," he said. "You going to ask me up for a nightcap?"

"Nope," she said. "A shared pizza is enough intimacy for one night. Let me get the bill; the Company can afford it."

"Okay," he said cheerfully. "My alimony payment is due next week and I'm running short."

"Need a few bucks till payday?" she asked.

He stared at her. "You're a sweetheart, you are," he said. "Thanks, but no thanks. I'll get by."

She paid the check and they dashed through a cold rain to his car, an old Pontiac she figured should be put out to stud. But the heater worked, and so did the radio. They rode uptown listening to a medley of Gershwin tunes and singing along with some of them. Wenden's voice might have been a rich, resonant baritone, but he had a tin ear.

He pulled up outside the Bedlington and turned to her. "Thanks for the pizza," he said.

"Thanks for the company, John," she said. "I'm glad I bumped into you."

She started to get out of the car, but he put a hand on her arm.

"If you change your mind," he said, "I hope I'll be the first to know."

"Change my mind? About what?"

"You and me. A little of that divine harmony."

"Good night, Detective Wenden," she said.

8

Clayton Starrett, flushed with too much rich food and good wine, stood patiently, waiting for his wife to finish cheek-kissing and air-kissing with all her cohostesses in the hotel ballroom. Finally she came over to him, smile still in place. Eleanor was a plain woman, rather bony, and her strapless evening gown did nothing to conceal prominent clavicles and washboard chest. But parties always gave her a glow; excitement energized her, made her seem warm and vital.

"I thought it went splendidly," she said. "Didn't you?"

"Good party," he said, nodding.

"And the speeches weren't too long, were they, Clay?"

"Just right," he said, although he had dozed through most of them. "Can we go now?"

Most of the limousines had already departed, so theirs was called up almost immediately. On the ride home she chattered animatedly about the food, the wine, the table decorations, who wore what, who drank too much, who made a scene over a waiter's clumsiness.

"And did you see that twit Bob Farber with his new wife?" she asked her husband.

"I saw them."

"She must be half his age—or less. What a fool the man is."

"Uh-huh," Clayton said, remembering the new Mrs. Farber as a luscious creature. No other word for her—luscious!

Charles, clad in a shabby bathrobe, met them at the door. He told them that both Mrs. Olivia and Miss Felicia had retired to their bedrooms. At Eleanor's request, he brought two small brandies to their suite, closed the door, and presumably went about his nightly chores: locking up and turning off the lights.

Clayton loosened his tie, cummerbund, and opened the top button of his trousers. He sprawled in a worn velvet armchair (originally mauve) and watched his wife remove her jewelry. He remembered when he had given her the three-strand pearl choker, the black jade and gold bracelet, the mabe pearl earrings, the dragon brooch with rubies and diamonds set in platinum. Well, why not? She was a jeweler's wife. He reckoned a woman who married a butcher got all the sirloins she could eat.

Eleanor came over to his chair and turned her back. Obediently he reached up and pulled down the long zipper. He saw her pale, bony back.

"Losing too much weight, aren't you, hon?" he said.

"I don't think so," she said lightly. "You know the saying: You can never be too rich or too thin."

She went into the bedroom to undress. He sipped his brandy and thought of Bob Farber's new wife. Luscious!

Eleanor returned pulling on a crimson silk bathrobe. Before she knotted the sash, he saw how thin she really was. There was a time, before their son died, before Eleanor changed, when to watch her dress and undress in his presence was a joy. He had cherished those moments of warm domesticity. But now all the fervor had disappeared from their intimacy. His joy had dried up, just as Eleanor's body had become juiceless and her passions spent on table settings for charity benefits.

She took one sip of her brandy, then handed him the glass. "You finish it," she said. "I'm going to bed."

She swooped to kiss his cheek, then went back into the bedroom. He knew she would don a sleep mask and insert ear stopples. He suspected the mask and plugs were intended as armor, to protect herself from unwanted physical overtures. That didn't offend him, though it saddened him; he had no intention of forcing himself upon her. His last attempt, almost two years ago, had been a disaster that ended with tears and hysterical recriminations.

He finished his brandy, put the glass aside, and drank from Eleanor's. He saw the bedroom light go out, and wondered how much longer he could endure this marriage that was all form and no content.

Since meeting Helene Pierce, he had become concerned about age and the passing of time. It seemed to be accelerating. My God, here it was Christmas again! A year almost over, so quickly, gone in a flash. He felt the weight of his years: His mind was sharp as ever, he was convinced, but the body inexorably slowing, gravity claiming paunch and ass, vigor dulled and, worst of all, his capacity for fun dwindling—except when he was with Helene. She restored him: the best medicine a man could want.

Bob Farber had done it, and so had a dozen other friends and acquaintances. It was easy to make crude jokes about old goats and young women, but there was more to it than a toss in the hay and proving your manhood. There was rejuvenation, a rebirth of energy and resolve.

It would be difficult, he acknowledged. He would have to move slowly and carefully. If he could not win his mother's approval, at least he would need her neutrality. As things stood now, she was, in effect, the owner of Starrett Fine Jewelry, and he could not risk her displeasure.

As for Helene, he could not see her rejecting him even if he was old enough to be her father. In addition to her physical attractions, she had a sharp mind, a real bottom-line mentality. He knew of no other lovers she had, and while he was no Adonis, he offered enough in the way of financial security to convince her to disregard his age. And, of course, Turner Pierce was dependent on Starrett Jewelry for a large hunk of his income. He could count on Turner's endorsement.

Eleanor would be saddened. Naturally. But there were many women in Manhattan, in their circle, who had endured the same experience. There was nothing like a generous cash settlement to cushion the shock.

Clayton finished the brandy, rose and stretched. The matter would demand heavy deliberation and prudent judgment. But he thought it was doable and needed only a clever game plan to make it a reality.

He went to bed, thought more of his decision and how it might be implemented. And never once, in all his speculation, did he put a name to what he planned. Just as, not too long ago, people spoke of cancer as the Big C, because naming the tragedy was too shocking. So Clayton Starrett never said, even to himself, "Divorce." Or even the Big D.

9

The Company's Hartford office opened officially at 9:00 A.M., but Dora knew Mike Trevalyan arrived every morning at eight to get his day's work organized. She called him early on his private line and grinned to hear his surly growl.

"Tough night, Mike?" she asked.

"No tougher than usual. I had to go to a testimonial dinner for a cop who's retiring. A very wet party. What's up?"

She told him what she wanted: Run Brian Callaway through the computer and see if there was anything on him. And get her some inside poop on Starrett Fine Jewelry: who owned it, their assets, revenues, profits, and so forth.

"Callaway will be easy," Trevalyan said. "I should have an answer for you later today. Starrett will take some time. It's a privately held company, so there won't be much public disclosure. But I have some contacts in the jewelry trade, and I'll see what I can dig up."

"Thanks, Mike," Dora said. One of the things she liked about her boss was that he never asked unnecessary questions, like, "What do you need this stuff for?" She couldn't have answered that.

She had an appointment at noon with Helene and Turner Pierce. It gave her enough time to have a leisurely New York breakfast (lox and cream cheese on bagel) and then wander about the selling floors of Starrett's store on Park Avenue. Miniature Christmas trees were everywhere, decorated with gold tinsel, and muted carols were coming from concealed speakers. There were few customers, but not a single clerk came forward to ask, "May I help you?"

Dora spent almost an hour inspecting jewelry in showcases and silver, crystal, and china on open display. All price tags were turned facedown or tucked discreetly beneath the items. But Dora knew she could never afford the things she liked—except, perhaps, a sterling silver barrette in the shape of a dolphin.

She arrived at Helene Pierce's apartment house a little before noon. It was a shiny new high-rise on Second Avenue, all glass and rosy brick with a gourmet food shop and a designer's boutique on the street level. The doorman wore a plumed shako and military cape of crimson wool. Inside, the concierge behind a marble counter wore a swallowtail of white silk. Dora was impressed and wondered what kind of rent Helene Pierce was paying. Even if the apartments were co-ops or condos, she figured the maintenance would be stiff; plumed shakos and silk swallowtails cost. And so do elevators lined with ebony panels and antiqued mirrors.

The woman who opened the door of the 16th-floor apartment looked to be ten years younger than Dora, six inches taller, and thirty pounds lighter. She had the masklike features of a high-fashion model, her smile distant. She was wearing a cognac-colored jumpsuit belted with what seemed to be a silver bicycle chain. Her long feet were bare.

"Dora Conti?" she asked, voice flat and drawly.

"Yes, Miss Pierce. Thank you for seeing me. I promise not to take too much of your time."

"Come on in. My brother should be along any minute."

The apartment was not as lavish as Dora expected. The rugs and furnishings were attractive, but hardly luxurious. The living room had a curiously unlived-in look, as if it might be a model room in a department store. Dora got the feeling of impermanence, the occupant a transient just passing through.

They sat at opposite ends of a couch covered with beige linen and both half-turned to face each other.

"What a lovely building," Dora said. "The lobby is quite unusual."

Helene's smile was mocking. "A little garish," she said. "I would have preferred something a bit more subdued, a bit more elegant. But apparently people like it; all the apartments have been sold."

"It's a co-op?"

"That's correct."

"How long have you lived here, Miss Pierce?"

"Oh . . . let me see . . . It's been a little over a year now."

"I hope you don't mind my saying, but you don't talk like a New Yorker. The Midwest, I'd guess."

Helene stared at her, then reached for a pack of cigarettes on the end table. "Would you like one?" she asked.

"No, thank you."

"Do you mind if I smoke?"

"Not at all."

Dora watched her light up slowly, wondering if this lovely, self-possessed young woman was stalling.

"Yes, you're quite right," Helene said with a short laugh. "The Midwest it is."

"Oh?" Dora said, trying to keep her prying light and casual. "Where?"

"Kansas City."

"Which one? Missouri or Kansas?"

"Missouri. Does it show?"

"Only in your voice," Dora said. "Believe me, your looks are pure Manhattan."

"I hope that's a compliment."

"It is. Have you ever modeled, Miss Pierce?"

"No. I've been asked to, but—" There was a knock at the hallway door. "That must be my brother. Excuse me a moment."

The man who followed Helene back into the living room was wearing a mink-collared cashmere topcoat slung carelessly over his shoulders like a cape. There was a hint of swagger in his walk, and when he leaned down to shake Dora's hand, she caught a whiff of something else. Cigar smoke, she guessed. Or perhaps brandy.

"Miss Conti," he said, smiling. "A pleasure. What's this? My sister didn't offer you a drink?"

"Sorry about that," Helene said. "Would you like something—hard or soft?"

"Nothing, thank you," Dora said. "I'll just ask a few questions and then be on my way."

The Pierces agreed they had attended a small cocktail party at the Starrett apartment the night Lewis had been killed. And no, neither knew of any enemies who might have wished the older Starrett dead. It was true he was sometimes a difficult man to get along with, but his occasional nastiness was hardly a reason for murder.

"How long have you known the Starretts?" Dora asked, addressing Turner.

"Oh . . . perhaps two years," he replied. "Maybe a little longer. It began as a business relationship when I landed Starrett Jewelry as a client. Then Helene and I met the entire family, and we became friends."

"What kind of business are you in, Mr. Pierce?"

"I'm a management consultant. It's really a one-man operation. I specialize in computer systems, analyzing a client's needs and devising the most efficient setup to meet those needs. Or sometimes I recommend changing or upgrading a client's existing hardware."

"And that's the kind of work you did for Starrett?"

"Yes. Their new state-of-the-art systems integration is just coming on-line now. I think it will make a big difference in back-room efficiency and give Starrett executives the tools to improve their management skills."

That sounded like a sales pitch to Dora, but she said politely, "Fascinating."

"I haven't the slightest idea what my brother is talking about," Helene said. "Computers are as mysterious to me as the engine in my car. Do you use computers in your work, Miss Conti?"

"Oh yes. The insurance business would be lost without them. I'd like to ask both of you an additional question, but first I want to assure you that your replies will be held in strictest confidence. Has either of you, or both, ever noticed any signs of discord between members of the Starrett family? Any arguments, for instance, or other evidence of hostility?"

The Pierces looked at each other a brief moment.

"I can't recall anything like that," Turner said slowly. "Can you, sis?"

She shook her head. "They seem a very happy family. No arguments that I can remember. Sometimes Lewis Starrett would get angry with Father Brian Callaway, but of course the Father is not a member of the family."

"And even then Lewis was just letting off steam," Turner put in swiftly. "I'm sure he didn't mean anything by it. It was just his way."

"What was he angry about?" Dora said.

Turner rose from his armchair. "May I have one of your cigarettes, sis?" he asked.

Dora watched him light up, thinking these two used the same shtick to give themselves time to frame their replies.

Turner Pierce was a tall man, slender and graceful as a fencer. His complexion was dark, almost olive, and he sported a wide black mustache, so sleek it might have been painted. He had the same negligent manner as Helene, but behind his casual attention, Dora imagined, was something else: a streak of uncaring cruelty, as if the opinions or even the suffering of others were a bore, and only his own gratification mattered.

"I believe," he said carefully, "it concerned the contributions Olivia was making to Father Callaway's church. It was nonsense, of course. The Starretts have all the money in the world, and the Father's church does many worthwhile things for the poor and homeless."

Dora nodded. "And I understand Mrs. Eleanor is quite active in charity benefits. It seems to me the Starrett women are very generous to the less fortunate."

"Yes," he said shortly, "they are."

"Felicia Starrett as well?" she asked suddenly.

"Oh, Felicia has her private charities," Helene said in her flat drawl. "She does a lot of good, doesn't she, Turner?"

"Oh yes," he said, "a lot."

They didn't smile, but Dora was conscious of an inside joke there, a private joke, and she didn't like it.

"Thank you both very much," she said rising. "I appreciate your kind cooperation."

Turner stood up, helped her on with her bulky anorak. "It's been a pleasure meeting you, ma'am," he said. "If there's anything more you need, my sister and I will be delighted to help."

She shook hands with both: identical handclasps, cool and limp. She walked down the marble-tiled corridor to the elevator, thinking those two were taking her lightly; scorn was in their voices. And why not? They were elegant animals, handsome and aloof. And she? She was a *plump-mobile,* not quite frumpy but no *Elle* cover girl either.

It was in the elevator that she decided to start a new diet immediately.

She spent the afternoon Christmas shopping. She selected a nice pipe for her father who, since her mother's death, was living alone in Kennebunkport and refused to leave town, even for a visit. And she bought scarves, mittens, brass trivets, soup tureens, books of cartoons, music boxes, hairbrushes, and lots of other keen stuff. She paid with credit cards, had everything gift-wrapped and mailed out to her and her husband's aunts, uncles, nieces, nephews, cousins, and friends. She still didn't find anything exactly right for Mario.

She had dinner in a restaurant in the plaza of Rockefeller Center: the best broiled trout she had ever eaten. She had one glass of Chablis, but when the dessert cart was rolled up, her new resolve vanished and she pigged out on a big chocolate-banana mousse. And then punished herself by walking back to her hotel, convinced the calories were melting away during her hike.

The desk clerk at the Bedlington had a message for her: Call Mike Trevalyan. She went up to her suite, kicked off her shoes, and phoned. Mike sounded much friskier than he was that morning, and Dora figured he had had one of his three-martini lunches.

"This Brian Callaway you asked about," he said. "Is he a big, beefy guy, heavy through the shoulders and chest, reddish complexion, lots of charm and a hundred-watt smile?"

"That's the man," Dora said. "You found him?"

"Finally. In the alias file. His real name, as far as we know, is Sidney Loftus, but he's used a half-dozen fake monikers."

"Is he a preacher?"

"A *preacher?*" Trevalyan said, laughing. "Yeah, I guess he could be a preacher. He's already been a used-car salesman, a psychotherapist, an investment advisor, and—get this—an insurance consultant."

"Oh-oh," Dora said. "A wrongo?"

"So twisted you could screw him into the ground. According to the computer, he's never done hard time for any of his scams. He's always worked a deal, made restitution, and got off with a suspended sentence or probation. Then he blows town, changes his name, and starts another swindle. About five years ago he put together a stolen car ring. If you couldn't keep up the payments on your jalopy, or needed some ready cash, you'd go to him and he'd arrange to have your car swiped. He never did it himself; he had a crew of dopers working for him. The car would be taken to a chop shop, and by the time the insurers got around to looking for it, the parts were down in Uruguay. The cops infiltrated the ring and were twenty-four hours away from busting Sidney Loftus when he must have been tipped off because he skipped town and hasn't been heard of since, until you asked about him. You know where he is, Dora?''

She ignored the question. ''Mike,'' she said, ''this stolen car ring— where was it operating?''

''Kansas City.''

''Which one? Missouri or Kansas?''

''Missouri.''

''Thank you very much,'' said Dora.

10

Despite working for Starrett Fine Jewelry for forty years, CFO Solomon Guthrie knew little about the techniques of jewelry making. All he knew were numbers. "Numbers don't lie," he was fond of remarking. This honest man never fully realized how numbers can be cooked, and how a Park Avenue corporation based on fiddled data might have no more financial stature than an Orchard Street pushcart.

But despite his naiveté, Guthrie could not rid himself of the suspicion that something was wrong with the way Mister Clayton was running the business. All those new branch managers. That new computer systems integration that Sol didn't understand. And the tremendous purchases and sales of gold bullion. He couldn't believe any jewelry store, or chain of stores, could use that much pure gold. And yet, at the end of each month, Starrett showed a nice profit on its bullion deals. Guthrie was bewildered.

Finally he phoned Arthur Rushkin, who had been Starrett's attorney almost as long as Sol had slaved over Starrett's ledgers.

"Baker and Rushkin," the receptionist said.

"This is Solomon Guthrie of Starrett Jewelry. Can I talk to Mr. Rushkin, please."

"Sol!" Rushkin said heartily. "When are we going to tear a herring together?"

"Listen, Art," Guthrie said, "I've got to see you right away. Can you give me an hour this afternoon?"

"A problem?"

"I think it is."

"No problem is worth more than a half-hour. See you here at three o'clock. Okay?"

"I'll be there."

He stuffed a roll of computer printout into his battered briefcase and added a copy of Starrett's most recent monthly statement. Then he told his secretary, Claire Heffernan, that he was going over to Arthur Rushkin's office and would probably return by four o'clock.

He had no sooner departed than Claire strolled into the office of Dick Satterlee.

"He's gone to see the lawyer," she reported.

"Thanks, doll," Satterlee said.

"Party tonight?" she asked.

"Why not," he said, grinning.

The moment she was gone, he phoned Turner Pierce. Turner wasn't in, but Satterlee left a message on his answering machine, asking him to call back as soon as possible; it was important.

Solomon Guthrie knew he'd never get a cab, so he walked over to the offices of Baker & Rushkin on Fifth Avenue near 45th Street. It was an overcast day, the sky heavy with dirty clouds, a nippy wind blowing from the northwest. Christmas shoppers were scurrying, and the Salvation Army Santas on the corners were stamping their feet to keep warm.

Rushkin came out of his inner office to greet him in the reception room. The two men embraced, shook hands, patted shoulders.

"Happy holidays, Sol," Rushkin said.

"Yeah," Guthrie said. "Same to you."

The attorney was the CFO's age, but a different breed of cat entirely. A lot of good beef and bourbon had gone into that florid face, and his impressive stomach was only partly concealed by Italian tailoring and, if the truth be told, an elastic, girdlelike undergarment that kept his abdomen compressed.

He settled Guthrie in an armchair alongside his antique partners' desk, then sat back into his deep swivel chair and laced fingers across his tattersall waistcoat. "All right, Sol," he said, "what's bothering you?"

Guthrie poured it all out, speaking so rapidly he was almost spluttering. He told Rushkin about the new branch managers; Clayton's plan to make every Starrett store autonomous; the new computer system that Sol couldn't understand. And finally he described all the dealing in gold bullion. Long before he ended his recital, Rushkin was toying with a letter opener on his desktop and staring at the other man with something close to pity.

"Sol, Sol," he said gently, "what you're complaining about are business decisions. Clayton is president and CEO; he has every right to make those decisions. Is Starrett losing money?"

"No."

"Making money?"

"Yes."

"Then Clayton seems to be doing a good job."

"Look," Sol said desperately, "I know I've got no proof, but something's going on that just isn't kosher. Like those gold deals."

"All right," the attorney said patiently, "tell me exactly how those deals are made. Where does Starrett get the gold?"

"We buy it from overseas dealers in precious metals."

"How do you pay?"

"Our bank transfers money from our account to the dealers' banks overseas. It's all done electronically. By computer," he added disgustedly.

"Then the overseas dealer ships the gold to the U.S.?"

"No, the dealers have subsidiaries over here. The gold is warehoused by the subsidiaries. When we buy, the gold is delivered to our vault in Brooklyn."

"How is it delivered?"

"Usually by armored truck."

"Good security?"

"The best. Our Brooklyn warehouse is an armed camp. It costs us plenty, but it's worth it."

"All right," Rushkin said. "Starrett signs a contract to buy X ounces of gold. You get copies of the contract?"

"Naturally."

"The subsidiary of the overseas dealer then delivers the gold to Starrett's vault. The amount delivered is checked carefully against the contract?"

"Of course."

"Have you ever been short-weighed?"

"No."

"So now Starrett has the bullion in its vault. Who do you sell it to?"

"To our branches around the country. Then they sell it to small jewelry stores in their area."

"Correct me if I'm wrong, but I presume because of its size, resources, and reputation, plus the volume of its purchases, Starrett buys gold at a good price from those overseas dealers."

"That's correct."

"And tacks on a markup when it sells to its branches?"

"Yes."

"Which, in turn, make a profit when they sell to independents in their area?"

"Yes."

Arthur Rushkin tossed up his hands. "Sol," he said, laughing, "what you've just described is a very normal, conventional way of doing business. Buy low, sell high. You get complete documentation of every step in the procedure, don't you? Contracts, bills of lading, shipping invoices, and so forth?"

"Yes. On the computer."

"And the final customers—the small, independent jewelry stores—have they ever stiffed you?"

"No," Guthrie admitted, then burst out, "but I tell you something stinks! There's too much gold coming in, going out, floating all over the place. And some of those small shops that buy our gold—why, they weren't even in business a couple of years ago. I know; I checked."

"Small retail stores come and go, Sol; you know that. I really can't understand why you're so upset. You haven't told me anything that even hints of illegal business practices—if that's what you're implying."

"Something's going on," Guthrie insisted. "I know it is. We're buying too much bullion, and too many independent stores are buying it from us. Listen, what do they need it for? Everyone knows pure gold is very rarely used in jewelry. It's too soft; it bends or scratches. Maybe twenty-four-karat or twenty-two-karat will be used as a thin plating on some other metal, but gold jewelry is usually an eighteen- or fourteen-karat alloy. So why do these rinky-dink stores need so much pure stuff?"

Arthur sighed. "I don't know, but if their checks don't bounce, what the hell do you care what they do with it? Sol, what is it exactly you want me to do? Talk to Clayton? About what? That he's making money for Starrett by dealing in gold bullion?"

Guthrie opened his briefcase, piled the statement and computer printout on the attorney's desk. "Just take a look at this stuff, will you, Art?" he asked. "Study it. Maybe you'll spot something I can't see." He paused a moment, then almost shouted, "You know what Clayton did the other day?"

"What?"

"Gave me a fifty-thousand-dollar-a-year raise."

"Mazeltov!" Rushkin cried.

Sol shook his head. "Too much," he said. "It doesn't make business sense to give me so much. And he gave it to me right after I complained about what's going on at Starrett Fine Jewelry. You don't suppose he did it so I'll keep my mouth shut, do you?"

The attorney stared at him. "Sol," he said, "I've got to tell you that sounds paranoid to me. In all honesty, I think you're making something out of nothing."

"Just look over this printout, Art—will you do that for me?"

"Of course."

"And please don't tell Clayton I came to see you. Well, you can tell him if he asks; my secretary knows I came here. But don't tell Clayton what we talked about."

"Whatever you say, Sol."

The CFO stood up, tucked the empty briefcase under his arm. "I'm going to keep digging," he vowed. "I'll find out what's going on."

Rushkin nodded, walked out to the reception room with Guthrie, helped him on with his coat. "Keep in touch, Sol," he said lightly.

When the outside door closed, the lawyer turned to the receptionist and stared at her a moment.

"Too bad," he said.

"What's too bad, Mr. Rushkin?"

"Growing old is too bad, for some people. They can't keep up with new developments, like computers. They resent younger people coming into their business and doing a good job. They want things to remain the way they were. Change confuses them. They get the feeling the world is passing them by, and they start thinking there's a conspiracy against them. Don't ever grow old, Sally."

"Do I have a choice?" she asked.

He laughed. "I have to meet Mr. Yamoto at the Four Seasons bar," he said. "That means I won't be back this afternoon. There's a pile of computer printout on my desk. Will you put it away in a filing cabinet, please."

"Which filing cabinet?"

"I couldn't care less," Arthur Rushkin said.

11

Mrs. Eleanor Starrett sat at a white enameled table in Georgio's Salon on East 56th Street, having a set of false fingernails attached. Next to her, Dora Conti was perched uncomfortably on a small stool on rollers. Across the table from Mrs. Starrett, the attendant, a buxom lady from Martinique, bent intently over her gluing job, saying nothing but not missing a word of the conversation.

"So sorry I couldn't meet you at home," Eleanor said, "but I'm due at Tiffany's in a half-hour to select door prizes for a benefit. With the holidays coming on, it's just rush, rush, rush."

"That's all right," Dora said, wondering how this woman could pull on gloves with rocks like that on her fingers. "I just have a few questions to ask."

"I really don't understand why the insurance company is investigating my father-in-law's death. I should think that would be a job for the police."

"Of course it is," Dora said. "But the policy is so large and the circumstances of Mr. Starrett's death so puzzling, we want to be absolutely certain the claim is, ah, unemcumbered before it is paid."

"Well, the poor man could hardly have stabbed himself in the back, could he?" Eleanor said tartly. "Which means, I suppose, that you think one of the beneficiaries may have done him in."

"Mrs. Starrett," Dora said, sighing, "no one is accusing anyone of anything. We would just like to see the murder solved and the case closed, that's all. Now, do you know of any enemies Lewis Starrett had? Any person or persons who might wish to harm him?"

"No."

"How did *you* get along with him?"

Eleanor turned her head to look directly at her questioner. "Dad—that's what I always called him: Dad—could be a dreadful man at times. I'm sure you've heard that from others as well. But for some reason he took a liking to me, and I got along with him very well. Olivia and Clayton and Felicia suffered more from his temper tantrums than I did. And the servants were targets, too, of course. But he never raised his voice to me. Perhaps he knew that if he had, I'd have marched out of that house and never returned."

"I understand Father Brian Callaway was sometimes the cause of his anger."

"My, my," Mrs. Starrett said mockingly, "you have been busy, haven't you? Well, you're right; Dad couldn't stand the man. The fact that Olivia was giving the preacher money infuriated him. He finally forbade her to give Father Callaway's so-called church another red cent."

"And what was his argument with the servants?"

"Oh, that was a long-running civil war. Stupid things like Charles' fingernails were too long, the Sunday *Times* had a section missing, Clara was using the good wine to cook with—picky things like that."

"Did they ever threaten to quit?"

"Of course not. They're being very well paid indeed, and though I wouldn't call them incompetent, they're far from being super. Just adequate, I'd say. If they quit, who'd pay them what dad was giving them—plus their own little suite of rooms as well."

"I understand you're very active in charity benefits, Mrs. Starrett."

"I do what I can," she said in a tone of such humility that Dora wanted to kick her shins.

"Does your sister-in-law ever join in these activities?"

"I'm afraid Felicia's favorite charity is Felicia. We get along. Period."

"But not close?"

"No," Eleanor said with a short bark of laughter. "Not close at all."

"Could you tell me something about Helene and Turner Pierce. How long have you known them?"

"Oh, perhaps a couple of years."

"How did they become friends of the Starrett family?"

"Let me think . . . " Eleanor considered a moment. "I do believe Father Callaway brought them around. He knew them from somewhere, or maybe they were members of his church—I really don't recall."

"And how do you get along with them?"

"Excellently. I admire them. They are two attractive young people, very *chic,* very *with* it. And it's a pleasure to see a brother and sister so affectionate toward each other."

"More affectionate than Clayton and Felicia?"

Eleanor stared at her. "No comment," she said.

Dora rose from the low stool with some difficulty. "Thank you for your time, Mrs. Starrett," she said. "You've been very helpful."

"I have?" the other woman said. "I don't know how."

Dora left the beauty salon, went next door to a small hotel, and used the public phone in the lobby.

"The Starrett residence," Charles answered.

"This is Dora Conti. Is any member of the family home? I'd like to speak to them."

"Just a moment, please."

It took longer than a moment, but finally Felicia came on the line, breathless.

"Hiya, kiddo," she said. "Listen, I can't talk right now. Gotta run. Heavy lunch date."

"Wait, wait," Dora said hastily. "I just want to know if it's okay if I come over and talk to Charles and Clara for a few minutes."

"Of course," Felicia said. "I'll tell them to let you in and answer your questions. 'Bye!"

Dora walked over to Madison Avenue and boarded an uptown bus. It had turned cold, almost freezing, and everyone was bundled up; the bus smelled of mothballs. Traffic was clogged, and it took almost forty-five minutes before she arrived at the Starrett apartment. Charles opened the door and led the way into the kitchen where a short, stout woman was standing at the sink, scraping carrots.

Clara Hawkins looked as dour as her husband. Her iron-gray hair was pulled up in a bun, and her lips seemed eternally pursed in a grimace of disapproval. She was wearing a soiled apron over a dress of rusty bombazine, and her fat feet were shoved into heelless slippers. What was most remarkable, Dora decided, was that Clara had a discernible mustache.

No one offered her a chair so she remained standing, leaning against the enormous refrigerator. She looked around at the well-appointed kitchen: copper-bottomed pots and pans hanging from an overhead frame; a Cuisinart on the counter; a hardwood rack holding knives and a butchers' round; a double-sink of stainless steel; gleaming white appliances; and glass-doored cupboards holding enough tableware to feed a regiment.

"I just have a few questions," Dora said, addressing Charles. "I understand that on the evening Mr. Starrett was killed, there was a cocktail party for family and friends."

He nodded.

"Where was it held—in the living room?"

"Mostly," he said. "That's where I served drinks and canapes. But people wandered around."

"You mean they all weren't in the living room constantly during the party?"

"They wandered," he repeated. "Only Mrs. Olivia remained seated. The others stood and mingled, went to their bedrooms to fetch something or make a phone call."

Clara turned from the sink. "Sometimes they came in here," she said.

"For more ice, or maybe for another drink while Charles was busy passing the tray of hors d'oeuvres."

"Were there any arguments during the party? Did anyone make a scene?"

Wife and husband looked at each other, then shook their heads.

"How long have you been with the Starretts?" Dora asked, bedeviled by the fear that she wasn't asking the right questions.

"Seven years, come March," Charles replied. "I started with them first. Then, about a year later, the cook they had left and Clara took over."

"Both of you get along well with the family?"

Charles shrugged. "No complaints," he said.

"I understand the late Mr. Starrett had a short temper."

Again the shrug. "He liked everything just so."

"And when it wasn't, he let you know?"

"He let everyone know," Clara said, turning again from her task at the sink. "He was a mean, mean man."

"Clara!" her husband warned.

"Well, he was," she insisted. "The way he treated people—it just wasn't right."

"Speak only good of the dead," her husband admonished.

"Bullshit," Clara said unexpectedly.

Hopeless, Dora decided, realizing she was getting nowhere. These people weren't going to reveal any skeletons in the Starretts' closet, and she couldn't blame them; they had cushy jobs and wanted to hang on to them.

She took a final look around the kitchen. Her gaze fell on that hardwood knife rack attached to the wall. It had eight slots. Two were empty. She stepped to the rack, withdrew a long bread knife with a serrated edge, and examined it.

"Nice," she said.

"Imported," Charles said. "Carbon steel. The best."

Dora replaced the bread knife. "Two are missing," she said casually. "What are they?"

Clara, at the sink, held up a paring knife she was using to scrape carrots. "This is one," she said.

"And the other?" Dora persisted.

Charles and Clara exchanged a quick glance. "It was an eight-inch chef's knife," he said. "I'm sure it's around here somewhere, but we can't find it."

"It'll probably turn up," Dora said, knowing it wouldn't.

12

Mike Trevalyan had frequently urged Dora to use a tape recorder during interviews. Most of the investigators on his staff used them, but she refused.

"It makes witnesses freeze up," she argued. "They see that little black box and they're afraid I'm going to use their words in court, or they might say something they'll want to deny later."

So she worked without a recorder, and didn't even take notes during interviews. But as soon as possible she wrote an account of her conversations in a thick spiral notebook: questions asked, answers received. She also made notes on the physical appearance of the witnesses, their clothing, speech patterns, any unusual gestures or mannerisms.

She returned to the Bedlington after her session with Clara and Charles Hawkins and got to work writing out the details of her meeting with the servants and with Mrs. Eleanor Starrett. That completed, she slowly read over everything in the notebook, all the conversations and her personal reactions to the people involved. Then she phoned Detective John Wenden.

He wasn't in, but she left a message asking him to call her at the Bedlington. She went into the little pantry and poured herself a glass of white wine. She brought it back into the sitting room and curled up in a deep armchair. She sipped her wine, stared at her notebook, and wondered what Mario was doing. Finally she put the empty glass aside and read through her notebook again, searching for inspiration. Zilch.

She went downstairs for an early dinner in the hotel, and had a miserable meal of meat loaf, mashed potatoes, and peas. At that moment, she mournfully imagined, Mario was dining on veal scaloppine sautéed with marsala and lemon juice. Life was unfair; everyone knew that.

She returned to her suite and, fearing Wenden might have called during her absence, phoned him again. But he had not yet returned to his office or called in for messages. So she settled down with her notebook again, convinced those scribbled pages held the key to what actually happened to Lewis Starrett—and why.

When her phone rang, she rushed to pick it up, crossing her fingers for luck.

"Hiya," Wenden said hoarsely. "Quite a surprise hearing from you."

"How so?" she asked, genuinely puzzled.

"The way I came on to you the other night; I thought you'd be miffed."

"Nah," she said. "It's good for a girl's ego. When the passes stop, it's time to start worrying. My God, John, you sound terrible."

"Ah, shit," he said, "I think I got the flu. I have it all: sneezing, runny nose, headache, cough."

"Are you dosing yourself?"

"Yeah. Aspirin mostly. I get these things every year. Nothing to do but wait for them to go away."

"Why didn't you call in sick, stay home, and doctor yourself?"

"Because three other guys beat me to it, and the boss got down on his knees and cried. You feeling okay?"

"Oh sure. I'm healthy as a horse. John, I was hoping to see you tonight, but I guess you want to get home."

"Not especially. I feel so lousy I don't even want to think about driving to Queens."

"That's where you live?"

"If you can call it that. What's up?"

"A couple of interesting things. Listen, if you can make it over here, I'll fix you a cup of hot tea with a slug of brandy. It won't cure the flu but might help you forget it."

"On my way," he said. "Shouldn't take more than twenty minutes or so."

She put a kettle on to boil, set out a cup and saucer for him, and then went into the bathroom to brush her hair and add a little lip gloss, wondering what the hell she was doing.

When Wenden arrived, carrying an open box of Kleenex, he looked like death warmed over: bleary eyes, unshaven jaw, his nose red and swollen. And, as usual, his clothes could have been a scarecrow's castoffs.

She got him seated on the couch, poured him a steaming cup of tea, and added a shot of brandy to it. He held the cup with both hands, took a noisy sip, closed his eyes and sighed.

"Plasma," he said. "Thank you, Florence Nightingale."

"You should be in bed," she said.

"Best offer I've had today," he said, then sneezed and grabbed for a tissue.

"Now I know you're not terminal," she said, smiling. "Anything new on the Starrett case?"

"Nothing from our snitches. We've checked the whole neighborhood for three blocks around. No one saw anything or heard anything. We searched every sewer basin and trash can. No knife. We've got fliers out in every taxi garage in the city. The official line is still homicide by a stranger, maybe after an argument, maybe by some nut who objected to Starrett's cigar smoke—who the hell knows."

"Uh-huh. John, did you see the medical examiner's report?"

"Sure, I saw it. I love reading those things. They really make you want to resign from the human race. The things people do to people . . . "

"Did the report describe the wound that killed Starrett?"

"Of course."

"How deep did it go—do you remember?"

He thought a moment. "About seven and a half inches. Around there. They can never be precise. Tissue fills in. The outside puncture was a slit about two inches long."

Dora nodded. "I think you need another brandy," she said.

"I'll take it gladly," he said, sneezing again, "but why do I need it?"

"I went up to see the Starretts' servants today. We talked in the kitchen. There's a knife rack on the wall. Nice cutlery. Imported carbon steel. One of the knives is missing. An eight-inch chef's knife. We have one at home. It's a triangular blade. Close to the handle it's about two inches wide."

Wenden set his cup back on the saucer. It rattled. "How long has it been missing?" he asked, staring at her.

"I didn't ask them," Dora said. "But when I noticed it, Clara and Charles glanced at each other. I think it probably disappeared at that cocktail party the night Starrett was killed, but the servants didn't want to come right out and say so."

"Why didn't you lean on them?"

"How the hell could I?" she said angrily. "You're a cop; you can lean. I'm just a short, fat, housewife-type from the insurance company. I've got no clout."

"All right, all right," he said. "So *I'll* lean on them. If the knife disappeared on the night of the murder, that opens up a whole new can of worms."

"It also clears three in this cast of characters," she said. "Olivia and the two servants stayed in the apartment for dinner and presumably were still there when Lewis went for his walk. Did you check the whereabouts of the others at the time of the killing?"

The detective looked at her indignantly. "You think we're mutts? Of course we checked. They all have alibis. None of them are rock solid, but alibis rarely are. Felicia was at a new restaurant down on Spring Street. Confirmed by her date—a twit who wears one earring. Helene and Turner Pierce were at a theatre on West Forty-sixth Street. They have their ticket stubs to prove it. Father Callaway was down at his church, passing out ham sandwiches to the homeless. He was seen there. Eleanor and Clayton Starrett were at a charity bash at the Hilton. Sounds good, but there's not one of them who couldn't have ducked out and cabbed back to East Eighty-third Street in time to chill Lewis. They all knew his nightly routine. Hey, what do I call you?''

"Call me? My name is Dora.''

"I know that, but it's too domestic. Will you be sore if I call you Red?'' She sighed. "Delighted,'' she said.

"Could I have another brandy, Red?''

"You're not going to pass out on me, are you?''

"Hell, no. I'm just getting my head together.''

She brought the brandy bottle and set it on the cocktail table in front of the couch.

"Help yourself,'' she said.

"Some for you?''

"No, thanks,'' she said. "I'm not driving to Queens.''

He laughed and poured more brandy into his teacup. "I could make that trip even if I was comatose, I've driven it so many times. Okay, let's assume someone at the cocktail party lifted the knife. Eliminate Olivia and the servants; that leaves us with six possibles.''

"Here's my second goody of the evening,'' Dora said. "Remember I told you I was going to ask my boss to run Father Brian Callaway through our computer.''

"Sure, I remember. Come up with anything?''

"His real name is Sidney Loftus. He's a con man with a sheet as long as your arm.''

"Oh-oh. Anything violent?''

"I don't know. I told you our data base includes only insurance fraud. You better run Callaway, or Loftus, through your records.''

"Yeah, I better.''

"And while you're at it, do a trace on Helene and Turner Pierce. I asked my boss, but we have nothing on them in our file.''

"Why should I check out the Pierces?''

"Callaway's most recent scam was a stolen car game in Kansas City, Missouri. That's where Helene Pierce comes from.''

"How do you know?''

"She told me.''

Wenden studied her a moment, then shook his head in wonderment. "You're something, you are. Red, how do you get people to talk?''

"Sometimes you tell things to strangers you wouldn't tell your best friend. Also, I come across as a dumpy homebody. I don't represent much of a threat, they think, so they talk.''

"A dumpy homebody,'' he repeated. "I'm beginning to believe you're more barracuda.'' He sneezed again, wiped his swollen nose with a tissue.

"All right, I'll ask for a rundown on Callaway and the Pierces. I warn you it's going to take time; Records is undermanned and overworked, like the rest of the Department."

"I can wait," Dora said. "That insurance claim isn't going to get paid until I say so."

He took a deep breath, put his head back, stared at the ceiling. "I guess I shouldn't be surprised that a member of his family or a close friend might have iced the old man; it happens all the time. But I thought those people were class. What do you figure the motive was?"

"Money," Dora said.

"Yeah," Wenden said, "probably. When money comes in the door, class goes out the window. Every time."

She laughed. "I didn't know you were a philosopher."

"How can you be a cop and not be a philosopher?" He lowered his head, stared at her with bleary eyes. "I lied to you, Red."

"How so?"

"I told you I wasn't going to pass out. Now I'm not so sure."

"Whatever," she said, "you're in no condition to drive. I have an extra bedroom; you can sack out in there."

"Thanks," he said.

"What time do you want to get up?"

"Never," he said. "Give me a hand, will you."

She helped him to his feet and half-supported him into the bedroom. He sat down heavily on the edge of the bed.

"Can you undress?" she asked him.

"I can get my shoes off," he said in a mumble. "That's enough. I've slept in my clothes before."

"I never would have guessed," she said. "Want more aspirin?"

"Nope. I've had enough."

"I'd say so. I'm not going to wake you up in the morning. Sleep as long as you can. It'll do you the world of good."

"Thanks again, Red. And listen . . . " He tried a grin. "You don't have to lock your bedroom door."

"I know that," she said.

But she did.

13

Solomon Guthrie lived alone in a six-room apartment on Riverside Drive near 86th Street. The prewar building had gone co-op in 1974, and Guthrie had bought his apartment for $59,500. His wife had told him it was a lot of money—and it was, at the time. And why, she had asked, did they need so much space since their two grown sons had moved away: Jacob, an ophthalmologist, to Minneapolis, and Alan, an aerospace designer, to Los Angeles.

But Solomon didn't want to give up an apartment he loved and in which he and his wife had lived most of their married life. Besides, he said, it would be a good investment, and it turned out to be exactly that, with similar apartments in the building now selling for $750,000 to a million.

Then Hilda died in 1978, of cancer, and Solomon was alone in the six rooms. His sons, their wives and children visited at least once a year, and that was a treat. But generally he lived a solitary life. After all these years it was still a wrench to come home to an empty house, especially on dark winter nights.

Every weekday morning Guthrie left his apartment at 7:30, picked up his *Times* from a marble table in the lobby, and walked over to West End Avenue to get a taxi heading south. An hour later and it would be almost impossible to find an empty cab, but Solomon usually had good luck before eight o'clock.

This particular morning was cold, bleak, with a damp wind blowing off the river. He was glad he had worn his heavy overcoat. He was also wearing fur-lined gloves and lugging his old briefcase stuffed with work he had taken home the night before. One of the things he had labored over was a schedule of Christmas bonuses for Starrett employees.

Solomon arrived at the southwest corner of West End and 86th Street, stepped off the curb, looked uptown. There was a cab parked across 86th, but the off-duty light was on, and the driver appeared to be reading a newspaper. He moved farther into the street to see if any other cabs were approaching. He raised an arm when he saw one a block away, coming down West End.

But then the cab parked across 86th went into action. The off-duty light flicked off, the driver tossed his newspaper aside, and the cab came gunning across the street and pulled up in front of Solomon. He opened the back door and crawled in with some difficulty, first hoisting his briefcase and newspaper onto the seat, then twisting himself into the cramped space and turning to slam the door.

"Good morning," he said.

"Where to?" the driver said without turning around.

"The Starrett Building, please. Park Avenue between Fifty-sixth and Fifty-seventh."

He settled back and unbuttoned his overcoat. He put on his reading glasses and began to scan the front page of the *Times*. Then he became conscious of the cab slowing, and he looked up. Traffic lights were green as far as he could see, but his taxi was stopping between 78th and 77th streets, pulling alongside cars parked at the curb.

"Why are you stopping here?" he asked the driver.

"Another guy going south," the driver said. "You don't mind sharing, do you?"

"Yes, I mind," Guthrie said angrily. "I'm paying you full fare to take me where I want to go, and I have no desire to stop along the way to pick up—"

He was still talking when the cab stopped. A man wearing a black fur hat and short leather coat came quickly from between parked cars and jerked open the passenger door.

"Hey!" Guthrie cried. "What the hell do you think—"

But then the stranger was inside, crouching over him, the door was slammed, and the cab took off with a chirp of tires.

"What—" Guthrie started again, and then felt a sear in his abdomen, a flash of fire he couldn't understand until he looked down, saw the man stab him again. He tried to writhe away from that flaming blade, but he was pressed back into a corner, his homburg and glasses falling off as the man stabbed again and again, sliding the steel in smoothly, withdrawing, inserting it. Then he stopped.

"Make sure," the driver said, not turning.

"I'm sure," the assailant said, and pushed Guthrie's body onto the floor. Then he sat down, wiped his blade clean on Solomon's overcoat, and returned the knife to a handsome leather sheath strapped to his right shin.

The cab stopped for the light at 72nd Street. When it turned green, it went south to 71st, made a right into the dead-end street, drove slowly between parked cars to a turnaround at the western end.

The cab stopped on the curve and the two men looked about casually. There was a woman walking a Doberman farther east, but no one else was on the street.

"Let's go," the driver said.

Both men got out of the cab and closed the doors. They paused a moment to light cigarettes, then walked toward West End Avenue, not too fast, not too slow.

14

"How do you feel?" she asked.

"Still got the sniffles," John Wenden said, "but I'll live to play the violin again. Actually, I feel a helluva lot better. It was the tea and brandy that did it."

"It was a good night's sleep that did it," Dora insisted. "You were whacked-out. Want to take a hot shower?"

"You bet."

"Help yourself. There are plenty of towels. If you want to shave, you can borrow my razor. I'll even throw in a fresh blade."

"Thanks, but I'll skip. I keep an electric shaver in my office; the beard can wait till I get there. Sorry I crashed last night, Red."

"You're entitled. While you're showering I'll make us a cup of coffee. But it'll be instant and black. Okay?"

"My favorite brew," he said.

She was preparing coffee when she suddenly thought of what to buy her husband for Christmas. An espresso machine! One of those neat, shiny gadgets that make both espresso and cappuccino. Mario, a coffee maven, would be delighted.

They stood at the sink and sipped their black instant. Wenden looked at her reflectively.

"You think Father Callaway was the perp, don't you?" he said.

Dora shrugged. "I think he's the front-runner. You're going to check him out, aren't you? And the Pierces."

"Oh sure. I'll start the ball rolling as soon as I get back to my desk. What're you doing today?"

"I've got a ten o'clock appointment with Clayton at the Starrett Building. It was the only time he could fit me in."

"What do you expect to get from him?"

"I'm getting confusing signals on how the Pierces became such good friends with the Starrett family. Whether it was before or after Turner Pierce landed Starrett Fine Jewelry as a client and designed their new computer system. I'd also like to know if Father Callaway made the introduction."

He looked at her admiringly. "You're a real sherlock. You enjoy your job?"

"Oh hell, yes."

"What does your husband think of your being a gumshoe?"

She flipped a hand back and forth. "He doesn't mind what I do. What he doesn't like is my being away from home so much. It means he has to cook for only one—which isn't much fun. Mario is a super chef. Do you prepare your own meals?"

"Not exactly," Wenden said. "I have a cook—Mrs. Paul. Listen, Red, I've got to run. Thanks again for the brandy. And the shower. And the coffee. I owe you."

"Just remember you said that," Dora told him. "I may call in my chits."

"Anytime," the detective assured her.

She let him kiss her cheek before he left.

She spent a few minutes straightening up the suite, not accustomed to maid service. Then she went out into a raw morning. It was too cold to hike all the way, so she took a Fifth Avenue bus south and then walked east to Park Avenue, stopping frequently to look in the shop windows on 57th Street.

She was on time for her appointment but had to wait awhile in a cramped reception room. Most of the magazines on the cocktail table were jewelry trade journals, but there was one copy of *Town & Country*. Leafing through it, Dora spotted a full-page Starrett ad. It showed a magnificent necklace of alternating white and yellow diamonds draped across a woman's bare breasts (the nipples hidden). The only print on the page, in a small, discreet script, read: *Starrett Fine Jewelry. Simply Superior.*

A secretary with an English accent ushered her into Clayton Starrett's office at about 10:15. He bounced up from behind his desk, beaming and apparently chockablock with early-morning energy.

"Good morning!" he caroled, shaking her hand enthusiastically. "Sorry to keep you waiting. The Christmas season, you know—our busiest time. Here, let me take your coat. Now you sit right here. Dreadful office, isn't it? So dark and gloomy. I'm having the whole place done over. Bright colors. Much livelier. Well, I hope you've brought me good news about the insurance."

"Not quite yet, Mr. Starrett," Dora said with a set smile, "but we're getting there. We'd like the mystery of your father's death cleared up before the claim is approved. As I'm sure you would."

"Of course, of course," he cried. "Anything I can do to help. Anything at all."

He seemed in an antic mood, and she decided to take advantage of it. "Just a few little questions. Really extraneous to my investigation, but I like to dot the *i*'s and cross the *t*'s. Could you tell me how you and your family met Helene and Turner Pierce?"

He was startled by the question, then sat back, tapped fingertips together. "How did we meet the Pierces? Now let me see . . . I think it was a few years ago. Yes, at least two. Father Callaway was over for dinner and I happened to mention something about the inadequacy of our computers. The Father said he had just the man for me, a management consultant who specialized in designing and upgrading computer systems. So I said to send him around. He was Turner Pierce, and he's done a marvelous job for us. And through Turner I met his sister Helene. A charming couple. They came over for dinner several times, and we all became good friends."

"I see," Dora said. "And did you investigate Turner's credentials before you—"

But then the phone on Starrett's desk jangled, and he looked at it, frowning.

"Damn it," he said. "I told my secretary to hold all my calls. Excuse me a moment, please."

He leaned forward, elbows on the desk, and picked up the phone. "Yes? Who? All right, put him on." He looked up at Dora, puzzled. "A police officer," he said. Then: "Hello? Yes, this is Clayton Starrett. That's correct. What? What? Oh my God! When did this happen? Oh God, how awful! Yes, of course. I understand. I'll be there as soon as possible."

He hung up. He stared blankly at Dora, and she rose to her feet, fearing he might collapse. He was stricken, face broken and sagging, eyes wide and staring, lips trembling.

"The police," he said, voice cracking. "They say Solomon Guthrie has been killed. Murdered."

"Who?"

"Sol Guthrie, our chief financial officer. He's been with Starrett forty years. A good friend of my father."

He began to blink rapidly, but it didn't work; tears overflowed. He wiped them away angrily with the back of his hand.

"How was he killed?" Dora asked.

"Stabbed to death. Like father. Oh, this lousy, rotten city! I hate it, just hate it!"

"It's not only New York, Mr. Starrett. It's happening everywhere."

He nodded, stood up, took a deep breath. "I've got to go. The police asked me to come to, uh, where Sol was found. They want me to, uh, identify the body. West End Avenue and Seventy-first Street. Yes, that's what he said."

Dora moved behind the desk to put a hand on his arm. "Mr. Starrett, would you like me to go with you? Perhaps it would be a little easier if you weren't alone."

He looked at her, face twisted. "Would you do that? Thank you. Yes, please come with me. I'd really appreciate it. Listen, there's a bottle of Scotch in that sideboard over there, and glasses. Would you pour us a drink while I call down and have my driver bring the car around."

She poured him a stiff shot of whiskey, but none for herself. He finished on the phone and downed his drink in two gulps. Then he coughed, and his eyes began to water again.

"Let's go," he said hoarsely.

On the drive uptown he kept his head turned away from her, staring out the limousine's tinted windows at the mean streets of his city.

"How old a man was he, Mr. Starrett?"

"Sol was sixty-three."

"Married?"

"A widower. He has two grown sons, but they don't live in New York. They'll have to be notified as soon as possible. I hope we have their addresses in our personnel file."

"The police will find them," Dora assured him. "Did they say if the killer had been caught?"

"They didn't say."

"What do you suppose he was doing there—where his body was found?"

"Probably on his way to work. He lived on Eighty-sixth and Riverside Drive."

They found West 71st Street blocked by two uniformed police officers. Clayton Starrett identified himself and the limo was allowed to move slowly down to the far end of the block. There were squad cars, an ambulance, a van from the police lab, all parked in a jagged semicircle around a yellow cab with opened doors. Crime scene tape, tied to trees and iron fences, held back a small throng of gawkers.

A burly man wearing a plaid mackinaw, ID clipped to his lapel, came over to them.

"Mr. Starrett?"

Clayton nodded.

"I'm Detective Stanley Morris. I spoke to you on the phone. Thanks for helping us out. We need positive identification. This way, please."

He took Clayton firmly by the arm and started to lead him toward the cab.

"Can I come?" Dora asked.

The detective stopped, looked back at her. "Who are you?"

"Dora Conti. I'm a friend of Mr. Starrett."

"Did you know the victim?"

"No," she said.

"Then you stay here."

Left alone, she looked about and saw John Wenden leaning against the door of a squad car, talking to a uniformed officer. She moved around to his line of sight and waved her arm wildly. He spotted her and came over, face expressionless.

"What the hell are you doing here, Red?" he asked her.

"I was in Clayton's office when he got the call. I thought he should have someone with him."

"How did he take the news?"

"Total shock. And he wasn't faking. This Solomon Guthrie—he was stabbed?"

Wenden nodded.

"Like Lewis Starrett?"

"No. From the front. And more than one wound. Several, in fact."

"Same kind of knife? An eight-inch triangular blade?"

"I doubt it. It looks more like a kind of stiletto, but we won't know for sure until the autopsy."

"Any leads?"

"Nothing worth a shit."

"What about the cab?"

"It was stolen early this morning from Broadway and Seventy-ninth. The driver parked for a minute to run into a deli to pick up a coffee and bagel. He left his motor running—the schmuck! When he came out, the cab was gone. It ended up here."

"Robbery?"

"Doesn't look like it. Guthrie's wallet and credit cards are all there. And a gold Starrett pocket watch. Nothing was touched. He was carrying a briefcase full of Starrett business papers. That's how come Clayton was called."

Dora shook her head. "I don't get it. Clayton says he was probably on his way to work. Then the driver turns in here, goes to the dead end, stops, gets out of the cab, opens the back door, stabs his passenger to death, and walks away. Do you believe it?"

"No," John said, "it doesn't fit. The victim would have plenty of time to scream or get out the other side of the cab or put up a fight. But there's no sign of a struggle. I'm betting on two perps: the driver and another guy in back with Guthrie."

"A planned homicide?"

"I'd guess so. Probably professionals. A contract killing most likely. They knew exactly what they were doing. The lab crew is vacuuming the cab now. They'll be able to tell us more. What does this do to your theory that Father Callaway offed Lewis Starrett?"

"Knocks it into left field," Dora admitted. "The chairman and principal stockholder of Starrett Fine Jewelry gets stabbed to death on East Eighty-third Street. Then the chief financial officer of Starrett gets knifed on West Seventy-first. You don't believe in coincidences, do you?"

"Hell, no. Not in this business."

"So where does that leave your official theory that Lewis Starrett's death was a random killing by a stranger?"

"Right next to yours," he said, "out in left field. It seems obvious the two homicides are connected, and Starrett Jewelry is probably the key. So now we start searching through their files for fired employees or someone who might have a grudge against the company and decided to knock off its executives to get even."

"You going to put a guard on Clayton?"

"We can't baby-sit him twenty-four hours a day. Haven't got the manpower. But we'll warn him and suggest he beef up security at his stores and hire personal bodyguards for himself, his family and top executives. He can afford it. Oh-oh, here he comes now."

Clayton Starrett, supported by Detective Stanley Morris, returned to the limousine. He was almost tottering; his face was ashen.

"I'll ride back to his office with him," Dora said, "or to his home, if that's where he wants to go. Listen, John, will you call me tonight if anything new breaks on this case?"

"I'll call you tonight even if nothing breaks," Wenden said. "Okay, Red?"

"Sure," Dora said. "I'm glad you shaved. Keep up the good work."

15

"I'm ready," Felicia Starrett said.

"You're always ready," Turner Pierce said, and she giggled.

The bedroom of Turner's sublet in Murray Hill was like the rest of the apartment: dark with heavy oak furniture, worn oriental rugs, and drapes of tarnished brocade. On every flat surface was artfully arranged the owner's collection of porcelain figurines: shepherds, ballerinas, courtiers, elves and fairies—all in pinks and lavenders.

Few of Turner's possessions were in view: mostly scattered newspapers, magazines, and computer trade journals. A closed Compaq laptop was on the marble sideboard and, in the bedroom, a bottle of Tanqueray vodka was in an aluminum bucket of ice cubes alongside the bed. Also thrust into the bucket was a clump of baby Vidalia onions.

Felicia rose naked from the crumpled sheets, stood shakily. She put hands on her hips and drew a deep breath before heading into the bathroom.

Turner stretched to pour himself a wineglass of chilled vodka. He selected one of the onions and began to gnaw on the white bulb. Felicia came from the bathroom, tugging snarls from her hair with a wide-toothed comb. She paused to pull on Turner's shirt, then sat on the edge of the bed and watched him drink and chew his onion. He offered her the glass of vodka, but she shook her head.

"Not my shtick," she said, "as you well know. Where did you learn to make love like that?"

"My mother taught me," he said.

She laughed. "Not your sister?"

"No, she taught dad."

Felicia laughed again. "You bastard," she said, "you always top me. Listen, I'm going to make you an offer you can't refuse."

"Oh?" he said, dropping an ice cube into his vodka.

"When the insurance money comes in, I'm going to have a cool million. I own ten percent of Starrett Fine Jewelry, and that pays me about fifty grand a year in dividends. And when mother shuffles off, I'll be a very, very wealthy lady."

"So?"

"I want to buy you," she said. "I'm proposing, you stinker. Marry me, and you'll be set for life. I'll sign any kind of a prenuptial agreement your shyster comes up with."

He showed no sign of surprise or shock; just began to nibble on the green onion top.

"Why would you want to do that?" he asked.

"Because I'm tired of alley-catting around. I'm tired of one-night stands. I'm tired of burned-out men who are scared of making a commitment. I'm tired of living in my father's house, now my mother's. I want my own home and my own man. I'm about ten years older than you— correct?"

"More like fifteen," he said casually.

"Swine!" she said. "But what the hell difference does age make? I'm as young as you in bed. Right or wrong?"

"Right," he said.

"You betcha. There's nothing you've asked me to do that I haven't done. I can keep up with you. The body's not so bad, is it?"

"The body's good," he acknowledged.

"It should be—the money I spend on it. I may not be a centerfold, but I'm not a dried-out husk either. And you'll be getting financial security for the rest of your life. What do you say?"

He poured more vodka, and this time she lifted the drink from his fingers and took a gulp. She grimaced and handed back the glass.

"What would your family say?" he asked. "Your mother? Clayton?"

"Screw my family," she said wrathfully. "I've got my own life to live. I can't keep living it the way they want me to. I'll bet you don't let Helene run your life."

"Your mother could disown you," he pointed out.

"Not without a helluva court fight," Felicia said. "If she dies and I don't get half the estate, some lawyer is going to earn mucho dinero representing me. But that's all in the future. Right now I've got enough loot so that you and I could live the lush life. Well?"

"Interesting proposition," Turner said. "I'll have to think about it."

"Sure," she said. "Run it through your little computer and see if it doesn't make sense. Now let me prove that marrying me would be the smartest deal you ever made."

He finished his vodka, set the empty glass on the floor. "I have something for you," he said. "Want it now?"

"I thought you'd never ask," she said. "Where is it?"

"Top bureau drawer."

"How much?"

"A gram."

"You darling!" she cried.

16

Two days before Christmas, Dora Conti went home to Hartford, lugging an espresso machine in a bulky carton. She had spent more than she intended, but it was a marvelous gadget. Not only did it make espresso and cappuccino, but it also ground coffee beans. And it had enough shiny spigots, valves, dials, and switches to keep Mario happily busy for days while he learned to brew a perfect cup of coffee.

Before she left New York, Dora called John Wenden. He reported there was nothing new on either the Lewis Starrett or Solomon Guthrie homicides. The Department was checking out all discharged employees of Starrett Fine Jewelry, but it was going to be an arduous task.

"We got their employment records," Wenden said, "but there's been a big turnover in the last two years. This is going to take a long, long time."

"Did you get anything from Records about Callaway or the Pierces?"

"Not yet. They say they're working on it, and if I push them, they're liable to get pissed off and stall just to teach me a lesson. That's the way the world works."

"Tell me about it," Dora said. "I have the same problem in my shop."

Then she told him she would return to Manhattan on January 2nd and would call him when she got back. She wished him a Merry Christmas and a Happy New Year.

"Likewise," John said.

So she went home, feeling guilty about leaving him alone for the holidays, and thinking what an irrational emotion that was. But he seemed such a weary, lost man that she worried about him and wished she had bought him a Christmas gift. A maroon cashmere muffler would have been nice. But then she wondered if NYPD detectives wore mufflers.

Mario was at work when Dora arrived home, so she was able to conceal his gift in the back of her closet. In the living room he had erected a bushy six-foot Douglas fir and alongside it, brought up from the basement, were boxes of ornaments, tinsel, garlands, and strings of lights. There was a big bottle of Frascati in the fridge, and in the wine rack on the countertop were bottles of Lacrima Cristi, Soave, Valpolicella, and—Dora's favorite—Asti Spumante.

They had a splendid holiday, all the better because they spent it alone. On Christmas Eve they made love under the glittering tree because it seemed a holy thing to do. Mario gave her a marvelous tennis bracelet, and even if the diamonds were pebbles compared to the rocks that Starrett women wore, Dora thought it the most beautiful gift she had ever received, and her happiness was doubled by Mario's joy with his new espresso machine.

During the remainder of the week, Dora went to the office every day and wrote a progress report on the word processor, consulting her spiral notebook to make certain she could justify her surmises and conclusions. She left the nineteen-page report on Mike Trevalyan's desk late one evening, and the next morning she was summoned to his office, a dank chamber cluttered with files and bundles of computer printout tied with twine. The air was fetid with cigar smoke; during crises or explosions of temper, Trevalyan was known to keep two cigars going at once.

He was a porcine man with small eyes, a pouty mouth, and all the sweet reasonableness of a Marine drill instructor. But the Company didn't pay him an enormous salary for affability. They *wanted* him to be irascible, suspicious, and to scan every insurance claim as if the money was coming out of his own pocket. He had worked as a claims adjuster all his life, expected chicanery and, it was said, was furiously disappointed when he couldn't find it.

"This case," he said, pointing his cigar at Dora's report, "it reeketh in the nostrils of the righteous. There's frigging in the rigging going on here, kiddo, and I'm not paying a cent until we know more."

"I agree," Dora said. "Too many unanswered questions."

"The cops think it was a disgruntled ex-employee taking out his grudge on Starrett executives?"

"That's what they think," she said.

"You know what's wrong with that theory?" Trevalyan demanded.

"Of course I know," Dora said. "It doesn't account for the knife disappearing from the Starretts' apartment, maybe on the night Lewis was killed. That's the first thing I want to check out when I get back to New York."

"This Detective Wenden you mention—he should have seen that. Is the guy a bubblehead?"

"No, he's just overworked, running a half-dozen homicide cases at the same time. He happens to be a very experienced and conscientious professional.''

Trevalyan stared at her. ''You wouldn't have the hots for this guy, would you?''

''Oh Mike, don't be such an asshole. No, I haven't got the hots for him. Yes, we are friends. You want me to make an enemy of the detective handling the case?''

''Just don't get too close,'' he warned. ''It's your brains I'm buying, not your glands. If he's as overworked as you say, he might try to sweep the whole thing under the rug.''

''No,'' Dora said firmly, ''John would never do that.''

''Oh-ho,'' Trevalyan said, mashing out his cigar butt in an overflowing ashtray, ''it's *John,* is it? Watch yourself, sister. This big-city slicker may be warm for your form, and is feeding you just enough inside poop to keep you coming back to him. And meanwhile he's working an angle you haven't even thought of.''

''You're crazy!'' she said angrily. ''It's me that gave him the scoop on the missing knife and Callaway's record. I'm way ahead of him.''

''Keep it that way,'' Trevalyan advised, lighting a fresh cigar. ''If he's not playing you, like you claim, then you play him. Don't tell him everything; just enough to make him want to cooperate. What else are you planning when you get back to Sodom on the Hudson?''

''A couple of things,'' Dora said. ''Mostly I want to dig deeper on how Father Callaway fits into the picture. Like where was he and what was he doing the morning Solomon Guthrie was stabbed to death.''

''You think Callaway did it?''

''I'm not sure about Guthrie, but I think there's a good possibility he killed Lewis Starrett.''

Trevalyan inspected the glowing end of his cigar. ''What was his motive?''

''I haven't figured that out yet. I guess Starrett said some nasty things to him, but nothing dirty enough to trigger a murder.''

Mike looked up at her and laughed. ''Dora, you better read your own report again. Callaway's motive is in there.''

''What?''

''You heard me. Your report includes a very logical reason why Callaway might have iced Lewis Starrett.''

''Mike, what *is* it?''

He shook his head. ''You find it; it's your case. And keep an eye on that New York cop. I still think he's trying to get in your drawers.''

''Where the hell were you when God was handing out couth?'' she said indignantly.

''Waiting for seconds in the cynics' line,'' he said. ''Now let's go drink some lunch. Your treat.''

He was exaggerating, of course; they actually had food for lunch: thick corned beef sandwiches with french fries and a schooner of beer each at an Irish bar near the Company's headquarters. And while they lunched, Mike told her what he had been able to pick up about Starrett Fine Jewelry, Inc.

Little was known because it was a privately held corporation, and public disclosure of its structuring and current financial condition was not required. But through rumors and hearsay, Trevalyan had learned that Olivia, Clayton, and Felicia each owned ten percent of the stock. Lewis had owned seventy percent which, presumably, would go to his widow.

"So as of now," Dora said, "Olivia really controls the whole shebang."

Mike nodded. "From what I hear, back in the 1950s and '60s, Starrett Fine Jewelry was a cash cow. That's when they opened all their branch stores. Then, beginning about ten years ago, their sales and profits went down, down, down. The problem was a-g-e. Their clientele was getting older, putting money in annuities and Treasury bonds instead of diamonds. And the baby-boomers were doing their jewelry shopping at trendier places. They thought Starrett was old-fashioned and stuffy. So about two years ago Lewis went into semiretirement and turned over the reins to Clayton.

"Well, Clayton's first year at the helm was a disaster. He brought in a bunch of kooky designers and started pushing a line of what was really horribly overpriced costume jewelry. Not only did it not attract the yuppies, but it turned off what few old customers were left. Starrett was drowning in red ink, and there was talk in the trade that they might end up in Chapter Eleven. Then, about a year ago, Clayton turned the whole thing around. He got rid of all the designers with ponytails and went back to Starrett's classic fine jewelry. He fired most of his branch managers and brought in young hotshots who knew something about modern merchandising. And he started trading bullion, buying gold overseas at a good price and selling it to small independent jewelers in this country at a nice markup. From what I heard, Starrett is back in the bucks again, and everyone is happy."

"Except Lewis," Dora said. "And Solomon Guthrie."

"Yeah," Trevalyan said, "except them. Have you talked to Starrett's attorney yet?"

"Not yet, but he's on my list."

"He probably won't tell you a thing, but it's worth a try. Ask him if Lewis kept a bimbo on the side."

Dora stared at him. "Why should I ask him that?"

"Just for the fun of it. You never know."

She sighed. "All right, Mike, I'll ask him. Now I'm going to pay for our lunch. But I warn you, I'm putting it on my expense account."

"Suits me," Trevalyan said.

On New Year's Eve, Dora and Mario walked to their church for a noon service. Afterwards, they went looking for Father Piesecki and found him in the church basement where he and a fat altar boy were gilding a plaster saint. They told him about the open house they were having that night and urged him to stop by.

"I'll try," he said, "but I have four other parties to visit."

"Homemade kielbasa," Mario said.

"I'll be there when the doors open," Father Piesecki promised.

It was a wild and wonderful evening, with friends and family members coming and going. Most of the guests brought a covered dish or a bottle, so there was plenty to eat and drink. Neighbors had been invited to fore-stall complaints about the noise. Father Piesecki showed up with his accordion and never did get to those four other parties.

No one got too drunk or too obstreperous, and if the Christmas tree was knocked over during a violent polka, it was soon set aright. Even Mike Trevalyan and Mario's trucker friends were reasonably well-behaved, and the worst thing that happened was when Dora's elderly uncle dropped his dentures into the punch bowl.

Mario started serving espresso from his new machine at 1:00 A.M., but it was almost three o'clock in the morning before the last guests went tottering off. It was an hour after that before the remaining food was put away, empty glasses and scraped dishes stacked in the sink, ashtrays wiped clean, and Dora and Mario could have a final Asti Spumante, toast each other, and fall thankfully into bed. They didn't make love until they awoke at eleven o'clock on January 1.

She returned to New York the following day. Manhattan was still digging out from a five-inch snowfall, but that was pleasant; garbage on the sidewalks was covered over, and the snow was not yet despoiled by dog droppings. Streets had been cleared, buses were running, and the blue sky looked as if it had been washed out and hung up to dry.

She called John Wenden from her suite at the Bedlington, but it was late in the afternoon before he got back to her.

"Hey, Red," he said, "how was the holiday?"

"Super," she said. "How was yours?"

"No complaints. I drank too much, but so did everyone else. How's your D.O.H.?"

"My *what?*"

"Your D.O.H. Dear Old Hubby."

"My husband is fine, thank you," she said stiffly, and Wenden laughed.

"Listen, Red," he said, "I finally heard from Records. What they dug up on Father Brian Callaway is pretty much what you told me: real name Sidney Loftus, small-time scams and swindles but no violent crimes. He's never done a day in the clink—can you believe it? Nothing on either Turner or Helene Pierce. That doesn't mean they're squeaky clean, just that they've never been caught. Let's see, what else . . . Oh yeah, I had a nose-to-nose talk with the Starrett servants.

They finally admitted the eight-inch chef's knife disappeared the evening Lewis Starrett was killed.''

''John,'' she said, ''I thought you were convinced Lewis and Solomon Guthrie were murdered by an ex-employee.''

''Convinced? Hell no, I wasn't convinced. But when two guys from the same company get iced, it's S.O.P. to check out former employees who might be looking for revenge. It's something that has to be done, but there's no guarantee it's the right way to go.''

''I'm glad to hear you say that. So you still think it might have been someone at that cocktail party?''

''It could have been Jack the Ripper for all I know,'' the detective said. ''What's your next move?''

She thought a moment, remembering Trevalyan's warning not to reveal too much. ''I don't know,'' she said. ''Just poke around some more, I guess.''

''Bullshit,'' Wenden said. ''Unless I miss my guess, you're going to investigate where Callaway was at the time Solomon Guthrie took his final ride in a yellow cab.''

''I might do that,'' she admitted.

''Don't hold out on me, Red,'' he said, ''or I'll bring this beautiful friendship to a screeching halt. Forget about Callaway; I've already checked him out. He was in a hospital the morning Guthrie was offed.''

''A hospital? What for?''

''Minor surgery. I'd tell you what it was, but I don't want to make you blush. Let's just say he's now sitting on a big rubber doughnut. Anyway, there's no possibility he could have aced Guthrie. Disappointed?''

''Yes,'' Dora said, ''I am.''

''Welcome to the club,'' John said. ''How about lunch tomorrow?''

''Sure,'' Dora said. ''Think you can stand hotel food again?''

''I can stand anything,'' he said, ''as long as it's free. Can you make it early? Noon?''

''Fine.''

''It'll be good seeing you again,'' he said. ''I've missed you, Red.''

''And I've missed you,'' she replied, shocked at what she was saying. Then: ''John, what's the name of Starrett's attorney?''

''Oh-ho,'' he said, ''the wheels keep turning, do they? His name is Arthur Rushkin. Baker and Rushkin, on Fifth Avenue. That's another one you owe me.''

''I'll remember,'' she promised.

''See that you do,'' he said, and hung up.

She called Baker & Rushkin on Fifth Avenue, explained who she was and what she wanted. She was put on hold for almost five minutes while ''Mack the Knife'' played softly in the background. Finally Arthur Rushkin came on the phone. Again she identified herself and asked if he could spare her a few minutes of his time.

"I have to be in court tomorrow," he said, "but I should be back in the office by four o'clock. How does that sound?"

"I'll be there, Mr. Rushkin."

Then she dug out a copy of the progress report she had submitted to Trevalyan. She reread it for the umpteenth time, searching for what Mike had said was a logical motive for Callaway killing Lewis Starrett. She still hadn't found it, and thought maybe Trevalyan was putting her on; he was capable of a stupid trick like that.

But this time she saw it and smacked her forehead with her palm, wondering how she could have been so dense.

17

Turner had warned Helene of Clayton's reaction to Solomon Guthrie's death and had suggested the spin she put on it.

"You'll have no trouble," he predicted. "Most people believe what they *must* believe, to shield themselves from reality."

"But not you," Helene said.

"Oh no," Turner said airily. "I take reality raw à la sauce diable. Delicious, but it might make you sweat a bit."

Still, it was no easy task to convince Clayton that Guthrie's murder had been a simple mugging gone awry. He admitted that such senseless killings occurred every day on the hard streets of New York, but Helene could see that guilt gnawed; he could not rid himself of the notion that somehow he had contributed to Sol's death, that he was in fact an accessory. That was the word he used: accessory.

Finally she ignored Turner's instructions on how to handle this crybaby and resorted to a more elemental and effective method: She took him to bed. Within minutes sorrow was banished, guilt forgotten, and he was exhibiting the frantic physical ardor of a man who had been brooding too much on mortality.

She understood his passion was death-driven, but no less enjoyable for that. Afterwards, though, she had to listen to his banal maunderings on how fleeting life was; how important it is to "Gather ye rosebuds while ye may"; how no man on his deathbed had ever said, "I should have paid more attention to business"—all hoary clichés Helene had heard dozens of times before, usually from older men.

But this time the peroration was different.

Lying flat on his back, legs together, arms at his sides, staring at the ceiling for all the world like a stripped corpse being fitted for a shroud, Clayton declared:

"I've decided to change my life. Change it completely."

It was said in a challenging tone, as if he expected opposition and was prepared to overcome it.

"Change it how, Clay?" she asked.

"I'm going to leave Eleanor. People are supposed to grow closer together in a marriage; we've grown farther apart. We're strangers. I don't know her anymore, and she doesn't know me. It's not the way I want to spend the rest of my life."

"Have you said anything to her?"

"No, not yet. Before I do, I want to get mother's reaction. And yours."

"Mine?" Helene said, fearing what was coming. "I have nothing to do with it."

He turned his head on the pillow to stare at her. "You do. Because if mother approves—or at least is neutral—and I leave Eleanor, I want to marry you."

She was nothing if not an accomplished actress, and her face and voice displayed all the proper reactions: shock, pleasure, dubiety. "Clay," she started, "I'm not—"

But he held up a palm to stop her. "Wait a minute; let me make my case. First of all, my marriage has become unendurable. That's a given. And I see no possibility of the situation improving. Absolutely not. So no matter what you decide, my life with Eleanor is finished. You mustn't think you're responsible for the breakup. It would have happened even if I had never met you."

"Shall I get us a drink?" she asked.

"No, not yet; I don't need it. Helene, I know I'm twice your age, but surely there are other things more important. We think alike, laugh at the same things, get along beautifully, and we're building up a lot of shared memories, aren't we?"

"Yes."

"I may not be the world's greatest stud, but I'm not a complete dud, am I?"

"It's all I can do to keep up with you," she assured him, and he smiled with pleasure.

"The most important thing is your future," he said earnestly. "Your financial future. And that I can guarantee. I know that if I wasn't helping you out, you'd be depending on your brother's generosity. But how long do you want to do that? And what if he suffers financial reverses—it's always possible—then where are you? What I'm offering you is security, now and for the future. You must think about your future."

"Yes," she said, "I must."

"Marry me, and we can draw up some kind of agreement so that even if I die suddenly or our marriage doesn't work out, you'll be well taken care of. I know how much you enjoy the good life. This is your chance to make certain you can keep enjoying it."

"You're quite a salesman," she said with a tinny laugh. "I think I better have a drink now. May I bring you one?"

"Yes," he said. "All right."

Naked in the kitchen, leaning stiff-armed on the countertop, she wondered how she might finesse this complication. She wished Turner was there to advise her, but then she knew what he'd say: stall, stall, stall. Until they could figure out the permutations and decide where their best interest lay.

She poured vodka over ice, added lime wedges, and carried the two glasses back to the bedroom: a proud, erect young woman with a dancer's body and appetites without end.

She handed Clayton his drink, then sat cross-legged at the foot of the bed.

"I won't say anything about your leaving your wife," she said. "I've never suggested it, have I? Never even hinted at it. It's really your decision and none of my business. But I don't understand why you feel you must marry me. Why can't we continue just the way we have been? I'm perfectly content."

He shook his head. "First of all, I happen to be a very conventional man. Tradition and all that. If I'm to have a long-term relationship with a woman, it should be legal; that's the way I was brought up. Second, for purely selfish reasons I want you for my wife. I want to be seen with you in public, take you to the theatre and parties, hear you introduced as Mrs. Clayton Starrett. I don't want people smirking and whispering, 'There's Clay with his floozy.' That wouldn't reflect well on Starrett Fine Jewelry. Bad public relations."

"I can see you've given this a lot of serious thought."

"Yes, I have," he said, missing the irony completely, "and I think you should, too. I don't expect an answer this minute, but if you think it over carefully, I know you'll see the advantages, especially security-wise."

"You don't mind if I tell my brother about this, do you?"

"Of course not," he said with a rapscallion grin. "I was counting on it. I know how close you two are, and I'm betting he'll be all for it. He'll tell you it's the smart thing to do: look out for Numero Uno."

She didn't reply.

He finished his drink and climbed out of bed. "Listen, I've got to get back to the office. Things are in a mess since Sol passed. Dick Satterlee has taken over and is doing what he can. But Sol carried a lot in his head, and it's going to take a while to get things straightened out."

After he was dressed, he tugged a small suede pouch from his side pocket and tossed it onto the bed. "Two carats. Pear-shaped. There's a tiny inclusion in the base but you'll never notice it."

"Thank you," she said faintly.

"I hope the next stone I give you will be in a solitaire," he said. "And I promise it'll be larger than two carats."

"Clay," she said, "do you love me?"

He waved a hand. "That goes without saying," he said, and bent down to kiss her.

After he was gone, the door locked, bolted, and chained behind him, she added the new diamond to her hoard and sat staring at the glittering heap. She didn't want to call Turner immediately. She needed time to think, to plan, to figure the best way to look out for Numero Uno.

18

The snow had melted, but the gutters were awash with garbage and some street corners were small lakes. But having gained almost five pounds during the holiday at home, Dora decided the walk downtown would do her good. This was after lunch with John Wenden during which she virtuously nibbled on a small tuna sandwich and drank nothing but tea.

"Are you sick?" John asked.

"Diet," she explained. "My New Year's resolution."

"I made one, too," he said, swilling his beer. "To cut out the beer."

Strangely, they spoke little of the Starrett case at lunch. Mostly they exchanged memories of Christmases past when they were children and the world was bright with hope and their dreams without limit.

"That didn't last long," Wenden said. "By the time I was ten I knew I would never be president, of anything."

"Even as a kid I was chubby," Dora said. "All the beautiful, popular girls chose me for a friend because they didn't want any competition."

"No one chose me for a friend," he said. "I've always been a loner. Maybe that's why my marriage flopped."

"Do you ever see your ex?"

"No," he said shortly. "I hear she's been dating a barber from Yonkers. Serves her right."

Dora laughed. "I think you should get married again, John."

He brightened. "My first proposal this year!"

"Not me, dummy," she said. "I'm taken."

"Not even for a week?" he asked, looking at her.

"Not even for a night. You just don't give up, do you?"

"You've never cheated on your husband?"

"Never."

"He wouldn't know. It would be an act of charity."

"It would be an act of stupidity," she said.

Plodding downtown, trying to leap over puddles and avoid a splashing from passing cabs, Dora thought of that luncheon conversation and smiled at John's persistence. It was a compliment, she supposed, to have a man come on so strongly. But it was worrisome, too, and she wondered how the hell Mike Trevalyan had guessed immediately what Wenden's motives were, without even meeting the guy. Maybe, she thought shrewdly, because Trevalyan had similar desires.

Men, she decided, were born to perpetual hankering. Except Mario, of course. Right? Right?

She was early for her appointment with Arthur Rushkin and walked over to the Starrett store on Park Avenue. There were few shoppers, and most seemed to be browsing, wandering about to examine the showcases of diamond rings, gold watches, brooches set with precious gems and, in particular, one fantastic three-strand choker of emeralds and rubies that, Dora guessed, probably cost more than the Contis' bungalow in Hartford.

On the way out she picked up a small, slick-paper leaflet: an application for a charge account. It also included a short history of Starrett Fine Jewelry and listed the addresses of all the branch stores. Dora slipped it into her shoulder bag, to be added to the Starrett file, and then headed for the attorney's office on Fifth Avenue.

She waited only five minutes in the reception room before Arthur Rushkin came out, introduced himself, shook her hand, and asked if she'd care for coffee. She declined, but was pleased with his hearty friendliness. If he was putting on an act, it was a good one.

He got her seated alongside the antique desk in his private office, then relaxed into his big swivel chair. He laced fingers across his bulging paisley waistcoat and regarded her with a benign smile.

"It's *Mrs.* Conti, isn't it?" he asked.

She nodded.

"I hope you won't be offended, Mrs. Conti, but after you called I made inquiries about you. I like to know something about the people I meet with. Perhaps you'll be happy to learn that you are very highly regarded. The people I spoke to praised you as a very intelligent, professional, and dedicated investigator."

"Yes," she said, "I am happy to hear it."

"I suppose," he said, still smiling, "your job is to make certain, before the claim is approved, that none of the beneficiaries was involved in the death of Lewis Starrett."

"That's part of it," she said cautiously.

"And what have you discovered?"

"Nothing definite," she said. "There are still many unanswered questions. Mr. Rushkin, do you know of any enemies Lewis Starrett had who might have wished him harm?"

He shook his head. "Lew could be a very difficult man at times, but I know of no one who disliked him enough to plunge a knife in his back."

Dora sighed. "That's what everyone says. And the whole situation has been further complicated by the murder of Solomon Guthrie."

Rushkin stopped smiling. "Yes," he said in a low voice, "I can understand that." Then he was silent for such a long time that she wondered if he was waiting for her to speak. Finally he rose, walked over to the windows facing Fifth Avenue. He stood there, staring out, his back turned to her, hands thrust into his trouser pockets.

"A hypothetical question, Mrs. Conti," he said, his deep voice a rumble. "If I was to reveal to you material that might possibly—and I repeat the word *possibly*—aid in your investigation, and should that material result in your uncovering *possible* evidence of wrongdoing and illegality, would you feel impelled to present that evidence to the authorities?"

"Of course," she said instantly.

He whirled to face her. "I would never, of course," he said sternly, "ask you *not* to. After all, I am, in a manner of speaking, an officer of the court. But what would your reaction be if I were to ask that if you did indeed uncover what you considered incriminating evidence, you would be willing to reveal that evidence to me before you took it to the police?"

She pondered that a moment. Then, lifting her chin, she said decisively, "I think not, Mr. Rushkin. This is no reflection on your trustworthiness or on your ethics, but I must consider the possibility that the evidence I find might implicate someone close to you, someone to whom you feel great personal attachment. In which case, revealing the evidence to you before it's turned over to the police might possibly—and I repeat the word possibly—result in the quick disappearance of the suspect."

Rushkin smiled wryly. "The praise of your intelligence was justified," he said, and came back to sit down again in his swivel chair. He fiddled with a pen on his desk, and she noted the sag of the heavy folds in his face and neck. He was a man she would ordinarily label "fat-faced," but sorrow gave his fleshy features a kind of nobility.

"I have had a problem these past few weeks," he confessed, not looking at her. "A problem you may feel is ridiculous, but which has cost me more than one night's sleep. The question is this: To whom do I owe my loyalty? In this whole sad affair, who is my client? Was it Lewis Starrett? Is it the Starrett family or any member thereof? And what of the Starrett employees, including Sol Guthrie? Whom do I represent? I have come to a conclusion you may find odd, but I have decided that my client is the one that pays my bills. In this case, it's Starrett Fine Jewelry, Incorporated. My client is a corporation, not the several owners or employees of that corporation, but the corporation itself, and it is to that legal entity that my responsibility is due."

"I don't think that's odd at all," Dora said. "He who pays the piper calls the tune."

"Yes," Rushkin said, "something like that. My wrestling with the problem was made more difficult because of my personal relationship with Lewis Starrett and Solomon Guthrie. They were both old and dear friends, and I don't have many of those anymore. I would not care, by my actions, to impugn their reputation or distress their families. I believe they were both men of integrity. I would like to keep on believing it."

"Mr. Rushkin," Dora said softly, "there is obviously something you know about this case that is bothering you mightily. I suggest you tell me now what it is. I cannot promise complete and everlasting confidentiality because I may, someday, be called to testify about it in a court of law. All I can tell you is that I'll make every effort I can to treat whatever you tell me as a private communication, not to be repeated to anyone without your permission."

He nodded. "Very well," he said, "I accept that."

He then told her that a few days before his murder, Solomon Guthrie came to that very office, "sat in that very chair where you're now seated, Mrs. Conti," and voiced his suspicions that something illegal was going on at Starrett Fine Jewelry, Inc. He had no hard evidence to back up his accusation, but he was convinced skulduggery was going on, and he felt it probably involved Starrett's trading in gold bullion.

"He described to me exactly how the trading is done," Arthur Rushkin told Dora, "and I could see nothing wrong with it. It seemed like a conventional business practice: buying low and selling high."

"Did Mr. Guthrie name any person or persons he suspected of being involved in the illegalities?"

"He didn't actually accuse anyone," the attorney said, "but he certainly implied that Clayton Starrett was aware of what was going on."

Rushkin then related how Solomon Guthrie had left a large bundle of computer printout and pleaded with the lawyer to review it and perhaps discover evidence of thievery, fraud, embezzlement—whatever crime was being perpetrated.

"I filed it away and forgot about it," Rushkin confessed. "Then Sol was killed, and you can imagine the guilt I felt. I dragged it out and spent hours going over it, item by item. I found nothing but ordinary business transactions: the purchase and sale of gold bullion by Starrett Fine Jewelry during the last three months. I was somewhat surprised by the weight of gold being traded, but there is ample documentation to back up every deal."

Rushkin said he had then called in a computer expert, a man he trusted completely, and asked him to go over the printout to see if he could spot any gross discrepancies or anything even slightly suspicious. The expert could find nothing amiss.

But, the attorney went on, he could not rid himself of the notion that the printout was, in effect, Solomon Guthrie's last will and testament and he, Rushkin, would be failing his client, Starrett Fine Jewelry, by not investigating the matter further.

"Yes," Dora said, "I think it should be done. Tell me something, Mr. Rushkin: Did anyone at Starrett know that Solomon Guthrie had come to your office?"

The lawyer thought a moment. "He asked me not to tell Clayton Starrett of his visit, but then he said his secretary—Sol's secretary—knew he was coming over here."

"And other than what he thought might be on the computer printout, he had no additional evidence to prove his suspicions?"

"Well, he did say that Clayton had raised his salary by fifty thousand a year. I congratulated him on his good fortune, but Sol was convinced it was a bribe to keep his mouth shut and not rock the boat. He was in a very excitable state, and I more or less laughed off what I considered wild and unfounded mistrust of his employer. I think now I was wrong and should have treated the matter more seriously."

"You couldn't have known he'd be killed. And there's always the possibility that his suspicions had nothing to do with his murder."

"Do you believe that?" Rushkin demanded.

"No," Dora said. "Do you?"

The lawyer shook his head. "I told you I feel guilt for ignoring what Guthrie told me. I also feel a deep and abiding anger at those who killed that sweet man."

"Clayton Starrett?" she suggested.

Rushkin glared at her. "Absolutely not! I'm that boy's godfather, and I assure you he's totally incapable of violence of any kind."

"If you say so," Dora said.

The attorney took a deep breath, leaned toward her across his desk. "Mrs. Conti, I want to hand over the printout to you. Perhaps you can find something in it that both the computer expert and I missed. Will you take a look?"

"Of course," Dora said. "A long, careful look. I was hoping you'd let me see it, Mr. Rushkin. But tell me: How do you think possible illegality in the gold trades relates to the death of Lewis Starrett?"

He shrugged. "I have no idea. Unless Lew found out something and had to be silenced."

"And then Solomon Guthrie found out that same something and also had to be silenced?"

He stared at her. "It's possible, isn't it?"

"Yes," Dora said. "Very possible."

Sighing, Rushkin opened the deep bottom drawer of his desk and dragged out the thick bundle of computer printout. He weighed it in his hands a moment. "You know," he said, "I don't know whether I hope you find something or hope you don't. If you find nothing, then my guilt at treating Sol so shabbily will be less. If you find something, then I fear that people I know and love may be badly hurt.''

"It comes with the territory," Dora said grimly, took the bundle from his hands, and jammed it into her shoulder bag. "Thank you much for your help, Mr. Rushkin. I'll keep in touch. If you want to reach me, I'm at the Hotel Bedlington on Madison Avenue.''

He made a note of it on his desk pad and she started toward the door. Then she stopped and turned back.

"You knew Lewis Starrett a long time?" she asked.

Rushkin's smile returned. "Since before you were born. He was one of my first clients.''

"My boss told me to ask you this: Did he have a mistress?"

The smile faded; the attorney stared at her stonily. "Not to my knowledge," he said.

Dora nodded and had the door open when Rushkin called, "Mrs. Conti." She turned back again. "Many years ago," the lawyer said.

She waited a long time for the down elevator and then descended alone to the street, aware of how a lonely elevator inspired introspection. In this case, her thoughts dwelt on how fortunate she was to give the impression of a dumpy hausfrau. If she had the physique and manner of a femme fatale–private eye, she doubted if Arthur Rushkin, attorney-at-law, would have revealed that his beamy smiles masked an inner grief.

She hustled back to the Bedlington, clutching her shoulder bag as if it contained the Holy Grail. Double-locked into her corporate suite, she kicked off her shoes, put on reading glasses, and started poring over the computer printout, convinced she would crack its code where two others before her (men!) had failed.

She scanned it quickly at first, trying to get an overview of what it included. It appeared to be a straightforward record of gold purchases abroad; shipments of gold by the sellers' subsidiaries in the U.S. to Starrett's Brooklyn vault; sales of bullion by Starrett to its branch stores; sales by the branches to small, independent jewelers in their areas.

Then she went over it slowly, studying it carefully. The documentation was all there in meticulous detail: numbers and dates of sales contracts, shipping invoices, warehouse receipts, checks, and records of electronic transmission of Starrett's funds overseas. Dora reviewed every trade, even double-checking addition, subtraction, and percentages with her pocket calculator. Everything was correct to the penny.

Suddenly, at about 9:30 P.M., she realized she was famished; nothing to eat all day but that measly tuna sandwich at lunch. She called downstairs hastily and caught the kitchen just as it was about to close for the night. She persuaded an annoyed chef to make her two chicken sandwiches on wheat toast—hold the mayo. While she awaited the arrival of room service, she brewed a pot of tea, using three bags.

And that was her dinner: sandwiches that tasted like wet cardboard and tea strong enough to strip varnish from a tabletop. As she ate, she started again on the computer printout, going slowly and methodically over every trade, looking for any evidence, however slight, of something awry. She found nothing.

By midnight her eyesight was bleary and she gave up. She took a hot shower, thinking that perhaps Solomon Guthrie had been imagining wrongdoing. And if there was something amiss, as Mike Trevalyan had suggested, she couldn't find it in Starrett's gold trades.

But she could not sleep; her brain was churning. She tried to approach the problem from a new angle. If Arthur Rushkin, his computer expert, and she had been unable to find anything wrong in the *details* of the printout, perhaps the corruption was implicit in the whole concept of bullion trading. Maybe there was a gross flaw, so obvious that they were all missing it, just as Mario sometimes said, "Where's the dried oregano?" when the jar was in plain view on the countertop. Then Dora would say, "If it had teeth, it'd bite you."

At 2:00 A.M. she got out of bed, turned on the lights, donned her reading glasses again. This time she flipped through the printout swiftly, trying to absorb the "big picture." She saw something. Not earthshaking. And perhaps it was innocent and could easily be explained. But it was an anomaly, and frail though it might be, it was her only hope.

She searched frantically through her shoulder bag for that folder she had picked up at Starrett Fine Jewelry the previous morning: the charge account application that also listed the addresses of Starrett's branch stores. She checked the location of the stores against the computer printout.

Then, smiling, she went back to bed and fell asleep almost instantly.

19

"This kir is too sweet," Helene Pierce complained.

"You were born a woman," Turner said, "and so you're doomed to eternal dissatisfaction. Also, it's a kir royale. Now eat a grape."

He had frozen a bunch of white seedless grapes. They were hard as marbles, but softened on the tongue and crunched delightfully when bitten.

The Pierces were slumped languidly in overstuffed armchairs in Turner's frowsy apartment, having returned from lunch at Vito's where they had pasta primavera, a watercress salad, and shared a bottle of Pinot Grigio. Now they were sodden with food and wine, toying with the kirs and frozen grapes, both smiling at the memory of their rice-and-beans days.

"I have something to tell you," Helene said.

"And I have something to tell *you*," he said. "But go ahead; ladies first."

"Since when?" she said. "Anyway, Clayton asked me to marry him."

Turner's aplomb shattered. He drained his glass.

"When did this happen?" he asked hoarsely.

"A few days ago."

"Why didn't you tell me immediately?"

"No rush," she said. "He has to ask mommy's permission first."

"Sure," Turner said, "she owns the company now. He's really going to divorce Eleanor?"

"That's what he says."

"Shit!"

"My sentiments exactly," Helene said. "How are we going to handle it?"

"Before we compute that, I better tell you *my* news; it'll give you a hoot. Felicia wants to marry me."

They stared at each other. They wanted to laugh but couldn't.

"This family's doing splendidly," Turner said with a twisted smile. "What did Clayton offer?"

"Financial security. A prenuptial agreement on my terms."

"Pretty much what Felicia offered me. There's a lot of loot there, kiddo."

"I know."

"Damn it!" he exploded. "Things were going so great, and now this. How long can you stall Clayton?"

She shrugged. "As long as it takes him to get a divorce. If Eleanor hires a good lawyer, it could be a year. Stop biting your nails."

He took a deep breath. "It means we'll have to revise our timetable. Another year on the gravy train and that's it."

"What about Felicia?"

"I'll think of something."

"You want to cut and run right now?" she asked curiously.

He shook his head. "It took a lot of time and hard work to set up this deal. It's just beginning to pay off; I'm not walking away from it. And besides, if I split, Ramon would be a mite peeved."

"The understatement of the year," she said.

He nodded gloomily. "I'll figure out how to handle Felicia; it's Clayton I'm worried about."

"You worry too much," she told him. "Leave it to me."

"If you say so," he said doubtfully, and went into the kitchen to mix more kir royales.

Helene straightened up in her armchair, lighted a cigarette slowly. She heard him moving about, the gurgle of wine, clink of glasses. She looked toward the kitchen door, frowning.

She had caught something in his voice that disturbed her. Not panic— not yet—but there was an uncertainty she had never heard before. He was the one who had taught her self-assurance.

"Just don't give a dam'," he had instructed her. "About *anything*. That gives you an edge on everyone who believes in something."

And that's the way they had played their lives; amorality was their religion, and they had flourished. And as they thrived, their confidence grew. They thumbed their noses at the world and danced away laughing. But now, it seemed to her, his surety was crumbling. She imagined all the scenarios that could result from his weakness and how they would impact on her life.

He brought fresh drinks from the kitchen, and she smiled at him, thinking that if push came to shove, she might have to make a hard choice.

20

Dora awoke the next morning convinced that her brainstorm of the previous night had been exactly that: a storm of the brain. Now, in the sunny calm of a new day, it seemed highly unlikely that the peculiarity she had spotted in the computer printout had any significance whatsoever. There were a dozen innocent explanations for it. It was a minor curiosity. It would lead her nowhere.

But still, she reflected glumly, it was all she had, and it deserved, at least, a couple of phone calls. So she dialed Arthur Rushkin. He wasn't in his office yet, and Dora continued calling at fifteen-minute intervals until, at about 10:30, she was put through to him.

"Did you find anything?" he asked eagerly.

"Not really," she said, wondering if dissembling was part of her job or part of her nature. "I just have a technical question, and I was hoping you'd be willing to give me the name of that computer expert you consulted."

"I don't see why not," Rushkin said slowly. "His name is Gregor Pinchik, and he's in the Manhattan directory. He has his own business: computer consultant for banks, brokerages, credit card companies, and corporations."

"Sounds like just the man I need."

"There are two things you should know about him," the attorney went on. "One, he charges a hundred dollars an hour. And two, he's an ex-felon."

"Oh-oh," Dora said. "For what?"

"Computer fraud," Rushkin said, laughing. "But since he's been out, he's discovered there's more money to be made by telling clients how to avoid getting taken by computer sharpies like him. Shall I give Pinchik a call and tell him he'll be hearing from you? That way you won't have to go through the identification rigmarole.''

"It would be a big help. Thank you, Mr. Rushkin."

Then she phoned Mike Trevalyan in Hartford.

"Are you on to anything?" he asked.

"Not really," Dora said again, "but something came up that needs a little digging. Mike, remember when you were telling me about Starrett Fine Jewelry? You said that about a year ago Clayton Starrett fired most of his branch managers and put in new people. And about the same time he started trading in gold bullion."

"So?"

"Starrett has fifteen branches in addition to their flagship store in New York. What I need to know is this: Which of the branch stores got new managers a year ago."

"I'm not sure I can get that," Trevalyan said, "but if it's important, I'll try."

"It's important," Dora assured him.

"How come I always end up doing your job for you?"

"Not all of it. The other thing I wanted to tell you is that I'm going to hire a computer consultant."

"What the hell for?"

"Because I need him," she said patiently. "Technical questions that only an expert can answer."

"How much does he charge?"

"A hundred dollars an hour."

"What!" Trevalyan bellowed. "Are you crazy? A hundred an hour? That means the Company will be paying twenty-five bucks every time this guy takes a crap!"

"Mike," Dora said, sighing, "*must* you be so vulgar and disgusting? Look, if you needed brain surgery—which sometimes I think you do—would you shop around for the cheapest surgeon you could find? You have to pay for expertise; you know that."

"Are you sure this guy's an expert?"

"The best in the business," she said, not mentioning that he had done time for computer fraud.

"Well . . . all right," Trevalyan said grudgingly. "But try to use him only for an hour."

"I'll try," she promised, keeping her fingers carefully crossed.

Her third call of the morning was to Gregor Pinchik, whose address in the directory was on West 23rd Street.

Dora gave her name and asked if Mr. Arthur Rushkin had informed Pinchik that she'd be phoning.

"Yeah, he called," the computer consultant acknowledged in a gravelly voice. "He tell you what my fees are?"

"A hundred an hour?"

"That's right. And believe me, lady, I'm worth it. What's this about?"

"I'd rather not talk about it on the phone. Could we meet somewhere?"

"Why not. How's about you coming down here to my loft."

"Sure," Dora said, "I could do that. What time?"

"Noon. How does that sound?"

"I'll be there," she said.

"It's just west of Ninth Avenue. Don't let the building scare you. It's being demolished, and right now I'm the only tenant left. But the intercom still works. You ring from downstairs—three short rings and one long one—and I'll buzz you in. Okay?"

"Okay," Dora said. "I'm on my way."

The decrepit building on West 23rd Street had scaffolding in place, and workmen were prying at crumbling ornamental stonework and brick facing, allowing the debris to tumble down within plywood walls protecting the sidewalk.

Dora nervously ducked into the littered vestibule and pressed the only button in sight: three shorts and a long. The electric lock buzzed; she pushed her way in and cautiously climbed five flights of rickety wood stairs, thinking that at a hundred dollars an hour Gregor Pinchik could afford a business address more impressive than this.

The man who greeted her at the door of the top-floor loft was short, blocky, with a head of Einstein hair and a full Smith Brothers beard, hopelessly snarled. But the eyes were alive, the smile bright.

"Nice place, huh?" he said grinning. "I'm moving to SoHo next week, as soon as they bring in power cables for my hardware. Watch where you step and what you touch; everything is muck and mire."

He led her into one enormous room, jammed with sealed wooden crates and cardboard cartons. His desk was a card table, the phone covered with a plastic cozy. He used his pocket handkerchief to wipe clean a steel folding chair so Dora could sit down. She rummaged through her shoulder bag, found a business card, handed it over.

Pinchik inspected it and laughed. "I know the Company," he said. "Their computer system has more holes than a cribbage board. I got into it once—just for the fun of it, you understand—and looked around, but there was nothing interesting. Tell your boss his computer security is a joke."

"I'll tell him," Dora said. "You're a hacker?"

"I'm a superhacker," he said. "I protect my clients against electronic snoops like me. Which means I have to stay one step ahead of the Nosy Parkers, and it ain't easy. By the way, your first hour of consultation started when you rang the doorbell."

Dora nodded. "Mr. Rushkin tells me you reviewed the computer printout from Starrett Jewelry and found nothing wrong."

Pinchik made a dismissive gesture. "That wasn't real computer stuff," he said. "It was just data processing. You could have done the same thing with an adding machine or pocket calculator, if you wanted to spend the time.''

''But it was accurate?'' she persisted.

''Accurate?'' Pinchik said, and coughed a laugh. ''As accurate as what was put into it. You know the expression GIGO? It means Garbage In, Garbage Out. If you feed a computer false data, what you get out is false data. A lot of people find it hard to realize that a computer has no conscience. It doesn't know right or wrong, good or evil. You program it to give you the best way to blow up the world, and it'll chug along for a few seconds and tell you; it doesn't care. Did Rushkin say I've done time?''

She nodded.

''Let me tell you how that happened,'' he said, ''if you don't mind wasting part of your hundred-dollar hour.''

''I don't mind,'' Dora said.

''I've got an eighth-grade education,'' Pinchik said, ''but I'm a computer whiz. Most hackers have the passion. With me, it's an obsession. I was a salesman in a computer store on West Forty-sixth Street. I could buy new equipment at an employee's discount, and I was living up here paying bupkes for rent. I worked eight hours a day at the store and spent eight hours hacking. I mean I was writing programs and corresponding electronically with people all over the world as nutty as I was. I can't begin to tell you the systems I got into: government, universities, research labs, military, banks—the whole schmear.

''Now you gotta know I'm a divorced man. My wife claimed she was a computer widow, and she was right. She's living in Hawaii now, and I understand she's bedding some young stud who wears earrings, beats a drum, and roasts pigs for tourists. But that's her problem. Mine was that I had to send her an alimony check every month. Getting bored?''

''No, no,'' Dora said, thinking of Detective John Wenden and his alimony problems. ''It's interesting.''

''Well, those monthly alimony checks were killing me,'' Pinchik went on. ''I could have afforded them if it hadn't been for my obsession; all my loose bucks were going for new hardware, modems, programs, and so forth. So one night I'm up here noodling around, and I break into the computer system of an upstate New York bank. Just for the fun of it, you understand.''

''How did you get in?'' Dora asked curiously.

Pinchik gave her his bright smile. ''If you want to know the truth, lady, most bankers are morons. This was the case of a brand-new integrated computer system installed in an old bank that had more than twenty local branches. There were seven top bank executives who were given private access code words to the entire system. All right, you have seven guys who can tap into the system and move it any way they want anytime they want. Now you guess what passwords those seven guys selected.''

"Days of the week?" Dora suggested.

"Try again."

"The Seven Deadly Sins?"

"Try again."

Dora thought a moment. "The Seven Dwarfs?" she said. "From 'Snow White'?"

"Now you've got it," Pinchik said approvingly. "They thought they were being so cute. It's easy for hackers to break into so-called secure systems. It took me about ten minutes to get into this bank's records, using the password 'Dopey.' I was just looking around, reading all their confidential stuff, and I got this absolutely brilliant idea."

"And that's what put you in jail," Dora said.

"Yeah, lady," the expert said ruefully, "but it wasn't the idea; that was a winner. I just screwed it up, that's all. Here's how it worked. . . . The bank I invaded, like most banks everywhere, carried a lot of what they call dormant accounts. These are old savings and checking accounts that haven't had any action—deposits or withdrawals—for years and years. Maybe the depositor forgot he had money in that bank. Maybe he died and his heirs didn't know he had the account. Maybe he's in jail and doesn't want to touch it until he gets out. Maybe he's hiding the money from his wife or girlfriend. Or maybe he *stole* the money and parked it in a bank until the statute of limitations runs out. For whatever reason, these are inactive accounts that keep getting bigger and bigger as the interest piles up."

"But don't the banks have to advertise the accounts?"

"Sure they do, after a period of years. Then some of the depositors come forward. In most states, if the money isn't claimed after a period of X years, it goes into the state's general funds. So I saw all these dormant accounts on the records of that bank I invaded in upstate New York, and I thought 'Why not?' So every month I'd have Dopey transfer my alimony payment electronically to my ex-wife's account in a Hilo bank, making withdrawals from a large dormant account. The depositor didn't scream; no one knew where the hell he was. Maybe he was dead. And my ex didn't object; all she saw were those monthly payments coming in. The bank's books showed legitimate withdrawals with no evidence that they were being made by Dopey, who was me."

"You were right," Dora said, "it's a brilliant idea. What went wrong?"

"I did," Pinchik said. "Every month I would get into the computer as Dopey and instruct the New York bank to transfer the alimony payment electronically to the Hawaiian bank. What I should have done was feed instructions into the New York bank's computer telling it to make those payments *automatically* every month. It would have been an easy job, but I had other things on my mind and never got around to it. So one month I forgot to tell the New York bank to transfer the alimony money."

"Oh-oh," Dora said.

"Yeah, oh-oh," Pinchik said disgustedly. "It was my own stupid fault. My ex-wife didn't see her payment show up on her statement that month and asked her Hilo bank to check up on it. They contacted the New York bank and asked where the alimony money was. New York said, 'What alimony money?' Naturally my ex gave them my name—she wasn't ratting on me; she really thought it was my dough she was getting—and the New York bank discovered I didn't have an account there. One thing led to another, and I ended up behind bars. But it was a sweet deal while it lasted."

"You don't seem bitter about it."

The superhacker shrugged. "Don't do the crime if you can't do the time."

"Is there a lot of computer crime going on?"

Pinchik rolled his eyes. "More than you and everyone else realizes. Want a rough estimate? I'd guess a minimum of two or three *billion* dollars a year is being siphoned off by computer thievery, fraud, and swindles. And most of it you never hear about."

"Why not?"

"Because the victims—mostly banks—are too embarrassed by their idiotic carelessness to make public their losses. In most cases, even when the crook is caught, they refuse to prosecute; they don't want the publicity. They let their insurance companies cover the shortfall."

"Thanks a lot," Dora said. "That makes me feel great. Tell me something else: Is there a national list somewhere of all the computer thieves and swindlers who have been caught, even if they've never been prosecuted?"

"No, lady, I don't know of any data base that lists only computer felons. But I imagine the FBI's computerized files are programmed so they could spit out a list like that."

Dora shook her head. "The people I'm interested in aren't in the FBI files."

"Ah-ha," Pinchik said, trying to comb his tangled beard with his fingers, "now we get down to the nitty-gritty. You got people you suspect of being computer crooks?"

"It's a possibility. The NYPD has done a trace on them, and they have no priors. The Company's data base of insurance swindlers also shows nothing. I thought maybe, with your contacts, you could do a search and see if these people have ever been involved in computer hanky-panky."

"Sure, I could do that," the expert said, and then gestured around the littered loft. "But you caught me at a bad time. All that stuff in crates and boxes is my hardware, disks, files, and programs, packed up and ready to go. It'll be at least a week, maybe two, before I'm really back in business."

"I can wait," Dora said.

"Good. Meanwhile, if you give me names and descriptions, I can get started calling hackers I know on the phone. When I'm set up and functioning in my new place in SoHo, I'll be able to make it a more thorough worldwide search. How does that sound?''

''Sounds fine,'' Dora said. ''Please keep a very accurate record of the time you spend on it and your expenses. I've got a tightwad boss.''

''I meet them all the time,'' Pinchik said. ''Now let me turn on my handy-dandy tape recorder, and you dictate everything you know about these people. Be as detailed as you can, lady; don't leave anything out.''

So Dora spoke into his notebook-sized tape recorder, stating and spelling the names of Turner and Helene Pierce, mentioning their roots in Kansas City, MO, describing their physical appearance, and what little she knew of their ages, habits, Turner's occupation as computer consultant, their style of living, their accents, their connection with Starrett Fine Jewelry, their home addresses and phone numbers.

''And that's all I have,'' she finished.

''Enough to get me started,'' Gregor Pinchik said, switching off the recorder. ''The names mean nothing to me, but maybe one of my contacts will make them.''

''I'm staying at the Hotel Bedlington on Madison Avenue,'' Dora said. ''Can you give me weekly reports?''

''Nope,'' Pinchik said. ''A waste of time. If I come up with something, I'll let you know immediately. But there's no point in sending you a weekly report of failure.''

''How long do you think the search will take, Mr. Pinchik?''

He considered a moment. ''Give me three weeks to a month,'' he said. ''If I haven't nailed them by then, they're clean—guaranteed. Trust me.''

''I do,'' Dora said, rising. ''Send your bills to me at the Bedlington—all right?''

''Oh sure,'' he said. ''Those you'll get weekly. Depend on it. Nice meeting you, lady.''

21

The decorator stepped back to the office door, turned and examined her work through narrowed eyes. "Well, Mr. Starrett," she said, "how do you like it?"

Clayton, standing alongside his new stainless steel desk, looked around the refurbished office. "That painting over the couch," he said, "shouldn't it be a bit higher?"

"No," the decorator said decisively. "You're a tall man; the painting seems low to you. But it's actually at the eye level of the average person. The proportions of the wall composition are just right, and a Warhol over a Biedermeier lends a certain je ne sais quoi to the room."

"Yeah," he said, grinning happily, "that's exactly that I wanted—a certain je ne sais quoi. I think you did a beautiful job."

"Thank you," she said, and discreetly placed her bill, tucked into a mauve envelope, on a corner of his desk. She took a final look around. "I just adore the ambience," she breathed, and then she was gone.

Clayton thrust his hands into his pockets and strutted about the office a moment, admiring the black leather directors' chairs set at a cocktail table with a top of smoky glass. The entire office, he decided, now reflected the importance and prosperity of the occupant. As the decorator had said, the ambience was right: a wealthy ambience; good-taste ambience; up-to-date ambience.

He opened the mauve envelope, glanced at the statement, blanched, then smiled. His father, he knew, would have had apoplexy at a bill like that for redecorating an office. But times change, as Clayton well knew, and if you didn't change along with them you were left hopelessly behind.

And he had changed, was changing; he could feel it. He had lived in the shadow of his father so many years. He had been a follower, a lackey, really nothing more than a gofer. But now he was living his own life, he was *doing*. In the midst of his glittery office, he felt a surge that made him take a deep breath, suck in his gut, stand tall. Now he was *creating*— there was no other word for it.

He used his new phone, a marvelous instrument that had been coded with frequently called numbers so he had to touch only one button to call home.

"Charles?" he said. "This is Clayton Starrett. May I speak to my mother, please."

While he waited for her to come on the line, he slid into his "orthopedically correct" swivel chair that cushioned him like a womb. It was a sensual experience just to relax in that chair, enjoy its soft but firm comfort, close his eyes and drift, savoring the rewards of his creativity.

"Mother?" he said. "Clayton. Are you going to be in for a while? Good. Has Eleanor gone out? Also good. There's something important I'd like to talk to you about. I'll be home in twenty minutes or so. See you . . . "

He hung up briefly, then lifted the handset again and touched the button labeled H.P.

"Helene?" he said. "Clayton. Will you be in this afternoon? Oh, in about two hours. Good. I'd like to stop by for a few minutes. I won't be able to stay long; my advertising people are coming in later. Fine. See you . . . "

When he arrived home, Mrs. Olivia Starrett was in her flowery bedroom, seated at a spindly desk, working on correspondence. Clayton leaned down to kiss her downy cheek.

"I'll never get caught up," she said, sighing. "All the letters of condolence after father passed. And then Christmas and New Year's cards and letters. It's just too much."

"You'll answer them all," he assured her, pulling up a cushioned armchair too small for him. "You always do. Did Eleanor say when she'll be back?"

"I don't recall," his mother said vaguely. "Something about planning a dinner-dance on a cruise ship. Does that sound right, Clay?"

"Probably," he said. "I want to talk to you about Eleanor, mother. Eleanor and me."

Olivia removed her half-glasses and turned to him. "Oh dear," she said, "I do hope it's not a quarrel. You know how I dislike quarrels."

"I'm afraid it's more serious than that," Clayton said, and plunged right in. "Mother, you know that things haven't been right between Eleanor and me for several years now. Since little Ernie died, she's been a changed woman. Not the woman I married. You're intelligent and sensitive, mother; you must have realized that things weren't going well between us.''

Mrs. Starrett made a fluttery gesture. ''God's will be done,'' she said. ''We must learn to accept pain and sorrow as part of the holy oneness.''

''Yes, yes,'' Clayton said impatiently, ''but I can't go on living like this. It's—it's hypocritical. My marriage is a sham. There's just nothing to it. It's putting up a front at charity benefits and everything else is empty. I can't live that way anymore. It's tearing me apart.''

She stared at him, her big eyes luminous. ''Have you spoken to Eleanor about the way you feel?''

''Eleanor and I don't speak about *anything*. At least nothing important. We've become strangers to each other. Mother, I'm going to ask for a— for a *divorce.*'' The word caught in his throat.

He was returning her stare but had to turn away when he saw her eyes fill with tears. She reached out to put a soft hand on his arm.

''Please, Clayton,'' she said. *''Please.''*

He stood abruptly and stalked about the room, unable to face her. ''It's got to be done,'' he said roughly. *''Got* to be. Our marriage is a great big zero. Eleanor has her charity parties, I have the business to take care of, and we have nothing in common. We just don't *share*. I want a chance at happiness. At least a *chance*. Don't you think I deserve that? Everyone deserves that.''

''Have you considered a marriage counselor?'' she said timidly. ''Or perhaps you could talk to Father Callaway; he's very understanding.''

He shook his head. ''This isn't a temporary squabble. It goes deeper. We've just become incompatible, that's all. I know this is a shock to you, mother, but I wanted to tell you what I plan to do before I spoke to Eleanor about it. I wanted to get your reaction.''

''My reaction?'' she cried. ''Another death in the family—that's my reaction.''

''Come on!'' he said heartily. ''It's not that bad. People get divorced all the time and survive. Sometimes it's the healthiest thing to do. A loveless marriage is like a wasting disease.''

She lowered her head, looked down at her hands, twisted her wedding band around and around. ''What will you do then?'' she asked. ''Marry again?''

He had not intended to tell her. He had planned to take it a step at a time: inform her about the divorce at an initial meeting; then, after giving her time to adjust, he would tell her about Helene in another intimate conversation.

But now, because she did not seem unduly disturbed, he suddenly decided to go all the way, get it all out, thinking that she might be mollified if she knew that he wanted to remarry and would not be alone.

He sat down alongside her again and clasped her hands in his. "Mother, the first thing I want to do is end an impossible situation and divorce Eleanor. Believe me, she'll be well taken care of; she won't have a thing to worry about for the rest of her life. I'm talking about money worries. You know I'll make certain she's financially secure."

She nodded. "Yes, you *must* do that."

"Of course. And when the divorce becomes final"—he took a deep breath—"I want to marry Helene Pierce—if she'll have me."

Olivia raised her eyes to his, and he saw something that surprised him: a kind of peasant shrewdness. "How long has this been going on?" she asked.

He concealed his guilt by feigning bewilderment. "How long has *what* been going on? You've known Helene as long as I have. She and her brother have become good friends to all of us. I think Helene is a lovely, sweet, sensitive person—don't you?"

"She's awfully young, Clayton—for you."

He shook his head. "I don't think so. Perhaps *she* does. Naturally I haven't even hinted to her about the way I feel. Maybe she'll turn me down."

"She won't," Mrs. Starrett said, the peasant again. "She's not that foolish."

He shrugged. "But that's all in the future. I just want you to know that I hope to remarry. I have no intention of living the rest of my life as a bachelor. When I remember how happy you and father were for so many years, I know that marriage—the *right* marriage—is what I want."

"Yes," his mother said.

He leaned toward her, serious and intent. "I know this must come as a shock to you, and a disappointment. I'd do anything in the world to keep from hurting you. I love you, and I know you love me."

"I do, but I love Eleanor, too. What you're doing to her seems so—so unkind."

He gave her a sad smile. "You know what they say: Sometimes you have to be cruel to be kind. Eleanor will be happier without me."

"You don't know that."

"Mother! She'll still have her life: her friends, her charities, her benefits. And perhaps she'll remarry, too. That's possible, isn't it?"

"I don't think so," Mrs. Starrett said.

He straightened up, trying to keep anger out of his voice. "If you don't want me to divorce Eleanor, I'll continue that miserable marriage the rest of my life. Is that what you want? Doesn't my happiness mean anything to you?"

Then she did weep and bent forward to embrace him. "Yes," she said, sobbing, "oh yes, I want you to be happy. I'd give my life to make you happy."

"I know you would, mother," he said in almost a croon, soothing her, stroking her wet cheek. "What's most important to me is that this doesn't come between us. I don't want to risk losing your love, and if you tell me not to do it, I won't."

"No," his mother said, "I can't tell you that. It's your life; I can't control it. Clayton, please let's not talk about it anymore. Not now. I'm so shaken I can't think straight. I think I'll take an aspirin and lie down for a while."

"You do that. And try not to worry about it. I know it's hard for you to accept, but things will work out—you'll see."

He said again that he loved her and then he left. On the way down in the elevator he thought of additional arguments he might have used, but generally he was satisfied with the way things had gone. On the way to Helene's, he had his chauffeur stop at a florist's shop where he ordered a dozen roses to be delivered immediately to his mother with a signed card that read: "I love you most of all."

He was still energized when Helene opened the door of her apartment. He embraced her, laughing, and really didn't calm down until she persuaded him to take off his hat and coat and sit in a living room armchair while she poured him a vodka. He gulped it greedily as he told her of the conversation with his mother.

"She'll go along," he predicted confidently. "Maybe it knocked her for a loop at first, but she'll get used to the idea. I'll hit her again in a day or so, and gradually she'll accept it."

"Then she's not going to fire you?"

"No," he said, grinning, "I don't think so."

"I hope you're right, Clay," Helene said. "I'd hate to be the cause of a breakup between you and Olivia."

"You won't be. She thinks you're too young for me, but I told her that's your decision to make."

"And what did she say?"

"She said you won't turn me down; you're not that foolish."

Helene's smile was chilly. "Sometimes you and your family treat Olivia like she was a bubblehead. She happens to be a very wise lady."

"If you say so. Are you ready to become Mrs. Helene Starrett the day after my divorce is granted?"

"Oh Clay, that's months and months away. It seems to me you're rushing things."

"Look, if you're going to do something, then *do* it. You still haven't answered my question."

"You really want to marry me?"

"Absolutely!"

She came up close, pressed her softness against his arm, caressed the back of his neck. "Then why don't we go practice," she said throatily. "Right now."

"You're on," he said at once and stood up. He put his drink aside and began to take off his jacket.

"What about your advertising people, darling?" she said, unbuttoning his shirt.

"Let them wait," he said. "I own them; they don't own me."

22

The phone rang a little before eight o'clock, and Dora roused from a deep sleep. "H'lo," she said groggily.

"Did I wake you up, kiddo?" Mike Trevalyan said. "Good. That makes my day."

"Yeah, it would," she said, swinging her legs out of bed. "Is that why you called—just to wake me up?"

"Listen, you asked me to check on which managers got canned from which Starrett branch stores a year ago."

"You got it?"

"Nope, I struck out on that one. My contacts in the jewelry business were no help. I even had a researcher go through jewelry trade journals for the past few years, but she came up with zilch. Sometimes those magazines publish personnel changes in the business, but only when the company involved sends them press releases. I guess Starrett didn't want to publicize the firings."

"Thanks anyway, Mike. I appreciate your trying."

"How you coming on the Starrett claim?" he asked.

"Slowly," Dora said. "It gets curiouser and curiouser the deeper I dig. By the way, I found that statement in my report that gives a good motive for Father Brian Callaway killing Lewis Starrett."

Trevalyan laughed. "You should read your own reports more often. You think Callaway aka Sidney Loftus did the dirty deed?"

"I don't know," she said doubtfully. "He's got a perfect alibi for the Solomon Guthrie murder."

"Maybe the two killings aren't connected."

"Come on, Mike. The two victims were old friends and worked for the same company. There's got to be a connection."

"Then find it," her boss said. "Now go back to sleep."

"Fat chance," Dora said, but he had already hung up.

She sat on the edge of the bed yawning and knuckling her scalp. She reflected, not for the first time, that she really should do morning exercises. Maybe a few deep knee-bends, a few push-ups. The thought depressed her, and she went into the bathroom to take a hot shower.

She was standing in the kitchen, drinking her first decaf of the day and thinking of what Mike had said, when she realized where she might be able to get the information she wanted. She phoned Detective John Wenden and was surprised to find him at his desk.

"What are you doing at work so early?" she asked.

"I didn't get home last night," Wenden said. "We had a mini-riot down in the East Village, and all available troops were called in."

"What was the riot about?"

"About who can use a public park. How does that grab you? This city is nutsville—right? What's up, Red?"

"John, you told me the Department was going through employment records from Starrett Fine Jewelry to find someone who was fired and was sore enough to snuff Lewis Starrett and Solomon Guthrie."

"Yeah, we're working on it. Nothing so far."

"Well, about a year ago Starrett terminated a bunch of managers at their branch stores. Could you check the records and find out how many managers were canned and at which stores?"

"I could probably dig that out," he said slowly, "but why should I?"

"As a favor for me?" Dora said hopefully.

"Red, this isn't a one-way street, you know. It can't be caviar for you and beans for me. If you want that information, you better tell me what's percolating in that devious mind of yours."

She hesitated a moment. "All right," she said finally, "I can understand that. If you get me what I want, I'll tell you why I need it."

"You're all heart," Wenden said, sighing. "Okay, Red, I'll get the skinny for you. But only on condition that I deliver it in person. I want to see you again."

"And I want to see you."

"Just so you can pick my brain?"

She didn't answer.

"Well?" he said. "I'm waiting."

"No," Dora said faintly, "I just want to see you."

"That's a plus," he said. "A small plus. I'll let you know when I've got the info."

She hung up the phone, wondering why her hand was shaking. It wasn't much of a tremor, but it was there. To stop that nonsense, she immediately called Mario. There was no answer. He was probably at work, and he didn't like to be phoned there. So Dora had another cup of coffee and resolutely banished John Wenden from her thoughts. For at least five minutes.

She spent the day doing research at the public library on Fifth Avenue.

She started with the basics: The atomic number of gold was 79, its symbol was Au, it melted at 1064°C and boiled at 2875°. It had been discovered in prehistoric times and used in jewelry and coinage almost as long.

She then started reading about the mining and smelting of gold, and its casting into ingots, bars, and sheets, including gold leaf so thin (four millionths of an inch) you could tear it with a sneeze.

She took a break at 12:30, packed up all her notes, and went out into a drizzly day to look for lunch. There was a vendor on 42nd Street selling croissant sandwiches from an umbrella stand, and Dora had one ham and one cheese, washed down with a can of Diet Dr Pepper. By the time she returned to the library, she figured she was two pounds heavier, but half of that was in her sodden parka.

In the afternoon she concentrated on jewelry: how it was designed and fabricated, the metals and alloys used. By four o'clock, eyes aching, her shoulder bag crammed with photocopies and notes, she left the library, slogged over to Madison Avenue, and bused uptown to the Bedlington.

She peeled off her cold, wet clothes, took a hot shower, and popped a couple of aspirin, just in case. Then she made a pot of tea, put on her reading glasses, and settled down in her bathrobe to try to find some answers in her research. She found no answers, but she did find a new puzzle and was mulling over that when John Wenden called around 7:30.

"Miserable day and miserable night," he said. "You eat yet, Red?"

"No, not yet."

"Neither have I, but I wouldn't ask you to come out on a lousy night like this. You like Chinese food?"

"Right now I'd like anything edible."

"Suppose I stop by a take-out place and pick up some stuff. I'll get it to the hotel while it's still warm."

"Sounds good to me," Dora said. "I have a thing for shrimp in lobster sauce. Could you get some of that?"

"Sure, with wonton soup, fried rice, tea, and fortune cookies."

"You can skip the tea," she said. "I can provide that. But load up on the hot mustard."

"All right," he said. "See you in an hour."

She put all her research away in a closet and dressed hurriedly in a tweed skirt and black turtleneck pullover floppy enough to hide her thickening waist.

Monday starts the diet, kiddo, she told herself sternly. I really mean that.

She had a fresh pot of tea ready by the time John arrived. His coat and hat were pimpled with rain, and his ungloved hands were reddened and icy. Dora poured him a pony of brandy to chase the chill while she opened the Chinese food he had brought. All the cartons were arranged on the cocktail table in front of the couch, and Dora set out plates, cutlery, and mugs for their tea.

He hadn't forgotten the shrimp in lobster sauce, and there was also a big container of sweet and sour pork cooked with chunks of pineapple and green and red peppers. Also egg rolls, barbecued ribs, and ginger ice cream.

"A feast!" Dora exulted. "I'm going to stuff myself."

"Be my guest," Wenden said. "You're looking good, Red. Losing weight?"

Dora laughed. "You sweet liar," she said. "No, I haven't lost any weight, and I'm not about to if you keep feeding me like this. I'll be a real Fatty, Fatty, two-by-four."

"More of you to love," he said, and when she didn't reply, he busied himself with a barbecued rib.

"Let's talk business," Dora said, smearing an eggroll with hot mustard. "Were you able to get the information about which Starrett branch managers were fired a year ago?"

"Yeah, I got it. And you said you'd tell me why you want it."

"All right," she said. "Did you know that Starrett has been dealing in gold bullion for about a year now?"

"Sure, I knew that," Wenden said, filling his plate with fried rice and sweet and sour pork.

Dora was startled. "How did you know?" she asked.

He looked up at her and grinned. "Surprised that we're not total stupes? When Solomon Guthrie was knocked off, he was carrying a briefcase stuffed with company business papers. We went through it. Most of it was about Christmas bonuses for Starrett employees. But there was also a file on recent purchases and sales of gold bullion."

"Oh," she said, somewhat discomfited. "Did you do anything about it?"

"Wow!" he said, wiping his forehead with a paper napkin. "That mustard is *rough*. Sure, I did something about it; I asked Clayton Starrett what gives. He said the company buys the gold overseas at a good price and sells it to small jewelry stores around the country at a nice markup. He showed me his records. Everything looks to be on the up-and-up. Isn't it?"

"Maybe," Dora said. "I got hold of a computer printout showing all of Starrett's gold business for the last three months, and it—"

"Whoa!" the detective said, holding up a palm. "Wait a minute. Where did you get the printout?"

"Let's just say it was from a reliable source. Will you accept that?"

He ate a moment without answering. Then: "For the time being."

"Well, I went over the printout many, many times and finally found something interesting. In addition to its flagship store on Park Avenue, Starrett has fifteen branches all over the world. Seven of them are overseas, and eight are in the U.S., including Honolulu. All the gold bullion Starrett was selling went to the domestic branches, none to the foreign stores.''

Wenden showed no reaction. He helped himself to more fried rice. "So?'' he said. "What's that supposed to mean?''

"I don't know what it means,'' Dora said crossly, "but it's unusual, don't you think?''

He sat back, swabbed his lips with a paper napkin, took a swig of tea. "There could be a dozen explanations. Maybe the overseas stores buy their gold from local sources. Maybe there are hefty import duties on gold shipped to those countries. Maybe the foreign branches don't *need* any gold because they get all their finished jewelry from New York.''

"I guess you're right,'' Dora said forlornly. "I'm just grabbing at straws.''

"On the other hand,'' John said, leaning forward again to start on his ice cream, "you may be on to something. About a year ago nine branch managers, including the guy in Manhattan, were fired and replaced with new people. All the firings and replacements were in Starrett's U.S. branches, none in the foreign stores.''

They stared at each other a moment. Then Dora took a deep breath. "You got any ideas?'' she asked.

"Nope,'' Wenden said. "You?''

"Not a one. There could be an innocent reason for it.''

"Do you believe that?''

"No.''

"I don't either,'' he said. "Something fishy is going on. Do you know anything you're not telling me, Red?''

"I've told you all I know,'' she said, emphasizing the *know* and figuring that made it only a half-lie.

"Well, keep digging, and if you come up with any ideas, give me a shout. Someone is jerking us around, and I don't like it.''

She nodded, stood up, and began clearing the mess on the cocktail table. "John, there's leftovers. Do you want to take it home with you?''

"Nah,'' he said. "I'm going back to the office tonight for a few hours, and I won't be able to heat it up. You keep it. You can have it for breakfast tomorrow.''

"With the hot mustard?'' she said, smiling. "That'll start me off bright-eyed and bushy-tailed. Thank you for the banquet. You were a lifesaver.''

"Is the way to a woman's heart through her stomach?'' he asked.

"That's one way,'' she said.

Working together, they cleaned up the place, put uneaten food in the refrigerator, washed plates, cutlery and mugs. Then they returned to the living room and Dora poured them tots of brandy.

"John, you look tired,'' Dora said. "Well, you usually look tired, but tonight you look *beat*. Are you getting enough sleep?''

He shrugged. "Not as much as I'd like. Did you know that in one eight-hour period over New Year's Eve there were thirteen homicides in New York. Ten by gunshot.''

"That's terrible.''

"We can't keep up with it. That's why I don't give the Starrett thing the time I should be giving it. I'm depending on you to help me out.''

"I'll try,'' she said faintly, feeling guilty because of the things she hadn't told him. "Don't you get days off? A chance to recharge your batteries?''

"Yeah, I get days off occasionally. But they don't really help. I keep thinking about the cases I'm handling, wondering if I'm missing anything, figuring new ways to tackle them.''

"You've got to relax.''

"I know. I need a good, long vacation. About a year. Either that or a good woman.''

She nodded. "That might help.''

"You?'' he said.

She tried a smile. "I told you; I'm taken.''

"One of these days you'll be leaving New York—right? Whether the Starrett thing is cleared up or not. Whether the insurance claim is approved or not. You'll be going home to Hartford. Correct?''

"That's right.''

"So we could have a scene while you're here, knowing it's not going to last forever. Who'd be hurt?''

She shook her head. "That's not me.''

"Oh Red,'' he said, "life is too short to be faithful. You think your husband is faithful?''

She lifted her chin. "I think he is. But it's really his decision, isn't it? If he's going to cheat on me because he's a man or because he's Mario— that's his choice. No way can I affect it.''

"Would it kill you to learn he's been cheating?''

She pondered a moment. "I don't know how I'd feel. It wouldn't *kill* me, but I'd probably take it hard.''

"But you'd forgive him?''

"I probably would,'' she said.

"And if things were reversed, he'd probably forgive you.''

"Probably,'' Dora said, "but I don't want to find out. Look, John, you said life is too short to be faithful. But I think the shortness of life is all the more reason to try to make it something decent. I see an awful lot of human corruption on my job—not as much *violent* corruption as you see, thank God—so I want to try as hard as I can to be a Girl Scout. Maybe it's because I want to prove I'm superior to the creeps I deal with. Maybe it's because if I make the one little slip voluntarily, it'll be a weakening and the first small step down a steep flight of stairs. Whatever, I want to live as straight as I can—which can be a mighty tough assignment at times.''

"Is this one of them?'' he asked. "You and me?''

She nodded dumbly.

He finished his drink, rose, and pulled on his damp coat. He looked at her so sadly that she embraced him and tried to kiss his cheek. But he turned to meet her lips and, despite her resolve, she melted. They clung tightly together.

"You better go," she said huskily, pulling away. "Give me a break."

"All right," he said. "For now."

After he was gone, she locked the door and paced up and down, hugging her elbows. She thought of what he had said and what she had said—and what she *might* have said, and what the result of that would have been.

She knew she should dig her library research out of the closet and get back to trying to solve the puzzle it contained. But she could not turn her thoughts away from her personal puzzle: what to do about this weary, attractive man who for all his flip talk was serious. Yes, yes, he was a *serious* man and fully aware that he was on his way to burnout.

"And who appointed *you* his nurse?" she asked herself aloud.

23

Mrs. Olivia Starrett and Father Brian Callaway sat at the long dining room table and waited silently, with folded hands, while Charles served tea. He was using bone china from Starrett Fine Jewelry in their exclusive Mimosa pattern.

He offered a tray of assorted pastries from Ferrara, then left the platter on the table and retired, closing the door softly behind him.

"Very distressing news indeed, Olivia," Father Brian said, adding cream and sugar to his tea. "You must have been devastated."

"I was," Mrs. Starrett said, "and I am. We have *never* had a divorce in our family, on either side."

"Has he spoken to Eleanor yet?"

"Not to my knowledge. He said he wanted to tell me first. Clayton is a good son."

"Yes," Callaway said. "Dutiful. Was he asking for your approval?"

"Not exactly. He did say that if I forbade it, he would remain married to Eleanor. But I cannot order him to continue what he calls a loveless marriage. The poor boy is obviously suffering. Do have an éclair."

"I think I shall; they look delicious. And how do you feel about his marrying Helene Pierce if the divorce goes through?"

"And I think I shall have an anise macaroon. Why, I believe Helene is a lovely, personable young lady, but much too young for Clayton. However, he feels the age difference is of little importance. And I must confess I have a selfish motive for wanting Clayton remarried, to Helene or any other woman of his choice. Before I pass over, I would like to hold a grandchild in my arms. Is it wicked of me to think of my own happiness?"

He reached across the table to pat one of her pudgy hands. "Olivia, you are incapable of being wicked. And your desire for a grandchild is completely natural, normal, and understandable. Eleanor cannot have another child?''

"Cannot or will not,'' Mrs. Starrett said sorrowfully. ''She has never fully recovered from the passing of little Ernie. Do help yourself to more tea, Father.''

"What a tragedy,'' he said, filling their cups. ''But pain, sadness, and passing are all parts of the holy oneness. We must accept them and indeed welcome them as a test of our faith. For from the valley of despair the soul emerges renewed and triumphant. Do try a napoleon; they're exquisite.''

"But so fattening!'' she protested.

"No matter,'' he said, smiling at her. ''You are a very regal woman, Olivia.''

"Thank you,'' she said, glowing with pleasure. ''Father, may I ask a favor?''

"Of course,'' he said heartily. ''Anything you wish.''

"I suggested to Clayton that he might consult a marriage counselor or speak to you before his decision becomes final. If there is any way at all the marriage can be saved, I must try it. Would you be willing to talk to Clayton and give him the benefit of your experience and spirituality?''

"I would be willing,'' Callaway said cautiously, ''but would he?''

"Oh, I'm sure he would,'' Olivia said warmly. ''Especially if you told him it was my express wish that the two of you get together and try to find a solution to this problem.''

Callaway nibbled thoughtfully on a slice of panettone. ''I gather that the solution you prefer is that the marriage be preserved?''

"That is my preference, yes. But if, in your opinion, the happiness of both Clayton and Eleanor would be better served by a divorce, then I'll accept that. I trust your judgment, Father, and will agree to whatever you think is best.''

"It is an awesome responsibility, Olivia, but I shall do what I can. May I tell Clayton that you have told me all the details of your conversation with him?''

"Of course.''

"Then I'll see what can be done. I agree with you, dear lady, that marriage is a sacred trust and those vows may only be broken for the most compelling reasons. We were put on this earth to nurture one another, to *share,* and every effort must be made to keep intact that holy oneness.''

"I knew I could count on your understanding, Father,'' Mrs. Starrett said. ''You're such a comfort. Now do have more tea and perhaps a slice of the torte. I believe it's made with Grand Marnier.''

When Brian Callaway departed from the Starrett apartment, he paused a moment in the outside corridor to loosen his belt a notch. He then descended to the lobby and used a public phone to call Clayton at Starrett

Fine Jewelry. It was almost 4:30 and Callaway guessed the man would be ready to leave his office.

Clayton was cordial enough, and when the Father asked for a meeting as soon as possible, to discuss a personal matter of "utmost importance," he agreed to meet Callaway at the bar of the Four Seasons at five o'clock or a little later.

"What's this all about?" he asked curiously.

"I prefer not to discuss it on the phone," the Father replied in magisterial tones.

He was the first to arrive and quickly downed a double vodka. He then ordered a plain tonic water and was sipping that when Clayton Starrett appeared, smiling broadly. The two men shook hands. Clayton ordered a gin martini.

"I'm afraid I'll have to make this short," Clayton said. "We have another charity benefit tonight, and I have to go home to dress."

The Father nodded. "I'll be brief," he promised. "I've just come from having tea with your mother. She asked me to meet with you. She informed me of your intention to divorce Eleanor and hopes I may persuade you to change your mind."

Clayton stared at him for a startled moment, then drained his martini. "Mother told you everything I said to her?" he asked hoarsely.

Callaway nodded. "She did. And gave me permission to tell you that she had. Clay, this is very embarrassing for me. I really have no desire to intrude on your personal affairs, but I could hardly reject your mother's request."

"Did she also tell you I want to marry Helene Pierce?"

"She told me. Clay, what's the problem between you and Eleanor?"

The younger man took a gulp of his fresh drink. "A lot of problems, Father. I guess the big one is sex—or the lack thereof. Does that shock you?"

"Hardly," Callaway said. "I guessed that might be it. Eleanor is not an unattractive woman, but compared to Helene . . . " His voice trailed off.

"Exactly," Clayton said. "I want a little joy in my life."

"That's understandable. But what if you ask Eleanor for a divorce and then Helene turns you down? Your mother said you told her you haven't even hinted to Helene about the way you feel."

Starrett turned his glass around and around, looking down at it. "That wasn't precisely true. I have told Helene about the way I feel about her and what I plan to do."

"And what was her reaction?"

"I don't know why I'm telling you all this. I hope I can depend on your discretion."

"I assure you this conversation has all the confidentiality of a confessional booth."

"Some booth," Clayton said, looking around at the crowded, noisy bar. "Well, if you must know, Helene will marry me the moment the divorce is a done deal."

"She told you that?"

"Not in so many words, but I'm positive that's the way she feels. Even if the divorce takes a year, Helene is willing to wait. After all, it means status and financial security for her."

"It does indeed," Callaway said. "I think I'll have another drink if you don't mind. Perhaps a straight vodka on ice this time."

"Of course," Clayton said, and summoned the bartender. "Father, I appreciate your efforts—I know you mean well—but there's no way you can change my mind."

"I didn't expect to."

"How did mother sound when she told you about it. Is she still upset?"

"She is, and somewhat confused. She wants you to be happy, and she hopes to have grandchildren someday, but the very idea of a divorce in the family disturbs her. And, of course, she's aware of the distress Eleanor will suffer."

"So mother really hasn't made up her mind?"

"Not really. As a matter of fact, she said she would be willing to accept whatever recommendation I make."

Clayton's laugh was tinny. "In other words," he said, "my fate is in your hands."

"Yes," the Father said, and took a swallow of his vodka, "you might say that. My main aim in this affair is not to cause your mother any unnecessary pain. She is a splendid woman and has made very generous contributions to the Church of the Holy Oneness."

As he said this, Callaway turned to look directly into Clayton's eyes. "Very generous contributions," he repeated.

The two men, their stare locked, were silent a moment.

"I see," Clayton said finally. "You know, Father, I feel somewhat remiss in not having offered any financial support to your church in the years I've known you."

"It's never too late," the older man said cheerfully. "The Church of the Holy Oneness is constantly in need of funds. For instance, we hope to enlarge the church kitchen so that we may provide food to more of the unfortunate homeless. But at the moment that seems just a dream. I have obtained estimates and find it would cost at least ten thousand dollars to build the kind of facility we need."

Clayton had a fit of coughing, and the Father had to pound him on the back until he calmed enough.

"Of course," Callaway continued blandly, "I realize ten thousand is a large donation for any one individual to make. But perhaps a large New York corporation might be willing to contribute to the welfare of the city's poor and hungry."

"Yes," Clayton said, much relieved, "that makes sense. Would you be willing to accept a ten-thousand-dollar contribution from Starrett Fine Jewelry, Incorporated?"

"Gladly, my son, gladly," Callaway said. "And bless you for your generosity. The donation, of course, would be tax-deductible. And when may I expect the check?"

"I'll have it cut and mailed tomorrow. You should have it by the end of the week. And when do you plan to give mother your recommendation on my divorce?"

Father Callaway smiled benignly. "By the end of the week," he said.

24

Eleanor and Clayton Starrett sat at a round table for eight, and directly across from Clayton was Bob Farber's new wife. She was a petite young woman wearing a strapless gown of silver lamé, but all he could see above the starched tablecloth were the bare top of her bosom, bare shoulders and arms, bare neck, and head topped with a plaited crown of blond hair. It was easy to imagine her sitting there absolutely naked, amiably chatting with her husband, laughing, her sharp white teeth nibbling a shrimp.

He tried not to stare but, uncontrollable, his gaze wandered back. She seemed to him soft, warm, succulent. And beside him sat his hard, cold, bony wife.

He dreamed of the day when he might be seen in public with his new wife, Helene. He would wear her proudly: a badge of honor. Her youth, beauty, and sexuality would prove his manhood and virility. What a conquest Helene would be. What a trophy!

His wife kicked his shin sharply under the table. "You're allowed to blink occasionally, you know," she said in a low, venomous voice, smiling for all the other diners to see. "You keep staring like that and your eyeballs will fall into your soup."

"What are you talking about?" he said, injured.

Eleanor paid him no more attention, for which he was thankful. He sneaked continual peeks at Mrs. Farber and let his fantasies run amok. The candlelight gave her flesh a rosy glow, and he dreamed of Helene, a fireplace, a bearskin rug.

The remainder of the party was endured only by drinking too much wine. At least, he told himself, he had sense enough not to dance. Eleanor was a miserable dancer, stiff and unrhythmic, and Clayton didn't dare ask Mrs. Farber lest he might suddenly become frenzied, wrestle her to the floor, and then . . . He shook his head. He could, he reflected gloomily, get twenty years for what he was thinking. Just for *thinking* about it.

He put his wineglass aside and rushed out onto the terrace. He stood there, breathing deeply of the cold night air, until his brain cleared and his ardor cooled. Then he was able to think rationally, more or less, and felt frustrated that so much time—perhaps a year!—must elapse before his dreams might be realized.

Eleanor was silent on the ride home, and so was he. They remained silent when they were alone in their suite, and finally this embittered silence convinced him that now was the moment. If he was going to do it, then *do* it. So, as she was removing her jewelry, he said, almost casually, "Eleanor, I want a divorce."

Her reaction was totally unexpected. He had thought she might faint, scream, weep, or at least express disbelief. Instead, she nodded, continued to take off her jewels, and said coolly, "It's Helene Pierce, isn't it?"

"What?" he said, aghast. "What are you talking about?"

She stopped what she was doing and turned to face him. "You're really brainless, Clay—you know that? I knew it before we were married, and nothing you've done since has changed my mind."

"I swear to you," he said hotly, "Helene and I have never—"

"Oh, cut the bullshit," she interrupted in a tone of great disgust. "You've been banging her since the day you met. Do you take me for a complete idiot? I've seen the way you look at her. The same way you looked at Bob Farber's new wife tonight. Is that what gave you the idea, Clay?"

"I'm telling you there's nothing between Helene and me."

"Laughing at her feeble jokes," Eleanor went on relentlessly. "Agreeing with all her stupid opinions. Rushing to help her on with her coat. Any excuse to touch her. There's no fool like an old fool, Clay."

"I'm not old," he shouted at her. "And you're dead wrong about all those things. I was just trying to be a good host."

"Oh sure," his wife jeered. "That's why you made certain you sat next to her every time she came to dinner. Playing a little kneesy, Clay? Listen, don't ever get the idea that the wife is the last to know. The wife is the *first* to know. When her rotten husband starts being extra pleasant and accommodating. When he starts buying clothes too young for him and gets facials. That's you, Clay. You're really a moron if you think I haven't known what's been going on. Sure, you can have a divorce, sonny boy, but it's going to cost you an arm and a leg, now and forever."

"Believe me," he said wrathfully, "whatever it costs, it'll be worth it to dump a sour, dried-up hag like you."

Still she would not weep. "Oh, Helene will marry you," she said, showing her teeth in a mirthless grin. "That greedy bitch has a bottom-line mentality. I give it a year, and then she'll walk. That's *another* alimony check every month, Clay. Then you'll find a new conversation piece—and I do mean *piece*— and do it again, and keep on doing it until you grow up, which will be never. You're a victim of your glands, Clay.''

''Just have your attorney contact Arthur Rushkin in the morning,'' he said stiffly.

''With pleasure,'' his wife said. ''Before I get through with you, you'll be lucky to have fillings in your teeth. Did you tell your mother about this?''

''Yes.''

''Poor Olivia,'' she said. ''She's the one I feel sorry for. She's had more than her share of troubles lately. But she's a tough lady; she'll survive. I'm sure she already knew her only son was short-changed in the brains department. Now I'm going to bed, Clay, and I think it would be best if you slept somewhere else.''

He was outraged. ''Where am I going to go at this time of night?'' he demanded.

''You can go to hell,'' Eleanor spat at him. ''You miserable shit!''

25

Turner Pierce paced about Helene's apartment, head lowered, hands clasped behind him.

"My God, you're antsy," Helene said. "Calm down; it's only Sid."

"I have bad vibes about this," he said. "I reminded him we had agreed on no private meetings unless there was an emergency. He said this was an emergency, but he sounded so damned smug. I don't like the way he sounded."

"He's such a scamp," Helene said.

"A *scamp?*" Turner repeated. "Darling, the man is an out-and-out crook—and a slimy crook at that."

"It takes one to know one," she said, and he turned to make certain she was smiling. She was.

He sat down on the couch, took a swallow of his Stolichnaya. "At least we don't promise suckers everlasting life in the holy oneness. Now that's slimy."

"Yes," she said, still smiling, "we do have our standards, don't we. Did I ever tell you Sid has the hots for me?"

"That was obvious in KC. Did he ever make a move on you?"

"Once," she said, not smiling now. "I told him what I'd do to him if he tried anything. He backed off."

Turner glanced at his watch. "If he's not here in ten minutes, I'm splitting. I have a date with Felicia tonight."

"Where are you going?"

"Who said we're going anywhere?" he said.

"Have you figured a way to stall her?"

"I have, but you don't want to know it, do you?"

"Not really."

"What about Clayton?"

"I can handle him," she said. "He's pussy-whipped. All we want is another year—right?"

He nodded. "That should do it."

The phone rang and Helene picked it up. "Yes? That's correct. Send him up, please. Thank you." She hung up. "That was the concierge. Sid's on his way up."

"I'm not looking forward to this," Turner said.

The first thing Father Brian Callaway did when he entered the apartment, even before he removed his hat and coat, was to rip off his clerical collar. "That damn thing is going to cut my throat one of these days," he said.

"We should be so lucky," Helene said, and Sidney Loftus laughed.

"What a kidder you are," he said. "What're you guys drinking?"

"Stoli rocks," Turner said.

"Sounds good to me," Loftus said, rubbing his palms together. "With a splash of water, please."

Helene rose, sighing, and went into the kitchen. Sid sat down heavily on an armchair. The two men looked at each other with wary smiles.

"How's the church doing?" Turner asked.

Loftus flipped a palm back and forth. "Not hellacious but adequate," he said. "The take is good but I've got to live in that shithouse on Twentieth Street, kip in the back room, and ladle out slop to a bunch of crumbums."

"Why don't you move?"

The other man shook his head. "No can do. It's the reverse of a flash front, y'see. Living in that dump proves my spirituality. I couldn't live in a Park Avenue duplex and plead poverty, now could I?"

"Image-building," Turner said.

"You've got it," Sid said, nodding. "Very important in our game, as you well know. Thank you, my dear," he said, taking the glass from Helene. He raised it. "Here's to crime," he toasted. But he was the only one who drank.

"Sid," Turner said, "I've got a meeting to get to. What's this big emergency you mentioned?"

Loftus crossed his knees. He adjusted the crease in his trousers. He leaned back. He took a pigskin case from an inner pocket. He extracted a long cigarillo carefully. He lighted up slowly.

"An impressive performance," Turner said. "Keep it up and I'm going to waltz out of here. Now what's on your mind?"

"Business, business," Sidney said, shaking his head. "With you it's always business. You never take time to smell the flowers. Very well, I'll be brief. You know, of course, that Clayton Starrett is divorcing Eleanor."

"Who told you that?" Helene demanded.

He looked at her, amused. "Olivia," he said. "She tells Father Brian Callaway everything."

"My God," Turner said, "you're not porking the woman, are you?"

"Oh, dear me, no," Loftus said. "I am her confidant, her father confessor. She dotes on me."

"You've got a sweet little scam going there," Turner said.

Sid shrugged. "To each his own," he said. "And Olivia also told me that as soon as Clayton can give his wife the boot, he plans to marry Helene." He turned to her. "Congratulations, my dear," he said. "May all your troubles be little ones."

"Stuff it," she told him.

He smiled and took a swallow of his drink. "Too much water," he said. "Now this is the way I figure it . . . Clayton has told you, Helene, of his impending divorce and has already proposed. I'm sure you've discovered that Clayton is not the brightest kid on the block. He's easily manipulated, and I'm guessing that you'll play him along until his divorce comes through, and then you'll take a walk. Am I correct in my assumptions?"

Helene started to reply, but Turner held up a hand to silence her. "Suppose you are," he said to Loftus. "What's it got to do with you? Where do you come in?"

"Why," the other man said, "it seems to me unjust that only you two should profit from this unique situation. And profit mightily, I may add. After all, I was the one who introduced you to the Starrett family. Surely I deserve a reward."

Turner nodded. "I figured it would be something like that," he said, "you're such a greedy bugger. And if I was to tell you to go take a flying fuck at a rolling doughnut, what would be your reaction, Sid?"

Loftus sighed. "I would have to give the matter serious consideration. It's possible my decision would be that it was my bounden duty, as spiritual advisor to Olivia, to inform her of certain details in the background and history of you two charmers."

"Blackmail," Helene said flatly.

Loftus made a mock shudder. "That's such an ugly word, dearie," he said. "I prefer to think of it as a finder's fee. For helping you aboard the gravy train."

Turner smiled coldly. "You're bluffing, Sid," he stated. "It works both ways. We might find it necessary to tell the Starretts about *your* history."

"Would you really?" Loftus said, beaming. He took another swallow of his vodka. "To save you the trouble, I should tell you that Olivia is already aware of the indiscretions of my past. Not *all* of them, of course, but most. I told her, and she has forgiven me. Y'see, these religious mooches just love repentant sinners. They put their heaviest trust in the lamb who has strayed from the fold and then returned.''

Turner said, "I underestimated you, Sid."

"People sometimes do," Loftus said complacently, "and end up paying for it."

"And what do you feel would be a reasonable finder's fee?"

"Oh, I thought fifty grand is a nice round number."

"Fifty thousand!" Helene cried. "Are you insane?"

"I don't believe I'm ready to be committed," Sid said, then laughed at his own wit. "Actually, Helene, it is not an outrageous request, considering what you have taken and will take from Clayton before the divorce is finalized. And I haven't even mentioned your split, Turner, from that lovely finagle at Starrett Fine Jewelry. No, I don't consider fifty thousand unreasonable."

"In cash, I suppose," Turner said bitterly.

"Not necessarily, old boy. A donation to the Church of the Holy Oneness would do the trick. It's tax-deductible, you know."

"Uh-huh," Turner said. "You will allow us a little time to consider your proposal, won't you?"

"Of course," Loftus said heartily. "I didn't expect an immediate answer. I should think a week would be sufficient time to arrive at the only rational decision you can make. Thank you for the refreshment."

He rose and took up his hat, coat, and clerical collar. The Pierces remained seated. Sid nodded at them affably and started to leave. Then he turned at the door.

"Remember," he said with a ghastly smile, "no pain, no gain."

Then he was gone.

"I think I need another drink," Helene said.

"Me too," Turner said. "I'll get them."

She lighted another cigarette while he went into the kitchen. She looked with amazement at the ashtray filled with cigarettes they had both half-smoked and then stubbed out during Sid Loftus' shakedown.

Turner came back with the drinks. They sat close together on the couch and stretched out their long legs.

"You were right," Helene said. "He *is* slimy. Turner, couldn't we tip off the buttons about that phony church of his?"

"Negative," Turner said. "He'd know immediately who had ratted on him and cop a plea by giving them the Starrett Jewelry job. We can't risk that."

"We're not going to pay him, are we?"

"No way," he said. "If we did, it would just be a down payment. He'd bleed us dry."

"So?" she said. "What are our options?"

He turned to stare at her. "Not many," he said. "Only one, in fact. We've worked too hard to split our take with a bastard like Sid."

She nodded. "Could Ramon handle it?" she asked him.

"He could, but I don't want to ask him. First of all, it's a personal thing, and Ramon has no need to know about you and Clayton. Second, it would give him too much of an edge on me. I'm afraid we'll have to handle this ourselves, babe. You willing?"

"Hell, yes!" she said, and he kissed her.

26

Dora Conti figured she'd spend the day on Jewelry Row—West 47th Street between Fifth and Sixth—talking to merchants and salespeople, hoping to find answers to some of the questions nagging her. She was heading for the door when her phone rang, and she went back to answer it. The caller was Gregor Pinchik, the computer maven.

"Hiya, lady," he said. "Listen, I'm in my new place, my hardware is all hooked up, and after I check it out I'll be ready to roll. Probably by tomorrow. Meanwhile I've been making a lot of phone calls, trying to get a line on that Turner and Helene Pierce you gave me."

"Any luck?" she asked.

"Maybe yes, maybe no. There's a hacker in Dallas who's a good friend of mine. I've never met him, but we been talking on computers for years. He's paralyzed and works his hardware with a thing he holds between his teeth. You wouldn't believe how fast he is. Anyway, I asked him about this Turner Pierce, gave him the physical description and all, and he says it sounds like a young hustler who was operating in Dallas almost ten years ago. This guy's name was Thomas Powell, but the initials are the same so I figured it might be our pigeon. What do you think?"

"Could be," Dora said cautiously. "Wrongos who change their name usually stick to the same initials so they don't have to throw away their monogrammed Jockey shorts."

Pinchik laughed. "You're okay, lady," he said.

"What was this Thomas Powell up to?"

"Dallas hackers called him Ma Bell because his specialty was telephone fraud. He started out by developing a cheap whistle that had the same frequency the phone company used to connect long distance calls. You blew the whistle into a pay phone and you could talk to Hong Kong as long as you liked. He sold a lot of those whistles. Then, when the phone company got hip to that and changed their switching procedure, this Thomas Powell started making and selling blue boxes. Those are gadgets that give off tones that bypass the phone company's billing system and let you make free long distance calls. Listen, the guy was talented, no doubt about it.''

"Didn't they ever nab him?''

"My pal says he always stayed one step ahead of the law. For instance, he never sold the whistles or blue boxes to the end-user; he always sold to a crooked wholesaler who sold to crooked retailers who sold to the crooked customers. Powell was always layers away from the actual fraud. By the time the cops traced the merchandise back to him, he was gone.''

"Where to? Does your friend know?''

"He talked to a couple of local hackers and called me back. One guy says he heard that Thomas Powell took off for Denver when things got too hot for him in Dallas. I have some good contacts in Denver, and as soon as my machinery is up to speed I'm going to try to pick up Ma Bell's trail there. Okay?''

"Of course," Dora said. "It may turn out to be a false alarm, but it's worth following up. Did your Dallas friend say anything about Helene Pierce?''

"Nope. He says this Thomas Powell was a handsome stud with a lot of women on the string, but no one special. And no one in Dallas knew he had a sister; they thought he was a loner.''

"Keep after him," Dora said, "and let me know if anything breaks.''

"You got it, lady," Pinchik said.

27

The bistro was on 28th Street between Lexington and Third, and nothing about it was attractive. The plate glass window needed a scrub, the rolled-up awning had tatters, and one pane of beveled glass in the scarred door had cracked and was patched with adhesive tape. Inside, it was obvious the designer had striven for intimacy and achieved only gloom.

Sidney Loftus strolled in and looked about curiously. He was wearing a tweed sport jacket and flannel slacks under his trench coat, and the Father Callaway collar was missing. Instead, a silk foulard square was knotted rakishly at his throat. He saw Helene Pierce seated alone in a back booth, lifted a hand in greeting, and sauntered slowly toward her. Only two of the dozen tables in the restaurant were occupied and, except for Helene's, the eight booths were empty..

"Good evening, luv," Sid said lightly. He hung his coat on a wall hook and slid into the booth opposite her. "What an elegant dump. I can't believe you dine here."

"I don't," Helene said. "Probably instant gastritis. But the drinks are big. I'm sticking to Tanqueray vodka."

"Sounds good to me," Loftus said. He signaled a waiter, pointed to Helene's glass, held up two fingers. "I was surprised to hear from you," he said. "I figured Turner might call, but not you."

"I thought we should get together," she said, looking at him directly. "In some place that Turner isn't likely to visit and where you wouldn't be recognized."

"My, my," he said, "that does sound mysterious. Then Turner doesn't know we're meeting?"

"No, he doesn't."

"Uh-huh," Sid said, and didn't speak while the dour, flat-footed waiter served their drinks, placing the glasses on little paper napkins that had a black Scottie printed on the front.

"Charming," Loftus said, holding up the napkin with his fingertips. "Real class. Well, whatever your motives, dearie, I'm happy to have a drink with you without Turner being present. Where is the lad tonight?"

"If you must know," she said, "he's out of town trying to raise fifty thousand bucks: your finder's fee."

Loftus sampled his drink. "Good," he pronounced. "Not quite chilled enough, but good. I can't believe raising fifty grand will be a problem. I'm sure the two of you have the funds available."

"I don't think you fully understand, Sid," Helene said earnestly. "Those 'mighty profits' you mentioned have yet to be realized. I admit the potential is there, but so far the actual receipts have been anemic. Clayton pays my rent and he's given me a few pinhead diamonds, but that's about it. The business at Starrett Fine Jewelry will pay off eventually—no doubt about it—but right now the returns are practically nil. Don't get me wrong, I'm not pleading poverty, but Turner will have to get a loan to come up with the fifty G's. And that means heavy vigorish, of course."

Sid took another sip of his drink and smiled bleakly. "Don't tell me you invited me to haggle over the price, Helene. Haggling is so demeaning, don't you think?"

"No," she said, "no haggling. Turner will come up with the fifty thousand. We don't have much choice, do we?"

"No choice at all," he agreed.

"But Turner expects some of that to come out of my take," she said stonily. "I don't like that. Which is why I wanted to talk to you privately."

"No disrespect intended, luv, but you don't mind if I have the teensiest-weensiest suspicion that Turner may have sent you to set me up."

"Listen to my proposition first," she advised, "and then make up your mind."

"I'm all ears," he said, smiling, and summoned the waiter for another round.

They waited silently while their fresh drinks were brought and the waiter left. Then Helene leaned across the table. She was wearing a V-necked sweater of heavy wool in periwinkle blue, and as she leaned forward the neckline gaped and he could see tawny skin, the softness of her unbound breasts.

"Tell me the truth, Sid," she said, "what do you *really* think of me?"

He tried a smile that failed. "Why, I think you're an extremely attractive young woman. Beautiful, in fact. With all the equipment to make an old man forget his years and dream of pawing up the pea patch."

"You're not an old man, Sid," she said impatiently, "and cut out the physical stuff. You've been around the block twice; what's your personal opinion of who I am and how I operate?''

He started slowly and carefully. ''I think you're a very shrewd lady with more than your share of street smarts. I think you have a heavy need for the lush life. Ambitious. Money-hungry. With the morals of an alley cat.''

She burst into laughter, tossed her head back; her long hair flung out in a swirl. ''You've got me pegged,'' she said. ''I plead guilty.''

''There's nothing to feel guilty about,'' he told her. ''You're the female equivalent of Turner, or me, or any other shark in the game. It's just a little unusual to find those characteristics in a woman. But I'm not condemning you. *Au contraire,* sweetie pie.''

''As long as you know,'' she said.

''Know what?'' he asked, puzzled.

''What my motives are. I told you I resent the fact that some of your finder's fee is going to come out of my poke. I don't like that. I've worked too long on Clayton Starrett to turn over my take without trying to protect it. I also know you have eyes for me. You proved that in Kansas City.''

''So I did,'' he admitted, ''and you gave me the broom.''

''You still feel the same way?''

He looked at her approvingly. ''Could be. What's on your mind, luv?''

''As long as you know it's not mad, carefree lust.''

''That's a laugh,'' he said.

''It would be strictly a business deal,'' she said, looking steadily into his eyes. ''My chance of getting back some of my contribution to your finder's fee. Shocked?''

''Hardly,'' he said, returning her stare. ''It's in character. You're a tough lady, Helene.''

''Tough?'' she said. ''You know any other way to survive?''

''No,'' he said, ''I don't. So what you're getting at in your oblique way is that you'd like a kickback from what Turner pays me. For favors granted. Have I got it right?''

''You've got it right.''

''And what size kickback were you planning to ask for?''

She leaned forward again. The sweater neckline widened. ''I haven't even thought of it. I just wanted to try the concept with you. If you turned me down, that's it. If you're willing to play along, then we can work out the details. I'm a reasonable woman.''

He laughed. ''And I'm a reasonable man. We're two of a kind, we two. It's an interesting idea, Helene. Dangerous but interesting. If Turner ever finds out, we're both dead.''

''You think I don't know that? But I'm willing to take the risk. Are you?''

He looked down at his drink, moved it in slow circles over the tabletop. He looked up again at the slim column of her bare throat and caught his breath.

"I might be willing to take a flier," he said. "But then we're faced with the problem of logistics. Specifically, where and when?"

"I can hardly see us checking into the Waldorf, can you?" she said. "Or any other Manhattan hotel or motel. Either of us might be seen and recognized. And it can't be my apartment. I think Clayton is paying off the concierge to keep track of my visitors. I just can't chance it. That only leaves your place."

"My place?" he protested. "It's an armpit."

"I'm sure I've seen worse," she said, then finished her drink. "Let's go there now and clinch the deal. This one will be a freebie to convince you that you're making a smart move."

"It's practically a monk's cell," he warned her.

"That might be fun," she said.

He surrendered completely. "It will be," he assured her.

28

Arthur Rushkin had mentioned casually that after going over the computer printout, he had been "somewhat surprised" by the quantity of gold being traded by Starrett Fine Jewelry. Instead of being surprised, Dora thought grimly, he should have been shocked. But then the attorney hadn't spent a damp day doing research on gold in the public library, and he hadn't schmoozed with the shrewd jewelry merchants on West 47th Street.

The reaction of one of them, a tub of lard in a tight plaid suit, was typical. Dora inquired if the average jewelry store could use the weight of gold Starrett was allegedly selling, and he looked at her as if she had just landed in a flying saucer.

"Absolut imposs," he said in an accent she could not identify. "Total out of the ques, my lovely young miss. Never in a mill years or more."

He then went on to explain in his fractured English that the average jewelry shop made none of the items they stocked, but depended on distributors and wholesalers to keep them supplied. If they did repair work, they might keep a small inventory of gold wire, chains, clasps, settings, etc. But these would be 14- or 18-karat alloys, not the fine gold Dora was talking about.

"Then no jewelry store would need pounds or kilos of the stuff?" she asked.

"Ridic," he said. "Utter ridic. You want to build a Stat of Liber, God bless her soul, of pure gold? With that much you tell me, you could do it. But for a small store, not even grains or ounces of the fine. I speak the trut."

"I believe you," she said hastily, and other proprietors and salespersons she talked to told her the same thing.

So on a bright morning she sat in her hotel suite staring moodily at the mess stacked on the cocktail table: the computer printout, her library re-search, and her spiral notebooks.

She wondered where further investigation of Starrett's gold trading might lead. She questioned what, if anything, it had to do with the murder of Lewis Starrett and the beneficiaries' claim on his life insurance. That, after all, was her prime concern, and even if the gold trading turned out to be illegal but had nothing to do with Lewis Starrett's death, then she was just spinning her wheels.

She was still pondering her wisest course of action when the phone rang.

"H'lo," she said, almost absently.

"Hi, Red," John Wenden said. "I've got good news for you. I think we can drop the Starrett case."

"*What?*" she cried.

"Because if we just wait long enough," he went on, "everyone con-nected with it will get knocked off."

"John," she said, "what the hell are you talking about?"

"It just came over the Department wire," he said. "Early this morning, Sidney Loftus, also known as Father Brian Callaway, was found murdered in the back room of the Church of the Holy Oneness on East Twentieth Street."

"Oh my God," Dora breathed.

"There goes your favorite suspect in the Starrett kill," Wenden said. "Sorry about that, Red."

"Was he stabbed?" she asked.

"Now how did you guess that? This case has more knives than Hoffritz. Listen, I don't know any of the details, but I'm on my way there now. Will you be in this afternoon?"

"I'll make it a point to be."

"After I find out what went down, I'll give you a call or maybe stop by for a few minutes."

"Stop by," she urged. "I'll pick up some sandwich makings."

"Sounds good to me," he said. "I'm in a salami mood today."

"You'll get it," she promised.

After replacing the phone, she went back to staring at the stack of papers, not seeing them. Her first reaction to the news of Callaway's death was dread at how the killing might affect Mrs. Olivia Starrett. That poor woman had already suffered through the murders of her husband and a close family friend. Now she would have to endure the "passing" of a man who might have been a swindler but who undoubtedly served as her spiritual advisor and, Dora supposed, provided solace and counseling. Cal-laway's motives might have been venal, but Dora was convinced he was a comfort to Olivia, something she could not obtain from husband or family.

It was two o'clock before Wenden finally showed up, looking as exhausted and disheveled as ever. He stripped off a tatty mackinaw and flopped onto the couch. "I'm bushed," he announced, "and the day's hardly started."

Wordlessly, Dora brought him a cold can of Bud and popped it for him. He drank almost half without stopping, then took a deep breath.

"Thanks, Red. You're looking mighty perky today."

"I don't feel perky," she said. "What happened?"

"He was stabbed four or five times. Chest, stomach, ribs, abdomen. Then, for good measure, his throat was slit. Someone didn't much like the guy. The place was a butcher shop."

"You think it was one of those dopers or derelicts his church feeds down there?"

"No," the detective said, and stirred uncomfortably. "He was lying naked, faceup on his bed. And he was tied up."

"So he couldn't fight?"

Wenden stared at her. "He was spread-eagled. Ankles and wrists tied to the bedposts with silk scarves. Slipknots. He could have pulled loose. It was a sex scene, Red."

She looked at him, expressionless.

"A lot of guys go for that bondage stuff," John said, shrugging. "I've seen kinkier things than that."

"You think he was gay and picked up some rough trade?"

"That was our first thought, but now we're not so sure. It may have been set up to look that way. The crime scene guys are still working, vacuuming the whole joint. We'll know more when we get their report. Hey, I'm hungry. You promised me a sandwich."

"I'm sorry, John. I got so interested in what you were saying, I forgot. The sandwiches are already made. Salami on rye with hot mustard. And kosher dills."

"Oh yeah," he said, "I can go for that."

She brought out a platter of sandwiches covered with a damp napkin, and the pickles.

"You're not drinking?" he asked her.

"Maybe a diet cola."

"Will you stop it?" he said, almost angrily. "You've got this complex about being too fat."

"It's not a complex; I know I am."

"I don't think so," he said, and began to wolf down one of the thick salami sandwiches.

"John," Dora said, nibbling, "how do you figure this connects with the Starrett and Guthrie homicides?"

"I don't know that it does," he said, then looked up at her. "Do you?"

"Not really," she confessed. "But knives were used in all three."

"Different knives," he told her. "I can't say for sure until the ME does his thing, but I'd guess that the blade used on Callaway was different from the chef's knife that killed Starrett and the stiletto that finished Guthrie. A lot of shivs in this town, kiddo. The weapon of choice. They don't make noise.''

''But all three victims *were* connected,'' she argued. ''They knew each other. All were part of the Starrett circle.''

He started on a second sandwich. ''It could be a serial killer who just happened to pick three targets who were acquainted. I don't believe that for a minute. Or it could be someone with a grudge against the Starrett family and their friends and associates. So he's picking them off one by one.''

''Have you put guards on the Starrett apartment?'' she asked worriedly.

''Of course. But you know as well as I do how much good that will do. A determined killer can always find a way. And sooner or later, the guards will have to be withdrawn.''

''So you *do* think the same person, or persons, is responsible for all three murders?''

''It's a possibility,'' he admitted. ''Is that what you think?''

''To tell you the truth,'' she said, ''I don't know what the hell is going on.''

''You and me both,'' John said, and sat back, sighing. ''That hit the spot. This is probably the only solid food I'll have all day.''

''Take the leftover sandwiches with you,'' she said. ''I insist.''

''You'll get no argument from me,'' he said with a sheepish grin. ''I can use the calories. Listen, after I leave here, I'm going back to Twentieth Street. Callaway's murder wasn't my squeal, but I want to hang around the edges and see if the guys running it come up with anything.''

''Like what?''

''They'll check all the trash baskets, garbage cans, and catch basins in the area to see if they can find the knife. And they'll brace all the neighborhood stores, bars, and restaurants—flashing a photo of the dear, departed Father—to ask if he was in last night, and if so, was he with someone.''

''John, that'll take days.''

''At least,'' he agreed. ''Maybe weeks. But it's got to be done. Hey, you look sad. What's wrong, Red?''

''I am sad,'' she said. ''You know about what? I'm sad about Sidney Loftus, aka Father Brian Callaway. I know he was a swindler and con man. I know he was taking Olivia Starrett and other religious saps for every cent he could grab. He was *bad*. But I still feel sorry for him, dying that way.''

''That's a luxury I can't afford,'' John said. ''Feeling sorry. I let myself feel and I'm no good to the Department.''

''I don't believe that.''

''Believe it,'' he insisted. ''I'm like a surgeon. He goes to cut out a cancerous tumor, he can't feel sorry for the patient; it would interfere with his job. All he's interested in is if he's getting out the entire malignancy. He's got to think of the person under his knife as a thing. Meat. He can't be distracted by feeling sad or feeling sorry.''

"Is that the way you think of people—as things?''

"Only the bad ones. Sid Loftus was a thing, so I can't feel anything toward him. I don't think of *you* as a thing. You know how I feel about you.''

"How?'' she challenged.

"All the time,'' he said, and she laughed.

"You're a bulldog, you are,'' she said.

"It sounds like a line, doesn't it?'' Wenden said. "It's not. It's a very, very serious pitch. I think it would make us both happy. All right, so it would be a temporary happiness. Nothing heavy, nothing eternal. Just a great rush that doesn't hurt anyone. Is that so bad?''

"You don't know,'' she objected. "That it wouldn't hurt anyone. You can't predict.''

"I'm willing to take the risk,'' he said. "Are you?''

She was silent.

"Think about it,'' he entreated.

"All right,'' Dora said, "I will.''

29

He said his name was Ramon Schnabl, and no one questioned it or even considered inquiring about his antecedents. He was a serious man, and the few people who had heard him laugh wished they hadn't. He was reputed to be enormously wealthy which, considering the nature of his business, was likely.

He was an extremely short, slender man whose suits were tailored in Rome and his shoes, with an invisible build-up, were the creation of a London cobbler. Everything he wore seemed tiny, tight, and shiny, and it was said that the toilet seats in his Central Park South apartment were custom-made as he might fall through a conventional design.

He was not an albino, exactly, for his eyes were dark and there was a faint flush to his thin cheeks. But he was undeniably pale, hair silver-white, skin milky, and even his knuckles translucent. He favored platinum jewelry and double-breasted white suits that accented his pallidness. He also wore, indoors and out, deeply tinted glasses as if he could not endure bright light or garish colors.

Turner Pierce thought him a dangerous man, quite possibly psychotic. But Helene thought him a fascinating character. What attracted her, she said, was the contradiction between his diminutive size and the menace he projected. Ramon never threatened, but associates were always aware that the power to hurt was there.

His apartment was as colorless as the man himself. The living room had blank white walls, a floor of black and white tiles set in a checkerboard pattern, black leather furniture with stainless steel frames. Over the cold white marble fireplace was the room's sole decorative touch: the bleached skull of an oryx.

Ramon and Turner sat facing each other in matching clunky armchairs.

The host had provided glasses of chilled Évian water. He was both a teetotaler and rigidly antismoking. At the moment, his guest was wishing fervently for a cigarette and tumbler of iced Absolut.

"Matters are progressing well," Schnabl said in his dry, uninflected voice. "You agree, my friend?"

"Oh yes," Pierce said. "No problems."

"None?" the other man said. "Then tell me why you appear so troubled."

"Do I?" Turner said, wishing he could peer behind the dark glasses and see the eyes that saw so much. He tried a laugh. "Well, you know they say a man has only two troubles in this world: money and women."

"And which is yours?"

"Not money," Pierce said hastily. "No trouble there at all. I have a personal problem with a woman."

"Oh?" Schnabl said. "Surely not Helene, that dear lady?"

Turner shook his head.

"Then it must be Felicia Starrett, Clayton's sister."

Turner nodded, not questioning how Ramon knew. This little man knew *everything*. "Not a serious problem," he assured Ramon. "But she is inclined to be very emotional, very unpredictable."

"A bad combination, my friend. Vindictive?"

"I'm afraid the possibility is there."

"I thought she was dependent on you for her supply."

"She is," Turner said, "but it isn't working out quite as I had planned. She still wants more."

"More?"

"Me," Pierce said, realizing he was giving up an edge but not seeing any alternative.

"I understand, my friend," Ramon said, totally without sympathy. "You have a management problem."

"Yes," Turner said, "something like that."

"Perhaps stronger medicine is called for."

Pierce looked at him, puzzled. "Such as?"

Ramon regarded him gravely for a moment. Then: "I am introducing a new product line. Large crystals of methamphetamine that can be smoked. On the street it is called 'ice.' I believe it may be the preferred recreation of the 1990s; other products will become declassé. The great benefit of ice is that it produces euphoria that lasts twenty-four hours. It might prove to be the answer to your management problem."

"Thank you," Turner Pierce said humbly.

He met Felicia that night. They dined at Vito's, and he smiled at her blather, laughed at her jokes, and held hands when they strolled back to his apartment. A tumescent moon drifted in a cloudless sky, and the whole night seemed swollen with promise: something impending on the wind, something lurking in the blue shadows, ready to pounce, smirking.

"What a hoot," she chattered on. "Clay divorces Eleanor and marries Helene. And you and I tie the knot. One big, happy family! Right, Turner? Am I right?"

"You're right," he said. "We'll be the fearless foursome."

"Love it," she said, squeezing his hand. "The fearless foursome—that's us. We might even have a pas de quatre some night if we all get high enough. Would you go for that?"

"Why not," he said.

She wouldn't even let him pour brandies, but began removing her clothes the moment she was inside the door. But he was deliberately slow, something spiteful in his teasing. He did enjoy her need and his power, meaning to punish for all the trouble she was causing him. But his cruelties only aroused her the more, and she welcomed the pain as evidence of his passion. This woman, he decided, was demented and so trebly dangerous.

Later, he left her on the bed and went into the kitchen for his cognac. He returned to the bedroom carrying the brandy, a glass pipe, a small packet of crystal chunks. She looked at him with dimmed eyes, then struggled upright.

"What's that?" she asked.

"Something new for you," he said. "It's called ice. The latest thing. You smoke it."

"You, too?"

He held up the brandy. "This is my out," he said. "The pipe is yours."

She inspected the crystals. "Ice," she said. "Like diamonds."

"Exactly like diamonds," he told her. "It's the *in* thing. Everything else is declassé."

That's all she had to hear, being a victim of trendiness, and she packed the pipe with trembling fingers, clutching it tightly while he held a match. She took a deep puff and inhaled deeply with closed eyes.

The rush hit her almost immediately. Her eyes popped open, widened, and she sucked greedily at the pipe.

"Good?" he asked her.

She looked at him with a foolish smile and leaned back against the headboard. She continued to fellate the pipe but slowly now, sipping lazily.

He put a palm to her naked shank and was shocked at how fevered her flesh had become. She was burning up.

The crystals were consumed. Turner took the glass pipe from Felicia's limp fingers and set it aside.

Suddenly she began to laugh, convulsed with merriment. Energized, she rose swiftly from the bed, stood swaying a moment, still heaving with laughter. She rushed into the living room, staggering, banging off the walls, and returned just as quickly, before he could move.

"How do you feel?" he asked curiously.

She looked at him, laughter stopped. She pulled him onto the bed with a strength he could not resist.

"I am the world," she proclaimed.

"Of course you are," he agreed.

"The stars," she said. "Planets. Universe. Everything and all."

"And all," he repeated.

She flopped around and crammed his bare toes into her mouth. He pulled away, and again he felt her incredible heat and saw how flushed her face had become. He put a hand to her breast, and the heavy, tumultuous heartbeat alarmed him.

"Are you all right, Felicia?"

She began to gabble incoherently: unfinished sentences, bits of song, names he didn't recognize, raw obscenities. The jabber ceased as abruptly as it had started. He left her like that and went into the kitchen for another brandy.

She was still at it when he returned to the bedroom. But now her face was contorted, ugly, and she was panting. He sat on the edge of the bed and observed her dispassionately, noting the twitching legs, toes curled. She seemed to be winding tighter and tighter, her entire body caught up in a paroxysm.

Suddenly she shouted, so loudly that he was startled and slopped his brandy. Her body went slack and her eyes slowly opened. She stared at him blankly, not seeing him, and he wondered where she was.

"Felicia," he said, "I'm Turner."

"Turner," she repeated, and soft understanding came back into her eyes.

"You're in my apartment," he told her.

She looked at him with love. "Do you want to kill me?" she asked. "You may, if you like."

30

Mrs. Olivia Starrett, wearing a lacy bed jacket, sat propped upright by pillows, a white wicker tray across her lap. And on the tray, tea service and a small plate of miniature croissants, one half-nibbled away.

"He was such a *dear* man," she said, dabbing at her eyes with a square of cambric. "I would be even more desolated than I am if I wasn't inspired by his teaching. Accept all, he said, and understand that pain and suffering are but a part of the holy oneness. Are you sure you don't want a cup of tea, dear?"

"Thank you, no, Mrs. Starrett," Dora said. She sat alongside the canopied bed in a flowered armchair. "You have certainly had more than your share of grief lately. You have my deepest sympathy."

Olivia reached out to squeeze her hand. "How sweet and understanding you are. The passing of Lewis, Sol Guthrie, and Father Brian were sorrows I thought would destroy me. But then I realized that one cannot mourn forever. Does that sound cruel and heartless?"

"Of course not."

"One must continue to cope with life, the problems of the present, and worries for the future." She picked up the half-eaten croissant and finished it. "You told me you have no children?"

"That's correct."

Mrs. Starrett sighed deeply. "They are a blessing and a burden. Have you heard about Clayton? And Eleanor?"

"Heard about them? No, ma'am, I've heard nothing."

Olivia, alternately dabbing at her eyes and taking teeny bites of a fresh pastry, told Dora of her son's impending divorce.

"Eleanor has already moved out," she said.

Then she spoke of Clayton's plan to marry Helene Pierce.

"Much too young for him, I feel," she said. "But I do *so* want a grandchild. Father Callaway, the last time I saw him, told me I am not being selfish."

"He was right," Dora said. "You're not."

"Still . . . " Olivia said, and looked about vaguely. "Sometimes it is difficult knowing the right thing to do. Young people are so independent these days. They think because you are old you must necessarily be senile."

"You are not old, Mrs. Starrett, and you are certainly not senile."

"Thank you, my dear. You are *such* a comfort. Sit with me a while longer, will you?"

"Of course. As long as you like."

"I could never talk to Lewis. Never. Not about important things. He thought I was just chattering on. And he would grunt. I love Clayton, of course. He is my son. But I can't talk to him either. Clayton is lacking. There is no depth to him. I love depth in people, but Clayton is not a serious man. He floats through life. He has never been a leader. Sometimes he lacks sense. Eleanor knew that when she married him. Perhaps that's *why* she married him."

Dora listened to this rambling with shocked fascination. Shocked because she suddenly realized that Mrs. Olivia Starrett was not a flibbertigibbet, not just a soft, garrulous matron. There was a hard spine of shrewdness in her. Despite her religiosity she saw things clearly. She had depth and had been married to a man who grunted.

"Felicia . . . " Mrs. Starrett maundered on. "So unlucky with men. A pattern there. She has taste in clothes, music, art. But not in men. There her taste deserts her. All her beaux have been unsatisfactory. Weaklings or cads. I could see it. Everyone could see it. But not Felicia. The poor thing. So eager. Too eager. Now she is running after Turner Pierce. Oh yes, I know. A man much younger than she. It is not seemly." Her gaze suddenly sharpened. She stared at Dora sternly. "Do you agree?"

"You're right," Dora said hastily. "It's not seemly."

"You are such a bright, levelheaded young lady."

"Thank you, Mrs. Starrett."

"I wish you'd talk to Felicia."

Dora was startled. "Talk to her?"

"About her life, the way she's wasting it."

"But I'm not a close friend."

"My daughter has no close friends," Olivia said sadly. "Not even me. Perhaps she'll listen to you."

"But what could I possibly say to her?"

"Offer advice. Give her the benefit of your experience. Try to steady her down. Felicia has these wild mood swings. Sometimes she frightens me."

"Mrs. Starrett, she may need professional help. A psychotherapist."

"It may come to that," Olivia said somberly, "but not yet, not yet. Oh, she is such a desperate girl. Desperate! But she will not discuss her problems with me. And she refused to talk to Father Callaway. But you are near her age. Perhaps she will confide in you, and you may be able to help her. Will you try?"

"If you want me to," Dora said doubtfully, "but she may resent my prying into her personal affairs."

"She may, but please try. I know she is unhappy, and this business with Turner Pierce worries me. Felicia has been hurt so many times; I don't want her to be hurt again."

"All right, Mrs. Starrett, I'll try."

"It's my family," the older woman said fiercely, "and I must do everything I can to protect them. Even if I think them stupid or wrong, even if they cause me pain, I must protect my children. You do understand that, don't you?"

"Of course," Dora said, rising. "Thank you for giving me so much of your time. I wanted to express personally my condolences at Father Callaway's passing."

"It was sweet of you, and I appreciate it."

"Mrs. Starrett, did Eleanor leave an address or telephone number where she can be reached?"

"She's staying with friends. Charles has the address and phone number. He'll give them to you."

"Thank you. And I'll try to set up a meeting with Felicia."

Mrs. Starrett turned her head away and stared at the thin winter light at the window. "She didn't come home last night," she said in a whispery voice.

No one awaited Dora in the foyer, so she walked back to the kitchen. Charles and Clara Hawkins were seated at an enameled table, drinking coffee and sharing a plate of what appeared to be oatmeal cookies. Houseman and cook looked up when Dora entered.

"Good afternoon," Dora said briskly. "Mrs. Starrett said you could give me the telephone number for Mrs. Eleanor Starrett."

Charles nodded and stood up slowly. "I'll fetch it," he said, and left the kitchen. Dora figured he was going to get Olivia's approval before handing over the phone number.

"How are you today, Clara?" she asked brightly.

"Surviving," the woman said, and Dora decided this had to be the most lugubrious couple she had ever met. She wondered if husband and wife ever laughed or even smiled, and she tried to imagine what their sex life must be like. She couldn't.

"Clara," she said, "Detective John Wenden told me you think the eight-inch chef's knife disappeared during the cocktail party on the night Mr. Lewis Starrett was killed. Do you have any idea who might have taken it?"

"No."

"I'm not asking if you know definitely who took it. I don't want you to accuse anyone. I'm just curious about who *might* have taken it."

Clara stared up at her, and Dora saw again that discernible mustache and couldn't understand why in the world this dour woman didn't *do* something about it. A daily shave, for instance.

"I don't name no names," the cook said sullenly.

Dora sighed. "All right," she said, "I'll name the names. You just shake your head no or nod your head yes. Okay?"

Nod.

"Was it Clayton Starrett?"

Shake.

"Eleanor Starrett?"

Shake.

"Felicia Starrett?"

Shake.

"Helene Pierce?"

Shake.

"Turner Pierce?"

Shake.

"Father Brian Callaway?"

Nod.

Charles came back into the kitchen, carrying a scrap of paper. He looked at his wife accusingly. "You been shooting off your mouth again?" he demanded.

"She hasn't said a word," Dora told him. "I've been doing all the talking, about what a great chef my husband is."

"She talks too much," he grumbled, and handed over the slip of paper. "That's Mrs. Eleanor's phone number and address. West Side," he added sniffily.

"Thank you, Charles," Dora said. "Now would you get my hat and coat, please; I'm leaving. Nice to see you again, Clara."

"Likewise," Clara said.

Dora hurried back to her hotel, anxious to get to her notebook and record all the details of that surprising conversation with Olivia. Plus what she had learned from Clara's dumb show.

She filled two pages with notes that included all her recollections of what Mrs. Starrett had said and implied about the Clayton-Eleanor-Helene triangle and the Felicia-Turner relationship. If this entire case was a soap opera, Dora reflected grimly, it had a deadly plot. Too many corpses for laughing.

She went down to the dining room for dinner and ordered a tuna salad, trying to recall if this was her fourth or fifth diet since being assigned to the Starrett claim. Brooding on her futile attempts to lose poundage, she remembered what John Wenden had said about her increasing girth: "More of you to love." What a *nice* man!

She returned to her suite and called him. He wasn't in but she left a message, hoping he might get back to her before midnight. He didn't, so she called Mario. He wasn't home. There was nothing left to do but brush her teeth and go to bed in a grumpy mood, wondering what the hell her men were doing and imagining direful possibilities.

31

It was easy to fake it, with Clayton or any other man, and Helene Pierce had learned to deliver a great performance. She considered herself a "method" actress and her motivation was that growing hoard of unset diamonds.

The dialogue came easily:

"Oh, Clay, you're too much . . . you drive me wild . . . I can't get enough of you . . . Where did you *learn* these things?"

She left him hyperventilating on the rumpled sheets and went into the kitchen to pour fresh drinks from the bottle of Perrier-Jouët he had brought. The guy had good taste, no doubt about it, and there were no moths in his wallet. Helene wanted to play this one very, very carefully and, for once in her life, sacrifice today's pleasure for tomorrow's treasure.

He was sitting up when she returned to the bedroom with the champagne. He was lighting a cigar, but she was even willing to endure that.

"Here you are, hon," she said, handing him the glass.

She lay beside him, leaning to kiss his hairy shoulder. "You are something," she said. "One of these days you'll have to call 911 and have me taken to Intensive Care."

He laughed delightedly, sipped his champagne, puffed his cigar, and owned the world. "I can never get enough of you," he told her. "It's like I've been born again. Oh God, the time I wasted on that bag of bones."

"Eleanor?" she said casually. "What's happening there?"

"Like I told you, she's moved out. My attorney, Arthur Rushkin, doesn't handle divorces but he's put me in touch with a good man, a real pirate who's willing to go to the mat for the last nickel. That's the way things stand now: My guy is talking to her guy. Listen, sweetheart, this is going to take time. Are you willing to wait?"

"After what we just did," she said, looking at him with swimming eyes, "I'll wait forever."

"That's my girl," he said, patting her knee. "Everything will come up roses, you'll see."

He started talking about the way they'd live once they were married. A duplex on the East Side. Cars for each; maybe a Corniche and a Porsche. Live-in servants.

"Younger and more attractive than Charles and Clara," he said.

They'd probably dine out most evenings. Then the theatre, ballet, opera, a few carefully selected charity benefits. A cruise in the winter, of course, and occasional shopping trips to Paris, London, Milan, via the Concorde. They might consider buying a second home, or even a third. Vermont and St. Croix would be nice. World-class interior decorators, naturally. *Architectural Digest* stuff.

As he spun this vision of their future together, Helene listened intently, realizing that everything he described was possible; he wasn't just blowing smoke. Turner had told her how much Clay was drawing from Starrett Fine Jewelry as salary, annual bonus, dividends, and his share of that deal with Ramon Schnabl.

And Clayton had a million coming in when that claim on his father's insurance was approved. And when his mother shuffled off, he'd be a multi multi. So all his plans for the good life were doable, and she'd be a fool, she decided, to reject it for a more limited tomorrow with Turner.

"How does it sound to you?" Clayton asked, grinning like a little kid who's just inherited a candy store.

"It sounds like paradise," Helene said.

"It will be," he assured her. "You know that old chestnut: 'Stick with me, kid, and you'll be wearing diamonds.' In this case it's true. Which reminds me, I have another chunk of ice for your collection."

"You can give it to me later," she said, taking the cigar from his fingers and putting it aside. "Let's have an encore first. You just lay back and let me do all the work."

When he left her apartment, finally, she had a lovely four-carat trilliant, a D-rated stone that was totally flawless. But before he handed it over, he subjected her to a ten-minute lecture on the four Cs of judging diamonds: color, clarity, cut, and carat weight.

After he was gone, she sprayed the entire apartment with deodorant, trying to get rid of the rancid stink of his cigar. Then she sat down with her fund of diamonds, just playing with them while she pondered her smartest course of action.

Turner was the problem, of course. She had a commitment there, and since the Sid Loftus thing, Turner had an edge that could prove troublesome. But she thought she knew how that could be finessed. She worked out a rough game plan, and as her first move, she phoned Felicia Starrett.

32

He insisted on taking her to a steak joint on West 46th Street.

"It's not a fancy place," he said. "Mostly cops and actors go there. But the food is good, and the prices are right. We'll have a rare sirloin with garlic butter, baked potatoes with sour cream and chives, a salad with blue cheese dressing, and maybe some Bass ale to wash it all down. How does that sound?"

"Oh God," Dora moaned, "there goes my diet."

"Start another one tomorrow," Wenden advised.

It was a smoky tunnel, all stained wood, tarnished brass lamps, and mottled mirrors behind the long bar. The walls were plastered with photos of dead boxers and racehorses, and posters of Broadway shows that had closed decades ago. Even the aproned waiters looked left over from a lost age.

"What have you been up to?" John asked, buttering a heel of pumpernickel.

"Nothing much," Dora said. "I went to see Mrs. Olivia Starrett to tell her how sorry I was about Callaway's death."

"How's she taking it?"

"She was sitting up in bed and looked a little puffy around the gills, but she's coping. She's a tough old lady."

She told the detective some of what she had learned. Some, but not all. Clayton and Eleanor were getting a divorce, and he wanted to marry Helene Pierce. And Felicia Starrett was playing footsie with Turner Pierce.

"Interesting," John said, "but I don't know what it all means—if anything. Do you?"

"Not really. Sounds to me like a game of Musical Chairs."

"Yeah," he said. "You want to hear about the Sid Loftus homicide now or will it spoil your dinner?"

"Nothing's going to spoil my dinner," she said. "I'm famished. If I never see another tuna salad as long as I live, it'll be too soon."

They finished their martinis hastily when the waiter brought big wooden bowls of salad and poured their ales.

"The knife that did him in wasn't like the ones that iced Starrett and Guthrie," Wenden said, going to work on his salad. "It was maybe a three- or three-and-a-half-inch blade. We figure it was a folding pocket knife, a jackknife. There must be jillions of them in the city. The big blade on this one was razor sharp."

"That wasn't in the papers," Dora said.

"We don't tell the media *everything*. Another thing we didn't release was that the crime scene guys and the lab think the perp may have been a woman."

Dora put down her fork and stared at him. "A woman? You're sure?"

"Pretty sure. They vacuumed up a few long hairs and particles of face powder."

"What color hair?"

"Black, but it may have been colored. We sent the hairs to the FBI lab to see if they can definitely ID the color and also what kind of shampoo or hair spray was used, if any."

They were silent while their steaks and baked potatoes were served. Dora looked down at her plate with amazement. "I'll never be able to eat all that."

"Sure you will," Wenden said. "I'm betting on you."

"So it *was* a sex scene?"

"Looks like it started out that way, but that's not how it ended. He hadn't had an ejaculation before he died. Too bad. A loser all around."

Dora ate in silence a few moments, pondering. Then: "Any cigarette butts?"

"Nope," Wenden said. "Just butts from those cigarillos he smoked. But when they took up the floorboards, guess what they found."

"Not Judge Crater?"

"About three grams of high-grade coke."

Dora paused with a forkful of steak half-raised. "You mean he was snorting?"

Wenden nodded. "Recently enough so that there were traces in his urine." He laughed. "What a splendid man of the cloth that old schnorrer was! Does Olivia Starrett still believe in him?"

"She seems to, and I didn't tell her any differently. Not even Callaway's real name or how he died. This steak is something else again, and I'm going to finish every bite."

"I thought you would. It's aged meat. They scrape off the green mold before they broil it."

"I hope you're kidding."

"Sure I am." He sat back and sighed. "Great food, and screw choles-terol. Now I'm going to have coffee and a shot of Bushmills Black, just to put the icing on the cake. How about you?"

"I'll have coffee, but Irish Whiskey is a little raunchy for me."

"Tell you what: Have a half-and-half of Bushmills and Irish Mist on the rocks. You'll love it."

"All right, I'm game. I hope you'll let me pay for all this, John. It'll go on the pad."

"Nope," he said. "It's my turn. You've fed me enough."

"Salami sandwiches," she scoffed. "This is *food.*"

They dawdled over their coffee and postprandial drinks.

"John," she said, "you think Loftus picked up some floozy off the street?"

He shook his head. "No," he said. "I don't see him as a guy who had to rent a hooker. Also, there was loose cash in the back room, credit cards, and some valuable jewelry, including a Starrett wristwatch. A streetwalker would have snaffled the lot. No, I think his playmate was someone he knew. Whoever it was went along with his kinky idea of fun. He couldn't have tied his own wrists to the bedposts."

"And then the party got rough?"

He stared at her. "Doesn't make much sense, does it? But that's the way it looks."

"Did your guys come up with anything at local bars and restaurants?"

"Negative. But as they say in the tabloids, the manhunt is widening."

"Was there any evidence that drugs had been done that night, before he was killed?"

He shook his head again. "The coke we found was in sealed glassine envelopes. There was nothing to indicate coke or anything else had been used. Analysis of his blood showed he had had a few drinks, but he wasn't drunk. How do you like *your* drink?"

She rolled her eyes. "Heavenly. I'd like to fill a bathtub with this stuff, roll around in it, and then drink my way out."

He laughed. "Talk about kinky! More coffee?"

"Maybe a half-cup. You working tonight?"

"No, I'm starting a forty-eighter. And I'm going to sleep all of it away."

"I hope so," Dora said. "You look beat. How do you feel?"

"A hundred percent better than I did two hours ago."

"A rare steak will do that."

"It's really a rare you," he said, looking at her. "You always give me a lift."

He drove her back to the Bedlington and double-parked outside.

"Thanks for a memorable dinner," she said.

"Thanks for sharing the memory."

"You want to come up for a nightcap?" she asked hesitantly.

"I'd love to," he said, "but I'm not going to. I've got a long drive ahead of me, and then I want to hit the sack. Raincheck?"

"Of course."

He turned sideways to face her. He put an arm along the back of her seat, not touching her. But she stiffened and continued to stare straight ahead through the windshield.

"I'll tell you something," he said, his voice sounding rusty. "You may not believe it, but it's the truth. When I first met you—and later, too—I know I pitched you, coming on like a hotrock. I figured a toss in the hay would be nice—why the hell not?"

"John," she said softly.

"No, let me finish. But now it's more than that. I think about you all the time. I dream up excuses to call you or see you, and then I don't do it. You know why? Because I'm ashamed of acting like a schmo by bugging you all the time. And also, I'm afraid of rejection. I've been rejected before and shrugged it off because I didn't give a damn. Now I give a damn. I don't know what I feel about you, I don't know how to label it, but I wasn't lying when I said that just being with you gives me a lift. It's like I'm hooked, and I get a rush every time I see you."

"Maybe it's because we're working together," she said quietly. "People who work in the same office, for instance, or on the same project, develop a special intimacy: shared work and hopes and aims."

"Sure, that's part of it," he agreed. "But I could be a shoe salesman or you could be a telephone operator and I know I'd feel the same way. It's more than just the job. This is something strictly between you and me."

Then she turned to look at him. "Don't think I haven't been aware of it. At first I thought you were just a stud looking for a one-night stand. Wham, bam, thank you, ma'am. But now I think you're telling the truth because my feelings toward you have changed." She laughed nervously. "I can even tell you exactly when it happened: when I suddenly realized I should have bought you a maroon cashmere muffler for Christmas. Nutsy—right? But as I've said many times, I'm married, and as I've said many, many times, happily married."

"And that's the most important thing in your life?"

"It was. Damn you!" she burst out, trying to smile. "You've upset my nice, neat applecart. You're the one who's making me question what really is important to me. I was *sure* before I met you. Now I'm not sure anymore."

They'd never know whether she kissed him first or he kissed her. But they came together on the front seat of that ramshackle car, held each other tightly, clinging like frightened people, and kissed.

He was the first to break away. "I'll take that nightcap now," he said hoarsely.

"No, you won't," Dora said unsteadily. "You'll drive home carefully and grab some Z's. And I'll go up to my bedroom by myself."

"It doesn't make sense," he argued.

"I know," she agreed. "But I need time to figure this out. Good night, darling. Get a good night's sleep."

"Fat chance," he said mournfully, and they kissed just one more time. A quickie.

33

"Hiya, lady. This is Gregor Pinchik."

"Hello, Mr. Pinchik. I'm glad to hear from you again."

"Mr. Pinchik! Hey, you can call me Greg; I won't get sore."

"All right, Greg. And you can call me Dora instead of lady; I won't get sore."

"Sure, I can do that. Listen, this guy you got me tracing, this Turner Pierce—it's really getting interesting."

"You've found out more about him?"

"I'm almost positive it's him. About five years ago or so a hacker shows up in Denver calling himself Theodore Parker. Same initials, T and P—right? Like Thomas Powell in Dallas. But in Denver he's got a wide black mustache just like you described, so I figure it's gotta be him."

"Sounds like it. What was he up to in Denver?"

"Still pulling telephone scams. But now he's selling access codes. Those are the numbers companies issue to their employees so they can call long distance from outside the office and have it billed to the company. Like a salesman on the road can call headquarters and have the charges reversed by punching out his access code."

"How did Theodore Parker get hold of the codes?"

"Oh hell, there are a dozen different ways. You invade a company's computers and pick them up. Or you buy software that dials four-digit numbers in sequence until you hit one that works. Or maybe you steal the salesman's code card. Then you're in like Flynn. It's easier when the company has an 800 number, but you can also get on their lines through their switchboard."

"And he was peddling the codes?"

"That's right. Mostly to college students and soldiers away from home, but also to heavies who made a lot of long-distance calls to places like Bolivia and Colombia and Panama and didn't want to run the risk of having their own phone lines tapped.''

''What a world!''

''You can say that again. Anyway, this Theodore Parker had a nice business going. He was even selling the codes to penny-ante crooks who were running what they call 'telephone rooms.' These are places you can go and for a buck or two call anyplace on earth and talk as long as you like. It would all be billed to the company that owned the access codes the crooks bought from Parker.''

''Beautiful. And what happened to him?''

''The Denver hackers I contacted told me the gendarmes were getting close, so Theodore Parker skedaddled. For Kansas City. How does that grab you?''

''I love it. Any mention of a woman skedaddling along with him?''

''I struck out there. Everyone says he was a loner, just like in Dallas. Plenty of women, but no one resembling Helene Pierce the way you described her. That's all I've got so far.''

''Greg, I've received your hourly bills and sent them on to the Company. But you didn't list the expense of all the long-distance calls you've been making or your modem time. The Company will pay for that.''

''They are. I'm using their access codes.''

''You stinker! Did you invade their computers again?''

''Nah. Listen, you can buy a long-distance access code on the street for five or ten bucks. But I didn't even have to spend that. Your Company's access codes are listed on an electronic bulletin board I use. I picked the numbers up from that. Well, I'm going to start on Kansas City now. I'll let you know how I make out.''

''Please. As soon as possible.''

''Nice talking to you, lady.''

Dora hung up smiling and then jotted a précis of Pinchik's information in her notebook. She sat a moment recalling her initial reaction to Turner and Helene Pierce: supercilious people with more aloof pride than they were entitled to. It was comforting to learn that Turner was apparently a two-bit lowlife scrambling to stay one step ahead of the law.

She glanced at her watch, then took a look in the full-length mirror on the bathroom door. She was wearing the one ''good'' dress she had brought from Hartford: a black silk crepe chemise that wasn't exactly haute couture but did conceal her tubbiness. She fluffed her red hair and vowed, again, that one of these days she was going to *do* something with it. Then she went down to the Bedlington cocktail lounge, hoping Felicia Starrett wouldn't be too late.

Surprisingly, she was already there, sitting at a corner table and sipping daintily from a tall pilsner of beer.

''Surely I'm not late,'' Dora said.

The woman looked up at her. "What?" she said.

"Have you been waiting long?"

Felicia shook her head. "I'm out of it, Nora."

"Dora. What's wrong? Are you ill?"

No reply. Dora looked at her closely. She was thinner, drawn. The cords in her neck were prominent enough to be plucked. Her nose had become a knuckle, and her stare was unfocused.

Dora went over to the bar and ordered a beer. While she waited, she observed Felicia in the mirror. She was sitting rigidly and when she raised the glass to her lips, her movements were slow, slow, as if she had planned every motion carefully and was dutifully obeying her mind's command.

She was wearing a belted cloth coat, buttoned to the neck although the cocktail lounge was overheated. And she had not removed her soiled kidskin gloves. She was hatless; her long black hair appeared stringy and unwashed.

Dora carried her beer back to the table. "Would you like something to eat?" she asked, taking the chair opposite. "Perhaps a sandwich?"

"What?"

"Are you hungry?"

"No," Felicia said, and looked about vaguely. "Where am I?"

Dora wasn't certain how to handle this. Felicia didn't appear drunk or high on anything else. But certainly she was detached. The woman was floating.

"The cocktail lounge of the Hotel Bedlington," Dora said. "I'm Dora Conti. Thank you for meeting me for a drink."

"A cigarette," Felicia said.

Dora fished a crumpled pack from her shoulder bag. But when she offered it, Felicia made no move to take a cigarette. Dora put the pack on the table.

"I see you're drinking beer," she said as lightly as she could. "No Chivas Regal today?"

The woman looked at her blankly. She said, "That's for me to know and you to find out."

Dora was shocked by this childish response. "Felicia," she said, "is there anything I can do?"

"About what?"

"Are you feeling all right?"

"I will be." She paused and slowly the focus of her eyes changed until she was actually looking at Dora. "I'm getting married," she said suddenly. "Did you know? Of course not; no one knows. But I'm getting married."

"Why, that's wonderful," Dora said. "Congratulations. Who's the lucky man?"

"I bought him," Felicia said, mouth stretched in an ugly grin. "I bought the lucky man."

Dora drank off half her beer, wondering whether to end this mad conversation as soon as possible or take advantage of this poor woman's derangement. "Turner Pierce?" she asked quietly.

"Oh," Felicia said, "I did tell you. I forgot. You know Turner?"

"We've met. I hope you'll be very happy."

"He knows how to make me happy." She leaned across the table and beckoned with a long forefinger. Dora bent forward to hear. "I'm naked," Felicia said in a low voice.

"Pardon?"

"Under my coat. I haven't a stitch on. Look." She opened two buttons, pulled the neckline apart. Dora saw bare breasts.

"Button up," she said sharply. "Felicia, why on earth aren't you dressed?"

"What's the point? I don't feel like it. I don't have to do anything I don't want to do. And mother can't make me." That bony forefinger beckoned again, and again Dora leaned forward. "Clayton is going to marry Helene. Good. You know why?"

"Why?"

"Because I thought Turner and Helene were making it."

"Felicia! They're brother and sister."

"So? But now it's all right. Turner is mine. I'll never give him up."

She said this so fiercely that Dora was saddened, fearing what might happen to this vulnerable woman. Felicia sat back and looked at her pridefully. "I've moved in with Turner. It's my home now."

"And when will the wedding be?"

The focus of Felicia's eyes flattened, the aimless stare returned. "Soon," she said. "Real soon. I think I better go. Turner worries about me. He doesn't like me to be out by myself. He wants me with him all the time. Every minute."

"That's nice," Dora said not believing a word of all this. "Felicia, please, take care of yourself. And see your mother as often as you can."

"I don't think so. Do you have any money?"

Dora was startled. "I have a little with me."

"Could you give me a twenty for a cab?"

"Of course," Dora said. She took out her wallet and handed over a bill.

Felicia stood up, steadily enough, and unexpectedly proffered her hand. "I've enjoyed our little chat," she said formally. "So nice seeing you, and we must do this again very soon."

"Yes," Dora said.

Felicia turned away, then came back to put an arm across Dora's shoulders and lean close. "I call him the iceman," she whispered. "Turner. When we're getting it off, I say to him, 'The iceman cometh.' Isn't that hilarious?"

Dora nodded and watched her go, feeling horrified and helpless. An avalanche was beginning to move, and there was no way to stop it.

34

That demented conversation with Felicia Starrett spooked her. But it wasn't only Felicia, Dora acknowledged; the entire case involved befuddled and vexatious characters, all seemingly acting from irrational motives. Their lives were so knotted, ambitions so perverse, plans so Byzantine that she despaired of sorting it all out.

But then, she admitted ruefully, her own life was hardly a model of tidiness. John Wenden's confession—and implied plea—was never totally banished from her thoughts. An analysis of the way she felt about him was proving as frustrating as untangling the Starrett mishmash. She, whose thinking had always been so ordered and linear, seemed to have been infected by the loonies who peopled this case. She had caught their confusion and was as muddled as they.

Almost for self-preservation, she resolutely decided to concentrate her attention on Solomon Guthrie's computer printout and what it might reveal about the perplexing gold trading by Starrett Fine Jewelry, Inc. Now she was dealing with names, addresses, numbers, transactions: all hard data that had none of the wild emotionalism of the Starrett clan and their intimates.

She jotted a page of notes and planned a course of action.

She phoned the car rental agency used by the Company, identified herself, and gave her credit card number. She arranged for a Ford Escort to be brought to the Hotel Bedlington the next morning at 7:00 A.M.

She left wake-up call instructions at the hotel desk.

She was waiting on the sidewalk the following morning when the Escort was delivered. It was dark blue, had recently been washed, and the interior smelled of wild cherry deodorant.

She drove to LaGuardia Airport, parked, and waited twenty minutes before boarding the next Pan Am shuttle. Destination: Logan Airport, Boston.

She had a window seat on the port side of the plane and midway in the flight, above the cloud cover, she waved at the ground. The man seated next to her, reading *The Wall Street Journal,* looked up and asked curiously, "What are you waving at?"

"My husband," Dora said. "In Hartford."

"Oh," the man said.

She waited in line for a cab at Logan, then handed the driver the address she had written down. He read it and turned to look at her. "You sure you want to go there?"

"I'm sure," Dora said. "You can wait for me, then drive me back here."

"If we're alive," he said mournfully.

The address was in Roxbury, on a street that was mostly burned-out buildings and weed-choked lots. But there were three little stores huddled together, awaiting the wrecking ball. One was a bodega, one a candy store cum betting parlor. The third was Felix Brothers Classic Jewelry.

"This is it," the cabdriver said nervously. "If you're not back in five minutes, I'm taking off—if I still have wheels."

"I'm not going anywhere," Dora said.

She got out of the taxi and inspected the jewelry store. Ten feet wide at the most. A plate glass window half-patched with a sheet of tin. Glass so dusty and splattered she could hardly peer within. She saw a few empty display cases, a few chairs, one lying on its side. There was no use trying the door; it was behind a rusty iron grille and secured with an enormous padlock.

A man lounging nearby had watched Dora's actions with lazy interest. He was wearing camouflaged dungarees and a fake fur hat with earflaps that hung loosely.

"I beg your pardon," Dora said, "but could you tell me when the jewelry store is open."

The idler was much amused. "Cost you," he said.

Dora gave him a dollar.

"It ain't never open," the man said.

"Thank you very much," Dora said, and hastily got back in the cab.

"Thank God," the driver said, and gunned away.

She took the next shuttle back to New York. She reclaimed the Ford Escort and drove into Manhattan. She left her car for the Bedlington doorman to park and went up to her suite. She immediately called John Wenden.

"Got a minute?" she asked.

"All my life," he said. "What's up?"

"Listen to this . . . " she said, and related her day's activities. Then: "John, that place isn't even a hole-in-the-wall. It's a falling-down dump. It's never open. No stock and no customers. It's a great big nothing."

"So?"

"Two months ago the Starrett Fine Jewelry branch store in Boston sold Felix Brothers Classic Jewelry more than a million dollars' worth of pure gold."

"Son of a bitch," the detective said.

35

He sat ripping the baguette apart with jerking fingers, rolling the dough into hard little balls and tossing them aside.

"Turner," Helene said, "what *are* you doing?"

He looked down at the mess he had made. "Jesus," he said, "I'm losing it."

He was about to say more, but then the waiter served their veal chops and angelhair pasta. The bartender brought over a chilled bottle of Pinot Grigio and showed the label to Turner. He nodded, and the bottle was uncorked and poured.

"Now calm down and eat your dinner," Helene said.

Turner tried a bite of veal, then pushed his plate away. "I can't make it," he said. "You go ahead. I'll have the wine and maybe a little pasta."

Helene ate steadily, not looking up. "What's she on?" she asked.

"Ramon gave me some new stuff he's distributing. Smokable methamphetamine. Called ice. He said it would be a great high, and it is. Lasts for hours. But Ramon didn't tell me about the crash. Disaster time."

"Then cut her off," Helene advised.

"I can't. You're hooked with the first puff. The stuff is dynamite. I had her move in so I can keep an eye on her. The woman is dangerous—to herself and to me."

Helene looked up frowning. "Dangerous? You mean suicidal?"

"Suicidal, homicidal, depression, hallucinations, delusions—you name it. She can't even talk clearly."

"You've got a problem, son."

"Thanks for telling me," he said bitterly. "I thought I could keep her quietly stoned. That's a laugh. She smokes the stuff and starts climbing walls. That stupid Ramon!"

Helene ate steadily. "If he's stupid," she said, "how come he's so rich?"

"That's where you're wrong," Turner told her. "The richest men I've known have been the dumbest. It has nothing to do with intelligence. The ability to make money is a knack, like juggling or baking a soufflé."

"Uh-huh," Helene said. "Aren't you going to eat your chop?"

"I have no appetite. You want it?"

"About half. Cut it for me."

Obediently, he trimmed the chop on his plate, cut slices of the white meat, and transferred them to her plate.

"Thank you," she said. "So what are you going to do?"

"I don't know," he said fretfully, and went back to rolling balls of bread dough. "I tried to cut her off, and she went wild. Absolutely wild. She threatened me. Can you imagine that? She actually threatened me."

"Threatened you how?"

"Said she'd kill me if I didn't bring her more ice. And believe me, she wasn't kidding."

"You're scared?"

"Damned right I'm scared," he said, gulping his wine. "She's totally off the wall."

"Turner, maybe you better go to Clayton or Olivia and suggest she be put away for treatment."

"And have her tell them where she's been getting the stuff? No way! That would queer everything."

Helene finished her wine, took the bottle from the ice bucket, and re-filled Turner's glass and her own. "You want to close up shop and take off?" she said quietly.

"I don't know," he said. "I don't know what to do."

His head was down as he pushed the bread pills around the tablecloth. Helene sat back and regarded him closely. He was right; he *was* losing it. Skin sallow, puffy circles under his eyes, twitchy fingers. And he, who had always been such a dandy, now wore a soiled shirt, tie awkwardly knotted, unpressed jacket. She could almost *smell* his fear.

"How long can you keep her going?" she asked.

"God knows," he said. "I've got to be there when she crashes. If I let her out of the apartment, she might go home, and then we're dead. Helene, you have no idea what that stuff has done to her. She's lost weight, she can't sleep, I've got to bathe her like an invalid. When she's smoking, her body gets so hot I'm afraid to touch her. But when she's high, she just wants to keep going. It lasts for hours, sometimes a whole day. Then she falls apart and wants to kill herself. Or me—if I don't get her out of her funk. Which means more ice."

"Where is she now?"

"At my apartment. Locked in. I fed her some downers, hoping she'd sleep it off. I better get back. If she's set fire to the whole place, I won't be a bit surprised. Maybe you're right; maybe we better split. I can't see any way out of this mess.''

"Let's think about it,'' Helene said. "You go on home now. I'll finish my wine, maybe have an espresso, and take a cab home.''

"Will you pick up the tab?''

She looked at him. "Sure,'' she said.

He stood up and tried a smile. "Thanks, sweetie,'' he said. "I can always depend on you. We'll come out of this okay; you'll see.''

"Of course we will,'' she said.

She sipped her wine slowly, then had an espresso and a small apple tart. She paid the bill and overtipped, asking the waiter to go out onto Lexington Avenue and get her a cab. She was back in her apartment within a half-hour.

She looked up the unlisted number of Ramon Schnabl in her address book. But when she phoned, all she got was an answering machine. When it beeped, she gave her name, phone number, and asked Mr. Schnabl to call her at his convenience.

Then she phoned the Starrett apartment. Charles answered, and she asked if Clayton was there. The houseman said that Mr. Starrett was attending a business dinner that evening but was expected home shortly. Helene asked that he call her whatever time he arrived.

She made herself a cup of instant black coffee and took it to the living room desk. She went over her accounts, adding up her cash on hand and what she might expect from an emergency sale of those unset diamonds. She estimated the total, roughly, at about fifty thousand. That was hardly poverty, but it was very small peanuts indeed compared to her dreams.

She was finishing her coffee when the phone rang, and she let it shrill six times before she picked it up.

"H'lo?'' she said in a sleepy voice.

"It's Clay, honey. Did I wake you up?''

"That's all right, Clay. I've only been sleeping a few minutes. It was nothing important. I just wanted to tell you how much I love you and how much I miss you.''

"Hey,'' he said, his voice eager, *"that's* important! Did you really go to sleep so early?''

"There's nothing special on TV, so I thought I'd go to my lonely bed.''

"Listen'' he said, almost choking, "we can't have you going to a lonely bed. How's about if I pop over for a while? You can always sleep later.''

"Well . . . '' she said hesitantly, "if you really want to. I'd love to see you, Clay, but you must be tired.''

"I'm never *that* tired,'' he said. "I'll be there in twenty minutes.''

She undressed quickly, brushed her teeth, took a quick shower. By the time he arrived, she was scented and wearing a peach-colored silk negligee.

"Oh sweetheart,'' she said, embracing him tightly, "I'm *so* happy to see you. I know how busy you are, but I was hoping you'd come over tonight. I felt so alone. I really need you.''

He stayed for almost two hours. As he was dressing, he took out his wallet and gave her five hundred dollars.

"That's just walking-around money," he told her. "After the divorce comes through and we're married, I'll put you on the store payroll at a thousand a week. We'll call you a styling consultant or something like that. It'll be a no-show job, but if anyone asks we can say you check out competitors' displays and new designs."

"A thousand a week," she repeated. "Thank you, darling. You're so good to me."

After he left, she showered again, poured herself a brandy, and changed the sheets and pillowcases on her bed.

She went back to her accounts, and finished the evening by making a meticulous list of her diamonds and their carat weight. Then she went to bed. She lay awake a few minutes, thinking that Turner should have left money for their dinner. That young man was developing short arms and low pockets. Clayton Starrett was different.

36

Mrs. Eleanor Starrett was unexpectedly gracious on the phone.

"I'm *so* glad you called, *chérie*," she said. "I've never been busier in my life, but I can always find time for *you.*"

Dora thought that a bit much, but asked when and where they might meet. Well, Eleanor had an appointment for a massage at Georgio's Salon on East 56th Street at 11:30, and if Dora could meet her there, they'd have time for a nice chitchat.

Dora found her in a curtained back room, lying naked on a padded table and being worked on by a gigantic flaxen-haired masseuse.

"Pull up a chair, darling," Eleanor caroled. "We can talk while Hilda reduces me to a mass of quivering jelly. You really should do something with your hair."

"I know," Dora said.

"Such a gorgeous shade, but it *is* a mess. I'll ask Georgio to handle you personally. The man is *très chic* and does absolutely marvelous things with his magic scissors."

"Maybe some other time," Dora said. "Mrs. Starrett, I want to—"

"Oh, do call me Eleanor. I don't know why, but I feel I've known you for years and years. Dora—isn't it?"

"Yes."

"Well, Dora, when— Oh my God, Hilda, you're breaking my leg! Well, Dora, I'm sure you've heard I'm getting a divorce from Clayton, and that rat has to turn over a list of all his assets, so of course it's very important for me to know when he's getting that million from his father's insurance."

Now Dora could understand her gushy friendliness. "I really can't give you a definite date, Eleanor, but I'm sure it won't be much longer."

"I hope not. I want to hit that schmuck where he lives—and that means his bank account."

"I was sorry to hear about the divorce," Dora said.

"Don't be sorry, sweetie; be glad, because I certainly am. I should have dumped that moron years ago. He is *so* dumb. A dumb rat. Of course Helene Pierce isn't his first playmate. He's been cheating on me since the day we were married. And the idiot thought I didn't know!"

"Why did you put up with it?" Dora asked curiously.

Eleanor raised her head to look at her. "Everyone cheats, luv. It's hardly a capital crime, is it? If it were, there wouldn't be enough electric chairs in the world. There's nothing so terrible about cheating— I've had a few flings myself—but one should try to be discreet, don't you think? And ending a marriage just for the sake of a roll in the hay is definitely *de trop*. I mean, it just isn't done. Except by rat finks like Clayton Starrett. Well, I wish him happiness with his Barbie Doll. She'll take him for whatever he has left after I get through with him. Poor Clay will end up washing windshields at stoplights." She cackled with glee.

"Eleanor, one of the things I wanted to talk to you about was Felicia. I met her yesterday, and she seemed—uh, she seemed ill."

"Ill?" the other woman said with a harsh laugh. "Stoned out of her gourd, you mean. Felicia is a basket case. She really should be under professional care somewhere, but Olivia doesn't know what's going on."

"What *is* going on?"

"Oh, she's doing coke, no doubt about it. I think Turner Pierce turned her on, but if it wasn't him, it would be someone else. Felicia is lost. She's going to get into serious trouble one of these days."

"Why would Turner Pierce want to supply her with drugs?"

"What a child you are! Felicia is hardly poverty-stricken, is she, and Turner has expensive tastes. As I well know. One of those flings I mentioned, I had with Turner. But I soon gave him the broom. A very, *very* grabby young man. Just like his sister."

"I thought you liked the Pierces. At our first meeting you were very complimentary."

"That was when I was a member of the family," Eleanor said bitterly. "Now I can tell the truth, and they can all rot in hell!"

When she left the salon, Dora stood on the sidewalk a few moments, gulping deep breaths. She needed that sense of a world washed clean, everything spotless and shining.

It wasn't Eleanor's vindictiveness toward Clayton that dismayed her; the scorned wife was entitled to that. Nor were the revelations of Felicia's addiction a shock; Dora had guessed that doomed woman was beyond her help—and probably any other Samaritan's.

But what really depressed Dora were Eleanor's blithe comments about cheating. Was she right? Did everyone do it? Was adultery no more serious than a mild flirtation at a cocktail party, and no more reason for marital discord than the toothpaste tube squeezed in the wrong place?

She walked west on 56th Street wondering if she was hopelessly naive, an innocent with no real perception of how the world turned and how people behaved. "What a child you are!" Eleanor had said, and perhaps, Dora acknowledged, she *was* a child, with all her notions of right and wrong the result of her teaching, and not wisdom distilled from experience.

She cut over to 54th Street and continued to plod westward, still brooding. Could she be right and everyone else wrong? It hardly seemed likely. John Wenden had said, "Life is too short to be faithful," and perhaps that was a universal truth that had somehow eluded Dora Conti, happily married and now questioning if her world was ridiculously limited.

She shook off these melancholic musings and looked about her. She stood on the corner of 54th Street and Eighth Avenue. This neighborhood was vastly different from the one she had just left. There was a police station, hemmed in by parked squad cars. Then there was a crowded stretch of tenements, garages, and low-rise commercial buildings.

She dodged traffic, crossed Eighth, and walked west on 54th, watching the numbers and realizing she still had a block or two to go.

When she told John about that empty jewelry shop in Roxbury, the detective had said, "Look, this gold-trading caper is yours. I have my hands full with the three homicides; I can't suddenly start chasing gold bars. Why don't you stick with it and see what you can come up with. I'm here and ready to help. Okay?"

Sure, Dora had told him, that was okay, and she went back to the plan of action she had outlined prior to her Boston trip.

She had the address of the vault of Starrett Fine Jewelry in Brooklyn, but it didn't seem worthwhile to investigate because she had no idea when a shipment of gold might be delivered. It made more sense to check out Starrett's main supplier of gold bullion, an outfit called Stuttgart Precious Metals, Inc., located on West Fifty-fourth Street in Manhattan. According to the computer printout, Stuttgart was the USA subsidiary of Croesus Refineries, Ltd., headquartered in Luxembourg.

Dora had expected to find Stuttgart Precious Metals in a blockhouse of a building, a thick-walled bunker surrounded, perhaps, by a heavy fence topped with razor wire, with armed guards in view. Instead she found a one-story concrete block building with no fence, no guards. It was located just west of Tenth Avenue and looked as if it had been built as a garage, with a small office in front and wide, roll-up doors leading to the main building. There was no sign.

Even more perplexing than the ordinariness of the physical structure was its air of dilapidation. It looked deserted, as if business had dwindled and bankruptcy loomed. A derelict was rooting in the garbage can outside the office door. Looking for gold bars? Dora wondered.

She had eyeballed the building from across the street. Now she marched resolutely up to the office door and pushed her way in. She found herself in a barren, wood-floored room with stained walls carelessly plastered and no chairs or other amenities for potential customers. There was a scarred wooden counter, and behind it, at an equally decrepit desk, a bespectacled, gray-haired lady sat typing steadily. There were no other papers or documents on her desk.

She stopped typing when Dora entered, and looked up. "Yes?" she said in a crackly voice.

"Is this Stuttgart Precious Metals?" Dora asked.

The woman nodded.

Dora had prepared a scenario.

"My husband and I have a small craft shop in Vermont," she said, smiling brightly. "We design and fashion one-of-a-kind jewelry pieces, mostly gold and sterling silver in abstract designs. We've been buying our raw gold and sterling in Boston, but I had to come to New York on business and decided to find out if we could get a better price on metals down here."

The woman shook her head. "We don't sell retail," she said.

"Well, it's not actually retail," Dora said. "After all, we are designers and manufacturers. We sell to some of the best department stores and jewelry shops in the country."

The woman didn't change expression. "How much gold could you use in a month?" she asked. "Ounces? We sell our metals in pounds and kilos. Our gold comes from abroad in bars and ingots. Too much for you, girlie."

"Oh dear," Dora said, "I'm afraid you're right; we wouldn't know what to do with a pound of pure gold. Listen, one other thing, I walked over from Eighth Avenue, and it occurred to me that someday we might consider opening a small workshop and showroom in Manhattan. Does Stuttgart own any other property in the neighborhood?"

"We don't own," the woman said, "we lease."

"Oh dear," Dora said again. "Well, I guess I'll just have to keep looking. Thank you for your time."

The woman nodded and went back to her typing.

Dora was lucky; she caught an empty cab that had just come out of an Eleventh Avenue taxi garage. But traffic was murder, and it took an hour to get back to the Bedlington. She went immediately to her suite and kicked off her shoes. Then she phoned Mike Trevalyan in Hartford.

"Gee, it's good to hear from you," he said. "Having a nice vacation?"

"Come on, Mike, cut the bullshit. I need some help."

"No kidding?" he said. "And I thought you called to wish me Happy Birthday."

"I have two words for you," Dora said, "and they're not Happy Birthday. The computers in our property and casualty department use a data base that covers all commercial properties in our territory—right?"

"Oh-oh," he said. "I know what's coming."

"There's this business on West Fifty-fourth Street in Manhattan called Stuttgart Precious Metals, a subsidiary of an outfit registered in Luxembourg. Stuttgart leases their premises. I'll give you the address, and I need to know who owns the property and anything else you can find out about Stuttgart: the terms of the lease, how long they've occupied the place, and so forth."

"What's this got to do with the Starrett insurance claim?"

"Nothing," Dora said breezily. "I'm just having fun."

After he calmed down, she gave him the address of Stuttgart, and he promised to get back to her as soon as he had something.

"Miss me?" he asked her.

"I sure do," she said warmly. "What's your name again?"

She hung up on his profanity and then, a few minutes later, phoned Mario, and they talked for almost a half-hour. Dora got caught up on local gossip and told Mario how much she missed him and their little house.

"It's the home cooking you miss," he said.

"That, too," she agreed.

"When are you coming back?"

"Soon," she promised. "Have you been behaving yourself?"

"As usual," he said, which wasn't *exactly* what she wanted to hear.

But the talk with her husband cheered her, and she went to bed resolved to forget all about people with sloppy morals; nothing could equal the joy of a happy, *faithful* marriage.

But sleep did not come easily; her equanimity didn't last, and she found herself questioning again. So she got out of bed to kneel and pray. It was something she hadn't done for a long while, and she thought it was about time.

37

Felicia Starrett was not a stupid woman, but introspection dogged her like a low-grade infection. She was aware—continually aware—that her life lacked some essential ingredient that might make it meaningful, or at least endurable. Her mother never ceased to remind her that a loving mate and a happy marriage would solve all her problems. That advice, Felicia thought wryly, was akin to telling a penniless, starving bum that he really should eat good, nourishing meals.

But it was true, she admitted, that her relations with men had soured her life. She was still in her teens, with the arrogance of youth, when she began to offer money or valuable gifts to men. This pattern continued after she was graduated from Barnard and, in an effort to find the cause of this curious behavior, she read many books of popularized psychology. But none offered clues as to the reason she continually met (or sought?) men who accepted her largesse casually as if it were their due.

At various periods of self-analysis she had ascribed different motives for her compulsive generosity. First she thought it was a power ploy: She wanted to dominate men. In fact, she wanted to *own* them, reduce them to the role of paid servitors. Finally she concluded that she gave money because she was unable to give love. She was fearful of commitment, recognized the deficiency, and lavished gifts as a substitute.

But recognizing the cause did nothing to ameliorate her unhappiness. And so she surrendered to addictions: caffeine, nicotine, alcohol, a variety of drugs, and eventually cocaine, in an endless search for the magic potion that would provide the joy life had denied her.

She thought her search had finally succeeded when Turner Pierce provided ice, the smokable methamphetamine. Here was a bliss that turned her into a beautiful creature floating through a world of wonders. The high was like nothing she had ever experienced before.

But there was a heavy price to pay. The crash was horrendous: nausea, incontinence, dreadful hallucinations, fears without name, and frequently violence she could not control. But Turner—the darling!—was always there to minister to her and, when the worst had passed, to provide more of those lovely crystals in a glass pipe, and then she soared again.

She was vaguely aware of vomiting, weight loss, respiratory pain, thundering heartbeat, and heightened body temperature. But she became so intent on achieving that splendid euphoria that she would have paid any price, even life itself, if she might slip away while owning the world.

But death held no lure, for there, always, was Turner, who had promised to marry her, an act of love that made her happiness more intense. So joyful was she that she was even able to acknowledge the beauty and beneficence of Helene—a woman she had formerly mistrusted—who came once to help Turner bathe her and wash her hair. And also clean up the apartment, which Felicia, during a vicious crash, had almost destroyed, slashing furniture with a carving knife, breaking mirrors, and smashing all those cute china figurines belonging to the landlord.

So she alternated between ecstasy and despair, hardly conscious of time's passage but, in her few semilucid moments, realizing with something like awe that she would soon be a married woman and finally, at last, her life would be meaningful.

38

Dora drove around the block twice, and then around two blocks twice. Finally, three blocks away, she found a parking space she hoped she might be able to occupy, but it took ten minutes of sweaty maneuvering to wedge the Escort against the curb. She locked up and walked back to Gregor Pinchik's building in SoHo. She didn't even want to *think* about the eventual problem of wiggling the Ford out of that cramped space.

The computer maven had the top floor of an ancient commercial building that had recently been renovated. There were new white tiles on the lobby floor, and on the walls were Art Deco lighting fixtures with nymphs cavorting on frosted glass. The original freight elevator—big enough to accommodate a Steinway—had been spruced up with crackled mirrors and framed prints of Man Ray photographs.

Pinchik's loft was illuminated by two giant skylights that revealed a sky as dull as a sidewalk. But there was track lighting to fill the corners, and Brahms played softly from an Aiwa stereo component system that had more knobs, switches, gauges, and controls than a space shuttle.

"How about *this,* lady?" Gregor cried, waving an arm at his equipment.

He gave Dora what he called the "fifty-cent tour," warning her not to trip on the wires and cables snaking across the floor. He displayed, and occasionally demonstrated, a bewildering hodgepodge of computers, monitors, printers, modems, tapes and disks, telephones, fax and answering machines, digital pagers, hand-held electronic calculators, and much, much more.

"I'm a gadget freak," the bearded man admitted cheerfully. "If it's electronic, I gotta have it. A lot of this stuff is junk, but even junk can be fun. Now you sit down over here, and I'll get you caught up on the adventures of our pigeon."

Dora sat in a comfortable swivel chair, and Pinchik perched on a little steel stool that rolled about on casters. He settled in front of a monitor and punched a few buttons with his stubby fingers.

"I put the whole file on one tape," he said. "You know what I collected in Dallas and Denver. Now we'll get to the new things."

Typed lines began to reel off across the screen, and Pinchik leaned closer to read.

"All right," he said, "here's the scoop I got from my hacker pals in KC. Our hero showed up in Kansas City after leaving Denver. Now he's Turner Pierce. Same initials, but who the hell knows if it's his real name."

"Still got the mustache?" Dora asked.

"Still got it. And he's still on the con. The reason the KC hackers knew so much about him was that he set up what was apparently a legitimate business. Office, secretary, letterheads, advertisements—the whole schmear. He called himself a computer consultant and designer of complete systems for any size business, large or small. He was one of the first in that field in KC, and he made out like gangbusters. First of all, he knew his stuff, and he never tried to sell a client more hardware than he needed. Of course Pierce was probably getting a kickback on the equipment he *did* recommend, but that was small potatoes. He lined up some hefty clients: a bank and its branches, a local college, an insurance company, a chain of retail shoe stores, and a lot of factories, distributors, supermarkets, an entire shopping mall, and so forth."

"So he went legitimate?"

"That's what everyone thought. At first. Then there was a string of computer swindles. The bank took heavy losses in cash, and the shoe stores and distributors lost merchandise delivered and logged in as paid for, though payment was never actually made. And the insurance company found itself paying off claims on policies it had never written."

"Don't tell me, Greg," Dora said. "I can guess."

"You got it," Pinchik said, nodding. "All those victims had computer systems installed by Turner Pierce Associates, Inc. What he was doing was leaving what we call a 'trapdoor' in every system he designed. In its simplest form this would be an access code, maybe just a single word or a six-digit number, that would enable a bandit to get into the system from outside, rummage around in all the records, and clip the business the way he wanted for as much as he wanted."

"And that's what Turner was doing?"

The computer expert shook his shaggy head. "Nope," he said, "he was too smart for that. He followed the same pattern we saw him use in Dallas and Denver. He never did the dirty deed himself, but he sold those trapdoors to guys greedier and dumber than he was. When all those crimes came to light, some of the actual crooks were nabbed and convicted, but Pierce folded his tent and quietly slipped away."

"Greg, some of those guys who were convicted must have tried to plea bargain by giving the prosecutor Turner Pierce's name."

"Sure, they fingered him as the guy who sold them access to the computer systems. But what evidence did the prosecutor have to come down on Pierce? No evidence. Just the accusation of an indicted criminal. There was no case against Pierce that would hold up in court, so he was advised to get out of town."

"And he came to New York."

"That's it," Pinchik agreed, then pressed more buttons on his console. "But I haven't told you the juiciest part yet. Wait a sec." He stood to peer more closely at the screen. "Yeah, here it is. You remember I told you that when Pierce set up his business in Kansas City, he had an office, a secretary, everything seemingly legit."

"I remember."

"The secretary was a tall, luscious lady with the first name of Helene."

"His sister!" Dora cried.

"I guess," Pinchik said. "The description I got matches the one you gave me. And when Turner Pierce lammed out of Kansas City, Helene disappeared at the same time, so I guess she came to New York with him."

"I guess she did," Dora said.

Pinchik sat down again on his little stool and wheeled around to look at her. "But I haven't given you the icing on the cake," he said, his face expressionless. "Before this Helene went to work in Turner Pierce's office, she was a hooker."

Dora stared at him a moment. Then: "You're sure?" she asked huskily.

He nodded. "I got the same data from two different sources, and I think it's for real. She was a hooker all right. But I don't mean she walked the streets or leaned against lampposts. My guys tell me she was more like a call girl, a high-priced call girl. She had some very important men as regular customers, and when a convention came to town, she did okay."

Dora took a deep breath. "Do you mind if I smoke?" she asked.

"Only if you give me one," Pinchik said. "I'm all out."

They lighted up and sat a few moments in silence, staring at the ceiling. "It's a wonderful world," Dora said finally.

"You can say that again," Pinchik said.

"It's a wonderful world," Dora said again, smiling. Then she lowered her gaze to stare at the grizzled man, the gadget freak who could use electronics to strip people naked. "Tell me, Greg: You're a been-around guy, what's your take on Turner Pierce?"

Pinchik regarded the glowing end of his cigarette. "I fell once. I knew it was wrong while I was doing it and, God willing, I'll never fall again. But this Pierce comes across as a natural-born outlaw. He just doesn't give a damn. Look, the guy is smart. When it comes to computers, he may even be close to a wunderkind. If he had gone straight, he might have been a zillionaire by now. But like I said, he just doesn't give a damn. No laws or rules for him. He bulls his way through life, and if someone gets hurt, that's tough shit. Excuse my language, lady.''

"I've heard worse.''

"Also,'' Pinchik said, "I think he could be very, very dangerous. Remember that.''

"I'll remember,'' Dora promised.

Pinchik dropped his cigarette butt to the tiled floor and ground it out under his heel. "So now we've got Helene and Turner Pierce in New York. I guess that ends my job—right?''

"No,'' Dora said, "not yet. Will you get back to your contacts in Kansas City and see if you can find out more about Helene Pierce. Like where and when she was born, why she gave up on being a call girl to team up with her brother—anything you can find out.''

"Sure, I can do that. I have a few sources in KC I haven't tapped yet.'' He laughed suddenly. "And one of the hackers, I know for sure, is into the city's computers. He has access to all their records.''

"Why would he want to invade city hall?'' Dora asked curiously.

Pinchik shrugged. "Just for the fun of it. Because it's *there*. The same reason people climb Mt. Everest.''

"The other thing,'' Dora said, "is a man named Sidney Loftus. He's dead now, but he died as Father Brian Callaway, a preacher who invented his own religion. I think he was in Kansas City at the same time as the Pierces, and I'd like to find out if they knew each other.''

"Okay, let me get a tape recorder, and you give me all you've got on Sidney Loftus, including his physical description, and I'll see what I can dig up.''

When Dora returned to her Ford Escort, she discovered the car parked tightly ahead had disappeared, and she had no trouble pulling out and heading uptown. She took this as a good omen: An apparently intractable problem had been solved by chance or a smiling Almighty.

"Thank you, God,'' she said aloud. "Now see what You can do about clearing up the Starrett mess.''

When she arrived back at the Bedlington, there was a message for her at the desk: She was to call Michael Trevalyan in Hartford as soon as possible. She went up to her suite, made herself a cup of tea and opened a fresh package of Pepperidge Farm cookies: Orange Milanos, her favorite. Then she phoned.

"You sure threw me a curveball,'' Trevalyan said aggrievedly. "That Stuttgart Precious Metals, the dump on West Fifty-fourth Street, I had it looked up by a computer guy in the property and casualty department.''

"And?''

"Like you said, Stuttgart leases. The lease was signed about two years ago and runs for five years with an option to renew on the same terms.''

"Who owns the building and land?''

"An outfit called Spondex Realty Corporation."

"Never heard of them," Dora said. "Did you?"

"Will you just shut up for a minute," Trevalyan said wrathfully, "and let me finish. The computer whiz in property ran a trace on Spondex and found out it's owned by R. L. Jessup Investments, another corporation. Now the computer guy got interested because it began to smell. You know when there's a paper trail like that, someone's trying to cover up. Anyway, the ownership of the property on West Fifty-fourth was traced back through four corporations and finally came to rest at a holding company that owns real estate in LA and New York, a shipping line, a boutique in Palm Beach, a big coffee plantation in Colombia, a ranch in Wyoming, and God knows what else."

"What's the name of the holding company?"

"It's called Rabl Enterprises, Ltd. And this will kill you: It's registered in Luxembourg. Isn't that where Stuttgart's parent company is registered?"

"You got it, Mike," Dora said. "And it *is* beginning to smell. Who's the owner of Rabl Enterprises?"

"It's set up as a limited corporation. Maybe a dozen shareholders. It's not listed on any exchange. The chairman of the board, president, and chief executive officer is a guy named Ramon Schnabl. I guess that's where they got the name of the holding company: first two letters of his first name and last two letters of his last name. We've gone through all our data bases, but there's nothing on Ramon Schnabl."

"All right, Mike. Thanks for your help. I'll take it from here."

"Does that mean we'll be able to deep-six the Starrett insurance claim?"

"I don't know what it means," Dora said worriedly, "if anything."

"Well, watch your tail, kiddo. That chain of corporate ownership makes me suspect someone may be playing hardball. Don't do anything foolish."

"Why, Mike," Dora said, "you're concerned about me. How sweet!"

"Ahh, go to hell," he said gruffly, and hung up.

Dora rushed to her spiral notebook and jotted down all the names she could recall from that telephone conversation. Then she called Detective John Wenden, but he was in a meeting and not available. She left a message and went back to her notebook, scrawling a condensed version of everything she had learned from Gregor Pinchik that morning. She was still scribbling when the phone rang and she grabbed it up.

"Hiya, Red," Wenden said. "I only got a few minutes. What's happening?"

"I'll make it fast," Dora said, and told him about her visit to Stuttgart Precious Metals on West 54th Street, and how the Company had run a computer search to discover who owned the property and, after following a complex corporate trail, had come up with the name of a holding company registered in Luxembourg.

"Does the name Ramon Schnabl mean anything to you?" Dora asked. There was no reply.

"John?" Dora said. "Are you there?"

"Listen," Wenden said, his voice suddenly urgent, "do me a favor, will you? Don't do another thing about Starrett's gold trading. Not a thing, you understand? Don't go back to that place on West Fifty-fourth. Don't ask any more questions about it. Don't even mention Starrett's gold trading to *anyone* until I get back to you. Okay? Will you promise to lay off until I call?"

"John, is this important?"

"Is life important? Will you promise not to make a move until you hear from me?"

"All right," Dora said faintly. "If you say so."

"I love you, Red," Wenden said.

39

Despite what Turner had said, Helene Pierce equated wealth with intelligence. Smart people made big money; that was a given. Now, seated in the colorless living room of Ramon Schnabl's minimalist apartment, she stared at his dark glasses and wondered what secrets those cheaters concealed. This little man in his tight, shiny white suit could pass as a Palermo pimp, but he was, she knew, a Croesus who would never be listed in the Forbes 400.

"What a pleasure to see you again, dear," he said in his bloodless voice. "I was surprised—delighted but surprised to hear from you. Does Turner know you're here?"

The question was so sudden and sharp that Helene was startled. "No," she said, "he doesn't. I thought it best not to tell him."

Schnabl nodded. "I certainly shan't," he said, no hint of humor in his tone. "You wish to discuss something concerning Turner?"

"And you," Helene said.

He waited, patient and silent, sipping his chilled Évian water.

"You know, of course," she said, wishing desperately for a cigarette, "that Turner is involved with Felicia Starrett."

"I am aware of their relationship."

"I'm afraid it may be a problem," Helene said.

"A problem? Felicia or Turner?"

"Both. She is totally hooked, and trying to control her is beginning to affect Turner's judgment. And not only his judgment but his personality, even his physical appearance. To put it bluntly, Ramon, the man is falling apart."

"I am extremely sorry to hear that, dear. I wish only the best for Turner, just as I do for you. Are you suggesting that his behavior is becoming somewhat, ah, erratic?"

"It's come to that," Helene said, lifting her chin but never taking her stare away from those tinted glasses. "But I think Felicia is the more immediate danger. She's irrational. She trashed Turner's apartment. And when she crashes, she's completely psychotic."

"What a shame," the little man said, sighing. "The price we pay for our pleasures. Well, this is disquieting news, dear. Have you any suggestions as to how this distressing situation may be remedied?"

Helene took a deep breath. "Did you know Clayton Starrett is getting a divorce?"

"I have heard something to that effect."

"He wants to marry me when his divorce is final."

Schnabl showed no surprise. "I see. And do you wish to marry him?"

"Yes. I mention this personal matter only to convince you that if you should decide to eliminate Turner . . . from your plans," she added quickly. "If you should decide to eliminate Turner from your plans, I wanted you to know that it need not affect the Starrett deal. I can control Clayton."

"And why should I want to, as you say, eliminate Turner?"

"Because he is going through a very bad time with Felicia. It has changed him. He is not the man he was six months ago, or even six weeks ago. He is no longer dependable. And, of course, Felicia represents an even greater threat. There is simply no telling what that insane woman might do. Another factor you may wish to consider: If Turner was out of the picture, you would save his share of the Starrett take. I assure you I have no desire to inherit it. Clayton is making quite enough for the two of us."

"You are not only a lovely woman, dear, but you are wonderfully shrewd. I like that."

Helene started to speak, but Schnabl held up a hand to silence her. He turned his blank stare toward the bleached oryx skull hanging above the cold fireplace. They sat without speaking for a few moments.

"I think not," Ramon said finally, turning his head toward Helene again. "The timing is not right. As you may or may not know, Turner is presently engaged in setting up an operation in New Orleans similar to the Starrett arrangement. It is important to me that this project be completed and brought on-line. Then we have discussed a third organization headquartered in Tucson, Arizona, which is rapidly becoming an important distribution center. No, my dear, I'm afraid I cannot grant your request."

"It wasn't a request," Helene said stonily. "It was merely a suggestion I thought would be to your benefit."

"And yours, too, of course," Schnabl said. "I do appreciate your concern, and I shall certainly keep a close watch on Turner's behavior. If, as you say, he has become undependable, then I may be forced to revise my decision. But for the time being, I intend to take no action. Sorry."

"There's nothing to be sorry about," Helene said. She stood and gathered up hat, gloves, purse, coat. "I just thought you should be aware of the true situation so you might act in your own best interest."

Finally, finally, he smiled: a horrible grimace, a death's-head grin. "We all act in our own best interest, dear. It's the mark of a civilized man. And woman," he added, staring at her.

She cabbed home to her apartment, furious but controlling it because she had already prepared a fallback scenario in case Schnabl couldn't be manipulated. He couldn't, and now she would have to do it herself. She was not daunted by that prospect.

Her spirits rose when the concierge handed her a package that had just been delivered by a messenger from Starrett Fine Jewelry. Helene hugged it to her breast in the elevator; she knew what it contained.

That night she and Clayton were going to attend a charity dinner-dance at the Waldorf, the first time they would be out in public together. Helene had bought a new evening gown: a strapless sheath of lapis-hued sequins. And Clayton had promised to lend her a necklace from Starrett's estate jewelry department.

"Remember, it's only a loan," he had said, "for one night. It has to be returned to the store—unless some woman at the party will kill for it and can come up with the two million five it costs. In which case you get a commission."

"I understand," Helene said.

She tore open the package with trembling hands, lifted the lid of the velvet case, caught her breath. It was a magnificent strand of ten splendid sapphires, each gem set in a pyramid of diamonds, the pyramids linked with 18K gold. Helene guessed the total sapphire weight at about 75 cts. and the diamonds at 50 cts.

She took off jacket and blouse and clasped the necklace about her throat. It was beautifully designed, and lay flat and balanced on her bare skin. She stood before the mirror, turned this way and that, admired the sparkle of the gems, the glow of the gold. This was the kind of adornment for which she was destined. She had always known it. All she had ever needed was a break—and Clayton Starrett was it.

She spent a long time bathing, doing her hair, applying makeup, stepping carefully into the sequined sheath, donning the satin evening pumps. Then she locked that wondrous necklace about her throat and saw in the mirror the woman she had always wanted to be.

She went downstairs carrying a silk trench coat. The stretch limousine was waiting. Clayton was standing alongside on the sidewalk, smoking a cigar. When he saw her, he tried to speak but something caught in his throat. She recognized the longing in his eyes.

"I feel like Cinderella," she said, laughing, "on her way to the ball."

"But midnight will never come," he proclaimed. "Never!"

At the Waldorf, they sat at a table for ten. All the other men seemed to be suppliers to Starrett Fine Jewelry, and they and their wives treated

Clayton with the deference a good customer deserved. They were no less ingratiating toward Helene, admiring the necklace, her gown, even the shade of her fingernail polish. She basked.

It was a black-tie affair and, looking about the big dining room, Helene saw nothing but wealth and finery. Flash of jewels. Scent of expensive perfumes. It seemed to be a room without worries, without grief or regrets. This was, she decided, what life should be.

Later, during the dancing, she was introduced to many people: admiring men and sharp-eyed women. She conducted herself demurely, murmured her thanks for compliments, held Clayton's hand and let him exhibit her proudly: his newest and most valuable possession.

The band played "After the Ball" at 2:00 A.M., but it was almost another hour before they had a final glass of champagne, reclaimed their coats, and waited for their limo to be brought around. They returned to Helene's apartment through a soft snowfall that haloed the streetlamps and added the final touch to a fairy-tale evening.

"I'd love to come up," Clayton said huskily, "but I can't. Heavy schedule tomorrow, and besides, I had too much to drink. I better get some sleep."

"Oh Clayton," she said sorrowfully, immensely relieved and gripping his hand tightly, "the first disappointment of a really fabulous night."

"It *was* super, wasn't it? Darling, you were the belle of the ball. I've never heard such praise. All the guys wanted your phone number, of course, but I told them you were taken."

"I am—with you," she said and kissed him fiercely.

"Oh God," he said, almost moaning, "what a life we're going to have!"

"Do you want the necklace now?" she asked.

"No, you keep it till tomorrow. I'll send a messenger around in the morning. Helene, I love you. You know that, don't you?"

She kissed him again as an answer, then went up to her apartment alone, the collar of her trench coat raised to hide the necklace. She undressed swiftly, realizing she would have to shampoo before sleeping to rid her hair of the smell of Clayton's cigars.

She stroked the necklace softly as it lay on her suede skin. It was an enchantment, an amulet that would protect her from failure and bring her nothing but good fortune.

So bewitched was she by this extraordinary treasure that never once did she remember that it would be taken away by a messenger in the morning.

40

Dora Conti was beginning to get a glimmer, just a faint perception of what was going on. She cast Sidney Loftus and the Pierces as the sharks and the Starretts as their wriggling prey. But who was doing what to whom remained murky. Dora even drew a diagram: boxed names linked by straight or squiggly lines. It didn't help.

Then Detective John Wenden called.

"Hey, Red," he said with no preliminary sweet talk, "there's a guy I want you to meet: Terence Ortiz, a detective sergeant. We call him Terrible Terry."

"All right," Dora said, "I'll play straight man: Why do you call him Terrible Terry?"

"He's in Narcotics," Wenden said, "and he shoots people. Listen, can we stop by tonight? Late?"

"How late?"

"Around eight o'clock."

"That's not late," Dora said. "I rarely go to bed before nine."

"Liar!" he said, laughing. "See you tonight."

Terry Ortiz turned out to be a short, wiry man with a droopy black mustache that gave him a melancholic mien. But he was full of ginger and had a habit of snapping his fingers. When he was introduced, he kissed Dora's hand, and the mustache tickled.

"Hey," she said, "would you guys like a beer?"

"The sweetest words of tongue or pen," Ortiz said.

"Except for 'The check is in the mail,' " Wenden said.

"Yeah, except it usually ain't," Ortiz said. "I'll settle for a beer."

He was wearing a black leather biker's jacket and black jeans. When he took off the jacket, Dora saw he was carrying a snub-nosed revolver in a shoulder holster. She brought out cans of beer, a bag of pretzels, and a saucer of hot mustard. They sat around the cocktail table, and Terrible Terry slumped and put his boots up.

"I got maybe an hour," he announced, "and then I gotta split. If I don't get home tonight my old lady is going to split *me*."

"Where do you live, Sergeant Ortiz?" Dora asked politely.

"Terry," he said. "The East Side barrio—where else? Let's talk business."

"Yeah," John said, "good idea. Red, tell Terry how you came up with the name of Ramon Schnabl."

She explained again how she asked her boss to run a computer check on the ownership of the premises occupied by Stuttgart Precious Metals on West 54th, and eventually the paper trail led to a Luxembourg holding company headed by Schnabl.

"Uh-huh," John said, "and who was the first owner you turned up— the outfit that leased the place to Stuttgart?"

"Spondex Realty Corporation."

The two detectives looked at each other and laughed.

"What are you guys giggling about?" Dora demanded.

"After you mentioned the name of Ramon Schnabl," Wenden said, "I remembered your telling me about that trip to Boston you made and how the store in Roxbury looked like a deserted dump. So just for the hell of it, I called the Boston PD and asked them to find out who owns the building occupied by Felix Brothers Classic Jewelry. Guess what: It's owned by Spondex Realty Corporation."

Dora smacked her forehead with a palm. "Now why didn't I think to check that out?"

"Because you're an amateur," Wenden said. "Talented and beautiful, but still an amateur."

Dora let that slide by—temporarily. "And who is this Ramon Schnabl," she asked, "and what's his racket?"

"Terry," John said, "that's your department. You tell her."

"Ramon Schnabl is very big in the drug biz," the narc said. "Very, *very* big. The guy runs a supermarket: boo, horse, snow, opium, crack, hash, designer drugs from his own labs—you name it, he's got it. He's also got a vertical organization; he's a grower, shipper, exporter and importer, distributor, wholesaler, and now we think he's setting up his own retail network in New York, New Orleans, and some of his field reps have been spotted in Tucson, Arizona. The guy's a dope tycoon."

"If you know all this," Dora said, "why haven't you destroyed him?"

Terry snapped his fingers. "Don't think we haven't tried. So has the Treasury, the FBI, and the DEA. Every time we think we have him cornered, he weasels out. Witnesses clam up. He doesn't kill rats, he kills their families: wives, children, parents, relatives. Drug dealers are willing to do hard time rather than double-cross Ramon Schnabl. He is not a nice man."

"No," Dora said. "But if he's such a big shot in drugs, what's his interest in precious metals and jewelry stores?"

"Beats me," Wenden said. "I thought about gold smuggling, but that doesn't make sense; gold is available everywhere, and the market sets the price. Also, gold is too heavy to smuggle in bars and ingots. Got any ideas, Terry?"

"*Nada,*" Ortiz said, and finished his beer. "I thought maybe he might be bringing in gold bars with the insides hollowed out and stuffed with dope. But that wouldn't work because, like you said, gold is heavy stuff and someone would spot the difference."

"So?" John said. "Where do we go from here?"

"This is too juicy to drop," Ortiz said. "I think maybe I should take a look at Stuttgart Precious Metals. It could be just a front, and instead of gold, their vault is jammed with kilos of happy dust. I'll case the joint, and if it looks halfway doable, maybe we should pull a B and E. John?"

"I'm game," Wenden said.

Ortiz turned suddenly to Dora. "You got wheels?" he asked.

"A rented Ford Escort," she said.

"Lovely. We may ask for a loan."

"If you need a lookout," she said, "I'm willing."

"I love this woman," Terry said to Wenden. "*Love* her." He stood up, pulled on his jacket and a black leather cap. "I'll check out Stuttgart and let you know. Thanks for the refreshments. You coming, John?"

"I think I'll hang around awhile," Wenden said.

The narc raised his hand in benediction. "Bless you, my children," he said. He took two pretzels from the bag and left.

Dora laughed. "He thinks we have a thing going," she said.

"I thought we had," John said. "May I have another beer?"

She brought him a cold can. "John, I didn't want to say anything while Terry was here, but you look awful. You've lost weight, and even the bags under your eyes have bags. Aren't you getting any sleep?"

"Not enough. I have to go for a physical next month, and the doc will probably stick me in Intensive Care."

"I worry about you," she said.

"Do you?" he said with a boyish smile. "That's nice. Listen, enough about me; let's talk about the big enchilada: the three guys who got capped. You hear anything new?"

Dora told him about her conversations with Felicia and Eleanor, and how the former planned to marry Turner Pierce. She told him nothing of what she had learned from Gregor Pinchik and his merry band of hackers.

"You think Felicia is hooked?" Wenden asked.

"Definitely. She should be under treatment right now."

"Where is she getting her supply?"

"Eleanor says Turner Pierce is her candyman. But Eleanor is so bitter about the divorce, I don't know if she's telling the truth."

John shook his head. "We find coke under the floorboards in Father

Callaway's pad, Felicia is snorting the stuff, and now Ramon Schnabl, a drug biggie, turns out to have some connection with Starrett's gold trading. Maybe it all fits together, but I don't see it. Do you?''

"Not yet,'' Dora said. "Do *you* have anything new on the three homicides?''

He brightened. "Yeah—we finally got a break. At least I hope it's a break. Remember I told you we were checking out all the stores, bars, and restaurants in the neighborhood of the Church of the Holy Oneness, to see if Loftus-Callaway had been in the night he was offed. We finally got to a scruffy French restaurant on East Twenty-eighth Street, and an old waiter there says he thinks the good Father was in that night.''

"John, it's taken a long time, hasn't it?''

"You think it's an easy job, that you just walk into a joint, flash a photo of the dear departed and ask if he was there at a certain time on a certain date, and then people tell you? It's not that simple, Red. Clerks and bartenders and waiters have so many customers, they forget individual faces. And also, it's hard to find out who was on duty that particular night. And then it turns out that one of the waiters has been fired, or quit for another job, or maybe moved out of the state. And then he's got to be tracked down. Believe me, it's a long, ass-breaking job, and chances are good it'll turn out to be a dead end. But it's got to be done. So as I said, we finally found this restaurant on East Twenty-eighth where a waiter remembers Callaway being in the night he was killed. The reason the waiter remembers him was that the noble padre didn't leave a tip. The moral of that story is: Never stiff a waiter.''

"Was Callaway alone or with someone?''

Wenden looked at her admiringly. "You're pretty sharp—you know that? I'm sorry for that crack I made about you being an amateur. But I did say you were a talented and beautiful amateur. That helps, doesn't it?''

"Some,'' Dora said, but it still rankled. "Who was Callaway with?''

"The waiter says he sat in a booth with a young woman. But the waiter is so old that to him a 'young woman' could be anyone from sixty on down.''

"What's your next move?''

"I went to Mrs. Olivia Starrett and got photographs of Eleanor, Felicia, and Helene Pierce. They're color Polaroids taken at a dinner party last Christmas at the Starretts' apartment. I'm having blow-ups made, and I'm going back to that waiter and see if he can pick out one of them as the woman who sat in the booth and had drinks with the recently deceased. It's a long shot, but it's all I've got.''

"It sounds good to me,'' Dora said enthusiastically. "I think you're doing a great job.''

"Tell that to my boss,'' the detective said mournfully. "He thinks I'm dragging my feet. Actually, I'm dragging my tail. Order me to go home, Red, and get some sleep.''

"Go home and get some sleep."

"Yeah," he said, "I should. Remember the night you let me crash here?"

"Not tonight, John," Dora said firmly.

"You don't trust me?"

"I don't trust either of us. Besides, you're too bushed even to go through the motions."

"You're right," he said, groaning. "I feel like one of the undead. Well, thanks for everything, Red."

"John, drive carefully."

He stared at her with eyes heavy with weariness. "No decision yet, huh?" he said.

"Not yet."

"But you're thinking about it?"

"All the time," she said, almost angrily.

"Good," he said. "It would work for us, Red, I know it would."

They embraced before he left, hugged tightly, kissed long and lingeringly. Finally Dora pushed him out the door and turned her head away so he wouldn't see the tears brimming.

She cleaned up the pretzel crumbs, still snuffling, a little, and dumped the empty beer cans. She took up her pen and notebook but sat for several moments without scribbling a word. After a while she was able to stop brooding about John Wenden and concentrate on what she had learned from ballsy Terry Ortiz.

She figured he'd probably go ahead with a break-in at Stuttgart Precious Metals, and John would help him, and so would she. She knew what they would find—and it wasn't drugs. But she'd never tell the detectives what she had guessed; it would bruise their masculine egos. Let them go on thinking she was an amateur.

41

Numbers had always fascinated Turner Pierce. He even gave them characteristics: 1 was stalwart, 3 was sensual, 7 was stern, 8 was lascivious. But even without this fanciful imaging, numbers had the power to move the world. Once you understood them and how they worked, you could exploit their power for your own benefit.

But now, in his elegant, number-ordered universe, a totally irrational factor had been introduced. The presence of Felicia Starrett was like the "cracking" of a functioning computer by the invasion of a virus. The software he had designed to program his life was being disrupted by this demented woman.

He was quite aware of what was happening to him. It was as if he had caught Felicia's unreason. His linear logicality was constantly being ruptured by her drug-induced madness, and his reactions were becoming as disordered as her hallucinations and paranoia. He knew his physical appearance was deteriorating and his work for Ramon Schnabl suffering from neglect.

Her speech was becoming increasingly incoherent. She had lost the ability to control her bladder and bowels. Her rages had become more violent. She had lost so much weight that her dry, hot skin was stretched tightly over white knobs of bones. Turner was chained to a convulsive skeleton whose paroxysms became so extreme that he was forced to restrain her with bands of cloth. But even when fettered to the bed, her thrashings were so furious he feared her thin bones might snap.

It was only when she smoked a pipe of ice that these frightening displays of dementia were mollified. But then her body temperature rose so high, her breathing became so labored, her heartbeat so erratic, that he panicked at the thought she might expire in *his* bed, in *his* apartment. His life had not been programmed to handle that eventuality.

He phoned Ramon Schnabl, twice, intending to ask if an antidote existed that might return Felicia to normality. His calls were not returned. He then phoned Helene and, trying not to sound hysterical, asked her to come over and baby-sit "the patient" so he could get out of that smashed and fetid apartment for a while, have a decent dinner, and try to jump-start his brain in the cold night air.

Helene, not questioning, said she'd be there as soon as possible.

"Thank you," Turner Pierce said, not recognizing his own piteous voice.

Felicia Starrett dwelt in a world she did not recognize. It was all new, all different: colors more intense, sounds foreign, smells strange and erotic. She heard herself babbling but could not understand the words. She wasn't aware of who she was or where she was. Her new world was primeval. She remembered a few things in brief moments of lucidity: an aching past and a glorious future when she would marry Turner Pierce and everything would be all right. Forever and ever. She stared about with naked eyes.

Once, in Kansas City, when she had repulsed Sid Loftus, he had said to her, "You're not deep, you're shallow." Then he had added, "But wide." Helene Pierce had never understood what he meant by that. If he was implying that she was incapable of reflecting on the Meaning of Life, he was totally wrong; Helene often had deep thoughts. She was not, after all, a ninny.

Experience had taught her that life was dichotomous. People were either staunch individuals, motivated solely by self-interest, or they were what might be termed communicants who devoted their lives to interactions with families, spouses, friends, lovers, neighborhoods, cities.

It seemed to Helene the choice was easy. Being a communicant demanded sacrifice of time and energy—and life was too brief for that. Being a self-centered separate demanded less sacrifice but more risk. You were on your own, completely. So she began to equate the communicant with timidity and the individual with courage. She had, she told herself, the balls to go it alone. Gamble all, lose all or win all.

Then Turner phoned and asked her to come to his apartment and watch over nutty Felicia while he took a break. Hearing the panic in his voice— she was sensitive to overtones when men spoke—Helene immediately agreed. She recognized at once that it was an opportunity that might not soon occur again.

As she prepared to leave, she reviewed the scenario she had devised. It had the virtue of simplicity. It was direct, stark, and she figured it had a fifty-percent chance of success. But her entire life had been a fifty-fifty proposition; she was not daunted by a coin flip.

And so she started out, excited, almost sexually, by what she was about to do.

*   *   *

Turner had the apartment door locked, bolted, chained; it took him a moment to get it open.

"My God," he said in a splintered voice, "am I ever glad to see *you,* babe. Come on in."

Helene tried not to reveal her shock at his appearance: haunted eyes, sunken cheeks, unshaven jaw, uncombed hair. Even his once meticulously groomed mustache had become a scraggly blur. His clothes were soiled and shapeless.

She said nothing about the way he looked but glanced about the disordered apartment with dismay.

"Turner," she said, "you're living in a swamp."

"Tell me about it," he said bitterly. "I've tried to clean up, but then she goes on a rampage again. And I obviously can't hire someone to come in with a raving lunatic in the next room."

"She's in the bedroom?"

He nodded. "I've had to tie her to the bed. It's for her own safety," he added defensively. "And mine."

"How's she doing?"

"At the moment she's sleeping. Or unconscious; I don't know which. She had a pipe this afternoon. If she comes out of it tonight she'll be groggy for a few hours before she crashes. Think you can handle it?"

"Of course," Helene said. "Get yourself cleaned up, go have a good dinner. I'll be here when you get back."

"Thanks, babe," he said throatily. "I don't know what I'd do without you. What's it like out?"

"Absolutely miserable. Snow, sleet, freezing rain. Cold as hell and a wind that just won't quit."

"Maybe I'll run over to Vito's and grab a veal chop and a couple of stiff belts. Make me a new man."

"Sure it will," Helene said.

He went into the bathroom, and a moment later she heard the sound of his electric shaver. She didn't go into the bedroom but made a small effort to straighten up the living room, picking books and magazines from the floor, setting chairs upright, carrying used glasses and plates back to the kitchen. She took a look in the refrigerator. Nothing much in there: two oranges, a package of sliced ham, some cheese going green. There was a bottle of Absolut in the cupboard under the sink, but she didn't touch it. She didn't need Dutch courage.

Turner appeared looking a little better. He had shaved, washed up, put on a fresh shirt, brushed his hair and mustache.

"Two things," he said. "Keep the front door locked and don't, under any circumstances, untie her. She may beg you to turn her loose, but don't do it. You just don't know what she'll do. I'll be back in an hour."

"Take your time," Helene said.

After he left, she bolted the front door and glanced at her watch. Then she went into the bedroom. It was a malodorous place, furry with dust, and overheated. Illumination came from a dim bulb in the dresser lamp. The rug was littered with scraps of torn cloth, newspapers, a few shards of broken glass. And there were great, ugly stains.

Felicia Starrett, eyes closed, lay under a thin cotton sheet despoiled with blotches of yellow and brown. Her breathing was shallow and irregular; occasionally little whimpers escaped from her opened mouth, no louder than a kitten's mewls. Her wrists were bound together with a strip of sheeting. Her ankles were similarly shackled, and a long, wide band of cloth had been run under the bed, the two ends knotted across her waist.

Helene thought she looked in extremis, that her next small breath might be the last. She pulled a straightback chair to the bedside, touched one of those bound claws lightly.

"Felicia," she said softly.

No response.

"Felicia," she repeated and stroked a blemished, shrunken arm. "Felicia, dear, can you hear me?"

Eyelids rose, not slowly but suddenly; her eyes just popped open. Helene leaned closer.

"Felicia," she said gently, "it's Helene. Do you recognize me, darling?"

Eyes swung to her, but the focus was somewhere else.

"Water," Felicia said, trying to lick dry lips.

Helene went back to the kitchen, found a plastic cup, filled it with tap water, brought it to the bedroom. She held it to those parched lips while the fettered woman gulped greedily. She finished it all, turned her head aside and spewed it all over the pillow, bed, floor.

"Never mind," Helene said, controlling her own nausea at the sight, "we'll try again a little later. Is there anything you want, Felicia?"

Rheumy eyes turned to her. "Helene?" the woman asked.

"Of course! I'm Helene, dear, here to help you. How do you feel?"

"I'm sick."

"I know, Felicia, but you're going to be better real soon."

"Where's Turner?"

"He had to go out for a little while, but he'll be back before you know it."

Felicia looked down at her bound hands lying atop the soiled sheet. "Untie me," she said in a scratchy voice.

"Not right now, dear. Maybe when Turner gets back. Would you like to try a little more water now? Maybe an orange would taste good. There's a nice cold orange in the fridge. I'll get it and peel it for you."

She returned to the kitchen again, and, after searching a few moments, found where Turner had hidden the knives: on the top shelf of the cupboard over the range. Helene selected the long, pointed carving knife, the one Felicia had used to slash the furniture. She brought the knife and orange back to the bedroom.

She sat calmly, slowly slicing rind from the orange with the sharp blade, letting the peelings drop to the floor. She was aware that Felicia was watching her every move.

"There we are!" Helene said brightly, holding up the naked orange. "Doesn't that look nice? Would you like a piece right now?"

"Where's Turner?" Felicia repeated.

"He had to go out for a little while," Helene said again, "but he'll be back soon. You love Turner, don't you, darling."

Felicia blinked her eyes, tried to moisten her cracked lips. She attempted to speak, once, twice, and finally croaked, "We're going to get married."

"That's what I wanted to talk to you about," Helene said, hunching closer. "Now listen to me, dear, and try to understand what I'm saying."

She spoke slowly, distinctly, for almost ten minutes, repeating everything until she was satisfied the other woman had heard and comprehended, even dimly. There was no reaction, no objection. But Felicia's mouth sagged open again, eyelids shut as suddenly as they had opened.

"I'm going now, dear," Helene said. "Turner will be back soon. But let me untie you first."

Rather than attempt to loosen the tight knots, Helene used the carving knife to slice them through. Felicia lay motionless. Helene left the peeled orange and knife on the sheet alongside that flaccid body in its mummy posture.

"I hope you're feeling better real soon, darling," she said lightly. "Do take care of yourself."

Then she went swiftly into the living room, grabbed up hat, coat, purse, and left the apartment. Outside, she bent forward against the wind, the gusts of stinging hail, and walked westward as rapidly as she could.

He had unbelted his trench coat to get at his keys.

When he entered the apartment, it was almost completely dark.

The only illumination was a weak light coming from the bedroom.

He turned to flip on the wall switch.

His coat swung open.

"Helene!" he called. "I'm home!"

The knife went in just below his sternum.

The force of the blow slammed him back against the closed door.

The blade was withdrawn and shoved in again.

Again.

Again.

In shock, body burning, he looked down at the blood blooming from his wounds.

He looked at the naked wraith crouched in front of him.

Dimly he saw her lips drawn tight in a tortured grin.

He glimpsed a matchstick arm working like a piston.

He felt the blade penetrate.

Scorching.

He tried to reach out to stop that fire, but his knees buckled.

He slid slowly downward until he was sitting, legs thrust out, hands clamped across his belly, trying to dam the flood.

She would not stop, but bent over him, stabbing, stabbing.

Even after he was dead, she continued to poke with the knife, in all parts of his body, until she was certain he had ceased to exist.

42

"It's *perfect* weather!" enthused Detective Ortiz. "All the precinct cops will be in the coop, and all the bums will be in cardboard cartons under a bridge somewhere."

"What's the setup, Terry?" Wenden asked.

"There is no setup. No security guards and no alarms that I could spot. The place is Swiss cheese. We go in through the front door. I could pick that lock with a hairpin. Then we're in the office. A back door leads to the warehouse. I got a quick look at that, and there's nothing but a push-bolt as far as I could see. Listen, we'll be in and out of that joint before you can finish whistling 'Dixie.' "

"You got it all straight, Red?" Wenden said. "You drop us at Tenth Avenue and Fifty-fifth. Then drive around the block. Park as close to Stuttgart as you can get. If you have to double-park, that's okay, too. Give us two blasts of your horn if you see something that could be a problem. Okay?"

"A piece of cake," Dora said.

She was driving the Ford Escort. The two detectives, dressed in black, sat in the back. The windshield wipers were straining, and Dora leaned forward to peer through slanting rain, fierce flurries of sleet.

"If you guys are going to be so quick," she said, "maybe I better keep the motor running. I wouldn't care to stall out and have to call the Triple-A."

"Good idea," Terrible Terry said. "You got a full tank?"

"Of course," Dora said, offended. "This isn't my first criminal enterprise, you know."

"Love this woman," Ortiz said, *"Love* her!"

Traffic was practically nil. No buses. A few cabs. A civilian car now and then. They saw a snowplow heading up Eighth Avenue and a sander moving down Ninth. Dora pulled across Tenth Avenue on 55th Street and stopped.

"Have a good time," she said.

The two cops climbed out of the car.

"Twenty minutes," Ortiz said. "But if we're late, don't panic."

"I never panic," Dora said. "I'll be waiting for you."

She drove slowly around the block, being careful to stop for red lights. She found a parking space almost directly across the street from Stuttgart Precious Metals. She turned to watch the two men come plodding down 54th, bending against the wind but taking a good look around. Dora thought they must be freezing in their leather jackets. They were the only pedestrians, and no vehicles were moving.

She saw them pause, glance about casually, then saunter up to Stuttgart's front door. Both bent over the lock. Ortiz was true to his word; they were inside within a minute. The door closed behind them. Dora turned on the radio. She caught a weather forecast. It didn't sound good: rain and sleet turning to snow. Accumulations of up to two inches expected in the city, four inches in the suburbs. She lighted a cigarette and waited.

Nothing occurred and she was disappointed; a little high drama wouldn't have been amiss. Less than twenty minutes later, the two men came cautiously out of Stuttgart's front door. They paused a moment while Ortiz fiddled with the lock. Dora turned on her lights, and the cops came trotting across the street and climbed into the back of the Escort.

"Jee-*sus!*" Ortiz said. "It was cold in that dump."

Dora opened the glove compartment, took out a brown paper bag, handed it back to them. It contained a pint of California brandy.

"Something to chase the chill," she said.

"Did I tell you I love this woman?" Terrible Terry said to Wenden. "*Love* her!"

They opened the bottle and handed it back and forth as Dora pulled out and started back to the Bedlington.

"Not too fast, not too slow," Wenden warned.

"I know the drill," Dora said crossly. "How did you guys make out?"

"Drive now, talk later," he said.

She didn't offer another word on the trip back to the hotel. The two detectives conversed in low voices in the back, but she paid no attention. She was almost certain she knew what they had found at Stuttgart.

The cops had flashed their potsies and left John's heap in the No Parking zone in front of the hotel. Dora double-parked, cut the engine, lights, and windshield wipers. The snow was beginning, but it was a fat, lazy fall; the flakes looked like feathers in the streetlight's glare.

She turned sideways, looked back at them. "Find any drugs?" she asked.

"Not a gram," Ortiz said.

"Gold bars?"

Both detectives laughed.

"Oh yeah," John said, "we found stacks of gold bars. As a matter of fact, we even took shavings from one of them with my handy-dandy Boy Scout knife. Want to see?"

He dug a hand into his jacket pocket, then stuck an open palm forward for Dora's inspection. She saw what she expected to see: thin curls of a dull pewterish metal.

"What the hell is that?" she asked, all innocence.

"Lead," John said. "Starrett Fine Jewelry has been dealing in lead bars."

"Shit!" Terry said disgustedly. "You'd think a high-class outfit like Starrett would have the decency to coat their lead bars with genuine gold. But no, those bars were *painted,* with five-and-dime gilt. Can you believe it?"

"I don't get it," Dora said, willing to give them their moment of triumph. "Why are Starrett and Ramon Schnabl schlepping gold-painted lead bars all over the country?"

"It's a be-*yooti*-ful scam," John said. "Here's how we figure it works: Cash from Schnabl's drug deals is carried by courier to cities where Starrett has branch stores and delivered to the managers. They buy gold from Starrett in New York and pay with the drug money. Starrett headquarters, in turn, transfers the money electronically to their overseas gold suppliers, all owned by Schnabl."

"But there is actually no gold at all," Dora said. "Just lead bars they keep moving back and forth to get apparently legal documentation in the form of bills of lading, shipping invoices, warehouse receipts, and so forth."

"You've got it, Red," Wenden said. "The whole thing is just a scheme to launder drug money, get it out of the country in what appear to be legitimate business transactions."

"But what's the reason for Felix Brothers Classic Jewelry in Boston," Dora asked, "and all those other little jewelry shops?"

"Fronts," Ortiz said. "Set up by Schnabl so, on paper, the Starrett branch stores can show they have legit customers for all that gold they're buying from New York. And maybe some of those holes-in-the-wall are also banks for local drug deals."

Dora thought a moment. "Clayton Starrett must be in on it."

"You better believe it," John said. "Up to his eyeballs. And the branch managers hired a couple of years ago. And probably the guy running Starrett's Brooklyn vault. They're all involved and getting a piece of the action. Solomon Guthrie was too honest to turn. But he knew something was going on that wasn't kosher, so he got whacked. By Schnabl's hatchets."

Dora shook her head. "You've got to admit it's slick. I wonder who dreamed it up."

Wenden said, "My leading candidate is Turner Pierce, the computer genius. It would need computers to keep track of purchases, sales, expenses, and then come up with a bottom line every week or so."

"If it really was Turner Pierce," Dora said slowly, "you think his sister knew about it?"

"Helene? Of course she knew. Had to. And she's going to marry Clayton Starrett, isn't she? That keeps the fraud a family secret; no outsiders allowed."

"John," Ortiz said, "we'll have to bring the *federales* in on this."

Wenden slumped. "Say it ain't so, Terry."

"It is so. This caper is interstate and international with the electronic movement of big money. It's going to take an army of bank examiners, lawyers, accountants, and computer experts to sort it out and make a case. We just don't have enough warm bodies. We'll have to notify Treasury, the DEA and FBI."

"Aw, shit," Wenden said, "I guess you're right. But make sure that Red here gets the credit." He smiled and leaned forward to pat Dora's arm. "There wouldn't be any case at all if she hadn't started snooping."

"There's enough glory to go around," Dora said. "What's your next move, John?"

"Go back to the office, alert the Feds, and start the wheels turning. But before they get their act together, maybe I'll look up Turner Pierce and have a cozy little chat."

"I think I'll come along," Terry said. "If we lean hard on him, he might rat on Ramon Schnabl. I want to see that *bastardo* in Leavenworth, playing Pick-Up-the-Soap in the shower."

"I know why Guthrie was capped," Wenden continued, "but I'd like to find out why Lewis Starrett and Sid Loftus were put down. It all connects somehow to the gold trading plot and laundering of drug money."

Dora made no response.

"Listen," Terrible Terry Ortiz said to her, "maybe I never see you again, which is a big sorrow for me. I just want you to know you are one lovely lady, and it was a pleasure to make your acquaintance." He leaned forward to kiss her hand. "And take care of *mi amigo,*" he added, jerking a thumb toward Wenden. "He deserves a break."

Dora nodded, but said nothing as they climbed out of the Ford, got into John's clunker, and drove away. She maneuvered her car into the spot they had just vacated in the No Parking zone. Then she went into the Bedlington, told the night clerk what she had done, and asked if the doorman would take care of the Escort when he came on duty.

The clerk assured her that her car was okay right where it was and handed her two messages, both from Gregor Pinchik. Please call him as soon as possible, at any hour of the day or night. But it was then close to 2:30 in the morning, and all Dora wanted was to hit the sack and grab some Z's.

Upstairs, she made herself a warm milk. She sipped it slowly while she reflected on the night's events and how they might or might not affect the insurance claim she was supposed to be investigating. She felt like someone in search of honey who finds herself enveloped in a swarm of buzzing and ferocious bees. But she could not flee; that would be unprofessional.

She wondered if she stuck to this case, to all her assignments, because of the raw human emotions they revealed. Perhaps her own personal life was so staid and commonplace that she needed to share the excitement of other people's travails, just as poor Felicia Starrett needed a periodic fix. And maybe that, after all, was why the possibility of an affair with John Wenden had not been instantly and automatically rejected. She yearned for something grand in her life, something that might shake her up, even if it left her frustrated and tormented.

She felt a terrible temptation to dare.

43

Dora had intended to sleep late, but when the phone jangled her awake she glanced at the bedside clock and saw it was only 8:00 A.M.

"H'lo?" she said drowsily.

"Good morning, lady. Gregor Pinchik here. Listen, something came up I think you should know about. Can you come down here right away?"

She groaned. "In this weather?"

"What weather?" he said. "The sky is blue, the sun is shining, and all the avenues have been scraped."

"You can't come here, Greg?" she asked hopefully.

"Nope. There's something on the screen you've got to see."

"All right," she said. "Give me an hour."

She brushed her teeth, combed the snarls out of her hair, and pulled on sweater and tweed skirt. Shouldering her big bag, she rushed out. Remembering the parking problem on her previous visit to SoHo, she decided to leave the Escort wherever it was and take a cab downtown.

Pinchik had been right: It was a brilliant morning, crystal clear, and what snow remained was rapidly turning to slush as the sun warmed. Traffic was mercifully light, and she was seated in Pinchik's loft a little after nine o'clock. Greg provided coffee and buttered bagels, for which Dora was grateful.

"You eat and I'll talk," he said. "I got some interesting stuff. There are no secrets anymore. Privacy is obsolete—did you know that? Anyway, first of all, that lowlife you told me about, Sidney Loftus: He was involved in a lot of shady deals and used a half-dozen phony names."

"I know," Dora said. "The Company has him on Red Alert because he was running an insurance swindle. What I wanted to know was whether Loftus knew Turner and Helene Pierce in Kansas City."

"Sure he did," Pinchik said. "As a matter of fact, he steered a few clients to Pierce for his computer consulting service—for a commission, of course. One of the clients he landed for Pierce was a guy who owned a string of bars, fast-food joints, and hot-pillow motels. Now get this! It later turned out this same guy was dealing dope. After he was indicted, the KC papers called him a kingpin in the Midwest drug trade. That's the kind of riffraff Loftus and the Pierces were associating with. Nice people, huh, lady?"

"Not exactly pillars of society," she agreed. "Did you get any reports that Loftus and the Pierces were using drugs themselves?"

He shook his head. "I got nothing on that, but the stuff was easily available to them if they wanted it. Now about Helene Pierce and her history before she showed up as a hooker. She came from a little farm town in Kansas and moved to the big city after high school, hoping to become a rich and famous movie star. She had the looks, I guess, but not the talent. She did some modeling for catalogues and such, and then she drifted into the party circuit, and before long she had her own plush apartment and was on call."

Dora sighed. "Hardly a unique story."

Pinchik stared at her. "I saved the best for last. Her real name is Helene Thomson."

Dora returned his stare. "I don't understand, Greg. Her brother's name is Turner Pierce. Different fathers? Adopted? Or what?"

"Lady," he said softly, "they're not brother and sister. They're husband and wife. Turner Pierce married Helene Thomson. They're still married, as far as I know."

Dora took a deep breath. "You're absolutely sure about this, Greg?"

"I told you I know a KC hacker who's cracked city hall. Take a look at this."

He switched on one of his computers, worked the keyboard, and brought up a document on the display panel. He gestured and Dora leaned forward to look. It was a reproduction of a marriage license issued four years previously to Helene Thomson and Turner Pierce.

Dora reached out to pat the computer. "Deus ex machina," she said.

"Nah," said Pinchik, "it's an Apple."

She cabbed home, thoughts awhirl, wondering where her primary duty lay. Warn Felicia? Inform Olivia? Tell Clayton? Or keep her mouth shut and let those loopy people solve their own problems or strangle on their craziness. One person, she decided, who *had* to know was Detective John Wenden. If he and Terry Ortiz were going to brace Turner Pierce, knowing of his "secret" marriage to Helene might be of use.

Her taxi was heading north on Park Avenue, had crossed 34th Street, when it suddenly slowed. Dora craned to look ahead and saw a tangle of parked police cars, fire engines, and ambulances spilling out of a side street. A uniformed officer was directing single-lane traffic around the jam of official vehicles.

"Something happened," her cabbie said. "Cop cars *and* fire engines. Maybe it was a bombing. We haven't had one of those for a couple of days."

"That's nice," Dora said.

The moment she was back in her hotel suite she phoned Wenden. He wasn't in, so she left a message asking him to call her as soon as possible; it was *extremely* important.

Then, faced with the task of entering Gregor Pinchik's revelations in her notebook, she said aloud, "The hell with it," kicked off her shoes and got into bed, fully clothed, for a pre-noon nap. She had never done that before, and it was a treat.

But a short one. For the second time that day she was awakened from a sweet sleep by the shrilling phone.

"John," Wenden said. "What's *extremely* important?"

"I've got to tell—" she started.

"Wait a minute," he interrupted. "There's something I've got to tell *you*. I'm calling from a drugstore on Lex. I've just come from Turner Pierce's apartment in Murray Hill. He's dead as the proverbial doornail. Stabbed many, many times—and I do mean *many*. There goes my cozy little chat. I told you if we waited long enough everyone in this case would get whacked out."

"In Murray Hill?" Dora said. "I went by in a cab. There were fire engines."

"Yeah," he said, "that's how Pierce was found. Felicia Starrett iced him last night and then, this morning, set the place on fire. Neighbors smelled smoke and called in the alarm."

"Is Felicia alive?"

"If you can call it that. She was naked and looked like last week's corpse. And so zonked out on drugs that she couldn't do anything but dribble."

"Are you sure she killed him?"

"Red! She was still gripping the knife, so hard that we had to pry her fingers loose. They took her to Bellevue. Maybe when she gets detoxed she'll be able to tell us what happened. Listen, I've got to run."

"Wait!" Dora cried. "I didn't tell you what I called about. Turner and Helene Pierce weren't brother and sister; they were married."

"What?" he yelled. "Are you positive?"

"Absolutely. I saw a copy of their marriage license. John, do me a favor. Even if it looks certain that Felicia stabbed Turner, check out Helene's whereabouts last night. Okay?"

"Yeah," he said tensely, "I better do that. Thanks for the tip, Red. I'll get back to you later today."

"When?" she demanded.

"Look, I've got a million things to do. I don't know when I'll get a break."

"Sooner or later you've got to eat," she argued, "or you'll end up in

Bellevue with Felicia. John, I'll stay in all day. You call me when you have time, stop over, and we'll grab a bite in the cocktail lounge downstairs. It'll give us a chance to compare notes.''

"That makes sense," he said. "You'll hear from me."

Dora spent the afternoon scribbling in her notebook, happy that she wouldn't be making many more notes. The tangled skein was unraveling, and what she didn't know, she could guess. She even dragged out that nonsensical diagram she had drawn with the names of all the involved characters in boxes connected by straight or squiggly lines. But now the connections seemed clear to her, and infinitely sad. She wondered if all humans are born with an innate capacity to screw up their lives.

John called a little after five o'clock, said he was going to shove his job for an hour, and didn't care if the entire island of Manhattan slid into the Upper Bay while he was off duty. Dora brushed her hair and went down to the cocktail lounge. She took the table which she and Felicia Starrett had occupied during their first meeting.

But when Wenden entered, he went directly to the bar and asked for a shot of rye. He tossed it down, then ordered a bottle of beer and brought it over to Dora's table.

"You'd think I'd be used to seeing clunks, wouldn't you?" he said angrily. "I'm not. But at least I don't upchuck anymore. My God, Red, I can't tell you how bad it was. Not only the remains but also that madwoman. And the apartment—a shithouse!"

"John, you're wired," Dora said, putting a hand on his arm. "Sip your beer and try to settle down. I'll order club sandwiches. All right?"

"Whatever."

He seemed to be operating on pure adrenaline, and she wondered if he might collapse when the rush faded.

"You were right," he said, speaking rapidly and gulping his beer. "I checked with the concierge at Helene's apartment house. She left the place last night about eight o'clock and didn't return until two in the morning. The guy said she was soaked through and looked like she had been walking in the storm. I don't know what that means—do you?"

"That she was at Turner's apartment last night. Will you dust the knife handle for prints?"

"What good will that do? I told you we had to twist it out of Felicia's hand. If there were other prints on it, they'd be smeared to nothing."

"Then check cups and glasses," Dora urged. "I'm sure you'll find Helene's prints."

"So what? She'll claim they were made weeks ago during a visit."

"Then vacuum the place," Dora said desperately. "You may find some long hairs—just like the ones you found in the room where Sidney Loftus was killed."

Wenden glared at her. "Are you trying to tell me that Helene knifed Turner Pierce?"

"No," Dora said, "I don't believe that. But I do think she went there last night."

"What for?"

"To tell Felicia that she was the wife of the man Felicia hoped to marry. She knew what condition that poor woman was in and figured to push her over the edge. Helene may not have actually stabbed Turner, but she guided the knife. She wanted her husband dead."

John took a deep breath, blew it out, and slumped in his chair, suddenly slack and relaxed. "You may be right," he said quietly, "but it's not illegal for a wife to tell another woman that her lover is already hitched."

Then they were silent while their fat club sandwiches were served. John stared at his.

"I'm not sure I can handle that," he said. "My stomach is still churning."

"Try," Dora pleaded. "You need it. You look like death warmed over."

He took a small bite, chewed determinedly, and swallowed. He waited a moment, then smiled and nodded.

"I'm going to be okay," he said. "Tastes good. About those hairs found in the back room of the Church of the Holy Oneness—you're probably right about Helene being there on the murder night. I took the photographs over to that waiter at the Twenty-eighth Street restaurant, and he definitely identified Helene as being the woman Loftus was with the night he was blanked. But that's all circumstantial, Red. A waiter's ID and a couple of hairs—we'd never get a conviction out of that."

"You mean," Dora demanded hotly, "she's going to go free?"

Wenden nodded. "Unless we can come up with something more than we've got. Besides, I'm not so sure Helene did it. I still think the Lewis Starrett, Sol Guthrie, and Sid Loftus homicides were all related and connected somehow to the laundering of drug money."

Dora ignored her sandwich. "Detective Wenden," she said as calmly as she could, "you're full of you-know-what."

"All right," he said equably, "you tell me what you think went down."

"There were four homicides," Dora began. "Four deaths. Four different killers. And four different motives.

"One: Lewis Starrett was murdered by Sidney Loftus, then using the name of Father Brian Callaway. His motive? Eleanor Starrett told me in our first meeting. I put it in my report but didn't see the significance until my boss in Hartford caught it. Lewis had ordered his wife not to give another penny to Callaway's phony church, and Olivia was the good Father's heaviest contributor. No way was that swindler going to lose his richest sucker. So he offed Lewis with the chef's knife taken from the Starrett apartment on the night of the cocktail party. He knew Lewis's death would leave Olivia an even wealthier woman.

"Two: The murder of Solomon Guthrie. You're right about that one;

Sol sensed something was fishy about Starrett's gold trading, probably made a fuss about it to Clayton, and took his suspicions to Arthur Rushkin, the attorney. When Clayton, Turner Pierce, and Ramon Schnabl heard about that, they got rid of the threat to their operation by getting rid of Guthrie. I imagine Schnabl provided the hit men; it had all the marks of a professional contract kill.

"Three: Sidney Loftus. This is the iffiest one of the lot, and I admit my ideas are mostly guesswork. Sid Loftus and the Pierces were buddy-buddy in Kansas City, and he had to know they were married. But in New York he had his church scam going and they were clipping the Starretts, so all the sharks were making a nice buck and no one rocked the boat. But then Clayton announced he was going to get a divorce and marry Helene. Loftus saw the chance for a profitable shakedown and put the bite on the Pierces. They weren't about to sit still for blackmail and decided to eliminate their old pal Sidney. Helene made a date with him, maybe promising sex, and put him down in the back room of his fake tabernacle.

"Four: the stabbing of Turner Pierce. I've already told you how I think that went. Turner was going nuts trying to keep Felicia under control with drugs—probably supplied by Ramon Schnabl—and Helene figured who needs Turner? With her hubby out of the picture she really could marry Clayton Starrett with all the goodies that promised. So she egged on Felicia to do the dirty work for her. I think that's the way it happened. One of the reasons I'm sure Helene did it is that I just don't like the woman."

Dora finished, sat back, and waited for Wenden's critique.

"Are you going to eat your sandwich?" he asked.

"Half of it," she said. "You want the other half?"

He nodded, and she lifted it carefully to his plate. They both began chomping.

"I like your ideas," John said. "Everything you say makes sense. If you're right, the Lewis Starrett file is closed because the killer, Sid Loftus, is dead. As for nailing the guys who aced Guthrie, I don't think there's much chance of that unless someone rats on Schnabl, which I don't see happening. And as for Loftus's murder, I'm just as convinced as you are that Helene is the perp, but right now there's not enough evidence to charge her, let alone indict and convict. And maybe she did trigger the stabbing of Turner by Felicia but, as I told you, what she did might have been wicked and immoral but it wasn't illegal. Felicia will get treatment for her drug addiction, and I doubt if she'll do time for an act committed when she was, as her lawyer will claim, temporarily insane while under the influence of dope supplied by the man she killed after learning he had betrayed her. So, as far as I can see, there were four brutal killings, and no one is going to spend a day in jail for any one of them."

"What happened to justice?" Dora cried.

"The law is one thing," Wenden said with a strained smile, "and justice is another. Unless you believe in divine retribution. And if you do, there's a bridge in Brooklyn you may be interested in buying."

"I hate it!" Dora burst out. "Just hate it!"

"The guilty not being punished?" John said. "I have to live with it. Every day."

They had finished their sandwiches and now sat back, gripping empty beer glasses, looking at each other.

"I suppose this just about winds it up for you," John said.

Dora nodded. "I have things to do tomorrow. Then I'll probably take off early Friday morning."

"Back to Hartford?"

"Uh-huh. I think I'll drive home. I can turn in the Escort up there."

"Can we have dinner tomorrow night?"

"Sure," she said. "I'd like that."

"When I called you from Lexington Avenue this afternoon I spotted an Italian restaurant. There was a menu in the window, and it looked okay. The place is called Vito's. Want to try it?"

"I'm game for anything," Dora said.

"I hope so," Wenden said.

44

Attorney Arthur Rushkin came from his inner office to greet her with a beamy smile, looking spiffy in houndstooth jacket and suede waistcoat, a butterfly bow tie flaring under his suety chin.

"Mrs. Conti!" he boomed, shaking her hand. "How nice to see you again. I was hoping you'd stop by."

"I'm leaving tomorrow morning," she told him, "and felt I owed you a report."

He took her anorak and hung it away. Then he ushered her into his private office and got her settled in the armchair alongside his antique partners' desk. He lowered his bulk into the leather swivel chair.

"Mr. Rushkin," Dora said, "I assume you're aware of what's been going on the last few days."

He nodded. "Sadly, I am. Starrett Fine Jewelry and all its branches have been closed. Temporarily, I hope. After that dreadful business in Murray Hill—aren't the tabloids having a field day?—Felicia is receiving medical treatment. The last I heard is that she will survive, but recovery will be a long and arduous process. And expensive, I might add."

"And Clayton?"

The attorney twisted his face into a wry grimace. "My godson? He has not yet been charged, but it's only a matter of time. At the moment he is being questioned by representatives of the U.S. Attorney's office. I can't represent Clayton—there would be a potential conflict of interest there— but I've been able to obtain for him the services of an extremely capable criminal defense attorney. On his advice, Clayton is answering all questions completely and honestly. He can't do much less; the authorities have already seized Starrett's business records, including those dealing with the fraudulent gold trading."

"Do you think Clayton will go to prison, Mr. Rushkin?"

The lawyer linked fingers across his thick midsection and sighed deeply. "I'm afraid so. But if he continues to cooperate, his punishment may be more lenient than you might think. The authorities are not interested in Clayton Starrett so much as they are in Ramon Schnabl, the drug dealer. If Clay helps them put Schnabl behind bars, I think they'll be inclined to settle for a light sentence and a heavy fine. I do believe a deal will be made."

"I intend to see Mrs. Olivia Starrett before I leave. How is she taking all this? Have you spoken to her?"

"I have indeed, and the woman's resilience is amazing. She'll be all right. Mrs. Conti, I have a fairly complete understanding of how the gold trading was jiggered, but I have less knowledge of the homicides it spawned. Can you enlighten me?"

Dora repeated the explanation of the four killings she had given Wenden. The lawyer listened intently, and when she finished he sighed again and shook his great head so sharply that his jowls wobbled.

"Of course a lot of that is supposition," Dora pointed out. "Some of it can never be proved."

"But I suspect you're right," Rushkin said. "It's a depressing example of chronic greed. That's the disease; violence is a symptom."

"What makes me furious," Dora said, "is that Detective John Wenden doesn't think there's much chance of Helene Pierce going to jail for what she did."

"Policemen have a tendency to be gloomy," the attorney said with a wintry smile. "Quite understandable." Then he leaned across the desk toward Dora. "Let me tell you something, Mrs. Conti. The law is like the Lord: It giveth and it taketh away. In re Helene Pierce, I think it quite likely that the prosecutors may feel she had guilty knowledge. In other words, she was fully cognizant of the gold trading fraud—indeed she profited from it—but did not inform the proper authorities as required. I believe Clayton will testify as to her involvement."

"Are you sure?" Dora asked anxiously.

Rushkin laughed. "Congreve wrote of the fury of a woman scorned. I assure you, Mrs. Conti, a scorned woman's virulence can be matched by the bitterness of a middle-aged man who realizes he has been played for a fool, a patsy, by a piece of fluff half his age. Oh yes, I think Clayton will be more than willing to testify against Helene Pierce. And if the guilty-knowledge ploy doesn't hold up in court, the government has another arrow in its quiver. I'm sure the IRS will be interested in learning if Helene declared all those gifts of money and diamonds that Clayton gave her. In addition, the idiot bought her co-op and was paying the maintenance by check. That left a paper trail the IRS will be happy to follow. No, I don't believe Helene Pierce will cha-cha her way to freedom."

"That makes me feel better," Dora said. She rose and slung her shoulder bag. "I hope you no longer feel guilty about Solomon Guthrie. You gave me his computer printout, and eventually that led to the solution."

The attorney was suddenly somber, his meaty features sagging. "I am not entirely free from regret, but at my age I can't expect to be. Mrs. Conti, thank you for all your efforts on my behalf and on behalf of Starrett Fine Jewelry. I intend to write to your employer expressing my deep appreciation of your excellent work as strongly as I can."

Dora smiled shyly. "You don't have to do that, Mr. Rushkin."

"I know I don't *have* to," he said, "but I *want* to. If you ever tire of your job and decide to relocate to New York, please let me know. I can promise you that your investigative talents will be well rewarded here."

"Thank you, sir," she said. "I'll keep it in mind."

Out on Fifth Avenue, in a frigid drizzle, she wondered why she was grinning and walking with a bouncy step. Then she realized it was because her professional performance had been praised and she had been offered a job. That did wonders for the old ego and supplied confidence for the meeting with Mike Trevalyan in Hartford the following day. That tête-à-tête, she knew, would be a brannigan.

Just for the hell of it, she walked over to Park Avenue. As Rushkin had said, the flagship store of Starrett Fine Jewelry was shuttered. The display windows were stripped of gems, and a sign proclaimed: CLOSED UNTIL FURTHER NOTICE. But Dora was amused to note it didn't deter a mink-swathed matron who was shading her eyes to peer within and furiously rattling the knob of the locked door.

She bused up Madison Avenue, then walked over to the Starrett apartment on Fifth. Charles, looking as funereal as ever, let her enter and left her standing in the foyer while he shuffled away to announce her arrival.

Mrs. Olivia Starrett was sharing the chubby love seat with a diminutive man swaddled in a voluminous white djellaba. He popped to his feet when Dora entered, his robe swung briefly open, and she caught a quick glimpse of skinny shins half-covered with black socks suspended from old-fashioned garters.

"Dora!" Olivia said. "I'm *so* happy to see you, dear. I want you to meet the Maharishi Ziggy Gupta, a very wise man who is teaching me the spiritual truths of the Sacred Harmony."

The little man grinned and bobbed his head at Dora. She nodded in return.

"Pliz," he said, "forgive my language, but I am mostly happy to be making your—your—" He turned to Olivia for help.

"Acquaintance," she suggested.

"Yiss," the Maharishi said. "Your acquaintance."

Dora smiled and nodded again. "Mrs. Starrett," she said, "I just wanted to stop by to offer my sympathy. I know the events of the past few days must be a terrible burden. Is there anything I can do to help?"

"How sweet of you," Olivia said. "But with Ziggy's instruction I am learning to endure. Think of life as a great symphony, and all of us are but individual notes. To know the Sacred Harmony we must contribute our personal sorrows and joys so that the holy music rises to heaven and is pleasing to God."

"Iss so," the guru said, grinning. "For He is the Great Conductor who leads us with His stick."

"Baton," Olivia said. "I can't tell you what a comfort the Maharishi has been to me. He has come from Bombay to bring America his inspiring message of hope and redemption. We were just discussing how we might set up a school in New York, The Academy of the Sacred Harmony, so more pilgrims may achieve spiritual tranquillity by learning how each of us can add to the symphonic universe."

"Yes," Dora said, dazed. "Well, I must be going. I'm happy to see you in good spirits, Mrs. Starrett."

"I am contributing my note," Olivia said with a beatific smile. "To the chords that shall become part of the exalted rhapsody. Did I say that right, Ziggy?"

"Eggsactly," he said, grinning.

Dora fled, found her parka in the foyer closet, and left that apartment. She refused to laugh at Olivia's hopeless hope. That long-suffering woman was entitled to any solace she could find.

When she exited from the elevator, she saw Eleanor Starrett come striding across the lobby, gripping a furled umbrella as if she'd like to wring its neck. She spotted Dora, rushed up, squeezed her arm tightly.

"Did you just see Olivia?" she demanded.

Dora nodded.

"Is she up and about?"

"She's doing fine."

"Thank God!" Eleanor cried. "She's got to give me some money. Did you hear about Clayton?"

"Yes, I heard."

"They can fry that moron in the electric chair for all I care," Eleanor said angrily, "but what about *me?* My lawyer says the government will claim there was a pattern of racketeering, and if he's convicted Clay will be subject to RICO penalties. Do you know what that means? I'll tell you what it means—that they can take everything he's got: money, cars, real estate, jewelry, the fillings in his teeth. So where does that leave *me?* What kind of a settlement am I going to get if the government strips that imbecile down to his Jockey shorts? You know what it makes me? A bag lady rooting in garbage cans for my *déjeuner.*"

Dora stared at her in astonishment, then noted the Starrett pearl choker at her throat, the Starrett gold brooch on her lapel, the Starrett tennis bracelet of two-carat diamonds, the several Starrett rings of emeralds, sapphires, rubies.

"Boohoo," Dora said mockingly, turned, and walked away.

45

She took special pains with her grooming that evening, brushing her hair until it gleamed, snugging on her "good" dress, adding the bracelet Mario had given her for Christmas. Finally she dabbed on a wee drop of Obsession—and wondered why she was tarting herself up. She hadn't been so nervous since her first prom, and breaking a fingernail did nothing to calm her down.

Wenden had wanted to pick her up at the hotel, but not knowing how their dinner-date might end, Dora thought it wiser to have her own transportation. So she drove over to Vito's in the Escort—and then had to park two blocks away and walk back.

John was already there, seated at a small bar just inside the door. He, too, had obviously made efforts to spruce up. His suit was pressed, shoes shined, shirt fresh, tie unstained, and he even had a clean white handkerchief tucked into his breast pocket. Dora thought he looked quite handsome.

They had extra-dry martinis at the bar, then carried refills to the back of the dining room. The detective was on his best behavior, anxious that she was satisfied with their table, holding the chair for her, asking if the room was too cold. Too hot? Too bright? Too noisy?

"John," she said, smiling, "it's just fine. I like it, I really do."

The waiter brought menus, and with no hesitation they both ordered broiled veal chops, pasta with *salsa piccante,* and a salad of arugula and endive. The wine list was left at Wenden's elbow, but Dora said she'd settle for a glass.

"Or two," she said. "I've got to get up early, and I have a long drive ahead of me. John, what's happening with Clayton Starrett?"

"Singing like a birdie," he said. "Ortiz thinks we're really going to nail Ramon Schnabl this time. He's already been charged, but he's out on bond. The judge made him turn in his passport, but Terry is keeping an eye on him just in case.''

"What about Helene Pierce?''

"She came in voluntarily for questioning and wouldn't even admit she was at Turner's apartment the night he was offed. I'd love to get a few of her hairs to see if they match up with the ones we found at the Loftus scene, but I don't know how to do it.''

"Does she have a cleaning woman?''

Wenden looked at her. "I don't know. Why?''

"Maybe a cleaning woman could get you a few hairs from Helene's brush.''

He laughed. "Your brain never stops clicking, does it, Red. Well, it's worth a try. Ah, here's our salad. Wine now?''

"A glass of white with the salad,'' Dora said, "and a glass of red with the veal. And that's it. Definitely.''

They started on their salads, along with chunks of hot garlic toast from a napkined basket. They were both hungry and didn't talk much while they were eating. John did say, "You look very attractive tonight,'' and Dora said, "Thank you. So do you,'' and they both laughed and reached for more garlic toast.

The veal chops were just the way they wanted them: charred black on the outside; white, moist, and tender inside.

The pasta sauce was a little more *piccante* than they had expected, but the red wine arrived in time to cool their palates. Dora attacked her food with fierce determination, and Wenden was anything but picky. They finished and sat back, staring with bemusement at the denuded chop bones.

"Think we could get in the *Guinness Book of World Records*?'' John asked. "Fastest time for demolishing double veal chops.''

"A scrumptious meal,'' Dora said.

"Dessert?''

"No, no, and no!'' she said. "It's diet time again.''

Wenden said nothing. She was conscious that he was staring at her, but she would not, could not raise her eyes to his. But she was aware that the lightheartedness of the evening was waning.

John consulted the wine list, then summoned their waiter.

"A bottle of Mumm's Cordon Rouge, please,'' he said. "As cold as you can make it.''

Then Dora looked at him. "Hey,'' she said, "why the celebration?''

"Not a celebration,'' Wenden said. "A wake. The answer is no, isn't it, Red?''

She nodded. "You're a good detective.''

"It's a downer,'' he said. "I imagined you had a thing for me.''

She reached out to cover his hand with hers. "I love you, John,'' she said quietly. "I truly do. But I also love my husband.''

"I'm not sure," he said, trying to smile, "but that may be illegal."

His reply, even in jest, angered her. "Can't I love two men at the same time? Why not? Men can love two or more women at the same time, and frequently do. What am I—a second-class citizen?"

He held up his palms in surrender. But then the waiter brought their chilled champagne and glasses. They were silent while he went through the ceremony of uncorking the bottle. He poured a bit into John's glass and waited expectantly. But John handed it to Dora.

"You first," he said.

She sampled it. "Just right," she proclaimed.

The waiter filled their flutes, left the bottle in a bucket of ice, and departed. They raised their glasses to each other in a silent toast.

Dora said slowly, "I wish I could explain to you the way I feel in a clear, logical way, but I can't. Because this is something that's got nothing to do with logic. It's a mishmash of emotions and fears and upbringing and education and God knows what else."

"But the bottom line is no," he said.

"That's right," Dora said decisively. "I'm not going to bed with you. But you've got to believe me; I do love you."

They both smiled sadly.

"Look at us," Dora said. "Me, an overweight housewife. You, a burned-out cop. I wish I could understand it, but I can't."

"It happens," John said. "Do you have to understand it? Can't you just accept it?"

"I do accept it," she said. "The love part. Not the infidelity. It's not so much wanting to be faithful to Mario, it's wanting to be faithful to myself. Does that make sense?"

"No," he said, and filled their glasses again.

"Listen," Dora said, almost desperately, "let me take a stab at it. I'm a Catholic. I went to a parochial school. My husband is a Catholic. But neither of us has been to confession for I don't remember how long. Our Catholic friends don't go either. So I don't *think* fear of sin has anything to do with it. But maybe, deep down inside me, it does because of the way I was raised, and I'm just not conscious of it."

"All right," Wenden said, "assuming it's not fear of sin, then what *is* it?"

"It's a lot of things," she said, "and I'm sure you'll laugh at all of them. Look at the people we've been involved with: the Starrett crew and their pals. All of them cheating like mad. You've got to admit they're a scurvy lot; they give adultery a bad name. They make it so *vulgar*. Someone once said morality is a luxury few can afford. Well, *I* can afford it, even if it costs me.

"That's one thing. Another is that it scares me. It really does. I said I love you, and that's the truth. But what if we get it off together, and I like it. Then we drift apart, for whatever reason, and I say to myself, 'Hey, that wasn't so bad. As a matter of fact, it was *fun*. I think I'll find myself another lover.' Then I'm on my way to bimbo-land. It could happen, John.''

''What you're saying is that you don't trust yourself.''

''You're exactly right; I don't trust myself. I don't dare take the chance. If that makes me a coward, then I'm a coward.''

''Or smart,'' he said with a twisty grin. ''Well, Red, I guess you've been doing a lot of heavy thinking about this, and that's kind of a compliment to me. But did you also think about how you might feel tomorrow, next week, next year, ten years from now? No regrets?''

She leaned across the table to stroke his cheek. ''You shaved for me,'' she said. ''How nice! Let me tell you something, John. It's like you're driving along a highway. You know where you're going. Then you see a side road leading away. It looks great. All leafy. Beautiful. You're tempted to turn off and explore it. Find out where it goes. But you don't. And maybe you think of that side road a lot in the years to come. Regret is too strong a word, but the curiosity is there. You may never stop wondering where that road led.''

He reached for the champagne bottle and poured what was left into their glasses.

''That's what will happen to me,'' Dora said. ''What will happen to you?''

''Nothing,'' he said. ''Which is what usually happens to me. Oh, I'll survive. I've been unhappy before, and I'll be unhappy again. You've been unhappy, haven't you?''

''Yeah,'' Dora said. ''Like right now. Listen, John, why don't you come up to Hartford and visit with us for a weekend—or as long as you like. We've got an extra bedroom.''

He stared at her. ''I don't think that would be so smart, Red—do you?''

''No,'' Dora said miserably, ''I don't.''

John lifted the champagne bottle and tried to pour. It was empty, and he shoved it, neck down, into the melted ice.

''The bubbles are gone,'' he said.

46

She returned to Hartford the following morning and went directly to the office. She composed her final report on her word processor. Then Dora filled out the forms all claims adjusters were required to submit. She dumped all her papers on the desk of Mike Trevalyan's secretary and went back to her cubicle. She put her feet up on her desk, drank a diet cola, and smoked too many cigarettes.

The summons didn't come until late in the afternoon, and when she walked into Trevalyan's cluttered office, she knew the shit was going to hit the fan; he had two cigars going at once.

"You're approving the claim?" he shouted at her. "You're actually *approving* it?"

"Of course," she said calmly. "None of the beneficiaries had a thing to do with the murder of Lewis Starrett. You want to fight it? You want a lawsuit? Be my guest."

"And look at this!" he howled, waving a fistful of her expense account vouchers. "What the hell were you doing—buying food and booze for every cop in New York?"

"If you read my report," Dora said, "you know what I was doing: helping to break up a fraud for laundering drug money and helping to solve four homicides. Aren't you happy to see a little justice done?"

"Screw justice!" Mike said wrathfully. "All I know is that this is going to cost the Company three million smackers. And what do you think the Accounting Department is going to say when I submit those humongous bills from your so-called computer expert, that Gregor Pinchik. They'll have my balls for hiring that guy."

"Oh Mike, don't be so cheap. Gregor provided the key to the whole case. Look, you want to come out of this smelling like a rose?"

He looked at her suspiciously. "What the hell are you talking about?"

"Pinchik didn't bill for his long-distance calls or modem time because he used our telephone access codes. They were on an electronic bulletin board he subscribes to. But he admitted he's been into our computers and rummaged around. If he can do it, then any smart hacker can do it. Persuade the Company to hire Pinchik as a consultant, to upgrade our computer security with state-of-the-art safeguards. If we don't do it, it's just a matter of time before we start paying out claims to some larcenous hacker who's invaded our records."

Trevalyan thought about that a moment. "Yeah," he said finally, "you got a point there, kiddo. Listen, how about us going out for some food and talking about what I should put in my memo to the brass."

"No, thanks," she said. "I want to get home to Mario."

"You just want one of his gourmet dinners," Mike said grumpily.

Dora smiled serenely. "There's a lot to be said for home cooking."

THE EIGHTH COMMANDMENT

◆

1

Men treat me with amusement, women with sympathy. My name is Mary Lou Bateson, but the nickname "Dunk" followed me from Des Moines to New York City. I am almost six-two—in my bare feet. When I wear heels, I loom—or so a man once told me.

"Don't worry about it, Dunk," Daddy advised. "People look up to you."

That will give you an idea of his quirky sense of humor. That, and the fact that he named my three brothers Tom, Dick, and Harry. I suppose that if I'd had two sisters, we'd be Faith, Hope, and Charity.

About that "Dunk" . . . Both my parents were tall, and all my brothers were over six-six before they were fifteen years old. If you think that means basketball, you're right. We had a barrel hoop nailed to the garage as long as I can remember. Having no sisters, and, being too tall to have close girlfriends, I joined my brothers in their daily practice.

We divided into teams of two, Tom and Dick flipping a coin to decide partners. The loser got me. But I worked as hard as they. And after months of striving to master the dunk shot, I succeeded well enough to earn my nickname. Everyone called me Dunk.

My brothers were stars in high school, and I played center on the girls' team. We won all kinds of tournaments, and our home was filled with trophies. Mother kept an album of newspaper clippings about our exploits. The *Register* referred to me as "the lofty, spindly Dunk Bateson." I know they meant it kindly, but it hurt.

The same year that story appeared, I wore a bikini to a pool party and overheard a girl say, "It looks like two Band-Aids on a broomstick." And I endured the usual chaff: "How's the weather up there?" and "Do you get many nosebleeds?" Sometimes people can be cruel without really meaning to be.

I tried to grin my way through all this. Wore my flats and kept telling myself not to slump. But it is difficult being a *very* tall girl. And the fevered attentions of *very* short boys are no help either. I didn't have a date for our high school prom. I went with my brother Harry and his date, a cute, cuddly blonde who came to his belt buckle. Everyone thought they made an adorable couple. If I had shown up with a male midget, we'd have been laughed off the dance floor. It's not fair.

My brothers got athletic scholarships to prestigious universities. I ended up at Chase, a small liberal arts college that had no organized women's athletic activities except field hockey. I had already decided that my competitive dunk shot days were over.

Chase was a four-year vacation from the realities of life. I breezed through the required courses, and in my last two years took a heavy dose of art history and appreciation. I hadn't the slightest idea what I wanted to do with my life. But just to be on the safe side, I learned how to type and operate a personal computer. You never know.

The high point of my career at Chase was losing my virginity. I must have been the only nineteen-year-old virgin in the state of Iowa. It happened in the grass under an old billboard that advertised: "Coca-Cola: The Pause That Refreshes." Daddy would have liked that.

Clutching my sheepskin, printed in Latin that I couldn't understand, I went home to Des Moines and played some lazy driveway basketball with my brothers. Late in August, with a cash graduation gift from my parents, I headed for New York City, determined to seek fame and fortune. Or at least find a man who might sweep me off my big feet. A *tall* man.

This was several years ago, but even then it was hard to find reasonable rental apartments. Now it's impossible. Anyway, I ended up in a closet on West 76th Street. It was before the West Side became Madison Avenue-ized, and there was a small-town flavor about Columbus and Amsterdam that I liked. Also, my apartment was so small that I could furnish it in Salvation Army Traditional for less than $500.

So there I was, living in glittery Manhattan, and too poor to do much else than sightsee, eat tunafish sandwiches, and agonize over the *Times* want ad pages as if they were reprints from *Remembrance of Things Past*.

I had a number of discouraging interviews, none of which led to anything much. For a while I sold men's gloves at Macy's, worked behind the counter at Chock Full o' Nuts, and addressed envelopes for a mail order company that sold a baldness remedy and a wrinkle remover.

My personal life during this period was something less than ecstatic. I met a few men, who seemed to be hungry and lecherous, in that order. We usually settled for tunafish sandwiches. I had no close women friends. I suppose I was lonely, but there was so much in Manhattan, so many things I wanted to see and do, I can't honestly say I was unhappy. I resolutely avoid self-pity.

I had a brief affair (about six weeks) with a man a few years older and a few inches shorter than I. He told me he wasn't married, but he had been out in the sun a lot the previous summer, and his hands were still tan. Except for a pale strip around his ring finger. He always took off his wedding band before he met me. I never told him I knew.

But he was handsome and amusing. I knew it couldn't last—but that was all right. I often wondered why he started up with me in the first place, and then decided it was for the same reason some men climb mountains: because I was *there*.

Also, there are certain men who seek the outré in their personal relationships: very tall women, very short, the very obese, those exceedingly ugly or, for all I know, the crippled and the blind. The whole subject is too depressing to think about.

Anyway, we broke up after six weeks (no tears), he went back to his wife, and I went back to the want ads. I answered a very short one requesting résumés be sent to a box number by anyone interested in becoming a secretary-assistant-salesperson for a numismatist.

As a kid, I had collected Indian head pennies and buffalo nickels in an empty pickle jar; that was the extent of my knowledge about coins. But nothing ventured, nothing gained, so I sent off my résumé with a covering letter. I remembered I answered a half-dozen ads in a similar fashion that weekend, and had no high hopes for any of them.

But two weeks later I received a letter from the numismatist asking me to come in for a personal interview. I was tempted to dash to the library and bone up on the history of coinage, but then decided it would be a waste of time. A few days of cramming would never convince him I was an expert. If he wanted to hire me, he'd have to live with my ignorance.

His name was Enoch Wottle, and he had a small, dusty shop on West 57th Street. It was really a hole-in-the-wall kind of place with one narrow, barred show window. The entrance was kept locked, and when I rang the bell, he peered at me from behind a torn green shade. I held up the letter I had received. He examined it carefully, then opened the door just wide enough for me to slip through.

He stared up at me, smiled, and said, "You're hired."

I worked for Enoch Wottle for almost three years, the two of us alone in that dim, cramped shop filled with locked glass cabinets and a safe in the back room as big and heavy as a bank vault. We started out as Mr. Wottle and Miss Bateson. Within six months we were Enoch and Dunk.

He was the dearest, sweetest man who ever lived. Pushing seventy, with a nimbus of snowy white hair surrounding his skull like a halo. He was terribly afflicted with arthritis, could hardly handle the coin tongs, which was why he had advertised for an assistant after working by himself so many years.

He had been a widower for twenty of those years, and now lived alone in a dinosaur of an apartment house just a block from his store. His only child, a son, was married and lived in Arizona. He was constantly urging the old man to come out and spend his remaining days in a hot, dry climate.

But Enoch resisted. His shop was his life, he told me, and giving it up would be the final surrender to age and mortality.

"Don't you want to see your grandchildren?" I asked him.

"I see them," he said. "Occasionally. I talk to them on the phone. I carry their photographs in my wallet."

I don't think he was a wealthy man, but I'm sure he was well-off. I know he was generous to me. I started out at just a little over minimum wage, but at the end of my three years with Enoch, I was doing very well indeed, had moved into a larger apartment with new furniture, and was buying my clothing and shoes at tall girls' shops. Expensive.

Wottle's was a strange sort of business. No off-the-street trade at all. But he had a faithful clientele, most of whom he served by phone or letter. So noble was his reputation and so trustworthy his judgment, that customers bought valuable coins on Enoch's say-so, without ever seeing their purchases until they arrived by mail or messenger.

He, in his turn, bought from collectors, other commercial numismatists, or at coin auctions all over the world. Most of this by phone, mail, or cable. After a while I started making weekly deposits at the bank for him and saw how profitable Wottle's Coin Shop actually was. He made no effort to minimize his success or hide it from me.

Although he dealt in all kinds of metal and paper money, tokens, and even a few medals, his specialty was ancient Greek coins, and most of his income was derived from buying, selling, and trading those little bits of minted gold, silver, copper, and bronze.

He taught me so much. I learned all about dekadrachms, tetrobols, and trihemitartemorions. (Try humming that last on your old kazoo!) I learned to distinguish electrum from purer forms of gold and silver. I even learned to judge between Extremely Fine and Very Fine, and between Fair and Mediocre. Close distinctions indeed.

Once Enoch tried to explain to me the fascination of those ancient Greek coins. It was a dusky November evening, and we were having a final cup of tea and a biscuit before closing up and going home.

He sat behind his battered desk in a wing chair so worn and burnished that the leather had a mirror gleam. He looked with quiet satisfaction at the glass cabinets containing his coins. The disks twinkled like imprisoned stars. He knew their history, and the men who had minted them, worked for them, fought for them, died for them. A wonderful people who lived short, harsh lives but never lost their capacity for joy or their love of beauty.

Those old bits of metal he loved were at once a link to the past and a promise of the future. In a way he could not define, Enoch Wottle saw his coins as proof of immortality. Not his own, of course, but of the human race. When great thoughts had been forgotten, great wars ignored, great art scorned, and monuments of stone crumbled to dust, money would survive.

That evening I think he infected me with his passion.

It couldn't last. His arthritis became progressively worse. And then came the summons from the landlord. The entire block, including Wottle's Coin Shop, was to be demolished so that a luxury high-rise could be erected. It was time to go. Enoch was not bitter—or claimed not to be.

"Off to Arizona," he said, trying to smile. "I'll close up and sell my stock to Fletcher Brothers on Lexington Avenue; they've been after me for years. The important thing is—what are we going to do with you?"

I kissed his cheek and held him tight.

What he did for me was beyond expectations, even my most fantastical hopes. Three months' salary as severance pay; a gift of his cherished library, including rare and gorgeously illustrated volumes on Greek coinage; all his catalogues of coin auctions of the past several years.

Best of all, he made several impassioned phone calls to old friends, and by the time I put him on the train to Arizona (he refused to fly), he had obtained a promise of a job for me with Grandby & Sons, the old, respected auction house on Madison Avenue. I was to work in the estate and appraisal department as resident numismatist.

And that was where my Great Adventure began.

2

"My name is Felicia Dodat," she said, looking up at me in amazement. "It is spelled D-o-d-a-t, but pronounced Do-day. Please remember that. I will supervise your work at Grandby and Sons."

I nodded brightly. I loathed her on sight. She was everything I could never be: petite, shapely, and dressed with a careless elegance that drove me right up the wall. She was dark, with a bonnet of black hair as soft as feathers, olive skin, brilliant makeup. I could understand why men might drool over her, but I dubbed her a bitch from the start.

"You will be responsible for all coin appraisals," she said sharply, tapping blood-red talons on her glass-topped desk. "Occasionally it may be necessary for you to go out of town to appraise an estate. You understand?"

Again I nodded, beginning to feel like one of those crazy Chinese dolls with a bobbing head.

"Unfortunately, our space is limited, and I cannot assign you your own office. You will have to share with Hobart Juliana, who handles stamps, autographs, and historical documents. I should tell you at once that he is gay. Does that offend you?"

"Not at all."

"Good. Then let's get you settled in so you can go to work at once."

Sweet lady. I tramped after her down a long decorated corridor furnished with raddled settees, end tables with cracked marble tops, and oil paintings of dead fish. She stopped before a solid oak door equipped with a small judas window.

"This will be your office," Felicia Dodat said severely. "Since you and Hobart will be examining valuable consignments at your desks, this door is *always* kept locked. Is that clear?"

My nodding was giving me vertigo.

She rapped briskly. In a moment the judas was opened, an eye peered out at us. The door was unlocked, swung open.

"Hobart," my boss said, smiling winsomely, "this is your new roommate, Miss Mary Lou Bateson. I'm sure the two of you will get on just marvelously. Show her the ropes, will you, dear?"

Then she was gone, I was inside, the door locked again. He turned to me and said, "My name is Felicia Dodat. It is spelled D-o-d-a-t, but pronounced Do-day. Please remember that."

It was such a perfect impersonation in tone and manner that I cracked up. He smiled and held out his hand.

"Hobie," he said.

"Dunk," I said.

"Dunk? As in doughnut in coffee or basketball in hoop?"

"Basketball," I said.

"Ah. Well . . . welcome to the zoo."

He had a little coffee-maker next to his desk, and we each had a cup. Mine paper and his a porcelain mug with DOWN WITH UP printed on the side.

"You better bring in your own mug," he advised. "About the boss, she's a pain in the ass—as you've probably noticed—but she can be dangerous, too, so do try to get along. She handles estates and appraisals, so she's a power to be reckoned with. Got a lot of clout with god."

"God?"

"Stanton Grandby. Who owns the whole caboodle. He and his multitudinous family. He's the great-grandson of Isaac Grandby, who founded the house way back in eighteen hundred and something. You'll meet him eventually, but Felicia Dodat is the one you've got to please. The office gossip is that dear Felicia has something going with Stanton Grandby. We all keep asking, 'Does Felicia do dat?' "

He gestured about our office, which seemed enormous to me after three years in Enoch Wottle's cubby. Hobie pointed out that we'd each have a window, overlooking a splendid airshaft. Each a massive desk, pine worktable, wooden file cabinets, glassed-in bookshelves. All a wee bit decrepit, but serviceable nonetheless.

"What happened to my predecessor?" I asked.

"Fired," Hobie said. He looked at me. "I don't mean to put you down, Dunk, but I fear she was just a bit too attractive. God was showing interest, and Madam Dodat took offense."

"Oh-ho," I said. "Like that, was it?"

"Just like that."

"Well, Felicia has nothing to fear from me."

"She would," he said, "if god had any sense."

"That's the nicest compliment I've had in years," I told him, and we smiled at each other, knowing we'd be friends.

Grandby & Sons dated from 1883—and so did most of the furnishings. We may have been installed in an elegant townhouse on Madison Avenue, just south of 82nd Street, but the place looked like a recently opened time capsule: velvet drapes, Tiffany lamps, Victorian love seats covered with moiré, and ornate clocks, chinoiserie, and mind-boggling objets d'art that had been purchased outright as part of estates and had never been sold.

Another office joke was that everything in Grandby's was for sale except the loo. Not true, of course. But I admit the surroundings were somewhat discombobulating. All that old stuff. It was like working in a very small Antwerp museum.

But I loved Grandby & Sons, and my career went swimmingly. I learned a lot about my new profession, didn't make any horrible mistakes, and was able to contribute my share to the bottom line by bringing to auction a number of coin collections from old customers of Enoch Wottle.

Although nowhere near as large and splendid as Sotheby's or Christie's, Grandby's really was a pleasant place to labor, especially for Hobart Juliana and me in our locked office. We were very *small* specialists, since most of Grandby's sales were paintings, sculpture, drawings, silver, prints, jewelry, antique weapons and armor—things of that sort. Coins and stamps came pretty far down on the list; there was no great pressure on us to show big profits.

So we were pretty much left with our tongs, loupes, magnifying glasses, and high-intensity lamps. A casual observer, admitted to our sanctum, would have thought us a couple of loonies: Hobie studying a scrap of gummed paper, and me examining a tiny chunk of bruised metal. Both of us exchanging muttered comments:

"Look at that watermark!"

"It's been clipped; what a shame."

"Unperforated; that's a blessing."

"Roman copy."

"They *will* use hinges."

"Silver hemidrachm of the Achaean League. Very nice."

Occasionally we would get so excited with a "find" that Hobie would summon me over to his worktable to take a look at an expertly forged signature of Herman Melville, or I'd call him to my side to admire the exquisite minting of a tetradrachm that dated from 420 B.C. and showed an eagle with wings spread, and a crab on the reverse.

I suppose we were a pair of very young antiquarians. All I know is that we shared an enthusiasm for the past, and liked each other. That helped to make our work pleasurable. Sometimes we went out to dinner together—but not often. Hobie's live-in lover was insanely jealous and suspected him of harboring heterosexual tendencies. He didn't.

Hobie was a slight, fair-haired lad with a wispy manner and a droll sense of humor. He dressed beautifully, and gave me some very good advice on clothes I might wear to minimize my beanstalkiness. I reckoned he and I got along so well together because the world considered us both bizarre creatures. For different reasons, of course. We had a kinship of discrimination—but our friendship was real.

I had been at Grandby & Sons for a little more than two years when one morning—late April, rainy and gusty: a portent!—I was summoned by Felicia Dodat. She was wearing a particularly oppressive perfume, flowery and sweet, and her office smelled like a greenhouse.

Following Hobie's advice, I had kept my relationship with dear Felicia on a cool, professional basis. We were warily cordial with each other, and if she was occasionally snappish, I laid that to the pressures of her job. She never joked about my formidable height, but she had a way of looking at me—her eyes starting at my feet, then slowly rising as if she was examining Mt. Everest—that I resented.

"Do you know a man named Archibald Havistock?" she demanded.

"Havistock? No, I'm not familiar with the name."

She gave me one of her dagger glances. "He owns what seems to be a very large, valuable collection of antique coins. Almost five hundred items with an insured value of two million. I'm surprised you've never heard of him."

"Miss Dodat," I said, as patiently as I could, "*no* one knows the names of the world's biggest coin collectors. For security reasons they buy and sell only through agents, attorneys, or professional coin dealers. You never see their names mentioned at auction or anywhere else. Sometimes they're known in the trade by nicknames. 'Midas,' for instance, is a Saudi Arabian sheikh. Nobody knows who he is. A woman called 'The Boston Lady' is reputed to own one of the finest collections of antique Greek coins in the country. 'The Man from Dallas' is another. These people work very hard to keep their names secret. When you possess that much wealth in portable property—a two-million-dollar collection of antique coins could be carried off in a small, brown paper bag—you don't wish to have your name and address publicized."

"Why don't they put their coins in a bank vault?"

I looked at her in astonishment. "Because they want to look at them, touch them, dream over them. Most of these people don't invest in antique coins for profit. They're hooked on the beauty, history, and romance of the mintage."

She made a gesture, waving away everything I had said as of no importance. "Archibald Havistock," she repeated. "He wishes to put his entire coin collection on the block or sell outright. I'm sure he has contacted Christie's and Sotheby's, and probably other houses as well. I have here a copy of his insurance inventory. I want you to go over it very, very carefully and give me an accurate estimate of what you feel Grandby's might earn if the collection was consigned to auction or whether we'd be better off buying outright."

"Miss Dodat, I can't do that without making a physical examination of the coins. Even an insurance inventory can be inaccurate. Values in the coin market change rapidly.''

"Then make arrangements to see them,'' she said crossly. "He lives in Manhattan, so it shouldn't be difficult. Here—it's all yours. I'll expect your report within a week.''

She held a folder of documents out to me. I took it and tried to smile, wondering if I should curtsy. I started out.

"By next Friday!'' she cried after me.

Hobie was down in Virginia, appraising the value of a stamp collection left to his heirs by a recently deceased nonagenarian. Grandby's provided this service to executors for a fee even though we might not be selected to offer the property at auction or be given the opportunity to buy outright.

So I had the office to myself that morning. I poured a mug of black coffee—my mug had I TAKE CANDY FROM STRANGERS printed on the side—and started going over the inventory of Archibald Havistock's coin collection.

In my business, there are collectors and there are accumulators. The former are people of taste and discernment, who have an educated knowledge of the history, provenance, and intrinsic value of what they acquire. Most of all, they buy through love. Accumulators are greedy addicts who buy everything, without regard to rarity and condition, and are only concerned with the bottom line (catalogue value) of their collections. Which often turns out to be woefully inflated when they try to sell.

It was immediately obvious to me, studying the inventory, that Archibald Havistock was a very discriminating collector indeed. His list included some real beauties, but the insurance estimates were dated four years previously and did not allow for inflation or the recent runup in antique coin values.

The gem of the collection, a real museum piece, was a silver dekadrachm dating from about 470 B.C. It was a famous coin, one of great classics of Greek mintage. It was called the "Demaretion" and judged as being in Extremely Fine condition. I consulted my catalogues and discovered the most recent Demaretion in similar condition to come on the market had sold for almost a quarter of a million dollars. The value in the insurance inventory was given as only $150,000. I felt Grandby's could auction this coin for a possible $350,000.

I read the covering letter addressed to Grandby & Sons, picked up the phone, and called Mr. Archibald Havistock.

3

In my eager wanderings about Manhattan I had discovered it to be a borough of neighborhoods, the most disparate side by side: poor and wealthy, ugly and lovely, raucous and sedate. And within those districts, even a single block could have a distinctive character that set it off from its neighbors, a weed in a nosegay of posies or a rose in a clump of nettles.

Archibald Havistock lived in a unique East 79th Street block that had not yet been given a transplant of glass and steel high-rises. The elephantine brick and stone apartment houses, all looking like armories, seemed to have settled into the earth since they were built fifty years ago. They gave the appearance of solid, dull permanence, and one supposed the occupants of those seven-, nine-, and eleven-room suites had taken on the character of their surroundings.

The lobby, paneled in varicose-veined marble, was a small Grand Central Station, with a codger behind the desk as patterned as the marble. I announced my name, he picked up a house phone and announced my arrival to Mr. Havistock, then announced the apartment number to me. It was all as formal as a court investiture.

The man who opened the apartment door didn't look like an Archibald to me; he looked more like a Tony or a Mike. Actually, he turned out to be an Orson. So much for my perspicacity. He introduced himself as Orson Vanwinkle, Mr. Havistock's nephew and secretary. We shook hands. A damp experience.

He was a dark, saturnine fellow with a beaky nose: a perfect Iago with that kind of menacing handsomeness I suppose some women find attractive, but which makes me slightly queasy. Also, his cologne smelled like Juicy Fruit.

I followed him down a muffled corridor, noting a series of etchings on the walls. They all seemed to be of Liverpool at low tide. Not too exciting. But then Vanwinkle ushered me into a chamber that *was* startling: a den-library from another era. Slate-tiled floor almost hidden by a buttery Oriental rug. Walnut paneling. Heavy velvet drapes swagged back with cords as thick as hawsers with tassels. Oil paintings in gilt frames (including two original Hoppers). Crystal and silver on a marble-topped sideboard.

And on deep, built-in oak shelves, a number of glass-topped display cases. The Havistock coin collection.

The man behind the enormous partners' desk rose to greet me with a wintry smile. A blocky figure draped in a gorgeous suit of dove-gray flannel with a hairline red stripe. White silk shirt with a bow tie: polka-dotted blue. His vest had white piping—the first time I had ever seen that. Hair silvered to a sheen, and eyes a cold, cold azure.

"Miss Bateson," he said in diapason tones, holding out a manicured paw, "I am Archibald Havistock. Delighted to make your acquaintance."

I had an instant reaction: I was meeting a personage. Later, I tried to analyze my awe, and decided it was due to his carriage, voice, grooming, and his *presence*. He just gave the impression of being a very important man. In control. Even in less admirable surroundings, I think he still would have conveyed the feeling of power and distinction. He was so *complete*.

And—as if he needed it!—he was beautiful, in the way certain older men sometimes are. A heavy face with crinkly laugh lines. Full mouth. Solid jaw. And, of course, the silvered hair and ice-cube eyes. He could have posed for Chairman of the Board of the Universe. His cufflinks were little enamel reproductions of a Picasso. I'm sure he thought them an amusing whimsy.

We all got ourselves seated. I was across that double-width desk from Mr. Havistock. Orson Vanwinkle sat behind me on a straight-back chair near the door. Almost like a bodyguard or security agent.

I began to explain that before Grandby & Sons could make an estimate of what his collection might bring at auction, or was worth in an outright sale, I had to make a personal inspection and appraisal of the individual coins. He held up a pink palm and favored me with another cheerless smile. Something sad about that smile.

"I understand completely," he said. "As I'm sure you've guessed, I have contacted a few other auction houses, and they all work the same way. Would you like to get started now?"

I had brought along what I called my "doctor's bag"—for out-of-the-office appraisals. It was a little black valise packed with a small high-intensity lamp, loupe, huge magnifying glass, silk gloves, tongs, a few of the latest catalogues, and a kit of chemicals in vials, used to test metal content. I spread all this paraphernalia on my half of the desk facing Mr. Havistock. Orson Vanwinkle rose to his feet and brought the first display case, placing it gently in front of me.

Now I must describe in exact detail how the Havistock Collection was mounted since it led to such important and dramatic consequences.

There were 497 items in the collection, including the Demaretion. They were housed in display cases approximately 24 by 16 inches. Each case was divided into forty-two velvet-lined compartments, one coin to each. And every little topless box bore a small pasted number corresponding to the numbers on the insurance inventory.

If my arithmetic is correct, you will see that the 497 coins could be accommodated in twelve display cases, with seven empty compartments. Explanation of that in a moment . . .

The first display case Orson Vanwinkle placed on the desk before me was completely filled. I spent a moment examining the case, running my fingertips lightly over the oiled teak sides, the solid brass hardware: recessed hinges and lock.

"The case," I said, looking up at Archibald Havistock. "It's splendid!"

"Yes," he said, and his smile had more warmth. "Custom-made for me by Nate Colescui in Greenwich Village. The best man for that kind of work in the city. Orson, will you unlock, please."

Vanwinkle took a ring from his pocket, selected a small, intricately tooled brass key, and unlocked the case in front of me. He raised the glass lid (framed in teak) and made certain the lid support was holding. I went to work, the copy of the inventory at my elbow.

It became quickly apparent that whoever had done the insurance appraisal knew the business: the condition ratings were, in my opinion, almost completely accurate. I disagreed on only 17 of the 497 items, and in 12 of them, the coin deserved a higher rating, and only 5, in my judgment, should have had a lower: from Very Fine to Fine, or from Fine to Fair. But at current values of antique coins, the whole collection was woefully underinsured.

I was there almost three hours, and it was a perfect delight. Only another numismatist could understand how I felt. The beauty of those coins! Miniature sculptures. Profiles of gods and goddesses. Horses and chariots. Birds and fish. Beasts and gargoyles. And so many nameless young men with faces of such joyous hope that I almost wept from the sight of them. All gone.

During those three hours, Havistock or Vanwinkle occasionally left the room. But never both at the same time; one of them was always present during my appraisal. I didn't blame them a bit. With those display cases of treasures unlocked, I preferred to have a witness present to testify that I had not suddenly swallowed an exquisite silver obol.

And finally, the thirteenth case . . .

It was laid before me by Orson Vanwinkle as if it was the pièce de résistance of a cordon bleu chef. If he had popped off a domed cover and shouted, "Voilà!," I wouldn't have been a bit surprised.

There it was, all by its lonesome, the Demaretion centered in its own case.

No mistaking it: a chunky silver dekadrachm, about the size of an American half-dollar. On the obverse, a trotting quadriga with a standing charioteer. Nike flies above, crowning the horses. Below, a lion springs. On the reverse, four dolphins swim about the profile of Artemis, who wears an olive wreath.

I am not going to tell you this is the most beautiful of all ancient Greek coins—in my opinion, it is not—but it is lovely enough, with crisp minting (the horses' legs are especially well done), and, of course, its rarity adds to its allure. That, and the romantic story of how the Demaretion came to exist. But I'll tell you about that later.

I looked up from my examination to find Archibald Havistock examining *me*. Again, that distant smile . . .

"Do you like it?" he asked in his deep rumble.

"It's splendid!" I burst out. "Up to now I've only seen it in photos—but they don't do it justice."

He nodded. "It's perfection. I bought it thirty years ago, paying more than I could afford at the time. But I had to have it."

Thus speaketh the true collector. They'll sell their mothers to possess something you or I might think a bauble or an incomprehensible daub of paint on canvas. But in this case I agreed with the owner; the Demaretion was a treasure.

I left shortly after, promising Mr. Havistock he would have an appraisal from Grandby & Sons within a week, including recommended reserve values. (When the final bid is lower than these floor prices, the items are removed from auction.)

I was conducted down that gloomy corridor to the front door by Orson Vanwinkle, who insisted on shaking my hand in parting, holding it just a wee bit too long in his clammy grasp. I will not say the man was slimy, but I believe he might have laughed at a homeless dog in the rain.

I went back to my office and set to work. I saw at once that attempting to auction 497 individual coins would be too time-consuming—and counterproductive. A better method would be to divide the coins into lots by period: Archaic, Classical, and Hellenistic, and by country of origin: Gaul, Spain, Sicily, Britain, etc. (Those ancient Greeks got around!)

After dividing the bulk of the coins into lots which I thought might attract specialized collectors, I withheld fourteen items to be sold individually. Including the Demaretion, of course. I then started estimating reserve and top values of each lot and the fourteen individual coins. It took me four days.

While I was laboring, Hobart Juliana returned to our lair from Virginia with fascinating tales of life amongst the gentry. We went out to lunch together, and I told him about the Havistock Collection, the biggest appraisal I had ever handled. Hobie was even more excited than I.

"Dunk, that's marvelous!" he enthused. "If you can bring it off, it'll mean mucho dinero for the house and probably a raise for you."

"Not a chance," I said gloomily. "If I can win it, Madam Dodat will take all the credit."

"No way!" he said determinedly, shaking his head. "You happen to be sharing an office with the best little rumormonger at Grandby and Sons. You bring in the Havistock Collection, and I'll make sure everyone in the place, including god, knows that it was due to your talent, intelligence, perseverance, and keen, analytical judgment."

I laughed and gripped his hand. It was good to have someone on my side, rooting for me. In other circumstances we might have . . . Oh, well, why talk about it.

I went in early and stayed late every night. Then went home, thawed and ate a "gourmet" dinner, and went to bed. I wrestled with the sheets, my brain churning, and finally fell asleep dreaming of drachms and trihemiobols, and a standing charioteer leaning forward to goad four elegant horses. What kind of dreams were those for a normal, healthy American female? Feh!

I met my self-imposed deadline, and delivered to Felicia Dodat a handsomely typed appraisal that included estimated reserve and top values on twenty-two lots and fourteen individual coins ($350,000 for the Demaretion). I left it up to Dodat, god, and the accountants to figure out an offer to make to Archibald Havistock if he wanted to sell his collection outright.

"Thanks," Felicia said briefly, tossing my manuscript aside.

"When do you think we might have an answer?" I ventured.

"When we get it," she said shortly, and I had a brief, violent desire to wire-brush her seamed pantyhose. That woman brought out the worst in me.

Nothing happened for almost two weeks. I gloomed around the office, hardly able to answer my correspondence or do appraisals on the little bits and pieces of large estates that came across my desk. Hobie counseled patience, patience, and more patience.

"The one thing you don't want to do," he told me, "is to bug Madam Dodat. Treat it casually. Make her think that appraising a two-million-dollar collection is just routine, and you couldn't care less if Grandby's gets it or not. Play it cool, Dunk."

But I couldn't play it cool; the Havistock coins meant too much to me. Especially that gorgeous Demaretion. I found myself gallivanting madly all over town for distraction, to movies, art galleries, new restaurants. Then coming home to sip a big shot of raspberry-flavored brandy so I could sleep at night.

Finally, into the third week, on a bright, sunshiny May afternoon, crisp and clear, I took Hobie's and my coffee mugs into the ladies' room, hoping to scour them clean of their accumulated crud.

Felicia Dodat was standing before one of the mirrors, preening, touching her raven hair, stroking her eyebrows with a fingertip.

I put the two coffee mugs into a sink and ran hot water into them. Soaked a paper towel and started to scrub them out.

"I understand they call you 'Dunk,' " Felicia said, still staring at herself in the mirror, turning this way and that.

"That's right."

"Dunk," she repeated. "What an odd name."

I didn't say anything.

She raised her skirt to tug up her pantyhose. I would never do that in front of anyone, woman or man. Then she smoothed down her skirt and inspected herself again. I swear she nodded with approval.

"Dunk,"̈ she said again, and laughed.

She started out, then paused at the door.

"Oh, by the way . . . " she said, as if she had suddenly recalled a detail of no importance. "Did I tell you we got the Havistock Collection?"

4

New problems never encountered before: the logistics of moving the Havistock Collection from the owner's apartment on East 79th Street to the basement vault of Grandby & Sons on Madison Avenue. Stanton Grandby had signed the auction contract, but I got the donkeywork.

I met four times with Mr. Havistock, Mr. Vanwinkle, a representative of the insurance company carrying a policy on the collection, and a burly gentleman from the armored truck service that was to make the actual transfer. We finally agreed on a plan and assignment of responsibilities that seemed to please everyone.

The move would be effected in this manner:

Archibald Havistock would seal the thirteen display cases holding his collection with strips of masking tape on all four sides, plus a blob of sealing wax near the lock which he would imprint with a heavy silver signet ring he sometimes wore.

I made a mild objection to this form of sealing, fearing it would mar the surface of those lovely teakwood cases. But Mr. Havistock stated he would have no need for the cases after his collection was sold, and in any event they could easily be refinished.

I would stand by, a witness to the sealing process to insure that each case contained the requisite number of coins. After sealing, each case would be slid into a protective Styrofoam outer container in which, I was told, Nate Colescui, the casemaker, had delivered his handicraft. Each container would be plainly marked with large pasted labels: Mr. Havistock's name and address, ditto for Grandby & Sons, and heavy numerals, 1 to 13.

After I had witnessed the loading of the Styrofoam containers and *their* sealing with masking tape, the men from the armored van service would take over. With armed guards in attendance, they would take the thirteen containers down to ground level via the freight elevator. Once they were loaded into the truck, the driver would sign a receipt. A copy to Mr. Havistock, a copy to the insurance company, a copy to Grandby & Sons.

I would then scurry back to my office—by cab, if I could find one; I was not allowed to ride in the armored truck. I would oversee the unloading of the thirteen containers and their safe storage in our vault. When all thirteen cases were accounted for, I would sign a receipt—copies to everyone—and the Havistock Collection became the responsibility of Grandby & Sons.

It all sounded so simple and logical.

I should mention at this time that during the planning sessions I met two more members of the Havistock family: wife, Mabel, and unmarried daughter, Natalie (called Nettie). In addition, I was told, the Havistocks had a married son and daughter-in-law, Luther and Vanessa Havistock, and a married daughter and son-in-law, Roberta and Ross Minchen.

But when the collection was moved, I was personally acquainted only with Archibald Havistock, nephew Orson Vanwinkle, wife Mabel, and daughter Nettie.

Mabel Havistock was a square, chunky matron with bluish hair and the jaw of a longshoreman. She was the sort of woman, I thought, who probably wore a brown corset with all kinds of straps, laces, buckles, and snaps. She looked somewhat ogreish, but I must admit she was civil enough when we were introduced, though her cold glance immediately pegged me as the costume jewelry type. Her pearls were real.

I liked Natalie, the unmarried daughter, much more. She was the "baby" of the Havistock family, and a wild one. The T-shirt and stone-washed jeans type, with a mop of uncombed dirty-blond curls and an unbra-ed bosom that made me reflect once again that life is unfair.

Nettie and I spoke briefly, but really hit it off, discovering we were both pizza mavens. She asked to stop by Grandby & Sons to learn how the auction of her daddy's coins would be organized. I told her to come along anytime. I wanted to witness Felicia Dodat's reaction when this fast-talking, sandal-clad wildebeest descended on her.

Anyway, the date of the Great Move finally arrived: a rare Tuesday in June that only needed birdcalls on Manhattan streets to make the morning perfect. I took it as a good omen, that the day would end as splendidly as it began.

I alerted our vault manager and was happy to see he had already made space for the Havistock Collection. Then I sauntered over to East 79th Street and was delighted to find the armored truck had already arrived, right on schedule, and was parked in the service alley alongside the apartment house. A bored driver sat slumped behind the wheel.

The antique concierge knew me by now, and gave me a limp wave of a plump palm as I went directly to the elevator bank. I rode up to the 9th floor. In the corridor was parked a four-wheeled dolly from the armored truck. Two uniformed and armed guards were sitting on it, smoking, and looked up as I arrived.

"All set?" I asked brightly.

"We'll never be setter," one of them said. "Let's get this show on the road."

I was admitted to the Havistock apartment by an employee I had never seen before: a stringy, dour-faced lady swaddled in black bombazine with white apron. Maid? Housekeeper? Cook?

"I am Mary Bateson from—" I started.

"They're in the back," she growled, jerking a thumb over her shoulder.

So I walked down that depressing corridor by myself, wondering if I had announced, "Hi! I'm Ma Barker, and I've come to steal the Havistock Collection." Would she have growled, "They're in the back," and shown me where to go? Probably. So much for tight security.

They were awaiting me in that splendid library, both busy sealing the thirteen display cases. Orson Vanwinkle was neatly cutting strips of masking tape, and his uncle was just as neatly applying them to sides and lids. If Archibald Havistock felt any sadness or depression at seeing his collection go on the block, he gave no sign. As I said, he was a very contained man.

I had brought along two inventories, the insurance company's and my own, and I checked carefully to make certain every coin was in its correct compartment in its correct case. As I okayed each case, Vanwinkle applied a thick blob of warmed sealing wax to the front junction of lid and case, and Mr. Havistock pressed his signet ring firmly. Then Vanwinkle slid the sealed display case into its properly labeled Styrofoam box, closed that with masking tape, and the deed was done.

I lingered over case thirteen, staring through the glass at the Demaretion. It twinkled back at me.

"Aren't you going to miss it?" I asked Mr. Havistock.

He shrugged and tried to smile. "As someone said, you spend the first half of your life collecting things, and the second half getting rid of them."

Then the Demaretion was gone, its own display case slid into the Styrofoam container marked thirteen, and sealed. I prepared to depart.

"I'll send in the armored truck guards," I said. "I want to get downstairs to make certain all the cases are brought down safely, and get my receipt."

"I think I'll come along," Orson Vanwinkle said, smiling thinly, "to get *our* receipt."

The two of us waited near the truck in the service alley. In about ten minutes the armed guards appeared, pushing the loaded dolly. The thirteen cases were put into the armored van. The driver ticked them off carefully on his loading list, then signed a receipt for the shipment. One copy to me, one copy to Orson Vanwinkle.

"See you at the auction," I said to him blithely.

"Before that, I hope," he said with a smarmy smile.

Boy, was he ever right!

I was lucky enough to grab a cab almost immediately, buzzed back to the office, and got things organized for the reception of the Havistock Collection. Grandby & Sons employed its own security force, and I recruited the Chief and two stalwarts to stand by for the arrival of the armored truck.

When it pulled up in front of the townhouse, our guards did sentry duty as the Styrofoam containers were unloaded and carried down to the basement vault. I took up station at the opened vault door as they were brought in. Thirteen, tape unbroken. I counted them again. Thirteen, tape intact.

I then signed a receipt for Grandby & Sons and handed it to the driver of the armored truck. He and his two minions disappeared. The Havistock coins were now safely tucked away in our vault, the door thick enough to stop a cruise missile, but so perfectly hinged and balanced that I could move it with one hand.

Hobart Juliana came down, laughing, to bring me a mug of hot black coffee.

"Got 'em?" he said cheerfully.

"Safe and sound," I said. "Am I ever glad that's over. Look at my hands; I'm shaking."

"Calm down, Dunk," he advised. "Your part of the job is finished."

"I guess," I said, just beginning to realize that my connection with the Havistock Collection had ended. Now it was all up to the sales staff and auctioneer.

"Hobie," I said, "I want to show you something that'll knock your eyes out. The Demaretion. A work of art if ever there was one."

I set my coffee mug aside. Slid container thirteen from the stack and pulled back the masking tape. Opened the Styrofoam box and gently withdrew the sealed teakwood case. I cradled it in my arms, held it out to Hobie.

"Just take a look at that," I said.

He glanced down, then raised his eyes slowly to my face. Something happened to his expression. It congealed.

"At what?" he said in a low voice.

I stared at him for a second or two, then looked down at the sealed display case.

It was empty. The Demaretion was gone.

You know the opening words of Dickens' *A Tale of Two Cities*? "It was the best of times, it was the worst of times ... " That last part was written for me: it was the worst of times.

Later, Hobie told me that he was afraid I was going to faint when I saw the Demaretion had disappeared. He moved closer so he could grab me if I began to crumple.

"It wasn't that you turned white," he said. "You turned absolutely *livid*, as if someone had kicked you in the cruller."

Disbelief was my initial reaction. Then bewilderment. Then anger. Then cold guilt when I realized what I had done: signed a receipt for a $350,000 coin that was not in Grandby & Sons' vault. Goodbye to job, career, reputation. I had visions of a lifetime in durance vile. Plenty of days, and nights, to try to solve the puzzle of how the Demaretion had been stolen from a sealed display case within a taped container.

When we sounded the alarm, everyone came running. That was all right; I wanted plenty of witnesses to the fact that the teakwood display case still had all its seals intact, including that blob of wax bearing the imprint of Archibald Havistock's signet ring. Then the question was asked: Was the Demaretion in the case when it was sealed?

I swore it was. People looked at me. I would not weep.

Stanton Grandby, god, was a plump, pouty man who dressed like a penguin. I could tell from his pursed lips and glittering eyes that he was computing what this catastrophe was going to cost the family business.

Grandby & Sons carried heavy insurance, of course, to cover disasters of this nature. But the money loss didn't bother god so much as the damage done to the reputation of the house. Who would be eager to consign coins, stamps, paintings, and sculpture to Grandby's if it was bruited about that valuable antiques disappeared from the premises?

I was set to work examining the other twelve display cases, peering through the glass lids without disturbing the seals. The collection was complete—except for the Demaretion. Then god, in whispered consultation with Felicia Dodat, decided to inform Archibald Havistock of the loss, and the New York Police Department, Grandby's insurance company, Mr. Havistock's insurers, and the armored truck service that had made the transfer.

"And we better phone our attorneys," Stanton Grandby added, glancing at me wrathfully. "This is a mess, and we need legal advice."

The remainder of that day was horrid, a monstrosity I find hard to recall, it was so painful. A detective team from the NYPD was first on the scene, followed by the burly man from the armored truck service, followed by representatives from the two insurance companies involved. Last to arrive was Lemuel Whattsworth, junior partner of the law firm of Phlegg, Sample, Haw, Jugson, and Pinchnik, attorneys for Grandby & Sons.

I must have told my story at least a half-dozen times, relating the exact details of how the coins were inventoried, displayed in the compartments, and how I witnessed the sealing of the display cases, their packing in Styrofoam, and the taping of those boxes. Six times I vowed to high heaven that I had seen the Demaretion sealed in its own case and slid into container thirteen.

Curiously, this repeated recital of what had happened did not anger me or bore me or offend me. In fact, I welcomed going over the facts again and again, hoping I or someone else would spot a fatal flaw in the preparations for the move of the Havistock Collection and cry, "Ah-ha! There's where you went wrong. That's how it was done."

But I didn't see it, and neither did anyone else. It was impossible for the Demaretion to disappear. But it had.

Finally, dusk outside and streetlights on, all my interrogators departed, and I was left to ponder the enormity of what had befallen me. I wanted, more than anything, to call Archibald Havistock, apologize, and commiserate with him on the theft of that prize I knew he cherished. But Lemuel Whattsworth had told me, in no uncertain terms, to have no communication whatsoever with Mr. Havistock or anyone else in his household.

Hobart Juliana—bless him!—refused to desert me during that dreadful day, and comforted me between my question-and-answer sessions with all those investigators. Then the office lights being switched off by departing staffers and night security guards, he said:

"Dunk, have you got a couch in your place?"

"A couch?" I said dispiritedly. "Of course I've got a couch. Why?"

"I don't think you should be alone tonight. Let me come home with you. I'll sleep on the couch."

"Oh, Hobie," I said, "you don't have to do that."

"I know I don't *have* to do it, but I *want* to do it. Please let me."

"All right," I said helplessly.

"Do you have anything to eat in the house?"

"Some frozen dinners."

"That'll do splendidly. Anything to drink?"

"Some wine. Vodka. Raspberry brandy."

"Loverly. Let me make one phone call, and then we'll take off."

It was a long phone call in a low voice I couldn't overhear, but I knew he was explaining to his roommate why he wasn't going to be home that night.

Hobie was so good to me; I don't know how I could have endured that night without him. He prepared the Lean Cuisine, poured the wine, served me, and did the dishes. Later we sat quietly, sipped a little brandy, and without prompting I told my story once again, and we went over it all, step by step.

Hobie shook his head. "I can't see anything you should have done that you did not do. It sounds absolutely foolproof to me."

"But someone copped the Demaretion."

"Yes," he said sorrowfully, "someone did."

"What do you think will happen to me, Hobie? Am I the number one suspect?"

"Maybe not number one," he said cautiously. "But you better be prepared for some nasty digging into your private life. The insurance companies are not going to pay out without a very, very close investigation. And the New York cops will be just as thorough. You're in for a tough time, Dunk.''

"I didn't steal it, Hobie. You know that, don't you?''

"Of course I know it. And you couldn't even if you had wanted to. You never touched that damned coin today, did you?''

"Never. Not once. Just looked at it.''

"Well, there you are. But someone touched it.''

Then I began to weep. Hobie came over to the couch, sat close, put an arm about my shoulders.

"Come on, Dunk,'' he said. "You're a strong lady, I know you are. You'll survive. Those smart cops will find out who did it, and you'll be completely cleared.''

"You really think so?'' I said, snuffling.

"Absolutely.''

He was such a sweet man. A wraith, with his fair hair and pale skin. So slight and frail. But when it came to the bottom line, he was a substantial man, a mensch, sympathetic and understanding and offering support at the moment in my life when I needed it most.

The day had been a trial for both of us, and after a while I brought out sheets, a pillow, blanket, and made up the couch.

"You're going to wake up with a sore back,'' I warned.

"Not me,'' he said. "I can sleep anywhere. That's what comes from having a pure heart.''

I took him into my arms. He barely came up to my chin.

"You do have a pure heart,'' I told him. "Thank you for all you've done for me. I love you, Hobie.''

"And I love you, Dunk. Try to sleep. Things will look better in the morning.''

I hoped, but I doubted. We exchanged a chaste kiss, and I went into the bedroom. I don't know whether it was the strains of the day or the raspberry brandy, but I fell asleep almost instantly. A dreamless sleep. But when my alarm went off and I awoke, things seemed no brighter, and I dreaded what shocks the new day might hold for me.

5

Lemuel Whattsworth, the attorney, was a thinnish man: thin face, thin body, thin voice. Even what he had to say was thin, being composed mostly of *whereas, heretofore, notwithstanding*, and similar expressions designed to make the eyeballs glaze over.

There we were, gathered in the conference room: Whattsworth, Stanton Grandby, Felicia Dodat, and me, awaiting judgment. The lawyer was attempting to explain the possible results (the *ramifications*) of the loss of the Demaretion.

Trying to follow his crazy lecture, I gathered that no lawsuit had yet been filed, but he guessed (*intuited*) that Archibald Havistock would not claim the $150,000 for which he had insured the Demaretion, but instead would demand $350,000 from Grandby & Sons, since that was the estimated value of the coin stated in the auction contract Havistock had signed with Grandby's.

"Naturally," Whattsworth said, "in fact, indubitably, his insurer will heartedly concur with this course of action. The receipt for the coin was signed by a representative of Grandby and Sons"—here a cold stare in my direction—"so legally this house is responsible. Grandby's, in effect, stated an item of value was on the premises when, in fact, it was not."

A little more of this, I thought, and I'd go bonkers.

"Investigations are under way," he droned on, "and we can but hope this grave offense will be satisfactorily resolved with the perpetrator of the theft brought to justice. Until that eventuality is finalized, it is my considered judgment that Miss Mary Lou Bateson be granted an indefinite leave of absence, without salary, until this distressing matter is explicated. Such a course of action will, in some small way, serve to protect the professional reputation of Grandby and Sons."

"And make me look like a thief," I said hotly.

"Not at all," he said in his tinny voice. "It is merely a temporary measure designed to avoid the rumors and confusion that would inevitably result from your continued employment. After all, Miss Bateson, you *are* deeply involved in this sad incident, and I am sure you can appreciate the need for Grandby's to, ah, distance itself from your involvement."

I looked at god and Felicia Dodat, hoping to find support and encouragement. Nothing. Stanton Grandby stared back at me blankly, and Madam Dodat was busy examining the vermilion lacquer on her talons.

So that was that. I was cast adrift, and went back to my office to pack up my coffee mug and few other personal possessions. I was scribbling a short note to Hobart Juliana, telling him of my expulsion, when there was a hard rap on the corridor door. I peered through the judas and saw, held up for my inspection, the gold shield and ID of a New York Police Department detective. I unlocked.

He was about my height, which made it easy to look into his startling electric blue eyes.

"Al Georgio," he said. "Can I come in and talk to you a few minutes about the theft?"

"I've already talked," I said. "Yesterday. At length. To two of your men."

"I know," he said. "I have their reports. But this thing was dumped on me, and I have a few questions I'd like to get cleared up before we prepare a statement for you to sign. Okay?"

"Sure," I said, "come on in. Coffee? In a plastic cup."

"That would be great," he said. "Sugar and milk if you've got it."

I poured us coffee and gave him packets of Sweet 'n' Low and some non-dairy creamer we kept around for visitors.

"You just caught me," I told him. "Another five minutes and I'd have been gone. I've been canned."

"So I heard," he said. "But not canned; just a leave of absence."

"Without pay," I said bitterly.

He shrugged. "Such is life in the great city."

He was a big, rumpled man who looked like he had been sleeping in his clothes. About thirty-seven to forty years old, I guessed—around there. A face like a punched pillow, except for those sharp eyes. And a smile of real warmth. I thought he was a charmer. Also, I thought he might be hung over.

"So," I said, "what can I tell you?"

"Who was in the Havistocks' apartment when you witnessed the packing of the coins?"

"Mr. Archibald Havistock and his secretary, Orson Vanwinkle, who is also Havistock's nephew. And a woman let me into the apartment. I had never seen her before, but she was dressed like a maid or housekeeper."

Detective Georgio took out a little pocket notebook and flipped a few pages. "Housekeeper," he said. "Ruby Querita. Her brother's in the slammer on a drug bust."

I looked at him in astonishment. "You guys do move, don't you?"

"Occasionally," he said. "You saw no one else on the premises?"

"Only the two guards from the armored truck service. They were waiting in the outside corridor. I never saw more of the apartment than the hallway and the library where the coins were kept. But I got the impression it was an enormous place."

"It is," he said. "Eleven rooms, three bathrooms. And there were a lot of people there you didn't see."

"I met Mrs. Mabel Havistock and Natalie, their younger daughter. But I didn't see them yesterday."

He consulted his notebook again. "They were there. And the son, Luther Havistock, and his wife, Vanessa. Also the older, married daughter, Roberta Minchen and her husband, Ross. The whole family was going to have lunch together."

"An occasion?"

"Sort of. It was Mrs. Havistock's birthday."

"Oh, God," I said despairingly. "The burglary must have put a damper on the festivities."

"Robbery," he said. "Yes, I guess it did. When Havistock put the Demaretion in the display case, did he—"

I held up a palm. "Whoa. He didn't put the coin into the case. It was already in there when I inspected it."

"So there was no possibility of sleight of hand? A little juggling?"

"Absolutely not. The Demaretion was in its case. I examined it through the glass lid."

"It was the real thing? Not a counterfeit?"

"It was the real thing."

"And you saw the case sealed?"

"I did."

"And the case put into the Styrofoam box?"

"I saw that, too. Then the container was closed with masking tape. That tape was still intact when I opened it in our vault."

"The container was already labeled? Marked with the number thirteen?"

"That's correct."

He looked up suddenly from the jottings he had been making in his notebook. "Who do you think did it?"

I was startled. "I haven't the faintest idea."

"That makes two of us," he said, giving me that melting smile again.

He really was a most attractive man. A little frazzled around the edges, like a worn French actor, but all the more comfortable for that. I mean he wasn't trying to be anything he wasn't. His heavy face, wrinkled clothes, his slouch, the way he moved—everything about him said, "What you see is what you get."

He finished his coffee and stood up. He looked at the catalogues, books, knitted cap, a pair of snow boots, etc., all piled on my desk.

"Hey," he said, "you clearing out? Going to take all that stuff home?"

"That's right."

"Where do you live?"

"Isn't that in your little black notebook?" I asked.

"Sure," he said cheerfully. "West Eighty-third Street. I've got a car outside. Can I give you a lift to your apartment?"

I was wary. "Detectives aren't mad rapists, are they?"

"Not me," he said. "I haven't got the energy."

He helped me down to the street with all my junk, got it stowed in his double-parked, faded blue Plymouth, and drove me home. Then he helped carry everything inside.

"I have some vodka," I offered.

"I'll pass," he said. "But I could stand another coffee—if it's not too much trouble."

"All I've got is instant. Black."

"My favorite vintage," he said.

When Hobart Juliana had left my apartment early that morning, I had folded his sheet and blanket and stacked them atop his pillow on the couch. They were still there, and I knew Detective Al Georgio noticed them. But he didn't say anything.

I made him a cup of instant decaffeinated. He blew on it to cool it. My father used to do that.

"Tell me about the coin," he said. "Please."

I described the Demaretion, and then showed him an exact-size photograph in one of my catalogues.

"Doesn't look like much," he said.

"It is much," I said indignantly. "A beautiful example of classic Greek minting."

"How come it's worth so much?"

"Rarity. It's a real museum piece. And the quality of the minting. Also, there's a story connected with it. It was made in Sicily when the Greeks occupied the island. Gelon, the Greek commander, defeated attacking Carthaginians at the battle of Himera in Four-eighty B.C. I guess Gelon was going to cut off all their heads, or something—he was supposed to be a genuine bastard—but his wife, Demarete, interceded on behalf of the Carthaginians, and Gelon softened the surrender terms. In gratitude, the Carthaginians gave Demarete a gold wreath in the value of a hundred talents. From this, she had minted a series of big coins, dekadrachms, that were named for her. How do you like that romantic tale?"

He looked at me thoughtfully. "I thought this coin was silver."

"It is. Not pure silver, of course. That would be too soft for a coin. But an alloy with a high silver content."

"Well, if this Demarete got a gift of gold, how come she had silver coins made? Why didn't she have the wreath melted down and have gold coins minted?''

I laughed. ''You really *are* a detective, aren't you? A lot of numismatists have asked the same question. Some of them think the story is pure hogwash. Some keep looking for a gold Demaretion. But no such animal has ever turned up. Just the silver variety.''

''How many are there?''

''In the world? Maybe a dozen. Possibly fifteen. Those are the known ones. There may be others in private collections no one knows about.''

He shook his head. ''Crazy business. What's a talent of gold worth?''

''About six thousand drachms. Ask what an ancient Greek drachm is worth in today's money—or an ancient Syrian shekel—and you'll get a million guesses. But no one really knows exactly.''

He sighed. ''I suppose all I've got to know is that the missing Demaretion was insured for one-fifty big ones and valued by Grandby's at three-fifty. That's grand larceny no matter how you slice it.''

I stared at him. ''You don't think I stole it, do you?''

He stared back at me. ''I'm just starting on this thing,'' he said quietly. ''I'd like to be able to tell you, No, I don't think you did it. But I can't say that. Right now everyone in the Havistock family and everyone connected with the transfer of the coins is a possible perpetrator. Including you. You can understand that, can't you?''

''I guess,'' I said miserably. ''But for what it's worth, I didn't do it. I could never do anything like that. I love coins too much.''

He threw his head back and roared with delight. ''That's one hell of an alibi,'' he said.

Then I laughed, too, realizing what I had said.

''Where do you go from here?'' I asked him. ''What's the next step?''

He sobered. Frowned. ''I think I better meet with Havistock and the secretary, Vanwinkle, and get their story on how the transfer was made.''

''They'll verify everything I've told you.''

''Will they?'' Then, suddenly: ''I'd like you to be there. If they say something that doesn't check with your recollection of what went on, I want you to speak up in their presence. Sometimes a confrontation of witnesses can help.''

I considered that for a moment. ''Grandby's attorney told me to have absolutely no contact with Havistock, but that was when I was an employee. I'm on leave of absence now, without pay, and I want more than anything else to clear my name. All right, I'll go along with you.''

''Good,'' he said. ''I'm glad you feel that way.''

''Listen,'' I said, ''apparently we'll be seeing more of each other, so what do I call you? Detective Georgio. Mr. Georgio?''

''Al will do fine,'' he said. That smile again.

''Al? For Albert?''

He may have blushed. At least he looked up into the air over my head.

"Alphonse," he said in a low voice.

I didn't laugh. "People call me Dunk," I told him.

"Dunk? For basketball?"

I nodded.

"That's cool," he said. "I follow the Nets." He stood up to leave. "Thanks for the coffee. I'll give you a call when I set up a meet with Havistock and Vanwinkle. Okay?"

"Fine," I said. "I can make it anytime. I've got nothing else to do."

He moved to the door.

"Al," I called, and he turned back. "Have you got any idea at all how someone got the Demaretion out of that sealed display case within a taped box?"

He grinned without mirth.

"Dunk, my old man was with the Department all his life. Mostly on what they called the Bunko Squad in those days. Scams and cons and the Gypsy Handkerchief Drop, and a hundred other tricky swindles. He taught me a lot. Everyone wants to know how it's possible to steal a coin from a sealed case within a taped container. It's not possible. No one copped that coin by itself. The whole box was switched."

6

That afternoon, about two o'clock, I got a phone call that added another potato to the stew.

A man's voice: "Miss Mary Lou Bateson?"

"Yes," I said. "Who is this?"

"My name is John Smack. I'm with Finkus, Holding, Incorporated. We're the—"

"I know who you are," I interrupted. "You handle the insurance for Grandby and Sons. I spoke to a man from your company yesterday, Mr. Smack. I told him all I know about the theft of the Demaretion."

"Uh-huh," he said. "That was Ed Morphy, the salesman who services Grandby's account. I'm an investigator, and I'd like to ask you a few more questions, if I may. At your convenience, of course."

I sighed. No end to it. "I'm just as anxious to get this cleared up as you are," I told him. "When and where do you want to meet?"

"I'm calling from Grandby's. I was hoping to catch you in your office, but I understand you're on leave of absence."

"Not through choice," I said, and he laughed.

"Only temporary, I'm sure. Any chance of my coming up to your place right now? I have the address. I could be there in twenty minutes."

"All right," I said, "come ahead. I hope you have some identification."

"A business card," he said. "But if you have any doubts, please call Stanton Grandby or Felicia Dodat; they'll vouch for me."

But instead, after we hung up, I phoned Hobart Juliana, having no great desire to chat with god or Madam Dodat. I asked Hobie to check and find out if John Smack really was an investigator for Finkus, Holding, Inc. Hobie called back in five minutes and said Smack was legitimate.

"They call him Jack Smack," he said. "How do you like that?"

"Unreal," I said.

"I miss you already, Dunk," Hobie said sorrowfully. "The place isn't the same without you."

"And I miss you, too, dear," I said. "Maybe if all these hotshot detectives get results, I'll be back before you know it. I like that job, Hobie, and I want to keep it."

"I know."

"And besides, I need that paycheck—even with all the deductions."

"Listen, Dunk," he said anxiously, "if you get the shorts, don't be bashful about asking me for help. I have a few dekadrachms I can lend you."

"Wise guy," I said, laughing, and hung up.

Jack Smack turned out to be a very elegant young man indeed. About thirty-five, I judged, and a few inches taller than me. His suit of raw black silk showed Italian tailoring, and he was wearing Aramis, which always turns me on.

I offered him refreshments, and he opted for a vodka on the rocks with a splash of water. I didn't have a drink, figuring I better keep a clear head.

"No doubt about the coin being the genuine Demaretion when the case was sealed?" he asked me.

"No doubt whatsoever."

"You saw the case sealed, and then you saw it put into the box, and *that* was taped?"

"Correct."

"And the next time you saw container thirteen was when the armored truck delivered it to Grandby's?"

"Correct again."

He uncrossed his knees, crossed them in the other direction. He fussed with the hanging trouser leg to make certain the crease was unwrinkled. Then he sipped his vodka reflectively, tinking the rim of the glass gently against his white teeth.

Really a beau ideal: slender, graceful, with all the right moves. A wry smile—but that may have been part of his act. There *was* a certain theatricality about him; I had the sense of his being always *on*. But that didn't diminish his attractiveness. He was possibly, I thought, the handsomest man I had ever seen—except for my oldest brother, Tom, who could have been minted on the obverse of a Greek drachm with a laurel wreath around his head.

"I understand Al Georgio is handling the case for the cops," he said suddenly.

I nodded. "You know Detective Georgio?"

"We've worked on a few things together," he acknowledged.

"Do I detect a slight note of hostility in your voice?" I asked him.

"Slight," he admitted, coming down hard on the irony. "But it's got nothing to do with Al personally. I really like the guy. It's just that he's police, and I'm insurance, and sometimes the two don't see eye-to-eye."

"I can't understand that," I said. "Both of you want the same thing, don't you? To catch the crook."

"Sometimes," he said, "but not always." He leaned forward, forearms on his knees, holding his drink with both hands. Very serious, very intent. "Look," he said, "here's how it works: Say a goniff steals something. Call it a painting we've insured for a hundred grand. The cops go to work trying to find out who did it. Now the guy who stole the painting will be lucky to get ten percent from a fence. That's ten thousand dollars. So he contacts us and makes a deal. We pay him say, twenty thousand, and he returns the painting to us. He gets double what a fence would pay him, and we're out twenty grand—which is a hell of a lot better than paying out a hundred grand in insurance."

I stared at him. "How long has this been going on?" I demanded.

He laughed. "Since property insurance was invented. Actually, the thief isn't stealing something of value; he's kidnapping it and holding it for ransom. The cops hate it, because when we pay ransom, the crook strolls away whistling a merry tune."

"I can see why the police would dislike deals like that," I said. "But doesn't it cost insurance companies a bundle?"

"So we raise premiums," he said, shrugging.

"You think that's what might happen with the Demaretion?"

"It could."

"Has anyone called you, offering to sell back the coin?"

"Not yet," he said. "Hey, I came here to ask you questions, and it seems to me you're doing all the asking."

"Go ahead," I said. "Ask away."

He grinned ruefully. "Can't think of anything else. We seem to have covered all the bases. At Grandby's, they told me you're called Dunk."

"That's right."

"May I call you Dunk?"

"Sure."

"Only if you call me Jack. I admit Jack Smack sounds like caramel popcorn, but I've learned to live with it. I hope we can work together on this thing, Dunk. I know you've been put on unpaid leave of absence—which was entirely unfair and unwarranted in my opinion—and you'll want to clear your name. So maybe if the two of us can put our great brains together on this, you'll be back to work before you know it."

He smiled winsomely. A hard guy to resist. Al Georgio was charming, too, but Jack Smack was charming *consciously.* Every woman over the age of four is able to spot the difference. Which doesn't mean we're able to resist the deliberate charmer.

He got up to go, then paused for a moment. Dramatic effect.

"By the way," he said casually, "no one lifted a single coin from a sealed display case within a taped container. I think the container itself was switched."

After he was gone, I reflected that I had met two tall, handsome men in the last few hours—so the day wasn't a total loss. But I recognized angrily my own stupidity at not seeing that stealing container thirteen and substituting a similar box (sans Demaretion) in its stead was the only way the robbery could have gone down.

Two male investigators, Georgio and Smack, had seen it at once. And I, witness and participant, had been racking my poor, feeble brain trying to imagine how it had been done. It was humiliating.

I have always been a competitive type; I suppose those driveway basketball games with my brothers contributed to that. Anyway, I was determined to show Georgio and Smack that I wasn't just another pretty face; I had brains. Feminism had nothing to do with it; it was *personal.*

I reasoned this way:

I accepted their theory that container thirteen had been switched. It was the only way the Demaretion could have been stolen. But when I exhibited the empty display case to Hobie in Grandby's vault, it was absolutely identical to all the other teakwood cases with glass lids that housed the Havistock Collection. I was willing to swear to that.

Which meant there had to be at least fourteen display cases—right? And an empty extra, sealed, was substituted for the one containing the Demaretion.

Now then . . . what was the name of the guy Archibald Havistock said had made the cases? "The best man for that kind of work in the city," he had told me. First name Nate—that I remembered. But the last name? Calesque? Colliski? Callico?—something like that. And he worked in Greenwich Village. I grabbed up the Manhattan telephone directory and Yellow Pages, and started searching.

It took me about fifteen minutes, but I found him: Nathaniel Colescui, custom carpentry, with a shop on Carmine Street. I pulled on beret, suede jacket, shoulder bag, and rushed out. Practically sprinted over to 86th Street and Broadway. Took the downtown IRT. All the short people in the subway car stared at me, but I was used to that.

I got off at Houston Street and walked back to Carmine. Colescui's shop wasn't hard to find. It was right next to a pub-type restaurant that had a legend gold-leafed on its window: FOUNDED IN 1984. That tickled me—but I guess when a restaurant lasts two years in Manhattan, it's something to brag about.

Colescui's window didn't brag, it just said: CUSTOM CARPENTRY. EVERYTHING TO ORDER. Inside, it smelled pleasantly of freshly sawed wood, and there was a fine mist of sawdust in the air. The middle-aged black woman pounding away at an ancient typewriter at the front desk was wearing a hat, and I could understand why.

She stopped her typing when I came in. "Hep you?" she asked.

"I'd like to inquire about having a display case made," I said. "For coins."

She swung around on her swivel chair and yelled into the back room. "Nate!" she screamed. "Customer!"

I heard the diminishing whine of a power saw switched off. Then a twinkly gnome of a man came out of the back, pushing goggles up onto his bald skull. He was wearing a leather apron over what looked like a conservative, three-piece business suit, plus white shirt and jacquard tie. And all of him—scalp, eyebrows, suit, apron, shoes, everything—was coated with sawdust, as if someone had gone over him with a shaker, sprinkling vigorously.

He couldn't have been more than five feet tall. He looked up at me, smiled, and said, "Now if you and I had a son, he would be just right."

"Great idea," I told the old man. "When do you want to start?"

"Oh-ho," he said. "A fresh lady. I like fresh ladies. Clara, did you hear that? When do you want to start, she asks me."

"I heard," the typist said, then addressed me. "Don't listen to him; he's all talk and no do."

That made the little guy laugh. His method of laughing was to clamp his dentures, press his lips tightly together, close his eyes and shake. His whole body bounced up and down.

When the seismic disturbance was over, I said, "Mr. Colescui?"

"The same," he said, "but a fresh lady like you can call me Nate."

"Nate," I said, "I came to ask about having a display case made for my coin collection. Do you do things like that?"

"Everything I do," he said. "Display cases, tables, chairs, bookcases, picture frames—whatever. What size display case you thinking of?"

"I was at a friend's house the other night," I said, faintly ashamed of myself for scamming such a nice man in this fashion, "and he kept his coin collection in beautiful cases he said you had made for him. I was wondering if I could get one case like those he had."

"Oh-ho," Nate Colescui said, head tilted to one side. "And what was this customer's name?"

"Havistock. Archibald Havistock."

He went to a battered file, pulled open the top drawer, began rummaging through folders. "Habley, Hammond, Harrison . . . Yes, here it is: Havistock." He withdrew the file, opened it, began reading, holding it close to his nose. "Oh my yes, I remember this now. Several years ago. A *big* order. The finest teak, tempered glass lids, velvet lining, recessed brass hardware. Everything the best." He peered up at me in a kindly way. "And expensive."

"How expensive?" I asked him.

"Mr. Havistock paid four hundred dollars a case. But as I say, that was several years ago. I'm afraid it would be considerably more today. Say six hundred a case." He must have seen my shock, for he added, "Of course I could make the same size case in pine, maybe maple or cherrywood. Put the hardware on the outside. Skimp a little here and there. Make it affordable."

"But it wouldn't look like Mr. Havistock's cases."

"No," he said, with an understanding smile, "it wouldn't."

"Well, that's that," I said, sighing. "I had no idea they cost that much."

He shrugged. "A lot of work. Dovetail joints. Everything just so."

"How many cases did Mr. Havistock have made?" I asked casually. He consulted the file again. "Fifteen."

"Wow," I said. "My poor little coin collection isn't worth that much. Well, thank you for your time and cooperation, Nate. If I ever decide to have a case made, I'll bother you again."

"No bother," he protested. "It's always a pleasure to talk to a fresh lady like you. Stop in anytime."

I left the shop and tramped north to Sheridan Square. The day had started out balmy, but now there was an edge to the wind, and the blue had disappeared behind a screen of muddy clouds. Pedestrians were beginning to hustle, and I noticed several were carrying furled umbrellas. That always amazed me about New York: It can be a perfectly clear day, then clouds come over, it begins to drizzle, and suddenly everyone has an umbrella—except me.

But the possibility of getting caught in a shower, and having my suede jacket spotted, didn't concern me half so much as those fifteen display cases Archibald Havistock had purchased. Thirteen of them housed his original collection. That left two empty extras, presumably stored in the Havistock apartment.

If one of the extras was missing, it would be proof positive that it had been substituted for the case containing the Demaretion. I was gloating over my newly discovered talents as a detective when I stopped abruptly in the middle of the sidewalk, stunned by the realization that the thief might have removed the Demaretion and left its case with the other extra. Result: two empty cases, just as there should be.

But then, resuming my brisk walk to the subway station, I reflected that if the crook had done that, the case he replaced would show signs of having been sealed: the residue of sealing wax and masking tape. Unless the thief had been clever enough to have the case refinished.

Groaning, I began to appreciate the complexity of the detective's art.

All those imponderables, what-ifs, and possibilities. I felt a grudging admiration for Al Georgio and Jack Smack. But then, if they could pick their way through a thicket of facts, fantasies, and suppositions, so could I, and I resolved to continue my new career as Girl Detective.

It turned out to be the most important dunk shot I ever tried to sink.

7

Al Georgio picked me up in his grungy blue Plymouth. He waited until we were in traffic, heading for the Havistock apartment on East 79th Street, then he let me have it.

"What the hell do you think you're doing?" he demanded.

"What?" I said, startled.

"Why did you go down to see Nate Colescui yesterday?"

"Oh . . . " I said confusedly. "Oh, that. Well, I wanted to find out how many display cases Havistock had. Because that empty case was the real thing. So if it was substituted . . . " My voice trailed away.

"Leave the detecting to the professionals, will you?" he said angrily. "I go down to Carmine Street this morning and find you and Jack Smack have been there before me. Colescui doesn't know what the hell is going on. He gets three people asking about Havistock's cases."

"I'm sorry," I said humbly. "I just wanted to find out where the extra came from."

"Ahh . . . " he said disgustedly, "I'm not sore at you. It's my ego that's suffering. Because you and Smack thought of it first and got there before me. No harm done. I called Havistock. Yes, he bought fifteen cases. He had two extras, kept in a closet in his bedroom. I asked him to check. He came back on the phone and said there's only one extra case now. One is missing. That was the empty switched for the Demaretion case."

I thought about it for a while.

"That clears me, doesn't it?" I asked him. "I couldn't have known about the extra cases. And even if I had, how would I know he kept them in his bedroom closet? He never mentioned them."

"Oh, you're clean," he said. "As of now. And, for the same reasons, so are the guys on the armored truck."

"Well, then . . . " I said, trying to puzzle it out, "who does that leave?"

"The family," Al Georgio said. "As they say in dick shows on TV, it was an inside job."

We drove through Central Park in silence for a while. Then:

"I'm sorry I yelled at you, Dunk," he said.

"That's all right, Al," I said. "I really didn't mean to interfere with your job. I was just so anxious to clear myself."

"Sure, I can understand that. But don't do any more prying on your own. Someone committed a crime. I don't want to scare you, but when you're dealing with big bucks like this, anything can happen."

"You mean I could be in danger?"

"People do wacky things when a lot of money is involved. And a lot of years in stir."

I didn't believe him. Was I ever wrong!

"When we talk to these people," he went on, "let me carry the ball. You tell your story as honestly and completely as you can. Then I'll see how they react and take it from there."

"Whatever you say, Al," I told him.

We all met in the living room of the Havistock apartment, a cavern I had never seen before. I mean the place was a mausoleum, swaddled in brown velvet, and I had to resist an impulse to take off my beret and look around for the open casket. If an organ had started to boom "Abide with Me," I wouldn't have been a bit surprised.

Awaiting us were Archibald Havistock, wife Mabel, married daughter Roberta Minchen with husband Ross, Orson Vanwinkle, and a lady introduced as Lenore Wolfgang, Mr. Havistock's attorney. She was almost as tall as I, but blockier: a real linebacker wearing a black gabardine suit that looked like it had been hacked out of a hickory stump.

We all shook hands, showed our teeth, and got seated on those horrendous velvet couches and obese club chairs. Not at all daunted by the crowd, Detective Georgio took charge immediately, and orchestrated the entire interview. I had to admire his stern, no-nonsense manner.

"I am going to ask Miss Bateson," he said, "to relate in detail, to the best of her recollection, exactly what happened on the morning the coin collection was packed and shipped to Grandby's. Please do not interrupt her. When she has finished, I will ask you, Mr. Havistock, and you, Mr. Vanwinkle, if your memories of that morning differ in any appreciable degree from her account. Miss Bateson?"

So I began my recital again, as familiar to me now as "Barbara Frietchie," which I memorized in the 5th Grade: "Up from the meadows rich with corn, Clear in the cool September morn . . ." As I spoke, almost mechanically, I looked from face to face, zeroing in on daughter Roberta Minchen and hubby Ross.

She was a dumpling, swathed in a high-collared, flowery chiffon, loose enough to hide the bulges. A florid face with popping eyes and pouty lips.

Her hair was cut short, which was a mistake. I thought she had a kind of blinking, rabbity look. Maybe that was due to her incisors: big and glistening.

Husband Ross was one of those solemn young men, prematurely bald, who comb their thinning locks from one side to the other. Awfully pale, with the grave look of a professional mourner. I remember that he cracked his knuckles until his wife reached out to stop him. While I was delivering my spiel, I had a sudden, awful vision of those two in bed together, and almost lost the thread of my discourse.

I finished and looked brightly at Al Georgio.

"Thank you, Miss Bateson," he said. "Very complete." He turned to Archibald Havistock. "Now, sir, does your recollection of the events differ from what you've just heard?"

Havistock stared at me, expressionless, heavy jaw lifted. "No," he said decisively. "Miss Bateson has given an accurate account."

"Mr. Vanwinkle?" the detective asked. "Any corrections or additions?"

"Oh, I don't think so," the secretary said, with a languid wave. "It happened just as she says."

Al Georgio took out his pocket notebook, a ballpoint pen, and made a few jottings. It seemed to impress everyone—except me. Then he sat back, crossed his knees, took a deep breath.

"All right," he said. "Now we're at the point when Miss Bateson and Mr. Vanwinkle leave the library and the taped cases and go out into the corridor to send in the armored truck guards. Correct?"

"Yes," I said, "that's how it happened."

"You showed them where to go, and then the two of you went down to the street to supervise the packing of the armored van?"

"Not exactly," Orson Vanwinkle said. "Miss Bateson was outside when I conducted the two guards into the library."

"Oh?" Georgio said. "And when you brought the guards into the library, was Mr. Havistock still there?"

The attorney, Lenore Wolfgang, spoke up: "What is the purpose of this line of questioning?" she demanded.

Georgio looked at her stonily. "The purpose of this line of questioning is to find out who stole the Demaretion. Mr. Vanwinkle, when you accompanied the guards to the library, was your uncle there?"

"Ahh . . . no," the secretary said. "He was not."

The detective turned to Havistock. "Is that correct, sir?"

"Yes, yes," he said, somewhat testily. "The whole family had gathered, so I came into the living room, here, to see how everyone was getting along."

"It was my birthday," Mrs. Havistock said. "We were going to have a little party."

"In other words," Georgio said, "no one was in the library with the coins until Mr. Vanwinkle returned with the guards to start them loading the boxes. Is that right?''

He looked at them all. No one answered.

''Mr. Havistock, how long were you gone from the library?''

''A minute or two. No more than that.''

''Mr. Vanwinkle, from the moment you left the library until you returned with the guards, how much time elapsed?''

''Couldn't have been more than two minutes. Then my uncle reentered the library. He supervised the loading of the dolly. I went back to the outside corridor, rejoined Miss Bateson, and we both went down to the street to oversee the loading of the armored van.''

Georgio was jotting furiously in his notebook. Then he looked up. ''In other words, the packed coins were unattended in the library for a period of approximately two minutes?''

''I regret to say,'' Archibald Havistock declaimed in his resonant voice, ''you are correct. It was my fault. I should never have left them alone.''

The detective ignored that. ''When you came into the living room, sir, who was present?''

Havistock frowned. ''Hard to remember. People were milling about. Some going into the kitchen to sample things the caterer had brought.''

''The caterer?'' Georgio said sharply. ''When did the caterer arrive?''

''Oh, that was at least two hours previously,'' Mrs. Havistock said. ''All cold dishes. The delivery men were long gone before Miss Bateson arrived, and they started packing the coins.''

''Okay,'' the detective said. ''Scratch the caterers. Let's get back to who was here, in the living room, when Mr. Havistock came in from the library. Were you here, Mrs. Havistock?''

''I was,'' she said firmly. Then, hesitant, ''I think I was. Part of the time. I may have stepped into the kitchen to see how Ruby was getting along.''

''Mrs. Minchen, were you here?''

''Right here,'' she said in an unexpectedly girlish voice. ''Exactly where I'm sitting now.''

''Well, not exactly, darling,'' her husband said. ''We were both sitting on the chocolate couch—remember?''

''And where was young Miss Havistock during the two minutes her father was in this room?''

''She was here,'' Mrs. Havistock said.

''And where were your son and his wife—were they also in this room during that two-minute period?''

They all looked at each other helplessly.

''Look here,'' Archibald Havistock said angrily. ''I told you we were all milling about. People were sitting, standing, moving to the kitchen, mixing a drink for themselves. I deeply object to your line of questioning.

You're implying that a member of my family might have stolen the De-maretion.''

Al Georgio slapped his notebook shut with a smack that startled us all. He glared at them. ''The armored truck guards couldn't have done it,'' he said, addressing Havistock. ''Miss Bateson couldn't have done it. Who do you want me to suspect—the man in the moon?''

''I resent that,'' Lenore Wolfgang said.

''Resent away,'' the detective said, standing up. ''This is only the beginning. I'll be back.''

He started out, then stopped suddenly and turned back to Havistock. ''Who knew you kept the two extra display cases in your bedroom closet?'' he demanded.

For the first time Mr. Havistock appeared flustered. He could hardly get the words out. ''Why . . . '' he said, almost stammering, ''I suppose everyone did. All the family.''

Georgio nodded grimly and stalked out. I rose hastily and ran after him.

When we were back in his car, he said, ''How about some lunch, Dunk? A hamburger?''

''Fine,'' I said. ''I'll pay for my own.''

''Okay,'' he said cheerfully. ''I know a good place over on Lex. They make British burgers. With bacon.''

So that's what we had. Sitting at a minuscule table for two alongside a tiled wall, munching burgers, popping French fries, and sipping tea out of glasses.

''I think it went good,'' Al Georgio said. ''I shook them up, got them looking at each other. They're beginning to wonder: Which one did it?''

''Orson Vanwinkle did it,'' I said.

''Why do you say that?''

''I don't like him.''

Al almost choked on a piece of bacon, he laughed so hard. ''Beautiful. I take that to the DA, and he kicks my ass out the window. Why don't you like Vanwinkle?''

''He's a snaky character.''

''How could he have pulled it? He was never alone with the sealed cases.''

''Somehow he did it. I'll find out.''

''Who the hell are you—Nancy Drew?'' Then, suddenly, surprising me, ''How about dinner tonight?''

I stared at him. ''Are you married, Al?''

''Divorced,'' he said. ''Almost two years now.''

''Children?''

''A girl. Sally. Would you like to see her picture?''

''Of course.''

He dug out his wallet, showed me a photo in a plastic slipcase.

''She's a beauty,'' I said. And that was the truth.

"Isn't she?" he said, staring at the photo. "She's going to break a lot of hearts."

"How old is she?"

"Going on twelve."

"Do you see her often?"

"Not as often as I'd like," he said miserably. "I have the right to two weekends a month. But this lousy job . . . That's why my wife divorced me. It's not easy being married to a cop. The job comes first."

"All right, Al," I said, "I'll have dinner with you tonight. Do I have to dress up?"

He laughed. "You kidding? Look at me. Do I look like a dress-up kind of guy? The place I'm taking you to isn't fancy, but they've got the best linguine and clams in New York."

So I wore my usual uniform: pipestem jeans, black turtleneck sweater, suede jacket and beret. Al said I looked like a Central American terrorist; all I needed was a bandolier. He was wearing one of his rumpled suits with all the pizzazz of a bathrobe. I had never met a man so completely without vanity. I found it rather endearing.

It was a scruffy trattoria he took me to, in Little Italy, but after I got a whiff of those marvelous cooking odors, I knew I had found a home. The moment we entered, the owner came rushing over to embrace Al, and the two men roared at each other in rapid Italian. Then the owner, a man with a white mustache big enough to stuff a pillow, turned his attention to me.

He kissed his fingertips and started chattering away again. All I caught were two "bella's" and one "bellissima!"

"He says," Al translated, "that if you are willing to run away with him, he will desert his wife, six children, and eleven grandchildren."

"Tell him not before I eat," I said.

Al relayed the message, and the old guy slapped his thigh, twisted the curved horns of his mustache upward, and rolled his eyes. Forty years ago he must have been a holy terror with the ladies.

We finally got seated, and even before we ordered, the owner brought us glasses of red wine.

"Homemade," Al told me. "In the basement. It's got a kick."

It did, but was so smooth and mellow, I felt I could drink it all night. "How did you ever find this place?" I asked.

"I was born two blocks away. It was here then. Same wine, same menu. Even some of the same waiters. It hasn't changed a bit, and I hope it never does."

We had a memorable meal: a huge platter of seafood linguine, with clams, baby shrimp, slivers of crabmeat, and chunks of lobster. I could have filled a bathtub with that sauce and rolled around in it. The fresh, crunchy salad was special, too, and afterward we had cappuccino with tortoni, and Al taught me how to float a spoonful of the ice cream atop the coffee. Heaven!

The owner brought us two little glasses of Strega, and after a taste I was ready to move into that restaurant and never leave. I told Al how much I enjoyed the dinner, and he nodded absently.

"Listen, Dunk," he said, "you met that Natalie Havistock, didn't you?"

"Nettie? Sure, I met her."

"What was your take?"

"A wild one. The hippie of the family. She just doesn't fit in with the others. But I like her."

"You get along with her okay?"

"Of course. She came up to the office one day to learn how the auction would be organized. Then we went out for pizza together."

"Uh-huh," he said, looking over my head. "I should tell you she runs with a rough crowd. Some of them are into drugs and some into guns. We've got a special unit that keeps an eye on gangs like that, hoping to grab them before they do something stupid—like blowing up the Statue of Liberty."

"Nettie?" I said, shaking my head. "I can't believe it."

"Oh, yes. She and her pals are a bunch of fruitcakes."

"You think they could have stolen the Demaretion?"

"Possible, but I doubt it. It's not their style. They'd go for a bank or armored van—something where they could wear ski masks and wave sub-machine guns around. How about you giving Nettie a call. Maybe having lunch with her."

"What for?"

"Pump her. I got nowhere with her. She's a throwback to the nineteen sixties; I'm a cop so therefore I'm a pig. But you say the two of you hit it off. So maybe she'll talk to you. About her family. The conflicts and so forth. In a family that big there's got to be jealousies. Grudges. Undercurrents. I'd like to know about them."

I stared at him, trying to smile. "And all the time I thought you invited me out to dinner to enjoy the pleasures of my company."

He leaned toward me. "That's the truth, Dunk. That's exactly why I asked you out. If you don't want to brace Nettie, just tell me, and we'll forget about the whole thing."

"You're something, you are," I said. "Well, you warned me—with you the job comes first. All right, I'll try to see Nettie. Only because I'm as anxious and curious about this thing as you are."

"Fine," he said. "Try to meet her tomorrow if you can."

"What will you be doing?"

"I've got an appointment to talk to Luther and Vanessa Havistock."

"If I tell you how I make out with Natalie, will you tell me what you learned from Luther and Vanessa?"

He held out a big, meaty hand. "It's a deal," he said, and we shook on it. "I've got some reports to do tonight," he continued. "I better get you home. Look, Dunk, I was being honest when I said I invited you out just to enjoy your company. I like being with you. You believe that, don't you?''

"I guess.''

"Can we have dinner again, or lunch, or whatever?''

"Sure," I said. "I'm a forgiving soul. Just keep feeding me like tonight and I'm all yours.''

That charming smile again. "And I'll bet you didn't gain an ounce. I envy people like you. Look at my gut. Isn't that disgusting?''

He double-parked in front of my brownstone and we sat a few minutes, talking about the Havistocks.

"Right now it's a can of worms," Georgio said. "But within a few days I hope we'll be able to eliminate a few possibles, and things will look simpler.''

I stared at him in the gloom. "Why are you doing this, Al?''

He was astonished. "It's my job.''

"I know that, but I think there's more to it. It's almost like a crusade with you.''

He shrugged. "I just don't like wise-asses who think they can get away with murder—or even get away with copping an antique Greek coin. I hate people like that—the ones who go elbowing their way through life, thinking the laws are for other people but not for them.''

"You get pleasure from putting them behind bars?''

"Not pleasure so much as satisfaction. It just seems right to me.''

"You're a deep, deep man," I told him.

"Me? Nah. I'm just a cop running to suet. You'll see Nettie tomorrow?''

I sighed. "Yes, I'll see Nettie tomorrow. Thanks for the marvy dinner.''

I leaned forward and kissed his cheek. I think it shocked him. But he recovered fast enough.

"Thank you," he said: "You're a sweet lady, Dunk.''

I stood on the sidewalk until he pulled away. We both waved. I turned to the doorway of my brownstone. A man came out of the shadows. I took a deep breath and opened my mouth, prepared to scream.

"Hi!" Jack Smack said. "Have a pleasant evening?''

"You bastard," I said wrathfully. "You scared the hell out of me.''

"Did I?" he said, grinning. He held up a brown paper bag. "Look what I've got—a glorious bottle of Finlandia vodka. For you. How's about inviting me in for a nightcap?''

8

Jack Smack lounged on my couch, one arm extended along the back, his legs crossed. That night he was wearing a Norfolk suit of yummy gray flannel, soft broadcloth shirt with a silk ascot at the open neck. Tasseled loafers buffed to a high gloss. What a nonchalantly elegant man!

"Where do you buy your clothes?" I asked him.

"Thrift shops," he said, with a snort of laughter.

He was working on a double vodka on the rocks. After all I'd had to drink at dinner, I settled for a cup of black coffee. He didn't scare me, but I recognized a kind of wariness in my feelings toward him. I wasn't sure what he wanted, and decided not to listen to his pitch with a muzzy mind.

"I don't suppose," he said with a lazy smile, "you'll tell me what Al Georgio said about the Havistock case tonight."

"You're right. I won't tell you."

He uncrossed his legs, leaned forward, suddenly serious and intent.

"I'm glad to hear that, Dunk," he said solemnly. "Glad to hear that you're discreet. Can I depend on you not to repeat to Al what I tell you?"

"Of course," I said. "But I think it's silly. The two of you should be working together. Exchanging information and all that."

"Mmmm," he said. "Sometimes it doesn't work out that way. Sometimes it's best that we do our own thing. My company got an anonymous letter this morning. Typewritten on cheap bond. Postmarked Manhattan. The writer wants to know if we'd be interested in buying back the Demaretion."

I sat up straight, excited. "My God, Jack, do you think it's legitimate?"

He shrugged. "Seems to be. The forensic lab we use went over it. The typewriter was an Olympia standard. No usable prints on the letter. They think it was written by a man.''

"How do they know that?"

"Wording. Phrasing."

"How much does he want for the Demaretion?"

"Didn't say. Just asked if we'd be interested in buying."

"Well, if you are, how do you get in touch with him?"

"Cloak-and-dagger stuff. We occupy the ninth floor of a building on Third Avenue and Eighty-third Street. If we're interested in buying, we're to close the venetian blinds on the entire floor. If the writer of the letter sees them closed any working day within the next week, he'll send us another letter stating his price."

"Are you going to do it?"

He shrugged again. "Maybe, maybe not. Right now it's being debated by the top brass. It could be a fake, you know. A colossal con. So meanwhile I'm to continue my investigation."

"And how are you coming along with that?"

He flipped a palm back and forth. "Bits and pieces. A little here, a little there. The brother of the housekeeper, Ruby Querita, is in the pokey on a drug charge. That could be something. And the youngest daughter, Natalie, runs with a bunch of wild-assed loonies. That could be something." He turned on the charming smile. "And I know you found out about those two extra display cases Archibald Havistock had made."

I nodded, figuring he heard about my visit to Nate Colescui.

Suddenly he was serious and sincere again. "That was good thinking on your part, Dunk. You were ahead of me and Al Georgio."

His quick switches of mood, levity to solemnity, were confusing. I wondered if he was doing it deliberately, to keep me rattled and unsure. I wanted to prove to him that he wasn't succeeding.

"Is there a typewriter in the Havistock apartment?" I asked him.

He smiled coldly. "That's a sharp brain you've got there, kiddo. Your mama didn't raise you to be an idiot. Yes, there's a typewriter in the Havistock apartment. But it's an IBM Selectric, not an Olympia. Vanwinkle uses it for correspondence. So the letter we got must have been typed somewhere else. That would be easy; there are hotels in the city where you can rent a desk and typewriter by the hour."

I saw his glass was almost empty and took it from his hand. I brought it into the kitchen, refilled it with ice cubes and a really stiff jolt of Finlandia. If he was trying to unsettle me with his mercurial changes of mood, I could play my own game—get him befuddled enough to tell me more than he intended.

"Jack," I said, handing him the bomb, "when you're assigned to an investigation like this, where do you start? What's the first thing you look for?"

"Motive," he said promptly. "Someone needs money—right? So they steal something of value."

I shook my head. "Not necessarily. Not when you're talking about antique coins or paintings or rare documents. Sometimes they're stolen not from greed, but because the thief wants to *own* them. It's the collector's instinct: to possess an object of great rarity and beauty. He doesn't want to make a profit from it; he just wants to look at it, devour it with his eyes, and think, 'Mine, mine, *mine*!'"

"You think that's what happened to the Demaretion?"

"It's possible. A private collector may have hired a thief, for a fee. Then the coin disappears into his safe. I mean, what else are you going to do with it? Jack, it's so *rare*. No reputable dealer is going to handle a Demaretion without wanting to know where it came from and how the would-be seller came into possession."

He stared at me thoughtfully. "That's an angle I hadn't considered: a contract theft engineered by a private collector with a mad desire to own the coin. But that anonymous letter we got knocks that theory into a cocked hat, doesn't it?"

"Not necessarily. Suppose a rich collector pays a professional thief ten thousand to lift the Demaretion. The crook succeeds, but then he finds out what the coin is really worth. So he says to himself, Why should I take all the risk for this piddling fee when I can get five or ten times as much from the insurance company. So he double-crosses the guy who hired him and contacts you."

"Dunk," he said admiringly, "you have a devious mind. I like that. I hope we can work closely together on this. I need the benefit of your expertise."

"What's in it for me?" I said boldly.

"The sooner we get it cleared up, the sooner you go back to work at Grandby's, with maybe a fat raise in gratitude for the help you provided. Isn't that enough for you?"

I thought a moment. Then: "Yes, it's enough."

"Then we can work together?"

I nodded.

"The first thing I'd like to get from you," he said, "is a list of coin dealers all over the world. We want to get letters out to them to be on the lookout for someone trying to peddle a hot Demaretion. Can you provide a list like that?"

"Sure," I said. "No problem. I'll just lend you the most recent directory of the Association."

"Fine," he said, then hesitated a moment. "Something else I'd like you to do—if you're willing."

"What's that?"

"Have a private meeting—a talk, lunch, dinner, whatever—with Orson Vanwinkle, the secretary."

"Why him?"

Jack Smack sat back, frowning. "I don't really know, except that there's something cheesy about the man."

"I agree. I don't like him."

"I can't see how it's possible that he could have lifted the coin, but I get bad vibes from that guy. There's something phony there; he doesn't ring true."

"I can't just call him and ask him to take me out to lunch."

"I know that," Smack said, "but there must be some way you can work it; you're a brainy lady. Think about it and see if there's any way you can talk to him in private. Did he come on to you?"

"Maybe," I admitted. "But maybe that's the way he treats all women."

He nodded. "Think about it," he repeated. "If you decide to do it, give me a call, and we'll talk about what we want to get out of him." Then, out of the blue: "Would you like me to stay the night?"

I glared at him. "No, I would not like you to stay the night."

"Okay," he said equably. "If you don't ask, you'll never know—right? You got a guy, Dunk?"

"Several," I said, lying in my teeth.

"I wish you'd add me to the list," he said. "I'm single, own a Jaguar, and know how to make Beef Wellington." Again that warm smile that melted my knees. Oh, God, he was so handsome! "This has nothing to do with our business, Dunk. This is between you and me."

"Oh, sure," I said.

He drained his drink and stood up—steadily. So much for my plot. Did I want him to leave? Did I want him to stay? If he planned to confuse me, he was doing one hell of a job.

"I'll get your bottle," I told him.

"Oh, no," he said, "that's for you. Maybe you'll invite me in again for a drink."

"Anytime," I said. Was that me talking?

At the door, he turned and kissed me. On the lips. It was nice.

"Out you go," I said, gasping.

"Sure," he said, staring into my eyes. "Don't forget about Vanwinkle. I've got a feeling there's something there."

Then he was gone. I locked, bolted, and chained the door. I was still shaken by that kiss. The swine! The lovely swine!

Undressing slowly, I pondered all the happenings of that eventful day: the meeting at the Havistocks', lunch with Al Georgio, dinner with Al in Little Italy, and finally the set-to with Jack Smack.

I found myself grinning. Because I had been living such a placid existence and hadn't realized how lonely and bored I had become. Now I was meeting new people, becoming involved with strong passions—and I loved it. Suddenly my life seemed cracked open, full of emotions I had never felt before. I suppose it was the normal process of learning, but at the time it seemed to me a delightful revelation—like tasting caviar for the first time.

Before I went to bed, I had a little bit of Jack Smack's vodka with grapefruit juice. Just what I needed, because later, warm and snug, waiting for sleep, I reflected, giggling, that with two tall, good-looking New York guys wanting to jump on her bones, little ol' Mary Lou Bateson of Des Moines was doing okay.

9

That morning with Nettie Havistock was one of the most discombobulating experiences of my life. When I finally got through (her private number at the Havistock apartment was busy for more than an hour), she said she'd be "charged" to see me, and suggested we do some shopping together and then have lunch. She told me to meet her at the toiletries counter of Saks 5th.

She showed up in a costume that threw me for a loop. From bottom to top: scruffy Adidas running shoes, heavy knitted leg warmers over baggy jeans, a T-shirt with SLIPPERY WHEN WET printed on the front, and over that a denim vest festooned with ribboned military medals. A man's fedora, sweat-stained, was crammed atop her fuzzy blond curls. And over her shoulder hung a leather, Indian-type bag with buckskin fringe, decorated with beads and shells.

"Hi, hon," she said blithely, ignoring my wide-eyed stare. "I'm not looking for anything in particular. Just thought we'd mooch around and see what's new."

So I tagged after her, all over the main floor of Saks. It took me about five minutes to realize she was shoplifting. Small stuff: bars of imported soap, silk scarves, a man's tie, a gold-plated chain. She was so casual and practiced that I knew she had been at it a long time. She slid the stuff inside the waistband of her baggy jeans or just scooped it into her capacious shoulder bag. Wandering, smiling, chatting over her shoulder at me . . .

I was terrified. I wanted to turn and bolt. I just couldn't believe it. I knew she could easily afford all those things she was boosting. Kleptomania? Was that a legal defense? I looked about nervously, certain that at any moment we would be apprehended by store detectives and marched off in shame.

"That should do it," Nettie said brightly. "Let's go get something to eat."

We walked over to Madison, Nettie nattering on and on. But I wasn't listening; I was debating with myself whether or not to mention her criminal behavior, what my reaction should be, how it might affect my relations with her and the investigation of the Demaretion theft.

"That stuff I lifted," she said with a roguish smile. "Want any of it?"

"No, thanks," I said hastily.

She laughed. "I don't need that crap," she said. "It's just a game. I give it all away."

"What if you get caught?"

"Daddy will pay off," she said confidently. "He always has." I felt sorrow for Archibald Havistock, that complete man. His solid manner concealed what must have been harrowing family problems.

We had lunch in a crowded luncheonette on Madison Avenue, pushing our way to the rear past the cashier's desk, a take-out counter, and a jumble of little tables. We finally found seats in the rear, close to the kitchen doors, waitresses rushing in and out.

"This is a new place," Natalie Havistock said, looking around. "It's a setup."

That comment made me uneasy, but I didn't dare ask what she meant. We finally ordered chicken salad plates with iced tea, and while we were waiting for our food, Nettie fished a crimped cigarette from her shoulder bag.

"My first today," she said, holding the cigarette up for my inspection. "Want one?"

"I think I'll pass," I said.

"Good stuff."

"Nettie, do you know what you're doing?"

"Nope," she said cheerfully. "Do you know what you're doing?"

"Not really," I confessed.

"Well, then . . . there you are."

She lighted her homemade cigarette, and when I got a whiff of that sweetish smoke, I hoped none of the nearby diners would start a ruckus. None did.

"Nettie," I said, "I feel terrible about your father losing that coin."

"He can afford it," she said casually. "Besides, he'll collect from the insurance company, won't he?"

"I suppose so. But the insurance value is outdated. Today the coin would be insured for much, much more."

"Then it's no big deal. The cops think someone in the family lifted it, don't they?"

I nodded.

"Not me," she said. "What would I do with that stupid coin?"

I just couldn't understand her. One minute she's showing no remorse for her shoplifting pranks, and the next minute she's shrugging off her father's loss of the Demaretion. I didn't know what she was revolting against. Family? Society? Or maybe herself.

But then our food arrived. Nettie handed the stub of her cigarette to the waitress.

"A little tip for you, luv," she said, smiling.

The waitress took the roach, sniffed it, and said, "Thank you, dear. Just what I need."

That could never happen in Des Moines. Or could it?

I looked at her as we ate our salads. A thin, nervy young girl (twenty-two? twenty-four?) with brittle energy: sharp movements, quick gestures. I got the impression of unhappiness there, some deep despair cloaked by a bright smile and brisk manner. But sadness in her eyes that all the blue eyeliner couldn't conceal.

"Ruby Querita?" I asked. "Could she have done it?"

"Ruby? Not a chance. Her brother's a doper, but she's a straight arrow. Works her ass off to keep her boy in private school. The kid's a mathematical whiz."

"Who then?"

Nettie shrugged. "Ross Minchen, my brother-in-law, is a wimp. I can't see him lifting anything more valuable than an ashtray from McDonald's. Roberta is just as dreary."

"Certainly not your mother."

Nettie laughed. "Don't be so sure. Don't let the blue hair fool you; there is one tough lady. But why should she steal the coin? The way I hear it, most of what Daddy owns is in her name already."

I realized how little I knew about the source of the Havistocks' wealth.

"Your father is retired?"

"Semi. He owned a textile company. Knitting mills and things like that. Then he sold out to a bigger outfit. But he's still on salary as a consultant. And Luther works for them. That was part of the deal."

"What about Luther. Could he have done it?"

She paused, fork halfway to her mouth. "Possibly," she said thoughtfully.

"I've never met your brother."

"He's got problems. Mainly his wife, Vanessa. She's a barracuda. Lives up to and beyond his income. Runs him ragged."

"I gather you don't like her."

"You gather correctly, Dunk. She's a real bitch."

"Could she have stolen the coin?"

"Wouldn't put it past her. She loves money. But she wouldn't do it herself; she'd get a man to do it for her. She's got eyes for anything in pants, with a fat wallet in the hip pocket. She was coming on to Ross Minchen, and it got so bad that finally Daddy had to tell Vanessa to lay off. It's a fun thing with her. She likes to stir guys up. Gives her a feeling of power, I guess.''

"Is she attractive?"

"Like a snake. Yes, I suppose you could call her attractive. I can't see it—I think she's chromium-plated—but men take one look at her and unzip their flies.''

I laughed. "What about Orson Vanwinkle? Did he unzip his fly?''

She drained her iced tea before she answered. "Orson is a schmuck. He thinks he's God's gift to women, but he's a schmuck. He came on strong with me once—I mean really physical. But I gave him a knee in the balls, and that was the end of that. You know, in a lot of ways he's the male equivalent of Vanessa. I think they're both a couple of hustlers.''

"You think there's something between them?"

"Vanessa and Orson? I doubt that. He's got no money, so Vanessa wouldn't be interested. I've seen them together many times, and never noticed anything going on. Mutual suspicion, maybe. They both know what they are; it takes one to know one. A couple of cruds. Well . . . '' she said, pushing her plate away and sitting back, "how do you like that rundown on the Havistocks? Just your average, normal, well-adjusted American family—right?''

"Nettie," I said, feeling guilty, "I really didn't mean to pry. But I'd like to get this whole thing cleared up so I can get my job back.''

"Sure, sweetie, I can understand that.''

"If you had to name someone in the family as a prime suspect, who would it be?"

She thought a moment, digging with a fingernail at a fragment of chicken caught in her teeth. "Orson Vanwinkle," she said finally. "Or my brother, Luther.''

"Why them?"

"They're both hurting for money," she said.

Then the waitress brought our bill. "Thanks for the roach, honey," she said to Nettie. "It hit the spot.''

Natalie Havistock grabbed the check. "You leave," she told me. "Go out to the street; I'll be along in a few minutes.''

"I want to pay my share," I said, fumbling with my purse.

"Forget it," she said. "Just go!''

So I went, past the tables, the take-out counter, the cashier's desk. I waited on Madison Avenue. It was almost five minutes before Nettie came out. She was carrying a white paper bag. We walked a half-block, and she dumped the bag in a refuse basket.

"Coffee and bagel," she said. "Who needs it?''

"Nettie," I said, "what *are* you doing?''

"Our lunch bill came to almost fifteen bucks," she said. "So I stopped at the take-out counter, bought coffee and a bagel for two bucks. I palmed the lunch bill and gave the cashier the take-out check for two bucks and paid that. No strain, no pain. Lousy organization in that place.''

"What about a tip for the waitress?''

"She got the roach, didn't she?''

"Nettie,'' I said, "you're awful.''

"That's right,'' she said, grinning. "And I love it.''

We kissed cheeks, promised we'd stay in touch, and she popped into a cab on Madison. I wondered how she was going to con the driver. I shouldn't have laughed, but I did. I decided to walk all the way home. I had a lot to think about.

It was a dynamite day in Manhattan: a velvety June afternoon with a muskmelon sun in a washed sky and a breeze just cool enough to tingle. It was a long hike back to West 83rd Street, but I still had calf and thigh muscles from my dunk shot days, and it felt good to stretch them.

I had now lived in New York for several years, but never ceased to marvel at how thronged the city was. Mobs of people! I saw Manhattan as one big, overcrowded basketball court. The only way for a pedestrian to make progress on those jammed sidewalks was by bobbing, ducking, weaving. I was good at that, and went dancing home, darting and spinning, imagining I was dribbling an inflated spheroid all the way.

But that was physical and mechanical. While I played games on the ganged sidewalks, my mind was wrestling with the Havistock family and what Natalie had told me. Her frankness was amazing; I could never be that open about *my* family to an acquaintance. And I certainly had less dramatic revelations to divulge.

I couldn't decide whether Nettie's casual disclosures were motivated by rancor toward parents, siblings, and inlaws, or whether she had a more devious reason. Perhaps she was trying to direct guilt elsewhere—her own guilt. I found that hard to believe, but it was possible.

I finally decided that her lack of discretion might be (probably was) due to an abiding hatred and disgust of hypocrisy. So open and forthright herself, she could not endure dissembling in others. She really was an idealist—or at least a romantic.

Al Georgio had accused me of acting like Nancy Drew. Now I was making like Sigmund Freud!

I stopped at a neighborhood grocery and picked up a blueberry yogurt and a plastic container of fresh salad. Also, on impulse, two cans of Schaefer beer. I toted my purchases home, kicked off my shoes, and popped one of the beers.

Slumped on the couch, I went over again what Nettie had told me about the Havistocks. A rogues' gallery! But in all honesty, I could not see any one of them as the Demaretion thief.

I was debating whether or not I had the energy to wash my hair when the phone rang. It was Al Georgio. He sounded harried and tense.

"Listen,'' he said, "you see Natalie Havistock today?''

"Yes, we had lunch together."

"Good. I'm seeing Luther and Vanessa at six o'clock. He gets home from work then, and I want to catch the two of them together. I figure it'll take about an hour; no more than that. You said you're a pizza maven—right? How's about I pick up a pepperoni and maybe a jug of red ink, and I'll show up at your place around seven-thirty or eight—like that. You tell me about Nettie, and I'll tell you about Luther and Vanessa. Okay?"

"Sure," I said, "come ahead. But make the pizza half-anchovy; that's my favorite."

"All that salt isn't good for you."

"And all those garlicky spices aren't good for *you*."

"All right, all right," he said, laughing. "You get the heart attack, I get the ulcer. See you later, Dunk."

He showed up a little before eight, lugging a big pizza box and a half-gallon of Chianti in a raffia cozy. As usual, he looked lumpy and disheveled. And weary. His heavy face sagged, but those electric blue eyes were sharp enough.

"Tough day?" I asked him.

"They're all tough," he said. "But I didn't come here to whine; let's eat."

We sat on the couch and pulled the cocktail table close. I provided wineglasses and paper napkins. We gobbled and we swigged. Not an elegant dinner, but I loved it.

"You first," he said. "About Nettie . . . "

So, between chomps of pizza and gulps of Chianti, I told him the whole story, not omitting the shoplifting spree and the scam in the luncheonette. He laughed at that.

"What a character she is," he said. "A real flake."

"She is that," I agreed. "But I don't think boosting in Saks means she lifted the Demaretion."

"Mmm," he said. "Maybe, maybe not. What else?"

I repeated everything Nettie had told me about the Havistock family. Al listened carefully, not interrupting me and not interrupting the destruction of his half (pepperoni) of the pizza.

"You've got good recall, Dunk," he said, sitting back and swabbing his mouth with a paper napkin. "And everything you've told me ties in pretty much with what I've picked up about the Havistocks. You think Nettie is clean?"

"I think she is, Al. She may be a nut, but I just can't see her stealing from her own father."

He brooded awhile. "Maybe it wasn't her idea," he said finally. "I told you about the gang of crazies she runs with. Her lover is a black stud who wears a red beret and one gold earring. He might have pushed her into it."

I sighed. "She's a mixed-up kid."

"Oh, sure," he said. "So am I. So are you. But we don't rip off Saks Fifth Avenue. The first thing you learn in the detective business, Dunk, is not to let your personal likes or dislikes influence your thinking. Nettie could be guilty as hell. Will you buy that?"

"All right," I said shortly, certain he was wrong. "Now tell me about Luther and Vanessa."

"They're just about what Nettie told you. Luther is a victim. A loser. Vanessa is a real femmy fa-tally." He said that with wry, deliberate mispronunciation. "She even came on to *me*, for God's sake. A slob like me."

"You're not a slob, Al," I said.

"No," he said, "and I'm not Cary Grant either. I knew what she was doing, Dunk, but I've got to tell you, there is one exciting woman."

"Beautiful?"

"Different. Striking. She just gives the impression of being available. She's not obvious about it. Doesn't show her thighs or flash her boobs— nothing like that. As a matter of fact, she was dressed conservatively. But she just exudes sex. I think what Nettie told you was right: Vanessa gets her jollies from teasing. I felt sorry for her husband."

"What kind of a man can he be to let her get away with that?"

"He's defeated. But so much in love with her—or infatuated, or obsessed, or whatever you want to call it—that he'd never think of dumping her."

"Al, do you think if she told him to steal the Demaretion, he'd do it?"

"If she told him to slit his throat, he'd do it. Dunk, you've got to meet this woman. She's something, she is."

"When I asked Nettie to name who she thought stole the coin, she said Luther or Orson Vanwinkle. She said they were both hurting for money."

"I can believe it about Luther. You should see their apartment. Park Avenue and Sixty-fourth. And the jewelry she was wearing! She had one ring that could feed a Puerto Rican family for ten years. He works for the conglomerate that bought out Archibald Havistock's textile company. If Luther makes seventy-five grand a year, he's lucky. But believe me, Dunk, a hundred grand a year wouldn't cover that apartment and Vanessa's jewelry and all the paintings and the Mercedes and the summer house in Montauk. Unless Daddy is helping him out, I think the guy is overextended. He's got that bankrupt look about him: pale, tremors of the hands until after the second drink, lips pressed together, high-pitched laugh. I've seen it all before in people trying to hang on to their style of living when they haven't got two nickels to rub together."

"So maybe copping the Demaretion could be the answer to all his troubles."

"It sure as hell would help," Georgio said, nodding. "He's got the motive, all right. But I haven't figured out yet how he could—"

The phone rang and he stopped talking. I have a wall phone in my kitchen, and an extension on a table in the bedroom. Like a complete idiot, I went to the kitchen. Al could easily overhear.

"Hello?" I said.

"Hi, luv," Jack Smack said breezily. "Can you talk?"

"Not very well," I said.

"Oh-ho," he said, "company. Al Georgio?"

"I'm busy," I said.

"Call you tomorrow," he said, and hung up.

I went back to the living room.

"Jack Smack?" Al asked.

I couldn't lie to him. I nodded miserably.

"That's okay," he said. "You're entitled. I know you're not carrying tales."

"I'm not!" I said hotly.

"I *know* that," he repeated patiently, trying to smile. "Jack has got his job to do, too."

Still, there was constraint.

"So . . . " I said, "where do you go from here?"

He shrugged tiredly. "Dig deeper. Try to find out who would profit most. This thing is a can of worms. And I'm getting a lot of flak. You've been reading the papers? The tabs love it. Who stole the priceless Greek coin? The Department is leaning on me."

"I can imagine," I said. "Have some more wine; there's plenty left."

"Splendid idea," he said, and this time his smile was warm and charming again. He topped off my glass and filled his.

"Where do you live, Al?" I asked him.

"Queens," he said. "Basement apartment. My ex got the house. But I'm not complaining; I've got a place to sleep."

"You cook for yourself?"

"Of course. When I get the chance. I happen to be a good cook."

"I'll bet you are," I said. "Italian stuff?"

"Mostly. I can gussy up chicken breasts until you'd swear you were eating veal."

"Stop it," I said. "I'm gaining weight just listening."

He looked at me. "If I invited you out, would you come for dinner?"

"Just try me," I said.

"Thanks, Dunk," he said. "You're good people."

I took the empty pizza box and used napkins out to the kitchen and dumped them in the garbage can. I couldn't have been gone more than a minute. When I went back to the living room, Al Georgio was fast asleep; it happened that quickly. His chin was down on his chest, he was breathing deeply, and the wineglass he was holding was tilting dangerously.

I lifted the glass gently from his fingers and set it aside. I turned off the overhead light and switched on a table lamp next to the only comfortable chair I owned: an oversized wing with enough soft pillows to make snuggling easy. I put on my half-moon reading glasses and dug out the needles, wool, and the Afghan I had been working on for the past four months.

I enjoyed needlework. Great therapy. Once you learn how, grasp the basic pattern of what you're doing, your hands fly, almost of their own volition. It's a pleasure to be creating something, and it's so automatic that your thoughts can soar. I've heard of women who knit sweaters while they watch TV soap operas. I believe it.

The Afghan I was working on was just a big shawl in an open, boxy pattern. Light blue. Not as deep as Al Georgio's eyes—more of a sky blue, an azure. So while Al dozed, my needles went clicking quietly away, and I could think about the lives of the Havistocks, much more tangled than my skeins of wool.

The complexities of that one family amazed me. And fascinated, too, I admit. My life, so far, had been simple and straightforward. Problems and troubles, of course, but nothing cataclysmic. Not even very dramatic. Now I was plunged into the operatic existence of the Havistocks—or so it seemed to me. I was playing a small role—extra or walk-on. But I found it exciting.

I called to mind all the members of the Havistock ménage, trying to decide which one was the thief, because Georgio and Jack Smack both thought the crime had been committed by a family member, and I agreed. Al had told me not to let my personal likes or dislikes influence my thinking—but he was a man, and I was a woman, and I wasn't certain he was correct. Men have this big love affair with logic, but cold reason can't explain everything.

So I just let my instincts roll, and decided Orson Vanwinkle did it. Or if he didn't steal the Demaretion personally, he was involved in the theft. Why did I believe that? Because he had a clammy handclasp and treated me in a lewd, insinuating manner. That was enough to condemn him. He was what my grandmother used to call a lounge lizard.

I was working on the puzzle of how Vanwinkle might have switched display case number thirteen, when Al Georgio roused. His head snapped up, he looked about, stupefied with sleep.

"My God," he said. "What's the time? How long have I been out, Dunk?"

"About a half-hour."

"Sorry."

"Don't apologize," I said. "You obviously needed it."

"Where's the john?" he said. "Maybe some cold water on my face will help."

He came out of the bathroom shaking his head ruefully. "I don't know what happened to me."

"The wine," I said.

"Nah. We didn't even put a dent in the bottle. I think I better get home and sack out for about eight hours."

"You're sure you want to drive?" I asked anxiously. "You can sleep here on the couch if you like."

That melting smile again. "Thanks, Dunk, but I better not. You may never get me out of the place."

"I'll take that chance."

He laughed and came over to kiss my cheek. "I like you in glasses," he said.

"You do?" I said, astonished, peering up at him over my half-moons. "Why do you say that?"

"I don't know," he said, shrugging. "Somehow they make you look more sexy."

"Then I'll wear them all the time," I said. "Al, most of your wine is left; take it with you."

"No way. You keep it. It'll give me an excuse to come back."

"Anytime," I said, and remembered I had told Jack Smack the same thing. Dunk Bateson—the femmy fatally!

At the door, Al said, "Thanks for the hospitality. And the nap. Next time I'll try to be a little more alert." Then: "Why are you looking at me like that?"

Sometimes, I had learned, you can stagger men with complete honesty.

"I was wondering," I told him, "if you had asked to spend the night, not on the couch but in my bed, what I would have said."

He took me in his arms, pressed. He was very warm, solid, comforting. He touched my hair.

"When you decide," he said, "may I be the first to know?"

"Absolutely," I promised.

"Ah, Dunk," he said, almost groaning, "what the hell is going on here?"

"I'm not going to worry about it," I said. "Are you?"

He moved away and stared at me. "There's more to you than meets the eye," he said.

"That's right," I agreed. "I'm not just another pretty face."

We both broke up and, like imbeciles, shook hands firmly before he left.

10

Have you ever had an experience like this:

You're trying to remember the name of an old friend, or the title of an old tune, or who played the male lead in an old movie—and you can't recall no matter how much you worry it, no matter how many names and titles your mind suggests. You go to sleep, still stymied.

Then you wake up in the morning—and there it is! Your brain worked while you slept and dredged up the recollection you sought.

I had related the details of the packing and transfer of the Havistock Collection from East 79th Street to Grandby & Sons on Madison Avenue at least a dozen times, to various people. And I had gone over the sequence of events in my own mind another dozen times. In all those retellings, I had searched for something missed, something that I, and everyone else, had overlooked that might provide a vital key to the mystery.

I sat up in bed the next morning, wide-awake, knowing what had been missed, and furious with myself for not having seen it before. But then, as far as I knew, no one else had either.

I showered, washed my hair, and wondered for the hundredth time what I could do with my mop. It wasn't short and it wasn't long; it just sort of hung there with no wave, no curl. And for the hundredth time I vowed that as soon as I got a few bucks ahead, I'd surrender myself to a hairdresser—someone named Louis or Pierre—and let him do with me what he would.

I looked at my Snoopy watch, but it was too early for Hobart Juliana to be in the office, too early for me to confirm the Great Revelation that had brought me sitting upright in bed that morning. So I went out, bought a buttered bagel and the *Times*, came back and made a cup of instant decaf.

I kept watching the kitchen clock, and at 9:30 I called Grandby & Sons, hoping Hobie wasn't off somewhere on a field appraisal. But he was there and sounded delighted to hear from me. We chatted and laughed for almost ten minutes, and I got caught up on all the latest office gossip at Grandby's, including the rumor that Felicia Dodat had been to a plastic surgeon and was contemplating a fanny lift.

Then I turned serious and got down to the reason for my call.

"Hobie," I said, "something has come up, and I need your help."

"Of course," he said immediately. "Anything."

"On the day the Havistock Collection was shipped, I came back to Grandby's to accept delivery. I stood in the vault and signed a receipt for the thirteen cases. Then you came down, bringing me a coffee. Remember? I wanted you to see the Demaretion, so I opened the thirteenth container and slid out the display case. That's when we saw the Demaretion was missing. Is all that correct, Hobie?"

"Exactly," he said, picking up on my earnestness and not joking anymore. "That's just how it happened; I'll swear to it."

"All right. Now, when I held the empty display case out to you, do you remember how it was sealed?"

"Sure. There were strips of masking tape on all four sides, overlapping the glass lid. And in front, near the lock, there was a blob of sealing wax on the junction of lid and case. The wax had an imprint. You said it had been made by Havistock's signet ring."

"You're positive of that, Hobie? You saw the wax seal and you saw the imprint?"

"Absolutely."

"Thank you, darling," I said. "I saw it, too. I just wanted confirmation."

Silence. Then . . .

"And that's all you're going to tell me, Dunk?" he said, disappointed.

"For the time being. Until I check it out."

"You're onto something, aren't you?"

"I think so. I think I've found something important. Talk to you later, dear, and thanks for your help."

I hung up before he could ask more questions. I sat back, sipped the tepid remains of my coffee, and went over again what I had discovered.

That thirteenth display case I had shown to Hobie in Grandby's vault had been sealed in just the way he recalled. And the patch of wax had been imprinted with Mr. Havistock's signet ring, in exactly the same manner the wax seals on the other twelve cases had been imprinted. I would testify to that in a court of law.

Going by masculine logic—I admit it comes in handy, occasionally—that meant:

1. Archibald Havistock had used his signet ring to seal an empty display case.

Or 2. Someone had stolen or "borrowed" the ring to seal an empty display case.

Or 3. There was a duplicate, one or more, of the signet ring, and the copy had been used to seal the empty case.

And Al Georgio hadn't seen it! And Jack Smack hadn't seen it! I confess I laughed aloud with delight. The great detectives! And knew immediately I wasn't going to tell either of them. Not yet. I had the ball now, and I remembered the feeling: rush down the court, timing, lift, and the slam-dunk. When everything went perfectly, there was no thrill like it.

And best of all, I now had a reason—my reason—for calling Orson Vanwinkle: I had to find out about that stupid signet ring. I thought a long time about how I should handle it. I didn't want to *lie* to anyone, exactly, but I didn't want to blab either.

The first thing I did was hunt up Jack Smack's business card. I called, but a secretary with an English accent said he was out of the office, but if I'd leave my number, she'd have "Mr. Smeck"—that's how she pronounced it—get back to me as soon as possible. He called two minutes later, so he must have been in the loo—right?

"Dunk!" he said. "Good morning. Sorry I disturbed your tête-à-tête last night."

"That's all right," I said. "No harm done. Jack, I've decided to try to have a meeting with Orson Vanwinkle."

"Good," he said. "Glad to hear it."

"I figured I'd call him and say how devastated I am by the loss of the Demaretion—which I am—and be very apologetic, and ask him to convey my regrets to Mr. Havistock. How does that sound?"

"He won't believe a word of it," Smack said promptly. "He'll think you're warm for his form and just called to set up a meet. That guy's got an ego that doesn't end. But that's okay; we can use that."

"Well, what do you want me to get out of him? I'm not going to enjoy this."

"I know that, Dunk, but if I didn't think you could handle it, I wouldn't have suggested it. If he comes on too strong, just tell him to get lost. I'd like to learn two things: One: Have there been any other thefts from the Havistock apartment, like silver, plate, cash, pieces of art—small things that could easily be carried out. I'm thinking of Natalie now; she's capable of lifting stuff like that to keep her sewing circle in grass. Two: Are Ross Minchen and Vanessa Havistock having a thing? I picked up some scuttlebutt that suggests they might be making nice-nice together. If anyone would know, it would be Orson Vanwinkle. He's the kind of guy who gets pleasure from knowing everyone is as rotten as he is."

"All right, Jack," I said, "I'll try to find out. No guarantees."

"I understand that. And I want you to know that I appreciate what you're doing to help me. Can I call you later, Dunk?"

"No," I said, "I'll call you. After I see Vanwinkle—if I do."

"Maybe we can have dinner tonight."

"Maybe," I said.

In for a penny, in for a pound; so I called Orson Vanwinkle, determined to be sorrowful and regretful. I asked timidly if he would convey my apologies to Archibald Havistock on the loss of his Demaretion.

"Sure, doll," Vanwinkle said, with what I can only describe as an Evil Chuckle. "I'll tell the old man. Hey, how's about you and me getting together?"

As my grandmother said—a lounge lizard.

"Such as?" I asked.

"Let me take a look at my schedule. Ah, yes, I have a business lunch at the Four Seasons at one o'clock today. Silly things: tax shelters and all that. I should get them off my back in time to meet you at the Four Seasons' bar at three o'clock. We'll have a drink or two and tell each other the stories of our lives. How does that sound?"

"Sounds fine," I said faintly. "All right, I'll be there. You will tell Mr. Havistock how sorry I am?"

"Trust me, babe," he said, and hung up.

In that short conversation I had been "doll" and "babe." Could "sweetie" and "chick" be far away?

Now's a good time to tell you something about the geography of my apartment, because it has a lot to do with what transpired in the next few weeks.

It was a basement (or ground floor) apartment that you entered by coming down three steps from the sidewalk (past the plastic garbage cans) in a short hallway. A staircase led to the upper five floors of the brownstone. My pad was at the end of the ground-floor corridor.

It was called a "garden apartment" (ha-ha), but it did have a back door giving access to a small patch of desert shaded by one noble ailanthus tree. I had tried to grow other things in that sad, scrabbly scrap of earth. Forget it.

You came into my place via a short hallway, just wide enough for a narrow sideboard and two nothing chairs. The bedroom was on your right. Straight ahead was the living-dining room area: large enough, I admit, but with a ceiling so low I was always afraid of scraping my scalp. The little john was to the left of that, and to the right was the compact kitchen with a barred door that led to my "garden."

I'm not complaining, mind you. It was rent-regulated; I was lucky to have it, and I knew it. In Des Moines, we had a three-story detached house with five bedrooms, three bathrooms, and a kitchen almost as large as my entire West 83rd Street manse. Plus a two-car garage. Plus a front lawn and a backyard. But I tried not to think of all that.

Anyway I had three or four hours to kill before my date with Orson Vanwinkle, so I decided to spend them cleaning. Housework is just as mechanical as needlework, but not nearly as rewarding or creative. Because you have to do it over and over; it's never finished.

I stripped to bikini briefs, covered my hair with a plastic shower cap, and set to work. Straightening. Washing. Vacuuming. Dusting. What a drag! Is there anything duller? I've heard that some women enjoy it. Nuts. The only good thing about it is that it's brainless; you can slave away while your thoughts and dreams take off.

I didn't spend those three hours puzzling the conundrum of the missing Demaretion; I spent them comparing the personalities and physical attractions of Al Georgio and Jack Smack. I even went so far, I confess, to say aloud "Mary Lou Georgio" and "Mary Lou Smack."

But you must understand that I was unmarried, pushing the Big Three-Oh, and beginning to wonder where I'd be in five or ten years. Still manless with only an ailanthus tree for company? So sure I fantasized, imagining all kinds of crazy scenarios.

It seemed to me that Al was a true-blue kind of guy, solid and steady. I knew I could trust him, and, if I needed anything, he'd be there. But his job! He told me it came first; it was the reason for his divorce. How could any woman deal with that kind of competition?

Jack was a tap dancer, slight and debonair. The only way a wife could keep him from straying would be to nail him to the bed. The guy was a conscienceless Romeo; I just knew it. But still, he was *soo* handsome and had so much sex appeal it was coming out his ears. You couldn't fault him for that; it's the way he was.

So I spent those housecleaning hours in silly reveries, enjoying every minute. You must realize that having one man in my life to daydream about was an Event. Two men were a Blessing. I didn't count Orson Vanwinkle; he was a Disaster.

It came time for me to shower (again) and get ready for my meeting with the Disaster. I won't bore you with the problems women of my height have in dressing attractively. Hobart Juliana gave me the best advice: Keep it simple. Solid colors. No plaids, no patterns. Avoid ruffles, ribbons, bows, and little girl fanciness. Stick to a chemise silhouette that hints of what's underneath but doesn't reveal. And if you've got no boobs (I hadn't—to speak of), show your back. I had a good strong, muscled back; I knew it. Sometimes I wished I could go through life in reverse.

Anyway, for my cocktail date with Vanwinkle, I wore a loose sheath of black silk crepe. Cut high in front and low enough in back so that a bra strap would have shown if I had worn one—which I didn't. Also, black lace pantyhose, and a single strand of carved wooden beads I had bought in a Mexican place in Greenwich Village. They were kitschy, but I liked them.

I must have done something right, because when I showed up at the Four Seasons' bar (fifteen minutes late—deliberately), Orson Vanwinkle almost fell off his barstool to greet me.

"Hey, hey," he said, with a lip-smacking grin, "you look ravishing—and if there weren't any people around, I would."

He leaned forward and upward to kiss my cheek while I wondered how many times he had used that line.

It didn't take me long to realize he was smashed: eyes slightly out of focus, speech a bit slurred, tottery on his feet—and even wavering when he was sitting down. That must have been some business lunch.

He was working on a big drink: dark brown liquid on the rocks. I didn't know what it was, but it looked lethal. I decided that if I was going to get any information out of him, I better do it quickly before he became comatose.

"What'll you have, sweetie?" he asked, putting a heavy hand on my knee. "I'm having a double cognac to settle the old tumtum. Join me?"

"Just a glass of white wine, please."

He snapped his fingers at the bartender. I hate it when men do that.

When my drink was served, he insisted on clinking his glass against mine. "Here's to us," he burbled. "I have the feeling this is going to be the beginning of a beautiful friendship."

He was such an *oozy* character I could hardly stand it.

"Mr. Vanwinkle—" I started, but he interrupted by putting a finger on my lips. That was nice. I wanted to run out immediately and get a shot of penicillin.

"Orson, chick," he said. "Call me Orson. Or better yet, Horsy. That's what my best friends call me."

"Why Horsy?"

He giggled. "It's a long, dirty story. I'd tell you, but I don't know you well enough—yet."

I stared at him, thinking he wasn't a *bad*-looking man, despite that beaky nose. He was beautifully shaved—something I always noticed about men—and his olive skin looked like felt. He dressed expensively, with a lot of gold glitter. Actually he would be a reasonably attractive package—if only he could learn to keep his big fat mouth shut.

"Orson," I said, "the theft of the Demaretion has really upset me, and I'd like to see it cleared up. I've been put on leave of absence until the crook is caught, so I have a personal interest in getting the case solved. The detectives seem to think someone in the household might be responsible. I wanted to ask you: Have there been any other robberies? Like silver, plate, cash, bric-a-brac—things like that?"

He bleared at me a moment, then squinched his eyes as if he was thinking deeply. "Noo," he said finally, "can't recall anything recent. About five years ago a temporary maid lifted fifty bucks from Mama Havistock's purse, but there haven't been any rip-offs since then that I know about."

I shook my head in mock amazement. "That's a very unusual family."

"Unusual?" he said, and moved his lumpy hand on my knee a little farther up. "Bunch of wackos. I'm related, you know, but not on *that* side of the family, thank God. They should all be going to a shrink. Maybe they could get a wholesale rate. Ready for another drink?"

"Not yet, thank you. But you go ahead."

He snapped his fingers again, and when the bartender turned, pointed to his empty glass. He watched the brandy being poured with the careful attention of the serious drinker. Then he picked up the filled glass and sipped delicately, demonstrating that he was an epicure and not a boozer. Hah!

"Oh, I don't think the Havistock family is *that* bad," I said. "Of course, I haven't met all of them. Vanessa, for instance."

"A slut," he said darkly. "She is not one of my favorite human beings."

"I've heard some wild stories about her."

"You can believe all of them, honey. Did you know she's got a tattoo?"

"You're joking?"

He held up a palm. "Scout's honor. I haven't seen it myself, but I have it on *very* good authority. An informed source, you might say. I won't tell you where it's, uh, located; you wouldn't believe it. Slut. She thinks she invented sex and has a patent on it. She leaves me cold."

Which meant, I supposed, that at some time in their relationship Vanessa Havistock had rejected Orson Vanwinkle. He reminded me of men who, when a woman rebuffs their advances, assume the woman is a lesbian. Of course. The fact that the guy has bad breath, a complexion like the surface of the moon, and wears white socks has nothing to do with it.

"Yes," I said thoughtfully, "I heard she comes on strong."

"To men, women, doorknobs, and cocker spaniels," he said with a nasty laugh. "She even came on to Ross Minchen, who could be president of the International Association of Nerds. But the old man soon put an end to that."

It was the second time I had heard that story; Nettie had told me the same thing at lunch.

"So there's nothing between them now?" I asked. "Vanessa and Ross Minchen?"

"Nada," he said. "At parties he still sniffs around her like a yak in heat, but she won't give him a tumble. Listen, the old man told her to lay off, and he controls the bucks. She's smart enough not to cross him."

So now I had discovered what Jack Smack had asked me to find out. It was time to do some sleuthing on my own—before the blitzed Horsy Vanwinkle fell off his barstool.

But I had waited too long. He stood suddenly, swaying, and drained his new drink, just chugalugged it straight down. I thought, next stop Intensive Care.

"Let's go," he said thickly.

"Go?" I said, Little Miss Innocence. "Where?"

"My place," he said with a wolfish grin. "We'll listen to some Sinatra tapes and let nature take its course."

"Don't you have to get back to work?"

"I work when I feel like it," he said, boasting, "and I play when I feel like it."

Dunk, I told myself, you've got problems.

I won't tell you all the aggravations of the next hour. Well, yes, I will tell you: Getting him to pay the bill at Four Seasons' bar—with a credit card, of course; I was a business expense. Then half-supporting him down the stairs to the street. His Juicy Fruit cologne overwhelmed me.

Then, outside, it took forever to get a cab, while Horsy leaned against the Seagram Building and sang "My Way" in a froggy tenor to the great amusement of passersby. And then in the taxi, he refused to tell the driver, or me, where he lived. I finally had to pluck his wallet from his inside jacket pocket as he giggled and tried to embrace me. I got his address from a card that testified he was a paid-up member of Club Exotica—whatever that was.

When I told the driver our destination, on East 85th Street, he said, "You sure you want to go there, lady? I think I should deliver this nut to Bellevue."

There wasn't enough cash in the wallet to pay the cab fare, so I had to make up the difference. I wasn't in a happy mood when I dragged him out of the taxi and implored him to straighten up and fly right. As a matter of fact, I came close to leaving him in a collapsed heap on the sidewalk and letting him survive on his own. But I was determined to find out about Archibald Havistock's signet ring.

He lived on the third floor of a six-story gray stone townhouse. Getting him to fish out his keys from his trouser pocket was a Keystone Kops comedy in itself, with grapplings, staggerings, and foiled embraces.

I finally got the keys, opened the front door, and wrestled us both inside. There was an elevator, thank God, and I propped him against one wall while we went up. More strugglings and fumblings outside his door, but at last we were inside and I had succeeded in getting this calamity safely home and still conscious.

"Got to see—" he said with a glassy grin, and went rushing for what I hoped was the john. Maybe, I prayed, the idiot would upchuck the business lunch and all that brandy and would return to me sober and chastened. No such luck.

Meanwhile I looked around at a trendy pad right out of *Playboy*. Stainless steel, glass, director's chairs in blond leather, imitation Motherwells on white walls, zebra rugs, enough electronic equipment to blow a dozen fuses, a fully equipped bar with wet sink—well, you get the picture. I didn't peek into the bedroom, but if it had mirrors on the ceiling I wouldn't have been a bit surprised.

It wasn't the glitz that shook me so much as the cost of all that flash in a townhouse on East 85th Street. Either Vanwinkle was making a giant salary as secretary to Archibald Havistock, or he was independently wealthy, or he had a secondary source of income that paid very well indeed.

And yet, when I asked Natalie Havistock if there was anything doing between Vanessa and Orson Vanwinkle, she said she doubted it. "He's got no money, so Vanessa wouldn't be interested." That's what Nettie had said.

Jack Smack had been right: There was something cheesy about the man.

Mr. Roquefort himself came staggering out of the bedroom, and I didn't know whether to laugh or to cry. He had put on a red velvet smoking jacket with black satin lapels and sash, a silk ascot clumsily knotted at his throat, a paisley square spilling out of his breast pocket. I suppose it was his seduction uniform, but with his loopy smile and shambling gait, he looked like a clown.

"Now then . . . " he said, "first things first . . . "

I thought he might fall over at any moment, but he navigated his way to the bar without bumping into any of the furniture. He poured himself a tumbler of brandy and a beer stein of warm white wine for me. If he had any ice available, he either forgot it or didn't want any dilution.

He collapsed on a couch shaped like two enormous red lips and patted the cushion beside him. "You sit here, babe," he said.

I took my schooner of wine and sat on the lips—at a wary distance. Sitting on that crazy couch was an unsettling experience. I expected the mouth to open up at any moment and swallow me down.

"Music," he said, looking about vaguely. "Sinatra tapes."

"Later," I said. "Why don't we just talk for a while."

"About what?" he said, looking at me blearily.

I told you he wore a lot of gold glitter, and he did. Chunky little ingot links on his cuffs, a Piaget Polo with gold strap, a gleaming identification bracelet on the other wrist—the chain heavy enough to anchor the *QE2*. And on the third finger of his right hand, a square gold ring set with a sparkling diamond.

That was my cue.

"What a beautiful ring you have," I said.

He looked down at it. "Two carats," he said, nodding. "Flawless."

"You do all right," I said, laughing lightly. "And all Mr. Havistock has is that sad little signet ring."

"Oh, hell, he doesn't *wear* that. It's a clunker. A piece of junk. I think Mama gave it to him when they got married. He just keeps it around."

"Keeps it around?" I said. "Where? If it has such sentimental value for him, you'd think he'd wear it or keep it locked up."

"Nah," Orson Vanwinkle said. "It's either on his desk in the library or maybe in his jewelry box in the bedroom. He's not *that* sentimental."

Which told me what I hadn't wanted to hear: Anyone in that freaky family would have easy access to the signet ring.

"Listen," Horsy said, "you're not drinking. You still have your drinkee-poo. Come on, let the good times roll. Let's have a party."

"Sure," I said, "why not? But let me take a look at your marvelous apartment."

I rose, wandered behind him, and succeeded in dumping half my wine in the planter of an inoffensive ficus tree. I figured that within a day or two the poor thing would be dead—or maybe it would be twice as tall.

"Beautiful apartment," I said. "Just splendid."

"You like it?" he said, beginning to mumble. "Wanna move in—temporarily?"

"Oh, Horsy," I said, "you sweep a girl off her feet."

I glanced at him to see how he was taking this bit of mild whimsy and to my horror I saw he was listing badly. He was slowly, slowly slumping sideways, his whole body leaning limply. I hastily came around in front of him and lifted the glass of brandy from his fingers.

I watched, fascinated, as he became hors de combat—you should excuse the expression. Within a moment he was completely out, eyes closed, breathing stertorously. His upper torso had fallen sideways onto the crimson lips. I lifted up his legs, made him as comfortable as I could, and looked down at him.

"Oh," I intoned aloud, "how have the mighty fallen." But he didn't stir.

I cabbed home, and had just enough money to pay the driver, though I had to undertip him.

"Sorry about that," I said, "but it's all I have."

"That's okay, lady," he said cheerily. "Give us a kiss and all is forgiven."

"Catch you next time," I said hastily, and scurried into my sanctuary, locking, bolting, and chaining the door behind me.

I slumped into my favorite chair, brooding about the last few hours. I was surprised to find I felt a little more kindly toward Orson Vanwinkle. Sympathy, I guess. The poor poop. Trying so hard to be something he could never be. But pity didn't stop me from wondering about his flashy wealth. Where *was* his money coming from?

That was exactly the same question Jack Smack asked when he called a few hours later. I gave him a rundown of my afternoon with Orson Vanwinkle, leaving out only the business about Havistock's signet ring. That was *my* baby. But I told Jack everything else, including Horsy's fervid pantings and grapplings.

Smack totally disregarded that. "Where *is* the guy getting his loot?" he said. "Not from his secretarial job. I can't believe dear old Uncle Archibald pays that much. I'll have to look into it."

"Will you tell me what you find out?" I asked him.

"Sure, Dunk," he said. "We're partners, aren't we? And there's nothing between Vanessa and Orson?"

"No romance, if that's what you're thinking. He kept calling her a slut, and I think he was sincere."

"Curiouser and curiouser," Jack said. "By the way, we closed all the venetian blinds on our floor like the anonymous letter writer wanted, signaling our willingness to make a deal, but we haven't heard anything more from him. Not yet. Hey, Dunk, how about some dinner tonight?"

"No," I said promptly, "thank you, but I can't make it."

"Sure," he said, not at all put out. "We'll make it another time. Have a good evening. I'll be in touch."

A minute later I was wondering why I had rejected him. I was all dressed up with no place to go, and he was a handsome, dashing guy. Considering the state of my checking account, I could have used a free dinner.

I think my quick decision had something to do with that afternoon with Orson Vanwinkle. I had enough of men for one day. I was tired of the hassle. I suppose that sounds stupid, that a brief encounter with a drunken idiot could sour me on the entire male sex, even for one evening, but that's the way it was.

So I got out of my silk sheath, Mexican beads, and black lace pantyhose, and pulled on my ratty flannel bathrobe with the frayed cord. I had a can of Campbell's chicken soup and a salami sandwich. *Bas cuisine.*

And spent a lonely and forlorn evening. Sometimes I don't understand myself.

11

They sat as solidly as Easter Island statues—Mr. Archibald Havistock and Mrs. Mabel Havistock—grim-visaged monoliths glowering at me. I won't say I was frightened, but I was awed.

Both were stiffly erect, and I wondered if, in private, they ever allowed themselves the pleasure of slumping. Probably not. In their world it simply wasn't *done*. She so hard, square, and chunky; he so impeccably groomed and complete. They could have posed for "Urban American Gothic"; both had steel in them, and not a little arrogance.

I had received a phone call from Orson Vanwinkle about ten o'clock that morning. No indication of hangover, no apologies. And he spoke in such circumspect tones I was certain someone was standing at his elbow.

"Miss Bateson," he said, "Mr. and Mrs. Havistock would like to meet with you here at their apartment at eleven-thirty this morning. Will that be satisfactory?"

"Meet with me?" I said, startled. "What for?"

"Ah . . . to discuss a matter to your advantage. Will you be able to make it?"

"Okay," I said breezily, "I'll be there."

I was greeted at the door by housekeeper Ruby Querita, dour as ever, and ushered into that Frank Campbell living room. And there sat Archy and Mabel, planted, as if they had grown to their velvet club chairs, unable or unwilling to rise and greet me.

They wasted no time getting down to business. Mrs. Havistock carried the ball. I admired the way she lifted her chin as she spoke. It almost smoothed out the wattles. Almost.

"Miss Bateson," she said crisply, "you impress me—you impress *us*, my husband and me—as an intelligent and alert young lady."

She paused, and I didn't know whether to simper or dig a toe into their Aubusson and mutter an "Aw, shucks."

"I am sure," she continued, "you are aware of the activities of Detective Georgio of the New York Police Department and Mr. John Smack, who represents the insurance company covering the loss of the Demaretion by Grandby and Sons."

"I know both men," I said cautiously.

"Then I am sure you are aware that both feel the theft was committed by a member of my—by a member of our family."

"Ridiculous!" Archibald Havistock said angrily.

I said nothing.

"There are two factors to be considered . . . " Mrs. Havistock went on. "First, while any member of this family is under suspicion, recompense for the loss of the Demaretion will be delayed. Second, we deem it a personal insult that a family member should be suspected. All that dreadful publicity! I was brought up, Miss Bateson, to believe that a lady's name appeared in the public print only three times: when she was born, married, and died. I absolutely deny that any Havistock could be capable of such a crime. Archibald, do you agree with me?"

"Absolutely," he boomed out in his resonant voice.

"What I—what we would like to propose," Mrs. Havistock said, "is that we employ you in a private capacity. To investigate the robbery of this valuable piece of property."

It took me a couple of ticks to realize she was talking about the Demaretion. It was like calling the Mona Lisa "a valuable piece of property."

Then as my resentment faded, astonishment set in. They wanted to hire *me* to find out whodunit! I was as shocked as if I had been floored under the basket while going up for a dunk shot. Apparently she took my shaken silence for doubt or rejection because she started the hard sell:

"We know that you are on leave of absence from Grandby's, so your time is your own. We can promise you complete cooperation—not only from my husband and myself, but from all the members of our family. Naturally, we expect to pay for your services. We feel that neither of the two official investigators has your knowledge of the inside world of numismatics."

By that time my wits had settled back into place. "Mrs. Havistock," I said, "if you wish to hire me to investigate the theft of the Demaretion, I'd be happy to take the assignment, and be very appreciative of your trust in me. But if you're hiring me to give your entire family a clean bill of health, that I cannot do. I would like the job—but with no guarantees that I won't find a family member guilty."

They turned slowly to stare at each other. If a signal passed between them, I didn't see it.

"Look, Mrs. Havistock," I argued, "you and your husband have complete faith in the loyalty of your family. That's very commendable, but you can't expect me to become a partner in any cover-up, if one becomes necessary. That I won't do, and the deal is off. But if you're willing to give me carte blanche, tell me to try to find out who stole the Demaretion, and let the chips fall where they may, then yes, I would accept—but only under those conditions.''

''Archibald,'' she said, troubled, ''what do you think?''

''Let's do it,'' he said. ''I think Miss Bateson's conditions are reasonable.''

''Very well,'' she said, lifting her heavy chin again, ''we will employ you with the understanding that there will be no restrictions on your investigation. We will pay you four hundred dollars a week, plus expenses, for a period of one month. At the end of that time we will meet again to review your progress and determine whether your investigation should continue under the same terms, or whether your employment should be terminated. Is that satisfactory?''

''Yes, it is,'' I said promptly, ''as long as you can promise me the cooperation of all the members of your family.''

''I can promise you that,'' Archibald Havistock said grimly. ''In return, I ask only that in the unlikely event you discover a member of the family is the thief, I will be told before you take your information to the authorities.''

I nodded, never imagining the horrendous results of my casual agreement.

So we settled things, and he went into his den-library and returned with a check for four hundred dollars, which I accepted gratefully. We then decided it would be best if they reported to Al Georgio and Jack Smack that I had been employed as their private snoop, and ask both men to cooperate with me fully.

''How do you intend to start?'' Mr. Havistock asked curiously.

I didn't have to ponder that. ''I think I've met all your immediate family except for Mr. and Mrs. Luther Havistock. I would like to talk to your son and daughter-in-law this evening, but it would help if you'd call them first, explain who I am and what my job is. Then I'll call for an appointment.''

''I'll arrange it,'' Mrs. Havistock said decisively. ''You'll have no problem there. They will see you.''

What a gorgon! But I hadn't the slightest doubt that she would deliver. This was one grande dame, and when she said, ''Jump!'' the other Havistocks asked only, ''How high?''

They both had the decency to rise when I departed. We shook hands formally, and I promised to deliver periodic verbal reports on my progress. We all agreed it would be best to put nothing in writing.

When I exited from the living room, Orson Vanwinkle was waiting for me in that muffled corridor. He might have been listening at the living room door or peering through the keyhole; I wouldn't have put it past him.

He conducted me to the outside door, looked about warily, then clamped a hot hand on my shoulder, leaning forward to whisper:

"Was it as good for you as it was for me?"

"Unforgettable," I told him.

He gave me a smarmy smile.

I hadn't been home more than an hour when the phone calls started coming in. The first two were from Al Georgio and Jack Smack. I thought both men would be outraged at my accepting employment as a private detective to inquire into a crime they were investigating, but they seemed to accept my new job with equanimity.

"Look," Al said, "you'll be able to get closer to the family than I can with a badge. We'll trade information, won't we?"

"Of course," I said. "I'm counting on it."

"We're still partners, aren't we?" Jack Smack asked. "I'll keep you up to speed on what I'm doing, and you tip me on anything you dig out. Okay?"

"Of course," I said. "I'm counting on it."

Their reasonableness surprised me. Until I decided that neither of them considered me a threat. What investigative experience did I have? I was just a long drink of water with a passion for pizza and more energy than brains. They might use me, but I don't think either of them took me seriously. That was all right; if they wanted to believe me a lightweight, I'd go along with that. It had something to do with catching more flies with honey than you can with vinegar.

The third phone call was from Vanessa Havistock, and it wasn't as pleasant. As a matter of fact, it was downright snarly.

"I have been informed," she stated in icy tones, "that my husband and I are expected to meet with you this evening and answer your questions about the burglary."

"Robbery," I said. "I hope it won't be too much of an inconvenience, Mrs. Havistock. I can make it at any time you suggest, and I promise you it shouldn't take long."

"We have already answered endless questions by the New York City detective and that man with the odd name from the insurance company. How much longer are we to be harassed in this manner?"

I could feel my temper beginning to simmer, but I was determined to play it cool. Making an enemy of this woman would get me nowhere.

"I know how distressing it must be for you, Mrs. Havistock," I said meekly. "But really, no one wishes to harass you. All we're seeking is information."

"But I know nothing about it. Absolutely nothing."

"You were there when the coin was taken," I pointed out. "At the birthday party planned for your mother-in-law. It's possible you noticed something that made no impression on you at the time, but which might provide a vital clue in solving the crime.''

A two-beat pause, then . . .

"You really think so?'' she said thoughtfully. "That I might know something I don't know I know?''

"It's quite possible,'' I said earnestly. "That's why I'm so anxious to talk to you and your husband. To refresh your memories and see if we can uncover something that will help end this dreadful affair.''

"It's been a nightmare. All those tabloid stories . . . Even my hairdresser wants to talk about it. Oh, very well,'' she said, reverting to her petulant tone, "we'll see you at six-thirty this evening. We'll give you an hour. No more.''

She hung up abruptly. I was looking forward to meeting that vixen. I decided to dress in my dowdiest, like Eliza Doolittle, the guttersnipe, before Professor Higgins converts her to a grand lady. I wanted Vanessa Havistock to feel immediately superior to me, to underestimate me and believe she had nothing to fear.

I made the fourth telephone call. Because the Havistocks were paying expenses, I called Enoch Wottle in Tucson, Arizona. Since he left New York, we had corresponded frequently, exchanging letters at least once a month. I often asked his advice on numismatic matters, not so much that I needed it, but because I wanted him to feel his perception and experience were still valued.

But this was the first time we had talked together in almost three years, and it was a touching experience for both of us. I know I cried a little, and I think he was similarly affected. We spent the first few minutes getting caught up on personal matters: his arthritis, my lack of suitors, his son's home and the grandchildren.

"Enoch,'' I said, "tell me the truth: how do you like Tucson?''

He sighed. "Manhattan it ain't,'' he said with heavy good humor. "You want a hot pastrami sandwich at two in the morning, where do you go?''

I laughed. "Enoch, you never in your life ate a hot pastrami sandwich at two in the morning.''

"I know,'' he agreed, "but in New York you know it's *there*.''

Then I got down to business. I had already written him about the loss of the Demaretion, and he had read about it in the newspapers and numismatic journals to which he still subscribed. Now I brought him up to date on recent happenings, including my employment by the Havistocks. He cautioned me about that.

"Dunk, darling,'' he said, "you are dealing here with someone who took the risk of stealing something worth a great deal of money. That can only mean someone desperate. I beg you, be very, very careful. People stupid enough to commit such a crime may do even more reckless things. Do not endanger yourself.''

"Don't worry about me, Enoch,'' I said. "I can take care of myself.''

Ah, the optimism of the innocent!

Then I told him I had supplied Jack Smack with a list of coin dealers all over the world, and his insurance company was getting out letters of warning, asking for information on anyone trying to peddle the stolen Demaretion.

"Now you know that's not going to do much good," I said. "There are some dealers who'll do anything to turn a buck, especially if they're buying for a client. The Demaretion could disappear into a private collection and never be seen again."

"I'm afraid you're right," he said mournfully.

I told him that I knew he had many old friends in the trade, and asked if he could call or write the most knowledgeable of his contacts and see if he could pick up any information, or even gossip, about a Demaretion coming on the market.

"The Havistocks will pay all expenses," I said, "but I admit it'll be a lot of work for you."

"Work?" he said. "Not work but a pleasure. Of course I'll do it. I'll get started today. You know, by now that dekadrachm could be in Sweden, Saudi Arabia, Iceland—anywhere. Smuggling a single coin across borders is the easiest thing imaginable. You put it in your pocket with your other coins. What customs inspector wants to look at small change? Of course, Dunk, I will be happy to see what I can find out. It will give me something to do. My son insists I play shuffleboard. I *hate* shuffleboard."

Then I told him of the anonymous letter Finkus, Holding, Inc., had received, purportedly from the crook, asking if they'd be interested in a buy-back. They had signaled an affirmative but, as far as I knew, had not yet received a second letter.

"I don't know," Enoch Wottle said dubiously. "It sounds like a con game to me. After a major theft like this by some big shark, the barracudas gather around, hoping to pull a smaller swindle. But you never know. Dunk, this is a fascinating chase. I will do what I can to help. Please call me as often as you like. And reverse the charges."

"Nonsense," I said airily. "I'm on an expense account. Goodbye, Enoch, dear, and stay well."

"I survive," he said philosophically. "At my age that's an accomplishment."

I spent the remainder of that afternoon mentally drafting the questions I wanted to ask Luther and Vanessa Havistock. Actually, I had little hope of learning anything startling from either of them, despite what I had told Vanessa of the possibility of her knowing something vital she didn't realize she knew.

What I wanted, most of all, was to meet them personally and get a splanchnic reaction. I had done the same thing with Roberta and Ross Minchen, and temporarily decided they were the wimpiest of wimps. But from what I had heard about Vanessa Havistock, she was cut from a different bolt of cloth. Gold lamé.

Natalie had called her a bitch. Al Georgio said she exuded sex. Orson Vanwinkle had insisted she was a slut. With a tattoo. Location not specified. And, from all accounts, father Archibald Havistock had to intervene to forestall a family scandal when rapacious Vanessa came on to Ross Minchen.

(But could she sink nine out of ten foul shots with one hand? I could.)

So I dressed like a ragamuffin for my meeting with Mr. and Mrs. Luther Havistock, feeling in a merry mood and wondering if I should take along a pen and pad and take notes as they answered my questions. I decided against it, figuring they'd speak more freely if they knew their words weren't being recorded for posterity.

Also, they'd think I was a complete incompetent. Let them.

12

Al Georgio had given me a hint of the richness of that Park Avenue apartment, but I wasn't prepared for its *splendor*. It made my modest pad look like a subway locker, and completely outclassed the Havistock home on East 79th Street and Orson Vanwinkle's *Playboy* spread on 85th. As Al had wondered, where *was* Luther's wealth coming from?

A panic sale of the stolen Demaretion?

A little gink greeted me at the door, dressed in a kind of uniform, combination chauffeur-houseman. It was deep purple whipcord with a starched white shirtfront and lilac bow tie. Different. I think he was from India, Thailand, Korea, Cambodia, Vietnam, or possibly Detroit—someplace like that. I know he had a purple eyepatch and hissed.

He ushered me into a living room that wasn't as large as Grand Central Station. Not quite. Very plushy, and so big I couldn't take it all in at one glance. I just had an initial impression of money, money, money. Original paintings, leather, glass, chrome, ankle-deep rugs, concealed lighting, crystal, brass, porcelains—it was a stage set, designed to accommodate a dozen actors.

They were standing when I entered, each with a glass in one hand, a cigarette in the other. Hi, there, Noel Coward! But they were affable enough, not bothering to shake hands but offering me a martini (Stolichnaya in Baccarat crystal, I noted) which I declined, and got me seated in an enormous pouf of buttery suede about ten feet away from where they took their seats on a couch upholstered in zebra skin—or maybe it was giraffe. Anyway, it was exotic as hell.

"I'm sorry to intrude upon you like this," I began humbly, "but I'm sure Mr. Havistock has informed you that—"

"Mabel," Vanessa interrupted sharply.

"Mrs. Havistock has informed you that I have been employed to try to discover what happened to the Demaretion, and in the process, hopefully, to clear members of the family of any complicity in the theft."

"It's ridiculous!" Luther burst out. "No one has accused any of us. It's an insult. Just because Father can't collect on the insurance . . . "

His voice trailed away, and I had a moment to take a close look at him. Not very prepossessing. A tall, attenuated man who seemed to have lost weight since he had that pinstripe tailored for him; it hung as slackly as a wet tent. Thinking it might be his first preprandial drink, I looked for the tremor Al Georgio had mentioned, and saw it.

Al thought Luther Havistock was a man teetering on the edge of economic disaster. That wasn't my take. I saw a man sliding into emotional collapse: vague stare, uncontrollable tic at the left corner of his mouth, endless crossing and recrossing of his knees, that high-pitched laugh Al had heard, and a broad, pale forehead slick with sweat that he kept swabbing with a trembling palm.

In better condition, he would have been presentable. Not as handsome as Archibald, but pleasant enough. He had a small echo of his father's firm jaw, full mouth, and ice-blue eyes. But all in a minor key, reduced and brought low. I had an absurd notion of a stalwart house, buffeted by the elements and allowed to molder and decay. No maintenance. That was Luther Havistock's problem: no maintenance.

I took them through that morning and afternoon when the Havistock Collection was packed and the Demaretion disappeared. They answered all my questions readily enough, and substantiated what Al Georgio, and I, had already learned from Mr. and Mrs. Archibald Havistock.

"You must realize," Vanessa said, staring with amusement at my denim muumuu, "it was a party day. The whole family was there. People were standing, sitting, mixing drinks, milling about. It's impossible to remember where any one person was at any particular time."

"But do you remember your father-in-law coming into the living room for a few moments before the shipment of the collection began?"

"That I remember very well. He asked if everyone was present and having a birthday drink. Then he went back to the library."

"I remember it, too," Luther said. "Father came in to play the host for a few minutes."

"Did either of you see Mr. Vanwinkle conduct the armed guards into the library to start loading the coin collection for the transfer to Grandby's?"

"No," Vanessa said. "The living room door to the corridor was open, but I didn't notice anything. Did you, dear?"

"No," Luther said. "Nothing."

I wasn't willing to give up. "Did either of you, at any time, notice anything odd or out of the ordinary that morning? Anything that you might have shrugged off at the time, but could have some bearing on what happened?''

They looked at each other.

''Not me,'' Luther said, wiping his damp brow. ''I didn't see anything.''

''Nor did I,'' Vanessa said. ''Unless—No, it's too silly.''

''What was it, Mrs. Havistock?''

''Well, as you probably know, the party was catered. The food had been delivered a few hours previously. All cold things. I remember wandering into the kitchen to see what we would be eating. I expected Ruby to be there, preparing the buffet. But she wasn't there. Some of the caterer's platters had been unwrapped, and some had not. As if she had left the kitchen in the middle of getting things ready.''

''Do you recall when this happened—your visit to the kitchen? Was it before or after Mr. Archibald Havistock came into the living room?''

She looked at me directly, not blinking. ''I honestly can't recall.''

''And what did you do after you noticed that Ruby Querita was not there?''

''I took a piece of divine Brie from one of the uncovered platters and went back into the living room nibbling on it.''

''And was Mr. Archibald Havistock in the living room when you returned?''

''I honestly don't remember. Oh, I don't suppose it means anything at all. Ruby could have gone to the front door to let someone in, or maybe she was in the john—there are a dozen innocent explanations of why she wasn't in the kitchen. But you said you wanted to know *everything*,'' she added brightly, ''so I thought I'd mention it.''

Quite a woman. She was wearing a Halston sheath that would have paid my rent for two months: a tube of shimmering bottle-green satin that hung from a single shoulder strap and touched her body lightly at bosom and hip. Nothing raunchy about it, but it hinted.

She was almost as tall as her husband, but while his shrunken frame spoke of desiccation, drained of vitality, she was bursting with vigor. I could understand why men found their senses reeling and eyeballs popping. As Detective Georgio had said, she exuded sex. But there was nothing obvious about her, nothing of the hooker.

She sat demurely, ankles crossed, hands clasped in her lap. But there was no missing the ripe curves of her full body. She was not beautiful. ''Striking'' is the word, with long, gleaming black hair parted in the middle, falling close in raven wings. Witchy. A coffin face saved from hardness by full, artfully colored lips. She made Felicia Dodat look like a Boy Scout.

It may have been pure bitchiness on my part, and envy, but I found her a little vulgar. There was a looseness about her that's hard to explain. She was certainly not blowsy, but I could see why men might immediately imagine her naked. Animal! That was it! She had an animal quality. In bed she might be a voracious tiger. In anger, I could see her snarling, spitting, clawing.

"Mrs. Havistock," I said boldly, "would you say that yours is a happy family?"

"Oh, my," she said, laughing lightly, "that *is* a personal question. All families have skeletons in the closet, don't they? But generally speaking, I'd say yes, ours is a happy family. Wouldn't you say so, Luther?"

"Yes," he said, busy refilling his martini glass from a crystal pitcher.

My ploy of arousing her disdain and contempt, of getting her to underestimate me, seemed to be getting nowhere. She could not have been more gracious or cooperative. Why did I have the feeling she was at least one step ahead of me?

Perhaps it was her jewelry that numbed me. With that bottle-green Halston sheath, she wore matching diamond choker, earrings, and bracelet. Nothing garish or ostentatious, mind you, but absolutely overwhelming. And she wore all that ice casually, as if each glittering stone was a merit badge.

Before I was rendered dumb by jealousy, I tried once more to get through that chromium plating Natalie had mentioned.

"Mrs. Havistock, can you think of anyone, within or outside the family, who might be capable of stealing the Demaretion? Either from need of money or from motives of revenge or whatever."

She frowned for a moment, considering. "I honestly can't," she said finally. "Can you, Luther?"

"No," he said.

It suddenly occurred to me that in the past fifteen minutes she had used the adverb "honestly" at least three times. Maybe that was her way of talking, an affectation. But mother taught me to be suspicious of people who keep assuring you how honest they are. "I wouldn't lie to you" and "To tell you the truth . . ." Hang on to your wallet then, mother had said, and count your rings after you shake hands.

I knew I wasn't going to get anything more from Vanessa and Luther. I rose, thanked them for their kindness and cooperation, and moved toward the door. Then that woman did surprise me. She came close, took my arm, gave me a smile that gleamed as brightly as her diamonds.

"I like you," she said. "Could we have lunch?"

"Thank you," I said, shocked. "I'd enjoy that very much."

"I'll give you a call," she said, squeezing my bicep, and the purple eyepatch with the hiss showed me out.

I had Lean Cuisine spaghetti dinner that night, with some greens picked up at the salad bar at my local deli. I also had two glasses of red wine from the jug Al Georgio had left. So when he called around ten o'clock, I was in a mellow mood.

"How's the private eye doing?" he asked.

"No hits, no runs, no errors," I said. "At least I hope that last is correct. I saw Luther and Vanessa this evening."

"Oh?" he said. "That's interesting. I'd like your take on those two. And I've got a couple of goodies for you. Listen, I've finished up all the typing I had to do, and I'm on my way home to Queens. How's about I stop at your place—no more than half an hour, I swear—and we compare notes?"

"Sure," I said, "come ahead. I just had some of your wine so I owe you. Did you have dinner tonight?"

"Yeah, I ate."

"What did you have?"

"A cheeseburger. At my desk. With a chocolate malt."

I sighed. "Al, that's no way to eat."

"Tell me about it," he said. "See you in about fifteen minutes, Dunk."

He looked wearier than ever, and accepted a glass of his red wine gratefully.

"You're working too hard," I told him.

"Ahh," he said, "it comes with the territory. So how did you make out with Vanessa and Luther?"

I gave him a complete rundown. He listened intently, not interrupting. When I finished, he rose to refill his wineglass.

"That business about Ruby Querita being absent from the kitchen— that's pretty thin stuff, Dunk."

"I know it is."

"But I'll check it out. Ruby's brother, the guy in the clink on a drug rap—well, his lawyer is filing an appeal on the grounds of new evidence. Lawyers cost money. So maybe Ruby saw a chance of grabbing some big bucks. It doesn't listen—I don't think she's got the brains to pull it—but I'll give it a look-see. What did you think of Luther?"

"You said you thought he was in a financial bind, a potential bankrupt. Maybe. But I thought he's heading for an emotional crackup. Al, the guy is barely functioning."

"Yeah," he said, staring at me, "you may be right. And Vanessa?"

"Were you attracted to her?" I asked him.

"Of course I was," he said gruffly. "I told you she came on to me. And even if she hadn't, I'd have been jolted. She's a lot of woman."

"She is that," I agreed. "But there's more there than meets the eye. She wants to have lunch with me. She says she likes me."

"Don't tell me she's coming on to *you*?"

"No, nothing like that. I think she just wants to know what's going on. She's figuring on becoming bosom buddies, excuse the expression, so she can pump me. Which makes me wonder why. Al, you said you had things to report."

He loosened his tie, slumped deeper into the couch.

"A few things," he said. "The FBI came in on this. It's a local crime
so they've got no jurisdiction. But anytime there's a heist like this—big
cash or art work or, say, something small or valuable—they figure there's
a good chance of it having been hustled across the state line for fencing,
so they're interested. They weren't heavy about it—just wanted to know
what was going on, and would I keep them informed, and did I need any
help—ya-ta-ta-ta. The usual bullshit. No problem. Then we got in touch
with Interpol. They're ready to cooperate—which will add a little muscle
to those letters Finkus, Holding is sending out. That's Jack Smack's insurance company. Did you know they're contacting coin dealers all over
the world?"

I nodded.

"Sure you did," he said without rancor. "And I suppose you know
they got a letter from the crook, or someone who says he is, asking if
they'd be interested in a buyback?"

I nodded again.

"Well, they signaled yeah, they'd be interested, and today they got a
second letter. The guy wants two hundred grand for the Demaretion."

I looked at him, shocked. "Al, how do you know all this? Don't tell
me that Jack told you."

He tried to laugh. "That guy wouldn't give me the time of day. No, he
didn't tell me. But I have a contact at Finkus, Holding. One hand washes
the other."

"Two hundred thousand?" I said, still astonished. "Isn't that a lot for
a thief to ask from the insurance company?"

"A lot?" he said. "It's ridiculous!"

"What do you think Finkus, Holding will do?"

"Try to bargain him down. They might spring for a hundred Gs—but
I doubt it. They'll wait until the crook realizes he's got no other option
except to take the coin to a fence and hope he can get ten percent. Then
he'll settle. I still say it isn't a professional goniff. It's someone in the
family."

"Yes," I said, "I think you're right. Al, I could scramble you some
eggs if you're hungry."

"No," he said, face creasing into that warm smile. "Thanks, Dunk, but
I'll skip. But I'll have a little more wine if you don't mind."

"Help yourself. It's yours."

I watched him as he sat brooding on the couch. Such a big, tired, *solid*
man. Like Luther Havistock, he needed maintenance and wasn't getting
it. I had never felt in a more comforting mood.

"Al," I said, "the last time you were here I said something about your
staying the night in my bed—if you made the pitch. You said that when
I decided, you wanted to be the first to know. All right, you are. Stay the
night?"

He smiled wanly. "You're a sweetheart, you are. I'd love to, Dunk.

But I'm beat, I need a hot shower, and more than anything else I need sleep. I wouldn't be any good for you.''

"Let me be the judge of that," I said. "Go take your shower."

Bodies are nice. I know that probably sounds inane, but it's true. Bodies are warm and smooth and slide on each other. I'm not talking about sex; I mean holding and hugging and saying silly things. You take your clothes off and you start giggling, don't you? Well, I do. Maybe not laughing out loud but feeling like it.

Al was wrong; he was *very* good for me. There's a lot to be said for snuggling. Closeness. That was what I had been starved for. He was no Adonis, but I was no Venus. If he had a layer of suet over hard muscles (those cheeseburgers and chocolate malts!), I was all twigs and splinters, being stretched out and bony.

Maybe it was our physical disparateness that put us in such a good mood. There was nothing heavy about what we did; it was just cuddling and kissing and touching. I think he was as hungry for it as I was. The intimacy. It doesn't always have to be sweat and shouts. It can be smiling affection.

We did some frivolous things, I suppose, but at the time they seemed important to me, and I think they were important to him. But there were no fervid avowals of passion—nothing like that. I suppose you'll think it was just a casual one-night stand, but it wasn't. It was *significant.*

I touched a reddish scar on his ribs. "What's that?" I asked.

"A guy shot me."

"Did it hurt?"

"No," he said, "it felt good."

He kissed my hipbones, which have a nasty habit of poking up the skin. Then he kissed my stomach, which is flat and hard as a board.

"Pregnant," he said. "Definitely pregnant."

"Bite your tongue," I said.

"No," he said. "Yours."

And he did.

That's the way it went. Just a man and a woman who had found a temporary cure for loneliness. I thought he'd conk out first, but I fell asleep before he did. I half-awoke once during the night to find I was all entwined about him, spoon fashion. I groaned with contentment, and pulled his warm, heavy body closer.

In the morning, fully awake, I discovered he had been up, dressed, and was gone. On my bedside table was a sheet torn from his notebook. It read: "I love you, Dunk."

That troubled me.

13

Next stop: Wimpsville . . . or so I thought.

It was Saturday, and I called Roberta and Ross Minchen, hoping to make an appointment to see them that afternoon. I expected grumbles and hostility, but Roberta couldn't have been more agreeable.

"Of course we'll see you," she said. "Mother told me you had been hired, and Ross and I think it's a marvelous idea. We do hope you can get this mess cleared up as soon as possible. But I'm afraid seeing you this afternoon is out of the question; we're in the middle of preparing for a little party we're having tonight. Listen, I have a fabulous idea! Our guests won't be arriving until eight-thirty or nine—around there. Why don't you come over, say, an hour earlier or so, and we'll have a nice chat. Then you stay on for the party. I think you'll like our friends."

"That's very kind of you, Mrs. Minchen, but—"

"Roberta."

"Roberta. But I wouldn't want to intrude."

"Nonsense! You won't be intruding at all. Please say you'll come early and stay for our little gala. Who knows—you may meet a fascinating man!"

Her effusiveness was hard to resist, but I was doubtful about spending an entire evening at the Home of the Wimps. But then I reckoned I could stay for one drink, and if it was too much of a drag, make a hasty exit, pleading a fierce migraine, the unexpected onset of menarche, or *something*.

"All right, Roberta," I said, "I'll be there. Thank you. Is it a dress-up party?"

"*Au contraire,*" she said gaily. "Very informal. Wear whatever you like. I just know everyone's going to *love* you!"

Then she giggled inexplicably. That giggle should have warned me that everything wasn't quite right at the House of Minchen—but how was I to know? How could anyone have known?

They lived in a lumpy apartment house on East 80th Street that was almost back-to-back with the Havistocks' building on 79th. It even had a similar lobby, with ancient attendant, frowsty odor, and walls of marble that might have been salvaged from Pompeii.

Even more startling was that the Minchens, a young couple, had apparently decided to make their apartment a smaller replica of the Havistocks'. Or perhaps they had furnished it totally with hand-me-downs. But there were the same brown velvet chairs and couches, stifling drapes, and suffocating bric-a-brac, whatnots, and a number of succulent plants that needed dusting.

But the most surprising thing, and quite out of character in that necropolis, was the largest television set I had ever seen—really an enormous screen. And atop cabinets on both sides, two videocassette recorders, and a portable video camera with power pack attached. Curious.

Roberta and Ross met me at the door, the soul of affability. They were both dressed informally: he in sport jacket, slacks, open-necked shirt, and loafers; she in a flowered print jumpsuit, zippered down the front, which, considering her dumpling body, gave her the look of a female Winston Churchill—or maybe an oversized Kewpie doll.

They were not the most attractive people I had ever met—he *would* crack his knuckles, and apparently they never called each other anything but ''dear'' or ''darling''—but they were hospitable enough, got me seated in one of those hot, overstuffed armchairs, and insisted I have something to drink. I settled for a glass of chilled white wine. I thought they were both drinking watered vodka. Later I discovered it was neat 94-proof gin.

As usual, I started out playing humble, explaining that while I had no desire to pry into their private lives, solving the puzzle of the missing Demaretion did, of necessity, demand the answers to some personal questions.

''For instance,'' I said, addressing Ross Minchen, ''I don't even know what your occupation is. Are you in textiles—like your father-in-law and brother-in-law?''

''Oh, no,'' he said quickly, ''nothing like that. I'm vice president of the Digman-Findle Corporation. We do plastic extrusions.''

I didn't want to reveal my ignorance by asking him what the hell *that* was.

''He practically runs the company,'' his wife said brightly. ''Don't you, dear?''

''Well, not quite, darling.'' he said modestly, patting his long, thinning locks to make certain they were concealing his baldness.

I didn't have the chutzpah to ask him what his income was, but I figured the vice president of *anything* was doing okay dollarwise. Besides, everyone had said that at one time Vanessa had come on to Ross. Would a luxury-loving lady like that have cut her eyes at a guy who was destitute? Doubtful.

So I got down to the nitty-gritty, taking them over the events of that morning and early afternoon when the Demaretion disappeared. They said what everyone else had told me: there were a lot of people there, all mingling and moving about, and it was difficult, if not impossible, to say where any one individual was at any particular time.

I asked them the same question I had asked Vanessa and Luther Havistock: Did either of them notice anything unusual or unexpected that morning? They looked at each other, then shook their heads; no, they had not.

I had a sinking feeling that as a detective, I was a washout. It wasn't so much that people were lying to me, but that I was asking the wrong questions.

"Look," I said desperately, "I hope you understand that whatever you tell me will be held in strictest confidence. Neither of you will be quoted as the source of anything you might say. Now, with that in mind, I should tell you that Detective Al Georgio of the New York Police Department, and John Smack, investigator for Grandby's insurance company, both think a member of your family was involved in the theft of the Demaretion. If what they believe is true—and I emphasize that *if*—who in the family do you think might possibly be guilty?"

Again they stared at each other: he so pale, solemn, with the intent frown of a pallbearer; she with that blinking, rabbity look, eyes popping, lips pouting.

"Orson Vanwinkle," Ross Minchen said finally. "He's capable of it. The man is a rotter."

Rotter? When was the last time you heard someone use that word? But I didn't laugh.

"It was Natalie, darling," Roberta Minchen said to her husband. "Definitely Natalie." Then she turned to me, incisors gleaming. "I hate to throw suspicion on my own sister, but let's face it, she's a disgrace. Those so-called friends of hers . . . I happen to know she's into the drug scene. Hopheads are always in need of money, aren't they?"

I was saved from answering by the front door chimes. The Minchens leaped to their feet.

"Our guests!" Ross cried.

"You'll just *love* these people," Roberta assured me. "They're so different."

Within the next thirty minutes, four married couples arrived, all about the Minchens' age. I was introduced to everyone, and to this day cannot remember a single name—which is all right with me.

You would think, wouldn't you, that in any gathering of five couples there would be at least *one* lovely woman and *one* handsome man? I'm not saying strangers should be immediately judged by their physical attractiveness—God knows I'm no beauty—but let's face it, isn't comeliness the first thing that makes us think someone may be worth knowing when we meet them for the first time?

Not that all the Minchens' friends were ugly; they were not. But the men seemed shaped like milk bottles—remember how they looked?—and the women appeared to be down comforters tied in the middle. The men were balding, with a shocking assortment of smutchy complexions, tics, and scraggly mustaches. The women wore too much makeup, inexpertly applied, and instead of laughing, most of them whinnied.

I was ready to get out of there as soon as decently possible, but then I decided to stay awhile. It wasn't their sparkling personalities—they had none at all—it was their conversation. It was in a kind of inside code they all understood, but which was pure Lower Slobbovian to me. It went something like this:

"Wait'll you see what *we* brought!"

"Ours is better!"

"Harry says it's the best yet!"

"It's got to win an Academy Award!"

"Martha tells me I have a knack for it!"

"Three on one—come on, that's a little much!"

While this chatter continued, all with exclamation marks, the host and hostess ladled out the drinks. I had one more glass of white wine and nursed it, but the others guzzled like there was no tomorrow. One geezer who was trying to grow a beard and wasn't succeeding latched onto me and gave me a total examination, head to foot.

"Oh, my," he said, showing tarnished teeth. "I hope you're going to join our group. We need a wild card!"

What the hell?

This went on for almost an hour, and everyone was into their second or third round of booze, when Ross Minchen shouted, "Showtime!" And immediately several others echoed, "Showtime! Showtime!"

We all got seated, me included, facing the huge TV screen. Lights were dimmed, and Ross fussed with one of the VCRs, sliding in a cassette. By this time I realized I wasn't going to see *The Sound of Music* or *Gone With the Wind*. I didn't.

It was porn all right, the hardest of hard-core. But if that wasn't numbing enough, the performers were Roberta and Ross Minchen and their happy little band of flakes. The color was great, the sound was professional, and there they all were on the silver screen doing things which never occurred to me that people could do or wanted to do.

I mean, I've read Havelock Ellis and Krafft-Ebing, and in a bemused kind of way I can understand why someone might have a mad passion for an oak tree or go around sniffing an old piece of leather, but this stuff was *gross*. They were such *ordinary* people—business and professional men, career women and housewives—and really, seeing them naked, doing those things, wasn't exciting at all. It was scary and it was sad.

When they started the second cassette, I decided I better get out of there before viewing ended and new filming began. I thought I was leaving unobtrusively; they all had their eyes glued to the screen and were busy with muttered comments and nervous laughter. But Roberta caught up with me at the door and clamped a tight hand on my arm.

"I know this is all new to you," she whispered, "but you'll be back, you'll be back!"

I gave her a weak smile and edged out the door.

"It was Natalie," she called after me. "She's *obscene!*"

I got home as quickly as I could, stripped and showered. Soaped a long time and stood under a hard spray, washing it all away. I didn't let myself think of what I had seen. I kept repeating nursery rhymes: "Mary, Mary, quite contrary . . . "

But later, in my shabby flannel bathrobe, sipping a vodka from Jack Smack's bottle, I *had* to think about it and ponder the vagaries of human beings. All of us. It was very unsettling. Foundations seemed to be cracking, and I had to remember one-on-one basketball in a Des Moines driveway to keep my mind from whirling off into the wild blue yonder.

I had no idea what effect the Minchens' aberrant behavior had on the disappearance of the Demaretion—if it had any effect at all. It was just another revelation of a family that was coming to look like a collection of misfits, totally unlike the personae they presented to the world.

Are we all like that? Ordinary and presentable, even wimpish, in public, and then, in private, something different and perhaps monstrous? Was I like that?

I think that was what depressed me most about the evening. Those stupid porn films were funny, when I thought about them, but the worst thing was that they made me doubt myself, and what I might be capable of. Just seeing those unhappy people in frantic action brought me down to their level.

14

I suppose I should have immediately told Al Georgio and Jack Smack about the Minchens and their coven of wife-swappers, but I just couldn't do it. I think I was too ashamed to relate what I had seen, not knowing how to describe it in polite terms. Also, at the time I didn't see what possible connection it might have with the stealing of the Demaretion.

So I didn't call either of them, and hoped to spend a quiet Sunday at home, cozying up with a five-pound *New York Times* and enjoying a breakfast treat of cream cheese, lox, and onion on a bagel. Then I intended to do some *very* deep thinking about the Havistocks, try to sort out my impressions, and see if I could devise a theory on who broke the Eighth Commandment and copped the coin.

But it was not to be the leisurely day I had planned.

First, Al Georgio phoned. He was on his way to pick up his daughter, Sally, and they were going to spend the day in Central Park, then take in a movie, and go to a new West Side restaurant that was reputed to have the best barbecued ribs in town. Would I like to come along, spend the day with them?

"Al," I said, "when was the last time you saw your daughter?"

"About a month ago," he admitted.

"Then she wants to spend the day with *you*. The two of you—alone. She'd resent me, and quite rightly. Maybe some other time, Al; I'd love to meet her. But I have a feeling that today she'd like to have you for herself, and I'd just spoil things."

He sighed. "You may be right. I know she's all excited about today."

"Of course she is. You haven't seen her in a month, and she was beginning to wonder if her father had deserted her. Now the two of you go out and have a wonderful day."

"Okay," he said, "we will. Thanks, Dunk."

I hoped that would be the last interruption of my Sunday tranquillity, but it was not to be. The phone rang again. This time—surprise!—it was Archibald Havistock.

"Miss Bateson," he said in his diapason, "I would like to have a brief private meeting with you, and this would be an ideal time. Mrs. Havistock and the Minchens have gone to church, and Ruby Querita doesn't work on Sunday. May I impose on you and ask you to come over now? It shouldn't take long. Would that be an inconvenience?"

"Of course not, Mr. Havistock. I'll be there as soon as possible."

"Take a cab," he said.

What else? He was paying expenses.

He met me at the apartment door himself and conducted me into the den-library where I sat across from his swivel chair at that enormous partners' desk. He excused himself, disappeared, and came back a few moments later with a silver tray laden with coffee pot, paper-thin china cups and saucers, silver spoons, pink linen napkins, creamer, sugar, a bowl of butter balls, a plate of warm miniature croissants, and a pot of Dundee's orange marmalade.

"Beautiful," I said, eyeing that attractive brunch and forgetting my lost bagel. "I won't have to eat another thing all day."

That distant, somewhat chilly smile appeared again as he poured me a cup of steaming black coffee. "Help yourself," he urged. "The croissants are from a new patisserie on Lexington Avenue. I think they're quite good."

It was before noon on a Sunday morning, but he was dressed for a board of directors' meeting—or maybe a Congressional hearing. I think he was the most impeccably groomed man I had ever met. I mean he *glistened*—from his silvered hair to his polished wingtips. I wondered if he had his shoelaces ironed.

"I'm not going to ask you for a progress report," he said, and I had the odd notion that he could shatter a champagne glass with that voice if he let it out at full power. "I realize you have only started your investigation. But there are two things I wanted you to be aware of. First of all, it was my wife's suggestion that you be employed as our private investigator. Initially, I was opposed, feeling it best to leave the solution of the theft to professional detectives. Your knowledge of ancient Greek coins didn't seem to me a sufficient reason."

"I can understand your feeling that way, Mr. Havistock. They've certainly had more experience in detection."

"But then, when I learned that members of my family were under suspicion, I changed my mind. I find it most distressing, Miss Bateson, that any of my children, their spouses, or our employees might be guilty of stealing the Demaretion. So I acceded to my wife's wishes, in hopes that you might be able to reassure us that no Havistock could or would do such a thing."

"I told you, sir," I said, "I can't give you any guarantee on that."

He waved my demurrer away. "I understand that. I also appreciate your agreeing to come to me first with the name of the culprit, if it proves to be a family member, before going to the authorities. The second thing I wished to discuss with you is this: Orson Vanwinkle has informed me that you asked him questions about my signet ring. Was he correct?"

Now that was a shocker. I could have sworn that Horsy was so smashed he would never remember any of our conversation. I thoughtfully buttered and marmaladed another of those delicious croissants.

"Mr. Vanwinkle is correct," I acknowledged. "I did ask about your ring."

He nodded, regarding me gravely. "I wondered about your interest, and then I realized . . . Whoever substituted the sealed empty case for the one containing the Demaretion must have had access to my signet ring since it was used to imprint the wax seal. Am I right?"

It was my turn to nod. Besides, I couldn't speak; my mouth was full.

He clapped his hands together with mild delight, and this time his smile had real warmth. "Very, very clever of you, Miss Bateson. And those so-called professional detectives still haven't grasped the significance of the ring. My wife is right; we did well to employ you. You are a very intelligent, perceptive young lady, and I now have high hopes that you may succeed if Georgio and Smack fail. My only objection is that you did not come to me directly with your questions about my signet ring instead of asking Mr. Vanwinkle."

I dabbed at my lips with a pink linen napkin, so starched it could have been balanced on its edge. "I didn't want to bother you, Mr. Havistock."

"No," he said, shaking his great, leonine head, "I will not accept that. When my wife and I asked you to investigate members of our family, we were quite willing that we—my wife and I—should be questioned as well as the others. I want to make that perfectly clear to you: Mrs. Havistock and I expect no preferential treatment whatsoever."

"All right," I said, pouring him and myself more coffee, "I'll go along with that, and I'm happy to hear you say it. Now, about the signet ring . . . Is there one—or more?"

"Only one, to my knowledge."

"Do you wear it?"

"Very infrequently. But I value it—a gift from my wife."

"Where do you keep it?"

"Sometimes here," he said, pulling open a small drawer at the side of his desk. "Sometimes in my jewelry case in the bedroom. That's where it is at present."

"So anyone in the household might have borrowed it temporarily?"

He sighed. "I'm afraid so. I use it rarely—to seal documents and things of that sort. It's never locked up or hidden. Yes, anyone who knew of its existence would have easy access to it.''

I gave him a wan smile. ''Just as they had easy access to the two unused display cases in your bedroom closet.''

''Yes. That, too. I can't tell you how painful I find all this, Miss Bateson, but the more I learn about the crime, the more I tend to agree with Georgio and Smack: a family member was involved. It is not a pleasant prospect to contemplate.''

''You want the Demaretion back, don't you?'' I asked.

He looked at me in astonishment. ''Of course. It is a glorious work of art.''

''I agree. I don't want it to disappear into some private collection where it'll never be seen again.''

''You think that's what will happen?''

''Unless we find it first. Mr. Havistock, how would you characterize your relations with your family? Intimate? Close? Distant? Cold?''

He looked at me queerly, those azure eyes glittering. ''I have tried to be a good paterfamilias, and I would be the first to say I haven't always succeeded. My own father was a stern, despotic man, and I suspect I learned too much from him. Times change, and I should have changed with them, but I wouldn't or couldn't. More harshness, more discipline, was not the answer. I should have been more sympathetic, more understanding when the children were young. It was my failure. It was my fault.''

Suddenly he was no longer the complete, self-assured man but, by admitting guilt and weakness, someone much more human and likable.

''I have no children,'' I said, ''so I'm not qualified to give advice. But the time comes, I suppose, when you have to kick them out of the nest and hope they can fly.''

''Yes,'' he said sadly, ''that time comes. Most of mine seem to have dropped—like stones.''

''I think you're exaggerating,'' I told him boldly. ''They may not have come up to your expectations, but they are living their own lives. You must allow them to make their own mistakes. How else can they learn?''

He didn't answer, but I had the feeling that he was aware of the frailties of all his children—and his nephew as well—and spent too much time brooding on what he might have done differently to ensure their success and happiness.

I cabbed home from that meeting with a lot to ponder. But I resolutely finished the Sunday *Times*, wishing I had accepted Al's invitation to spend the day with him and his daughter. Then I did some laundry, slurped a blueberry yogurt, and prepared to spend the evening watching TV, with maybe a brief trip out into the living world to have a hamburger or a slice of anchovy pizza.

But I canceled all those noble plans and did something exceedingly

foolish. I phoned Jack Smack, really hoping he wouldn't be in. But he
was.

"Hey, Dunk!" he said, sounding genuinely glad to hear from me.
"How're you doing?"

"All right. I'm not interrupting, am I?"

"Hell, no. I'm just sitting here counting the walls."

I wanted him to know this was a professional call—nothing personal.
"Something came up on the Demaretion case, and I thought you'd be
interested."

"Oh?" he said. "Maybe we shouldn't talk about it on the phone. Listen, Dunk, have you had dinner yet?"

"Not yet," I said, hating myself.

"There's a new place over on the West Side that's supposed to have
the best barbecued ribs in town. Want to try it?"

"No, no," I said hastily. "Pork makes me break out in splotches."

"Okay," he said equably, "then how about this scenario: I'll run out
and pick up a couple of strip steaks and Idaho potatoes. I've got the
makings for a green salad. Meanwhile you cab down here—I'll pay the
freight. I'm in a loft in SoHo. We'll have dinner, talk about the Demaretion, and after that, we'll let nature take its course."

I didn't like that last; it scared me.

"All right," I said faintly.

His loft looked like a factory: High Tech with everything in metal and
Lucite. But he had a fully equipped kitchen—the largest compartment in
the place. (The bathroom was the only enclosed room.) The bed, I noticed
nervously, seemed to be double futons on the floor. Soft, plump, and
lascivious.

He had a microwave, and fifteen minutes after I arrived he served up
a yummy meal on a table of milk glass supported on black steel saw-
horses. He also provided a bottle of super Cabernet. This lad knew how
to live. Sour cream and chives with the potatoes, of course. He didn't
miss a trick.

While we gobbled our food, I told him about the signet ring, and what
Vanwinkle and Archibald Havistock had to say about it.

He stopped eating long enough to slap a palm onto the tabletop. "God
damn it!" he said wrathfully. "I missed that, and I'll bet Al Georgio did,
too." Then he looked at me admiringly. "Dunk, that was good thinking.
You've got a talent for investigation."

"Well . . . maybe. But it doesn't amount to anything. I mean, anyone
in the family could have used that ring."

"I know," he said, "but I should have seen it. I'm supposed to be the
professional. Anything else?"

"No," I said, deciding not to tell him about the Minchens' hobby.
"Nothing."

"Well . . . " he said, working on his salad. (Too much salt in that salad.)

"We got another letter from our anonymous crook. The guy wants two hundred grand for the Demaretion. No way!"

"What will you do now, Jack?"

"Haggle."

"How will you do that? By letter? Phone calls?"

"This guy is very clever. He sends us print-free letters from different zones in Manhattan. Practically impossible to trace. We reply by coded Death Notices in the *Times*. I know it all sounds like cloak-and-dagger stuff, but it works. In case you're interested, we're going to offer him twenty-five thousand."

"You think he'll accept?"

"No," Jack said, "I don't think he will. He's got us by the short hairs, and he knows it. We'll probably settle for fifty Gs—around there. Meanwhile I'll keep gnawing at it. I may catch up with him before the payoff. Well . . . enough about business. I have some chocolate tofutti in the fridge. Interested?"

"Thanks," I said, "but not really."

"Me neither. But I also have some Rémy Napoléon—and that I *am* interested in."

"Jack, do you eat like this every day?"

"Of course not," he said. "I'd be a balloon if I did. I usually thaw something frozen. One of those complete gourmet dinners that tastes like glue. But once or twice a week I like to cook."

"For yourself?" I asked.

"Sometimes," he said, giving me that wisenheimer grin that implied sexual goings-on and probably didn't mean a damned thing—I told myself.

We collapsed on those yielding futons and sipped our cognacs from small jelly jars.

"I have Tiffany snifters," he said, "but occasionally I like to use these, to remind me where I came from."

"And where was that?"

"Poverty," he said, laughing shortly. "I've made it, Dunk—so far— but I want to keep remembering the time when a peanut butter sandwich was a treat."

I had absolutely no idea if he was telling the truth or putting me on. I did know the man was a consummate actor. He told amusing stories in a dozen dialects. His movements could be as graceful as a ballet dancer's steps or so gauche that they broke me up. He seemed driven to entertain, and I must say he succeeded. I never enjoyed myself as much. Couldn't stop giggling.

"You know," he said, taking the empty jelly jar from my fingers and putting it aside, "a friend of mine—a great cocksman—once told me that the best way to seduce a woman is to make her laugh. Do you think that's true?"

I considered. "It's a start," I said.

The problem was that when we were naked, flouncing around on those pads, he was still the entertainer. I didn't want to think of how many women he had been with to learn all the things he knew. He certainly educated *me*. He was such an expert—but somehow divorced, not really involved. Like an actor who has played the same role too many times.

All those reflections came later. At the time, I was whirled away, brain detonated, unable to concentrate on anything but his physical beauty and skill and what he was doing to me. I was one long, throbbing nerve end, and he knew how to tickle it. What a craftsman he was! I loved him. I hated him.

He drove me home in his Jaguar.

15

I was beginning to learn how detectives worked. You couldn't sit at home or in your office and wait for people to come in and tell you things; you had to have the gall to go after them, pry, ask embarrassing questions, nag them, and generally make a nuisance of yourself.

I could do all that. Not only was I being paid for it (plus expenses), but I really loved the Demaretion and resented its theft. Also, someone had made a fool out of me—getting me to sign a receipt for an empty display case—so I had a personal interest in this affair. Revenge!

I retained that dauntless mood while I phoned Mrs. Mabel Havistock on Monday morning, asking if I might see her as soon as possible. If she was surprised or discomfited, her voice didn't reveal it. She said she'd see me at precisely two o'clock that afternoon—in royal tones suggesting that I was being granted an audience with the queen. I thanked her meekly. So much for fearlessness.

My bravura mood got another jolt when the mail was delivered a little after noon. Three catalogues, bills from New York Telephone and Con Edison, and a plain white envelope. Just a typed Mary Lou Bateson on the front, with my address. No hint of the sender.

Inside, a single sheet of white paper. Typed in the middle in capital letters: LAY OFF—OR ELSE. No signature.

Very melodramatic, and very scary. My first reaction was an instant resolve to take the first plane back to Des Moines and spend the rest of my life practicing dunk shots in the driveway.

Second reaction: fury. What son of a bitch was trying to frighten me off the Demaretion case? How dare he! Third reaction: Call the police, which I did. It took me almost a half-hour to locate Detective Al Georgio. I told him about the anonymous threat.

"I'll be damned," he said slowly. "Plain white paper?"

"Yes."

"The whole thing typed?"

"Yes."

"You handled it?"

"Of course I handled it. How else could I read it? I tore open the envelope, took out the sheet of paper, unfolded it, and read it. How could I do that without handling it?"

"All right, all right," he said soothingly, "don't get your balls in an uproar. I'll pick it up and have it dusted. And you know what we'll get? Zip, zero, and zilch. Sounds to me like the kind of letters Finkus, Holding has been getting: plain paper, no prints, typed on an Olympia standard. Well, we'll see . . . You know what this means, don't you, Dunk? You're getting close."

"Close to *what*?" I wailed. "Al, I haven't found out a damned thing."

"What have you been doing? Who have you talked to?"

Then, because I had already told Jack Smack and was trying very hard not to favor either of them, I told Al about the signet ring and Vanwinkle's and Archibald Havistock's answers to my questions. His reaction was the same as Jack's.

"Jesus Christ!" he said disgustedly. "I'm a dolt. I should have picked up on that. Nice work, Dunk. But they both said everyone in the family had access to the ring?"

"That's right."

"Well, it's hard to believe the ring business was enough to trigger your black-spot letter. It must be something else."

He paused and for a moment I was tempted to tell him how Roberta and Ross Minchen got their jollies. Then I decided that since it had nothing to do with the Demaretion heist, Al had no need to know.

"What are you doing today?" he asked me.

"Seeing Mrs. Havistock in about an hour. I want to talk to everyone who was in the apartment on that morning."

"That sounds sensible. And safe enough."

"After I talk to her, it'll only leave Ruby Querita. I'll get to her next."

He was silent. Then:

"Dunk, watch your back. Don't press too hard. I don't like that letter you got. It scares me."

"Well, it sure scares the hell out of *me*."

"Want to move into a hotel? Change your phone number? I can't provide 'round-the-clock protection; you know that."

"No, I'll go along just the way I've been doing. Maybe I've heard something that threatens the crook—but what it could be, I have no idea. Al, how was your day with your daughter?"

"Wonderful," he said. "Just perfect. I told her about you. She said she'd like to meet you."

"That's sweet. And I'd like to meet her. Next time you see her—okay?"

"You better believe it. And Dunk, do be careful."

"I intend to be."

"You've got my home phone number and where I can be reached during the day. Don't be bashful; call me anytime."

"Thanks, Al," I said gratefully. "I'm hoping I won't get myself in a crisis situation, but if I do, it's nice to know you're there."

"I'm here," he said.

What a splendid June day it was! Rare sky, beamy sun, kissing breeze. Manhattan isn't all graffiti and dog droppings, you know. Sometimes the light and the shining towers can make you weep with pleasure. It was like that when I started out early and strode across Central Park to the East Side. I didn't even look behind me. Nothing could frighten me on a day like that.

Except possibly the matriarch of the Havistock clan. If Mrs. Mabel didn't have bones in her corset, she sat as if she had: stiffly erect, spine straight. I wondered how long it had been since she had allowed that spine to touch the back of a chair. All in all, a very stern, domineering matron, and to avoid being completely intimidated, I had to keep reminding myself that this ogress had been the one who suggested my employment as the Havistocks' private investigator.

I had been admitted to the apartment by Ruby Querita, who gave me a small smile, signifying, I supposed, that she now recognized me as a friend of the family. But halfway down that gloomy corridor, Orson Vanwinkle brushed her aside and took over as usher.

"Hi, doll," he said with his lupine grin. He also stroked my cheek, and I knew blossoms would never bloom there again. "Madame Defarge is waiting for you," he said, jerking a thumb toward the living room. "Going to have a nice chin-chin?"

I nodded.

"About what?"

"About who stole the Demaretion," I said, looking at him directly.

"Oh, that old thing," he said, not at all disconcerted. "Just a hunk of metal as far as I'm concerned. The insurance company will pay off; you'll see." Then he leaned closer and lowered his voice. "When are you and I going to have another scene?"

"Scene?"

"You know—fun and games."

I swear the man was certifiable. But that didn't make him any less dangerous. I walked away from him and entered the living room where I found her majesty sitting bolt upright on one of those loathsome brown velvet couches. She graciously beckoned me to sit beside her.

She was wearing a lavender scent—what else? I would have bet her dresser drawers were packed with sachets.

"I don't like your hair," she said, staring. "You really must do something with it."

"I know," I said miserably. "I intend to have it styled one of these days."

"Do," she said. "I can give you the name of a good man. Now then, what did you wish to speak to me about?"

Not exactly a propitious beginning, but I plunged right in, explaining that I was interviewing everyone who was present in the apartment on the morning the Demaretion was taken.

"I have already related my activities on that morning to Detective Georgio. You were present. I answered all his questions."

"*His* questions, ma'am. Mine are of a more personal nature."

She looked at me coldly. "Such as?"

"Detective Georgio and insurance investigator John Smack are convinced that a member of your family took part in the theft. Both are experienced men and would not make such an accusation lightly. Would you care to name one or more family members you think might possibly be involved?"

She made a sudden, distraught movement of one hand: a wild, jerky wave. "I will not point the finger of suspicion at anyone. Certainly none of my kin."

"As you wish, Mrs. Havistock. But you have employed me to discover the truth, and your refusal to cooperate, no matter how well-intentioned, just makes my job more difficult. All right, let's skip family members and talk about employees. How long has Ruby Querita worked for you?"

"Almost ten years now."

"You trust her?"

"Absolutely."

"I understand her brother is in prison."

"That has nothing to do with Ruby. I have complete confidence in her."

"She works six days a week?"

"Five, plus a half-day on Saturday."

"She cooks and cleans."

"Cooks mostly, and does some light housework. Twice a week a man comes in from a commercial service to dust and vacuum. And once a month we have a crew from the same service to give the apartment a good going-over, including washing the windows and scrubbing down the bathrooms."

"Were any of these commercial cleaners here on the morning the Demaretion was taken?"

"No, they were not."

"But they were aware of your husband's coin collection?"

"I'm sure they were. It was on open display in his library. I spoke to him several times about that, asking him to put the coins in a bank vault, but he would not."

"Numismatists are like that, ma'am," I said softly. "They like to have their collections readily available where they can see them, examine them, enjoy them. Whose idea was it to sell your husband's collection?"

"His. And I agreed. We are presently engaged in revising our estate planning, and rather than attempt to break up the collection amongst our heirs, with so many coins to each beneficiary, it seemed simpler to sell the collection and add the proceeds to the assets of the estate."

"Then I gather your husband is no longer an active collector."

"That is correct. I think he made his last purchase about five years ago. And since then he has sold off a number of items. At one time I think he had more than six hundred coins."

"Oh?" I said, surprised. "I wasn't aware of that."

"I fail to see what these questions about my husband's collection have to do with the disappearance of the Demaretion."

"Probably nothing," I admitted. "But I'm trying to learn as much as I can, in hopes that something small will lead to something bigger, then to something larger yet, and eventually we'll get to the truth of the matter. Mrs. Havistock, I respect your decision not to single out a member of your family as a possible suspect, but I wish you would reconsider your decision. It might speed things up considerably if you'd be willing to give me a hint—no matter how tiny. I assure you I won't treat it as proof of guilt, or even as an accusation. It will simply be a lead that will enable me to make a more thorough and efficient investigation. Won't you name *someone* you think might have been involved?"

I was watching her closely. As I made my plea, her heavy features began to sag. It was like putting a wax mask too close to a flame. But in this case it was flesh that was melting, all her features softening and flowing downward. It was a dreadful thing to see because it left her with nothing but sadness and tragedy, eyes dulled, resolve gone, strength fled.

"No," she said in a low voice, "I will name no one."

So that was that.

I was in the outside hallway, waiting for the elevator. It arrived, and who should pop out but Natalie Havistock, frenetic as ever. She looked like she was dressed for a masquerade. The item I remember best was a mess jacket of soiled white canvas emblazoned with military shoulder patches.

"Hey, Dunk!" she said. "Getting much these days?"

Then she embraced me and lurched up to kiss me on the lips—which I could have done without.

"What'cha been doing in the morgue?" she asked, and I had to laugh; she was so right.

"Talking to your mother, Nettie."

"Mommy dearest? She's been in the doldrums lately. Something's been eating her, and I can guarantee it ain't a man. Listen, hon, would you like to go to a party tonight?"

"A party?" I said, startled. "What kind?"

"A party-party. A bash. An orgy. Down in the East Village. Hundreds of people. Plenty of booze and grass. Maybe a line of coke if you know the right people. How about it?"

"Will your boyfriend be there?"

"Akbar El Raschid? That's what he calls himself. His real name is Sam Jefferson. You've heard about him, have you? Hell, yes, he'll be there. If you don't like the scene, you can split. Okay?"

I agreed. She opened her bulging shoulder bag and took out a gold ballpoint pen and pigskin notebook. I wondered what store she had honored with her light-fingered presence. She scribbled the address, tore the sheet away, and tucked it into the pocket of my suede jacket.

"Try to make it," she urged. "You'll have a ball."

"What time does it start?"

"It'll open up around nine, but these things don't get moving until midnight. Wear your chastity belt."

"Thanks a lot," I said. "You're really making it sound attractive."

"Nah," she said, laughing. "You won't have to put out. Unless you want to. Listen, Dunk, you got a couple of extra bucks I could borrow?"

I thought swiftly. "I've got a five you can have."

"Five is alive!" she cried. "But twenty is plenty! Pay you back one of these days. Remind me."

So I handed over a five-dollar bill, figuring I could always fiddle my expense account and get it back from her father. Then she dashed into the apartment, and I waited patiently for the next elevator.

What do you wear to a party-party, a bash, an orgy in the East Village? Not basic black with pearls, that's for sure. Besides, I didn't own basic black and pearls. So I settled for jeans and a long-sleeved white "bullfighter's shirt." It had a ruffled front and was cut low enough to show cleavage—if I'd had any. And my suede jacket, of course.

I had no idea how to get to that address by bus or subway, so I cabbed down. After all it *was* part of my investigation; I wanted to get a line on Nettie's boyfriend. So it was a legitimate business expense—right?

The cabby wasn't happy about taking me to that neighborhood.

"Your life insurance paid up?" he asked.

Actually, when he dropped me and I looked around, the street didn't seem menacing at all. Maybe not as clean as West 83rd, but there were no corpses in the gutter, and there were even two scraggly ginkgo trees struggling to survive.

The party wasn't hard to find. It was only a little after ten o'clock, but the decibel count was soaring. They were playing a Pink Floyd tape—I think it was "The Dark Side of the Moon"—and the volume was turned up high enough to loosen your fillings.

There weren't "hundreds of people" there, but maybe they'd arrive by midnight when "things got moving." But the top-floor apartment—half-attic and half-loft—was crowded enough. Thirty or forty people, I reckoned, of three colors, five races, and four sexes. It was a sort of zonked-out United Nations.

Nettie hadn't exaggerated about the booze and grass available: plenty of both. Plus platters of brownies. But fearing those might be laced with hash, or something stronger, I passed. No one paid any attention to me, which was okay. I poured myself a little vodka in a plastic cup—no ice available—and surreptitiously turned down the volume on the cassette player. No one objected. As a matter of fact, I don't think anyone noticed. Maybe they were all tone-deaf.

I searched through the mob for Natalie but couldn't spot her. I did see a tall, lanky black propped against a wall, regarding the scene with amused contempt. He was wearing a red beret and had a single gold earring. Had to be Akbar El Raschid, née Sam Jefferson. Handsome lad with a little spiky Vandyke. I went up to him.

"I think we have a mutual acquaintance," I said.

"Allah?" he said, looking at me lazily. Then he straightened away from the wall and inspected me. "Hey, Stretch, you're a long one. Groupie for the Globe Trotters?"

"Not quite," I said. "The Celtics."

He snapped his fingers. "Got'cha," he said. "You're Dunk—right? Nat Baby told me about you. She says you're a foxy lady. Pleased to meet you, sweet mama."

"Did you steal the Demaretion?" I asked him.

If he was shocked or insulted, he didn't reveal it. "Who, what, where?" he said. "Oh, you mean that coin Nat Baby's papa lost. Nah, I didn't lift it. It was a *coin*. If I was to decide on a life of crime, coins would have no interest for me whatsoever. I'd go for the green. Worth more and easier to carry. Coins too heavy. You know us coons—we're lazy, sweet mama."

"This coin is worth a lot of loot."

"So?" he said. "You know how many bills you can pack in a little bitty suit satchel? Hey, how come you leaning on me? We just met, didn't we? Who you—Missy Sherlock Holmes?"

"I'm sorry," I said. "I apologize. But I'm getting paid to investigate the robbery. I'm asking everyone."

"Say no more. But look at me; I'm pure as the driven snow—right?"

His smile was hard to resist. He brought me another vodka, offered me a drag on the cigarette he was smoking—which I declined—and began a fascinating commentary on the people roiling about us.

"Look at them," he said. "They got to be first of the first. New fads, new fashions, new restaurants, new music. The Trendies, I call them. They can't stand to be second. Pick it up, try it out, drop it down, go on to something newer. Like pickled kiwi fruit maybe, or steaks grilled over dried cow flops. You dig? They run and run and run. What's new? What's the latest? Well, patricide is in. Oh, yeah? Well, then I got to kill my daddy. Next year it's matricide. There goes Mommy. No verities—that's their problem."

"Where did you graduate from?" I demanded.

He stared at me a long moment. "I got an MBA from Wharton," he said. "You going to hold that against me?"

"No, but why don't you *use* it?"

"I'd rather steal, sweet mama," he said, flashing the whitest choppers I've ever seen.

He was slender, loose, with a disjointed way of moving—like a marionette with slack strings. He seemed to be two men: flashy Harlem stud and sharp intellectual observer. I didn't know how seriously to take him. His talk could have been all taunts. Or maybe a mask for his despair. A complex character.

Then Natalie Havistock came rushing up and grabbed his arm—a proprietress.

"Hi, Dunk," she said. "Glad you could make it. This guy giving you his nigger jive? The Wharton MBA and all that? Bullshit! He's nothing but a field hand. Load that barge. Tote that bale."

He showed his teeth again, and cupped one of her heavy breasts. "Nah, honey mine," he said. "No jive. Dunk here asked me if I pinched your daddy's coin, and I admitted, yeah I did it. You and me, working together."

"Don't listen to him," Nettie advised. "He's flying tonight."

He was flying? *I* was flying! You could get a rush just by breathing that choky air. My brain was dancing a gavotte—and not just from the pot fumes. I couldn't decide how much Akbar El Raschid was putting me on. I thought, despite his indolent manner, he had a razor brain. What Netty called his nigger jive could have been an act, a devious way of concealing his guilt. I just didn't know.

As Nettie had predicted, by midnight the party was whirling, with new recruits arriving every minute. Someone turned up the volume on the cassette player, and my eardrums began to throb. A few people tried to dance, but most of the guests just stood swaying like zombies, smoking or drinking or both, looking about and grinning vacuously.

I circulated and talked to a few people. One was "into" primal scream, one was "into" Icelandic poetry, and one was "into" high colonics. With luck, I'd never see any of them again.

It really wasn't my kind of a do. Some of those guests were so *young*. When I was their age, I went to parties where we played Post Office and

Spin the Bottle. So I decided to take off. I still hadn't met the host or hostess, and knew that trying to make a polite farewell in that mob was useless.

I looked around for Natalie and finally spotted her in a corner, pressed up against Akbar El Raschid, gripping him by the lapels of his camouflaged field jacket. It was obvious she was angry about something. I could see she was yelling at him, leaning up to put her face close to his. She appeared furious, but he just looked down at her with his loopy smile.

It took me forever to find a taxi, and I wasn't overjoyed at roaming those mostly deserted streets at that hour. But I finally took a chance on a rusted gypsy cab and arrived home safely, so thankful that I overtipped the driver and said, "Have a nice day." At two in the morning!

When I unlocked the door, my phone was ringing, and I dashed for it. "Hello?" I said breathlessly.

"Dunk?" Al Georgio said. "Jesus, where the hell have you been? I was ready to call out the Marines. After that letter you got . . . "

"It was sweet of you to be concerned," I said. "I'm all right, Al. I went down to a party in the East Village to meet Natalie Havistock's boyfriend."

"The stud? Have a good time?"

"Not really."

"Learn anything?"

"First he said he had nothing to do with stealing the Demaretion. Then he said that he and Nettie did it together. I don't know what to believe."

"Yeah, the guy's a flake."

"When I left, they were having a big fat argument. I don't know about what. Probably doesn't mean a thing."

"Probably not."

"Al, did you know the Havistocks have commercial cleaners? A man comes in twice a week to vacuum, and once a month a whole crew gives the place a complete going-over."

"Yes, I knew that."

"Did you check them out?"

"Of course I checked them out. The second day I was on the case. What do you think—I walk around with my thumb up my—sure, I checked them out. Their alibis stand up."

"Just asking," I said humbly.

"That's okay, Dunk; ask anything you like. Now let me get some sleep."

"Al, thank you again for checking on me."

"You're welcome," he said gruffly.

I showered and shampooed to get the smoke fumes out of my hair. After I used my dryer, conditioner, and comb, I took a good look in the mirror. Mrs. Havistock had been right; I had to *do* something with it.

I fell into bed, thinking I'd be asleep instantly. But I wasn't. I kept flopping from side to side. Somehow I was convinced that I had heard something important that day, something significant. But what it was I could not recall. Finally I drifted into troubled slumber. I may have snored—I've been told I do that occasionally—but no man was there to give me an elbow in the ribs.

16

"Now you must call me Vanessa," she said in the kindliest way imaginable, touching the back of my hand with her bloody talons, "and I shall call you Dunk. Isn't that your nickname?"

I nodded, doing my best to smile.

She turned slightly and raised one finger. Immediately a waiter was at her shoulder, bending over deferentially—and also copping a peek down her bodice. She had that effect on every man within a fifty-foot radius: heads turned, chairs scraped and, I suppose, testosterone flowed.

"I shall have," she said precisely, "a very, *very* dry martini, straight up with a single olive. Dunk?"

"A glass of white wine, please."

"Nonsense," she said firmly. "No one drinks white wine anymore. And a kir royale," she said to the waiter. He nodded, grinning like an idiot, and scurried away. "You'll love it," she assured me. "Champagne and cassis." She looked around. "Isn't this a *fun* place?" she said.

I agreed it was, indeed, a fun place.

What it was, actually, was a fake Tudor pub on Third Avenue near 62nd Street. Beamed ceiling, plastered walls, pseudo-Tiffany lamps, everything burnished wood, gleaming brass, and red velvet. A stage set, with the menu written with chalk on a posted blackboard. Mostly steaks, chops, and things like broiled kidneys and sweetbreads. The prices were horrendous.

We were two of five women in the crowded joint. All the other customers were male, three-piece-suited money types who kept looking up from their mixed grills to take another long stare at Vanessa Havistock. When two men were lunching together, I figured one of them had to say, "We'll flip for them, Charlie. Loser gets the beanpole."

That morning phone call had been a surprise. I thought Vanessa was just being polite when she had asked, "Can we have lunch?" But no, there she was with an invitation to join her at the "fun place" on Third Avenue. I accepted promptly. I wore an old droopy shirtwaist, knowing there was no way I was ever going to outdress *her*.

It took me awhile to understand why she had selected that pub. Then I realized it was practically a men's locker room, with hearty guffaws, slapped backs, and vile cigars. Our Vanessa wanted to be where the boys were. That was okay; every grown woman should have a hobby, and she just *reveled* in the attention she attracted.

She ordered for both of us—naturally; she wouldn't trust me to know what I wanted. So we had cold sliced beefsteak, very rare, with a salad of arugola and watercress.

"Lots of protein," she said, patting my hand. What a *physical* woman she was. "Very good in the sex department. By the way," she added, "how *is* your sex department?"

"Fabulous," I said boldly.

"Glad to hear it," she said, knowing I was lying in my teeth.

The kir royale was super, and so were those slices of cold beef, so rare that I wondered if they had even warmed the cow. But Vanessa soon made it clear that this wasn't to be a purely social occasion.

"Tell me," she said casually, drizzling some olive oil over her salad, "how is your investigation coming along?"

"All right. I've talked to a lot of people."

"Oh?" she said, knifing her steak into smaller slabs. "Who?"

"Just about everyone. You and your husband, of course. Mr. and Mrs. Archibald Havistock. Roberta and Ross Minchen. Orson Vanwinkle. Natalie and her boyfriend."

"Oh, my," she said, "you have been getting around."

I was fascinated by the way she ate. Those sharp white teeth tore into meat, greens, and a crusty baguette with ferocious joy. Something primitive in the way she consumed food, and I thought my initial reaction had been on target: she really had a lot of animality.

"About Ross Minchen . . . " she said, busy with her lunch and not looking at me. "Don't you think he's . . . well, a wee bit *odd*?"

"Odd?" I said. "What do you mean?"

"Oh . . . " she said vaguely, "sometimes he does strange things."

I could have sworn right then that she knew about the Minchens' videocassettes, but I never mentioned them. "What kind of strange things. Vanessa?"

"Well . . . for one thing, he likes to compose pornographic haiku—those three-line Japanese poems."

"Ross Minchen can write Japanese?"

"Oh, no," she said, laughing merrily. "He writes them in English. Some of them are quite amusing. Like dirty limericks, you know—but different."

Weirder and weirder.

She ordered espresso for us and consulted the posted blackboard for desserts available. We agreed that everything offered sounded sinfully fattening, so we skipped. She took a pack of Kent III from her bag and held it out to me.

"No, thank you," I said. "I don't smoke."

"Smart you," she said. "I'm hooked." She extracted a cigarette, and instantly that infatuated waiter was at her side, snapping a lighter.

"Thank you," she said.

"My pleasure, madam," he murmured, and moved regretfully away.

"Isn't he sweet?" she said, in the tones she might have used to comment, "What a nice fox terrier." Then, smoking and sipping her coffee, she asked me my personal reactions to everyone in the Havistock family.

"I'm always curious to know what people think, meeting us for the first time," she said, an expert at the Wry Pout.

I knew she was pumping me, ever so tenderly, to learn what I knew about the theft of the Demaretion. I should have told her that what I had learned could have been engraved on the head of a pin.

I told her only what I was certain she already knew. I was determinedly discreet, and she listened without displaying any reaction until we got onto the subject of Orson Vanwinkle. Then her dark eyes glittered, she raised a hand to brush one of those wings of raven hair away from her face, and her expression became absolutely feral.

"Orson Vanwinkle is a vile, vile man," she said, very intensely. "And if I were you, I'd have nothing to do with him."

"I do have to question him," I said mildly.

"I suppose so, but never, *ever* trust him. He's alienated everyone he's known. Went through a dozen jobs before Archibald took pity on him and hired him as a secretary. What a mistake that was! The man's a creep. Ugh!" she added, shaking her shoulders with disgust.

She signaled for the bill, and when it arrived, she took a credit card from her brocaded handbag. "Isn't plastic wonderful!" she said, and I agreed it was wonderful. I thanked her for a delightful lunch, and she said we must do it again soon.

On our way out, the headwaiter, who apparently was an old friend, greeted her effusively. He thanked her for her patronage, and said he hoped to see her again soon. Then he kissed her fingers. I could swear he passed a small, folded piece of paper into her palm, but on the sidewalk, she fumbled in her purse to make certain she had her credit card, the little paper disappeared, and I wondered if I had imagined the whole thing.

"Got to leave you here, Dunk," she said. "My dentist is waiting. Nothing serious—just cleaning and a checkup, but I've put it off long enough."

"Thank you again for the lunch, Vanessa. I enjoyed it."

"We *did* have a good time, didn't we?" she said, and leaned up to kiss my cheek. "Ta-ta," she said.

I started south, figuring I might stop at Bloomingdale's to browse. I walked about twenty or thirty feet, then turned to look back. Vanessa was still standing in front of the restaurant, and when she saw me looking, we both waved. Then I continued south.

At 61st Street, I turned again and looked back. The sidewalk was crowded, but I thought I saw her walking rapidly north on the avenue. I reversed course and went after her. My legs are long, and I can move when I want to. I followed her up to East 65th Street.

It was the first time in my life I had ever ''shadowed'' anyone, but I had read enough detective mysteries to know the rudiments. Don't get too close. Don't fall too far behind. Use the show windows of stores as mirrors. If necessary, cross the street and tail from the other side. Try to be as nondescript as possible—a little difficult for a skinny six-two female with a mop of wild hair.

But she never looked back, so I figured I was a success. She crossed the avenue, walked quickly toward Second, and entered a brownstone in the middle of the block. Then I crossed the street and inspected the residence from the other side. No dentist's sign. No brass plaques at all. Nothing to indicate it was anything but private apartments. Vanessa Havistock was nowhere to be seen.

I walked to Second Avenue, crossed the street again, and returned west. Taking a deep breath, I ducked into the vestibule of the building she had entered. Took a quick look at the names listed on the bellplate. No dentists. But there was one L. Wolfgang. That could have been Lenore Wolfgang, Archibald Havistock's chunky attorney.

I started out for Bloomies again, wondering if L. Wolfgang was the name on the slip of paper the headwaiter had handed her, wondering if L. Wolfgang was someone else, wondering if she had gone into one of the other apartments in the brownstone to spend a few innocent minutes with a friend before seeing her dentist.

I didn't buy anything at Bloomingdale's, but I did pick up a steno's spiral notebook at a nearby stationery store. Then I went home and spent the rest of the afternoon writing down everything I knew about the disappearance of the Demaretion. It was time, I thought, to get things organized and make certain I had a record of events, conversations, and impressions before I forgot them.

It took longer than I expected it would—there was so *much*! I kept going back again and again to add recalled details. Finally, early in the evening, I read over what I had written and was reasonably certain I had included everything. But it didn't tell me a damned thing. I wondered how detectives like Al Georgio and Jack Smack could endure all those uncertainties and loose ends. I know they maddened me.

I poured myself a glass of red wine from Al's bottomless jug and put it on the floor alongside the couch. Then I lay down. That couch was only five feet long, so my bony ankles and feet hung over one end. I sipped slowly. Went over everything in my mind and couldn't see any pattern at all. I hadn't a clue.

Except that I had heard something of significance that hadn't registered. I hit my forehead with the heel of my hand, trying to jar my brain into awareness. It didn't work. I finished the wine and set the glass carefully aside so I wouldn't step on it when I got up. Then I napped. On the couch. I admit it.

I was awakened about eight o'clock by the ringing of a bell. I started up dazedly, thought it was the phone, then realized it was the front door. I padded over in my bare feet and stared out the peephole. One advantage of living on the ground floor was that I could see who was ringing my bell in the vestibule. Al Georgio. I buzzed him in.

"Disturbing you?" he asked.

"You woke me up," I said. "I was napping—can you believe it? At this hour?"

"I wish I was."

"Tough day?"

"The usual."

"Have you eaten?"

"Oh, sure. I had something."

"Don't tell me," I said. "A cheeseburger and a chocolate malt."

"Not tonight," he said with that boyish smile. "We sent out for Chink. Everything in cardboard containers. Delicious."

"I can imagine. Al, there's about enough of your wine left for a glass for each of us. How about it?"

"Sure," he said, "let's kill it."

He sat on the couch, rubbing his forehead wearily. "I've really got nothing to tell you, Dunk. It's all bits and pieces. But I wanted to stop by to see if you're okay."

"I'm fine."

"No more threatening letters?"

"Nope. For which I am thankful."

"I'll take the one you got along with me. Like I told you, we'll probably get nothing from it, but you never know. What have you been up to?"

"Had lunch today with Vanessa Havistock."

"Did you? Get anything?"

"Only that she doesn't like Orson Vanwinkle," I said, deciding not to tell him about that brownstone on East 65th Street. "But then, no one does."

"Yeah," he said, "the guy's not exactly Mr. Clean. He's got a sheet—did you know that?"

"A sheet?"

"Criminal record. Minor stuff mostly. Traffic violations. Complaints by neighbors about excessive noise. A charge of public drunkenness. A couple of suits for bad debts that he eventually settled. The heaviest is a rape charge that was dropped. He probably paid off. A nasty son of a bitch."

"He certainly sounds like it," I said slowly.

"But all that stuff dates from more than five years ago," Al said. "Since then he's apparently cleaned up his act."

"Since he went to work for Archibald Havistock."

"Yeah," Al said, staring at me, "I had the same idea. I guess he's making a nice buck now, and Archibald told him to shape up or ship out."

I shook my head. "A leopard can't change its spots," I said.

"And a bird in the hand is worth two in the bush," Al said. "How *are* you, Dunk? I've missed you."

"That's nice. And I've missed you, Al."

"This lousy job," he said, groaning. "I never have time to do what I want to do."

"Like what?"

"Live a little. See you. See my daughter. Enjoy."

"Al, do you think this Demaretion thing will ever get cleared up?"

He shrugged. "It's getting colder and colder. We can spend just so much time on it, then it goes into the file. It'll still be open, but with new stuff coming along every day, we've got to ration—"

But just then my doorbell rang again.

"Oh, God," I said, "now who can that be?"

"Jack Smack," Al said with a rueful smile.

He was right.

The greeting between the two men was cool.

"Hey, there," Smack said.

"How you doing?" Georgio said.

And that was that. No shaking of hands. A kind of wary, glowering hostility. They both sat on the couch. I brought Jack a glass of his vodka. If Al was surprised that I knew what Jack drank, he didn't show it.

"How's it going, Dunk?" Smack asked.

"I'm surviving."

"She got a threatening letter," Georgio said. "From the description, it sounds like it's from the same slug your company has been dealing with. Could we take a look at it Dunk, please?"

I brought out the letter. The two detectives moved closer together on the couch and examined the sheet of paper, holding it lightly by the corners.

"It's the same," Smack said. "I'd swear to it. Same paper, same typewriter, and the *o*'s are filled in, just like on the letters we got."

Georgio folded it up, put it back in the envelope, and slid it into his jacket pocket. "I'll have our lab guys give it a look," he said. "But I don't think they'll find any more than you got, Jack."

"They won't," Smack said. "We put some good people on it." He looked at me thoughtfully. "You know what this letter means, don't you, Dunk? A member of the Havistock family has to be involved. Who else would know you've been hired and are going around asking questions? Not an outside crook."

"I'll buy that," Al said. He turned to the other man. "Trade-off time?" he suggested.

"Sure," Jack said. "What have you got?"

"Financial stuff."

"Okay. You go first."

"Archibald Havistock is worth about six mil. But a lot of it is in raw land, and mostly in his wife's name. He's not exactly in what they call a liquid condition. Not hurting, mind you, but not sleeping on a bed of greenbacks either."

"Maybe that's why he decided to sell off his collection," I said.

"Wouldn't be a bit surprised," Smack said. "Well, son Luther *is* hurting. He's in hock up to his pipik. The apartment, the car, the summer home—all on high-interest loans. And his out-of-pocket expenses must be brutal."

"Like Vanessa's jewelry," I said.

"Right. I think Luther is on the ropes. He's making about sixty-five thousand a year in salary and probably spending twice that. Maybe Daddy is helping him out, but I doubt it."

"What about the Minchens?" I asked.

"They're in good shape dollarwise," Al Georgio said. "In addition to his salary, Ross is drawing against a trust fund. Not a big one but tidy. Enough to pay the rent every month. From what I hear, he's a tight man with a buck."

"Heard the same thing," Jack Smack said, nodding, "and I can't figure it. He's got a nice bank balance, but for the past two years or so he's been making some hefty cash withdrawals and no investments to show for it. Five and ten Gs at a time."

Georgio looked up sharply. "Regularly? On a monthly basis?"

"No," Jack said, "four or five times a year. But it could still be blackmail. As far as I can find out, he doesn't play the horses or keep a cupcake on the side."

Maybe, I thought morosely, Ross Minchen was spending it all on porn videotapes.

"We were talking about Orson Vanwinkle before you came in," Georgio said. "Now there's a case. Five years ago he was in brokesville, but now he's living the life of Riley."

"Right," Smack said. "And there isn't even any Mrs. Riley. I don't know where he's getting the loot, but he seems to be floating through life."

"Maybe Mr. Havistock is paying him a good salary," I said.

Jack shook his head. "I couldn't find out how much he's making, but it couldn't be enough to pay for Vanwinkle's toys. If his salary covers his brandy bills, it would surprise me. Did you get any skinny on the younger daughter?" he asked Georgio. "The born-again hippie?"

"She draws a sweet allowance," Al said. "A trust fund when she marries—if ever. I think most of her allowance goes to that spade lover of hers, and the other crazies she runs around with. She's supporting the whole kooky cell.''

Then we were all silent, looking at each other, then looking down at our drinks. I had a panicky moment when I wondered if the two men were trying to outlast each other, waiting for the rival to leave. If that were true, the three of us might be sitting there, wordless, when the sun rose over Brooklyn.

"Well," I said brightly, "if financial need was the motive for swiping the Demaretion, then Luther Havistock seems to be the best bet. Am I right?''

The two detectives nodded, not too confidently.

"It makes sense logically," Georgio said, "but I just can't buy it. Even assuming he could have made the switch when Archibald was in the living room, I still don't think he's got the balls for it.''

"I agree," Smack said, "but his wife has. Two desperate people. They could have been working together. She pushed him into it. That woman would steal the torch from the Statue of Liberty if she could figure a way to carry it.''

Silence again. I looked at them, sitting side by side on the couch. Al so heavy, solid, and dependable. Jack the tap dancer, slender, carefree, and oh so elegant. If I had my druthers—which? I honestly didn't know.

"Well . . . '' Georgio said, sighing and heaving himself to his feet, "I've got to be going.''

Smack finished his drink hastily. "Me, too," he said, rising. "It's been a long day.''

I watched with dismay as both of them moved to the door. *Both* of them! I wanted to knock their heads together. But instead I kissed their cheeks and smiled sweetly when they thanked me for the drinks. Then I locked, bolted, and chained the door. The idiots!

I washed the glasses, emptied the ashtrays, and went in to shower. I washed my damned hair furiously, then tried to do something with it. As Al would have said, zip, zero, and zilch. I put on my pajamas and there I was—alone in bed again. It was getting tiresome.

17

The next day was a roller coaster. It started up, then swooped into the pits, and ended on the heights again. A little shattering, but it wasn't dull.

For breakfast, I had cranberry juice, an English muffin with blackberry preserve, and decaf coffee while I plowed through the morning *Times*. Then I went back to my steno notebook and entered everything I had heard the previous evening from Al Georgio and Jack Smack on the financial status of the Havistocks. I was convinced if I was organized, efficient, eventually my detailed notes on the crime would reveal the solution. Ho-ho.

The first phone call of the day came from Hobart Juliana—which pleased me mightily. Not only because I wanted to keep our friendship intact, but also because he had some good news to pass along. We chatted awhile about what was going on in his life, in my life, and life in general, and then he sprang a surprise.

"Dunk," he said, "I heard some office gossip this morning on very good authority. It concerns you, so I thought you should know."

"What? What?"

"Well, apparently, from what I heard, the police detective and the insurance detective, both of them, came in to talk to god and Felicia Dodat. They swore there's absolutely no way you could have been involved in the disappearance of the Demaretion, and they said you should get your job back again, and it was cruel and unusual punishment to keep you on unpaid leave of absence."

It's possible that tears came to my eyes. "That was sweet of them, Hobie," I said.

"Yes," he went on, "and the powers that be said they'd discuss it with that old fart attorney, Lemuel Whattsworth, before they decided what to do. Anyway, Dunk dear, I wanted you to know that you have some clout on your side.''

''Thank you, Hobie,'' I said, all choked up. ''You're a darling to tell me about it. As soon as I get out from under, I'm going to call you for lunch. Okay?''

''You better,'' he said. ''I miss you, Dunk.''

Hobie missed me. Al Georgio missed me. That was comforting. I really wasn't alone. But what about Jack Smack—my one-night stand? He hadn't said he missed me. But that bastard probably didn't miss anyone.

I reflected on what I had just heard. I thought I knew why Georgio and Smack were trying to get my job back for me. After that stupid letter I received, they were concerned for my safety. So they figured if they got me reinstated at Grandby's, I'd give up my investigative work for the Havistocks and be out of the line of fire.

It *was* sweet of them, and I appreciated it. In fact, their kindness made me feel guilty about not telling them both about Vanessa's visit to the East 65th Street brownstone and the Minchens' porn parties. But I salved my conscience by deciding that they probably knew about that already.

I thought I understood their motives, but I wasn't certain I understood my own. If their plea to Grandby & Sons succeeded and I was put back on salary, would I give up my investigation of the Demaretion theft?

Never!

And why not?

Because I wouldn't be completely cleared until the real thief was caught. The moment I thought that, I realized how silly it was—pure rationalization.

The real reason I didn't want to give up the search for the Demaretion was because it was challenging, exciting, and I enjoyed it. It made me come face-to-face with how empty my life had been before this whole thing started.

Also, the investigation had enabled me to meet two interesting men who seemed to be attracted to me. As they say in New York, that ain't chopped liver!

I called the Havistock apartment, hoping to speak to the madame. I wanted to go over to East 79th Street and talk to Ruby Querita, but thought it politic to ask Mrs. Havistock's permission first. But Ruby herself answered the phone and told me the lady of the house wasn't in. Neither was Mr. Havistock. Neither was Orson Vanwinkle nor Natalie. So, remembering I had carte blanche from my employers to talk to anyone and everyone, I told Ruby I'd be right over to ask her some questions. And hung up before she could object.

She greeted me at the door pleasantly enough and led me into a kitchen that looked big enough to service a cruise ship. We sat at an enameled table, and Ruby busied herself peeling fresh garlic cloves while we talked.

That garlic odor was something. We had a neighbor in Des Moines who ate them raw, washed down with slivovitz. He was a friend, but not a *close* friend.

Ruby's dourness seemed to have lightened up since I first met her, and now she was almost companionable. I will not say she was ugly, but she was excessively plain—with a discernible mustache that didn't help things. I felt sorry for her. She looked like a woman who had worked hard all her life, knew nothing but the miseries, and didn't expect things to change much until she was put to rest.

I went into my spiel and took her through the events of that fateful morning. She answered all my questions readily enough. Yes, the caterer's men had brought the food for the birthday party, then left. The Minchens arrived. Natalie was there. Then Vanessa and Luther Havistock came in. Everyone was assembled.

People wandered in and out of her kitchen, mixing drinks, sampling tidbits. Ruby was aware of my arrival. And then the guards from the armored van were brought into the apartment by Orson Vanwinkle. She seemed to know everything that went on that morning.

"You were in the kitchen, here, all the time?" I asked.

She thought a moment. "No," she said finally. "Not all the time. A man comes with flowers—for the lady—I let him in. Then, also, I was in the living room. Also, I went to a back storage closet for a punch bowl and glasses. I was in and out."

It all added up to a big fat nothing. I had to keep reminding myself that she could be lying. It was difficult to believe.

"I understand your brother is in prison," I said softly.

She shrugged, concentrating on the garlic cloves, gently peeling away the silk with a little paring knife. "The devil's got him," she said quietly.

"The devil?" I asked.

She looked up at me, and suddenly those dulled eyes blazed. "He has forsaken our Saviour," she said with great intensity. "He must pay for his sins."

I took a deep breath. "I understand his case is being appealed. Are you helping him out, Ruby?"

She shook her head. " 'Vengeance is mine, saith the Lord.' "

"Ruby," I said, hunching toward her over the table, "who do you think stole the coin?"

"That I do not know," she said, looking down at what her fingers were doing, "but it is God's punishment on this house."

I was shocked. "Why should God want to punish the Havistocks?"

She stopped her work, raised her head, glared at me. "Because of their sins! They have sinned in the eyes of God Almighty, and they must suffer for their transgressions. Did they think their crimes would go unseen? Oh, no! Bitter is the fruit thereof. The first shall be last, and the last shall be first. A camel through the eye of a needle . . . Bring the innocent unto me.

And what shall it profit a man? Blood of the lamb. Be sure your sins will find you out. Set thine house in order. Whoever perishes, being innocent? Blessed are all they that put their trust in Him. The Lord is my strength and my shield.''

She finally ran down, and I rose hastily, thanked her for her cooperation, and practically ran out of there. I was really shook.

I walked home, and all along East 79th Street I looked up at the glittering windows of those big apartment houses and wondered what was going on inside. Suddenly they no longer seemed bastions of solidity, respectability, or even of rationality. They were just stone and steel façades, shining in the June sunlight. And within—darkness.

I was still gloomy when I arrived home and had to force myself to make notes on the interrogation of Ruby Querita. It was all religious gibberish, I acknowledged, but might there not be a germ of truth there? Ruby had been with the family a long time. She was in a position to know what was going on. So why her outburst? What were the awful sins of the Havistocks?

This was the kind of stuff I wouldn't dare repeat to Al Georgio or Jack Smack. They'd tell me Ruby was a nut, and I was even nuttier to take her seriously. But that was masculine logic at work again. Sometimes you sense things, you *feel* things, and I felt Ruby Querita wasn't entirely irrational; she knew something.

When I'm in an antsy mood like that, I have to eat, so I opened the refrigerator door and examined the possibilities. Depressing. I settled for a poor little potato that had already been baked and was now all shriveled. I heated it up and opened a can of brisling sardines. (Do you know what sardines cost these days!) I washed that gourmet lunch down with a can of diet cola. I really know how to live.

I spent the afternoon doing chores: took in some dry cleaning, picked up a pair of shoes with new lifts, bought some frozen dinners—Lean Cuisine and Stouffer's—a loaf of French bread, treated myself to a jug of Gallo Hearty Burgundy and, throwing caution to the winds, purchased a Sara Lee cheesecake with chocolate bits. Enjoy a little, I told myself— remembering that depressing lunch.

I was stowing away my vittles when the phone rang—and the day's roller coaster took its downward swoop. It was Al Georgio.

"You sitting?" he demanded.

"No," I said, "I'm standing up."

"Then hang on to something. I'm on East Eighty-fifth Street. The body of Orson Vanwinkle was found a couple of hours ago. The guy's stone cold dead in the market. Murdered. Shot to death.''

Silence.

"Dunk?" he said anxiously. "You there?"

"I'm here," I said faintly.

"I heard about it by accident. A buddy who knows I'm working the

Demaretion heist got it on the squawker and alerted me. The homicide guys took over; I'm just hanging around the edges.''

"Al, what happened?''

"Dunk, it's only two hours old; no one knows much. No signs of forced entry. Apparently shot twice in the head with a small-caliber weapon. That's all we've got so far.''

"Al,'' I said desperately, "you think this has something to do with the Demaretion?''

"You want me to guess? All right, I'll guess. Yes, it's got something to do with the theft.''

"Al, will you call me back if you learn anything more? Better yet, can you come over when you're finished? I've got some frozen dinners and wine. We can eat, and you can tell me all about it.''

"It may be late.''

"I don't care how late it is: *Please*, Al.''

"Okay,'' he said. "Meanwhile, watch yourself, Dunk. Looks like the guy who wrote you that swell letter wasn't kidding. Be careful.''

"I will be,'' I assured him, and when he hung up, I went around to check the locks on my windows and doors, still stunned from what I had heard. Orson Vanwinkle dead? Murdered? I didn't like the man, but no one deserves *that*.

I was so confused. Al said he thought it was connected to the Demaretion robbery, and I thought so, too. But how? I frantically consulted my notebook, looking for the magic clue. Found nothing, of course. So I popped two Anacin. I suddenly had a headache that just wouldn't end.

Al called again shortly after eight o'clock and said he was on his way, but he didn't show up until a little after nine. He was in a furious mood.

"Son of a *bitch*!'' he said angrily, flopping on the couch. "This really screws things up.''

"I don't suppose you've eaten today,'' I said. "Have you?''

"What? No, I haven't.''

"Have a glass of wine and try to unwind. I'll put some food on. Your choice is meatball stew or vegetable lasagna. Which will it be?''

"I'll go for the stew.''

"Good for you. Only three hundred calories. But we'll have Sara Lee cheesecake for dessert.''

"So who's counting calories? God *damn* it! I can't figure it. Why Orson Vanwinkle? Why him?''

By the time I put things in the oven, poured us glasses of wine, and went back into the living room, he had calmed down a little, but was still brooding.

"Tell me about it,'' I said. "What happened?''

He sighed. "We haven't got a hell of a lot. Vanwinkle had a cleaning woman who came in twice a week. She had a key to his apartment. The super of the building let her in the front door. She found the body and called nine-eleven. No signs of forced entry. So he let in someone he knew—right? Almost two grand in cash in his bedside table, so it wasn't a ripoff. Nothing else missing, as far as we can tell. He was shot twice in the back of the skull. Small caliber. Maybe a twenty-two. The ME guesses he died around midnight last night. Around there. We'll have to wait for the autopsy to be sure.''

I took a deep breath, feeling a wee bit queasy. ''Al, where do you go from here?''

''Not me. I'm not handling it, thank God. The homicide guys will try to trace his movements after he left the Havistocks' apartment yesterday afternoon. Around four-thirty. They've got a lot of work. They found his little black book. Plenty of names, addresses, and phone numbers. Mostly women. You're in it.''

''*Me?!*''

''That's right,'' he said, smiling bleakly. ''The guy was either a Casanova or thought he was.''

''Al, I swear I—''

He held up a palm. ''Hey, Dunk, I'm not accusing you of anything. I think you've got more sense than to play around with a creep like that. But you're in his book, so you can expect a visit from the homicide dicks.''

''What should I tell them?''

''The truth. No more, no less. Actually, he had a kind of steady girlfriend. A frizzy blonde who looks like a nineteen-twenties type. A real boop-boop-a-doop girl. A flapper. Not a brain in her head, but apparently they've been making nice-nice for almost five years. I think he's laying a lot of loot on her.''

''Where was she last night when he was killed?''

Georgio looked at me admiringly. ''You're really learning the drill, aren't you? She says she was visiting a sick aunt in Riverdale. They're checking it out.''

I glanced at my Snoopy watch. ''Our dinners should be thawed by now. Hungry?''

''Famished,'' he said.

We ate at my dinky dinner table, about as large as a bandanna. I had the vegetable lasagna, and Al had the meatball stew. Thank God for that loaf of French bread; he demolished it. But while we ate and drank, we couldn't stop talking about Orson Vanwinkle's murder.

''Who do you think hated him enough to do it?'' Al asked me.

''Probably everyone,'' I said. ''Natalie didn't like him. Vanessa called him a vile man. And then there's Ruby Querita . . . ''

I decided to tell him about my conversation with her early that morning. He listened intently, and he didn't seem to think me nutty to believe there might be something in what she said.

''These religious fanatics . . . '' he said, ''you've *got* to take them seriously. They'll massacre and say God told them to do it. Like Natalie's boyfriend, that born-again Muslim . . . Who knows what's going on in his tiny, tiny mind? But my big problem is that the homicide guys are going to be tramping all over my investigation of the Demaretion heist.''

''You still think the two are connected—the theft of the coin and Vanwinkle's murder?''

''Oh, hell yes,'' he said, sitting back, dunking a crust of bread in his red wine, then munching on it—I never saw anyone do that before. ''I think it's all one case. But I don't like the idea of being pushed aside by the homicide squad. God damn it, it's *my* baby.''

''Of course it is.''

''All I can do is trade with them,'' he said thoughtfully. ''One for one. If they're willing to cooperate, I'll cooperate.'' He looked at me with a bleak smile. ''Interoffice politics,'' he said, ''but that's the way things work. We're all trying to protect our backs and claim credit due.''

''That's understandable,'' I said. ''It was the same way at Grandby's. And talking about that, thank you for making a pitch to get my job back. You and Jack Smack.''

''Oh, you heard about that, did you? Well, we figured that after you got that threatening letter, it might be smart to try to get you out of the target area. Now, with Vanwinkle scragged, I think it's more important than ever. Dunk, give it up, will you?''

''No,'' I said instantly. ''The Havistocks are paying me to do a job, and I mean to do it.''

He stared at me. ''You might get your ass shot off,'' he said. ''You know that, don't you?''

''Not me,'' I said. ''Not enough ass to aim at.''

He laughed at that. ''You're always putting yourself down. You happen to have an elegant ass.''

''I think,'' I said, ''this would be a perfect time to have the cheesecake.''

I didn't ask him if he'd like to stay the night, and he didn't ask if he could. It was just generally understood.

He insisted he smelled like a goat and *had* to shower. So I gave him a fresh towel and let him go ahead while I cleaned up and washed the few dishes we had used. I took the wine jug and our glasses into the bedroom, turned down the lights, undressed, and slid between the cool sheets. It was delightful and frightening at the same time—if you know what I mean.

He wasn't half as expert as Jack Smack, but twice as sincere. I didn't have to wonder if he was putting on an act, or think of how many women he had been with to learn the things he knew. Al didn't know all that much. But he was tender and solicitous, and there was a kind of brutal power there that Jack could never have. All I can say is that we had us a time. A good time.

Later, sitting up in bed, both of us sipping wine, he said, "We just sinned. I'm Catholic—did you know that?"

"Going to confess what we did?"

"Nah," he said, laughing. "Why should I get a poor priest all stirred up? It'll be our secret. I guess I'm not a very good Catholic."

"I was raised a Methodist," I told him, "but after I came to New York I got out of the habit. I haven't been to church in I forget how long."

He patted the mattress. "This is as good a church as any, Dunk."

"I agree."

"After I got divorced," he said, "I played around some. Not a lot, but enough. Mostly one-night stands. Fun and games. Not very satisfying."

"No," I said, "it isn't."

"I like being with you, Dunk. I mean *really* like it. Not just the sex— though that was great. I mean talking and laughing. Being together. We can keep on doing it, can't we?"

"I'm counting on it."

"You have no special guy?"

"No," I said, "no one special."

"Well, I have no right to ask you to devote your entire life to me. That's too heavy. But I just wanted you to know that while I'm seeing you, I'm not going to do any tomcatting around. I guess I really am a one-woman man. I'm not telling you that to get you to change your way of living. Nothing like that. I just wanted you to know how I feel."

I turned to kiss his wine-sweet lips. "You're a dear man, Al, and I love being with you. But I can't make any promises I won't keep."

"I know that," he said, "and I'm not asking for any promises—except that you'll keep seeing me. For a while."

"*That* I can promise," I assured him. Then, because he was being so loving, I said, "Al, there's something I have to tell you."

"Hey, listen," he said, "you don't *have* to tell me anything."

"It's about the Demaretion. That case means a lot to you, doesn't it?"

"Oh, hell yes. A big theft. Important people. Lots of publicity. It would look good in my jacket if I broke it. Maybe a promotion. Especially now that Vanwinkle's murder is involved."

I sighed. "Then I think I better tell you . . . "

I described my evening with Roberta and Ross Minchen, their party, guests, and the torrid videocassettes. Then I told him about my lunch with Vanessa Havistock, and how she claimed an appointment with her dentist, but then had scurried to a brownstone on East 65th Street where there was an apartment in the name of L. Wolfgang.

"Maybe Lenore Wolfgang," I said. "Archibald Havistock's attorney. You met her at their place. Al, I don't know what all this means—if it means anything."

He had listened closely, never interrupting, and when I finished, he didn't say something stupid, like, "Why didn't you tell me this before?" Instead, he said, "You're becoming one hell of a snoop, Dunk."

Then he said the porn party at the Minchens was interesting, but not something he really wanted to get involved with.

"Pornography in the privacy of your own home is in a kind of gray area," he said. "We'd never get a conviction unless they're peddling the stuff, which I doubt. Still, it's good to know. I might be able to use it as a club one of these days. About Vanessa and the brownstone—now that *is* interesting. You didn't happen to get the number of the building, did you?"

"I'm afraid not," I said, ashamed. "I'm not such a supersleuth after all."

"That's okay," he said. "You're super in other ways. More important ways. Maybe in the next day or so you'll take a ride with me and point out the building. Okay? Then I'll find out if L. Wolfgang really is Havistock's attorney, and how long she's lived there, and what her connection is with Vanessa, and so forth and so on. It's a brand-new lead, and a good one. Thank you, Dunk."

"You'll let me work with you on this?" I asked anxiously.

"You better believe it," he said, turning to take me into his arms. "I'm not going to let you go now."

He was capable and I was eager, so we had an encore. Later we slept like babies. Well . . . maybe not *exactly* like babies. I heartily approve of twosies in one bed. I just hope I didn't snore.

18

The next morning—Al gone before I awoke—I looked in the mirror and decided that loving is good for the complexion. I don't mean I was radiant or anything like that, but I really did think that some tiny lines and wrinkles that had been worrying me had disappeared. Do you think sex is a kind of vanishing cream?

I had my usual skimpy breakfast and read every word in the *Times* about the murder of Orson Vanwinkle. It was a small front-page story with runover, and it didn't tell me any more than I already knew. Still, seeing it all in cold print was a shocker, and I remembered that poor idiot asking, "Was it as good for you as it was for me?"

Just as Al Georgio had warned, homicide detectives came knocking at my door. Two of them, one skinny, one fat—like Laurel and Hardy. I answered all their questions as honestly as I could, but to tell you the truth, they didn't seem too interested. They were going through the routine, but I got the feeling I had already been eliminated as a possible suspect. For which I was thankful.

While they were in my apartment (I gave them coffee), Jack Smack phoned, but I told him I was busy and would call him back. After the detectives left, I called Jack, but *his* line was busy. I finally got through to him a little after noon.

"What do you think?" he asked. "About Vanwinkle getting chilled. It ties in with the Demaretion—right?"

"I don't know for sure," I said, "but I guess it does. You think so?"

"Absolutely," he said. "No doubt about it. Why else would anyone knock off a nothing like that?"

I was determined to play no favorites, and whatever I had told Al Georgio I wanted Jack to know. I swear that at that point in time—where did I learn that phrase!—I had no preference.

"Jack," I said, "I have some things to tell you. Shall I give it to you now, over the phone, or . . . ?"

"No," he said promptly, "not on the phone. Let me look at my pad . . . How's about dinner late tonight?"

"No," I said, just as promptly. I wasn't about to become a shuttle-cock—you should excuse the expression. "I'm busy tonight."

"All right," he said equably. "Then how's about the Sacred Cow for cocktails? Around five o'clock. It's on West Seventy-second, not too far from where you live."

"Why there?"

"I like the place," he said. "Meet you there at five."

He hung up. I stared at the phone. He said and I did. I wasn't certain I liked that.

But other things happened that afternoon. I got a call from Enoch Wot-tle—dear old Enoch—and he didn't even reverse the charges.

"Dunk, love," he said, "how *are* you?"

"Oh, Enoch, I don't know how I am."

"I can understand," he said. "I read in the paper and heard on the TV. Orson Vanwinkle is murdered, who was personal secretary to Archibald Havistock, who owned the Demaretion that was stolen. I don't like that."

"I don't like it either, Enoch."

"Please, Dunk," he said, "don't get involved."

"Enoch, I *am* involved. I can't get out of it now."

He blew out his breath. "What a mess," he said. "Well, maybe what I have heard will help. This morning—it is still morning out here—no more than an hour ago—I got a phone call from an old friend in Rotter-dam. We have done business together, and I trust him. He is one of the dealers I contacted when you asked me to see what I could find out about a Demaretion being offered for sale. This Rotterdam man said he had a call from a dealer in Beirut. I have heard of this Beirut goniff. Very, very shady. He buys from grave robbers. His coins have no provenance at all. But he does very well selling to private collectors. Anyway, according to my Rotterdam friend, this Beirut man asked if he'd be interested in a Demaretion in Extremely Fine condition."

"Wow," I said.

"Yes, that was my reaction. How often does a Demaretion come on the market? Of course it could always be a new discovery, a piece found in a hoard in that part of the world. But the coincidence is too much. A Demaretion disappears in New York, and a Demaretion shows up in Bei-rut. Fascinating—no?"

"Fascinating, yes," I said. "Enoch, I hate to ask you for more favors—you've been so kind to me—but could you follow up on this? Try to find out if the Beirut dealer actually has the coin."

"I will do my best," he said. "Dunk, I must tell you I am enjoying this. It is very, uh, romantic. But please, I beg you, do not put yourself in danger. The people mixed up in this are not nice."

"I know that, Enoch," I said, "and I promise not to do anything foolish."

"Good," he said. "I love you, and I miss you."

Another man who missed me! It made my day. After I got off the line with Enoch, I did something I should have done before: I looked up L. Wolfgang on East 65th Street in the Manhattan telephone directory. No such animal. But there were two listings for Lenore Wolfgang, a residence on East 91st Street, and a business address on lower Fifth Avenue.

Just to make sure, I called Information and asked for the number of L. Wolfgang on East 65th Street. The operator told me sorry, it was an unlisted number. So that was that. Maybe Al Georgio could find out.

I entered what Enoch Wottle had told me about the Beirut dealer and the business about L. Wolfgang's unlisted number in my notebook. Then I sat back and stared at what I had written. Nothing. None of it came together. I didn't even have a crazy idea.

I was only a few minutes late getting to the Sacred Cow on West 72nd Street, but Jack Smack was already at the bar, working on a double vodka. Handsomest man in the place, without a doubt. He gave me a big *abrazo*, a kiss on the cheek, and held my hand. So maybe it wasn't just a one-night stand after all.

I ordered a white wine, despite Vanessa Havistock telling me it was unchic. Then I started babbling. I told Jack about Ruby Querita's religious mania and about Vanessa's visit to that East 65th Street brownstone with an apartment occupied by L. Wolfgang.

When I finished, Jack looked at me and shook his head in wonder. "You're a dynamite lady," he said. "Did you tell Al Georgio all this?"

I nodded.

"Fair enough," he said. "I already knew about Ruby's craziness, but what do you think the business about Vanessa means?"

"I have no idea. Absolutely none."

"I guess Al is going to check into that Sixty-fifth Street building."

"I imagine he will."

"Oh, he will," Smack assured me. "He's very thorough. A real professional."

"Jack," I said, "did your company get another letter from the crook?"

"No," he said, "and that's what worries us. We should have had a reply by now to the notice we put in the paper. Maybe the guy who's writing us really does have the coin, but isn't satisfied with our offer and doesn't want to haggle. Maybe he's trying to peddle it somewhere else."

"Beirut," I said.

"What?"

"Beirut," I repeated, and then told him about Enoch Wottle and his call to me that afternoon. Jack listened carefully, frowning.

"It just doesn't *sound* right," he said. "It's like two different guys are trying to sell the same merchandise. I mean, we were dealing with a man in New York—right? We could have come to terms; he had to know that. But no, he suddenly offers the Demaretion to a back-alley dealer in Lebanon. It doesn't make sense, Dunk.''

''I agree; it doesn't.''

He looked at me with a queer expression, then suddenly snapped his fingers. ''Unless,'' he said, ''unless . . . ''

''Unless what?''

''When did your friend in Arizona hear from his pal in Rotterdam?''

''This morning. An hour before he phoned me.''

''And when did the Rotterdam man get the call from the Beirut dealer?''

''Enoch didn't say, but I had the feeling it was very recently, and he called Enoch immediately.''

''Yeah,'' Jack said, looking at me with a twisted grin, ''I'll bet it was recently. I'll bet it was after Orson Vanwinkle got dusted.''

''What does that mean?''

''How does this scenario sound: Orson Vanwinkle cops the coin. He's been the guy dealing with us, and he's the guy who sent you the drop-dead letter. But then Orson gets killed. Now someone else has the coin. And he's dealing with Beirut. Does that listen?''

''Button, button,'' I recited, ''who's got the button?''

''Something like that. What do you think?''

''It could have happened like that,'' I said, ''except there's no way Orson could have switched display case thirteen.''

''Sure there is,'' Jack argued. ''Archibald was out of the library for a few minutes when Vanwinkle brought in the armored car guards. Orson could have made the switch right then.''

''Maybe,'' I acknowledged, ''but how could Orson have known that Mr. Havistock would be absent? That's where it falls apart, Jack.''

''Shit,'' he said disgustedly, ''you're right. Well, back to the old drawing board. Let's have one more drink, Dunk, and then I've got to run.''

''Heavy date tonight?'' I said casually, hating myself for asking it.

''Not so heavy,'' he said. ''Dolly LeBaron—Vanwinkle's sleep-in girlfriend. She's got herself an agent, and she's trying to sell her story to the tabloids. Her life with the murdered socialite—complete with intimate photos. Hot stuff. Isn't that beautiful?''

''Beautiful,'' I said. ''Al called her a boop-boop-a-doop girl.''

''Al's right,'' he said. ''She looks like she's ready to break into a Charleston at any minute.''

I got home, alone, about an hour later. Depressed. I told myself I was not, absolutely *not* jealous of Dolly LeBaron because Jack Smack was taking her to dinner. After all, hadn't he asked me first? Still . . .

I wasn't hungry—too many salted peanuts at the Sacred Cow—so I went back to my spiral notebook, rereading everything I had written and trying to make some sense out of it. Hopeless. Then I started thinking about Jack Smack's theory: two thieves involved. One steals the Demaretion and starts dealing with the insurance company. Then someone else gets possession of the coin and calls a disreputable Lebanese coin dealer for quick cash.

It sounded right, except that I still didn't think Orson Vanwinkle was the original crook. My mind was boggled. I was saved from complete mental collapse by a brief phone call from Al Georgio.

"Just got a minute," he said, "but I wanted you to know that last night was the best thing that's happened to me in God knows how long, and I thank you."

"Al," I said, "you don't have to—"

"Got to run," he said. "We're all jammed up here. Now they say Vanwinkle's apartment was tossed."

"Tossed?"

"Searched. Very cleverly done. But someone was looking for something."

"The Demaretion?"

"Could be."

"Al, there's something I've got to tell you. This morning I got a call from—"

"Phone you early tomorrow," he said, and hung up.

So there I was, bereft again. I thought of people I might call and yell, "Help!" But I got over that mood soon enough—I'm really an up person—and spent the rest of the evening just schlumpfing around, which is what I call doing unnecessary chores to keep busy, like changing the bedding, wiping out the ashtrays, and taking up the hem on a denim shirt. Swell stuff like that.

But I was thinking!

Mostly about Al's news that Vanwinkle's apartment had been tossed. That tied in with Jack Smack's theory that two thieves had been involved. Orson had been the first. Then someone had searched for and perhaps found the Demaretion.

Someone who was the second thief, and someone who was a murderer.

19

Al Georgio was true to his word and called me early in the morning—so early that I was still asleep.

"Oh, God," he said when he heard my grumpy voice, "I woke you up, didn't I?"

"That's okay."

"Sorry, Dunk. Want me to call you back?"

"No, no. I'm wide awake now."

"How many hours did you sleep?"

"About seven."

"You're lucky," he said. "I got three. I'm running on black coffee and bennies. Listen, Dunk, I'm going to be tied up all day, but there's a favor I'd like to ask."

"Shoot."

"Never say that to a cop. I'm not going to be able to drive you to East Sixty-fifth Street to get the number of that brownstone Vanessa Havistock went into—the one with the apartment rented by L. Wolfgang. Do you think you could get over there today, get the number, and give me a call? Leave a message if I'm not in. After I have the number of the building I'll be able to start checking records: who owns it, who leases the apartments, and all that jazz. Will you do it?"

"Of course, Al. I should have gotten the number when I was there. It was stupid of me to forget."

"Stupid you ain't. Dunk, last night you said you had something to tell me."

So once again I related the story of Enoch Wottle's telephone call from Arizona, the friend in Rotterdam, and the Beirut coin dealer who was trying to hawk a Demaretion.

"I'll be damned," Al said when I had finished. "This thing is getting as fucked-up as a Chinese fire drill—please excuse the language."

"I've heard worse," I said.

"Did you tell Jack Smack about this Enoch Wottle's call?"

"Yes, I did."

"What was his reaction?"

I told him about Jack's theory of there being two thieves—Orson Vanwinkle stealing the coin originally, then a second person getting possession of it and trying to peddle it in Beirut.

"The only trouble with it," I said, "is that I can't see how Orson could have switched display cases."

"I agree," Al said.

"But you did tell me his apartment had been searched."

"Looks like it, but there's no guarantee someone was hunting for the Demaretion. But they were looking for *something*. I told you there was about two thousand in cash in his bedside table, and that apparently wasn't touched."

"How did you find out the apartment had been searched?"

"Vanwinkle's little blond flapper told us. She slept over, usually on weekends, and knew where everything was kept. She swears the place was tossed."

"Al, I'd like to talk to her. Do you think I could?"

"Why not? She's not under arrest or being held as a material witness. Hell yes, talk to her; maybe you can get something that we missed. Give her a call. Her name's Dolly LeBaron, and she's in the book. Lives on East Sixty-sixth Street."

"East Sixty-*sixth*?"

"That's right. Just around the block from L. Wolfgang's brownstone. Isn't that interesting?"

"Yes," I said slowly, "interesting. Coincidence?"

"In my business," he said, "you learn not to believe in coincidences. See what you can find out, Dunk. Talk to you later."

He had a habit of hanging up abruptly without saying goodbye. But that was all right. At least he didn't say, "Have a nice day."

I showered, shaved my legs, dressed, and went out to buy the *Times* and a croissant. It was about 10:30 when I called Dolly LeBaron. Her "Hello?" was high-pitched and breathy, a little girl's voice.

I stated my name and explained that I was a friend of the Havistock family, had met Orson Vanwinkle several times, and wanted to express my condolences to her on his untimely demise.

"Wasn't it awful?" she said. "Absolutely the worst thing that's ever happened to me."

And to Orson, I thought.

"Miss LeBaron," I said, "I've been hired by the Havistock family to investigate the theft of a valuable coin that disappeared from their apartment. I thought it just possible that Orson might have mentioned it to you, and I was hoping we could talk.''

"About what?" she said.

Not too swift, this one.

"About the disappearance of the coin," I said patiently. "Could you give me a few minutes today? I promise it won't take long."

"Gee, I don't know," she said doubtfully. "My agent told me not to talk to anyone."

"This isn't a newspaper interview or anything like that, Miss LeBaron. Completely confidential.''

"I'm going to have my picture taken at noon," she said, then giggled. "In a bikini. It's going to be on the front page of something."

"Isn't that nice," I said.

"The red, I think," she said thoughtfully. "The knitted one."

I wasn't certain she had both oars in the water.

"How about three o'clock?" I urged. "I can come over to your place. It won't take long."

"Well . . . I suppose it'll be all right. What did you say your name was?" She had a slight lisp.

I repeated it.

"My name is Dolly LeBaron," she said primly.

"I know," I said. "See you at three o'clock."

Whew!

That gave me some hours to kill and, on the spur of the moment, I decided to call Hobart Juliana at Grandby & Sons and see if I could take him to lunch. He was delighted, and we made plans to meet at 12:30 at the health food place around the corner from Grandby's.

"My treat," I insisted. "I'll talk to you about the Demaretion theft and bill Archibald Havistock for the lunch."

"Okay," he said cheerfully.

We had mushburgers, alfalfa salad, and carrot juice. It was all so awful, it *had* to be good for you. Hobie got me caught up on office gossip. He reported that god had hemorrhoids, and Felicia Dodat was wearing green polish on her fingernails. Also, Hobie had brought in a fine collection of Mark Twain letters to Grandby's for auction.

"Hobie, that's wonderful!" I told him. "Congratulations. Have they replaced me yet?''

"Nope," he said, shaking his head. "I'm still all alone in our little cubbyhole. From what I hear, that asshole lawyer, Lemuel Whattsworth, told them not to reinstate you until the crook is caught and the fair name of Grandby and Sons is cleared. He said to hold your job in 'abeyance'— you know the way he talks."

"What are they doing about appraisals of coin collections?"

"Using independent dealers on a consulting basis. It's costing god a lot of money—which makes me happy. You know, Dunk, you and I should have been making another fifty a week.''

''At least,'' I agreed. ''Hobie, when is the auction of the Havistock Collection scheduled?''

''It isn't. The sale has been put on indefinite 'Hold.' With all the litigation going on—everyone suing everyone else or threatening to—all the attorneys got together and decided to postpone the auction until things get straightened out. The coins will remain in Grandby's vault.''

''That's awful,'' I said. ''I'll bet Archibald Havistock wasn't happy about it.''

''He wasn't. I understand he screamed bloody murder—and who can blame him? Now he hasn't got the coins and he hasn't got the money. But he really doesn't have a leg to stand on. You know the standard contract that Havistock signed. Grandby's can schedule the auction at their discretion provided it's held within twelve months after the delivery of the merchandise. Hey, Dunk, what do you think about Orson Vanwinkle's murder?''

''I don't know what to think about it.''

Hobie loves to gossip. He leaned across the table eagerly. ''Did you hear anything that wasn't printed in the papers?''

''A few little things,'' I said cautiously. ''Nothing important.''

He inched closer. ''I can give you a charming tidbit,'' he said, lowering his voice. ''Vanwinkle was a member of what we call Manhattan's gay community. Not an active member, just occasionally.''

''That's impossible!'' I burst out.

Hobie sat back. ''Believe me, Dunk, I *know*.''

''But he had a sleep-in girlfriend!''

''So? A lot of guys swing both ways. From what I hear, Vanwinkle was a nasty piece of goods. But he spent money like there was no tomorrow, so he was tolerated.''

After I left Hobie, promising to keep in touch, I still had about an hour to spare before my appointment with Dolly LeBaron. So I decided to walk over to her place, having a lot to think about. Also, I wanted to detour to get the number of that East 65th Street brownstone for Al Georgio.

I walked slowly because it was a steamy day. July was right around the corner and New York's joyous summer humidity was building up. The sky was smoky, pressing down, and the sun was all haze. I was happy I had left my suede jacket at home; it would have been too much.

I thought about my conversation with Hobart Juliana during that dreadful lunch. (No more carrot juice for me!) Curiously, I found that I wasn't disappointed or depressed to hear that I wasn't to be immediately reinstated, despite the pleas by Al Georgio and Jack Smack. Maybe I was having too much fun playing girl detective. And the fact that Grandby's hadn't hired a replacement was a faint reason to hope they were keeping my job open for me.

I was sorry that the Havistock Collection wasn't going to auction. I knew how disappointing that must be to Archibald, but I didn't attach any great significance to the postponement. Boy, was I ever wrong!

Much more interesting, I thought, was Hobie's revelation that Vanwinkle had been AC-DC. I had no idea what that meant to the twin investigations of his murder and the Demaretion robbery, but at least it was another clue to Orson's personality. I wondered if Al and Jack knew about it. And if they did—why hadn't they told me? Maybe they were trying to protect my tender sensibilities. It is to laugh!

I ambled along, trying not to raise a sweat, and noticed how the rhythm of the entire city had slowed. Not so many pedestrians rushing and shoving. Mostly they were sauntering, men carrying jackets over their arms. Even traffic seemed to be moving slower, and it might have been my imagination, but I thought taxi horns were muted and a dog day somnolence had descended on Manhattan.

I stopped first on East 65th Street and got the address of the L. Wolfgang brownstone. To make certain I wouldn't foul up my report to Al, I jotted the number in a little notebook I carried in my shoulder bag. Then I walked around the block to East 66th and found Dolly LeBaron's address. I stood on the sidewalk, staring up. This was no row house.

It was one of those high-rise glass and steel condominiums that were sprouting up all over Manhattan. This one soared forever, with a hard glitter, sharp edges, and the look of a Star Wars rocket ship about to blast off. The lobby was a clean subway station with palm trees, and the elevator was a sterile white cubicle that reminded me of a false molar. Sometimes I have weird reactions to my surroundings.

Dolly LeBaron lived on the 42nd floor—which would have been enough to give me a terminal attack of the jimjams. The hallway had all the charm of a hospital corridor, and even the apartment doors—plain, white, flat panels—looked like part of some gigantic maze. It really was a creepy place.

She opened the door herself.

"My name is Dolly LeBaron," she said, smiling brightly. "What's yours?"

"Mary Lou Bateson," I said for the third time, reflecting that she wasn't so great in the attention span department—or any other department demanding mental effort.

My first impression was one of shock—at how short she was. Couldn't have been more than five-two, and she was wearing heels. Otherwise, she was much as Al and Jack had described her: a young, petite blonde with frizzy curls, plumpish figure, and skin seemingly so soft and yielding that you'd think a touch would cause a bruise.

What they hadn't mentioned, and which perhaps I imagined, was a look of sweet innocence. A little girl in a woman's body. She was wearing a sashed wrapper in a hellish Oriental print, and there was no doubt, from the occasional flash I got of calf, thigh, and arm, that her body was almost completely hairless. *She* didn't have to shave her legs.

She led me into a one-bedroom apartment that dazzled, and I remembered my father's comment when we had visited a similar place in Des Moines. "Looks like a Persian *hoor*house," he had said.

Such a profusion of velvets, soft pillows, swagged drapes, mirrors, porcelain animals, ornate screens, serigraphs of female nudes on the walls, Art Deco female nudes on the tables, a plushy carpet (stained), and a leather rhinoceros bearing a hammered brass tray on its back. What, no incense?

We sat on a couch as saggy as a hammock, and she looked about vaguely. Wondering, no doubt, where she was. Who I was. What day it was.

"Thank you for seeing me, Miss LeBaron," I said. "It was very kind of you."

"Dolly," she said. "Everyone calls me Dolly. What do they call you?"

"Dunk," I admitted.

"Dunk," she repeated, and apparently it never occurred to her to question the derivation of that nickname. "Okay, Dunk."

"How did the pictures go?" I asked her. "You in the red bikini."

"Oh!" she said. "That was fun. This photographer said I had a marvelous body. He called me a vest-pocket Venus. Wasn't that nice?"

"Very," I said.

"He wanted to take some nudes to send to *Playboy*—test shots, you know—but my agent wanted to talk money first. Everything is money, isn't it?"

"It surely is," I agreed.

Even sitting on that droopy couch I towered over her and had to look down to meet her eyes. She was so small, soft, and vulnerable. I don't know why, but I thought of her as a victim. She seemed so defenseless.

"About Orson Vanwinkle . . . " I reminded her. "That's what I came to talk to you about."

"Wasn't it awful?" she said, wide-eyed. "Just awful."

"It was, Dolly. How long had you known him?"

"Oh . . . " she said uncertainly, "maybe five years. Maybe more."

"Was he good to you?"

"He sure was," she said. "But he really was a crazy guy."

"Crazy?"

"We had such crazy times together."

"I can believe it."

"I mean we were doing coke and *everything*."

"Dolly, did you tell all this to the police?"

She tried to recall. "I may have," she said finally. "I really don't remember. There were so many of them."

"How did you and Orson meet?"

"It was at a party. I think. Or maybe at a bar."

"What were you doing before you met him?"

"I wanted to be a disc jockey," she said. "A girl disc jockey. I thought that would be cute—don't you think so?"

"I certainly do."

"I love music. All kinds. Would you like to hear something? I have this marvy collection of tapes."

"Thank you," I said, "but not right now. Then you met Orson Vanwinkle. And . . . "

"He sort of took care of me."

"Was he generous?"

"Oh, yes! Horsy bought me this apartment. And let me furnish it. Isn't it beautiful?"

"It's lovely," I assured her.

"Yes," she said, looking about, "lovely. What do you think is going to happen to it now? I mean, it was in his name and all. He was paying the maintenance. Do you think he left it to me in his will?"

"I have no idea."

"Well, who cares?" she said with a bubble of laughter. "Now I'm beginning to make some money on my own. Maybe I can keep the apartment. Or meet someone . . . "

It was all so sad I wanted to weep.

"Dolly," I said, "do you have any idea of who might have wanted to kill him?"

"Oh, no," she said instantly. "He was such a sweet man. Crazy, but sweet."

"Did you love him, Dolly?"

"Well . . . " she said, her eyes drifting away, "we had this situation." I heard a slight lisp again.

"Did he ever talk to you about the theft of a coin from his uncle's apartment?"

She frowned, trying to concentrate, and I found myself frowning in empathy.

"No," she said finally, "I don't remember anything like that."

"But he always had plenty of money?"

"Plenty," she said, laughing gaily. "Last winter he bought me a ranch mink. And we were going away together."

"Going away? On a vacation? A cruise?"

"No. Forever. We were going to live on a French river."

"A French river? You don't mean the Riviera, do you?"

"Yes, that's right, the French Riviera. We were going there to live. He told me all about it. It's gorgeous, and you don't have to wear a bra on the beach."

"When were you going?"

"Real soon. Like in a month or so."

"That's a big move to make, Dolly."

"Well, Horsy said he was coming into an inheritance from a rich relative. I wish I had one, don't you? A rich relative?"

"I surely do. When did Orson first suggest that the two of you move to the French Riviera?"

"Oh, I don't know," she said, drifting again. "Maybe a few weeks ago. Listen, are you sure you don't want to hear some music? Horsy bought me a videocassette player. I've really got some groovy tapes."

"Maybe some other time, Dolly," I said, rising. "Thank you so much for letting me barge in."

She rose too, then unfastened her sash and spread the wrapper wide. She looked down at her naked body with what I can only describe as a puzzled look.

"You really think *Playboy* would be interested?" she asked.

I stared for a moment. "I really think they would," I told her.

"Maybe I should diet," she said.

"No," I said hastily, "don't do that."

She walked me to the door. What a pair we made! Female Mutt and Jeff.

"Come back soon," she caroled, giving me a sappy smile.

The moment I got home, I went to one of my illustrated coin books— for reasons I'll never understand. I stared at the photo of the Demaretion. To most people it would simply be a flat, round piece of metal, a medium of exchange. Enoch Wottle had taught me what it really meant, what avid collectors saw in it.

You thought of how old it was, how it had been minted, and the uses to which it had been put: dowry, bribery, ransom, tribute, rent, wages, investment, and on and on. Then you dreamed of all the people, now dead and gone, who had handled it.

If only that single dekadrachm could have talked! What a tale of human bravery, frailty, conquest, and defeat. Why, that one coin could have meant success or failure, joy or despair. The same might hold true for a U.S. dime. Take one out of your pocket right now, and let your fancies explode. Who owned it before you? What were their lives like? Was that lousy dime important to them? It might have meant the difference between life and death; it was possible.

And now here was the Demaretion, a piece of metal almost 2500 years old, affecting the lives of a disparate set of characters from would-be Bunny Dolly LeBaron to austere Archibald Havistock. There was magic in money, magic to move people, affect their lives and turn them in ways they had never planned.

I closed the coin book and sat staring at the ceiling. That talk with Dolly had really shaken me. First of all, her soft vulnerability, ignorant innocence, and unthinking trust were enough to make me rethink my own life—what I wanted and where I was going.

And also, what she had said gave me the glimmer of an idea so outrageous, so unbelievable, that I tried to put it out of my mind. But it wouldn't go, and I consulted my spiral notebook to prove it or refute it. I couldn't do either, so I finally solved all my problems: I took a nap.

I awoke, groggy, at about six o'clock, and switched on my air conditioner. It was an old, wheezy window unit, but it worked, thank God, and while it was reducing my apartment from sauna to livable, I went in to shower. Halfway through, the phone rang—doesn't it always?—and I dashed out. It was Jack Smack.

"Hi, Dunk," he said cheerfully. "What'cha doing?"

"Dripping," I said. "You got me out of the shower."

"Sorry about that," he said, not sounding sorry at all. "How do you feel about chili?"

"Love it," I said, remembering that tasteless mushburger at lunch.

"Good. There's a new Tex-Mex place on West Twenty-third. How's about meeting me there in, oh, about an hour? We'll do the whole bit: chili and rice with enchiladas, chopped onions and cheese, jalapeños, and a lot of cold Mexican beer. How does that grab you?"

"Ulcer time," I said, "but it sounds marvelous."

He gave me the address, and I went back to finish my shower. I wondered how much I should tell him, and Al Georgio, about what I had learned that day from Hobart Juliana and Dolly LeBaron. I was beginning to consider holding out on them—only because I was certain they were holding out on me. If it was going to be a three-way competition, I wasn't about to give anything away. If they wanted to trade, fine. But they'd get nothing for nothing.

The Tex-Mex joint turned out to be crowded, hot, smoky, and aromatic. We had to wait at the bar for almost a half-hour, but when we were finally seated, it was worth it; the food was really super. Hot, but not too hot. I mean steam didn't come out your ears, but the back of your scalp began to sweat.

We dug into our platters (liberally sprinkled with red-pepper flakes), and Jack Smack wasted no time . . .

"So tell me," he said, "how are you doing on the Demaretion?"

"Okay," I said cautiously. "Nothing earth-shaking. I talked to Dolly LeBaron today."

"Did you?" he said. "Learn anything?"

"Not much. Is she my competition?" I don't know why I asked that. It just came out, and I was ashamed.

He looked at me, amused. "No, Dunk, she's not your competition. No one is. Dolly is an airhead."

Unexpectedly, I came to her defense. "She's a sweet, dumb, innocent girl who has been exploited by men."

"Hey," he said, "don't go feminist on me. Dolly happens to be an amateur hooker. She could be selling gloves at Macy's if she wanted to.

But she goes through life depending on handouts from men. Maybe she'll marry one of them. I hope so. I hate to think of what'll happen to her when her bits and pieces begin to sag.''

He was right and I knew it, but I didn't want to hear it.

"I still say she's a victim," I said.

"Dunk, we're all victims," he said patiently. "Did she tell you anything?"

"Only that Vanwinkle had been very generous. He bought that condo apartment for her."

"That I knew," he said. "Where *was* the guy getting his bucks? His parents are dead. He inherited bubkes. But five years ago he started throwing money around like a drunken sailor. I'm still trying to figure out how he could have copped the Demaretion."

"He couldn't," I said.

Jack sighed. "It's a puzzlement," he admitted. "Did Dolly say anything else?"

I figured it was trade-off time. "Nothing important. What's happening on your end? Get any more letters from the New York crook?"

"Not a word. We put a man on that Beirut connection you told me about, but it's too soon to expect any results. Did you hear anything from Al Georgio about that East Sixty-fifth Street brownstone?"

He was pumping me, and I resented it.

"No," I said, "not a word." Then I decided to throw him a curve ball that could only confuse him further. Why should I be the only one all bollixed up? "By the way," I said casually, "did you know that Orson Vanwinkle was gay? Occasionally."

He stared at me. "You're kidding."

"I'm not. I heard it from a very reliable source."

"Jesus," he said, and drank off half a glass of beer. "That's another noodle in the soup. I swear to God I've never had a mishmash like this before. Dunk, have you got any ideas at all? No matter how nutty."

"None whatsoever," I said, lying, but looking at him steadily. "It's as much a jumble to me as it is to you."

"Yeah," he said disgustedly. "What the British call a balls-up. Let's have some sherbet or ice cream to cool our gullets."

We came out of the restaurant into a night that still held the day's shimmering heat.

"I'm parked around the corner," Jack said, leading the way.

He didn't walk; he danced along the street. Not actually, of course, but that's the impression he gave. Light-footed and light-hearted. Whenever I was with him, I had the feeling that he might just float up and away—he was that insubstantial.

When we arrived at his black Jag, he walked around it, inspecting wheels, glass, finish.

"Nothing missing," he reported happily. "No broken windows. No dents. No scratches. My lucky night."

It wasn't mine. I guess I had visions of going back to his loft and having a giggle on those crazy futons on the floor. But it was not to be. He drove me directly to my apartment, thanked me for an enjoyable evening, and gave me a chaste kiss on the cheek.

A perfect gentleman. The bastard!

20

The next morning, awake but still lying in bed, listening to my air conditioner cough and sputter, I thought of the previous evening with Jack. My feelings about him were really ambivalent, no doubt about it.

He was a gorgeous man, physically, and on the futons he was a tiger. Charming, good sense of humor, intelligent, mercurial enough to be interesting, and he owned a Jaguar and knew how to make Beef Wellington: What more could a growing girl want?

Except that the guy was a lightweight, a real tap dancer. If he had any capacity for emotional commitment to anyone or anything, he had never revealed it to me. I don't mean that I prefer solemn men, but I do like a soupçon of seriousness now and then. Jack the Smack seemed to float through life, bobbing on the current. Everything was a joke, and laughter was the medicine that cured all.

Still, he was good company and gave my life a lift: I couldn't deny that. So when the bedside phone rang, I half-hoped it was him, calling to apologize for not taking advantage of my good nature the night before. But it was Al Georgio.

"Morning, Dunk," he said. "Didn't wake you up this time, did I?"

"Nah," I said, "I've been up for hours." Slight exaggeration.

"You didn't call me, but I wondered if you had a chance to check the number of that East Sixty-fifth Street brownstone."

"Sure I did," I said, and gave him the address.

"Good," he said. "Thanks. Shouldn't take me long to check it out. I'll let you know if anything comes of it. We're still going around in circles on the Vanwinkle kill. The homicide guys visit you?"

"That they did. But I got the impression they were just going through the motions."

"They were," Al said. "I told them you were clean."

Then, because I had already told Jack Smack and didn't want to favor either of them, I said, "By the way, Al, in case you or the homicide men haven't discovered it yet, Orson Vanwinkle was gay."

Silence.

"Al?" I said. "Are you there?"

"I'm here. Where did you hear that?"

"From a reliable source. I guess he was bisexual."

"I guess he was," Al said, sighing. "That opens a whole new can of worms. Thanks for the tip, Dunk; we'll work on it. Now I'll give you one you won't believe."

"Try me," I said. "I'll believe anything."

"Vanessa Havistock has a record. Before she married Luther, she was Vanessa Pembroke. Ain't that elegant? Actually, her real name is Pearl Measley, and she's from South Carolina—but that's neither here nor there. She's got a sheet in New York. Want to guess what she was arrested for?"

"Indecent exposure?"

He laughed. "Close, but no cigar. It was loitering for the purpose of prostitution. No record of trial. Apparently she was charged and released. How do you like that?"

"Incredible."

"Yeah, it's an eye-opener. Call you later."

He hung up abruptly again, leaving me with another unconnected item to add to my spiral notebook. I wondered idly if a computer might be able to assimilate all this, hum for a few seconds, then spew out a beautifully logical solution to the whole puzzle. I doubted that could ever happen. Computers deal with facts. We—Al, Jack, and I—had to juggle tangled human emotions and passions. Which calls for instinct and judgment— does it not?

I showered, dressed, and went out for the morning paper and a hot bagel with a shmear of cream cheese. By ten o'clock I had devoured both bagel and *Times*, and was pondering what I might do that day to give the Havistocks their money's worth of investigation. Then my doorbell rang. I looked through the peephole, and there was Dolly LeBaron standing in the vestibule. I couldn't have been more discombobulated if it had been Martha Washington.

She came in, smiling bravely, carrying a shoebox-sized package in a brown paper bag that had been wrapped with yards and yards of wide Scotch tape. She was wearing a simple Perry Ellis dress that I had seen advertised for about $400. It was a muted pink linen, and she looked absolutely smashing.

"Hi!" she said brightly.

"Hi," I said. "How did you find me?"

"Well, after you left, I wrote down your name. Mary Lou Bateson— right?"

"Right."

"So then I looked you up in the telephone directory," she said triumphantly.

"Good for you," I said. "Would you like a cup of coffee—or anything else?"

"Nothing, thank you," she said formally. "But I appreciate the offer."

So we sat on the couch, side by side, looking at each other with glassy stares. She really was a cute little thing, all bouncy curves and wide-eyed innocence. I could understand Orson Vanwinkle's infatuation. This kid was a living toy, and I imagined if he suggested they swing naked from a chandelier, she'd giggle and say, "Okay."

"Listen," she said suddenly, "you're the best girlfriend I have."

That came as something of a shock. I had only met her once before, for a limited time. To me, that didn't add up to intimacy. Again I reflected that her back burners were not fully operative.

"Dolly," I said, as gently as I could, "surely you know other women. I've only talked to you once."

"No," she said, "you're the only one. Mostly I know men."

"What about your family?"

"They're in Wichita," she said. "We send cards."

That hurt because it reminded me that I hadn't written home in more than two weeks. I resolved the moment she left, I'd write a long, long letter to Mom and Dad in Des Moines, and mail it that very day.

"It's these phone calls, Dunk," she said, little frown lines appearing between her plucked eyebrows.

"What phone calls?"

"I get them all the time. Some during the day. Some wake me up."

"Man or woman?"

"Man."

"A heavy breather—or does he say anything?"

"Sometimes he says things."

"Sexual?"

"No. He wants to kill me. It's scary."

"Oh, my God," I said, remembering my threatening letter. "Did you call the phone company?"

"No."

"The police?"

"No."

"Why don't you change your number? Get an unlisted number."

"It wouldn't do any good," she said helplessly. "He'd find me."

Did she know who it was?

"Who? " I asked her. "Who'd find you, Dolly?"

A very brief pause, then: "I don't know."

"I have a friend who's a detective in the New York Police Department. Would you like to tell him about it? He's very understanding. Maybe he could do something about it."

"No," she said, "he couldn't help me. Because you're my very best girlfriend, I was hoping you'd do me a favor."

"Of course," I said. "Whatever I can."

She thrust that crudely wrapped package at me.

"It's some personal stuff," she said. "But it's valuable to me. I was wondering if you'd keep it. Just for a while."

"Dolly," I said, "I hate to take the responsibility. Don't you have a safe deposit box?"

"What's that? Well, whatever it is, I don't have it. It's just for a little while. I may go away," she added vaguely.

I didn't think she was on anything. I mean she wasn't doped up or anything like that. It was just that the things she said and did were slightly askew. Her gears weren't quite meshing.

"Can you hide it?" she pleaded.

I looked around my apartment hopelessly. "Maybe I can put it on a top shelf in a closet or cupboard somewhere. Put things in front to cover it. That's the best I can do. But, Dolly, I really wish you wouldn't ask me to do this."

"You're the only one I know," she said. "Please?"

I couldn't resist that. "All right. Will you come and take it back as soon as you can?"

"Of course!" she cried. "Just as soon as I can."

"But what if you don't? How long should I wait?"

She thought about that a long time. I could almost see the wheels turning as she labored with the mental challenge.

"A month?" she suggested.

"You'll come back and get it within a month?"

She nodded briskly.

"And if you don't?" I asked. "What do I do with it then?"

"Burn it," she said promptly.

"Burn it?"

"Put it in the insinuator." That's the way she pronounced it.

So if she didn't reclaim something valuable to her, something personal, I was to destroy it. Curiouser and curiouser.

She left that clunky package on the couch and stood up.

"I knew I could depend on you," she said, taking a deep breath. "I just knew it. You won't open it, will you?"

"Of course not," I said, insulted.

"I knew you wouldn't." She craned up to kiss my cheek. But she was so short, and I was so tall, that I had to bend down to take her peck. She smelled nicely of something sweet and fruity. A little girl's scent.

When she was gone, I came back into my living room to stare at that bundle and wonder what I was letting myself in for.

I picked it up and shook it gently. Naturally I suspected it might contain

the Demaretion. But who would be simple enough to wrap a single coin
in a shoebox? Not even someone as loopy as Dolly LeBaron.

Anyway, there was no rattle, no sound at all. Whatever was within the
package was well-swaddled. I hefted it. Surprisingly light. How much did
a bomb weigh? The moment I had that awful thought, I resolutely put it
out of my mind. Sweet, sappy Dolly would never do anything like that.
Would she? Unless she was just the messenger.

Other questions, other answers . . .

Should I open it?

Absolutely not. I gave her my word.

Should I tell Al Georgio and Jack Smack about it?

No.

Then what should I do with it?

Hide it—but only for the month she requested.

And then?

Burn it in the insinuator.

Carrying it rather gingerly, I wandered about my apartment looking for
a good hiding place that thieves with limited time might have trouble
finding. I finally settled on the top shelf of the metal cabinet in my kitchen,
above the sink. I tucked it far in the back, behind packages of pancake
mix and instant rice. Let the roaches have a field day on that Scotch tape.

I really did write that letter home—which made me feel virtuous. I
stamped it and ran outside to drop it in the corner box. A droopy day with
an army blanket over the city, rain threatening, and everyone frowning as
they mooched along. I was depressed and, other than the weather, couldn't
understand the reason.

Then I figured out it was that visit from Dolly LeBaron and the package
she had left in my care. That was a downer—and I didn't understand why.
But somehow it seemed as menacing as the creepy sky. I didn't like the
idea of being trusted custodian of a parcel, contents unknown. It could be
stolen goods, drugs, or anything else illegal. That made me a receiver,
didn't it? I could hear myself stammering to a judge, "Your Honor, I just
didn't know what was in it."

Before I got myself in a real snit, I decided to get out of the house and
do something. What I planned was to go up to the American Numismatic
Society and see if I could dig up any information on Archibald Havistock's
collection of ancient Greek coins. Oh, I knew what was in the Havistock
Collection, now languishing in the vault at Grandby & Sons. What I was
interested in were the coins Archibald had sold off, according to wife
Mabel, over the past five years.

So I shouldered my bag, locked up, and started out. I admit I wasn't
as alert as I should have been. I wasn't "living defensively," which is
what everyone says you must do in New York. Anyway, I didn't look
ahead, and so I failed to see the three guys lurking in the areaway beyond
the outer door. But they were obviously waiting for me.

The moment I was in the vestibule, caught between two doors, two of the thugs hustled in, and the third stood on guard with his back against the outer door. Here it is, I thought: my first mugging. Or worse. But it was not to be.

The two guys crowding into the vestibule with me were in their middle twenties, I guessed. Wearing punky outfits: running shoes, a lot of stone-washed denim and creaky black leather, studded bracelets, chain belts, sharks' teeth necklaces—the whole bit. I remember one of them had a gold tooth in front.

"Hi, there," gold tooth said, grinning.

I thrust my shoulder bag at them. "Take it," I said. "Just don't hurt me. Please."

"Nah," the other one said. He had a silly blond Stalin mustache. "We don't want your gelt. Mary Lou Bateson—right?"

I nodded frantically, absolutely determined not to wet my pants.

"Got a message for you," gold tooth said. "You should stop asking questions. You dig?"

I kept nodding.

"You're making a lot of people uncomfortable," mustache said. "So just be nice and lay off. It's healthier that way. For you."

Their voices were not particularly menacing. They spoke in quiet conversational tones. But what they were saying was all the more frightening for that. They talked like businessmen, professionals, offering terms on a sale or contract. I never doubted them for a moment.

"Listen," I started, "I don't—"

"No," gold tooth said, "you listen. Just walk away from it. The coin and everything and everyone connected with it. Give it up. It's got nothing to do with you—right?"

"We're being gentlemen, aren't we?" mustache added. "Very polite. We haven't touched you, have we? So you take our advice, and that's the way it'll stay. You keep poking your nose into things that don't concern you, and we'll have to come back."

"Then we might not be so polite," gold tooth said. "Then we might touch you. So-long, sweet mama."

And they were gone, whisking through the outer door, joining their guard, the three of them walking rapidly away. I watched them go, trying to breathe and gradually becoming aware of my shaking knees and trembling hands.

I went back into my apartment and found a miniature bottle of cognac I had been saving for medicinal purposes. Now was the time. It took me almost a minute to get that damned screw top off, but I finally managed, and drained the brandy out of that little bottle in three gulps. Then, gasping, I staggered to the couch, collapsed, and waited for my hypertension to ease.

I went over that brief encounter and had no uncertainty whatsoever about their threats; they meant what they said. They had looked perfectly capable of any kind of violence: knifing, bombing, rape, murder—you name it. I had been lucky. Those messenger boys would obey any orders. "You want us to toss acid in her face? Sure, boss."

But I'm a stubborn dame, and as fear faded, my indignation grew. The bastards! Did they really think I'd cave in that easily? And what was the reason for the whole megillah? Whoever sent them must have felt threatened by my investigation. But *why*, for God's sake? I hadn't learned anything that threatened anyone.

Unless I had heard something important that I wasn't aware of.

I reviewed the melodramatic dialogue with the two amateur Scarfaces. "Just walk away from it," gold tooth had said. "The coin and everything and everyone connected with it." No clue there. His warning included all I had done and every person I had met since going to work for Grandby & Sons.

But then, just before they had scuttled out, gold tooth had said, "So-long, sweet mama."

And who had first called me that? Sam Jefferson, aka Akbar El Raschid, Natalie Havistock's misanthropic boyfriend. But what did I know about *him*?

I went into the kitchen to make a call. I was reaching for the phone when suddenly it rang. I jerked my hand away as if I had touched something hot. Has that ever happened to you? Then I took the phone off the hook. Slowly.

"Hello?" I said cautiously, remembering Dolly LeBaron's problems.

"Ms. Bateson?"

"Yes."

"This is Lenore Wolfgang's secretary. Ms. Wolfgang would like to meet you this afternoon for a short time. Would that be convenient?"

"All right," I said. "When and where?"

"Here at our office. Three o'clock."

"I'll be there," I said.

"Please try to be prompt. Ms. Wolfgang has a very tight schedule today."

Screw you, ms., I thought, slamming down the phone.

So now I was being hassled by a lawyer's secretary, in addition to being muscled by goons in the vestibule of my home, getting a drop-dead letter in the mail, and being saddled with a mysterious package by the pea-brained mistress of a murdered bisexual lecher.

I think it was at that precise moment that, wrathful and tired of being pushed around, I decided no more Ms. Nice. I wasn't going to pass along *any* information to Al Georgio or Jack Smack. Fine, upstanding lads, but they weren't the ones being leaned on, and I had enough chutzpah to think I could take care of myself, solve my own problems, and to hell with all men, friends and enemies alike.

So, of course, the next thing I did was to make a call to a man: Hobart Juliana at Grandby's, asking for a favor.

"Hobie," I said, "remember your telling me that Orson Vanwinkle had this, ah, certain predilection?"

"Predilection?" he said, giggling. "What a sensitive way of putting it! Yes, I'd say he had a predilection."

"Is there any way you can find out if he had someone special? A regular?"

Short pause, then: "Is it important, Dunk?"

"It is to me."

"Then I'll try, dear. No guarantees. I'll make some phone calls. Will you be in today?"

"I have to go out this afternoon, but if you learn anything—or nothing—will you call me tonight?"

"Of course. Either way."

"You're a darling."

"I agree," he said. "And let's never eat mushburgers again."

"My sentiments exactly," I said.

Then I went back to my spiral notebook, bringing it up-to-date with all the happenings of that crazy day. By the time I finished jotting my notes, it was too late for my planned trip to the American Numismatic Society. So I had an endive salad with watercress and cherry tomatoes, and then sallied forth to keep my appointment with attorney Lenore Wolfgang. God forbid I should be late; her secretary would have the fantods.

What a bummer of a day it was: a drizzle that was half steam and a breeze that smelled like it was coming from some giant exhaust pipe. I wore a plastic raincoat, which was like being swaddled in cotton batting. I finally got a cab going downtown on Broadway, and the driver was playing a Willie Nelson tape on his portable. That lifted my spirits a little—but not enough.

Lenore Wolfgang had her office in one of those hunks of masonry on Fifth Avenue just north of 42nd Street: a big, brutal building. When you looked up, you had the feeling it might topple onto you at any moment. I searched the lobby directory and eventually found her listing: Getzer, Stubbs & Wolfgang. I rode up to the 36th floor in a bronze elevator that had been sprayed with a piny deodorant that was supposed to make you think you were in the north woods. Fat chance.

I got in to see her right away, which was a surprise; I was certain she'd keep me waiting. She shook my hand with the grip of a wrestler, then got me seated in a leather club chair in front of her clumpy oak desk. She sat in a swivel chair and parked her heavy cordovan brogues atop the desk. She had a wad of chewing gum stuck to the sole of her left shoe, but I didn't mention it.

She was wearing a dark flannel suit, man-styled shirt with a wide ribbon tied in a bow at the neck. No jewelry. Minimal makeup. The face was

big, fleshy, and a little overpowering. A very strong, hard woman. As tall
as I, but blockier. If I was a basketball player, she was a linebacker for
the Steelers. And if she smoked cigars, I wouldn't have been a bit surprised.

"I understand the Havistocks have hired you to investigate the theft of
the Demaretion," she started.

I didn't know if that was a statement or a question, so I said nothing.

"I advised against it," she said sternly, staring at me. "I think criminal
investigations are best left to the professionals, don't you?"

"In most cases," I agreed. "But in this one, the professionals seem to
agree that a member of the family is involved. The Havistocks are aware
of it, and I'm sure it's upset them. They wanted a personal representative
looking into it."

She stirred restlessly, recrossing her ankles and leaning forward to tug
her flannel skirt over her lumpy knees.

"Well . . . " she said finally, "I don't suppose it can do any great harm.
Have you discovered anything?"

"No," I said. "Nothing important. And the murder of Orson Vanwinkle
complicates matters."

"How so?" she said sharply. "You think he stole the coin?"

"It's possible."

She shook her head. "Can't see it," she said. "He was a vain, weak
man with no self-discipline whatsoever. But I can't see him as a common
thief. Defrauding old widows would be more his style."

A rather harsh opinion, I thought, of a homicide victim. But then he
couldn't sue for slander, could he?

"I would appreciate it," she continued, "if you would keep me informed on the progress of your investigation. Weekly reports, say."

She was backed by a wall of thick law books. All the furniture in her
office was massive. Colors were muted, brass shined, surfaces dusted.
Everything bespoke the solidity and majesty of the law. But I was not
about to let her muscle me. I had enough of that in the vestibule a few
hours ago.

"I don't think that would be wise," I said evenly. "I was employed
by the Havistocks. I promised them periodic progress reports. Whatever
they wish to tell you is up to them."

She took it well, merely nodding with no change of expression. "My
only reason for asking," she said mildly, "is that Archibald Havistock is
my client, and naturally I want to protect his interests."

"Naturally," I said. "How long has Mr. Havistock been with you, Miss
Wolfgang?"

"Oh," she said, "about five years now." Then she looked at me
strangely. "Why do you ask that?"

I shrugged. "No particular reason. Just an idle question."

She frowned, took her feet off the desk, and stood up. I rose also,

figuring this incomprehensible interview was at an end. But then she said
something that gave me a clue to the reason she had called me in.

"By the way," she said casually, "in addition to my office here and
my private apartment, a co-op, I also rent a small place on East Sixty-
fifth Street for the convenience of out-of-town clients and visiting friends.
This morning I received a call from the owner of the building saying he
had been contacted by a detective from the New York Police Department
who asked questions about the apartment, who leased it, who occupied it,
and so forth. Do you know anything about that?"

When I played high school basketball, I had always been better on
defense than offense.

"Not a thing," I said. "It's all news to me. But I suppose that since
the murder of Vanwinkle they're investigating everyone who knew him."

"Yes," she said thoughtfully. "I suppose they are. Thank you for coming in, Miss Bateson. I hope to see you again soon."

I got that bone-crusher grip again. When I went down to the street, the
drizzle was thickening, and there was no way I was going to get a cab on
Fifth Avenue. So I plodded over to Eighth on 42nd Street—not exactly a
scenic wonderland.

Traffic was murder, but on that slow ride home in a taxi that seemed
to have been stripped of springs and shock absorbers, I had time to think
about the interview with Lenore Wolfgang.

She was obviously worried about the brownstone apartment on East
65th. But her concern could be completely innocent. Who wants the cops
coming around and asking questions? On the other hand, she had gone
into unnecessary detail to explain why she leased living quarters in addition to her primary residence.

It was not until I was inside my own primary (and only) residence, the
door locked, bolted, and chained, that I recalled another little goody from
the conversation. I dug out my notebook to verify what I was thinking.

Wolfgang said that Archibald Havistock had been her client for about
five years. And Orson Vanwinkle had been Archibald's private secretary
for about five years, during which he started throwing simoleons around
like the money cow would never go dry. And Archibald had been selling
off coins in his collection for about five years. Al Georgio had told me
detectives don't believe in coincidences. So what cataclysmic event five
years ago triggered all the activity?

I've mentioned that I had a wild idea of what had been and was going
on, an outrageous notion I could hardly believe myself and which I certainly couldn't prove or even describe. But this latest intelligence from
Lenore Wolfgang made the cheese more binding. Things were beginning
to fit.

I have no clear recollection of what I did for the remainder of that
miserable day. I know Hobie Juliana called and said he hadn't been able
to discover anything specific about Orson Vanwinkle's gay contacts, but

would keep trying. And both Al Georgio and Jack Smack called, just to say hello. They didn't tell me anything, and I didn't tell them anything. Still, it was nice of them to check to see if I was still alive.

By evening it was pouring outside, so I ate in. I forget what it was— nothing memorable. Probably scrambled eggs or Cup-a-Soup: something like that. I tried watching television, but before I knew it, I was flipping pages of my notebook again, the TV set still flickering while I tried to make sense of all those random scribbles.

I went to bed early, thanking God I was inside a locked, bolted, and chained cage. The animals were all outside, prowling. I fell asleep listening to the gush of rain. It was a dreamless sleep. Granted only to the innocent and pure of heart. That's me. Damn it.

21

The next morning my phone kept ringing off the hook. *Four* calls before ten o'clock: a new world's record—for me at least. I was dazzled by this unexpected popularity, remembering when I had gone a week or two without a single call, and then, when I did get one, it was some guy trying to sell me an encyclopedia of the mammals of North America.

The first came from Roberta Minchen, all gush and giggles. She thought it would be *fun* if we had lunch at the Russian Tea Room at 12:30, and could I possibly make it?

If this was going to be another attempt to recruit me into her cast of bare-ass TV stars, I wanted no part of it. But then I reflected a free lunch was not to be scorned, and what could happen over vodka and blintzes? Besides, maybe I could get something new out of her. So I accepted.

The second call was from Hobie Juliana.

"Got something for you, Dunk," he said. "I don't know how accurate it is, but I thought I'd pass it along anyway. The late, unlamented Orson Vanwinkle, while alive, was having a thing with a black stud, a guy who went by one of those crazy Arabian names."

"Oh-oh," I said.

"Something wrong?" he asked.

"Hobie, it couldn't have been Akbar El Raschid, could it?"

"That sounds like it. Wears a single gold earring."

"And a red beret," I said.

"My God, Dunk, do you know him?"

"I think I've met the gentleman. Hobie, I just can't believe it. Orson and Akbar have got to be the oddest of all odd couples."

"Well, you never know," he said judiciously. "I told you Vanwinkle was throwing money around. That might have had something to do with it."

"Probably," I agreed. "Thank you so much for your help, dear."

"One of these days will you tell me what this is all about?"

"When I find out," I promised, "you'll be the first to know."

After we hung up, I pondered the implications of what I had just heard. Could Vanwinkle have been financing Akbar's merry little band of would-be revolutionaries? And if so, was Natalie Havistock aware of her boyfriend's liaison with her cousin?

Every time I learned something new, instead of diminishing the puzzle, it added to it. The whole thing grew and grew, like a blob that might eventually take over the world. Sighing, I added this latest intelligence to my notebook, reflecting that if things continued the way they were going, I might have to start Volume II.

The third call was one I never expected to get—from Felicia Dodat at Grandby's. She was all chirpy charm, couldn't have been sweeter, and carried on like a maniac about how they all missed me and couldn't wait until I returned. Uh-huh.

In fact, she went on, she and Mr. Grandby and attorney Lemuel Whattsworth thought it might be "productive" if I stopped by that afternoon, just for an "informal chat" to review my "situation."

And what situation is that? I wanted to ask—but didn't. I told her I had a lunch date and couldn't possibly meet her before three o'clock. She said that would be just fine, and she was looking forward to seeing me.

"Have you found a man yet, Dunk?" she asked, her snideness surfacing.

"Two of them," I told her, and hung up.

I knew exactly why the powers that be at Grandby & Sons wanted to have an "informal chat." They knew I was working for the Havistocks and wanted to pump me, find out what I had discovered. After all, Grandby's was still on the hook for the Demaretion, and the insurance company was in no hurry to pay off. I didn't imagine that state of affairs was doing god's hemorrhoids any good.

The final call of the morning was from Vanessa Havistock with *another* luncheon invitation. If this kept up I'd need a social secretary.

"Oh, I'm so sorry," I said, "but I already have a date for lunch."

"With a man, I hope," she said lightly.

Then, like an idiot, I told her: "No, as a matter of fact, it's with your sister-in-law, Roberta Minchen."

"Why, that's wonderful," she said immediately. "I'll give Bobbi a call and ask if I can join you. You don't mind, do you?"

"Of course not."

"Won't it be hilarious," she said. "We'll have a real hen party."

I didn't know if she was being ironic or not. With her, it was hard to tell.

"Now then," she continued, "another thing . . . Luther and I are having a very informal buffet dinner next Tuesday night, and we'd like so much to have you. Do you think you can make it?"

I was tempted to say, "Let me take a look at my appointment calendar." But I didn't have the gall. "Yes," I said, "I'd like that. Thank you very much."

"Lots of yummy food," she said. "Plenty to drink, and the handsomest men in Manhattan. I think you'll have a ball." She paused a moment, then: "Listen, Dunk, I have a wonderful idea. I'm on my way to Vecchio's on Madison Avenue to buy some new rags for the party. Could you meet me there at, say, eleven o'clock, and we'll pick out something wicked and scrumptious for me. We'll leave in plenty of time for lunch. How does that sound?"

Why did I have the feeling I was being manipulated?

"Sounds fine," I said faintly. "I'm supposed to meet Roberta at the Russian Tea Room at twelve-thirty."

"No problem," she said. "It won't take me that long to pick out something. And I'd really like to get your opinion. I trust your taste."

Bull*shit*!

Vecchio's was the kind of place where they took a good look at you through the plate glass door before they unlocked and allowed you to enter and blow a wad. It was an Italian boutique, Milanese, and if you could find a blouse under $600 or a dress under $2,000, it had to be last year's styles.

The doorman probably would have taken one look at my denim sack and turned away in horror, but I had walked over through Central Park, and arrived just as Vanessa was climbing out of a cab with a flash of bare thigh. The guard took one look at *her* and practically tore the door off its hinges.

Inside, an Adonis in a black silk suit came running forward to smother her hands with kisses. "Signora!" he kept crying. "Signora!"

"Down, Carlo, down, " Vanessa said, laughing. Then she introduced me.

"Signorina," he said, bowing. I didn't even get an exclamation point.

That was some lush joint. Polished marble floors, Corinthian columns, subdued lighting, and sinfully luxurious chairs and couches covered with lemony cowhide. Not a garment in sight. I gathered you told them what you were interested in, and they whisked things out of an inner stockroom to display for the signora's pleasure.

"Something splashy, Carlo," Vanessa said. "For a party. You know what I like."

"But of course," he said, turned, and snapped his fingers at two assistants hovering nervously in the background. "The red with sequins," he ordered. "The white Grecian drape. The fringed black."

They scurried, and hustled back with the three gowns. I'd have given my eyeteeth to own any of them, but of course I could never have gotten into them. I would have looked like an elephant in rompers.

Carlo exhibited them with dramatic flair, caressing the fabrics with his fingertips, shaking the hangers so the dresses billowed and swayed.

"Amusing," he said. "No?"

"What do you think, Dunk?" Vanessa asked.

"I love them all," I confessed.

"Mmm," she said, inspecting the gowns critically. "The drape is a little too full for me, and the sequined red is hookerish—don't you think?"

This from a woman with a record of loitering for the purpose of prostitution. It was to laugh.

She selected the fringed black: a short sheath with spaghetti straps, cut reasonably high in front and no back at all. Wear that thing backward and you'd be in *biiig* trouble. The fringe hung in tiers, and moved, swayed, flipped as the wearer walked.

"Let's try it on," Vanessa said, and I wanted to say, "*Both* of us?"

We went into a dressing room as elegantly appointed as a Roman vomitorium. All right, I'm exaggerating, but it *was* splendidly furnished, with more mirrors than a fun house. Vanessa began to undress, casually, which made me a little uneasy. Despite my basketball team experience, I've never been an uninhibited locker room type.

"Tell me," she said, unbuttoning, unsnapping, unhooking, "have you found out who ripped off the Demaretion?"

"No," I said, "I haven't."

"Orson's murder really shook me," she chattered on. "I didn't like the man—I told you that—but even so, I was devastated by his death. Do they know who did it?"

"They're investigating."

"Tell me about it," she said bitterly. "I had a two-hour session with the homicide detectives. My God, I hope they don't suspect *me*. I wouldn't hurt a fly."

A zippered fly? I was tempted to ask.

By then she was stripped down to high-heeled shoes, little white bikini panties, and nothing else. I'm one long hunk of cartilage, but she had a body that just didn't stop. I mean, it *gleamed.* Perfectly proportioned with a narrow waist, flare of hips, a luscious tush, and a really exceptional pair of lungs. Incidentally, I didn't see that tattoo Orson Vanwinkle had mentioned.

She inspected her practically naked body in the three-way mirror, turning this way and that, lifting her arms.

"What do you think?" she said. "Not so bad for an old dame—right? The thighs are still firm."

"So is everything else," I said.

She touched her breasts lightly, a brief caress. "There's a little silicone in there," she said, "but that's just between us girls. Do you think Orson did it?"

"What?" I said, startled. "Oh, you mean steal the Demaretion. No, I don't think he did it. He couldn't have."

"Natalie then," she said, her voice muffled as she pulled the fringed dress over her head. "She's nutty enough. Or Ruby Querita. There's a freak for you."

She was pointing fingers in all directions, and I wondered if she was just running off at the mouth or had good reasons for her suspicions. But maybe the theft of the Demaretion and Vanwinkle's murder were the most dramatic things that had happened in her life in a long time, and she was trying to keep the excitement alive. Good party talk.

She turned her back to me. "Zip me up," she ordered, and I did. Then we both inspected the result in the mirrors.

Some result! The dress looked like it had been painted on her, and the tiers of fringe made it sexier. I don't know why, but I thought of a strip-tease dancer with tassels on her pasties.

"What do you think?" Vanessa asked.

"Beautiful," I said. "But about an inch too long. They can take up the hem."

She looked at me with astonishment. "You're absolutely right," she said. "Will you call Carlo and the fitters, please."

Within minutes, there were four people hovering around her, clucking and murmuring and rolling their eyes. The hem would be shortened, certainly. "And perhaps, signora," Carlo said, "if I may suggest it, the straps taken up. Not a lot—no! A trifle. To fit snugly. Ah, what a glory!"

After things had been chalked and pinned, Vanessa undressed, dressed, and we moved out into the main room. She didn't even flash a credit card.

"Bill me, Carlo," she said gaily.

"But of course, signora," he said, bending to nibble on her fingers again. I may have been imagining it, but I could have sworn he passed her a little folded slip of paper—just like the headwaiter at that Tudor pub on Third Avenue. Then he released her hand and shook mine. "Signorina," he said, really not interested.

I never did find out what that fringed black cost. Probably more than my entire savings account at Chemical Bank.

I was willing to admit that Vanessa Havistock had a lot of talents, and one of them was obviously the ability to get a cab. She had no sooner stepped off the curb and held up one finger languidly than a Checker pulled up with a screech of brakes. I wish I had that gift.

On our way to the Russian Tea Room, she suddenly said, "Are you a close friend of Roberta's?"

"Close?" I said, surprised. "Hardly. I think I've seen her twice."

"Be careful," Vanessa said darkly. "She's not exactly the Flying Nun, you know."

Roberta Minchen was at a table, waiting for us. The Christmas decorations were still up, as always, in the back room. The place was already crowded, and the clack of conversation was rising.

"Look what I've got," Roberta said, giggling and holding up a glass. "Peppered vodka. It's delicious."

She was wearing one of her high-collared, flowery chiffons, and I tried not to remember what she had looked like in that videocassette I had seen. Not Academy Award material—unless all those men would nominate her for Best Supporting Actress.

Vanessa had her very, *very* dry martini straight up with a single olive, please, and I asked for a vodka gimlet. Then, to keep things simple, we all ordered the same luncheon: avocado stuffed with crabmeat salad. Kiddo, I told myself, you're *living*.

It took about three seconds for the talk to get around to the Demaretion robbery and Orson Vanwinkle's murder. The Havistock women thought both events were connected.

"It stands to reason," Roberta Minchen said, rabbity teeth gleaming. "I mean we were all living such a nice, peaceful existence, and then those two awful things happened, one right after the other. There must be a link between them."

"I agree," Vanessa said. "And I still think Orson was involved in stealing the coin. He was such a creep."

"Wasn't he?" Roberta said, blinking. "I just never did understand why Daddy kept him on. Do you know, Vanessa?"

"Why, no," she said tightly. "How in hell would I know something like that?"

That was my first intimation that there was a tension between the two. Maybe not outright hostility, at the moment, but a kind of wariness. The sparring kept up after our luncheon plates were served.

"Even Mother didn't like him," Roberta said. "But he was Archibald's nephew, and I guess she didn't want to say anything. Did you know his girlfriend, Vanessa? Dolly LeBaron?"

"I met her once," Vanessa said. "Once was enough. You had them over to your place, didn't you?"

"We tried to be friends. Briefly. But they really weren't our kind of people."

"Oh? I'd have thought you'd hit it off."

I was silent, listening to this dueling with fascination.

"He just drank too much," Roberta said. "And she's a flibbertigibbet."

"Do you really think so?" Vanessa said. "As I said, I only met her once, but my impression was that behind the Marilyn Monroe exterior was a real barracuda."

"It takes one to know one," Roberta said, smiling sweetly.

Vanessa stared at her coldly, then turned to me. "Have you met her, Dunk? Dolly LeBaron?"

"Yes, I've met her."

"What was your take?"

"Not too bright."

"Bright enough," Vanessa said grimly, "to latch on to Orson and take him for whatever she could get. That's where all his money went."

We were silent then, digging into our avocados. But the truce didn't last long.

"How is Luther?" Roberta asked. "The last time I saw him he looked so pale and thin."

"Luther is fine," Vanessa said.

"Is he still biting his fingernails?"

Vanessa glared at her. "Is Ross still cracking his knuckles?"

I prepared to push back my chair if dishes started flying. But their jousting remained verbal.

"After all," Roberta said, "Luther *is* my brother, and I *am* interested in his welfare. You shouldn't let him drink so much."

"Butt out," Vanessa said, her face becoming almost ugly with anger. "Just butt out. I don't tell you how to manage that nerd you're married to, do I? Advice from you I don't need."

"Ladies," I murmured, but it did no good.

"At least," Roberta said, "Ross is a good provider."

"I won't ask what he provides," Vanessa said nastily. "After all, you're paying for the lunch, and I never insult the woman who pays the bill."

"Or the man either," Roberta said. "You're always very sweet to the one who picks up the check."

"What that's supposed to mean?" Vanessa demanded.

"If the shoe fits, wear it."

Thank God the waitress arrived just then to remove our empty plates. I swear that if that snarling had gone on much longer, I'd have stood up and stalked out with as much dignity as I could muster. It was embarrassing. But the waitress saved the day, and we all ordered coffee, no desserts, in calm, controlled voices.

"Ruby Querita," Vanessa said, looking at Roberta with no expression. "What do you think?"

Roberta pouted her lips. "Yes," she said, "I think it's very possible she took the coin. Her brother's in jail, you know. She needs money to get him out."

They both turned to stare at me.

"And killed Orson Vanwinkle?" I said. "Why would she do that?"

"Maybe he saw her do it," Vanessa said. "He was going to turn her in to the cops, so she shot him."

"Yes," Roberta said, nodding wisely, "that makes sense."

Again I had the feeling of being pushed in directions I didn't want to go.

"It doesn't make sense to me," I said. "Letters were written to the insurance company, offering to make a deal: the Demaretion returned for cash. I don't think Ruby would be capable of that."

"Maybe she got someone to write the letters for her," Vanessa said.

"Now you're reaching," I told her. "Ruby is very religious. She lives by the Ten Commandments. I really don't think she'd steal."

"Then it was Natalie," Roberta said firmly. "She'd steal—as a kind of joke, you know. I hate to say it about my own sister, but she's capable."

What a family!

I was never so glad in my life when that awful luncheon finally ended. I told them I had an appointment uptown, and left them together on the sidewalk as soon as I decently could, after thanking Roberta for her hospitality.

"We must do it again soon," she said brightly.

In about 1998, I thought.

I walked away from them as fast as I could, not looking back. If they started pulling hair after I was gone, that was their problem. And if it came to a knockdown and dragout fight, I'd have bet on Vanessa; she was the ballsier of the two.

I had time to kill before my appointment at Grandby & Sons, so I sat for a while on a bench in Central Park. Then an ancient dodderer came along, dropped his newspaper in front of me, bent slowly to retrieve it, and tried to look up my skirt. Just an average day in the Big Apple. I rose hastily and strode over to Madison where the weirdos were younger and better dressed.

What a lunch that had been! But valuable, I thought. It gave me new insights into the stresses and pressures within the Havistock family. I didn't know what it all meant, but I never doubted for a moment that it was significant. If I could understand those enmities, I might be a lot farther along in finding out who copped the Demaretion and who knocked off Orson Vanwinkle.

Madison Avenue, from 57th Street northward, is really something: my favorite window-shopping tour. All the riches of the world: art galleries, boutiques, antique shops, jewelers, wine stores, swank hotels, and crazy little holes-in-the-wall where you could buy things like polo mallets, porcelain picture frames, and furniture made of Lucite. Bring money.

I still had a lot of Des Moines in me, and a street like this was an invitation to a world I'd never known. I couldn't help laughing, because I knew I'd never know it—but I could admire it. That didn't depress me. I was happy just to be able to goggle at all those baubles, dream, and go home to my Lean Cuisine. *Things* are nice, but they're not everything. Right?

I timed my stroll and got to Grandby & Sons a few minutes before three o'clock. If the meeting didn't take too long, I planned to stop in and give Hobie Juliana a big hug, in thanks for all his help.

We all met in Grandby's conference room, an austere chamber that needed only candles and a casket on a trestle to pass as a funeral parlor. We sat at wide intervals around a polished table, and lawyer Lemuel Whattsworth, Mr. Congeniality himself, opened the game.

"Miss Bateson," he said, "you have been employed by Archibald Havistock to investigate the theft of the Demaretion. Is that correct?"

I nodded.

"You realize, of course, that technically you are still employed by Grandby and Sons, on temporary leave of absence."

"Technically," I said. "Meaning I'm not getting paid."

"There is a conflict of interest involved here," he said, sucking his teeth happily. "It is quite possible that Grandby's and Archibald Havistock may, eventually, if this matter is not speedily and satisfactorily resolved, be in litigation re the loss of the Demaretion and recompense demanded for its reserve value as stated in the auction contract."

"So?" I said.

"Surely you can see the awkward position into which you are placing your legitimate employer," he droned on. "I refer, of course, to Grandby and Sons. You have, in effect, become a hireling of a party who may very well become our adversary in a court of law."

"Hireling?" I said. "Watch your language, buster. All I'm trying to do is clear my name."

Stanton Grandby, looking more like a plump penguin than ever, gave a little cough and tried to smile. He didn't succeed.

"What we'd really like to know," he said, "is whether or not you've made any progress in your investigation."

"Not much," I said casually, sitting back. Let them sweat.

"Dunk," Felicia Dodat said, "you have no suspect?" She really was wearing green nail polish.

"Oh, there are a lot of suspects," I said. "Too many. But if you're asking me if I know who stole the Demaretion, the answer is no, I don't."

They looked at each other, then all three looked at me.

"But you feel you *are* making progress?" Stanton Grandby asked anxiously.

I considered that. "Yes," I said finally, "I think I am. I've collected a lot of information. I agree with Detective Georgio and investigator Smack: the robbery was committed by a member of the Havistock family."

"Ah-*ha*," lawyer Whattsworth said with some satisfaction. "You're sure of that?"

"No," I said, "I'm not sure of anything."

His confidence evaporated. "How long," he asked in his papery voice, "do you anticipate your investigation will continue?"

"As long as it takes," I told him.

Again they exchanged glances. If a signal passed between them, I didn't see it.

"Under the circumstances," the attorney said, "it seems somewhat unfair to you that your income should derive solely from a party with whom Grandby's may very well find itself in an antagonistic position."

After digging through that tortured syntax, I gathered he was saying that I wasn't making enough money.

"I agree," I said.

"Therefore," he continued, "we suggest that you terminate your employment by Archibald Havistock. Your leave of absence will be ended, and you will be returned to a salaried position with Grandby and Sons. It will be understood that you shall be relieved of all your regular duties, allowing you to continue your investigation into the theft of the coin."

"No," I said promptly.

"No?" Stanton Grandby cried.

"No?" Felicia Dodat cried.

"No," I repeated firmly. "The Havistocks put me on salary after you people took me off. I promised them I'd do everything I could to solve the crime. I intend to keep that promise."

"But didn't they demand certain conditions?" the attorney said slyly. "That you weren't to investigate too closely members of the immediate family?"

"Absolutely not," I said. "I asked for a free hand, and I got it. The only condition to which I agreed was that, if a member of the family turned out to be the criminal, I would inform Mr. Havistock before I told the authorities. I assumed the reason for that was so he could arrange legal representation for the accused family member before he or she was arrested and charged."

"Yes," Whattsworth said dryly, "I would say that is a logical assumption. However, it is extraneous to the basic interests of Grandby and Sons. What I now propose is that you continue your employment by Archibald Havistock, if you insist, but at the same time you return to a salaried position with Grandby's. With the absolute understanding, of course, that we shall become privy to the results of your investigation at the same time you reveal those results to Mr. Havistock, and that you shall provide us with weekly written reports on your progress."

"Verbal reports," I said. "Not written. And not weekly reports, but periodically—whenever I've got something to tell you."

"Oh, Dunk," Felicia Dodat said sorrowfully, "you're being so difficult."

"Am I?" I said. "I thought I was being cooperative."

The lawyer looked at god. "Mr. Grandby," he said, "are you willing to accept those terms?"

The penguin squirmed. Then he nodded. "All right," he said.

"Oh, Dunk," Felicia caroled, "it's so nice having you back with us again."

I had two words for her, and they weren't Happy Birthday.

I stopped down to see Hobie Juliana and tell him the good news, but he was out of the office on an appraisal. So I left Grandby's and walked back home through Central Park, proud of the way I had handled that confrontation. I was now making *two* salaries with complete freedom to conduct the investigation any way I chose. A slam dunk!

I knew what Grandby's was after, of course, and why they had put me back on salary. If a member of Archibald Havistock's family was involved in the theft, they wanted to know about it as soon as possible. It would give them leverage in the anticipated lawsuit. Also, by paying me, they thought they were insuring against any possible cover-up on my part.

Not very complimentary to me, but understandable.

That night, mercifully free of phone calls—I had gibbered enough—I lay awake in bed a long time, thinking over the events and conversations of that day. But then I found I was not pondering the investigation so much as I was reflecting on myself, and what was happening to me.

I was changing, no doubt about it; I was aware of it. I won't say I was naive prior to my involvement with the Havistock Collection, but I was inclined to accept people at their face value, believing what they told me. I suppose I had lived a sheltered existence; crime and homicidal violence were things I read about in newspapers and novels, or saw in movies and on television.

But during the past weeks I had become intimately acquainted with what I guess you could call the underbelly of life. People *did* lie. They were *not* what they seemed. And they were capable of acting irrationally, driven by passions they could not control.

And my experiences with Al Georgio and Jack Smack were added evidence of how often the heart and glands overruled the mind and good sense. I suppose I should have learned all that at an earlier age, but I hadn't. Finally, finally I was suffering a loss of ingenuousness, if not innocence.

I was becoming, I thought, wiser, more cynical, street-smart. So something had been lost and something had been gained. But if you asked me what the bottom line was, I couldn't have told you.

22

After breakfast the next morning, I devoted myself to "choring," which is what, in my Iowa home, we called those endless boring tasks that had to be done: putting out the garbage, dusting, changing the linen, washing the sinks, etc. When I was satisfied with the way my apartment looked (it could have been more sparkling, but I lacked the willpower to tackle the windows), I left the house to pick up some dry cleaning.

This time I was careful to inspect the vestibule and areaway before I ventured out. On my way to the dry cleaners, I passed a newsstand and thought I might buy a copy of *Vogue* to see what I should be wearing, wasn't, and never would. But all thoughts of fashion fled when I glimpsed the screaming headline of the *Post*.

HIPPY SOCIALITE TRIES SUICIDE. And there was a photograph of Natalie Havistock with a dopey grin, wearing a beaded headband and earrings that looked like they had been snipped from the lid of a sardine tin.

I bought a *Post* and read the story on the sidewalk, oblivious to the people brushing by. It said that Natalie Havistock, younger daughter of wealthy tycoon Archibald Havistock (has there ever been a *poor* tycoon, I wondered), had been found unconscious in her bedroom at her parents' home on East 79th Street, apparently after ingesting alcohol and drugs that had not yet been identified.

She had been rushed to Wilson Memorial Hospital, only three blocks away, where, after treatment, doctors had pronounced her condition "stable." Her parents stated that no note had been found, and could give no reason for their daughter's attempted suicide.

I trotted home, errands forgotten, and called the Havistock apartment. Busy signal. Waited a few minutes and called again. Still busy. Waited.

Called. Busy. Finally, on the fourth try, I got through. Ruby Querita answered. I identified myself.

"How is Nettie?" I asked. "Have you heard anything?"

"*Nada*," she said dolefully. "They all at the hospital. I don't know how things are."

"All right," I said. "Thank you, Ruby. Maybe I'll go to the hospital myself and see what's happening."

Her voice dropped to a whisper. "I told you, didn't I? Sin and you must suffer. This family is marked. Didn't I tell you?"

"You told me, Ruby," I said, and hung up.

My idea of a hospital is a big shiny place with wide corridors, white walls, and tiled floors. Everything spotless and gleaming. Forget it. Wilson Memorial looked like a crumbling castle right out of *Young Frankenstein*. Gloomy, gloomy, gloomy. With narrow hallways, walls painted a sick brown, and worn linoleumed floors. I learned later it was a sort of temporary refuge for the terminally ill. I could believe it. If they weren't terminal when they were admitted, that place would push them over the edge.

The nurse at the lobby desk gave me a sad smile. I told her I'd like to see Natalie Havistock.

"Are you a member of the immediate family?" she asked.

"No," I said, "I am not. Actually, I don't want to see Natalie, but I have an important message for her father, Mr. Archibald Havistock. I understand he's here. As soon as I see him, I'll be on my way."

The scam worked.

"Room four-twelve," she said, handing me a pass. "Please make your visit as brief as possible."

"You better believe it," I said. "Hospitals depress me."

"Me, too," she said mournfully, which I thought was an odd thing for a nurse to say.

I found the dismal corridor outside room 412. I also found Ross Minchen sitting on a scarred wooden bench, cracking his knuckles like a maniac.

"Hello, Ross," I said.

He looked up, and it took him a couple of beats to recognize me. "Oh, hi," he said, not rising. "Dunk—right? How're you doing?"

"How is Nettie doing?"

"Okay, I guess. They pumped her out. They're releasing her at noon. Mabel and Archibald are in with her now. The cops took off."

"I thought Roberta and Vanessa would be here."

"They were," he said, "but they left. I think they had some shopping to do."

"And Luther?" I said. "Wasn't her brother here?"

"Luther? No, he didn't show up. I guess he's busy. I'm just waiting to drive them all back home. Then I've got to get to the office."

"Sure you do," I said, sitting down beside him. "I'll bet your work is piling up."

"It really is," he said, nodding. "Unless I'm there every day, you wouldn't believe how things pile up."

Mr. Wimp himself, with those scrawny locks of hair combed sideways across his balding skull. Hard to believe this guy was the producer of X-rated videocassettes. You'd have thought that knitting antimacassars was more in his line.

"Ross," I said, "have you any idea why Nettie would do such a thing?"

"Gee," he said, "I really don't. Of course, she runs with a wild gang. I mean, they're probably dropping dope and all that. I don't know what the world is coming to."

I didn't either.

Then stupid me, I had to ask: "Are you and Roberta going to Vanessa's party?" I heard myself saying it and could have chomped off my tongue.

"No," he said. "Is she having a party?"

"Probably not," I said hastily. "After this business with Natalie. It was a very vague thing. She'll probably call it off."

"We don't see much of them," he said, looking down at his big, spatulate hands. "Vanessa and Roberta don't get along."

"That's a shame," I said. "Families should stick together."

"Yeah," he said, "that's what I think. We tried to get Vanessa and Luther to join our, ah, little circle, but they weren't interested. How about you?" he said, brightening. "Have you thought about it?"

"Frequently," I said.

"And?"

"Still thinking," I told him.

"Nothing to it," he said. "It's fun—you'll see. We're having another do next Friday. Can you make it?"

"I'm not sure," I said then, swiftly, "Wasn't it awful about Orson Vanwinkle?"

He looked at me, unblinking. "The man was a crud," he said. "I don't mean I wanted him dead, don't get me wrong, but I can't be a hypocrite either and pretend I'm all broken up at his passing. I figure he got what he deserved."

"No one seems to have liked him," I said. "Except Dolly LeBaron."

"Oh, *her*," he said scornfully. "As greedy as he was. They were two of a kind. Listen, about next Friday, why don't you—"

But I was saved from more excuses when Mabel and Archibald Havistock came out of room 412. I rose and went to them.

"How is she?" I said anxiously.

"Much better," Mrs. Havistock said. "We're taking her home in an hour. Thank you for your concern and for coming by."

"How did you hear about it?" Archibald asked.

I reckoned he might as well know. "It's on the front page of today's *Post*," I told him.

"Oh, yes," he said bitterly, "it would be."

Ross Minchen was still seated on his wooden bench, playing a merry tune on his knuckles. I gently urged the Havistocks down the corridor, away from him. I moved them to the end of the hallway, to a window where we could look out at a shadowy airshaft.

They were two somber people, faces creased with sorrow. But they retained their dignity, both of them erect and steady. I admired their stalwartness. Both seemed capable of absorbing blows without flinching and without complaint. Well, I thought, they have each other, and that's how they survive.

"I promised you a progress report," I said. "If you feel this is a bad time for it, please tell me and we'll leave it for later."

"No, no," Archibald said. "Let's have it now. What have you found out?"

"First," I said, "I must tell you that Grandby and Sons have put me back on the payroll, with the understanding that I can spend all my time investigating the robbery. If you object to that, if you feel there's a conflict of interest involved, I want you to know that I'll reject their offer and work only for you."

He looked at me a long moment. "Thank you," he said finally. "You are a very straightforward young woman. I like that. No, I see no reason why you should not be employed by Grandby's at the same time you're working for us. Actually, we all want the same thing, don't we? Have you discovered who stole the Demaretion?"

"No, I have not. But I do feel I am making progress. Orson Vanwinkle promised his girlfriend that they'd soon be leaving the country permanently to live on the French Riviera. That certainly sounds like he expected to come into a great deal of money shortly, and makes him the Number One suspect."

Husband and wife exchanged glances, just the briefest of eye-flickers.

"But I don't believe it," I went on. "Mostly because I cannot possibly conceive how Orson could have switched display cases. It was a physical impossibility."

"Perhaps he had accomplices," Mabel Havistock said faintly.

"Who?" I demanded. "The guards from the armored van? Ruby Querita? I don't think so. Mr. Havistock, you were out of your library for perhaps two minutes. The switch had to be made then: a prepared empty display case, sealed with your signet ring, substituted for the case containing the Demaretion. It had to be done by someone in the family, someone present in the apartment for the birthday party."

"Not Nettie?" Mr. Havistock said, his magisterial features expressionless, ice-blue eyes revealing nothing. "Don't tell me it was Nettie?"

I didn't answer his question, but asked one of my own: "The *Post* story said Nettie didn't leave any note. Is that correct?"

Mabel nodded, eyes skimmed with grief. "We can't understand it," she said. "She was always such a bright cheerful child. Laughing and joking. Perhaps it was something we did. Or failed to do."

I had been debating with myself whether or not to tell them. But now, seeing that imposing woman suffering from a guilt trip, I thought I would.

"There are some things you should know," I said. "What I'm going to tell you is rumor and supposition. Nothing is proven. Orson Vanwinkle was bisexual. He had many homosexual encounters. This comes from a reliable source. Nettie's boyfriend is a black. Are you aware of that?"

"We are," Mr. Havistock said stonily.

"Her boyfriend was also one of Orson's homosexual contacts," I said. "I wish I could have spared you this, but I don't want you to blame yourselves for a situation over which you had no control."

They didn't crumple. If anything, they straightened, drew deep breaths. They seemed to have a source of stamina I wished I could have tapped.

"You're certain of this?" Archibald asked.

"Mr. Havistock, I'm not certain of *anything*. I'm just reporting what I've heard. That's what you're paying me for. But I think what I've heard is true. And it might possibly explain Natalie's suicide attempt. She discovered her boyfriend's, uh, sexual proclivities, argued with him about it, and he refused to change the way he lives."

"I don't understand," Mabel said, completely flummoxed. "Why would those two men have anything to do with each other? They belonged to different worlds."

"Money," I said promptly. "I think Orson was paying Akbar El Raschid and, through him, financing that gang of kooks Akbar commands. Maybe it was just the excitement Orson liked. The threat of violence. Radical chic."

Archibald Havistock thought about it a long time while we all stared out at that haunted airshaft. Then he turned to me.

"Possible," he said. "It's possible. Orson was what I'd call a flighty man. Not quite as steady as I would have liked. Are the police aware of what you've told us, Miss Bateson?"

"They're aware of Vanwinkle's sexual activities," I said. "Whether or not they know about his liaison with Nettie's boyfriend—that I don't know. They'll probably find out."

He nodded. "Do you have anything else to tell us?"

"No, sir, not at the moment. A lot of wild guesses, crazy ideas, rumors I've got to track down. But nothing that even resembles fact or evidence. Do you want me to continue my investigation?"

"Absolutely," Mrs. Havistock said. "We want to know the truth. Don't we, Archibald?"

"Yes," he said.

"All right," I told them, "I'll keep at it. Now I'd like to ask a favor of you."

They waited.

"May I go in to see Natalie? Just for a few minutes?"

They looked at each other.

"You won't disturb her?" Mrs. Havistock said. "Ask questions?"

"Of course not. I do like her and I want her to know I care."

"All right," Archibald said. "Just for a few minutes."

I started away from them, then turned back. I addressed Mrs. Havistock.

"Ma'am," I said, "the last time we spoke you mentioned that you and your husband are involved in estate planning."

"Yes," she said, "that's correct."

"Does that include the drawing up of new wills for both of you?"

"It does," Mr. Havistock said. "Why do you ask?"

"I don't know exactly," I said fretfully. "Except money seems to be the thread that runs through everything: the stealing of the Demaretion and the murder of Orson Vanwinkle. Have the wills been completed?"

"No," he said, "they have not."

I thought he was a little short with me, and I assumed he resented my intrusion into his private financial affairs. But I would not stop.

"Were members of your family aware that you were preparing new wills?"

"I assume they were," he said. "Don't you think so, Mabel?"

"I'm sure they were," she said. "We made no secret of it."

"Thank you very much," I said. "I'll get back to you the moment I have anything important to report."

23

Poor Natalie looked so weak and drawn, white as the sheets she was lying on. She held out a thin hand to me.

"I can't do anything right, can I?" she said.

"You're alive," I said, kissing her cold fingertips. "That's right. How are you, love?"

"Oh . . ." she said, "I don't know. I'm not thinking straight."

"You'll clear up," I assured her. "I just stopped in for a few minutes to say hello."

"It was sweet of you," she said. "Did you find out who boosted the coin?"

"Not yet."

"You will," she said. "You're a determined lady. The cops haven't found out who snuffed Orson, have they?"

I shook my head.

"Well, who cares," she said. "That little Barbie Doll of his—what's her name?"

"Dolly LeBaron."

"Yeah, a real dolly. She'll find another bankroll, and in a year—a year? Hell, within a month—the world will be rolling along without him. That's what's going to happen to all of us, isn't it?"

"Nettie, don't talk like that. Your mother and father are outside. They're really shook. They love you and want you to have a happy life. You're important to them."

"I guess," she said, sighing. "I've been a pain in the ass to them. Two different worlds—you know?"

"You made the front page of the *Post* today," I told her.

"I did?" she said, brightening. "Hot shit! Have you got it with you?"

"I have it at home," I said. "I'll save it for you if you can't get a copy. You're wearing a beaded headband and tin earrings."

"Oh, that old shot," she said. "It was taken years ago at the Slipped Disco. I was stoned out of my skull."

"You look like it," I said, and we both laughed.

She reached for my hand again. "Listen, Dunk, when I get back to the land of the living, can we see each other again?"

"Absolutely," I said.

"Promise?"

"Of course. I'm counting on it. If you promise me something first."

"What?"

"If you ever get in the mood to try something like that again, will you call me first?"

"Okay," she said, "I will."

We linked our little fingers, shook, and both of us said, "Pinkie square!"

I didn't know what it was—maybe the sultry July day or maybe that childish business of "Pinkie square!"—but on the way home I had a sudden, irresistible urge to chaw on a frozen Milky Way. And I wasn't even pregnant! Anyway, I stopped off to buy three of the candy bars. I put them in the freezer and waited patiently. I remembered they've got to be so hard you think you'll break your teeth—but you never do. The joys of my youth!

I was entering all the happenings of the morning into my notebook when I received my first phone call of the day. I thought it might be Al or Jack, alerting me to Natalie's attempted suicide. But it was Enoch Wottle, calling from Arizona. I was delighted.

"Enoch, dear," I said, "I love to hear from you, but you've *got* to call collect. I don't want you spending your money on my business."

"It's nothing," he said blithely. "I'm never going to outlive my bonds. Dunk, darling, how are you and what's happening?"

I gave him a précis of what had been going on, including my reinstatement at Grandby & Sons.

"Good," he said firmly. "They should be ashamed of themselves for putting you on leave of absence in the first place. Are you any closer to finding out who stole the Demaretion?"

"Closer," I said, "I think. But close doesn't help. I'm still not sure who did it, Enoch."

"But you suspect?"

"I suspect, but it's so crazy I don't even want to talk about it."

"All right," he said equably, "then I'll talk. I have something that might help. I checked with my friend in Rotterdam who, in turn, contacted that Beirut dealer. Dunk, from what everyone says—if they're telling the truth—that Demaretion being offered for sale is absolutely authentic. Provenance will be supplied during serious negotiations. It sounds legitimate to me, Dunk. Not the source of the coin,'' he added hastily. ''Not how the seller got hold of it. But the dekadrachm itself—that's not a fake. Does that help you?''

''I think so,'' I said slowly. ''I'm not sure how it fits in, but everything helps. Thank you so much, Enoch. You've been a treasure.''

''Now then,'' he said briskly, ''what's next?''

''What's next? Enoch, you've done enough for me. Spending your own money on phone calls and cables. I can't ask you to do anything more.''

''Ask!'' he urged. ''Ask! Dunk, sweetheart, let me tell you something. My life is drawing to a close; I know it. But what am I supposed to do, just sit and *wait*? So what I do for you, I do for myself also. To keep busy, to be needed, wanted—that is something at my age.''

My eyes teared. ''All right, Enoch,'' I said, ''you certainly can help. Who else has your knowledge and experience? Tell me: Why would a collector—not a speculator but a true collector—sell off part of his coin collection?''

He thought a moment. ''Financial need,'' he suggested. ''That would probably be the first motive. Some investments go wrong, the stock market takes a nose dive, he needs ready cash. So he sells off some coins. That would be the first motive. Another would be that he wants to upgrade his collection. He sells off the lesser mintages, maybe some duplicates, so he can buy higher quality.''

''But the true collector who sells and doesn't buy, doesn't add, that's unusual, isn't it, Enoch?''

''I'd say so, unless he's in a real money bind.''

''Archibald Havistock has been selling for the past five years,'' I told him. ''About a hundred items, maybe more. I'd like to find out how much he got for them. Not for individual coins, but the total. How do I do that? Go to the Society?''

''No,'' he said immediately. ''Privileged information. They wouldn't know—and if they did, they'd never tell you. Do you know who he dealt with?''

''No, I don't. But he's a wealthy man, Enoch. Very upright, very honest. He wouldn't deal with shlockers.''

''That means there are maybe a half-dozen people in Manhattan he'd go to. I know them all. You want me to check?''

''Would you?''

''I would and I will. This gives me something to do. I feel important.''

''You *are* important, Enoch, and I love you.''

''Why aren't you fifty years older?'' he said, groaning. ''We could make such beautiful music together.''

I laughed. ''Enoch,'' I said, ''you're a dirty old man.''

''I was a dirty *young* man,'' he said, ''and I haven't changed. Dunk, darling, as soon as I learn something, I'll get back to you. It may take some time.''

"I don't care how long it takes," I said, "but be sure and reverse the charges."

"All right already," he said, "I'll reverse. Thank you, Dunk."

After we hung up, I wiped my eyes. Sweet, sweet man. Thanking me. For what? I knew. I returned to my journal and continued entering all the latest intelligence I had garnered that day. Then I dashed to the refrigerator. The Milky Ways weren't yet hard enough, but I chewed on one with pleasure, remembering hot summer days in Des Moines when I was all legs and a stomach that could never be filled.

Would you believe I pigged down all three frozen Milky Ways that afternoon? I did, and I'm not ashamed of it. I should tell you that in spite of the Lean Cuisines I gobble, I'm blessed with a fantastic metabolism and can eat anything without putting on a pound. Sometimes I wish I could—in the right places.

Maybe all that sugar gave me energy, or maybe what I had heard that morning made me think I was making progress; whatever it was, I was in a charged mood and had no desire to spend the evening all by my lonesome. So I called Al Georgio.

And while I listened to his phone buzz, I wondered why I hadn't called Jack Smack. Did my choice indicate a preference—or was it just a chancy act with no significance whatsoever. I didn't know.

I had to wait almost three minutes before they located him and got him to the phone. He came on breathless and laughing.

"Hey there, Dunk," he said. "I was going to call you in a half-hour, I swear. How're you doing?"

"Surviving," I said. "How are *you* doing?"

"Surviving," he said. "I guess you heard about Natalie Havistock?"

"I read it in the *Post*. I went over to the hospital this morning and saw her."

"You did? They wouldn't let me in. She say anything about why she tried to off herself?"

"She didn't say and I didn't ask. I was with her for only a few minutes, and it was just girl talk. Anything new on the Demaretion?"

"Nah," he said disgustedly. "A lot of little bits and pieces that don't come together. The same goes for the Vanwinkle kill. The homicide guys are still checking out all the names in his little black book. I passed along your tip that he was AC-DC, and they're working that angle. Nothing yet."

"Listen, Al," I said, suddenly bold, "I'd like to take you to dinner tonight."

"You would?" he said. "That's the best offer I've had all year. What's the occasion?"

"I was put back on salary at Grandby's, and I'm still working for the Havistocks, so I want to celebrate. How about it?"

"Sounds great. But we'll go Dutch. Got any idea where you want to eat?"

"There's a new Chinese restaurant in the neighborhood I'd like to try. Over on Amsterdam. The menu in the window looks good. It's Szechwan. Too hot for you?"

"You kidding? I put Tabasco on my corn flakes. What are you giggling about? The joke wasn't that funny."

"The name of the restaurant . . . " I said. "It's called Hung Lo."

"My kind of joint," he said. "Pick you up about eight?"

"Try to park if you can," I said, "and we'll walk over. It's only two blocks away."

Hung Lo, although recently opened, looked like a million other Chinese restaurants in New York. But there were a lot of Orientals at the tables, which Al and I figured was a good sign. Also, the menu said you could have your food with or without monosodium glutamate, and you could designate mild, hot, or superhot.

"Let's go with hot," I suggested. "If it's not incendiary enough, we can always pepper it up. But if the superhot turns out to be too much, we're stuck with it."

So that's what we did, ordering eggrolls and barbecued ribs as small appetizers, wonton soup, and deciding to share our main dishes, shrimp with peanuts, shredded pork with garlic sauce, and servings of white and fried rice.

"And beer instead of tea," Al told the waiter. "Cold, cold beer. Okay, Dunk?"

"Just right," I said.

Maybe I was hungry despite those Milky Ways. I know Al seemed to be famished. We went through all that food like a plague of locusts. I had a bottle of Heineken, and Al had two. Then we had pistachio ice cream and opened our fortune cookies. Mine read: "Your fondest wish will come true." Al's was: "The wise man wants for nothing."

"The story of my life," he said. "That's what I'm getting—nothing."

I excused myself, telling Al I wanted to find the ladies' room. But I grabbed our waiter, paid the bill, and tipped him. Then I went back to our table.

"All set?" Al said. "I'll get the check."

"I took care of it," I said.

He looked at me, shaking his head. "You're sneaky, you know that? I said we'd go Dutch."

"That's what *you* said. I didn't agree."

He laughed, took up my hand, kissed the palm. "You're something, you are. The new woman."

"Not so new," I told him. "A little worn around the edges."

"You're worn?" he said. "I'm frayed."

We strolled slowly back to my place. He insisted on stopping off to buy a cold six-pack of Heineken. Which was all right with me. I could still feel the glow of the Szechwan cooking, and I was happy we hadn't ordered the superhot. My eyebrows would be charred.

We hadn't said a word about the Demaretion or the murder or Orson Vanwinkle all evening. I think we both wanted a brief respite from all that. So we chatted lazily about new movies, whether roast duck was better with mandarin oranges or black cherries, and the problems Al was having with his cleaning woman. She kept stealing his Future floor wax.

"I swear she's drinking the stuff," he said.

When we got home, he asked if he could make himself comfortable, and I said sure, go ahead. He took off his jacket and eased out of his shoes. He was wearing a knitted sport shirt with no animal insignia, which gave him a plus in my book.

No way was he ever going to be an elegant, dapper dude. He just didn't have the body, and he just didn't care. But there was something comforting in his lumpiness. Winston Churchill wasn't Beau Brummell, and neither was Pope John XXIII. But both men made you feel good just to look at them, they were so *solid*. They knew life wasn't to be taken lightly. The same with Al Georgio.

"I got a Sunday coming up with my daughter," he said. "I'd like you to join us. Will you?"

"You sure it will be all right?"

"No, I'm not sure," he said. "But let's try it."

"Okay."

"You like the beach?"

"Love it, but I've got to be careful. I freckle, get red, and then I peel."

"So you cover up," he said, shrugging. "Maybe we'll go to Jacob Riis. The water should be warm enough by now. Do you swim, Dunk?"

"Like a fish," I told him. "An eel."

"You're always putting yourself down. Does it bother you that you're so tall and slender?"

We were both working on cold beers, drinking out of the bottle. I took a deep gulp before I answered.

"Thank you for saying slender instead of skinny. It doesn't *bother* me, but I know it's there. When I look in the mirror. The way people sometimes stare at me. Trying to buy clothes that fit. But I can handle it."

"I figure you can handle just about anything," he said. "Fifteen years ago my waist size was thirty-two. Now it's forty. I've tried everything: diet, working out. Nothing helps. So I've learned to live with it. I know I'm a slob."

"You're not a slob," I said indignantly. "Don't say that. You're just a very, uh, robust man."

"That's me," he said. "Robust."

He said it so wryly that we both laughed, and that made our physical shortcomings seem unimportant.

"What about you, Dunk?" he said, staring at me. "What do you want? Marriage? The patter of tiny feet?"

"I don't know," I said, looking down at my beer bottle. "I really don't. I'm not sure I'm ready for all that yet. I want to *do* something first."

"Seems to me you've done a great deal."

"Not enough. Tonight my fortune cookie said my fondest wish will come true. Al, I don't even know what my fondest wish *is*. I'm just floating."

"Nothing wrong with that. I'm the same way. Sooner or later things will point us in one direction or another. No use trying to force it."

"That's the way I feel. Things will happen."

"They always have," he said. Then, suddenly: "May I stay the night?"

I knew that if I had said no, he'd have said, "All right." But I said, "Sure. I paid for dinner, didn't I?"

He cracked up. When he finally got his guffaws under control, he said, "I love you, Dunk, I really do. You're a lot of woman."

"You can handle it," I told him.

"I'm going to give it the old college try," he said.

He was ponderous in bed, almost solemn. It was obvious that sex was a serious thing to him. But it's nice to be with a man who doesn't think it's just recreation. Al thought it was important, and every kiss was a commitment.

Lord knows I wasn't an artful or practiced lover. Very little experience. So what Al brought to our coupling was new—for me. He was so—so *earnest*. Not clever but sincere. I'm not sure I'm telling this right, but he gave me more comfort than pleasure. Just snuggling in his strong arms gave me a feeling of relief and contentment.

As if I had come home.

24

I awoke the next morning and found Al had departed. He left a little note on my bedside table, a page torn from his pocket notebook: ''Thank you for dinner—and everything. Especially everything. Al.'' Sweet man.

By the time I bathed (bumping my noggin on the shower head, as usual) and dressed, I realized I had an enormous appetite that a bagel and a cup of coffee would never appease. I mean I was *ravenous*. There was a down-home diner over on Columbus Avenue, a scuzzy place, that on a scale of 1 to 10 ranked 1 for cleanliness and ambience and 20 for their country breakfasts. I decided I was going to have grits and fried bologna—and if you haven't tried it, don't knock it.

I went through my new drill of checking the vestibule and areaway before I went out. All clear. But when I got to the corner, there was Sam Jefferson, also known as Akbar El Raschid, leaning negligently against the mailbox. He flashed his white teeth at me.

''Morning, sweet mama,'' he said.

Then, when he saw my reaction—I didn't know whether to scream, run or both—he held up both hands, pink palms outward.

''Hey,'' he said, ''look. No shiv, no gun, no brass knuckles. All I want is a few minutes of your valuable time.''

''I already spent a few minutes,'' I told him. ''With two of your goons. The mustache and the gold tooth.''

''Yeah,'' he said, ''I know. That was stupid, stupid, stupid, and I apologize. Okay?''

''I don't like getting hassled.''

''You know anyone who does? How about it—friends again?''

I considered a moment, then: ''What do you want to talk about?''

''Nettie,'' he said. ''My main woman.''

"I'm on my way to breakfast," I said. "Grits and fried bologna. You want to come along?"

"Grits?" he said, his eyes glazing over. "Haven't had them in five years. Oh, yeah, let's go. The treat's on me."

In the greasy diner, sitting in a back booth, he looked around and then inspected the tattered menu.

"The cook has *got* to be a brother," he said. "Who else is going to offer ham hocks for breakfast? Sweet mama, if the food's as good as it sounds, I'm going to move right in. Let's go for broke."

So we both had field hand breakfasts with the best hashbrowns I've ever tasted and chicory-laced coffee that made you sit up and take notice.

"About Nettie," he said, digging into his grits, "you hear what happened to her?"

I nodded.

"Silly, silly woman," he said, groaning. "She had no call to do that."

"Apparently she thought she did. Your argument with her was about Orson Vanwinkle, wasn't it?"

"Oh, you know about that?" he said, not surprised. "So do the cops. They been around asking questions. Yeah, our little altercation was about that honky flake. You know, some flakes are crazy and funny. He was crazy and not so funny. A miserable shit if the truth be known."

"Then why did you have anything to do with him?"

He paused in his eating to stare up at me and rub a thumb and forefinger together. "Mon-eee. The mon-eee, sweet mama. That guy leaked green. You think I'd have given him the time of day if it wasn't for the gelt? I got big plans, and big plans need venture capital. That schmuck came up with the funds."

"And Nettie found out?"

"Yeah, she found out. She was the one who introduced us, but she didn't know he was a butterfly. She just thought he was a nutty drunk with an open wallet. Listen, Dunk, I want you to know—I didn't scrag him. And none of my lads did either."

"I believe you."

"Why should I want to knock off the golden goose? Someone else chilled him, and I really grieved. But only because the bank was closed. You dig? I'm telling you like it is."

"I believe you," I repeated.

"So . . . " he said, motioning the waitress over to refill our coffee cups, "my big problem now is Nettie. She means a lot to me."

"Does she?"

"I kid you not. I want to tell her how I feel, but I can't get through to her. I call her private number, but someone else answers and won't put her on. They got her sewed up."

"Do you blame them?"

"I guess not. I'm not the all-American boy they figured she'd grab.

But, at the same time, look at it from my point of view. I really do have
a thing for her and want to tell her so. That business with Vanwinkle was
just that—business. All I want to do is say to her how I feel. Then, if she
tells me to get lost, I'll get lost, and that'll be the end of that, I swear.''

''What do you want from me? What can I do?''

''Just call her. They'll let you talk to her. Tell her I'll be at the 787
number all afternoon. She knows what it is. If she wants to call me, that'd
be great. If she doesn't, that's her decision, and I'll abide by it. Will you
do that?''

I thought about it a moment. ''All right,'' I said, ''I'll try. But she may
not be in.''

''Keep trying,'' he urged. ''I'll be at the 787 number afternoons for the
next few days.''

I sat back, wiped my lips with a paper napkin, stifled a small belch.
''Tell me,'' I said, ''where was Orson Vanwinkle getting all his
money?''

''Beats the shit out of me,'' he said. ''Nettie and I used to talk about
it. I mean he was a secretary—right? But he had cash like you wouldn't
believe. And he was laying off a lot of it on that Miss Cuddles of his.
Maybe he was printing it in his bathroom—who knows? But he never had
the shorts, I can tell you that.''

I looked at him. ''You didn't like the man, he disgusted you, but you
went along for the money?''

He looked at me just as directly. ''That's right, sweet mama. If you
believe in something strong enough, then nothing you have to do makes
you turn back. You got a goal, and that's all that matters.''

''What's your goal?'' I asked him.

''A small thing,'' he said, flashing his teeth again. ''I just want to
remake the world, that's all.''

''Lots of luck,'' I said.

''You make your own luck,'' he said. ''I learned that a long time ago.
You'll call Nettie?''

''I'll try.''

''Good enough,'' he said. ''I do thank you. Something else I've got to
ask you: Are you tall or am I shrinking?''

I laughed. ''It's me,'' I said. ''Turn you off?''

''Au contraire,'' he said. ''If it wasn't for Nettie, I'd love to shinny up
you. But things being what they are, that'll have to remain a wild fantasy.''

''You better believe it,'' I told him.

When I got home, I called the Havistock apartment and asked to speak
to Natalie. Ruby Querita answered the phone and said that her parents had
taken Nettie to their family physician for a checkup; they would probably
all be home in an hour or so. I asked her to tell Natalie I had phoned and
to please call me back.

Then I settled down to read my morning *Times*. But I found my eyes rising from the paper to stare at the wall. What Akbar El Raschid had told me was pretty much what I had already figured, but where *was* Orson Vanwinkle's money coming from? My next step, I resolved, was to brace Archibald Havistock directly and ask him how much he was paying his private secretary. He might refuse to answer. But that in itself would be a kind of answer, wouldn't it?

Natalie did call back, almost two hours later, and said she was feeling a lot better, her mind had cleared, and she was determined to solve her problems one by one, instead of being overwhelmed by all of them at once.

"Good for you," I said. "That's the way to do it. Now I don't feel so guilty about giving you another problem."

I told her about my breakfast with her boyfriend and what he had asked me to do.

"So," I said, "if you want to talk to him, he'll be at the 787 number this afternoon. It's up to you."

"How did he look?" she said eagerly.

"He looked all right. The same way he looked when I met him at the party."

"Isn't he the most beautiful man you've ever seen?" she said breathlessly.

"He's very handsome."

"That crazy little beard of his," she said. "It drives me wild."

I had the unsettling feeling that since the Demaretion had been stolen, I had wandered into never-never land.

So far, most of my detecting activities had been limited to asking people questions and trying to make sense out of what they told me. I figured that's the way most professional investigators worked. I mean, how many detectives go crawling across a rug on their hands and knees with a big magnifying glass looking for clues? Interrogation was the name of the game.

But my questioning of the principals involved had resulted in more puzzles than solutions. One of the things that still bugged me was that East 65th Street brownstone apartment. Lenore Wolfgang had given me a facile explanation of why she rented it. But it didn't account for Vanessa Havistock entering the building.

Apparently Al Georgio had accepted the attorney's story. At least he hadn't told me differently. But then there were a lot of things I hadn't told *him*. I decided I'd try to find out a little more about Wolfgang's pied-à-terre.

So I cabbed over to the East Side on a muggy July afternoon, the whole city one big sauna. But I was too busy concocting a scenario to be bothered by the heat. What I planned to do was locate the superintendent of the building, and charm, wheedle, or bribe him into telling me if anyone occupied Lenore Wolfgang's apartment on a regular basis. Then I intended to describe Vanessa Havistock and ask if he had ever seen her on the premises.

Full of confidence, I strode fearlessly into the vestibule of the brownstone to check the number of the Wolfgang apartment. Instant shock. No Wolfgang listed. The space her name label had occupied was now just a little strip of bare brass. I stared at it, not believing.

It took me a few moments to recover. What *was* going on? To one side of the bell plate was a small sign: RING BASEMENT BELL FOR SUPER. I looked around; no basement bell. Then, getting my wits together, I went outside again and down three steps into the areaway. There I found the super's bell, pressed it, and improvised a fast new scam while I waited.

There were two doors, the outer a grille of forged iron in an attractive foliage pattern. It was locked. The inner door, a solid wood slab, was the one that was opened. The gorilla in a man's suit who stood there glared at me through the iron grille. He had the beginnings of a beard, but I didn't think it was deliberate; he had just neglected to shave—for almost three days.

"Good afternoon," I said, smiling brightly. "I heard there's an apartment available in this building."

"You heard wrong," he growled. "Nothing available."

He began to close his door.

"Wait a minute," I cried desperately. "Didn't Lenore Wolfgang move?"

"Yeah, she moved," he acknowledged. "But it's been rented. Lady, we got fifty people on a waiting list. At least."

I opened my shoulder bag, fished in my purse, pulled out a ten-dollar bill. I folded it lengthwise, poked it through the iron grille. He stared at it.

"What's that for?" he demanded. "I can't get you on the waiting list. You got to go to the owner. His name and address are in the vestibule." He pronounced it "vestabool."

I waggled the ten-dollar bill. "I don't want to get on the list," I said. "I just want a little information."

His hand struck like an adder, plucking the bill from my fingers.

"Yeah?" he said. "What?"

"When did Lenore Wolfgang move?"

"Coupla days ago. The new tenant moves in tomorrow. That's it?"

"Not for ten bucks, that's not it," I said indignantly. "Did you ever see a woman use Wolfgang's apartment? Tall, full-bodied, long black hair, lots of makeup and jewelry."

Something came into his eyes, a shifting of depth, a certain shrewd knowing. "Yeah," he said, "I seen a woman like that. Plenty times. A real looker."

"She used the Wolfgang apartment?"

He nodded.

"You ever see a man go up there when she was here?"

He stared at me. "No," he said, "I never seen no man with her."

He slammed the inner door. From which I concluded that someone had paid him more than I had. He was an honorable man—in his way.

I went home via bus, which was a mistake; it was a long, miserable, fume-choked trip. But I had a lot to think about. Vanessa *had* been using Wolfgang's place, as I originally suspected. And about a week after Al Georgio queried the building's owner, Lenore had given up her apartment—which, in Manhattan, is an act akin to hara-kiri.

The fact that Vanessa had been playing around came as no great surprise; I never figured her to be a one-man woman. And I couldn't see her having a lesbian relationship, especially with Lenore Wolfgang, who wore chewing gum on her shoe. No, Vanessa was having trysts with a man—or men—in that apartment. Was that where the money was coming from to pay for the jewelry, the summer home, that sumptuous Park Avenue apartment? Interesting idea: Vanessa reverting to loitering for the purpose of prostitution.

All this was supposition, of course—pure guesswork. But it did fit the facts, and the longer I considered it, the more logical it seemed. There was only one thing wrong: I couldn't see where it had any connection with the disappearance of the Demaretion. I should have considered a little longer and thought a little harder.

No phone calls for the rest of the day—which made me irritable. I wanted Al Georgio and Jack Smack to volunteer vital information that would enable me to solve the mystery to the applause of all. I realized how unfair that was—I wasn't telling them what I had discovered—but still it rankled. I was an amateur sleuth, and they were experienced professionals. You'd think they'd drop a few crumbs my way, wouldn't you?

I got myself in such a tizzy thinking about it that it took two hours of knitting to calm me down. Then I could laugh at my anger and admit that I better plan on solving the puzzle by myself or never solve it at all. Al and Jack had their own jobs and responsibilities. And I was sure they wanted the glory of breaking the case as much as I did.

That night, my stupid air conditioner making a racket, I lay naked between the sheets, reading the latest how-to book on "fulfilling your latent potential." I kept flipping the pages, looking for the magic secret that would enable me to become successful, irresistible, and shorter. I didn't find it.

I was listening to WQXR on my bedside radio with half an ear. I decided that after the midnight news, I'd turn off the radio, switch off the light, and wait for sleep.

Later, I was to reflect that I had been present when the Demaretion disappeared, Al Georgio had telephoned to tell me of Vanwinkle's death, and I had read of Natalie's attempted suicide in the daily press. Now I was to learn of the latest tragedy from the radio while lying naked in bed reading a self-improvement book. If that's not running the gamut, I don't know what is.

It was just a brief mention; the news announcer made no big deal of it. He merely said that the body of a young woman, apparently strangled, had been found in an East 66th Street apartment. The victim had been identified as Dolly LeBaron. The police said the slain woman had reportedly been a close friend of Orson Vanwinkle, whose recent murder was still under investigation.

After the initial impact of those words, I found I was weeping. That poor, silly girl with her red bikini and doomed dreams. She had told me I was her closest girlfriend, which was ridiculous, but now, hearing of her violent death, I thought it just might have been true, and wept the harder.

I didn't even begin to wonder how her murder might impinge on the investigations of the Demaretion theft and/or the Vanwinkle homicide. Only one thing concerned me. I flung out of bed, dashed bareass through the apartment, turning on lights as I went.

In the kitchen, I opened the cabinet over the sink and probed in back with trembling fingers. I was searching for that package Dolly LeBaron had left in my care.

25

I read the gory details in the morning papers. Dolly's body had been discovered by neighbors who noticed her door was ajar. She was lying on her back in the living room, wearing an opened Oriental happy coat, and nothing else. Police didn't believe she had been sexually assaulted, but awaited the autopsy for final determination.

That garish apartment was a shambles. Furniture had been overturned and slashed, closets and cupboards emptied, dresser drawers spilled, even the lid of the toilet tank removed. The killer had obviously been searching for something. (I could have told him where it was—in my kitchen.)

There was little data on Dolly's background, other than she was from Wichita and had come to New York to seek a career on the stage. There were some snide references to what had befallen her, including a mention that she was known as a "party girl," as if that was sufficient justification for what had been done to her.

The big angle in all the tabloid stories was her relationship with Orson Vanwinkle—both of them murdered within weeks. Dolly had been strangled and Orson shot, but the police were investigating the possibility that a single killer was responsible for both deaths. They had also found "quantities" of marijuana and cocaine in Dolly's trashed apartment.

Her parents were flying in from Kansas to reclaim her body after the autopsy was completed.

I stared at the front-page photos of Dolly in her red bikini.

She would have liked that.

I hardly had time to breakfast, read the papers, and wonder what it all meant when I got a call from Al Georgio. He was very abrupt.

"I just talked to Jack Smack," he said. "He's not involved in the Vanwinkle and LeBaron kills, but he thinks they're connected to the coin robbery. I think so, too. Maybe it's time the three of us sat down together and compared notes. How about it?''

"Yes," I said, "that makes sense to me. Where do you want to meet?''

"How about your place? Have any objection?''

"Of course not. When?''

"Noon today. We'll bring something to eat and something to drink, so don't go to any trouble.''

What they brought were three quarter-pounders and three cheeseburgers from McDonald's, plus enough French fries to stuff a pillow. Also, a cold six-pack of Michelob Light. We sat around my cocktail table, munching and sipping while we talked.

"The way things are going," Al said, "if we wait long enough, everyone connected with this case is going to get knocked off. Then all our worries will be over.''

"Al," I said, "was there anything about Dolly's murder that wasn't in the papers?''

"Not much, except there were no signs of forced entry. So she let in someone she knew.''

"Just like Vanwinkle," Jack said, nodding. "You're going on the theory that it's the same killer?''

"Seems likely," Al said. "Now we've got to go back and check everyone in Orson's little black book to find out where they were when Dolly was dumped.''

"Was anything stolen from her apartment?'' I asked him.

"The place is such a mess it's hard to tell. It must have taken at least a half-hour to do that much damage. Can you imagine? The killer chills Dolly and then stays on the scene for thirty minutes or more, tearing up the joint. He must have been desperate.''

"You think he found what he was looking for?'' Jack said.

"Who the hell knows," Al said roughly.

"The Demaretion?'' I suggested.

"Yeah," Al said, "it could have been that. Assuming Vanwinkle copped the coin. After he was snuffed, the killer searched his place and didn't find it. He figures Orson gave it to his girlfriend to hold for him. So the perp visits her place and goes through the whole drill again.''

"Perp?'' I said.

"Perpetrator," Al said. "Jack, what's new on your end?''

"Not a whole hell of a lot. Our contact in Lebanon says, yeah, that Beirut coin dealer is trying to peddle a Demaretion. It seems to be the real thing. But our man wasn't able to find out who the principal is.''

"Thin stuff," Al said. "Dunk, you got anything?''

"Did you check out that East Sixty-fifth Street apartment?'' I asked.

"I called the owner," he said. "Yes, it's rented by Lenore Wolfgang, Archibald Havistock's lawyer. She keeps it for friends and out-of-town clients. I haven't had time to dig any deeper than that.''

"I did," I said. "I went over there yesterday. Wolfgang gave up the apartment a few days ago. But while she had it, Vanessa Havistock used it frequently. The super wouldn't say if she was meeting a man there."

The two men stared at me, then turned to stare at each other.

"Now what the hell does that mean?" Al said.

"Nothing," Jack said. "It's garbage. So Vanessa was playing around. Big deal. I can't see it affecting anything."

That offended me. "Wolfgang's apartment was right around the block from where Dolly LeBaron was murdered. What's that—a coincidence?"

Al finished a cheeseburger, sat back, and opened his second beer. "All right," he said, "let's all blow a little smoke. Let's have some wild theories of what went down here. It doesn't have to be logical or touch all bases. Just a hazy idea of what happened. I'll start. I figure Orson engineered the Demaretion grab. He plans the whole thing, but someone else in the family makes the switch. My prime suspect is Luther Havistock, who's hurting for money. Then they argue about the split. Luther blows his cool and decides that since he actually lifted the Demaretion, he's entitled to a bigger share. So he scrags Orson and Dolly, looking for it. Now before you tear that story apart, let's have your own fairy tales. Jack, you go next."

Jack hunched forward over the cocktail table, popping French fries like they were vitamin pills. And he was still working on a quarter-pounder.

"I'll go along with your idea that there were two crooks involved," he said. "First of all, we get these neatly typed letters offering to make a deal on the return of the coin. Then suddenly the letters stop, and we hear someone's working through a Beirut dealer. That adds up to two different guys—right? I agree that Orson was involved—he probably wrote the letters to us and that threatening letter to you, Dunk—but I don't think his partner was Luther Havistock; I think it was the younger daughter, Natalie. And she was working for her screwball boyfriend, Sam Jefferson, who claims to be a born-again Muslim, Akbar El Raschid. Well, he may or may not be, but if he has Muslim contacts, what's a better place to peddle the coin than Lebanon. Doesn't that make sense?"

"I hadn't thought of that angle," Al Georgio said. "It's a possible. Dunk, let's have your daydream."

I really didn't want to tell them about my crazy idea because I thought they'd laugh at me and treat my solution with amused contempt. It was such a fragile flower that I didn't want it trampled before it had a chance to bloom. Also, I wasn't so sure about it myself.

"I'll go along with the two thieves theory," I said cautiously. "Vanwinkle was involved, no doubt about it. But I can't see either Natalie or Luther Havistock being the partner in crime. Natalie would steal from Saks Fifth Avenue, but I can't believe she'd steal from her own father. Call it woman's intuition or whatever you like, but I just don't think she's guilty. As for Luther, yes, he's in hock and seems to be close to a crackup, but do you really believe he's capable of killing two people? And if he did, who the hell is trying to sell that coin through the Beirut dealer? If it really is Archibald's Demaretion, then what's the point of murdering Orson and Dolly and searching their apartments trying to find it? No, there's someone else involved, someone who actually has the coin right now.''

''Oh, my God,'' Al said, groaning. ''Don't tell me you think there are *three* people involved.''

''I don't know,'' I said desperately. ''I suppose it sounds silly, but you've got to admit the coin was offered by the Beirut dealer *before* Dolly was killed.''

We all sat there, staring gloomily at each other. Then we reached simultaneously for more food and beer and busied ourselves, ruminating.

''You know what I think?'' I said finally, and the two detectives looked at me hopefully. ''I agree with both of you that the murders of Orson and Dolly are connected to the theft of the Demaretion. But analyze it. What, actually, *is* the connection? Because the robbery and the murders happened so close together, we assume they're linked. But when you look at it logically, the only connection is that all this is occurring in the same family. Archibald Havistock's favorite coin gets swiped. Then his private secretary, and the secretary's girlfriend, are killed. Let me ask both of you: Is there any real, hard evidence that Orson was actually involved in the theft?''

They thought awhile.

''No,'' Al admitted, ''nothing I can take to the bank.''

''He just seemed the most likely suspect,'' Jack Smack said. ''You think he *wasn't* involved, Dunk?''

''I didn't say that. But I'm not sure that stealing the coin was the reason for his murder. He led a wild life. Maybe there are other motives involved. I think we're all trying to neaten this thing up, trying to get the facts to fit our theories, and disregarding the facts that don't fit.''

''Thanks a lot,'' Jack said. ''You're giving me a lot of confidence.''

''I don't know what you're getting at, Dunk,'' Al said, frowning. ''Are you suggesting that the Vanwinkle and LeBaron homicides had nothing to do with the coin getting copped?''

''It's possible, isn't it? I guess I'm not explaining this very well, but it seems to me that there might be two crimes involved here. All right, Orson was the link between them. But isn't it conceivable that the killer searched his apartment, and Dolly's, for something other than the Demaretion?''

''For what?'' Al demanded. ''Drugs? We found them in Dolly's place. Easy to find, but they hadn't been touched.''

''Money?'' Jack suggested. ''Vanwinkle was supposed to be a heavy spender. Maybe we're trying to make something big out of what are really two run-of-the-mill burglary-homicides: a crook looking to make a cash score and panicking.''

"You don't really believe that, do you?" Al asked.

"No," Jack said, "I don't. The coin is mixed up in it. Somehow. Anyone got anything to add?"

We all stared at each other, expressionless and silent.

When I was a kid in Des Moines, after supper on Friday nights, my mother always went off to choir practice. Then my father, my three brothers, and I would sit around the kitchen table and play poker. We played for matches, and had a lot of fun.

I got to be a pretty fair poker player, mostly by learning to judge the strength of my father's and brothers' hands by their body language. When they were holding something good, they squirmed, blinked repeatedly, or maybe drummed their fingers. And when they were bluffing, their features froze; they thought they were giving nothing away.

Now, looking at Jack and Al, I had the feeling they were both bluffing. Not only were they not telling me all they knew, but they weren't telling each other either. That was all right; it saved me from having a guilt trip about what I was holding back.

"Well . . . " Al said, draining his beer, "I guess we've gone as far as we can go. No hits, no runs, and God knows how many errors. Let us all pray for a lucky break."

"Amen," Jack said. "If you look at this whole thing coldly, we're still on square one, aren't we?"

"I wouldn't say that," I protested. "It seems to me we've collected a lot of information."

"Oh, yeah," Al said, "but what does it all *mean?* Thanks for the use of the hall, Dunk."

He rose, Jack stood up, and the two of them moved toward the door. Al hung back a few steps and came close to me.

"Sunday?" he said in a low voice. "With my daughter?"

I nodded.

"Call you," he said.

Then they were gone, and I was left to clean up the mess from our lunch. But I really didn't mind. One quarter-pounder remained, and I wrapped it in aluminum foil and put it in the fridge. With a nice green salad, that would be my dinner.

I went back into the living room and took up my knitting while I did some heavy thinking.

Both detectives thought Orson Vanwinkle had been involved in the switch of the Demaretion display case. I did, too, but couldn't believe that was the reason for his murder, or Dolly's. Why search their apartments when the coin was being offered for sale in Beirut? What a puzzlement!

Jack Smack had come up with a fresh idea, suggesting that Akbar El Raschid was trying to peddle the coin in Lebanon because of his Muslim connections. A neat notion, but I didn't buy it. No logical objections—

just the way I felt. Natalie and Akbar might be a couple of screwballs, but I didn't think they were capable of the clever theft of the coin, let alone two cold-blooded murders.

Luther? A maybe, but I doubted it, for the reasons I had given Al and Jack. I admit I was going by my visceral reactions, but what else could I do? I didn't have the resources of the NYPD or Jack's insurance company to provide research. So I was on my own.

Who else might have conspired with Orson? Vanessa? Very, very doubtful. They had said they hated each other, and I believed it. The Minchens? What motive could dear Roberta and Ross have for killing Orson and Dolly? What about Ruby Querita? Now there was a possibility. She was such a religious fanatic that she might slay and call it God's vengeance.

But finally, finally, I had to face the cause of all this maundering. I was trying to postpone thinking about my most important decision. What on earth was I going to do with that crudely wrapped package Dolly LeBaron had entrusted to me? Sighing, I considered the options.

1. She had said she would reclaim it within a month. She obviously wasn't going to do that.

2. She had also said that in the event she didn't come back for that dumb package, I was to destroy it. Burn it in the "insinuator."

3. And she made me promise not to open it.

My thinking about all this was wild and disconnected. I really should burn the damned thing. But what if she had left it to someone in her will? I had vowed not to open it, but what if it held clues to the identity of her killer? To whom did I owe primary responsibility? To poor, dead Dolly? Should I follow her instructions to the letter, as honor dictated, or disregard them in hopes the Scotch-taped brown bag contained the answers to all my problems? A dilemma.

In the end, I solved it by doing nothing. I left the package where it was, not even looking at it or touching it, and I decided not to mention it to Georgio or Smack just yet. In poker terms, I guess you could call it my ace in the hole.

I spent a gloomy evening. I've told you that generally I'm an up-person—look on the bright side, think positively, things will turn out for the best. But I was down that night. I guess the actuality of Dolly's death really hit me. I couldn't mourn for Orson, he was such a slime, but Dolly was different.

I know everyone thought her a chippy, and I suppose she was. But she was also young, pretty, and hopeful, and it was hard to believe she had done anything in her life to explain or justify what had happened to her.

It made me think deep, deep thoughts about my own life, my hopes and dreams, and how they might all be brought low. No one likes to reflect on death—right? I mean, in our minds we all know we're mortal. But we push that away and concentrate on popcorn and balloons. Our own dis-solution is just too bleak to face.

I did something that night I hadn't done in years and years. I got down on my knees at bedside, pressed my hands together, bowed my head, and prayed for the immortal soul of Dolly LeBaron. I concluded by reciting the child's prayer that begins, "Now I lay me down to sleep . . . "

26

The raddled blue Plymouth was waiting for me when I popped out with my beach bag at eight o'clock on Sunday morning. Behind the wheel, Al Georgio in kelly green slacks and a sport shirt in a hellish plaid. In the back seat, daughter Sally, wearing jeans and a T-shirt, a blue ribbon tied about her long wheaten hair. A beauty!

"Hi!" she said when I climbed in front.

"Hi!" I said.

"Are you my daddy's girlfriend?" she asked.

"Nah," I said, "I'm just a stranger thumbing a lift."

"Boy oh boy," Al said, "I can see this is going to be one great day."

But on the trip out to Jacob Riis Park, it began to seem as if it might be exactly that—a great day.

I ignored Al and turned sideways in the passenger seat so I could talk to Sally. It wasn't difficult; she was a bright, voluble kid with opinions on everything.

"Why do you wear your hair like that?" she asked.

"Like what?" I said. "I don't wear it like anything. That's my problem."

She regarded me gravely, head tilted to one side. "I think you should have it cut short," she pronounced. "Like a loose feather cut—you know?"

"Not a bad idea," I acknowledged.

"Dad says to call you Dunk. Okay?"

"Sure," I said, "that's fine."

"How tall are you, Dunk?"

"Six-two, give or take a little."

"Are you a model?"

"I'm a model of something," I said. "I don't know what."

"You're pretty enough to be a model."

"And you're a sweetheart for saying it," I told her. "What's in the hamper?"

"Lunch," she said. "Fried chicken and potato salad. Father probably bought it all at some greasy spoon."

"Hey, come on," he said indignantly. "I made the chicken myself, and the potato salad comes from a very high-class deli."

"I was just kidding," his daughter said. "Also, some cheesecake, lemonade for me, and a bottle of wine for the old folks."

"Keep it up, kiddo," her father told her, "and you're going to be walking to Jacob Riis."

She giggled and threw herself back in the corner of the rear seat, hugging her knees.

"I'm wearing a bikini," she said. "What are you wearing?"

"A black maillot," I told her. "Norma Kamali."

"Is that the one cut high on the legs and no back?"

"That's the one."

"I love that suit," Sally said dreamily. "Maybe by next year I'll be big enough to wear it. If my old man will spring for it."

"You keep talking like that," Al said ferociously, "and you're not going to make next year."

She giggled again, and for the next hour she and I chattered about fashions, her schoolwork, boyfriends, rock groups, movie stars, television shows, and the pros and cons of washing your hair in beer. What a knowledgeable kid she was! And she wasn't shy about spouting off. Not in an obnoxious way, mind you, but firm and convinced. She really was a darling.

She was wearing makeup—not a lot, but some—which threw me a little. When I was her age, I'd have been kicked out of the house if I used perfumed soap. But the times, they are a'changing. And even without the lip gloss and a touch of eyeliner, she'd have been a beauty. She was going to break a lot of male hearts, and I was afraid she knew it.

"I think my father should get married," she said to me. "Don't you?"

"Will you cut it out, Sally?" Al said, laughing. "You promised to behave."

"I crossed my fingers behind my back," she said. "You didn't see me. Well, don't you think he should get married?"

"If he wants to," I said.

She thought a moment, frowning. "I think my mother might get married. She's got a boyfriend."

"Do you like him?"

"He's okay, I guess. But he wears a toupee. That puts me off—you know?"

"Whee!" Al said, banging the steering wheel with his palms. "It's Looney Tunes time, folks!"

We beat most of the heavy traffic and got out to Jacob Riis sooner than I expected. Al had a folding beach umbrella in the trunk, along with a big blanket and two beach chairs. He carried all that while I managed the wicker hamper. Sally scampered ahead of us. We set up about thirty feet from the shoreline, the sea reasonably calm and clear, sun shining, sky washed. A gorgeous day.

The moment we had the blanket spread, Sally kicked off her loafers, shucked T-shirt and jeans. Her little bikini was cute: a strawberry print with ruffles around the top and hips. What a bod the kid had! She was going to be a problem, but I didn't tell Al that.

She took off her hair ribbon and went running down to the water, blond hair floating back in the breeze.

"No swimming till I get there," Al yelled after her. Then he turned to me. "She can dog-paddle," he said, "but still . . . I hope you don't mind her, Dunk. What she comes out with."

"Mind her?" I said. "I love her. She'll never need any assertiveness training."

"That's for sure," he said. "She's so *bright*. Sometimes it scares me. Want to try the water or would you rather get some sun?"

"Swim first," I said, "then sun."

I heeled off my sandals and struggled out of my denim tent. Al stared at me.

"I know," I said. "I look like a black Magic Marker."

"You look beautiful," he said, and I think he meant it. I made no reference to his salt-bleached khaki shorts that almost came to his knees.

Sally stayed close to shore, floating around, never getting over her depth. Al and I went out a way. He swam like the kind of man he was, with a heavy, ponderous overhand stroke, wallowing a bit, but making steady progress. He had thick, muscled shoulders and arms, and I figured he could get to Europe if he put his mind to it.

We had a good swim, my first of the summer, then turned around and came back in. Sally was already spread-eagled on the blanket, all oiled up. I dried off, then spread on my Number 15 sunscreen. Al had a swarthy skin; he could get a better tan walking a block down Broadway than I'd get all summer.

The two of us sat on beach chairs under the umbrella. Al opened the bottle of chilled rosé, and we each had a paper cup. Good stuff.

"The ocean was great," I said. "Just great. Nothing like that in Iowa."

"Ever want to go back?" he asked me curiously.

"For a visit? Sure. But permanently? I don't think so. Not yet. How're you going to keep them down on the farm—and so forth and so on."

"I really don't know a hell of a lot about you," he said. "I mean your background and all. Before you came to New York."

"Ask away," I said. "If there's anything you want to know."

"No," he said, "not really. But then you don't know a hell of a lot about me, do you?"

"Nope," I said, "and I'm not going to ask. If you want to tell me, you'll tell me."

"You're so goddamned trusting," he said. "I could be Attila the Hun and you wouldn't know—or care."

"Will the two of you please lower your voices," Sally said severely from the blanket. "I'm trying to take a nap and don't wish to listen to your personal confessions."

"That's a crock," her father said, laughing. "You're listening to every word and you love it."

She giggled. "You're awful," she said. "If you weren't my dad, I wouldn't put up with you."

"You're stuck with me, babe," he told her, "and I'm stuck with you. Ain't it nice?"

"Yes," she said, sighing and turning over to tan her back. "It's nice, pop."

"I'll pop you," he said in mock anger, but she just smiled and closed her eyes.

Is there anything new you can say about a splendid July afternoon on the seashore? Warm lassitude. Lulling sound of the surf. A kissing breeze. The comfort of quiet broken by children's shouts. So relaxing that you think your bones are going to melt.

"I suppose," I murmured to Al, "if we did this every day, it would get to be a bore."

"You believe that?"

"No. Al, I've got to say something that's really going to shock you."

"What's that?"

"I'm hungry."

"I am, too," Sally yelled, leaping to her feet. "Let's eat!"

We moved the beach umbrella so it shaded the blanket, and we all sat on that. We gnawed the fried chicken Al had made (delicious!), spooned potato salad, and munched on celery stalks, radishes, and cherry tomatoes. Al had even remembered the salt and paper napkins. The man was a treasure.

When we were finished, Sally surprised me—and her father—by cleaning up and taking all our refuse to the nearest trash can.

"Oh-oh," Al said. "She wants something."

"Don't be a goop," she said crossly. Then, in a grand manner: "I may take a walk down the beach. By myself. Just to relax—you know?"

"Just to meet boys," Al said. "You know?"

"Father, sometimes you can really be gross!"

We watched her stalk away. She hadn't been down at the water's edge more than a minute before we saw two boys about her own age circle about her and draw closer.

"Will she be all right?" I asked anxiously.

"Don't worry about Sally," Al advised me. "She can take care of herself."

"I hope so."

"She'll stay close enough so I can keep an eye on her," he said. "You'll see."

She did exactly as he predicted. It was a joy to watch the young flirt at work. Running into the ocean up to her knees, dashing out with whoops of feigned horror at the chill. Laughing and hugging her elbows. Flinging her long blond hair about. The boys were enchanted.

"Is your ex really going to get married?" I asked Al.

He opened a second bottle of rosé. It was warmish, but we didn't care.

"Probably," he said. "She's got this regular guy. I've never met him, but from what I've heard from Sally and her mother, he's solid enough. I mean he's got a good job and all that. An accountant."

"How do you feel about it?"

He shrugged. "It's her life. The only thing that bothers me is that Sally will have a new father. Well, a stepfather. Maybe she'll forget all about me."

"No way," I told him. "She loves you; she's never going to let you go."

"You really think so?"

"Absolutely. Besides, you don't wear a toupee."

He smiled. "Yeah, there's that. I don't know what I'd do if I lost that kid. My life is rackety enough as it is. Without her, I'd really be drifting."

"No chance of getting back together with your ex?"

"Oh, no," he said immediately. "She doesn't want to be a cop's wife, and I can't blame her for that. It's what came between us: the job, the damned job. Lousy hours. And her worry. It's not that dangerous, but she thought it was. Every time a cop got killed, she'd cry for days. I'd tell her the percentages weren't all that bad, but she couldn't get it out of her head that some day an Inspector would show up on her doorstep and give her the bad news. A lot of cops' wives drink—did you know that?"

"No, but I can understand it."

"Still," he said, "it's my life. If I wasn't a cop, what would I be? A night watchman? Bodyguard for a rock star? Not president of General Motors, that's for sure."

We were back in our chairs under the umbrella. The sun glare bouncing off the sand was all I needed. I could feel my skin beginning to tingle. Pretty soon, I vowed, I'd wrap myself in denim.

Al's hand moved sideways. He held my fingers loosely. "What about you, Dunk?" he said. "Ready to settle down?"

"I don't know," I said, embarrassed and confused. "I really don't know what I want. For the time being I'm just floating. I figure if I'm that unsure, I better wait awhile until I'm more certain of what I want to do.''

"Yeah," he said, "that's wise. But don't wait too long. Time goes so *fast*! I remember when I was a kid in grade school, I thought vacation would never come. Time went so slowly. Now it whizzes by. Weeks, months, years. And then you wake up one day and say, What the hell happened? Where did it go?''

We sat awhile in silence, holding hands, watching Sally frolic on the beach with her two beardless lovers. They were tossing a Frisbee back and forth. Lucky kids. Little did they know that they were going to grow up and have troubles.

"By the way," Al said, "we finally got into Orson Vanwinkle's bank account. He had over a hundred thousand. Not bad for a secretary— wouldn't you say? Particularly when you consider how well he lived.''

"I would say. Did he leave a will?''

"No sign of one—the idiot. He had no close relatives. Just some cousins. I guess eventually it'll go to them, but meanwhile it'll be a lawyer's delight.''

"What about Dolly LeBaron?''

"She had about five thousand. No big deal. I guess Orson was paying her food bills and maintenance on the apartment and cash for her clothes— stuff like that. But apparently he wasn't laying heavy money on her. Not enough so she could build up a nest egg.''

"That's odd," I said. "He seemed to have enough money for a lot of other people.''

"Yeah," Al said, turning his head to stare at me. "Like Akbar El Raschid. Why didn't you tell me about that, Dunk? You knew, didn't you?''

"I knew," I admitted. "But there are a lot of things you don't tell me, aren't there?''

"Maybe," he said grudgingly. "Little, unimportant things.''

"Besides," I said, beginning to resent this, "I was the one who told you Orson swung both ways, wasn't I? I figured you'd find out about his connection with Akbar. And you did.''

"After a lot of work," he said. "You could have saved us time.''

I dropped his hand. "That's not my job," I said angrily, "to save you time.''

He groaned. "Jesus," he said, "what the hell are we doing? A beautiful day on the beach and we're squabbling about a couple of homicides. Now do you understand why my wife dumped me? I can't forget the job. I'm sorry, Dunk. Let's not even mention it for the rest of the day. Okay?''

"Fine with me.''

"Truce?" he said, taking up my hand again. "You're not sore at me?''

"How could I be sore at a guy who makes such scrumptious fried chicken?''

"The hell I did," he said. "I bought it at Sam's Chicken Chuckles around the corner from where I live."

I howled. "You're a bastard," I told him. "You know that?"

"Oh, sure," he said. "But I could have made it if I had wanted to. I just didn't have the time."

"Uh-huh," I said, "that's your story. I'll never believe you again."

"I only lie about unimportant things," he said. "Here comes Miss America of ten years from now."

Sally came dashing up to us. How come kids of her age never saunter? They always run at top speed. All that energy . . . I wish I had some.

"Any lemonade left?" she demanded.

"Shake the thermos," her father said. "It's your jug."

She drained it and got about a half-cup that she gulped down.

"So tell us, Cleopatra," Al said, "did you give them your phone number?"

"They live in Jersey," she said. "Can you imagine? Who needs that?"

"Better luck next time," he said.

We got about another half-hour of sun, then decided we better start back to beat the traffic. We packed up and moved to the parking lot. The car was an oven, and we had to leave the doors open awhile before we could get in. I sat in the back with Sally.

"What am I?" Al demanded. "A chauffeur?"

"Do a good job," I told him, "and we might give you a tip."

"A small one," Sally said.

We hadn't been on the road more than ten minutes when she slowly slumped sideways against me. I put my arm about her shoulders, and she snuggled in. She was asleep almost instantly, breathing deeply with just the tiniest snore. She smelled of suntan oil, salt, and youth. Lovely.

Al noticed all this in the rearview mirror and grinned. "Conked out?" he asked softly.

"She's entitled," I said.

"You want to? Go ahead."

"Not me," I said. "I just don't feel like it." Which was a fib. I swore the moment I got home I'd take a hot shower and flop into bed.

We drove back to Manhattan in almost total silence, except when Al cursed at someone who cut him off. He pulled up outside my brownstone and I gently disengaged my arm from around Sally. I had to massage it.

"I didn't go to sleep," I said, "but my arm did."

I moved away from Sally and she slid down until she was lying on the seat.

"Let her snooze," Al said, turning around. "I'll wake her up when I get her home."

I leaned across the front seat, took his face in my palms, kissed him on the lips. "Thanks for a wonderful day," I said. "It was super."

"It had its moments, didn't it? Do it again?"

"Just whistle," I said, "and I'll come a'running."

"Dunk . . . " he said.

"What?"

He had a strange expression, all twisted. I couldn't tell what he was thinking.

"Nothing," he said. "It'll go for another time."

"Whenever you say."

"Sally likes you; I can tell. You're two of a kind: a couple of nuts."

"You need women like us in your life."

"Tell me about it," he said. "You think I don't know? I'll wait here until you're inside."

I paused at my door to turn and give him a wave. He blew a kiss to me.

Old-fashioned. But nice.

27

I slept for about four hours that Sunday evening, completely whacked out from the fresh air and the sun. Then I woke, staggered into the kitchen, drank about a quart of water, and peeled and ate a chilled tangerine. Then I went back to bed—what else? I think the expression is "plum tuckered."

When I looked at myself in the mirror on Monday morning, I could see the sun lines of my maillot, but the burn was just a gentle blush. It didn't hurt, and I didn't think it was going to peel—which was a blessing. Just to make sure, I rubbed on some moisturizer. I hated to shed skin, like some old snake.

All in all, I was feeling pretty frisky. I made notes in my journal about what Al had told me of the money left by Orson Vanwinkle and Dolly LeBaron. Then I went out to pick up the morning paper and a brioche. Back home, I sliced open the brioche and slathered it with cream cheese and blackberry jam. That's living!

It became a busy day, which suited my mood exactly. I wanted to be *doing*. When the phone rang, I grabbed it up, thinking it might be Al Georgio, thanking me for the most exciting, memorable afternoon of his life. But it turned out to be Archibald Havistock—which was okay, too.

"Miss Bateson," he said, "I must apologize. With the confusion following my secretary's death and my daughter's, ah, recent incident, I fell behind in my personal accounts. I now see that I owe you for two weeks' employment. I am sorry for the oversight. I have written out the check. Shall I mail it to you or would you prefer to pick it up?"

"I'd like to pick it up, sir," I said promptly. "Mostly because I'd like the opportunity of talking to you for a few minutes. Would that be possible?"

"Of course," he said in that deep, resonant voice. "I expect to be in all day. Come over whenever you wish."

"And Ruby Querita," I said. "May I talk to her, too?"

A brief pause, then: "Yes, she'll be here."

"Thank you, Mr. Havistock," I said. "See you shortly."

I dressed with deliberate care: a high-necked, long-sleeved white blouse with a calf-length black skirt, not too snug. If I had put my hair up in a bun and stuck a pencil through it, I figured I could have passed as J. P. Morgan's secretary. That was the impression I wanted to give Mr. Havistock: a sober, industrious, dutiful employee. Little would he know that I had wolfed three frozen Milky Ways in one afternoon.

I took a final glance in the mirror and wondered if Sally could be right: a short, feathered hairdo might change my entire life. Nah.

I was at the door, ready to leave, when the phone rang again. That *had* to be Al. I dashed back.

"Mary Bateson?" a woman's voice asked.

"Yes."

"I have a collect call for you from Enoch in Arizona. Will you accept the charges?"

"Yes," I said. "Oh, yes."

"You are Mary Bateson?"

"I am."

"Thank you. Go ahead, sir."

"I did it!" he said triumphantly. "I called collect like you told me to."

"Bless you, Enoch," I said, laughing. "How *are* you?"

"If I felt any better," he said, "I'd be unconscious. And you, Dunk?"

"Feeling fine," I said.

Then I told him about my day at the beach, and he told me that he had been asked to write a monograph on Greek coinage of the Gaulish tribes for a numismatic journal. He sounded chipper—which was a delight.

"Enough of this chitchat," he said. "I spoke to my friends in New York who might have handled sales by Archibald Havistock over the past five years. As far as I could learn, he sold mostly through three dealers, which is unusual in itself."

"How so?"

"Why *three* dealers? Most serious collectors work through one man. You find someone you can trust, someone you like, and you stick with him."

"Not all dealers are like you, Enoch. Maybe he was just shopping around for the best price."

"Maybe. Anyway, from what I could learn, over a period of five years Havistock unloaded—are you ready for this?"

"How much?" I said eagerly. "Tell me!"

"Almost half a million."

"Wow! He must have had some good stuff."

"He did. The man apparently is, or was, a very dedicated and knowledgeable collector. Not a dog in the bunch. And, of course, the dealers did very well on what they bought from him or handled on consignment. So everyone gained. Still, it's hard to understand."

"What is, Enoch?"

"You spend a lifetime building up a fine collection and then you sell it off. So maybe he needed the money. But it's sad to break up a collection like that. He's not starving, is he?"

"Far from it."

"Well, there you are. Dunk darling, do you think this will help you find the Demaretion?"

"I don't honestly know," I said slowly. "It's another piece of information to put in my notebook, but what it means, I have no idea."

"All right," he said briskly, "that's taken care of. What's next?"

I cast about wildly for something he could do, knowing how important it was to him to be needed. Then I had an inspiration.

"There's one thing you might do, Enoch," I said. "Remember when a new client came into the shop, you always ran a credit check on him."

"Of course," he said. "It's best to know the reputation of the person you're dealing with. Is he trustworthy? Does he pay his bills? Do his checks bounce? Better to know beforehand."

"Could you run a credit check on Archibald Havistock?"

"Havistock?" he said, shocked. "He is a wealthy, reputable man."

"I know," I said, "but still, I'd like to learn more about his financial condition."

This was strictly make-work for Enoch. Al Georgio and Jack Smack had already investigated and told me about Havistock's situation: his income, the fact that most of his assets were in his wife's name. But it wouldn't do any harm to get another opinion.

"I'll try," Enoch said doubtfully. "You're wondering why he was selling off all those lovely mintages for the past five years?"

"That's it," I said gratefully. "Just a woman's idle curiosity."

"To tell you the truth," he said, "I'm curious myself. I'll see what I can do, Dunk dear."

After we hung up, with vows of love, I started out again. This time I made it.

It was a hazy, dazy day with an odor of sulfur in the air, and I immediately decided against walking over to the East Side. I caught a cab that was mercifully air-conditioned and smelled only of dead cigars.

When I first moved to New York, going from the West Side to the East was like going from Calcutta to Paris, but things had changed and were changing. The city (Manhattan) was becoming one big potpourri of boutiques, antique shops, unisex hair styling salons, and Korean greengrocers. In another five years, I figured, Broadway would have a branch of Tiffany's and Park Avenue would have massage parlors.

Ruby Querita let me into the Havistock apartment. As usual, she was dressed like one of the witches from *Macbeth*, but she gave me a defrosted smile and I touched her arm.

"How are you, Ruby?" I asked.

"Healthy," she said. "God be thanked. And you?"

"Hanging in there," I said. "Mr. Havistock is expecting me. Would you tell him I'm here?"

"I'll tell," she said, nodding.

"Anyone else home? Mrs. Havistock? Natalie?"

She shook her head.

"Well, after the lord of the manor is finished with me, could you and I have a little talk?"

I had never noticed before how piercing her eyes were.

"Yes," she said. "All right. I'll be in the kitchen."

"Your office," I said, trying a mild jape that fell flat.

Archibald Havistock rose to his feet when I entered the library. He motioned me to the chair facing that enormous partners' desk. It had deep kneeholes, like a tunnel, running through the two linked desks. You could hide a body in there.

We exchanged pleasantries, and he gave me a plain white envelope. That was so like him. He preferred not to hand over a naked check. Too crass. Money should be chastely concealed.

"Thank you, sir," I said, tucking the envelope into my shoulder bag without glancing at the contents. I could be as circumspect as he. "I wish I felt I was doing more to earn it."

He sat erect in his leather swivel chair. What a magisterial man! I swear that in a black robe he could have passed for a chief justice. But he was wearing a suit of gray flannel with a silken sheen, light blue shirt with white collar and cuffs, a subdued foulard tie. That silvered hair! Those icy azure eyes! Oh, God, I raved in my mind, if he was only thirty years younger or I was thirty years older.

"No progress?" he asked with a small smile.

"Well . . . " I said, not wanting to admit I was a total dolt, "I have made progress if that means collecting a great deal of information. But I haven't yet been able to put it all together, see a logical pattern to every-thing that's happened."

"I'm sure you will," he said. "My wife has great confidence in you."

His wife did? Did that imply that he didn't? Or was this my day for a paranoia attack?

He swung gently back and forth in his swivel chair. He was wearing a cologne—not Aramis; I know that—but something subtle and stirring. Maybe, on another man, I might have thought it a bit much, but he had the presence to carry it off. My impression was that he didn't give a tinker's dam about what other people might think of how he dressed, talked, lived. He had achieved a kind of serenity.

"Tell me," he said, "how do you keep track of everything you've learned? All in your mind?"

"I wish my memory was that good," I said, "but it isn't. No, I make notes in a journal. And add everything new I learn."

"Very wise," he said, nodding. "I keep a daily diary of business dealings, telephone conversations, conferences, and so forth. It can be very useful."

"I hope my notebook will be. Right now I can't make any sense out of it at all."

A small prevarication. It was beginning to come together.

"You said there was something you wished to speak to me about, Miss Bateson. Something special?"

"Just one question, sir. You may not want to answer it. Could you tell me how much you were paying Orson Vanwinkle?"

He stared at me and didn't answer immediately. Then: "This is important to your investigation?"

"I think it is."

"I see no reason why I shouldn't answer. He was paid eight hundred dollars a week. By check. So there is a paper trail if the police or anyone else wants to investigate. Why do you ask?"

"I don't know," I said fretfully. "Except that he seemed to be living on a scale far beyond eight hundred a week."

"I was aware of that," Mr. Havistock said, "and cautioned him about it more than once. But it did no good. As I think I told you, he was not a solid man. But he was my nephew, and I didn't wish to cast him adrift. And, I must say, he fulfilled his duties. But I warned him about his debts."

I didn't mention that dear old Horsy left a hundred grand when he shuffled off this mortal coil. Mr. Havistock would learn that soon enough—but I preferred he didn't hear it from me. I stood up.

"Thank you, sir. I appreciate your making time with—" Now there was a Freudian slip. But I caught it, I hoped! "Making time for me," I finished. "I'd like to talk with Ruby for a few minutes, if I may."

He rose and proffered his hand. "Of course. As long as you like."

We shook hands and exchanged distant smiles. His clasp was exactly like the man: cool, dry, firm.

When I found my way to the kitchen, I discovered Ruby Querita hunched over the stainless steel sink, snapping string beans and weeping. I put an arm about her shoulders.

"Ruby," I said, "what's the matter?"

She shook her head, not answering.

"Your brother?" I asked.

She nodded. "Life is unfair," she said.

I wanted to say, "So what else is new?" but I didn't.

"Ruby," I said, "you can be responsible for your own life, but not for other people's. Isn't that true?"

She nodded dumbly, ran cold water over the beans in a colander, and let them drain in the sink. Then she dried her hands on a kitchen towel and we sat down at the table. She had stopped crying.

I hunched forward, keeping my voice low. This was to be a confidential exchange of gossip—just between us girls.

"Ruby," I said, almost whispering, "the last time we spoke you hinted that the Havistocks had sinned, that the family was cursed. What did you mean by that?"

"I don't want to talk about it."

"Please do," I urged. "I'm trying to find out who stole the Demaretion. Everyone is under suspicion. That includes you. The police think you may be involved, that you took the coin to finance your brother's appeal. I know that's completely ridiculous, you wouldn't do anything like that, but you've got to help me to find out who actually did it. You can see that, can't you?"

She was silent.

"Whatever you tell me," I went on, "is strictly between you and me. I have a tight mouth. I'll repeat it to no one. But I've got to find out what's going on in this house."

"The daughter," she said. "Natalie. She runs around with bad people. She steals. Stays out all hours. Sometimes she is gone a day. Two. I think she takes drugs. She is wild. A black boyfriend. She doesn't go to church."

Nothing new for me there.

"And . . . ?" I prompted her.

"The other one, the older daughter, Roberta, she is married to an evil man. Evil! They do things—I will not tell you. But I hear them talking. Because I am a servant, they think I have no ears. But God will punish them."

I looked at her, wondering if Roberta and Ross had ever tried to recruit her for their TV spectaculars. It was hard to believe, but with people as flaky as the Minchens, anything was possible. If I learned they had cast a giraffe and a cocker spaniel, I wouldn't have been a bit surprised.

"That's awful, Ruby," I said, trying to sound shocked and disgusted. "To think things like that are going on."

"Oh, yes," she said. "But it is true."

"Do you think Mr. and Mrs. Havistock are aware of all this?"

She thought a moment. "About Natalie," she said finally, "they know. About their other daughter and her husband, I think they don't know, but they suspect. They have heard things. But how can you reject your children?"

"You can't," I said.

"No, you can't. So you must suffer. And hope eventually they will see the Light of God that makes a glory of our days."

"What about the son, Ruby? Luther and his wife. Do they behave?"

"That woman!" she burst out. "She is a devil! She shows herself—you know? She tempts men, leading them into transgression. No good will come from her. She has sold her soul."

"I heard," I said carefully, "that at one time she made a play for Roberta's husband, and Mr. Havistock had to break it up. Is that true?"

She nodded darkly. "And friends of the family. The men. And delivery boys. She likes to show her devil's power. She will burn in hell!"

I began to get just a little frightened. That kind of religious mania scared me. Keep thinking that way and you might decide to rid the world of evildoers by killing them. It was God's will, wasn't it?

"Ruby," I said, "can't Luther control his wife? Make her stop acting like that."

"He is not a man," she said scornfully. "He is a slave."

"A slave? To what?"

She cupped her two flat breasts under the black bombazine, making them jut. Then she reached under the table, and I could only guess that she was grasping her crotch. The gestures were undeniably gross, but there was no mistaking their meaning.

"He is a man possessed," she said. "And there is more," she added, staring into my eyes. "But so wicked, I cannot tell you."

And despite my pleading, she would say no more. So I left, needing a breath of even that sulfur-laden outside air to rid myself of the heavier fumes within the Havistock apartment. What a Gothic family that tribe had turned out to be!

I told myself that other than learning Orson Vanwinkle had been making eight hundred a week, I had heard nothing new. What Ruby Querita had related, I already knew, or had guessed. But her fanaticism had given the revelations an ominous weight. I walked quickly away from the Havistock manse before a thunderbolt came down from heaven and destroyed them all. That Ruby was getting to me.

I wondered what was so wicked that she wouldn't speak of it. Then I pondered my next move. I found a sidewalk telephone kiosk in working order (the third I tried), and called Hobart Juliana at Grandby & Sons. Thank God he was in.

"Hobie darling," I said cheerfully, "how *are* you?"

"Miserable," he said. "All alone and longing for company. *Your* company. When are you coming back to join me?"

"Soon," I said. "I hope. Hobie, I'm in your neighborhood, and I'd love to see you. I'd come up, but I'm afraid Madam Dodat might grab me and demand a progress report on my investigation. That I don't need. Could you sneak out for a little while? I'll buy you a drink at the Bedlington bar. How about it?"

"I'm on my way," he said happily.

It was so *good* to see him again; he really was a sweetheart. We sat in that dim, cloistered cocktail lounge (only one other customer), held hands, and Hobie got me caught up on all the latest office gossip. It was rumored that Felicia Dodat was going to have a tummy-tuck, and it was said that Stanton Grandby was taking pills for flatulence. Fascinating.

"What about you, Dunk?" Hobie said, almost nose to nose with me in the gloom. "Anything happening on the Demaretion?"

"I think so. I think I'm getting somewhere. But it's taking a lot of digging. Hobie, you've helped me so much, I hate to ask for another favor."

"Ask away!" he cried. "What are friends for?"

"Do you like intrigue?"

"Like it? I love it, love it, love it!"

"Well, there's this woman—Vanessa Havistock. She's married to Luther, Archibald's son. She's got this absolutely divine body and doesn't mind showing it."

"Couldn't care less," he said, grinning.

"I know," I said. "I'm just trying to describe her. Anyway, I suspect she's cheating on her husband. Everyone says she comes on to anything in pants—but that might be just malicious rumors. I mean she's beautiful, and people may resent her for that."

"Perhaps," he said. "Perhaps not. Where there's smoke, there's usually one hell of a fire."

"What I'd like to do," I went on, "is try to prove it out one way or another. She buys her clothes at an Italian boutique on Madison—Vecchio's. You know it?"

"Oh, yes. Bloody expensive."

"It is that. I think maybe the manager, a guy named Carlo, might be steering tricks her way. You understand?"

"I'm keeping up, sweet."

"Are you a good actor, Hobie?"

"Good? The stage lost a great star when I decided to devote my life to postage stamps. What do you want me to do?"

"Call her," I said. "She's in the book. Phone her and say you're from Wilkes-Barre or Walla Walla or some such place. Tell her you're in town for a business meeting, you're lonely, and would like to take a lovely lady out to dinner. Say that Carlo of Vecchio's suggested you call her."

"Oh, my God," Hobie said, "that's beautiful! Dunk, you're a naughty, naughty woman."

"I know," I said. "I want to get her reaction. If she hangs up on you, that's one answer. If she's interested, that's another."

"Do it right now," he said. "There's a phone in the lobby."

"She may not be in," I warned.

"Then I'll try later," he said, slid off the barstool and headed for the lobby. He had a kind of John Wayne sidle, and I never did figure out if it was natural or if he was kidding the world.

While he was gone, I wondered if I should have told him about Vanessa's arrest for loitering for the purpose of prostitution. Then I thought this test would be more legitimate if Hobie knew nothing of her police record.

He was back in less than five minutes, drained his kir, and motioned to the bartender for another.

"Was she in?" I asked.

"She was in, and she's guilty as hell. I told her I was Ralph Forbes—that's the name of my consenting adult—and I was from Tulsa, in town for a bankers' convention. Carlo of Vecchio's had suggested I might call her. Could she join me for dinner at Lutèce, and maybe a night on the town later? Cabarets, discos, piano bars—whatever turned her on. If she was an innocent, she'd have told me to get lost and hung up immediately. But oh, no. Dunk, I could almost hear her ears perk up."

"She agreed?" I asked eagerly.

"Of course not," Hobie said. "She's too smart for that. She gave me some jazz about canceling previous plans and she'd call me back. What she's doing, of course, is checking with Carlo at Vecchio's. Did he give her name to a Ralph Forbes from Tulsa?"

"When she said she'd call you back, what number did you give her?"

"The one on the pay phone I called from," Hobie said smugly. "What else?"

I leaned forward to kiss his cheek. "You're a genius," I told him. "But you think if Carlo had confirmed, she would have called back?"

"Absolutely," he said. "That lady is hot to trot. She's not the kind you pay in advance. She's the kind you get it off with, and then say, 'Oh, darling, you've made me so happy, I want to buy you a gift. But I don't know your sizes or tastes. If I give you money, will you buy yourself something nice and pretend it's from me?' She'll protest and then finally agree. A lot of women are like that—and more men than you can imagine. I've done it myself. It leaves you a small measure of self-esteem. Better than finding cash on the mantel after the guy has gone."

"Oh, Hobie," I said, gripping his arm, "you've been such a big help. When this is all over, I'm going to buy you the greatest dinner at the Four Seasons you've ever had in your life."

He took up my hand to kiss my fingertips. "I'll nudge you," he said. "But the dinner isn't that important. Just come back to share our office again. That'll make me happier than anything."

We stared at each other. Tender and sad.

"It's a crazy world," he said, "isn't it?"

"It is that," I said.

When we came out of the Bedlington, the air had freshened, and I decided I could walk home without fear of dropping from asphyxiation at the feet of Daniel Webster's statue. The long walk gave me a chance to think. Mostly about Vanessa Havistock.

The way she lived was so inexplicable to me. Married to a guy with a good job. Apartment on Park Avenue. Apparently all the money in the world. So why play the strumpet? Maybe that question contained the answer: she was *playing*. Her strident sexuality was a role. Blessed with sensual flesh, she was using it as a costume.

That began to make sense to me. It had little to do with the disappearance of the Demaretion, but I wanted to understand the people involved. Al Georgio had said Vanessa was actually Pearl Measley from South Carolina. I could extrapolate a lot from that: small-town girl adrift in the big city with nothing to sell but herself.

Then, maybe with memories of a deprived childhood, she gets hooked on *things*: jewelry, ball gowns, paintings, cars, a smart apartment and groovy vacation home—all the panoplies of wealth. But she never forgets where it all comes from—the luscious source.

That was how I saw her: not so much a greedy woman but one terrified by poverty and lack of status. She would, I thought, do anything to maintain her hard-fought and hard-won battle against life. She had vanquished Pearl Measley. Now she was Vanessa Havistock—and don't you forget it, buster!

And when I arrived home, sweated and aching pleasantly from my hike, I emptied my mailbox, and there was a letter from the lady herself: a cutesy invitation to a cocktail party and buffet dinner on Tuesday evening. "Wear whatever you like—or nothing at all!"

I wouldn't have missed it for the world.

I showered, shampooed, pulled on an oversized khaki shirt I had bought many moons ago at an army surplus store on Forty-second Street. It had been laundered so many times it felt like silk, and was so big it fitted like a burnoose. I padded around the house, wearing that and nothing else, feeling deliciously depraved.

I had just started adding notes on the day's events in my journal when I got a call from Jack Smack. He sounded slightly aggrieved.

"Where the hell you been, Dunk?" he demanded. "I've been phoning all day."

"I had lunch with Hizzoner," I told him, "and then I had to go down to the Federal Reserve to settle a squabble about interest rates."

He laughed. "Okay," he said, "I deserved that. How you coming on the Demaretion?"

"As the cops say, zero, zip, and zilch."

"Yeah," he said casually, "me, too. I think maybe my company better pay off. I don't see any happy ending to this thing—do you?"

"You never know," I said, determined he wasn't going to get anything from me without giving me something in return.

"I did come across one interesting item," he said. "Luther Havistock is seeing a shrink. Three times a week."

"Yes," I said slowly, "that *is* interesting. I think the poor man needs it. But it must be expensive."

"Maybe Daddy is paying the bills," he suggested, and then paused, waiting for the trade-off.

"That's possible," I said. "Perhaps that's why Archibald needed ready cash. Over the past five years he's been selling coins from his collection. Did you know that?"

Silence. Then . . .

"No," Jack said, "I didn't know that. Are you sure?"

"I'm sure."

"Do you know what his total sales were?"

"No, I don't," I said, surprised that I could lie so easily.

"Maybe I'll look into it," he said thoughtfully. "But enough about business; how about dinner tomorrow night?"

"Love to," I said, "but I can't. I'm going to a party."

"Can you take me?"

"I don't think I better."

"Oh-ho," he said without rancor, "it's like that, is it? Well, listen, if the party turns out to be a dud and you decide to split early, give me a call, will you? I'll be in all night."

"Sure," I said, "I'll do that."

"I'll keep a lamp burning in the window," he said cheerfully. "I'd really like to see you, Dunk."

"I'll try to make it," I promised. "I'll give you a call either way."

"You're a sweetheart—did I ever tell you that?"

"No, and it's high time you did."

He made a kissing sound over the phone and hung up. A nut. But a nice nut.

28

What a party that was! Almost exactly as I imagined sophisticated Manhattan soirées would be when I was sinking dunk shots in our Des Moines driveway. Elegantly dressed women. Handsome men. Champagne. Exotic food. Everyone saying clever things. The whole bit.

So why wasn't I ecstatic? Because there was something so *forced* about those twittering people. If Vanessa Havistock was playing a role, all her guests were, too. I mean everyone was *on*, flushed, nervy, trying to top each other's gags and put someone down. "Don't tell me you're still eating *kiwi*!"

I know what my father would have said about that bunch: "More dollars than sense."

My first shock came when I spotted Roberta and Ross Minchen standing close to the bar, smiling glassily and chatting animatedly with anyone who came near. Casting a new video classic, no doubt.

Their presence really surprised me. After that snarly standoff at the Russian Tea Room, I would have sworn Vanessa would never again give Roberta the time of day, let alone invite her and spouse to an expensive party. But there they all were, everyone apparently lovey-dovey and not a weapon in sight.

I looked around for host or hostess. I saw Vanessa talking seriously to—guess who? Carlo of Vecchio's, that's who. The Adonis looked splendid in a deep-red velvet dinner jacket, ruffled shirt, gold lamé butterfly bow tie. Too bad he was such an oozy man.

Then I located Luther, all by his lonesome in a corner, working on a drink so big it looked like an ice bucket. I pushed my way through the throng, smiling and nodding at all those sleek strangers. They couldn't have cared less. Finally I planted myself in front of Luther.

"Good evening!" I said brightly.

He stared, trying to focus. "Evening," he said. Then: "Oh, it's Miss Bateman."

"Bateson."

"Bateson, yes, sorry. Are you having a good time?"

"I just arrived, but it looks like a lovely party."

"Does it?" he said, looking around with a bleary stare. "I don't know any of these people."

"Sure you do. You know your sister and her husband."

"Oh, *them*. They don't count. But all the others . . . They come here, drink up all my whiskey, eat themselves sick, steal the ashtrays—who *are* they? Vanessa's so-called friends."

"Surely you know some of them."

"Don't want to," he said surlily. "Bloodsuckers. Leeches. I keep telling Vanessa, but she won't listen. She thinks they're the *in* people. They're in all right. In my house, in my booze, in my food." He laughed his high-pitched giggle, then thrust his schooner at me. "Do me a favor?" he asked. "Please? Get me a refill at the bar. I don't want to talk to the Munchens."

"Minchens."

"I call them the Munchens," he said, with that frantic laugh again.

He was even paler than when I last saw him: a ghost in a rusty tuxedo. But his hands weren't trembling, so I figured he was well on his way. I took his glass. "What are you drinking?" I asked.

"Gin."

"With what?"

"More gin. Make sure it's the ninety-four proof. But you don't have a drink. Aren't you drinking?"

"Not yet. But I'll get something for myself."

"Try the champagne," he advised. "Good stuff. Cost a bundle," he added gloomily.

At the bar, tended by a dwarf in a clown's costume, I was grabbed by Roberta and Ross with effusive joy. They insisted on kissing me—which I could have done without. We exchanged small talk. Small? It was *tiny!*—and I finally got away from them, carrying my glass of champagne and Luther's beaker of gin.

One advantage of being tall is that you have a great view of what's going on in a crowded room. I saw Vanessa moving amongst her guests, patting, hugging, smooching. She was flushed with excitement. Her long black hair was up in a coil, stuck through with two ivory chopsticks. The makeup, I knew, was a professional job. She was wearing the fringed dress from Vecchio's and looked absolutely smashing.

I was wearing my white poet's blouse and a skirt of what seemed to be a brocaded upholstery fabric. I had bought it in a thrift shop, and I loved it. It made me feel like an ottoman. My hair was in its usual wind-tunnel state.

I handed Luther his drink. "There you are," I said. "Double gin on the rocks. Ninety-four proof."

"Bless you," he said. "Do you think I should commit suicide?"

That was a stunner. How do you reply to something like that? Treat it as a joke? Take it seriously?

"I don't think you should," I said finally. "Why would you want to?"

"Oh, I don't know," he said vaguely. "I'd just like to *do* something."

He took a deep gulp of his drink. Some of it ran down his chin, and he wiped it away with the back of his hand.

"I like you," he said abruptly.

"Thank you," I said. "I like you, too."

"You do?" he said, surprised. "That's odd."

"What's odd about it?"

"Nobody likes me."

"Come on," I said, uneasy with this crazy conversation. "Your wife, your parents, your sisters, your friends—a lot of people like you."

He stared at me owlishly. "I don't think so," he said. "I think they endure me. I think I endure me. Hey!" he said, suddenly brightening. "You're looking for the coin—right?"

"Right."

"Find it yet?"

"No," I said, "not yet. Any idea who has it?"

"Probably Vanessa," he said with his high-pitched whinny. "She's got everything."

I took it as drunken humor. "Your wife is a very beautiful woman," I told him.

"Sure she is," he said. "Till midnight. Then she turns into a toad."

"Well, I think I'll wait around until midnight. That I've got to see."

"You'll see," he said, nodding solemnly. "You'll see."

I tried to change the subject. "Your parents aren't here tonight?"

"They rarely go out at night. They sit at home and stare at each other. Thinking."

I couldn't cope with this dialogue; it was becoming too unpleasant. "I think I'll find your wife," I told him, "and pay my respects."

"You respect her?" he said nastily. "That's a switch."

I touched his arm, smiled, and moved away. The guy was bonkers.

Vanessa gave me a big hug. She smelled divine.

"*So* glad you could make it, Dunk," she burbled. "Having a good time?"

"Wonderful."

"It *is* nice, isn't it?" she said, looking around. "Don't forget to eat. The buffet's in the other room. *Do* try the caviar on smoked salmon. Yummy! And by the way, you've already made a conquest."

Fat chance!

"I have?" I said.

"Carlo was looking for you. You remember Carlo from Vecchio's? I think the poor boy is quite smitten. He wanted to talk with you, but you were busy with Luther. What *were* the two of you chattering about for so long?"

She didn't miss much.

"Just laughing up a storm," I told her. "Your husband has quite a sense of humor."

"Does he?" she said dubiously. "I've never noticed it. Dunk, I've got to circulate and act like a hostess. Promise me you'll be nice to Carlo."

"Of course."

She leaned close to whisper in my ear. "I hear he's hung like a horse."

Then she laughed and moved away to greet some arriving guests. I slid through the mob into the dining room to inspect the buffet. Talk about your groaning boards! That one was wheezing, presided over by a chef in a high *toque blanche* wielding a long-handled fork and saber.

The pièce de résistance was a steamship roast beef, rare as anything. That platter was surrounded by a million calories in all kinds of side dishes: cold vegetables and fruits, appetizers and nibbles, obscenely rich desserts, and a melting ice sculpture of Leda and the Swan. What the swan was doing to Leda, I don't wish to say.

The chef, an elderly black man who could carve like a surgeon, prepared a plate for me with little bits of almost everything. Balancing all this, plus cutlery and a stiff linen napkin, and trying to keep my champagne glass upright, I looked around for a place to sit and eat. I was rescued by Carlo, who came up to me, laughing, and relieved me of my burdens. He led me out to the mirrored foyer where there was a small marble-topped table flanked by two lovely and extremely uncomfortable cast-iron chairs.

"You wait," he ordered, "I'll be right back."

And so he was, bearing his own plate of nothing but very, *very* rare roast beef and a few cold hearts of palm. He also had an unopened bottle of champagne clamped under one arm.

"Now then . . ." he said, seated himself opposite me, and expertly twisted out the champagne cork. He refilled my glass and poured his own. He sat back, crossed his legs, carefully adjusting the crease in his trouser leg. What a dandy!

"I am so happy to see you tonight," he said, watching me eat. "Happy to have the chance to speak to you."

"You are?" I said, concentrating on my food. Vanessa had been right; the caviar and smoked salmon was yummy.

"But of course," he said. "The other day at Vecchio's I could not talk. Not with the signora present. You understand?"

I nodded, not certain I *did* understand.

"I have always had this thing for tall women," he said, showing me a mouthful of white teeth that looked like Chiclets. "A secret passion."

I laughed, and he was offended.

"You doubt me?" he demanded.

"Of course not. It's just that I'm—embarrassed."

"That is natural," he said generously. "But I speak the truth. Dunk—may I call you Dunk?"

"Sure," I said. "Aren't you going to eat? The beef is delicious."

"Later," he said, "I think you and I could be—you know? Good friends. Very good friends."

"That's nice," I said. "You can't have too many friends, can you?"

He was puzzled. "I mean special friends," he said. It sounded like *speciale*.

I had a Swedish meatball on my fork, halfway to my mouth, but I paused, looking at him. I never doubted for a minute that Vanessa had put him up to this *seductio ad absurdum*—but why?

He took a sip of champagne, then stared at me over the rim of the glass with widened eyes. God, he was good! All I could think of was Rudolph Valentino in the tent, sex-crazed eyes glittering.

"We can see more of each other?" he whispered. "Dunk?"

"If you like," I said. "Why not? But it will be difficult. I'm very busy."

"Ah, yes," he said. "You are a detective—no?"

"Amateur," I said. "I really don't know a great deal about it."

He daintily cut up his rare beef into postage stamp slices. He had beautiful hands. The nails manicured, of course. Al Georgio's were bitten.

"I would like to be a detective," he said, keeping my champagne glass filled.

"Another secret passion?" I asked.

He looked at me sharply to see if I was ribbing him, but I kept my expression serious and interested.

"Yes," he said. "Another dream. I would wear an elegantly tailored trench coat—British, of course—and a black Borsalino turned down on one side. Very mysterious. Very menacing."

We both laughed, and I began to think he wasn't such a schlemiel after all.

"Tell me," he said, reaching across the table to spear one of my smoked oysters on his fork, "how does a detective work? You go around, ask questions, try to catch people lying?"

"Yes," I said, "something like that. You collect as much information as you can."

"But how do you remember it all?" he persisted. "What people have said, what they have done. Do you keep it all up here?" He tapped his temple with a forefinger.

"Nobody's memory is that accurate," I said. "Professional detectives file reports. I keep a notebook, just to make sure I don't forget anything. I write it all down.''

"Ahh," he said sadly, "then I cannot be a detective. I am very bad at writing. My poor mother in Tuscany complains bitterly. Why don't you write? she asks. But I am too concerned with other things.''

"You could find the time," I told him.

He shrugged. "Some people write, some people live. Dunk, I saw some tiramisu at the buffet. It is made with mascarpone. A dreamy dessert. Have you tried it?''

"No, I haven't. Good?''

"Delizioso," he said, kissing his fingertips. "Let me get us some.''

"Small portions," I pleaded. "I'm stuffed.''

"Very, very small portions," he said, standing up. He patted his flat stomach. "I must keep myself in condition," he said with a lewd smile.

I had been wrong; he *was* a schlemiel.

The tiramisu was heavenly—but so rich! The dry champagne helped, and so did Carlo—by dropping the hard-on role and becoming very amusing, telling me outrageous stories of some of the customers who came into Vecchio's, including a transvestite who spent a fortune on sequined cocktail dresses.

"A fantastic body," Carlo reported. "All silicone, of course. But still, she, he, it, is beautiful. Shall we join the party?''

I stood up—a bit unsteadily, I admit. Carlo grabbed my arm.

"All right?" he asked.

"Fine," I said. "It's the tiramisu.''

"But of course," he said. "It has brandy in it. Did I not mention that?''

Back in the mob scene, Carlo excused himself and drifted away, not to return. Whatever happened to his secret passion? I looked around for Luther Havistock. No sign of him. The Minchens were sticking close to the bar. Vanessa was still circulating, urging people to move to the buffet.

I went looking for a telephone. There seemed to be one in every room, but they were all in use—by guests calling friends in Hong Kong, no doubt. Finally, driven by need, I went into a bathroom, and there was a lovely mauve Princess phone. I called Jack Smack, called him three times, in fact, waiting for the other freeloaders at the party to get off the line. Finally I got through.

"Hey there, Dunk," he said genially. "Good party?''

"Good," I said. "Not great, but good. Champagne and super food. I'm a wee bit disoriented.''

"A wee bit disoriented," he repeated, laughing. "You mean you're dead drunk.''

"I am not dead drunk," I said indignantly. "And I resent the—What do I resent?''

"The accusation? The implication?''

"Yes," I said, nodding at the phone, "I resent the implication. Is your invitation still open?"

"Of course. Do you want me to come get you?"

"I am quite capable," I said loftily, "of navigating by myself."

"Of course you are," he said. "Promise to take a cab?"

"I promise."

"Promise not to talk to the driver?"

"Can I say 'Good evening' when I get in, and 'Good night' when I get out?"

"Only that," Jack said, "and nothing more. Promise?"

"Go to hell," I said, giggling, and hung up.

In my foggy state I still remembered that, as my dear mother had taught me, I must seek out the hostess and thank her for a lovely evening. But it was such a madhouse in the apartment—people sitting on the floor and gobbling from their buffet plates, a few passed-out drunks, two couples dancing to no music that I could hear—I decided to steal away like a mouse and write Vanessa a thank-you note the next day.

At the doorway, I turned and looked back, towering over the *walpurgisnacht*. In a corner behind the bar I noticed Vanessa, Roberta Minchen, and Carlo huddling together, thick as thieves. They were speaking seriously, not chattering, not smiling, and I suddenly had a sinking feeling that I had talked too much that night to Carlo, the demon lover.

Following Jack's instructions, I cabbed down to his loft in silence, sobered, and thoughtful.

29

"I want a quart of ice water," I told Jack. "Immediately."

"Water?" he said. "Cheap date."

But he brought me a pewter tankard of ice cubes and a glass pitcher of water. He filled the mug, waited while I gulped it down, then filled it again.

"Feeling better?" he asked.

"I drank too much, ate too much, talked too much."

"Welcome to the club," he said. "Who threw this shin dig?"

"Vanessa Havistock," I told him.

"Oh-ho," he said. "And I wasn't invited? I better change my deodorant. Learn anything?"

"Yes," I said. "I learned that Luther Havistock is a dingdong, right on the edge. May I take off my shoes?"

"Whatever turns you on," Jack said.

He was wearing sandals on bare feet, flannel bags, and a dress shirt with the sleeves rolled up and the tails hanging outside. What a casually handsome man! He made Carlo look like a mannequin. I mean Jack moved like a premier danseur. He could pick his nose and it would be a work of art.

"I know what you need," he said.

"Don't be so sure of yourself," I said.

"Do what Daddy tells you. Have exactly one ounce of cognac. Sip it very, very slowly. In twenty minutes you'll be a new woman, ready to run the four-forty. Trust me."

"Never," I said, "but I'll try the cognac."

He was right. The first sip burned, but after that it lulled, soothed, smoothed, and I began to get back to what I laughingly call normal.

"How was Vanessa acting tonight?" Jack asked. "Coming on to every guy in sight?"

"She was doing all right. If I was a man, I'd be interested."

He shook his head. "A barracuda," he said. "She scares me. I think I talked to her twice, and each time, after I left, I patted my hip to make sure my wallet was still there."

I laughed. "Don't tell me the great Romeo is frightened of a poor little old female?"

"Who said she's a female? Not a human female. She's an animal, and this Romeo never learned to work with a chair and a whip. Anything else happen at the party?"

I knew he was pumping me, but I felt so mellow I didn't care.

"The Minchens were there," I said. "Which surprised me. I went to lunch with Vanessa and Roberta, and it was a shouting match. I thought they were sworn enemies, but tonight was like old home week. Maybe they all starred in the same video porn flick."

He stared at me. "Dunk," he said, "what are you talking about?"

"I thought I told you," I said confusedly. "Or maybe I told Al Georgio. He just laughed. You might as well know about it."

So I related the story of my evening at the Minchens', and their efforts to recruit me into their circle of videocassette stunt men and women.

"And the Minchens were in them?" Jack said. "This wasn't commercial stuff you saw?"

"They were in them," I assured him. "It was homemade."

"Son of a bitch," Jack said thoughtfully. "Who would believe it? They look like Mr. and Mrs. Square. I've got a VCR, but I don't have any porn tapes. I never think of sex as a spectator sport. Want to watch *The Sound of Music*?"

"No, thanks."

"Good. I haven't got it. How about the original *King Kong*?"

"I never think of sex as a spectator sport. Jack, why are we wasting time talking about videocassettes?"

"Beats the hell out of me," he said. "I guess I was trying to be a gentleman."

"That'll be the day," I said.

He was *such* a lover. He turned me upside down and inside out. After he kissed my breasts, I said, "Now you must marry me." He laughed. A hollow laugh, I thought.

"Hey," he said, "you're free, white, and twenty-one."

"At least," I told him. "What comes next?"

"Probably me," he said, groaning and going back to work.

What a frolic that was! The tap dancer was so loving and funny and knowing. He knew just which switches to flick and buttons to press. I didn't want to think of how he had learned all that.

He was all over me. A wicked tongue. And absolutely no inhibitions.

Which made me respond in kind, of course. When you're in a foreign country, you try to adopt the customs of the natives, do you not? But he had some nerve calling Vanessa an animal; this kid was a tiger.

Later, when it was over, my heartbeat and respiration slowing, I was reasonably certain I wouldn't have to be admitted to Intensive Care. Jack was clever enough to hold me in a nice, warm, horizontal hug. He didn't miss a trick.

"So tell me," he said, "what do you think of the International Monetary Fund?"

I laughed and punched his arm. "I wish I could hate you," I told him, "but I can't."

"Why would you want to hate me?"

"Because you're no damned good."

"That's true," he acknowledged, "but then I never claimed to be a Boy Scout, did I? You know what I'm going to do now?"

"I'm afraid to ask."

"Have a beer," he said. "Be right back."

When he returned, he put the cold can of Pabst on my stomach.

"You bastard!" I gasped.

"Dunk, you said Luther Havistock was right on the edge. What did you mean by that?"

Just like Al Georgio. Neither of them could forget the job.

"I think there's a potential for violence there," I said. "He was somewhat smashed, but *in vino veritas*. He was talking wildly. About suicide, amongst other things. Including some disagreeable stuff about his wife. Not exactly what I'd call a healthy situation."

"He's hurting," Jack said. "Moneywise, I mean. You think that's why he's boozing?"

"That may be part of it. But there's more to it than that. Vanessa is leading him a merry chase and he just can't keep up."

"Yeah," Jack said, "that's my take, too. You think he swiped the Demaretion?"

"No. I don't think the poor man's capable of deciding what he wants for lunch, let alone engineering a clever caper. Jack, the guy is falling apart."

He looked at me strangely. "Bright lady," he said. "Dunk, I've got to apologize. When I first met you, I thought you were just another pretty face. I know differently now. You've got a brain."

"Is that why you lured me onto these crazy futons?"

"No," he said, laughing, "that had nothing to do with your brain. It was your belly button."

"My *what*?"

"It's an outsy," he explained. "Haven't seen one in years."

"You're a stinker," I said. "An A-Number One, dyed-in-the-wool stinker. May I have a sip of your beer?"

"A little one," he said, holding the opened can up to my lips. I got a small swallow. Then he carefully poured a few drops over my boobs and licked them off.

"Yum-yum," he said.

"Talking about brains," I said, "if you had one, you'd be dangerous."

"I happen to be a closet intellectual," he told me. "But there is a time and place for everything. Dunk, I hate to make this shameful confession, but I think you're nice people."

"I can endure you, too," I said. "Jack, do me a favor?"

"If I can."

"I forget whether it was you or Al who told me, but one of you said Ross Minchen has been making some hefty withdrawals from his bank account over the past few years. Could you find out where it's going?"

"Oh, boy," he said, "that's a tough one. If he wrote a check to someone, maybe I could trace it. If he took it in cash, it'll be practically impossible. I'll see what I can do. Why do you ask?"

"Money," I said. "That seems to be the thread running through everything: the theft of the coin and the murders of Vanwinkle and LeBaron. Admittedly some very heavy human passions were involved, but money looks like the motive."

"Speaking of heavy human passions . . . " he said, looking at me.

"Yes?"

"I have a heavy human passion."

"What a coincidence!" I cried.

It was bliss. He taught me so much. And in all modesty, I think I can say I improvised a little on my own. It was all so mindless and delightful. Fun and games, I suppose you'd call it, but it seemed to me there was more to it than that. There was a kind of wild, joyous, childish primitivism. Instead of a high-tech loft in SoHo, we could have been in a jungle or on a desert island. I mean we behaved like we were the last people on earth.

I lost all sense of time. I do remember that at one point, early in the morning, Jack roused long enough to say, "No way am I going to get up and drive you home."

"No way am I going to go," I said drowsily.

"See you at breakfast," he said, and we went back to sleep on the futons.

In the morning we showered together—and that was a giggle. Then Jack donned a terry robe, and I pulled on his white dress shirt with the rolled-up sleeves. He thawed some frozen croissants and we had those with lime marmalade. And lots of strong, black coffee—not instant or decaf. We didn't talk much. Mostly we just looked at each other and grinned.

It was almost eight o'clock before we shook off our dopey lassitude and were able to get dressed. Then Jack drove me uptown in his Jaguar. He double-parked outside my building.

"What can I say after I say I'm sorry?"

"Sorry about what?" I demanded.

He put a palm on my cheek, kissed me on the lips.

"Not a goddamned thing," he said.

"I concur in your opinion," I said, got out of the car, then turned back. "Jack, you'll check on Ross Minchen's bank withdrawals?"

"Sure."

"You're a darling."

"I'd be the last to deny it," he said, winking at me, then pulling away with a squeal of the Jag's tires.

I had two locks on my apartment door (plus an interior chain latch). The lower lock had a spring tang and the upper was a dead bolt. I never, but *never*, left the apartment without locking the bolt and double-locking the spring latch. It was a habit, and I always locked up, even before running down to the corner to mail a letter, to be gone for no longer than a minute.

Now, when I inserted my keys, I discovered the dead bolt was already unlocked and the spring latch not double-locked. I stood staring at the faceplates, unable to believe I had been so careless. I leaned closer to inspect the locks and door. No nicks, scars, or gouges. I remembered what Al Georgio had said of the Vanwinkle and LeBaron homicides: "No signs of forced entry."

I knew very well what I should do; the police had issued enough warnings. If you suspected there was an intruder in your home, *do not enter*. Call the cops or, at the very least, summon a burly neighbor to escort you inside. Every single woman living alone in New York knew that.

But, fearing the open locks were merely the result of my own stupidity, I opened the door a few inches and called, "Hello?" How's that for the acme of silliness? If there was a crook inside, did I expect him to carol back, "Hi, there!" But there was no answer. Just silence.

I cautiously ventured inside, then turned and locked, bolted, and chained the door behind me. Another idiotic mistake. If there was a thief on the premises, what good would locking the door have done? I should have left it wide open in case I had to beat a screaming and hysterical retreat. I just wasn't thinking clearly.

I moved slowly through the apartment, checking every room. Nothing. Then I tried the back door to my minuscule garden. It was still locked and chained, and, looking through the window, I could see no one lurking outside.

I went back to open closet doors, peer under the bed, and draw back the shower curtain. All clear. But, standing in the middle of the living room, hands on hips, looking around, I had a definite feeling that someone *had* been there. The door of the cabinet in my little sideboard was slightly ajar. I always made sure it was tightly latched to help keep out dust.

And other things weren't precisely in the position I had left them. The cushion on my armchair, for instance, had been flopped over; I could have sworn to that. And there was just something in the air of the place: a faint, strange scent signaling an alien presence.

The television set was still there. My two radios, my poor little jewel box, almost a hundred dollars in cash in the drawer of the bedside table— all untouched. Then I smacked my forehead with a palm, gave a groan of dismay, and went galloping into the kitchen to search the cabinet above the sink.

Dolly LeBaron's package was still there. Thank God!

I went back into the living room, flopped on the couch, and tried to make sense of it all. I knew, absolutely, that I was not being paranoid; someone *had* been in my apartment—but for what reason? Sighing, I gave up trying to figure it out, and decided to take my mind off the puzzle by entering all the things I had learned the previous evening in my spiral notebook.

Of course it was missing.

30

I called Al Georgio, and this time I was in luck; I got him on the first try.

"Al," I said, "I've got to see you right away."

He must have caught something in my voice because he immediately said, "Dunk, you okay?"

"I'm all right, but I've got to see you."

He didn't say any bullshit things like "Is it important?" or "Can't it wait?" He just said, "I'll be right there," and hung up. The man was a tower of strength.

I still wasn't thinking clearly. If I had been, I'd have peeled off my fancy party duds—poet's blouse and long, brocaded skirt—and pulled on jeans and a T-shirt. But it never occurred to me. So when Al arrived and looked me up and down, I was sure he guessed I had been out all night; he didn't carry a detective's gold shield for nothing. But he never mentioned my costume.

"You all right, Dunk?" he asked anxiously.

"I think so," I said. "I'm not sure. I made some coffee. Have a cup?"

"Love it," he said. "What happened? You look spooked."

We hunched over the cocktail table, sipping our hot coffee, and I told him all about it. He got up, went to my front door, and inspected it. Then he came back. "Dunk," he said, "those locks are cheese. I could crash this place with a hairpin, a nail file, and a plastic credit card."

"What should I do?" I said desperately.

"Get Medeco locks with big pry-plates around the face. Get a long jimmy shield for the jamb of the door. No guarantee, but it's better than what you've got. You say nothing was taken but your notebook?"

"That's right."

"What was in the notebook?"

"Everything," I said despairingly. "Everything I learned about the Demaretion robbery. Everything about the Havistock family. About the murders of Vanwinkle and LeBaron. Everything you and Jack Smack told me. Al, that notebook had everything I've been doing since this whole thing started. I'll be lost without it."

"Can you remember what was in it?"

"I'll try. I think I can, but there was so *much*. I needed those notes."

"I know," he said sympathetically. "I go back over my reports again and again, trying to find something I've missed."

"Can you do anything?" I asked hopefully.

"Like what? Have the place dusted for prints? A waste of time. Whoever grabbed your notebook was probably wearing gloves, and in and out of here in fifteen minutes. Where did you keep it?"

"In the upper drawer of the sideboard."

"Locked?"

"No."

He sighed. "It's gone, Dunk. And I doubt if you'll ever get it back. I can ask neighbors if they saw or heard anything, but that's the best I can do."

"Forget it," I said. "You're right; it's just gone."

"You think it happened last night?"

"Yes," I said. "I was out."

"Lucky you," he said casually. "Better than being home asleep when the guy broke in. Dunk, who knew you were keeping a notebook?"

I held my head in my hands, trying to think. "I told Enoch. That's Enoch Wottle, my friend in Arizona. You can scratch him as a suspect. I mentioned it to Archibald Havistock, and he could have repeated it to his wife."

"Yeah," Al said, "at the dinner table where Natalie and Ruby Querita might have heard."

I nodded miserably. "And I told a friend of Vanessa's last night. So she could have known about the notebook. And that means Luther, too. Also, the Minchens."

"Jesus Christ, Dunk, why didn't you take out a full-page newspaper ad to let everyone in New York know you were keeping notes on the Demaretion robbery."

"I talked too much," I agreed mournfully. "But who could have figured anyone would be interested enough in the stupid thing to steal it."

"Obviously someone who felt threatened by your investigation and wanted to find out exactly what you knew. Who's this friend of Vanessa's?"

"Carlo. He's the manager of a Madison Avenue boutique where Vanessa spends a bundle." Then I decided to come clean. "Al, I went to a party at Vanessa's last night. That's where I got a mite smashed and shot off my mouth about the notebook. I didn't get home until early this morning, so anyone at the party could have popped over here and grabbed it.''

Thankfully, he didn't ask me where I had been ''until early this morning.'' Maybe he knew—or guessed.

He finished his coffee and sat back on the couch. ''No use brooding about it, Dunk. You'd do better trying to remember your notes and figuring out what you might have had that drove someone to breaking-and-entering. Learn anything at the party?''

I told him what I had told Jack Smack, that Luther Havistock had been in a pitiable condition and, in my opinion, was close to violence. Also, that the Minchens had been present, to my surprise, and seemed to be palsy-walsy with Vanessa.

''I have no idea what that means,'' Al said. ''Do you?''

''Haven't the slightest,'' I said, not yet ready to tell him about my crazy theory. And unwilling, at the moment, to confess I had a mysterious package that belonged to Dolly LeBaron in my kitchen cabinet.

We sat in silence awhile. He seemed in no hurry to leave—which was fine with me. After what had happened, it was nice to have a big, husky cop on the premises.

''Anything new on the homicides?'' I asked.

''What?'' he said, coming out of his reverie. ''No, nothing new. We're up against a stone wall. Unless we get a lucky break, I'm afraid the whole thing will have to be put on the back burner.''

''You can't do that,'' I said hotly.

''No?'' he said with a sour grin. ''You know how many killings there have been in this town since Vanwinkle got snuffed? It's a problem of time and manpower, Dunk. We can't work one case for months or years. Besides, Vanwinkle and LeBaron are the homicide guys' headache. It's not mine. I've got enough to worry about, wondering if I screwed up on the Demaretion thing. My bosses aren't exactly enthusiastic about the way I've handled it—or mishandled it.''

''Jack Smack hasn't done any better,'' I pointed out. ''And neither have I. It's not your fault, Al.''

He gave me his slow, charming smile. ''Thanks for your loyalty; I appreciate it. Dunk, I talked to Sally on the phone last night. She said to say hello.''

''And hello to her. How is she?''

''Doing great in school. Getting good marks. And she's in a play where she gets to sing a song. She's all excited.''

''I can imagine.''

''You like her, Dunk?''

''Like her? What a question! I love her. She's a marvelous kid.''

''Yeah,'' he said, ''I think so, too. I just wanted to find out how you felt.''

Then he was silent again, sitting there like a slack giant, rumpled as ever. What he needed, I decided, was a loving wife who would wind him up every morning and send him off to work with a pressed suit, shined shoes, and a straight part in his hair. He needed sprucing and the knowledge that someone cared. He was beginning to show a hermit's disrepair. I didn't think he was a man who enjoyed solitude.

"Something on your mind, Al?" I asked him. "You seem awfully quiet."

"Yeah," he said, leaning forward with his elbows on his knees. "I've got something on my mind. Dunk, will you marry me?"

I used to believe it was a literary figure of speech to say someone's jaw dropped in amazement, but I could feel mine go *kerplunk*! I had just been thinking he needed a wife to straighten him out and give his life meaning. What a shock to learn I had been nominated.

"My God, Al," I said, "you can't be serious."

"Never more serious in my life. Hear me out, Dunk, before you laugh at me."

"I'd never do that, and you know it."

"Well, I'll give it to you straight. I've been thinking about it a long time. Since I met you and drove you home—remember? Let me give you the minuses first. I told you why my wife dumped me. She couldn't stand the pressures of my job. That's all right; I can understand that. But if you married me, the pressures would still be there. The job would come first. Lousy hours. Meals where I don't show up. Maybe gone for a day or two and all you get are phone calls. Not exactly what you'd term a storybook romance. Plus the possibility that some weirdo might blow my head off. A remote possibility—but still it's there. Also, I admit, I can be stubborn. You know—the Italian macho syndrome. I try to control it, but sometimes it gets away from me."

"You do okay," I told him.

"Do I?" he said. "Well, I try. And then there are a lot of little things that might drive a wife bananas. Like I think I'm such a hotshot cook and could be supercritical of what I'm given to eat. And I guess I'm not the neatest guy in the world. I'm trying to give you all the drawbacks, Dunk."

I smiled and took his hand.

"Now for the pluses," he said. "Such as they are. I make a good buck. Not great, but good. Maybe someday I can make lieutenant. Chancy, but it's a possible. The pension is better. If my ex gets married, which I'm praying for, then I'll be saving the alimony. I've got a few CDs—nothing to brag about. I'm in good health. Overweight, but healthy. I really can cook, and don't mind helping with housework if I've got the time. But the most important plus, Dunk, is that I love you. I really do. If we got married, I would never cheat on you. I wouldn't even *dream* about it. I would be with you always."

This was my first proposal of marriage, and I didn't know how to handle it. I was so confused that my best reaction, I figured, would be to delay, temporize, put off a decision until I could determine how I felt. But Al, bless him, made it easy for me.

"Look," he said, "I don't expect an immediate yes or no. You're a brainy lady and I know you'll want to think about it and weigh the pros and cons. I just wanted to make my pitch and let you know how I feel. Take your time. If you say no, I'm not going to stamp my foot and pout. It's your decision. If you say yes, I'll be the happiest son of a bitch in New York. But don't let the way I'm going to feel affect what you decide. You do what you think is best for you."

I had to kiss him. He was so honest, forthright, and solid. I never doubted his integrity for a moment. He was exactly the man he appeared to be. No sham. No playacting. What you see is what you get.

"Al," I said, "first of all, I thank you for even thinking about me that way. First time it ever happened to me, and it's great for a girl's ego."

"Listen," he said, "if you've got any questions, don't be afraid to ask them. You know, like my finances, bank balance, debts, and all that. Religion. I'll answer everything. Also, what about children? Do you want your own kids or don't you? These are things we'd have to work out if you decide to say yes. But let's put all our cards on the table first. I think that's the best way, don't you?"

"You bet," I said. "Al, just as you figured, I'm not going to give you an answer right now. I've got some heavy thinking to do."

"But you're not giving me a fast no?"

"You're right; I'm not."

"That's good enough for me," he said, rising. "And remember what I told you: Do what you think is best for you."

We embraced and I hugged him tightly. I tried to keep from weeping. I don't know why I felt like crying; a woman's first marriage proposal is hardly a reason for melancholy. I think it was just that, at the moment, I felt so tender and loving toward him.

When he was gone, and I had imprisoned myself with those cheesy locks, I finally got out of my party clothes and pulled on something more informal and comfortable. While I was doing this, moving as dreamily as a somnambulist, I thought of Al's offer and tried to imagine what my life would be like as Mrs. Al Georgio. Mrs. Mary Lou Georgio. Mrs. Dunk Georgio.

I couldn't see myself clearly in the role of a wife. I could easily see Al as a husband. Other than his rackety job, he seemed to have all the attributes of a good, solid, faithful mate. I knew he'd take the marriage vows seriously, especially that part about "till death do us part."

But what kind of a spouse would I make? I decided, sighing, that I'd never know until I gave it a go. I might have the best intentions in the world, but chance and circumstance have a way of fouling up the most sincere resolves. I guess, when you got right down to it, marriage frightened me. The big unknown. Who could predict if it would be a benediction or a curse? Not me.

So I tucked *that* decision into the back of my mind, letting it percolate awhile, and turned my attention to more immediate demands. How was I going to replace my missing notebook? I could do something about that, and started by running out to buy a yellow legal pad at our neighborhood stationery store. I also stopped at the deli to pick up a cold six-pack of Bud. I still had a thirst that wouldn't quit.

Back home, sipping from an opened can, I made brief jottings on the pad of everything I could recall that had been included in the stolen journal. You know, I think the attempted duplication of my original notes was a blessing in disguise. Because I'm sure I forgot a lot of meaningless details. Red herrings flopped at the wayside. There apparently was a kind of mental selection involved here: The things I remembered and scribbled down seemed to be significant and to have a logic and pattern I hadn't seen before.

My crazy theory didn't appear so demented after all. It was now a rational and verifiable explanation of everything that had happened. It took all the events into account and supplied motives and reasons for the puzzles that had been bedeviling me.

It even gave me a very good idea of what was in the late Dolly Le-Baron's mysterious package, now nestling amongst pancake mix and instant rice in my kitchen cabinet.

31

"I'm sorry, Dunk darling," Enoch Wottle said apologetically, calling from Arizona. "What I found out about Archibald Havistock's finances you could put in your eye and it wouldn't hurt a bit."

"That's all right, Enoch," I said. "I know you tried, and I appreciate it."

"The dealers I talked to made credit checks maybe four or five years ago. At that time his reputation was A-OK. They had no trouble with him whatsoever. So they saw no reason to investigate again."

"Of course not," I said. "Why should they? Enoch, thank you again for your help. I couldn't have done it without you."

"Done what?" he said sharply. "Dunk, you sound like you know something."

"Do I?" I said, wondering if Al's marriage proposal had given me confidence. "I'm not sure I know anything definitely, but I'm making some guesses that I think are on target."

"And you'll get the coin back?"

"I hope so."

"I hope so, too. However it comes out, you'll let me know?"

"Of course, dear. Thank you for calling."

He hadn't told me what I wanted to hear, but there was more than one way to skin a cat.

It was Thursday morning, and I was filled with vim and vigor, planning how I would spend a day that would, inevitably, end up with the total triumph of Dunk Bateson. It didn't turn out exactly that way.

I dug an old shopping bag out of my closet—a brown paper job with twine handles. I filled it with catalogues, books, a folding umbrella, a pouched plastic raincoat, a box of Alka-Seltzer, and my office coffee cup.

Then I set out for Grandby & Sons, stopping off at a liquor store en route to pick up a gift for Hobart Juliana: a bottle of Irish Mist, which he dearly loved.

He was delighted to see me, and even more delighted when I began to stow my belongings back into my desk and onto my bookshelves.

"Ma and Pa Kettle are back together again!" he shouted.

We celebrated by having a cup of black coffee and opening Hobie's gift to have a wee taste. A nice way to toast my homecoming.

"I've got to call Felicia," I told him. "Listen to this, Hobie. I think it's the first time I'm going to lie with malice aforethought."

"Welcome to the real world," he said, smiling.

I punched out Madam Dodat's intraoffice extension and waited impatiently while her snooty secretary put her on the phone.

"Dunk, darling!" she caroled. "How *nice* to hear from you. Do you have good news for us?"

"I think so," I said. "I'm downstairs in my office and I'd like to meet with you and Mr. Grandby if that's possible."

"Oh, dear," she said, "I'm afraid not. Stanton isn't in. It's his day for squash and a sauna."

The thought of god sitting naked in a sauna was more than I could bear. That glistening penguin!

"Is this a progress report, Dunk?"

"Something like that," I said.

"Then there's no reason why you can't tell me. I'll repeat it to Stanton just as soon as I hear from him."

"I don't think so," I said decisively. "I want him to be there. And it wouldn't hurt to have the lawyer present. Lemuel what's-his-name."

"Whattsworth."

"Yes. I'd like him to be there. Can you arrange it?"

"Well . . . " she said, obviously offended by my peremptory tone, "I'll see what I can do. How long will you be here?"

"About fifteen minutes."

"I'll try to get back to you before you leave," she said. "If not, I'll call you at home. Is it important?"

"Very," I said, and hung up, glorying in my boldness.

"What was that all about?" Hobie asked curiously.

"I need some information from them," I explained. "But if I told them what I wanted, they'd turn me down cold. So I implied that I have a progress report to deliver. That'll bring them running, hoping to learn something that might forestall a lawsuit by Archibald Havistock."

He laughed. "Dunk, you're becoming a *very* devious lady."

"I'm learning," I said. "Hobie, let's have another sip of that glorious elixir."

"As many as you like," he said, pouring into our coffee mugs. "It's like old times again, Dunk."

We parked our feet on our desks and raised our cups to each other.

"Hobie," I said, "one more favor? Please? The last, I swear."

"The *last?*" he said. "You mean this thing is finally unraveling?"

"I think it is. Keep your fingers crossed."

"I shall. What's the favor you want?"

"Just your opinion. When you were asking around about Orson Vanwinkle's activities, did you get the idea that he might be a man who would engage in—ah, how can I put this delicately?—in group sex?"

"Orgies, you mean?" Hobie said, grinning. "Oh hell, yes. Dunk, from what I heard, the guy was an absolute *freak*. He probably got it off with Doberman pinschers, for all I know. He was a wild one."

"Thank you, Hobie," I said gratefully. "When I write a novel about all this, you're going to get the biggest credit line in the book."

"Could you refer to me as Rodney instead of Hobart?" he said wistfully. "I've always fancied the name Rodney. Hobart sounds like a collapsed soufflé."

We laughed, and chatted of this and that. I was standing, ready to leave, when Felicia Dodat called back. She said she had arranged a conference with Stanton Grandby and Lemuel Whattsworth—and herself, of course—for 1.00 P.M. on the following day, Friday. Would that be satisfactory?

"It'll have to be," I said shortly, in my new assertive role. I was really beginning to enjoy throwing my weight around.

"So long, dear," I said, embracing Hobie. "I shall return carrying my shield or on it."

He gave me a look spangled with love. "Lots of luck, Dunk," he said.

"And I think Hobart is a perfectly marvelous name," I told him. "Live with 'Dunk' for a while, and you'll be thankful for what you've got."

I cabbed home, practically feverish with anticipation because I knew what I had to do next. I rushed into my apartment, closed the venetian blinds and drew the drapes—like an idiot!—and hauled Dolly LeBaron's package down from the top shelf of the kitchen cabinet.

I turned it over and over in my hands, inspecting it, hefting it. Then I fetched a pair of manicure scissors and started cutting all those windings of Scotch tape. I finally got the brown paper bag sliced open. Within was a shoebox, as I had suspected. The stamping on the end read: 4-B, RED.

I opened it as cautiously as if I had been defusing a bomb. Please, God, I prayed silently, let me be right.

Inside were wrappings and paddings of purple tissue paper. I peeled everything away slowly and carefully. Then I held the contents. The secret. I didn't know whether to shout with joy or weep with sadness.

But I *had* been right.

I didn't even want to think about it. I didn't want to ponder or question or analyze. Action was the name of the game. Full court press. Up and in. Dunk shot. Crowd roaring. The satisfaction of completing a class act. Nothing like it.

I started making phone calls. It took me almost a half-hour to get it set up, but I pushed it through, insisting.

When I got hold of Jack Smack, he said:

"Is this about Ross Minchen's bank withdrawals, Dunk? Forget it. He took out cash. There's no way to trace what he did with it. Blew it on slow horses or fast women—who knows?"

"That's not important now," I said impatiently. Then I told him what I wanted.

"Why does it have to be my place?" he complained. "I've got a million things to do here at the office."

"It *has* to be," I said. "At three o'clock. Trust me."

"All right," he said resignedly, "I'll be there."

Al Georgio was easier. "What's up, Dunk?" he said.

"Something interesting," I said. "It's going to help make you a lieutenant."

"Oh?" he said. "That I've got to hear. Okay, I'll be there. Give me the address."

So, a little after 3:00 P.M., we all met at Jack Smack's loft in SoHo, me carrying Dolly LeBaron's package, hugging it tightly as if it contained the plans for an atomic bomb, which, in a way, it did.

Both of the men looked at me like I was some kind of a nut.

"Dunk, what *is* this?" Al said gruffly.

I didn't answer him. I said, "Jack, you mentioned once that you own a videocassette recorder. Is that right?"

He looked at me, puzzled. At least he was smart enough not to say, "You know I do, Dunk. I wanted to play *King Kong* for you the other night when we made nice-nice." *That* would have raised Al Georgio's bushy eyebrows!

Instead, Jack said, "Yeah, I've got a VCR."

"Play this for us, will you?" I asked him, unwrapped the package, and handed him Dolly LeBaron's videocassette.

He inspected it. "What is it?" he said. "A travelogue of the Children's Zoo in Central Park?"

"If it is," I said, trying to laugh and not show my nervousness, "I'm going to spend the rest of my life wiping egg off my face. Just show it, will you?"

He warmed up the set, slid in the cassette, and we settled back. The videotape started. The colors were sharp, everything in focus, sound clear. It had played for about five seconds when Al Georgio shouted, "Holy Christ!" After that, we watched in silence.

It was what I had guessed: a sexual *pas de quatre* starring Roberta and Ross Minchen, Orson Vanwinkle, and Dolly LeBaron. It wasn't pretty, but it was explicit. The knowledge that two of the performers had been brutally murdered gave all those grunts and groans a surrealistic quality. But it was still an X-rated film. More foolish than exciting.

When it ended, Jack rewound the tape, slid the cassette out, and handed it to Georgio. "I think you'll want this, Al," he said. Then we sat there, saddened and depressed I think, staring at each other. Finally . . .

"Where did you get it, Dunk?" Al asked quietly.

I explained how Dolly LeBaron had come to my apartment shortly before she was killed and left the sealed package in my care.

"She made me promise to destroy it if she didn't come back for it," I said. "After she was murdered, I didn't know what to do, so I didn't do anything. But then I put a lot of things together and decided I better see what she had left with me."

I had thought that Al Georgio would scream at me for withholding evidence, but he didn't. "What things did you put together, Dunk?" he said.

"Vanwinkle was living high off the hog, spending much more than the eight hundred a week he was making as Mr. Havistock's secretary. So where was he getting it? He had the reputation of being a wild freak, a drunken sensualist. Even poor Dolly admitted they did crazy things."

"Okay," Al said, "I can take it from there. Orson and Dolly go to one of the Minchens' skin extravaganzas, and a tape is made of their gymnastics together."

"Blackmail," Jack Smack said. "Orson swipes the tape, the night it was made or maybe at a later session, and he begins to lean on the Minchens. That would account for Ross's bank withdrawals."

"Mr. and Mrs. Havistock were involved in estate planning," I added. "Rewriting their wills. Can you imagine what would have happened if Vanwinkle took the tape to Mabel and Archibald? As far as inheriting goes, Roberta and Ross would have been down the drain. So they paid Orson to keep his mouth shut. What else could they do? He had the tape."

Al Georgio rose and began to pace back and forth, hands in the pockets of his polyester slacks. "It listens," he said. "I like it. I like it very much. A scumbag like Vanwinkle isn't going to let up. Blackmailers never do. He increases the pressure. Finally, Ross Minchen decides he can't take any more of this; he's got to end it, once and for all."

"How's this for a scenario?" Jack chimed in. "Vanwinkle ups the ante and Minchen agrees. He goes to Orson's apartment. Vanwinkle lets him in, expecting payment. Instead, he gets two slugs in the head. Exit Orson. Then Minchen searches the apartment for the tape."

"But he can't find it," I said, putting in my two cents' worth, "because Vanwinkle had given the cassette to his girlfriend for safekeeping."

"You think Minchen finally figured that out?" Al asked me.

"Probably," I said. "Dolly told me she was getting threatening phone calls. Or maybe she decided to go into the blackmailing business on her own. With Orson dead, how was she going to pay for that apartment, the bikinis, and all her other swell stuff? However it happened, Ross Minchen, frantic now, went up to her place, killed her, and tore everything apart, looking for the tape. Again he didn't find it. Because it was in my kitchen cabinet.''

Al nodded with satisfaction. "Better and better," he said. "This is something I can take to the brass. Thank you, Dunk. You'll have to make a sworn statement of how you came into possession of the tape and what Dolly said to you. Okay?''

"Of course," I said.

"Fine. Then I'll be on my way to get the wheels rolling.''

"Arrest warrant?" Jack asked.

Al thought a moment. "It may not be necessary. With Minchen's bank withdrawals and this''—he held up the videocassette—"I think we can prove probable cause, considering the gravity of the crimes. But that's for the Department's legal eagles to decide. I'll let you both know how it turns out." He paused at the door. "Jack, do me a favor, will you?''

"What's that?"

"The next time you show a film, try to have some buttered popcorn.''

After he was gone, Jack brought an opened bottle of chilled soave from the refrigerator and poured us each a glass. We sat there, sipping, regarding each other without expression.

"You're really something," he said finally. "You saved Al's ass today—you know that? He was getting nowhere on the Demaretion case, but breaking the homicides will take the pressure off. How the hell did you do it?''

"I had the videocassette.''

"Sure you did, but you didn't know what was on it. As for the rest of the stuff, Al and I both knew as much as you did, but we didn't have the brains to put it together. You're really a wonder.''

"Thank you.''

"Now how about saving my ass?" he said. "What have the killings got to do with the disappearance of the Demaretion?''

"Nothing," I said. "Not directly. They were two different crimes.''

"Vanwinkle didn't steal the Demaretion?''

"No.''

"Then who did?''

I thought a moment. "Tell you tomorrow," I said.

He stared at me. "You're kidding.''

"I'm not. I've got one more piece to fit into place, and then I'll know.''

"What time tomorrow?''

"Ohh . . . how about three o'clock? At the Havistocks' apartment.''

"I'll be there.''

"It may turn out to be a waste of time, Jack. But if I can't sew it up, I'll tell you what I do have.''

"That's good enough for me. How about dinner tonight?''

"No, thank you. I've got to get home and do some things. I'll take a rain check.''

He accepted that. It was one thing I admired about him: he endured rejection and failure as calmly as success and triumph. But maybe he just didn't care.

I looked around at that big, spacious loft. Twelve-foot ceilings and a huge skylight. It was about twice the size of my pad. Everything was so open and airy. The Russian Ballet could do *Swan Lake* in there and never touch a wall.

"Like it?" Jack said, guessing what I was thinking.

"I sure do," I said.

"Want to move in?"

"I'd love to," I said. "When are you moving out?"

"I'm not," he said. "I want you to move in with me. Plenty of room. I'll even buy a regular bed."

I gawked at him. I couldn't believe I had heard correctly—but I had. He was looking at me intently, no smirk, and I wondered how I was going to handle this. Slap his face? Stalk out in injured silence? Break into girlish giggles?

"Jack, is this a joke?" I asked him.

"No joke. I like you, Dunk. I like being with you. If you feel the same way about me, why don't we try living together?"

"For how long?"

He shrugged. "As long as it lasts. Who can predict? You may want to move out after two days. I may want to evict you. But let's give it a try."

"What's the point?" I said.

"Does everything have to have a point? Don't you ever act on impulse, and damn the consequences? I do—all the time. And it turns out good more often than it turns out bad. I'll pay the rent and utilities. We'll go fifty-fifty on the food and booze. You can keep your apartment if you like. In fact, it would probably be smart. A safety net. But you'd be living here."

"Until you got bored," I said.

"Or until you did. This would be a two-way street. If you want to leave or I want you to leave, that's it—no explanations necessary. No excuses, no complaints. But I think we could have a hell of a time together—for as long as it lasts. I don't foresee any big arguments. We haven't had any yet, have we?"

"No," I said faintly, "not yet."

"I told you I like you, and I do. And I think you like me. Do you like me, Dunk?"

I had to nod.

"So it makes sense," he said. "It's really no big deal. But I'm tired of tomcatting around. And I imagine you'd like someone to come home to. Wouldn't you, Dunk?"

Again he forced me to nod. He knew me.

"Well, then," he said, "why don't we give it a try? What have we got to lose? You'll keep your apartment, keep your job. I'm not saying that living together will be all peaches and cream, but it might turn out to be something great.''

"But not marriage?"

He looked away. "A little early to be talking about that. They used to call it a 'trial marriage.' That's what I'm suggesting. What do you think?"

"You want an answer right now?"

"Oh hell, no," he said. "Take your time. Think about it. I do admire you. You're a very mental lady. And you're sensational in the sack. I think we're sexually compatible, don't you?"

I nodded again, thinking that if I kept this up, my head would come off.

"Consider it," he urged. "You'll be able to live your own life just as you have been doing. I will, too. We'll have our jobs. But we'll also have each other. A lot of laughs. That's something, isn't it?"

He was a good salesman. Also a handsome salesman. A charming, rakish salesman.

"I'll consider it," I agreed, shocked to realize that after all my drought years, I had a sudden deluge: two proposals (one legal, one illegal) in as many days.

"Sure," he said, "you do that. I'm not going to pretend to be anything but what I am: footloose and fancy-free. But if you can accept that, I think you and I could climb clouds."

"For a while," I said.

He shrugged again. He did a lot of shrugging. "Nothing's forever, is it?" he said. "Grab what you can: that's my philosophy. Am I wrong, Dunk?"

I glanced at my Snoopy watch and stood up. "I've got to get going."

"Drive you home?"

"No, thanks, I'll take a cab. I'm still billing Archibald Havistock for expenses."

"You'll think about it? Moving in with me?"

"Absolutely," I said. "I can guarantee I'll think about it."

"That's good enough for me," he said, and gave me a chaste kiss on the cheek before we parted. He was wearing Aramis again.

What an evening that was! I wanted to do some heavy thinking about the Demaretion investigation, but my personal problems kept intruding. Finally I gave up and wallowed in self-analysis, trying to face up to the decisions I had to make: accept Al's proposal or Jack's proposition. Or neither. I was determined to be very logical.

I thought I knew the two men well enough to make a rational choice. They were total contrasts: Al heavy, serious, solidly dependable. He would always be a hard worker and good provider. Jack was a lightweight, elegant and debonair, a man to whom irony was a way of life and commitments a curse.

Al needed a wife. Jack didn't need anyone. Al was a devoted father. Jack was a social chameleon. Al drove a spavined Plymouth. Jack drove a shiny Jaguar. Al wanted to legalize our relationship. Jack wanted a handy bed-partner. Al said he loved me. Jack said he liked me. Both men could cook.

You can see what a state my mind was in. Nutsville! I suppose I had something to eat that night, but I don't remember what it was. Probably bits and pieces of this and that. I do remember I did a lot of pacing, hugging my elbows and pondering about who I was and what kind of life I wanted. No easy answers to those questions.

I went to bed early, spent a sleepless hour wrestling the sheets, and then got up, sighing. I pulled on a robe, moved back into the living room, and took up my knitting. That was usually a sure cure for insomnia, but this time it didn't work. My brain kept churning, and I wished someone— mother, father, Enoch Wottle, anyone!—would appear and *tell* me what to do.

I looked up from my clicking needles, and the apartment had never seemed so empty, and I had never seemed so *alone*. I think it was at that moment I came to my Great Decision.

Then I could sleep.

32

I *do* remember what I had for breakfast on Friday morning because it was special. I figured it was going to be a momentous day in my life so I followed my mother's dictum: "When there's work to be done, it's best done on a full stomach." A debatable opinion—I can't see a trapeze artist loading up on spaghetti and meatballs before a performance—but nevertheless I believed it.

So I went to our local deli and treated myself to a double tomato juice, scrambled eggs, kippered herring, and home-fries, and English muffin with apple butter, and two cups of black coffee. Then I walked back to my apartment with the morning *Times*. I searched for some mention of the arrest of Ross Minchen, but there was nothing.

I put the paper aside to read later and began to scribble the day's schedule on my yellow legal pad. The timing of everything seemed right. The first thing I had to do, I decided, was to contact Al Georgio and get him over to the Havistocks' apartment for what might or might not be the grand dénouement.

But he called me before I could call him. He sounded absolutely awful.

"Al," I said anxiously, "what's wrong?"

"I've been up all night," he said in a growly voice. "Well, I did have about two hours' sleep on a cot with a mattress as thin as a stale pancake, but then they got me up and it started all over again. There's good news and there's bad news. Which do you want first?"

"Oh, God," I said, "I hate that stupid question. All right, I'll take the good news first. Maybe it'll give me strength for what's coming."

"Okay," he said. "We lowered the boom on Ross Minchen. He's behind bars right now, with his lawyer fighting to get him out. He hasn't admitted a damned thing, but we found a choice library of porn videocassettes in his apartment—all home movies. Plus a .22 revolver with two slugs missing from the cylinder. The idiot didn't even clean and reload—can you imagine? The DA's man is very high on this one. He says if ballistic tests prove out, he'll go for Murder One on the Vanwinkle kill. Even if Minchen plea-bargains—because he was being blackmailed, you know—he's still going to do time. Does that make you happy?''

"What about Dolly LeBaron?" I demanded.

"Well, that'd be a tough one to prove. If we can put him away for one homicide, won't that satisfy you?"

"I guess," I said, thinking of silly Dolly. Even her murder seemed of no interest to anyone.

"Now for the bad news," Al Georgio said. "A real shocker."

"Let's have it."

"I told you, didn't I, that if we waited long enough, everyone connected with this case would get knocked off and we could all go home. Well, it's happening. Vanessa Havistock is dead."

"Dead?" I said, beginning to tremble. "Al, I can't believe that."

"It's the truth, kiddo," he said. "I saw the body—and wish I hadn't. It happened early this morning. Four or five o'clock, the ME's man figures. She was murdered, but there's no mystery about it. Hubby Luther pulled the plug on her. Then he called nine-eleven and reported what he had done. He was sitting there, waiting, when the blues arrived. They read him his rights, but he didn't care; he admitted everything. I think the guy is cuckoo, and his lawyers will probably plead the same thing."

"How did he kill her, Al?"

"You don't want to know that, Dunk."

"I *do* want to know," I said fiercely.

"He beat her to death. With his fists and his feet. He destroyed her. You were right about him being on the edge. He finally went over."

"Ah, Jesus," I said, sickened and saddened. "The poor woman. The poor man. Poor us."

"Yeah," Al Georgio said, "I know what you mean. I hate to turn the day rancid for you, Dunk, but you'd have heard about it anyway, and I wanted to tell you the good news about Ross Minchen."

"Sure, Al," I said, "I understand. Thank you for calling. Are you going home now?"

"Nah," he said. "Wish I could, but I'm sitting in on the interrogations of the Minchens and Luther Havistock, so I'll be around and semi-awake all day."

"Good," I said. "Can you meet me at the Havistocks' apartment at three o'clock?"

He was silent a moment. Then:

"Got something good, Dunk?"

"I think so."

"On the Demaretion heist?"

"If all goes well. If I fall on my face I'll give you everything I do have. Jack Smack will be there, too."

"Hey," he said, "we're becoming like the Three Musketeers."

"More like the Three Stooges," I said.

"See you at the Havistocks' at three," he said, laughing, and hung up.

Al was familiar with violent, bloody death and could accept it stoically. But I wasn't and couldn't. So I shed tears for Vanessa Havistock. Not a lot, but some. I knew there was quality in life, and I supposed there was in death, too. I knew I had mourned more for Dolly LeBaron. Mindless Dolly had been a true victim. Vanessa had engineered her own destruction.

The two were contrasts, in looks, intelligence, life-styles. But there was something of each in the other. When I thought of it, Dolly was Vanessa when she was Pearl Measley and first came to the Big City from South Carolina to make her way. And Vanessa still had the wants and appetites of a country girl bedazzled by wealth and opportunity.

Now they were both dead, all their hopes and ambitions and greeds brought low. There was a moral there, I supposed, but I couldn't see it. All I could grieve was the waste: two lives ended too soon, annihilated by passions that went out of control and became sins.

Vanessa's murder by Luther Havistock added credibility to my theory of what had happened and increased my hopes of bringing the whole thing to a screeching halt. But I found no satisfaction in that. If I had been sharper, smarter, faster, perhaps I might have prevented the bloodbath. A sobering thought, and one I didn't wish to dwell on.

I tore all the annotated sheets from my pad, folded them up, and stuffed them into my shoulder bag. I started out for my appointment at Grandby & Sons, in no mood to be lied to, stalled, or bullied. I was determined to have my way.

We gathered in that funereal conference room. Felicia was wearing one of her "simple black frocks" that looked like it had been sprayed on her. Stanton Grandby wore his penguin's uniform. And Lemuel Whattsworth wore his usual earth-colored three-piece suit that seemed ready to mold. All three wore expressions of frozen interest in what I had to say.

"Well, Dunk," Felicia said with her chintzy smile, "I hope you have some good news for us."

I ignored her. "Mr. Grandby," I said, "has Archibald Havistock brought suit for the loss of the Demaretion?"

God looked to his attorney. "Litigation has not actually commenced," Whattsworth said cautiously. "However, the possibility still exists. We are, in my opinion, legally vulnerable for the loss of the coin since you, Miss Bateson, an employee of Grandby and Sons, signed the receipt."

He had to remind me of that—the wretch!

"But Mr. Havistock hasn't made any claim as yet?"

"Not at this point in time," the lawyer said.

I took the folded notes from my shoulder bag and made a great pretense of shuffling through them, pausing occasionally to read. All flimflam, of course. I knew what was in them and what wasn't.

"Mr. Grandby," I said, "do you have any plans to auction the Havistock Collection minus the Demaretion?"

"No," the penguin said. "Not until this thing is cleared up. Under the contract we have a year before the collection goes on the block."

"So, as of this date, Mr. Havistock has received nothing, and his collection is still in Grandby's vaults?"

"That is correct."

"Dunk," Felicia said, "what *is* this all about?"

Again I ignored her. How I loved it!

"Mr. Grandby," I said, "I know that it is standard operating procedure when someone comes to us with valuable property to be auctioned—be it furniture, paintings, coins, stamps, or whatever—a credit check is made to determine the reputation and trustworthiness of the client. I presume such an investigation was made of Archibald Havistock. Could you tell me what the results were?"

"That is confidential information," Lemuel Whattsworth said in his thin voice.

I stood up, jammed my notes back into my shoulder bag, and faced them defiantly.

"You're paying me to investigate the disappearance of the Demaretion," I said, in what I hoped were steely tones. "If you refuse to cooperate, that's your problem, not mine. I've asked you for information. If you refuse to divulge it, then I tender my resignation as of now, and you can face the possibility of paying for the Demaretion's loss on your own."

Stanton Grandby groaned. "For heaven's sake, Lemuel," he said, "tell her."

"I advise against it," the attorney said.

"Then I'll tell her," Grandby said. "Please, Miss Bateson, sit down. The credit check on Archibald Havistock was satisfactory. He was—is a rich man. But most of his wealth is in unimproved land which is in his wife's name. The only section of his credit report that gave us pause was that he was not in a very liquid condition. That is, he did not have a great deal of cash in relation to his total assets."

"I know what 'liquid condition' means," I said. I wasn't going to let him patronize me.

Now that the cat was out of the bag, the lawyer took over. "However," he said, "that is hardly an unusual condition of people seeking to auction property. Invariably they wish to convert their collections to cash. I fail to see how Mr. Havistock's shortage of liquid resources relates to the theft of the coin. If the Demaretion had been included in the auction, he would have gained more."

"That's true," I agreed. "A great deal more."

I think I had them thoroughly befuddled at that point—which suited me just fine. Let them suffer awhile. I thought I'd bring them out of their misery soon enough, but meanwhile I enjoyed their discomfiture. Such *stiff* people!

"Let me get this straight," I said. "If the Demaretion is not recovered, Grandby and Sons will have to recompense Mr. Havistock for its loss. But actually, your insurer, Finkus, Holding, Incorporated, will pick up the tab."

"That, essentially, is correct," Whattsworth said. "Minus the deductible, of course. Which I may say, without fear of contradiction, is a considerable sum."

"All that doesn't amount to a row of beans," Stanton Grandby said impatiently. And from that moment I began to like him—almost. "The dollar loss isn't going to kill us. What does hurt is the damage to our reputation. Grandby's has never had a scandal of this magnitude in our long and honorable history. People entrust valuable property to our care in the expectation that it will be guarded as if it was our own. If we are forced to admit carelessness or incompetence, the result will be similar to a run on a bank: people will simply lose confidence in our house. That I will not allow."

Then all three looked at me as if I was to be their savior, the Joan of Arc who would solve all their problems, temporal and spiritual.

"We'll see," I said, standing up again. "I thank you for your cooperation."

"Dunk!" Felicia Dodat wailed. "Don't you have *anything* to tell us?"

"Not at the moment," I said. "Things are moving too swiftly. I'm sure you are aware of the murder of Orson Vanwinkle, Mr. Havistock's private secretary. Last night, Ross Minchen, Mr. Havistock's son-in-law, was arrested and charged with committing that homicide. And early this morning Mr. Havistock's son, Luther, confessed to the brutal slaying of his wife. So you see, there is more to this than just the disappearance of an ancient Greek coin."

I left them stunned and shattered.

I had plenty of time to walk over to the Havistocks' apartment; it wasn't far. I hadn't called for an appointment because I thought I'd be put on hold; they'd be distraught and concerned only with the imprisonment of their son. But I was resolved to wait there until I could see Mabel or Archibald, or both. I owed them that.

It was a murky kind of day, the sky a swamp and the air as thick as pudding. No breeze at all; the poor, dusty leaves on the street trees weren't moving, and everyone seemed to go shuffling along, conserving their energy to breathe. Which was no great treat.

I had expected to find a gaggle of reporters outside the Havistocks' door, and perhaps a TV crew. But the hallway was empty. I rang the bell and waited. The door was opened cautiously a few inches, the chain still on. Ruby Querita peered out.

"Ruby," I said, "it's me. Can I come in, please?"

She let me enter, then hurriedly relocked, bolted, chained the door. "Lots of people come," she said. "I don't know who they are."

I nodded. "I can imagine. Big trouble, Ruby. More and more trouble."

She took a deep breath. I could see that she had been weeping. That dour face was creased with damp folds and wrinkles. All her features seemed drawn down, everything sagging with sorrow. I realized then that, despite her imprecations and predictions of doom, she loved this family and felt their hurts. I put an arm about her shoulders.

"Are you all right?" I said.

"I live," she said. "I try to understand God's justice."

We spoke in whispers, as if a corpse was laid out in the next room.

"Is anyone home?" I asked her.

"Natalie is in her room. She won't come out."

"Good. Make sure she stays there. Mr. Havistock?"

"He is at the lawyer."

"And Mrs. Havistock?"

"She is here. In the living room. She sits and stares. She will not eat."

"Ruby, would you tell her I'd like to talk to her? I'll wait here. If she doesn't want to see me, I'll go away."

The housekeeper drifted away. I had never before noticed how silently she moved. She was back in a few moments.

"She says to come in," Ruby reported. "Please, be very good to her. She is broken—like this." Ruby made a twisting gesture: two closed fists moving in opposite directions. "She tries to live—but I know."

"I'll try not to disturb her. Ruby, there are two men coming at three o'clock. Will you tell me when they get here? One is a police officer."

She stared at me. "Oh," she said. "Ah. Then it is the end?"

"I think so," I said. "I think it is finished."

I left her weeping, tears slowly dripping down those dark furrows in her cheeks.

When I entered that fusty living room, Mabel Havistock was seated on a severe ladder-back chair, pressed into it as if to support the rigidity of her spine. Her broad shoulders were square, the long jaw lifted. I saw no outward signs of that twisting motion Ruby had made; this woman had not been broken.

"Miss Bateson," she said with just the faintest hint of a wan smile, "thank you for coming by."

"Ma'am," I said, totally incapable of commiserating adequately, "I am sorry for your troubles."

She gave a sharp nod, but that heavy, corseted body did not relax for an instant. As usual, she was groomed to an inch, the blued hair precisely in place, the dress of flowered chiffon unwrinkled. Her eyes were as cold as ever, showing no signs of the strains she was enduring. How solid and craggy she was! She could have been right up there on Mount Rushmore.

"Please," she said, gesturing, "do sit down. Would you care for a cup of tea? Coffee? Anything?"

"No, thank you, Mrs. Havistock," I said, touched by her effort to act the gracious hostess. I sat in one of those obese club chairs facing her. I found myself at a lower level, looking up at her—which, somehow, seemed right. "Actually I came to see your husband, ma'am, but Ruby tells me he's out."

"Yes," she said, "he is consulting with the attorneys regarding our son Luther. I believe—we believe the boy was temporarily deranged and in need of, ah, professional help."

"I agree completely," I said. "The last time I saw him, I thought he was close to the breaking point."

She stared at me. "All my children," she said bleakly, but I didn't understand the significance of that. She shook her massive head slightly as if to clear her mind. "What was it you wished to see my husband about?" she asked.

The question made me acutely uncomfortable. I could have faced Archibald Havistock and told him the truth without flinching. But this woman—nephew murdered, daughter an attempted suicide, son-in-law arrested for homicide, son a confessed killer—surely I could not add to her sorrows; it would be too painful, for her and for me.

She must have guessed what I was thinking because she raised her heavy chin a trifle and said, "I am stronger than you think."

She gave me such a keen, shrewd look that, at that moment, I was certain, absolutely, positively, that she knew why I had come and what I had discovered.

"Mrs. Havistock," I said, feeling my face suddenly flushed with confusion and embarrassment, "you've known all along, haven't you?"

"Not known," she demurred, raising a cautionary finger, "but suspected."

I took a deep breath. What a family! Wheels within wheels.

"When I accepted your offer of employment," I said, "I agreed that if I discovered a member of your family was involved in stealing the Demaretion, I would come to you first before going to the authorities."

"I am aware of that," she said calmly.

"Then why in God's name did you hire me?" I cried out.

She touched that beehive of bluish hair. "I insisted on it because I thought you were an intelligent, persistent young woman. And perhaps because I considered that you might serve as a kind of avenging angel who would set right a wrong." She was silent a moment. Then: "A wrong that I didn't have the courage to set right."

How I admired her! What a blunt, honest woman. I could understand her conflicting feelings. Suspecting but not knowing, and not really wanting to know because the final realization might mean the end of her life as mother, wife, and dutiful matriarch of this dissolute family.

"I am not an angel," I told her. "As for avenging anyone or anything, I really have no interest in that. My initial motive for beginning the investigation was to clear my name. It was purely selfish. But then, I admit, I got caught up in the challenge of the search."

"And now it's at an end?" she said.

"Yes, Mrs. Havistock," I said, "it's at an end. I have asked Detective Al Georgio of the New York Police Department and insurance investigator John Smack to join me here. When they arrive, and when your husband returns, I think we better finish all this."

"Yes," she said, sighing, "it's time. When did you begin to understand what had happened?"

"Not for quite a while. There were too many loose ends, too many false leads. Then I got this crazy idea I could scarcely believe myself. But as time went on, it began to seem more and more logical. Not logical, perhaps, but understandable."

"Irrational!" she thundered. "Totally irrational! I should have told you my suspicions from the start. I acted like a weak woman."

"Not weak," I said. "Never. But you *are* a woman, wanting to protect your family, your marriage, your home. I don't blame you. No one can blame you."

There was a slight cough from the doorway. We looked up. Ruby Querita.

"Those two men," she said. "They're here."

"Please show them in, Ruby," Mrs. Havistock said as serenely as if she was inviting the entry of dignitaries.

Al Georgio and Jack Smack came in, bobbing their heads at us. I stood up.

"Ma'am," I said to Mabel Havistock, "I must talk to these gentlemen, explain to them what has happened. Perhaps it would be best if I spoke to them in the hallway or another room."

"No," she said decisively, "you may talk to them here, in my presence. I assure you I shall not be shocked or insulted."

"As you wish," I said.

I waited until Al and Jack got seated, side by side on one of those awful brown velvet couches. I turned sideways in my armchair so I could address them and still not ignore Mrs. Havistock. I wanted to note her reactions to what I had to say. I spoke as directly and concisely as I could.

"For the past five years," I said, "or perhaps more, Archibald Havistock had been having an affair with Vanessa, his son's wife. They met in that apartment on East Sixty-fifth Street, leased by Lenore Wolfgang, Mr. Havistock's attorney. I am sure he paid Vanessa for her sexual favors. I suppose they called the payments 'gifts,' but whatever you call them, she was getting a great deal of money out of him."

I paused to glance at Mabel. Her naturally florid complexion had paled, but her lips were tightly pressed, and she made no effort to interrupt my recital.

"I have good reasons to believe," I continued, "that Vanessa was also entertaining other men, and receiving cash 'gifts' from them as well. Whether Archibald was aware of those activities, I don't know. I suspect he was, but so sexually obsessed that he could not bear to give her up. The same was true of her husband. Luther must have known where all the money was coming from, but he was in thrall to his wife and endured her unfaithfulness. But he drank heavily; it was, literally, driving him out of his mind."

Al and Jack glanced at each other, both expressionless. Then they turned back to me. I had no idea how they were taking all this, but I supposed, being detectives, they would have a lot of questions to ask later.

"Now we come to Orson Vanwinkle," I went on. "He came to work as private secretary to Archibald about five years ago. Being the kind of man he was, it didn't take long for Orson to discover his boss was involved in an adulterous relationship with his daughter-in-law. So Orson began to blackmail him. To come up with the payments, Archibald had to sell off coins from his collection. The cash drain must have been horrendous. Not only was he paying Vanessa for those afternoons on East Sixty-fifth Street, but now he was paying Orson to keep his mouth shut. Do you wish to comment, ma'am?" I asked, turning to Mrs. Havistock.

"No," she said. "I have no comment."

I think that impressed Georgio and Smack more than anything: the wife was making no objections to this sordid tale of her husband's adultery. They began to believe it could all be true. I could see their increased interest in the way they leaned forward, waiting for more revelations.

"And then," I said, "Vanwinkle and his sappy girlfriend, Dolly LeBaron, went to one of the Minchens' filming parties, and Orson saw the opportunity to enlarge his blackmailing business. He stole the videocassette, put the arm on Ross Minchen, and had another source of income. No wonder he was living so well and throwing money around like it was going out of style."

"The Demaretion," Jack Smack said in a low voice.

"All right," I said, "now we come to the Demaretion. I think what happened is this: Orson decided to extort a final big payment from his two blackmail victims and then move abroad with Dolly to live happily ever after on the French Riviera. But that required a lot of loot, so you can imagine what he demanded. It proved to be too much for Ross Minchen, which led to his murdering Orson and Dolly. But Archibald Havistock is no killer; he concluded the best way to get rid of that devil Vanwinkle who was sucking him dry would be to pay him off and get him out of the country. The only way Archibald could come up with that kind of cash would be to put his coin collection up for auction. Then he could pay off Orson and have enough left to continue his liaison with Vanessa. Al, are you with me so far?''

"So far it listens, Dunk," Georgio said. "You're on a roll. Keep going.''

"Well, now it gets a little heavy," I said, "but bear with me. First of all, you have to understand the psychology of true collectors. They don't buy things for investment or profit, but because the objects are rare or beautiful or both, and they love them. Mr. Havistock was—is a true collector. It must have hurt him to sell off coins over the past five years, even if they were only duplicates or lesser items from the really fine collection he had put together. But now he had to sell off everything including the Demaretion. Surely it was anguishing for him to put on the block all those glorious mintages he had spent a lifetime amassing. But he went ahead with the auction contract. Then, at the last minute, he decided to hold out the Demaretion. He *couldn't* let it go, it was the gem of his collection. In his eyes it was priceless. And he figured that if he kept the Demaretion, he could collect on the insurance."

Jack Smack looked at me with astonishment. "Dunk, are you telling us that Archibald Havistock stole the Demaretion?''

"How can a man steal his own coin?" I asked. "What I'm saying is that Archibald prepared a sealed empty display case, properly taped inside a Styrofoam box and marked as package thirteen. Then he switched boxes. Who else could have done it? Not Orson Vanwinkle. He was with the guards from the armored van. Not anyone else in the family because they couldn't have known how the display case was sealed with wax imprinted with the signet ring, and how the outside box would be taped and numbered. No, Mr. Havistock made the switch.''

"And what did he do with the original box thirteen?" Al asked.

I shrugged. "Probably shoved it into that deep kneehole under his desk where he had kept the empty case. He made the switch, then strolled into the living room for a couple of minutes to chat with his family. Styrofoam box thirteen was loaded into the van, and it was only after I signed the receipt for the collection at Grandby's that we discovered the Demaretion was gone. Mrs. Havistock, do you agree that's the way it happened?''

"I don't know," she said stonily. "I cannot say if the details are correct. I do know my husband loved his coins. Especially the Demaretion. It is quite possible it happened as you described.''

"Wait a minute," Jack said. "Suppose Havistock did keep the Demaretion, then who wrote the letters to my company offering to make a deal?''

"Orson Vanwinkle," I said promptly. "When the coin disappeared, he knew immediately that only Archibald could have switched cases. He was smarter and faster than I was. But then he had a criminal mind and assumed everyone was as crooked as he. So he went to Mr. Havistock and demanded part of the insurance on the loss of the Demaretion. It meant nothing to Orson that Archibald loved that coin and wanted to keep it. So he wrote the letters to your company, Jack, to raise cash as quickly as possible, and he wrote that drop-dead letter to me.''

"So who was dealing in Lebanon?'' Al Georgio asked.

"Archibald,'' I said. "After Vanwinkle was killed, the letters to the insurance company stopped, and the Beirut dealer offered the coin. Mr. Havistock would know about him and his sleazy reputation. After all, Archibald had been involved in the collection of antique coins for many years; he probably knows everyone in the field. And if you're wondering why he tried to peddle the coin through the Beirut dealer, the answer is simple: he needed the money. Orson was dead, but there was still Vanessa and her 'gifts.' And Grandby's postponed the auction of the Havistock Collection in their vaults. And the insurance companies were dragging their feet on the payoff for the missing coin. A lawsuit might take years. So, in a word, Mr. Havistock found himself broke. Or at least cash-poor. He had to sell the coin if he wanted to keep Vanessa happy. It came down to a choice between a splendid treasure of ancient Greek mintage and the woman who obsessed him. Vanessa won—for a while.''

Then we were all silent, looking at each other. Mabel Havistock had remained stern and erect through much of my narrative, but now I noticed she was beginning to slump. Not slump so much, perhaps, as soften. No longer so hard, so unyielding. Hearing what she had feared spoken aloud had taken something out of her. I had hit her like a tabloid headline, and I knew it hurt.

"A nice story,'' Al Georgio said finally, "and I believe every word of it. But you know what we've got, Dunk?''

"Zero, zip, and zilch,'' I said, sighing.

"Right,'' he said. "Jack?''

"Nothing. His insurance company hasn't paid him a cent, and my company hasn't reimbursed Grandby's. So how can we scream fraud? At the moment we just can't nail him.''

"Hasn't he suffered enough?'' I said.

"No,'' Mrs. Havistock said. "Not enough.''

Al Georgio stared directly at her. "Ma'am,'' he said softly, "you know a wife cannot be compelled to testify against her husband. But if she volunteers, her testimony is judged just like that of any other witness.''

"I volunteer,'' Mabel Havistock said grimly.

"Volunteer for what?'' a resonant voice asked from the doorway, and we all looked up.

Archibald Havistock stood planted, regarding us with his ice-cube eyes. Al, Jack, and I stood and confronted him.

"Sir,'' Al said, "could we have a private talk with you, please?''

Havistock bristled. "By what right,'' he demanded, "do you invade my home and disturb my wife? I must ask you to leave at once.''

"Mr. Havistock,'' Al said pleasantly, "cut the bullshit. You'll either talk to us here and now or I'll take you down to the precinct house and we'll talk there. Is that what you want?''

The two big men locked stares, and it was Archibald who blinked. ''Very well,'' he snapped. ''Come into my library. Please keep it short.''

''It will be,'' Al promised. ''And sweet.''

We all moved out into the hallway and down to the library. Mrs. Havistock watched us go, her eyes filmed with tears. And for the first time I thought Ruby Querita had been right: she *was* broken.

Al took my arm and held me back for a moment. ''Who swiped your notebook?'' he asked in a low voice.

''I think it was Carlo, one of Vanessa's pimps. She probably had them all over the East Side.''

''What a woman,'' he said, shaking his head. ''She should have gone public and sold shares.''

In the library, without invitation, the three of us pulled up chairs in a semicircle facing Archibald Havistock as he sat in the swivel chair behind his desk. I took a good look at him.

He was impeccably dressed as ever, all pressed, creased, starched, and shining. The only sign of disarray was a single lock of his silvered hair that had fallen over his right temple. He kept brushing it back with his palm, but in a moment it would flop down again. I know it sounds fanciful, but that errant lock of hair symbolized for me the man's disintegration.

''I trust this won't take long,'' he said, speaking to Georgio.

''That depends on you,'' Al said. ''I'll start off by telling you what we've got.''

Then, a lot blunter and harsher than I had been, he repeated everything I had just recited in the living room. He kept it brief and toneless, making it sound like an official police report. I was impressed, but other than continually brushing his hair back with his palm, Mr. Havistock showed absolutely no signs of dismay. The thought occurred to me that I might be totally wrong. Oh, my God!

''So,'' Al Georgio concluded, ''I think the best solution to this whole thing would be if you turned the coin over to me. If you do that, I think it's safe to say there will be no arrest, no prosecution. Jack?''

''Not from our end,'' Jack Smack said. ''All we want is the return of the Demaretion.''

Archibald Havistock leaned back in his chair and regarded us with what I can only describe as a benign smile.

''A fairy tale,'' he said in his rich, boomy voice. ''Not a word of truth in it. Do you have any evidence at all to support this farrago?''

''You deny what I just told you?'' Al asked.

''Utterly and completely,'' Havistock said, leaning forward over his desk. ''If this nonsense was what you wanted to talk to me about, then I must ask you again to leave.''

Al sighed. ''Mr. Havistock, I know you've got heavy troubles. Your son and son-in-law are going to be charged with homicide. Your nephew and daughter-in-law are dead. Your daughter attempted suicide. Enough problems for any man. But if you keep jerking me around, I'm going to have to add to your troubles. I'll give you one last chance: Where's the Demaretion, Mr. Havistock?''

Archibald looked at him warily, seemed to consider a moment, but then shook his head. ''I assure you,'' he said, ''I do not have the Demaretion and I do not know where it is.''

''You want me to get nasty?'' Al said. ''I can get nasty.'' Then he gave me a lesson on what a professional detective can do with the resources of the NYPD behind him. ''Here's the program: First, I'm going to bring a photograph of you over to the super of that apartment on East Sixty-fifth. I'll lean on him, and no matter how much you paid him to keep his mouth shut, he'll admit that, yeah, you were there two, three, or four afternoons a week with Vanessa.

''Then I'm going to get copies of your cables to that coin dealer in Beirut. How else would you communicate with him—by postcard? Maybe you phoned. If you did, New York Telephone will have a record of the calls.

''Then I'm going to get a search warrant and tear this place apart. Even if I don't find anything, the neighbors will learn about it. Won't that be nice?

''Then I'm going to have another talk with poor, confused Luther, just to make sure that he knew his father was shtupping his wife.

''Then I'm going to pull in Carlo and any other pimps who delivered johns to Vanessa. The tabloids will eat it up.

''Then I'm going to ask the District Attorney to take a close look at the activities of Lenore Wolfgang, especially in leasing that love nest of yours. I don't know whether or not what she did was unethical, but it might be enough to get her disbarred.

''Then I'm going to ask the IRS to audit your returns—did you report the sale of those coins over the past five years?—and the returns of Vanessa, Luther, and everyone else in your family.

''And finally, just to add to your troubles, I think I'll have a long chat with Mrs. Havistock. That lady is ready to talk, and after what you've done to her and the family, I believe she'll tell the truth.

''See how nasty I can be, Mr. Havistock? Now do you want to keep insisting the whole thing is a fairy tale?''

Throughout Georgio's discourse, Archibald sat stiffly upright, propping himself with his two palms pressed onto the desktop. I saw no change of expression as Al heaped stone upon stone. But that lank lock of hair now hung across his forehead, almost covering one eye, and he made no effort to brush it back into place.

It was so quiet in that library that I could hear traffic noises on the street below, thought I heard the hoot of a tugboat on the East River, and did hear the drone of an airliner letting down for LaGuardia. No one spoke. We all waited.

Mr. Havistock, who had been staring stonily at Al Georgio, now turned his gaze to me. He looked at me a long time.

"Congratulations," he said finally with his wintry smile. "I tried to convince my wife not to hire you, but she insisted. I knew you were aching to find the coin. Someone had made a fool of you, and you wanted revenge."

"I would have given anything if it had turned out differently," I told him. "I admired you."

"Did you?" he said. Then, forlornly: "I wish I did."

"The Demaretion, Mr. Havistock," Al said impatiently.

He opened his top desk drawer, found a small key, then swung around in the swivel chair, his back to us. He leaned forward, unlocked a cabinet under those handsome bookshelves. He brought out a Styrofoam box, stood, and placed it on his desk. The tape had been removed, but I recognized it at once: box thirteen.

Mr. Havistock slid out the sealed teak display case with the glass cover. Then we all rose and bent over the desk. There it was.

That gorgeous, cursed coin! It loomed like a silver sun. So crisp, so strong. We all stared, mesmerized, and I thought of all the people who had owned it, even briefly. The loves, murders, treacheries, the sorrows and ecstasies—all that the Demaretion had seen and come through unclipped, unscratched, shining and complete.

"Is that it, Dunk?" Jack Smack asked.

"Yes," I said huskily, "that's it. It's beautiful, isn't it?"

I looked up at Mr. Havistock, but he would not meet my eyes and turned away.

"Thank you, sir," Al Georgio said briskly. "We'll take it along now."

He slid the display case back into the Styrofoam box, tucked it under one arm, and started out, motioning us to follow. He paused at the doorway and turned back for one final oratorical flourish.

"I leave you to the tender mercies of your wife, Mr. Havistock," he said. "Lots of luck."

It wasn't until we were down on the sidewalk in front of the apartment house that we stopped to grin at each other.

"Dunk," Al said, "you're a genius." And he leaned forward to kiss my cheek.

"A double-genius," Jack said, kissing the other cheek. "A triple-genius! Al, how do you feel about this female-type detective making us look like a couple of klutzes?"

"I love it," Georgio said. "I'm going to take all the credit at the Department for closing the file. Aren't you going to take all the credit with your company?"

"You bet your sweet ass," Jack said. "The coin has been returned; that's all we were interested in. Al, Havistock is going to walk, isn't he?"

"Sure he is," Al said. "What could we charge him with? All those things I threatened—so much kaka. I could have done all that, but it wouldn't have convicted him of anything. Just made his life more miserable than it is now. Let him walk; I've got the coin."

"If you're not going to arrest him," I said, "what do you need the Demaretion for?" And I whisked the box from under Al's arm. "It belongs to me. I signed for it."

He looked at me a moment, startled. Then he laughed. "You're right, Dunk, it's yours. Want us to escort you back to Grandby's?"

"Nope," I said, "I'm going to do this my way. If someone tries to mug me, you'll have another homicide to investigate. Not mine; the mugger's."

"Be careful, Dunk," Jack warned.

"Talk to you guys later," I said, and went breezing away.

It was late in the afternoon, and I knew my chances of getting a cab were nil. So I practically ran back to Grandby & Sons, hugging the Demaretion to what I laughingly call my bosom and trying not to shout with triumph.

I dashed up the stairs to my old office and banged on the door, then started kicking it. Hobart Juliana peered at me through the peephole, then unlocked.

"Dunk," he said, bewildered, "what on earth . . . ?"

"Look!" I yelled. "Just look at this!"

I slid the display case from the box and placed it on Hobie's desk. He bent over to inspect that single coin nestled on velvet in the middle compartment. Then he straightened and turned to me.

"Oh, my God," he said. "The Demaretion. Dunk, it's glorious!"

"Yes," I said, wanting to laugh and cry at the same time. "It's so lovely, so lovely."

He gave a whoop of delight, grabbed me, and we went dancing around the office, banging into tables and desks, holding each other and so excited and joyous I didn't think I could stand it.

Hobie stopped suddenly. "Let's go," he said. "We've got to impress Madam Dodat and god with your incredible victory."

So, with me carrying the display case, we sped into Felicia Dodat's office, barging by her indignant secretary. Felicia looked up, shocked by this sudden intrusion. I plunked the display case down on her desk.

"There it is," I said. "The Demaretion."

She stared at it a moment. "Oh, Dunk," she said, "isn't that *nice*! I must call Mr. Grandby. He'll be so *pleased*."

Within ten minutes there must have been a dozen people crammed into Felicia's office, all bending to examine that old Greek coin and laughing, kissing me, or shaking my hand. God was there, but all he could say was,

"Well, well, well." He kept repeating it: "Well, well, well." Everyone wanted to know how I had recovered it, but I just smiled mysteriously and winked. A great moment in my life. Dunk shot.

Finally Madam Dodat shooed everyone out of her office except for Mr. Grandby, Hobie, and me.

"All right, Dunk," she said, giving me her toothy smile, "now tell us how you did it."

I had my story ready. I told them that Archibald Havistock was an impassioned collector and, at the last minute, just couldn't let go of the Demaretion. I told them nothing of his relationship with his daughter-in-law or of his being blackmailed by his nephew. If the tabloids got hold of the story, everyone would know the details soon enough, but they weren't going to hear them from me.

They accepted my version readily enough, and we all agreed that true collectors were infected with a mania that could never be cured. Then the four of us formed a triumphal procession down to the vaults, god carrying the display case, and saw it safely locked away.

"Well, well, well," Mr. Grandby said, beaming, "I think this calls for a celebration. Will you join me for dinner?"

So we did, adjourning to the Bedlington dining room where we all had chateaubriand with the best béarnaise sauce I've ever tasted. And two bottles of champagne. My employer was acting in a most unpenguinlike manner. He even leaned over to whisper in my ear that I could expect a salary raise for my "remarkable efforts" on behalf of Grandby & Sons.

We parted about eight o'clock. God and Felicia Dodat went off together—to an apartment on East 65th Street, I wondered? Hobie and I embraced on the sidewalk, and I swore I would be in to work first thing Monday morning. Then he left to return to his consenting adult. I cabbed home alone.

There was nothing interesting in my mail—just bills and junk. So I kicked off my shoes and sprawled on the couch, beginning to feel a letdown after all the day's excitement. There was no reason I should have felt depressed—I had won, hadn't I?—but I did.

Then I realized what was saddening me was the fate of Archibald Havistock. I had thought of him as a statue, but now he was overturned, broken, and crumbling. I tried to understand how that could have happened. He was an intelligent and rational man; how could he have acted as stupidly as he did?

Perhaps it was male menopause. Perhaps it was nothing more than lust for a young, lubricious body. But I thought it was more than that. He was a deep man and must have known exactly how foolish it was to become enthralled by his son's wife, a doxy, and risk the happiness of his home. But he could not resist.

Suddenly it occurred to me that he might actually have been in love with her. It was possible. That reserved, magisterial, *complete* man may have, for the first time in his life, felt an overwhelming passion that gave new meaning to his life. He surrendered to that surge, not caring, because it was new to him and he had never learned to cope with such fervid emotions.

But whatever his motives or obsessions, nothing could excuse his illogical conduct.

I sighed and went into the bedroom to phone. I had two calls to make. The first to Al Georgio, telling that estimable man that no, I would not marry him. The second to Jack Smack, telling that flighty tap dancer that yes, I would move in with him.

You can be logical about other people's lives, but never about your own.